Darkest Fears T

Forever
With Him

Clair Delaney

REVIEWS FOR FOREVER WITH HIM

'Love always wins! Had to read the entire trilogy, one right after another. The angst, the forgiveness, and the passion were page turners from beginning to end. The cleverness of plot, the characters, and turncoat Stuart made for nailbiting intrigue. You won't go wrong buying these books today!' **Amazon**

'Wow…what an utterly compelling story! I found myself reading into the wee hours on the weekend and at every spare opportunity during the week. Clair Delaney will definitely be added to the list as one of my top 10 authors. I'm looking forward to reading more of her books in the near future.' **iBooks**

"Brilliant third book in this well written trilogy, I loved them all. Coral and Tristan fit so perfectly together. This trilogy captures your attention, not just a load of romance. It's got intrigue, psychology and the girly stuff as well. Loved it!" **Amazon**

"Sooo good! Beautiful story, beautiful ending. I love this trilogy. I love Coral, and I'm so in love with Tristan. This is the kind of trilogy that puts you on an emotional rollercoaster ride while transporting you to into their world, this author truly has a gift. Love, love, loved it! So sad it's ended " **LibraryThing**

"I love this story—456 pages of love, hardship and learning to trust." **Barnes & Noble**

'I can't believe it's ended, I want more…I'm a sad, sad girl right now. I love, love, loved this trilogy. I loved it was British, I loved the raw, honest style of writing that can have you crying one minute and laughing the next. I think this shows great promise in an author and I want more from her.' **Goodreads.**

'Magnificent! From the beginning this was so hard to put down. Epic romance. This author has become one of my favourites!' **Kobo**

'This is the third book in an enchanting love story. Lots of good writing and suspense here that has been lovely to read. I found myself glued to the book until the very end. I was rooting for Coral and Tristan who truly make this worth reading. Thumbs Up." **Amazon**

'I loved this book and I couldn't put it down. I finished the trilogy in a few days and I love the characters. I love Tristan and Coral.

I'm really recommending this one and for the writer you've done a very good job.' **5 stars – iBooks**

'Great love affair…a page turner! Glad it ended happily ever after.' **Scribd Library**

"A wonderful series conclusion. I loved this last book, and the entire trilogy, so much. Having travelled this road with Coral and Tristan, it's heartening to find things not only work out the way you want it to, but better. An excellent romance series that I would highly recommend." **Amazon**

'Great finale that had me gripped. This author can write romance, sex scenes and suspense. Coral and Tristan are most certainly in my heart and in my head. I'm actually getting a bit weepy writing this review as I remember all that happened in this one. Heart wrenching read that I highly recommend.' **5 stars – Scribd Library**

'If you are wondering whether or not to give it a go, don't, just buy it. Each book gets better and better as Coral and Tristan become more entwined in each others lives. My heart is overflowing with love after that happy ending in Forever With Him.' **Goodreads**

ALSO BY CLAIR DELANEY

Fallen For Him
Darkest Fears Trilogy Book One

Freed By Him
Darkest Fears Trilogy Book Two

A Christmas Wish
Darkest Fears Christmas Special Book Four

CONTENTS

Prologue 1
Chapter One 5
Chapter Two 14
Chapter Three 22
Chapter Four 30
Chapter Five 38
Chapter Six 49
Chapter Seven 59
Chapter Eight 68
Chapter Nine 80
Chapter Ten 93
Chapter Eleven 108
Chapter Twelve 128
Chapter Thirteen 144
Chapter Fourteen 163
Chapter Fifteen 179
Chapter Sixteen 195
Chapter Seventeen 212
Chapter Eighteen 227
Chapter Nineteen 246
Chapter Twenty 266
Chapter Twenty-One 285
Chapter Twenty-Two 304
Chapter Twenty-Three 326
Chapter Twenty-Four 341
Chapter Twenty-Five 360
Chapter Twenty-Six 378
Chapter Twenty-Seven 400
Chapter Twenty-Eight 418
Chapter Twenty-Nine 434
Chapter Thirty 449
Epilogue 468
About the Author 476

PROLOGUE

HE SITS ON THE park bench waiting. His brother is late – again. He takes another drag on his cigarette then looks down at his watch as he slowly blows out the smoke.

"Fucking asshole," he hisses, between gritted teeth and then takes another drag.

"Yo' bro!" His older brother shouts. He looks up and sees his older brother, Kane approaching. *Asshole! Just like dad!*

Dillon takes another drag and tries to his best to keep his temper in check. If it weren't for the fact that he needed his brother's money, he wouldn't have anything to do with him. But he's been made redundant again, and if he misses this month's rent, he's out on his ass, and the last thing he wants is to go back to living on the streets – *That part of my life is over!* When you've got a record, spent time inside, and you're a recovering alcoholic who had a major drug problem, not many people will employ you.

As he looks up again, he has to admit, Kane looks good. He's dressed in a designer suit and tie, his shoes are incredibly shiny, and he's changed his hair style, he has it gelled back into place like some sort of London gangster. Dillion can tell he's dripping with money.

Dirty money, he reminds himself. And he wants nothing to do with that.

Dillon looks down at his dirty fingernails, his tatty clothes, and once again has to reign in his temper – he'd love nothing more than to wipe the smug smile off his brothers' face. He shakes his head slightly and stares down at the ground. He could have gone down that road too, as Kane has and like his father before him. But he had to get away from his father's evil ways, or he was going to kill him – He couldn't stand being anywhere

1

near him in the end, so at fourteen years of age, he ran away from home, and he's never looked back.

Dillon is thirty now, a grown man. He's finally kicked the drugs and alcohol, and he's been clean for five years. Not that he had any help from his brother or his father, if they had offered, he would have told them both to go fuck themselves – *Calm Dillon, calm...*

He takes the last drag on his cigarette and stubs it out with his foot.

Kane reaches his brother, sits next to him and slaps him on the back. "How's it hanging?" he cajoles.

"How's it look?" Dillon snaps. *Fucking wanker!* "I need money." Dillon stares at his brother, holding eye contact, trying not to glare at him.

"How much?" Kane sighs clearly not interested.

"A thousand." Dillon clenches his jaw, he hates having to ask his brother for anything.

Kane looks around the park, thinking about his answer. He knows he's going to give him the money, it's not like his brother has called on him before, but he's always loved winding him up.

"What happened to your job?" He asks, trying not to smile.

"Redundancy," Dillon snaps.

"So you're being a good boy then?" Kane laughs, glancing at his brother. *Good boy!*

Dillon squeezes his eyes shut as memories of his childhood flood his mind. The bastards that touched him and made him do things he didn't want to do – his father being one of them. He grips his hands into fists, trying to stop the rage from spilling out of him. He knows Kane has said that word purposely, he used to hear it too, but Kane doesn't seem bothered by what happened to them back then, it doesn't seem to have affected him at all.

"Asshole," Dillon hisses.

Kane laughs loud and clear, throwing his head back as he does. Dillon glances up, and pictures his hands around his brother's neck, squeezing, tightening – Kane suddenly stops and stares down at his brother.

"You remember that girl with the weird eyes?" Kane asks.

Dillon shakes his head in exasperation. He doesn't give a fuck about any girl. "Kane, are you going to give me the money, or not?" he asks, staring ahead, trying to keep his temper in check.

"Relax bro, you got it – but do you?" Kane laughs.

"Do I what?" Dillon asks, turning to look at Kane's smug smile.

"Remember her? Fucks sake, you been smoking the whacky backy?" Kane asks.

"No." Dillon snaps, but he does remember her.

Kane starts laughing again. "You do remember?"

Dillon clenches his jaw. "What about her Kane?" He snaps, staring ahead again.

"I found her," Kane says.

Dillon turns and looks at him, surprised. "Why would you want to find her?"

"I wasn't looking you dipshit. I had a meeting, down in Brighton and out of the blue, there she was, all timid and shy, she wouldn't even look me in the eye."

Dillon cringes inwardly. He knows where Kane's going with this. "Leave her alone Kane, she hasn't done anything to you." He says, wondering if she's just as fucked up as he is.

"Too late," Kane laughs.

Dillon glares at his brother. "What's that supposed to mean?"

Kane smiles triumphantly at his brother. Dillon instantly knows that he's screwed her already. Dillon starts to feel slightly nauseous, he knows what kind of reputation his brother has and how he treats women.

"Did you hurt her?" Dillon asks.

"What do you care?" Kane laughs.

Dillon shakes his head and stares down at the floor, wishing there was something he could do for the girl with the weird eyes.

"You're fucking sick Kane," Dillon spits.

"They love it," Kane laughs, getting to his feet and buttoning up his suit jacket. "Be here, tomorrow, seven-thirty. I'll send someone over with the money." Kane looks down at his brother with disdain, then turns and walks away.

Dillon stares ahead, thinking of the past. He remembers clearly the girl with the weird eyes, he even remembers her name. Coral, like the coral blue sea, she was sweet. Dillon remembered how she saved him from a beating and showed him what to do, what they wanted from them both – she was kind. He was scared, and she took care of him and told him everything would be ok – not that it was. Dillon shakes his head, feeling sorry for the girl, and hoping Kane went easy on her…

CHAPTER ONE

SOMEONE IS TRYING to wake me by tapping my cheek…*No, stop it!* – I'm tired…so tired. My mouth tastes dry and rancid, and I hurt all over, I just want to go back to sleep. I can see a light trying to push through the darkness of my eyelids….*No stop!*

"Give her some time." I hear a woman's commanding voice say. "She's going to be pretty groggy, so don't crowd her. Coral, can you hear me?" She asks.

My cheek is being tapped again…*leave me the fuck alone lady!*

"Come on sweetheart, open your eyes," she says.

I blink my eyes open, then squint. It's too bright, and my surroundings are unfamiliar. I hear several gasps, and someone starts crying – *What's going on?*

"Can everyone please leave the room," she says. I hear a door open and close, I open my eyes and try to see who it is. "Welcome back," she says smiling down at me. I close my eyes again, the darkness is pulling me back under, and I want to go.

"Coral, stay with me, sweetheart. I need you to tell me how you're feeling?" she asks. I start blinking more rapidly as I try to work out, through the strange blurry haze; what's going on.

"Coral, please answer me. How are you feeling?" she asks again.

I squeeze my eyes shut and take a second to assess – my body hurts all over – *Why?*

"I feel like I've been hit by a truck?" I whisper. My voice sounds strange. I hear a deep voice curse – *Tristan?* I open my eyes and try to find him, but I can't see him, and I can't lift my head to search for him either.

"Coral, my name is Dr Green. You're in the hospital. Do you remember what happened?" she asks. *Dr Green? Hospital?* I have no idea what she's talking about. I feel so confused, disorientated...I squeeze my eyes shut and try to remember...but nothing comes to me. *Why am I in here?*

"Coral, please look at me," she asks, so I open my eyes and look up at her. She shines a bright light in each of my eyes, making me squint again, and then she starts feeling under my glands – prodding in places I'd rather she didn't prod!

"Are you in any pain?" she asks.

"Yes, I hurt all over," I whisper. *Why?*

"Yes, that's to be expected," she says smiling warmly at me. I watch her walk over to a machine and press a button. "That was for the nurse, her name is Jenny, and she's going to take care of you, ok?" I manage to nod in reply.

Dr Green walks back over to me, and presses another button. My bed starts to move, so I'm sitting more upright. I immediately spy an IV line in my right hand. *Ugh...I hate needles!* – The moment I think that it starts to burn and itch, it feels so sore...*I want it out of me!* I lift my left hand – it takes a hell of an effort to do so – and reach over to my right hand. In my dazed state, I try to pull at the needle, but the tape is stopping me.

"No Coral," she softly scolds. "That's your IV line." I look up at Dr Green, I can see her more clearly now, she has auburn hair, bright green eyes and a very freckly face. "Now, this may come as a shock to you, but I need to fill you in on what happened' – "I'd like to do that," I hear Tristan's low voice interrupt. I search the room for him, my eyes finally resting on the tall stature that has stood up and stepped forward...*Tristan?*

Our eyes lock, I frown back at him trying to work out why he looks so mad, his eyes are dark, really dark, like rich dark chocolate as he glares at me, then his stares emotionless at the doctor. I stare wide-eyed at my man – *What the hell has happened to him?* He looks completely washed out, dishevelled, like he hasn't slept in days; and he has a full beard.

How did that happen?

"Mr Freeman, I have to disagree' – "I know her, you don't. This isn't a debate, she'll hear it from me," he orders. The atmosphere in the room instantly drops ten degrees and is so silent you could hear a pin drop. The doctor stands back from the bed and puts her hands on her hips, she does not look happy.

"As you wish, but I'm putting it on record that I disagree," she says.

"Fine by me," Tristan snaps.

"Coral, are you happy for Mr Freeman to run through what happened?"

"Yes," I croak.

"Ok." She smiles warmly at me. Another lady enters the room, and as she does, I notice there's a big glass window to the right of the door and everyone is here, watching me. Gladys is tightly wrapped up in Malcolm's arms, as she chokes back tears; he looks pretty cut up too. Deb's and Scott are hugging Lily, who sleepily waves at me. Rob and Carlos are stood next to one another, their hands locked together, and they both look relieved as I catch their eyes, and George and Joyce are here too? They all look so tired and worn out.

What's going on?

"Hello Coral, my name is Nurse Jenny, are you feeling uncomfortable honey?" I look up at the strawberry blonde woman, with a soft round face and kind hazel eyes.

"Yes," I breathe.

"Coral, I'll see you soon." Dr Green says nodding to the nurse. I manage to raise my hand to wave her goodbye; she smiles at me as she exits the room.

"Alright now Coral, you should start feeling the pain relief any moment now." As Nurse Jenny says that, I get a warm, weird feeling flooding my veins, my body, making all pain disappear. "Are you thirsty honey?" Nurse Jenny asks.

"Very," I say, my throat feeling burned.

"Alright, I'll be back in a moment," she says and exits the room.

"Tristan," I croak, lifting my hand to him.

He's straight over to me, gently squeezing my hand. He looks like hell, what happened to him? I want to question it all, but the room starts to pull away from me, I feel like I'm slipping into a dark tunnel. I try really hard to fight against it, but it's no good, the darkness takes me away again…

I FEEL A HAND stroking my cheek, my forehead, and then softly stroke my hair. Then it stops, and the soft fingers are tracing my lips.

"Mmm…" It feels so nice.

"Coral…?" I hear Tristan's voice, it sounds soft, exhausted. I push myself to fight against the haze and blink my eyes open.

"Hey…" I croak, my throat feels so sore. "Where am I?" I ask blinking more rapidly.

"Hospital," he softly says. *Why am I in the hospital?*

"Um...I...which one?" I ask.

"Montefiore," he answers grimly.

I frown back at him in confusion – This does not look like a hospital; more like a hotel room. Light cream walls, and very modern looking, with white and pale blue furnishings.

"I don't know that one," I croak.

"You do, you just don't remember," he tells me. I open my eyes again. *This definitely looks like a hotel room.* I suddenly become aware that there's something attached to my face, some kind of tube, so I lift my hand to pull it.

"No baby, it's your cannula; it's helping you breathe." Tristan softly says, his hand stopping mine.

I close my eyes and swallow hard again. "Thirsty," I say. *Why do I feel so out of it?*

"Ok." I hear Tristan shuffling around then he's next to me again. "Open your eyes baby," he tells me, so I do. He's leaning over me with a cup and a spoon in his hand. "You're only allowed crushed ice for now." He dips the spoon in the cup and feeds me a small amount. He does that a few times, he's concentrating hard on the task, his brows furrowed together.

"Enough?" He asks after the fourth spoon.

"Yeah...Tristan…it hurts, I hurt all over, why?" I croak.

"Ok baby." I watch Tristan walk over to a machine and press a button. Fear ripples through me; fight or flight kicking in. My worst fear comes rushing to the surface – I'm being carted off to a fucking mental home just like my Mom. *Shit! I have to get out of here!*

"Tristan!" I panic. "Why am I in here?" I say breathlessly.

"Hey." He's instantly by side again. "You're ok now baby, I...I thought I'd lost you," he chokes.

"What was that button?" I ask. "Why am I in here?" My heart is racing against my chest, the machine behind me echoing its action. I look up at Tristan, he looks lost, confused, mortified.

"Coral please...calm down," he pleads.

"Answer my question then!" I bark, my voice breaking on me.

"It's nothing to worry about darling, I just called for the Nurse that's all. She'll be here in a moment to give you some painkillers. You...you don't remember why you're in here?" He asks, rubbing his hand across his face.

I shake my head in reply, then I really take a good look at Tristan. He has dark rings under his eyes, and he looks exhausted. He has no colour, his face is deathly white, and his eyes have lost all their sparkle, and he's grown a light beard. *How did that happen?* Then I notice a nasty gash across his forehead leading into his hairline. It looks like he has stitches.

"What happened to you?" I whisper reaching my hand up to his forehead.

"Never mind me," he answers brusquely. "But' – "No buts baby," he says, his eyes glistening over. He leans in and softly kisses my lips. I can feel the relief behind his kiss...*oh Tristan, what happened to you?*

"Tristan," I mumble. "Please...I still don't understand. How did I get here? I remember we were arguing..." I tell him, everything else is a blank.

"You don't remember anything after that?" He asks darkly.

"No." I frown. "Why? What happened?" I ask taking a deep breath. *Ouch, that really stung!* My lungs hurt – *Why does it hurt to breathe?*

"You... you came back," he snarls, his hands bunching into fists. "You were right, everything you told me Coral, it was all right," he growls.

I came back to what?

"I...I..." I blink around the room trying to remember. Then all of a sudden I get a flashback of running down the concourse – something happened to Bob?

"Bob!" I squeak in panic.

"He's fine, he's staying with Gladys," he tells me, softly stroking my cheek.

I instantly feel relieved that Bob's ok, but it still doesn't answer my question. "I still don't understand?" I whisper.

"We argued about Susannah, do you remember that?" he asks.

"Yes," I swallow hard. "You told me we were through...you told me to leave..." I stop, unable to say anymore. I'm not really sure how I feel about that now. I'm just so glad Tristan's here and that he's ok.

Tristan squeezes his eyes shut as though he's in pain. "I was *never* going to end it Coral!" He barks, then takes a deep calming breath. "I just needed to clear my head..." he stops for a moment. "When you left, you went to Rob's, and then you got a call from the police. Susannah had ransacked your studio and attacked Bob." I gasp aloud – *Susannah!*

"Tristan, she' – "Hey, it's ok, she can't hurt you or me," he says.

"She's gone?" I swallow hard, feeling relieved.

"Yes, after you left I called her and questioned her about what you'd found out." Tristan laughs sarcastically, shaking his head at himself. "She denied it all of course, then she turns up on my doorstep and admits it's all true, said she was quitting the company, and that she needed help. I invited her in, she poured us both a drink…I didn't think anything of it, but she drugged me with Rohypnol." He looks down at me, his jaw tensing several times. *She date rape drugged him? I wonder if she…?*

"She threatened to kill me if I didn't go upstairs, took me ages…I kept losing my balance, I was pretty out of it," he stops again, frowning deeply, then continues. "She told me to call you but I wouldn't; so she hit me over the head a couple of times," he says tracing the gash on his head. "I don't really remember anything else until you turned up."

I frown back at him. "I turned up?" I whisper in confusion.

"Yes, yes you did you brave, stupid girl," he says leaning down to kiss me again. "You're my heroine, you know that?" he smiles.

I stare back at him, searching his face, trying to understand it all. Then it starts coming back to me, one flash image after the other. Bob on the floor in my studio, the ambulance driving away, driving Rob's car, finding Tristan beaten, tied up, bleeding – just like the dream – then Susannah in Tristan's bedroom. But it still doesn't explain why I'm here?

"I…I remember finding you, you were bleeding," I say. Reaching up, I stroke his face again.

Tristan takes my hand in his and kisses it several times. "She shot you," he croaks, fighting back the tears. "You crazy girl, she was aiming at me, and you jumped in front of me!" *She shot me?*

Then I remember – clearly – Susannah was pointing the gun at me then she pointed it at Tristan. "I wasn't going to let her hurt you," I choke out, shaking my head. "Not for me." I try to move so I can hug him, but a sharp, shooting pain runs through my right lung and across my shoulder blade. It makes me wince in pain; I try not to cry out.

"God damn it Coral, keep still! Did you hear what I said? She shot you, you need to be careful, keep still!" He snaps.

Tears prick my eyes as it all comes crashing down on me. I saved Tristan, he's safe now, and Susannah is locked away somewhere, she can't hurt him now…she can't hurt him.

Tristan strokes my forehead as he hovers above me again. "Hey, there's no need for tears. I'm sorry I got mad," he murmurs, then gently kisses my forehead. I close my eyes I must be dreaming this, I must be!

Then I remember my mother. "Was it her Tristan?" I whisper, opening my eyes and staring up into his. "Did Susannah kill my mom?" I whimper. I'm not even sure if I want to know the answer to that one.

"No baby, Gladys told me it was heart failure."

"Oh." I choke back the tears that threaten again. Then I remember what Susannah stole from me. "My photograph!" I shout feeling incensed again that she took it.

"Coral, I really don't want you to worry about things like' – "Did they get it back?" I snap, feeling like I want to stamp my feet.

"Yes, it was found in her hotel room along with the photo of us. And they found a set of your keys on her when they arrested her."

"Good," I whisper. "That's good." I close my eyes again…I really do feel out of it. I hear the door open, and force my eyes open. A woman in a white coat walks in the room.

"Mr Freeman," she nods in his direction. "Well now...." she turns and smiles at me. "How are you feeling Coral?" she asks.

"Groggy, confused…" I don't really know what else to say.

"Do you remember me?" she asks.

"We've met?" I question, looking from her to Tristan for an explanation.

"Yes, yesterday morning. My name is Dr Green." I frown back at her.

"We did?" I say in surprise, I do not remember meeting her – *What's wrong with me?*

"Coral, has Mr Freeman explained why you are in here?"

I nod my head. "Yes, Susannah shot me," I whisper.

"And has Mr Freeman explained' – "Dr Green," he snaps, interrupting her. "I haven't had a chance to explain…everything." He adds.

They stare at one another for a moment. Dr Green doesn't look too happy, and I can see it on Tristan's face – whatever they are disagreeing about, Tristan will not budge.

Finally, she turns to me and smiles. "Coral, all your vital signs are looking good, you're healing quickly, but I'm afraid we're going to have to keep you in here a little while longer, I want to monitor you a little more. I want to be absolutely sure that all is as it should be before we send you home. If you have any further questions regarding this, or if you would like to speak to me about anything, just let Nurse Jenny know you want to see me," she says patting my hand.

"Nurse Jenny?" I question.

"Your nurse," she and Tristan both answer at the same time. *Uh-oh!* Something is definitely going on there.

"Ok, thanks…Dr Green." I smile weakly at her.

"You are very welcome Coral." She smiles back at me, shoots a disappointed look at Tristan then walks out of the room.

"What have you done?" I turn to Tristan with one eyebrow cocked up.

"Nothing," he says avoiding eye contact, so I know he's done something.

"Tristan!" I scold.

"It's not important," he says. He's not going to tell me, so I decide to leave it for now. I look down the bed and around the room – *Smells funny in here!* "What's wrong?" he asks.

I glance over at him. "A while longer…?" I say anxiously. "I hate hospitals," I add.

"I know, but like it or not you're staying. You're healing nicely, but they just want to be sure you're ok; so do I," he says frowning deeply and squeezing my hand.

"It was just a gunshot," I say, hoping he'll change his mind and take me home. "It doesn't hurt. I'm ok, you can take me home now." I wince as I try to move – *God damn it!*

"Don't do that Coral," he softly admonishes.

"Do what?" I feign innocence.

"Lie to me," he growls. "And stop thinking you have to be so tough all the time will you. Christ!" Tristan runs his hand through his hair in frustration.

"Sorry," I say, tears welling up again. "I don't mean to be difficult...." I choke.

"I know," he sighs and kisses me again. "Now go back to sleep, you need to rest."

"Why are you still here?" I ask.

"Where else would I be?" he asks incredulously.

"Tristan you should go home, get some rest, you look exhausted," I tell him. He just stares back at me, his big chocolate eyes, wide and weary. "You're not going to leave?" I whisper.

"No." He tells me firmly, then reaching up he gently strokes my hair.

"Am I dreaming?" I whisper.

"No." Tristan gazes down at me with those deep, soulful eyes of his.

"Am I dead?" I question.

"No." He states clearly.

"Prove it," I challenge.

Tristan leans forward and gently rests his forehead against mine. "Feel this?" He says, clutching my hand in his.

"Yes," I whisper, it feels heavenly.

"And this?" He says, kissing my forehead, I smile up at him. "I love you," he tells me. "More than life itself…when I thought I'd nearly lost you' – I press my fingertips against his full, soft lips. Now I know I'm not dreaming; I can smell his hypnotic scent invading all my senses….*He smells like home.*

"I love you too," I softly say, and slowly but surely his lips gently meet mine…

CHAPTER TWO

MY STOMACH GRUMBLES loudly making us both smile. I look up at Tristan; I guess the kissing is over for now.
"Hungry?" He asks.
"Yes, I feel like I haven't eaten in a week," I state.
Tristan frowns and looks down at our entwined fingers.
"What?" I question. "What are you looking so worried about?" He silently shakes his head at me. "Tristan!" I warn.
"You've been in here for a while baby, you took your time coming around after the operation." *Operation?*
"So what are you saying?" I whisper.
"You've been out cold for ten days baby." I frown back at him, then smile – *He's winding me up, he's got to be.* Lifting my hand to his lips, he softly kisses my knuckles. "Happy birthday darling." *Shit! He's telling the truth.*
"It's my birthday!?" I squeak in horror.
"Yes." Tristan kisses my hand again trying to soothe me.
"But...but, Gladys and Malcolm were getting married today!" I squeak, suddenly remembering that conversation.
Tristan shakes his head at me. "They've cancelled it, baby."
"What!?" I screech. The machine that I'm hooked up to starts rapidly beeping; echoing my anxiety.
"Coral, with everything that's happened, it was the last thing on their mind, don't you understand? You were shot baby, your heart..." Tristan stops for a moment and squeezes his eyes closed as though he's in pain, then he opens them and glares down at me. "They had to resuscitate you...you came back to us but you'd lost a lot of blood, so they had to give you a transfusion. Then they took you down to surgery, we all thought...prayed you would pull through," he takes another deep breath. "When you were wheeled into ICU after your op, we all breathed a sigh

of relief, but then you wouldn't wake up...I thought...." He takes a deep, steadying breath.

"It's been the most horrendous ten days of my life," he says, his eyes wide, weary and full of fear. "I thought you'd never wake up again," he says bowing his head as he chokes back tears.

"Tristan!" I gasp and pull him to me. I take his head and rest it on my chest, it hurts like hell, but I don't care; I need to comfort him. "Baby, don't cry, I'm here, and I'm not going anywhere," I say running my fingers through his thick, soft hair.

He lifts his head, and I see the fear and the pain behind his eyes, he's been to hell and back. He sniffs loudly, kisses me with his soft tear stained lips and puts his head back on my chest.

"Tristan, you look terrible. When was the last time you slept? I ask.

"I don't know..." he mumbles, looking up at me.

I place my hands on his cheeks. "Baby, when I get out of here I need you to be fit and healthy so you can look after me, not so exhausted that you'll get ill, now go home," I order.

"No!" he barks back.

"You're very stubborn," I mutter.

"Yes, just like you," he says cocking one eyebrow up at me.

I shake my head at him, trying to think of a way to get him home, he looks awful.

"Ok, I'll make a deal with you," I say.

"A deal?"

"Yes."

"Ok, I'm all ears," he says.

"We eat something because you look like you haven't had a decent meal in you for days, then you go home. I don't expect to see you until tomorrow morning, deal?"

"No, no deal," he says, shaking his head at me.

"Tristan!" I moan.

"I'm not leaving Coral, so drop it," he snaps.

I roll my eyes at him. "Fine!" I bob my tongue out at him.

"Fine!" he mimics me then smiles his cheeky grin.

"You're crazy," I say laughing and shaking my head at him.

"And hungry," he says.

"Tristan, there's no excuse for you not eating!" *Why the hell hasn't Gladys fed him up while I've been in here?*

"What are you hungry for beautiful?" He asks, ignoring my telling off.

"You," I tease.

His smile spreads from ear to ear. "As I am, for you my

darling," Tristan says, softly stroking my cheek, then he gets to his feet; he seems very tired and weary.

His face contorts as he stares down at my body, then he leans down, pulls the covers back, and lifts up my horrid, hospital nightgown. He plants a soft kiss on my belly – I notice a funny look in his eyes as he does this – then he slowly brushes his prickly jaw against my skin, it sends tingles to all the right places – *I so would right now, if I could.*

"Don't tempt me," I growl, running my hands through his hair.

"Tempt you?" he asks, brushing his stubble against me again.

"Just because I'm in the hospital and unable to move, doesn't stop me shagging your brains out!" I grumble. *He has no idea the effect he has on me.*

"Yes it does," he firmly says, kissing my belly once more.

"Get up here," I say, pulling on his hair. Tristan smiles shyly as I pull his lips down to meet mine. The machine suddenly goes silent as my heart splutters to a stop. *I still can't get used to the feel of his lips against mine.*

Tristan instantly stops kissing me, his lips frozen millimetres from mine. Then he looks across at the machine, just as my heart thuds a couple of times, then zooms into action. I blow out a deep breath.

"What was that all about?" he asks.

"You just...*drive me wild!*" I say against his lips.

"Wild, eh?" *Ok, he's enjoying this.*

"More than you'll ever know," I add.

"Ditto baby," he says sweetly, kissing me softly again.

"Tristan, I really want you to' – "I know what you're going to say," he interrupts. "And I'm not going anywhere, the only time I'm walking out of this hospital is with you in my arms," he states.

"Tristan, that's silly," I admonish.

"You nearly died Coral, so I don't think it's silly at all. Now, what are you hungry for?"

"I've told you. You!" I pout, wishing I could make love to him.

"Well, I'm afraid I'm off the menu for a while....so?" Tristan cocks his head to the side waiting for my answer. For some unfathomable reason I'm craving Macaroni Cheese, yet I never eat that stuff. *How odd?*

"Well?" Tristan pushes.

"Macaroni Cheese?" I answer.

"Sounds good," he chuckles.

"You like it too?" I question.

"Yes." Tristan kisses me again, then takes out his mobile and types up a text.

"What time is it?"

"Lunchtime."

"Who are you texting?" I ask.

"Stuart."

"Why?"

"To get us some food from the cafeteria, he's been here the whole time Coral, to get anything we need," he adds. *There's a cafeteria here?*

"He has?" I squeak.

"Yes, he's been worried about you too."

"Well he should take your sorry ass home, so you can shower, shave and get your butt into bed for some rest," I admonish. I don't want him to know, but I'm really worried about him, he looks terrible.

"You don't like the beard?" he asks running his hand across his jaw.

"Actually I do, I think it looks really sexy but' – "You do?" he says in surprise.

"Um...yeah," I smile. "Tristan, I think you're sexy with or without it, so do want you want to do baby. Keep it if you like it," I say smiling up at him. He smiles his shy smile, then shakes his head at me in wonder. "What?"

"Nothing, I just...Coral, I love that you care about me so much, that you think I should go home, but I can rest here," he says, patting the bed next to me.

"Yes, you can," I say smiling broadly at him. "And of course I care about you like that, I love you, Tristan, that's why I took a bullet for you. But now I think about it, maybe I shouldn't have," I say staring down at the bed. "It was a really silly thing for me to have done, and now I'm in pain, and I can't move, which means I can't bed you whenever I want to!" I say putting on a pretend pout, teasing him.

"Oh, baby..." He leans down to kiss me, chuckling hard against my lips.

"S'not funny!" I moan as it all starts to sink in – If I'm in this much pain lying still, there's no way any sex is going to happen! *God damn it!*

"Sex deprived?" he titters.

17

"You're going to have a lot of making up to do you know," I mumble.

His eyes glint wickedly. "Oh, it's a dirty job, but someone's got to do it," he chuckles.

"I'm glad it's you," I say.

"Yeah?" He croaks.

"Yes, you're my man baby. You make me feel safe, protected, loved. All those women that wanted you, I feel sorry for them. They lost out, but I got you, and I'll always remember that I'll never take you for granted." I say surprising myself.

Tristan loses his grin. His face falls, and his eyes grow dark. "Baby..." he chokes trying his best to hold me without hurting me. "It's always been you, always will be," he whispers then pulls back, gazing adoringly at me again - like I'm the air that he breathes. *God knows why?*

"How much longer do you think I'll have to stay in here?" I ask.

"You want to go home?"

"Yes, I want to go home."

"When you say *home*?" he questions.

My heart sinks. *Doesn't he want me with him?* "Well, I mean with you...I mean...well I can't go back to my studio...?" I say frowning deeply at him.

"You sure this is what you want?" He asks. I notice him swallow hard.

I sigh inwardly. "Tristan nowhere has ever been home to me. I mean...I love Gladys and Debs, and the house I was raised in, but...well, the first time I ever felt *at home*, was when I met you. So my *home* is where you are." Tristan silently nods as he digests this information, but I keep pushing because I want out of here. "I'll heal quicker there, I know I will. Please baby...." I stop remembering something. "Dr Andrews works here," I say hoping he'll sign me out.

"Coral, he's in a completely different department. He can't sign you out if that's what you're thinking?" My face falls. *I so want out of here!*

"But I'll see what I can do, I don't want you leaving' –
"Tristan, nothing is going to happen to me. I want to go home, I want to sleep in our bed, I want to sit on the sofa with you and eat home cooked food. Please baby, get me out of here." I beg.

"Sounds heavenly," he says. "I'll see what they say," he adds.

"I don't care what they say, I want out." I pout.

Forever With Him

"I know," he says kissing me again. "Let's eat and then I'll go talk to them."

I smile back at him. "Thank you, Tristan." I lean forward to kiss him and wince – *Fuck that hurt!* "Where's the nurse?" I ask, panting in pain.

"You need some painkillers?" Tristan asks I nod frantically at him. Tristan leans over and presses the button again. "She'll be here in a sec," he says squeezing my hand in his. "Nice deep breaths baby," he soothes.

I close my eyes briefly and concentrate on blocking out the pain. The door opens, and a nurse in a blue uniform enters.

"Hi Coral," she smiles. "Sorry about the delay, we're really busy today. You need some painkillers?"

"Please," I whimper.

"Alright honey," I watch her inject something into my drip. "You feeling better?" she asks, I nod back at her. "Ok, see you later." She smiles and walks out of the room.

"You know if we go home you'll have to take painkillers in tablet form, it won't be this easy," he tells me.

"Tristan, you're rich," I rightly point out. "I want a nurse and a drip at home," I say gritting my teeth. Tristan chuckles at my little rant, then we both look up as the door is opened again.

"Stuart!" I beam. Tristan is straight to his feet taking the tray off Stuart and placing it on the table in front of me – *It smells delicious!*

"How are you feeling Coral?" Stuart asks.

"Good thanks; you?" I smile.

"No complaints, glad to see you're awake," he says nodding once at me.

"Thanks, Stu," Tristan says.

"Can I get anything else for you?" he asks.

"Coral?" Tristan looks across at me.

"Yes, can you wait till were finished, then take Tristan home so he can shower' – "Coral, we've discussed this," he says, his eyes narrowed, a deep frown etched into his features.

"Fine!" I grumble.

"Fine!" He grumbles back at me.

Stuart smiles softly at me, nods to Tristan and discreetly disappears out the door. Tristan pulls the table closer to us. *Wow, that smells so good!*

"Honestly, you're so huffy sometimes," I say.

"So are you," he retorts. "Can we eat now?" he adds. He looks angry, which is making me want to laugh because he really does look pissed off – *Honestly, men and no food, not a good combination.*

"Eat!" I tell him, trying to hide my smirk.

"It's not funny Coral!" he barks.

"Fine, it's not funny!" I say, trying not to laugh.

Tristan shakes his head in frustration, removes the plastic top to each of our bowls, silently hands a spoon to me, and starts munching on his macaroni. I smile down at my poor baby, who's been through so much, and dig into my food. I have so many questions for him, there's so much to talk about, but this food tastes so good, I don't want to stop eating to talk.

It doesn't take long for us both to finish. Tristan places both our bowls down and pushes the table back down the end of the bed.

"Curl up with me?" I whisper, suddenly feeling drained.

"Here?" he questions.

"Yes please," I whimper, I need to feel him close to me.

Tristan shakes his head at me. "I don't want to hurt you."

"How are you going to hurt me?" I huff.

"I might turn over and catch you or something' – "Tristan please, I want to you to lie down next to me. Please..." I beg.

"Fine!" he answers frustratingly. I watch him kick off his trainers and climb in beside me – *Now I'm happy.*

"Bliss," I say laying my head on his shoulder, placing my hand over his heart.

"Yeah baby, this is," he sleepily answers and lifts his hand to cover mine.

I feel my eyes getting heavier and heavier as I try to hold onto the feeling of Tristan's body next to mine, but sleep soon comes, and I start to drift away, but just as I do, I get a really weird mental image of my mom. She's stood in front of my studio, and she's glowing and......*Shit! My mom!*

"Tristan!" My heart starts hammering against my chest again.

He leans up and looks down at me. "What's wrong baby?" he asks, a little panicked.

"My mom," I choke. "Did I miss the funeral?" I ask.

His face twists with sorrow – *Shit, I've missed it!*

"There wasn't one baby...she was cremated. When nobody turns up they..." He stops and runs his hand through his hair.

"So she doesn't even have a grave?" I squeak, tears threatening.

"Baby, if that's what you want we can do that, bury her

ashes even, whatever you want, I'll sort it," he tells me, stroking my cheek.

A few strays tears roll down my cheeks…I'll never see her alive again.

"Thank you, Tristan, with everything that's gone on…" I swallow hard. "You're too good to me," I whisper.

"No, I'm not," he argues. "You deserve it all baby," he adds.

I close my eyes and hold him to me. "I love you, Tristan, forever."

"And I you baby." I feel his lips meet mine and surrender to the feeling.

It's bittersweet.

On the one hand, I feel so sad about my mom and gutted that Gladys has cancelled her wedding, but the absolute up has to be that Tristan is alive, that he's here with me and that Susannah didn't kill him, and she could have, so easily. I squeeze him tight once more and snuggle up to him, my man, my wonderful man.

I take a few deep breaths, and before I know it I find myself drifting off…

CHAPTER THREE

I T FEELS LIKE I'VE been floating for a long time. I'm heading down towards my studio; it's weird how it doesn't feel like my feet are hitting the ground. As I reach the Marina, I start to notice that there aren't any people about, just the houses and the boats. I stop for a moment and look out to sea, but I can't see anything except thick, dense fog. I turn and look down the concourse, the fog lifts for a moment, and in the distance, I see a figure standing outside my studio. I squint trying to work out who it is, but I'm too far away. The moment I think that I zoom forwards and stop in front of my studio.

The unearthly figure is hard to look at, there's a bright white light surrounding it; it's almost blinding, suddenly the figure turns and stares at me, and I realise it's a woman.

"Hello Coral," she says, but her lips don't move.

I stare back at the woman. I think I recognise her, but I'm not sure.

"Mom?" I question and notice that my voice doesn't sound like me.

"You have to go back Coral," she tells me.

"Go back?" I question.

"You can't come with me," she says.

"Come with you? What do you mean?" I question.

She floats towards me and presses her hand against my cheek. "It was my time darling it's not yours. Tristan needs you."

I frown back at her. "But I want to go with you," I tell her. "I've missed you."

"I've missed you too darling, and I'm sorry. So, so sorry I didn't make it work for us." She opens her arms, and I fall into them.

"Oh, mom!" I'm instantly flooded with a feeling of peace

and absolute, unconditional love. "I don't want to go," I whisper. "If I do, I won't see you again, will I?" I look up at her.

"No baby girl, you won't see me again, not like this. But I'll always be with you, even if you can't see me, I'll be there."

"How do you know that?" I question.

"Because I've been watching you for a while now," she says smiling softly at me.

"You have?"

"Yes, I have." She takes my face in her hands. "Go now Coral, before it's too late," she says.

"No! I like it here." *I don't feel any pain, or hate or sorrow – just love.*

"Baby, it's time. I love you Coral, please forgive me." I try to hold onto her, but she takes a step back from me.

"No...mom..." In the next instance, she's slammed her hands against me, one across my heart and the other under my rib. *My god that hurt!*

She does it again – *Fuck, that really hurt, what's going on?* Suddenly, my whole world shifts, and I feel like I'm being pulled through a vacuum.

"She's back!" someone shouts. *Back? Where have I been?* I question, but no words come out. I hear more voices, people shouting at one another, I try to hear what they are saying, but they seem so far away. I try to open my eyes, but I feel myself slipping, the fog washes over me. I let it take me, hoping I'll see my mom again...

"SHIT!" I'M STARTLED awake. I feel like I've just popped into my body...*how odd?*

"Baby, what is it?" Tristan asks, hovering over me. I look around the room in desperation...I'm in the hospital? *Oh yes, I remember now.* Its pitch black outside, god knows what time it is. I turn back to Tristan who's lying next to me on the big hospital bed. "Baby, tell me," he pleads. "What's wrong?"

I shake my head, trying to understand. "Just a dream Tristan...I think?" I add.

Tristan wraps his arms around me, warming me up, I feel so cold. "Want to talk about it?" He softly asks.

"Yeah...no," I shake my head feeling unsure. "That was weird," I mumble.

"Tell me," he says. But I still feel so tired, so sleepy.

"I will," I whisper and I drift off again...

I BLINK MY EYES open and take a quick look around the room. There's a hazy, lemon light bleeding through the blinds at the window; it's dusk or dawn I'm not sure which. I notice Tristan is not on the bed with me anymore. I close my eyes and frown. I'm so disorientated, is it still last night? Have I slept through another day? I can hear the beeping of the machines behind me and try to sit up.

Pain – my body still hurts so much, I squeeze my eyes shut trying to block it out.

"Coral, can you hear me?" I groggily open my eyes. "Over here sunshine..." A soft voice chuckles, I turn my head and see Rob smiling down at me, then I look down at the bed, then to the small chair in the corner of the room – *Tristan's gone!*

"Where's Tristan?" I croak, feeling slightly panicked.

"Oh that's nice!" he scoffs jokingly. "*I* come to see you, but all you're interested in is Mr Fancy Pants!" he teases.

I start chuckling – *Ouch that really hurts!*

"Don't make me laugh!" I chuckle.

"Oops! Sorry, does it hurt?" he questions.

I cock one eyebrow up at him. "Seriously?" I say as sarcastically as I can.

Rob chuckles some more. "Hey, I was thinking, should I call you Cagney or Lacey?" he jokes.

"Oh very funny," I scoff.

We both start laughing again, but I wince and close my eyes for a second trying to control the pain.

"Rob...seriously, where is Tristan?" I say breathlessly.

"Relax, Gladys practically frogmarched him out of here so he can shower and get a meal inside him, he looks terrible. I'm so glad you met him Coral, he's got it so bad for you, aren't you the lucky girl!" He gazes down at me with a smug, satisfied smile, I grin back at him. "I said I would stay till he gets back," he adds.

I reach for his hand, my wonderful best friend is here, and he's ok. He grabs hold of my hand and squeezes it tight. "Thanks," I close my eyes again. "Is Carlos ok?"

"He's fine, he's worried about you but I sent him home, he's knackered. Everyone's been here since it happened." He tells me.

"Wish I was home," I grumble, looking up at him.

"Relax, Tristan's taken care of it. But seriously, what did you expect? Get shot and walk out of the hospital the next day? Honestly, woman, you need to get a grip!"

"Shut up!" I titter. "So what day is it?" I ask.

"Friday. Oh yeah...happy birthday for yesterday! Carlos and I came by with your present last night, but you and Tristan were both sleeping," he says.

"You did?" I say, I instantly feel cheered up.

"Yes, I was going to give it to you today but -" Rob stops himself by slapping his hand to his mouth.

"What?" I chuckle.

"Bollocks!" he hisses.

"Tell me, Rob," I chuckle.

"I can't, it'll spoil the surprise," he says with a guilty look.

"I don't like surprises," I grumble. "Besides, I know there is one now, so spit it out!"

Rob sighs deeply. "Gladys is going to kill me," he moans.

"No, she won't because she won't know I know. Come on Rob, tell me!"

"Well, when we were all here yesterday, with presents I might add, Gladys said we should give them to you when you get home, you know have a little surprise celebration."

I smile up at Rob. "She did?" I squeak.

Rob smiles back at me. "Yep, then Gladys came by this morning and spoke to Tristan, he had a -" Rob slaps his hand to his mouth again.

"What's Tristan up to Rob?" I chuckle.

"Stop asking me, you're going to get me into trouble!" he scolds lightly.

"Ok, but I get the gist of it!" *Hmm, I wonder what Tristan has planned?* Then I remember about Gladys's wedding. "I can't believe Gladys cancelled her wedding," I groan, feeling tears bubbling up again. "I feel so guilty that she has if I hadn't had got shot she would be on her honeymoon by now," I sniff.

"I know," he says squeezing my hand again. "But don't feel guilty about it Coral, you didn't know this was going to happen, and there's not a chance Gladys would have married without you being there!" He smiles and shrugs his shoulders.

"I guess," I grumble suddenly feeling ravenous. "What time is it?" I ask.

"Seven thirty," he chuckles. "Why?"

"I'm hungry," I answer. "Hey, don't you have a client this week?" I ask, wondering why Rob is here, he should be working.

"No, I cancelled it," he tells me.

"Rob' – "My best friend falls in love. Is stalked and broken into, she then quits her job and gets shot by some crazy psycho chick. The last thing I'm going to do is bugger off," he argues.

"Besides, you want Tristan helping you with bathroom breaks and showering while you're like this?" He questions, his head cocked to the side.

Showering – *Yes, absolutely!*

Bathroom breaks – *No, no way!*

"I didn't think so," he says reading my wide eyes. "So, I'm here like it or not."

"'K' fine!" I relent. "Not that you'll need to, Tristan's getting me a nurse," I say a little smugly.

"Posh bastard!" Rob chortles.

"Hey!" I squeak.

"Only kidding!" he laughs. "Now, I woke you up to tell you something very important."

"You have?" I ask.

He solemnly nods his head. *Uh-Oh!* Then a stupid ear to ear grin spreads across his face. "I've found your wedding dress!" he says clapping his hands together in excitement.

Wedding?

"I...I told you about that?" I whisper.

Rob frowns. "Er...no, Tristan did."

"He did?" I say surprised.

"Well...kind of," Rob says, biting his bottom lip.

"What's going on Rob?" I ask, feeling anxious.

Rob debates for a moment. "I guess I *should* tell you," he says, his face falling.

"Tell me what?" I whisper.

"Well...Tristan and I...sort of...well, we had an altercation." He says, guilt written all over his face.

"What!?" I bellow.

"Relax," he coos. "It was just a misunderstanding."

"A misunderstanding?" I question, he nods sheepishly at me. "Tell me everything!" I add.

"There's not really much to tell. I was mad, *he was livid*. We got into an argument about you' – "Me?" I interrupt.

"Yeah," Rob sighs. "I just...at the time, I didn't know he'd been drugged. I was mad that he'd let you..." Rob stops and takes a deep breath. "I thought he'd let you take that bullet and that's not right, that psycho woman would never have come into your life if it wasn't for him, it was his shit, he should have dealt with it." Rob stops short and stares out the window for a while.

"Rob, Tristan coming into my life is the best thing that's ever happened to me, I wouldn't change a thing." I softly say.

"I know," he sighs.

Forever With Him

"So, what happened? Why did you quarrel?"

"Like I said, I was blaming him for what happened to you, I didn't know..." he shakes his head. "I'm sorry I argued with him. Anyway long story short, in his furious rage, he sort of let it slip that well, he'd proposed, that you mean the world to him and, well, to be honest, he was in such a rage, I didn't get everything he said to me."

"Think hard Rob, I want to know." *I can't believe they've argued!*

Rob sighs again. "Um...well, he was angry that you did what you did, and that you didn't tell him or anyone else what was going on. He wished he'd have been able to protect you, he was angry with himself for not believing you - Look Coral, the point is, I didn't know all that, I didn't know you two were that serious. I can't believe you said yes!" he says, staring down at me with wide eyes.

"Oh!" I look up at Rob, my eyes reflecting his worry.

"What's wrong sunshine? Don't you want to marry him anymore?" Rob asks, looking a little worried at my wide-eyed expression.

"Yes, of course, I do. I...I just, with everything that's gone on...I haven't really thought about it," I say feeling shocked then I panic – *What if he's said something?*

"Rob, you haven't told anyone have you?" I ask my mouth going dry.

"No, only Carlos," he softly says.

"Oh, good," I breathe – Then something comes to me...a conversation....? Then I remember it. "Tristan's hiring a wedding planner," I say.

"What!" Rob bellows. "Well you can tell him to cancel it," he scoffs. "Honestly woman! How could you let him do that to me?"

I shrug then regret it, that hurt. "Rob, you buggered off, I couldn't get hold of you. I couldn't talk to you about all the..." I stop and shake my head. *What's the point?* "Do you want to be my wedding planner?" I ask.

"Of course," he snorts, rolling his eyes at me. "Who else would you choose?" he bites.

"No one," I say, smiling up at him, feeling totally relieved. Rob will sort it all, and it will be magical, I know it will. I involuntarily yawn, which hurts like hell – *Ok this 'everything hurts thing' better stop soon!*

"You really are out of it," he says, I nod my head in agreement.

"I think it's the painkillers, I keep falling asleep," I grumble.

Rob leans over to me and kisses my cheek. "Ok, you sleep sunshine. I'll look through more wedding magazines...Oh, we're going to have so much fun!" he says with animated glee, a slight chuckle escapes me – *Ouch, don't laugh Coral!*

I grab hold of him as he turns to sit down. "Rob," I take a deep breath. "Thank you, for everything...for being my best friend, for putting up with me," I stop and sniff. *I'm so glad he's ok.*

"Coral," Rob leans down, so he's inches from me, wide black eyes to sleepy coral blue. He clutches my hand in his again then starts to choke up – *Oh Rob! No, don't cry for me!*

"Don't ever do that to me again," he croaks. "I was so scared. For a moment, when you were down in surgery, I...I thought I would never see you again..." he breaks off and sniffs loudly.

"Now you know how I felt when you disappeared," I retort.

Rob looks guilty for like a nanosecond. "Yes, but I didn't have some lunatic trying to kill me," he argues.

"And I didn't know that she was a lunatic!" I argue back. "I was just as worried about you, you kept me in the dark' – "You kept me in the dark too, and you didn't tell anyone!" he interrupts shouting at me.

"You weren't here! How was I supposed to tell you, Rob?" I shout back.

"True, but you should have told someone," he retorts.

"Rob, we could argue about this all day. We were both wrong, you should have told me what was going on, and I should have told you, we both fucked up! Now can I go back to sleep?" I huff in frustration.

"You're right. And yes you can," he chuckles.

"It's not funny!" I bark, although I can't help the smile that starts to spread across my face.

"Maybe we should call you Wonder Woman?" he laughs.

"Rob!" I chuckle.

"Or one of those female characters from X-Men...I don't know the names," he says shaking his head, tittering away to himself.

"Stop it!" I scold, laughing even harder.

"Or Superwoman?" He adds, really chuckling now.

"Was there ever a Superwoman?" I question, trying not to laugh.

Rob cocks his head to the side. "I have no idea!" he laughs. "Ooh, I have another one. Maybe you should become a private investigator with a badge and a gun!"

"Rob!" I really start laughing now, and it really fucking hurts.

"Yeah, I could see you doing that," he chuckles in a high pitched tone. *He's so funny!*

"But seriously Coral, you jumped in front of him, took a bullet for him? What in god's name possessed you to do such a thing? It's supposed to be the man saving the woman you know, not the other way around!"

My heart instantly sinks to the pit of my stomach as I recall the event. Susannah looking so deranged, the gun in her hand, the very thought of losing Tristan...

"Hey," Rob soothes. "Don't look so worried. I'm sorry I mentioned it, it's just, well, it's the bravest thing I've ever known anyone do," he says.

"Rob, that's just not true," I say.

"Yes it is," he argues. "If anything like that ever happened to me, I hope I have Super-Coral around to protect me." I chuckle at him. "Hey, I just remembered. You're famous!" he squeals with delight.

"What?" I frown up at him.

"You're in The Argus," he tells me, standing up to pick up the local Brighton newspaper. "Wanna hear it?" he questions, I nod my head in reply...

CHAPTER FOUR

Rob smiles down at me and starts reading the article aloud.

"Mr Tristan Freeman, a resident of The Cliff, raised the alarm when an employee he suspected of mental instability arrived at his house on Monday night. Ms Johnson had been an employee of Mr Freeman's for several years but suffered a breakdown when she learned of his relationship with Miss Coral Stevens. According to reports, Ms Johnson had developed a psychotic obsession with Mr Freeman, and her intentions were clear, no one was to have him, but her.

"Once she gained access to the property, she drugged Mr Freeman with the well-known date rape drug, Rohypnol, and forced him to call his lover to the scene. Mr Freeman refused to do so, enraging Ms Johnson, who was armed with a small pistol. Ms Johnson attacked Mr Freeman and waited for Miss Stevens to arrive. We now know that moments before Ms Johnson arrived at Mr Freemans, she had in fact, gone to Miss Steven's studio, located on the Western Concourse at Brighton's Marina Village. Ms Johnson had ransacked Miss Steven's studio and attacked her ninety-three-year-old neighbour, Mr Bob Saunders.

"Miss Stevens was called to the scene, and according to the police officers on duty, she escorted her neighbour to the waiting ambulance, came back to her studio for a moment, then fled the scene. Reports have indicated that Miss Stevens had in fact, gone to Mr Freeman's property on The Cliff, to ensure his safety. Miss Stevens had been suspicious of Ms Johnson's behaviour and wanted to check her lover was safe.

"During her brave rescue of Mr Freeman, Miss Coral Stevens was shot by Ms Johnson just moments before she was apprehended. Ms Johnson was taken into custody and is reported to be staying at East Brighton Community Health Centre for

Psychiatric Evaluation where she will more than likely remain until her trial.

"Mr Freeman is said to have recovered well, while Miss Stevens recovers from her ordeal in the opulent Montefiore's private hospital. We'll bring you more on this breaking story in tomorrow's edition."

Rob chuckles and looks down at me. "What?" he asks, his face falling at my worried expression.

"She...she's still in Brighton?" I ask with wide eyes.

Rob chucks the paper on the floor and grabs my hand. "She can't get anywhere near you Coral. Besides, I'm sure they've got her drugged up to her eyeballs by now!" he snorts.

"Like that's going to help her," I snap.

"Why do you care what happens to her?" Rob quizzes, his head cocked to the side.

"She needs help Rob, not stuffing full of drugs." I intend to speak to Tristan about this. I know what I want to happen.

"Seriously?" he scoffs. "She tried to fucking kill you Coral, why the hell do you care what happens to her?" he barks.

"Rob, her husband, died in Iraq, and then she miscarried their baby. She was so sad about it all that she tried to kill herself, twice. I...I just want her to..." I break off.

Rob shakes his head at me. "You're crazy," he says with wide eyes. "I wouldn't give a fuck what happened to her," he spits.

"Rob, my Mom died in a fucking mental institution. I don't want that to happen to Susannah," I break off, trying to fight back the tears.

"Coral!" Rob gasps squeezing my hand again. "I'm so sorry, that was really insensitive of me."

"No, it wasn't. I understand your point of view, I just' –
"Shh, it's ok. You don't have to explain to me," he softly says.

The door suddenly opens, we both look up at the same time and see Malcolm walk through with Gladys right behind him, his whole body sags with relief when he sees me. Gladys hasn't looked up at me, which I'm glad of, it gives me a second to study her...and she looks terrible. She looks like she's dropped a stone in weight and she's so pale and gaunt, her eyes are all puffy and red, and she has deep, dark rings underneath them; she looks like she's aged ten years!

And for some strange reason, maybe the death of my biological mother, I suddenly realise that Gladys is my mom, she always has been, and always will be. She is everything a good mother should be, and at that moment I know, I feel the fundamental shift – I don't want to call her Gladys anymore.

"Mom!" I choke. Gladys looks up and stares back at me in disbelief.

Oh, mom! – Our eyes reflect one another as we both start crying, I cannot stop the tears from cascading down my cheeks.

"Coral!" she wails and comes rushing over to me, knocking Rob out of the way.

Gladys leans down and tries to hug me as best she can. "I thought I'd lost you," she cries out, gently stroking my cheek.

Rob laughs ay Gladys, steps over to the chair in the corner, sits down, pulls out a magazine and winks at me.

"I know, I'm sorry, but I'm ok mom," I choke out and hug her to me, we both cry some more –*God I love this woman!*

"Mom, I'm ok, don't cry," I say trying to soothe her, so she'll stop crying, which means I'll stop crying!

Gladys sits back up and sniffs several times. "Really mom, you're worrying me, you look terrible," I croak. Her bottom lip starts wobbling again. She lifts her hand to her mouth and chokes back more tears, then she takes a deep, steadying breath and pats my hand.

"Oh darling, it's so good to see you awake," she chokes. "I'm going to go clean myself up." She leans down and kisses my forehead, then scuttles off into the en-suite bathroom.

Malcolm comes over, sits on the edge of the bed, then leans down and kisses my cheek. "Hello Coral." He takes hold of my hand and squeezes it tight between both of his; he looks really upset.

"Hey, Malcolm..." I say, tears falling down my cheeks again. Malcolm picks up the box of tissues pulls several out, and taking me by surprise again, he gently dabs the tears away.

Oh...what a sweet thing to do...

I smile tentatively at him. "Gave us all a fright their Coral," he says smiling gently at me. "How are you holding up?" He softly asks.

"I'm good," I say smiling back at him – *I really do like him.*

"That's good to hear," he says his eyes glistening over – *Oh Malcolm, don't cry for me!*

Gladys comes back into the room, sits on the other side of the bed, and takes my hand in hers. "How are you feeling sweetheart, are you in any pain?" she asks, softly stroking my hand.

"No, they're keeping me pretty doped up," I say taking a

Forever With Him

deep breath and trying not to wince, it doesn't feel too good when I breathe deeply.

"Ok darling," she says.

"Is Bob ok?" I ask, remembering what happened to him.

"Yes dear, he's doing fine. He wanted to come and see you, but I told him to rest for a few more days and get his strength back."

"Good, that's good," I say. I start to choke up again, seeing them both...knowing their wedding could have been and gone. "I'm so sorry, to both of you. Tristan told me you cancelled the wedding, I'm so sorry," I sniff.

"Don't be," they both say. "Darling, it's absolutely fine," Malcolm tries to assure me.

"But you'll have lost the deposit and' – "Coral, get some perspective," Malcolm scolds – I shut the hell up, he doesn't look happy. "You nearly died," he reminds me.

Ok, that sounds like Tristan!

"Getting married has been the last thing on our minds. Seeing you healthy and back on your feet is our main priority now," he adds. *Oh!*

"Oh Coral!" Gladys starts wailing again. Malcolm smiles tenderly at me then rests his hand on Gladys's shoulder, she places her other hand in his and squeezes it tight. I'm so glad they've found each other.

"Are you thirsty darling?" Malcolm asks.

"A little," I reply. Malcolm stands, pours me a small glass of water and passes it to me. "Thanks." I take several sips, Gladys is still crying!

"Mom, you shouldn't be here, you look tired," I tell her. *I don't want her to worry herself to death.*

"I'll be here whenever I want to be," she argues. "Besides, I can't sleep, so it doesn't make any difference anyway," she says, choking up again.

"Mom," I take her hand in mine. "Don't worry, I'm ok. The doctor said I'm doing well and Tristan's here, you know if anything happened he'd call you straight away," I tell her.

"I know," she squeaks, squeezing my hand in hers. "But I...." she drifts off.

"What is it?" I ask.

"When we came by last night, I...I wanted you to wake up so I could talk to you and you were just, so still," she shudders. "Malcolm took us home, and I fell asleep on the sofa...I had this awful nightmare..." She stifles a couple of sobs back.

33

"Oh, mom!" I exclaim. I don't want her hurting.

Her face suddenly looks thunderous – *Uh oh!*

"Why on earth didn't you tell anyone what was going on?" She shouts, getting to her feet. I'm about to answer her, but she continues her tirade. "Tristan explained it all to us, I cannot believe you didn't tell anyone what was going on with *that* woman!" she spits, her eyes nearly popping out, her cheeks going from light pink to bright red.

"Mom, don't say that," I argue.

"Why ever not!" She shouts.

"Darling," Malcolm softly says. "Don't get upset with Coral, we've talked about this," he adds.

"Yes, well..." Gladys huffs, sitting back on the bed. I can tell she really wants to bollock me and Malcolm has told her she can't. *Good!*

"Mom, she was sick, she couldn't help it. She lost her husband and then her baby. I think that would be enough to push most people over the edge." I mumble.

"Coral!" Gladys bellows, jumping up from the bed again, her hands flying in the air – *Oh no! Now I'm in trouble!*

"She tried to kill you, *and* Tristan. When I think of what might have happened...what *could* have happened?" She screeches then slaps her hand over her mouth, trying to stifle the sob from escaping her.

"Mom, I think you should go home," I say, frowning at the floor. I don't need reminding that she could have killed Tristan. I don't need reminding of how scary it all was...*jeez!*

"You want me to leave?" She says, blinking back tears. *Now I feel guilty!*

"No, but you're getting yourself all worked up. Which is making me feel anxious, you need to relax, I'm going to be fine. I didn't know she had a gun, I wouldn't have..." I break off thinking about what I'm saying, and I have to question – Would I have still gone to find Tristan knowing she had a gun? I already know the answer to that one – *Yes, without doubt, I would have.*

"Mom, I love Tristan, and I would do the same thing again, even if I knew she had a gun. I've never loved anyone like I love him, and I would give up my life for his, but isn't that how it's supposed to be when you love someone?" I say.

Gladys is speechless...*well that's a first!*

"Tristan proposed mom," Gladys and Malcolm both gasp. "I said yes. I couldn't imagine spending the rest of my life with anyone else but him. He's everything to me, I love him so much." Gladys starts crying again and turns away to compose herself.

"Congratulations." Malcolm offers and leans down to kiss me again.

"Thanks." I squeak with tears in my eyes. *I guess it's official now!*

"You... you really love him that much Coral?" Gladys finally asks.

"Yes. I do." I can see she looks worried and I can understand her apprehension, Tristan, and I have only known each other for three weeks – well four with the one I've missed.

"Mom, I know I've only known him a short time..." I stop talking because Gladys has a Cheshire cat grin starting to appear on her face. "What?" I chuckle.

"You knew the moment you met him, didn't you?" she questions. I look away not wanting to share. "I knew it," she says. "Love," she adds holding her hand to her heart. "When it hits you, you just have to fall." I smile back at her with a stupid loved up grin on my face. I can't believe I've told her how I feel about Tristan, and that we're getting married, which makes me think of Gladys and her wedding.

"Mom, you have to get the Hilton on the phone." I turn to Malcolm. "Get another date, Malcolm. Maybe they'll have a cancellation? I don't want you putting this off for ages because of what's happened to me." Malcolm makes no move, so I know I have to push. "Malcolm, please..." I beg.

"We are not booking anything until you're better," Gladys tells me firmly. *No!*

"Tristan said I'm coming out today or tomorrow, if I can walk out of here, I can get to the Hilton, sit in a chair and watch you two say 'I do' so there!" I look across at Malcolm again. "Please," I beg again. "I'll be there, I know I will' – "Oh Coral! Don't be so silly, there's no way you're going to be out of here that soon." Gladys chides.

"Yes I will," I scoff. "Look, I have every intention of seeing you two get married, even if I'm only there for a few hours, then go home, you are making another booking today!" I bark. If I could stamp my feet, I would.

"But darling, I don't think we'll get another date," Gladys softly says.

"But you don't know that?" I argue. I turn to Malcolm, cock up one eyebrow and give him a look that says what-are-you-still-standing-here-for!

Malcolm smiles then stands up and takes his mobile out of his pocket. "I'll sort it Coral," he says and walks out the room.

I really hope they can get another date, sooner rather than later.

"Mom, you shouldn't have cancelled it without speaking to me first." I admonish.

"And how was I supposed to do that with you lying here... in this bed...unconscious, so still..." She starts choking up again. *I guess she has a point!*

"Well, let's hope they can get you another date," I say feeling guilty. After a few minutes Malcolm walks back in the room looking downhearted – *Great, no dates left!*

"No luck?" I grumble.

He looks across to Gladys then back to me. Taking a deep breath, he walks over to Gladys, gets down on one knee and takes her hand in his. "We have another date, Ms Stevens?"

Gladys gasps with glee. "Oh, Malcolm!" She cries and falls into his arms.

The biggest smile spreads across my face. I look across at Rob, who rolls his eyes at the whole situation, then throws the Hello magazine on the floor that's been hiding the Wedding magazine he's been secretly reading. He casually flicks a page and winks at me. *Git! I want to know what dress he's found.*

"When?" I ask Malcolm.

"In a month's time," he beams. "They have had a cancellation, just like you said Coral." *I better be back to normal by then!*

"Right, well now that's all sorted. I would like to know the whereabouts of my fiancé?" *I'm missing him so much.*

"He should be here shortly, we've only just had dinner. Tristan said he was going back to his to shower and change." Gladys says. – *Hmm, maybe he's fallen asleep?*

"I made my famous steak and ale pie," she adds rubbing her stomach.

My mouth instantly starts watering. "With puff pastry?" I question.

"Of course darling," Gladys beams.

My face falls. I could really eat that right now – *I'm ravenous!*

"You could have bought me some," I grumble.

"Are you even allowed it?" Malcolm questions.

I cock one eyebrow up at him. "Malcolm, right now I wouldn't care what was put in front of me." I look across at Gladys who is hiding a smile. "What?" I smile back at her.

"Well, when Tristan had dinner, he said he wanted to bring some here for you, so he could surprise you with it." Her eyes glow with love.

"He did?" I swallow hard at the lump that's formed. I miss him so much. I want him here with me now, my wonderful sweet, caring man.

"Yes darling, he did," she softly adds. "He really is a lovely man Coral, I hope..." she breaks off.

"What?" I ask. She looks across at Malcolm, he nods at her, gestures for Rob to follow him and they both leave the room... *Uh-oh!*

CHAPTER FIVE

I BLINK RAPIDLY at her, trying to suppress my anxiety.
"Mom, what's wrong?" I manage to whisper.
"Well, a few things actually darling." She says, coming back over to me and sitting on the edge of the bed – *Great! What have I done now?*
"Ok," I whisper. Gladys takes a deep breath, picks up my hand in both of hers and smiles warmly at me.
"Well, since what happened to you..." She closes her eyes for a second and composes herself. "Well, it's made me re-think a lot of things darling, and one of those things is Malcolm and I moving away, it's made me realise I don't want to' – "Mom, don't change your mind because' – "Hush!" she hisses, instantly silencing me.
"Now, what I mean is it's made me realise how much I really will miss you if I leave, but I'll miss Debbie, Scott & Lily too if I stay here. So Malcolm and I have talked about it, and we've come up with a solution. We are going to buy a place in Spain and one here, and we're going to split our time between the two; we both think it's a better option. I really don't know why we didn't think of it in the first place? We can still see our families and keep our friends here in the UK, and we'll have the time in Spain to make new friends, we're really looking forward to it," she says, smiling broadly. *No way!*
"Really?" I squeak in surprise.
"Yes darling, I love you so very much, and I don't want to miss out on seeing you so happy with Tristan. I want to spend more time with you both, as does Malcolm. He thinks you're lovely Coral, and I know he like Tristan too, thinks he's a fine young man." She says.
"Oh, mom!" I choke back more tears. *They're not leaving!*
"I know you didn't really want me to leave," she says. I look

Forever With Him

down at the bed, hoping she can't see I'm trying to hide the truth. "I know I'm right Coral," she whispers.

I look up at her and shake my head. "I...I just didn't want you to stay because of me," I whisper.

"Because you don't think you're worth it?" she wisely surmises. I go to answer her, but I can't find the right words to say. "Darling, look at me," she says, I lift my head and meet her eyes. "You really are worth it. You deserve love Coral, in every way. From me, Joyce, Malcolm, your sister, Tristan; and I know Rob and Carlos love you very much. Be honest Coral, did you want me to leave?"

"No, I didn't," I admit.

"Why didn't you say so?" She questions.

"Because you looked so happy with Malcolm, I wasn't going to spoil that for you."

"But darling, Malcolm is just a part of my life, not all of it. Don't you understand that?"

"Yes, I do understand that but' – "And that's the other thing I wanted to ask you. How *do* you feel about Malcolm?"

"I think he's great," I say, smiling up at her.

"That's not what I mean Coral." She says shaking her head.

"It isn't?" I question.

"No. You don't like men darling, which is understandable considering your past." I instantly stop breathing. "Which is why it took me so long to introduce him to you, but you seem, well, comfortable with him. Am I right?"

I slowly exhale and nod my head.

"Tell me what you think Coral, I'd love to know?" She says.

I take a deep breath and decide to be brave, let her know how I really feel.

"Well, we haven't known each other very long, but I already feel like...well, like, he's the father figure I never had. When I came over last week and Malcolm came down to the taxi with me, I felt so sad that you were leaving...both of you, but he was so protective of me. And at the barbeque, I watched him with Erin and Ellie, he's so thoughtful and caring towards them both, I just..." I shake my head feeling embarrassed.

"Go on darling." Gladys prompts.

"I know I've met Tristan who I love...so much, but the love that you get from a father is very different, and well, I didn't think I'd ever have that. I always thought you were happy on your own, but having Malcolm be like that with me feels..." I stop for a moment and try to think of the right words to say.

"It feels like the hole that's always been there is being filled, I guess. I have a wonderful mother and sister, but meeting Tristan and then Malcolm...it's like everything's come together at the right time, and I knew if I let them both in, I'd feel fulfilled. I'd be one of the lucky girls that have a real family, a mom, a dad and sister, and the bonus of a loving husband." I take a deep breath and look up at Gladys, she has silent tears streaming down her cheeks – *Mom, stop crying!*

"Mom!" I scold. "Stop it! You're going to start me off again!"

"Oh, I just never knew you felt like that darling." She squeaks.

"Everything happens for a reason." I quote her words back to her.

"Yes, darling." She says patting my hand again, she looks bone tired.

"Mom, please go home, get some rest. Rob's staying with me until Tristan gets back, all I'm going to do is eat, then sleep," I say feeling exhausted.

"Are you sure darling?"

"Absolutely positive," I say brightly. Malcolm knocks on the door. I wave him inside. Rob follows and plonks himself in the chair again.

"Come on Malcolm, take me home. My daughter needs her rest," she says looking so much brighter than before, she leans down and kisses me one last time. "Night darling, sleep well," she adds, hugging me to her.

"Night mom, please get some rest."

"I will," she sniffs.

"And please, don't worry. Give me your word that you won't worry?" I look up her, my eyes pleading.

"No more worrying," she says as she sombrely nods her head. "But I couldn't help it at the time darling! I feel better now I've seen you awake though," she adds, softly stroking my cheek.

Malcolm leans down and gives me a kiss goodbye. "Take care of yourself Coral," he whispers, then smiles and winks at me.

"Don't let her worry Malcolm," I whisper back.

"I won't," he says smiling broadly at me. They both say farewell to Rob, and I wave at them as they walk out the door. "Hey, have you eaten Rob?"

"Yes. Actually, Carlos and I were just at George's for tea." *Holy crap! George and Will, they don't know!*

"Where's my mobile?" I squeak in panic.

Forever With Him

"Tristan has it, why?" Rob answers.

"I need to call George and Will, so I can apologise to them both' – "Coral," Rob chuckles. "They've both been here to see you. The moment Tristan called me I let everyone know."

"Everyone?" I question.

"Yes, Gladys, Joyce, George, actually George was out, so I told Phil, and then I left a message for Will."

I sigh in relief. "Thanks, Rob, you're the best!"

"I know," he answers smugly.

"Yeah, I kind of love you," I say smirking at him.

"Love you too sunshine, now about this dress –" The door swings open, we both look up again and see Tristan walk through the door. I stop breathing. *My gorgeous man – he still looks so tired!* Then I'm hit with his fresh shower smell...*Hmm, Tristan, shower gel, and aftershave all mixed into one. Delicious!* I notice he's changed into jeans and a t-shirt, but his beard is still there.

Rob sighs. "Another time," he says getting up from his seat and shrugging into his jacket. "Behave," he whispers as he kisses my cheek. I stifle a giggle and watch him pick up his magazines. "Tristan, she's a mess," he laughs, teasing him.

"Oi!" I retort, wanting so badly to throw a pillow at him, but I know it'll hurt. "I won't be like this for long Delgado!" I warn.

Rob laughs and shakes his head at me, turning to leave he shakes Tristan's hand. "See you both later," he says.

"See you, Rob, thanks for today," Tristan says. *I guess they're friends again!*

"Anytime," he says. I wave at Rob as he heads out the door, he throws a wink at me then disappears from view.

"Thought you said you weren't leaving here without me?" I tease.

"Yes, well, I didn't plan on leaving, but Gladys is' – "A force of nature," I interrupt, giggling as I do.

"She certainly is, wouldn't take no for an answer. Makes a damn good pie though," he says, placing an empty plate in front of me.

I cross my arms and pout at the plate. "Did you eat my dinner, Tristan?"

"*Your* dinner?" he questions.

"Yes, Gladys said you were bringing some back for me, but all I can see is an empty plate," I say gesturing to it.

"You're grumpy when you're hungry," he states.

"Yeah, I know," I sigh. "I'm sorry, I don't mean to be, it's just all the talking, and I'm just so tired all the time, it's starting to piss me off. All I want to do is eat and sleep, I'm being very boring," I admit.

Tristan starts laughing at me.

"What?" I grumble.

"Ok, I'll stop teasing you," he chuckles.

Leaning down into the bag he brought with him, he re-appears with a round Tupperware box; it's lime green in colour and has two locks on it. Tristan pops the locks and carefully lifts off the lid, and there inside is my steaming pie, with mashed potatoes, broccoli and green beans. My stomach grumbles in appreciation.

Producing a spoon, Tristan starts to plate it all up for me, when he's done he clips the little container back together, leans down and reappears with a knife and fork and another little green container.

"What are those?" I ask.

"Thermal containers, Stuart got them from Argos," he says.

"He did?" I squeak in surprise.

"Yes," Tristan chuckles. He pops the caps on the little container, steam rises as he lifts the lid, I look down and see dark brown, thick, delicious gravy.

Tristan continues. "When he took me to Gladys's, she insisted he come in and eat too, which he did, and when I said about bringing some dinner over for you he said he'd used one of these when he last went camping, so he'd see if he could get hold of one. When he picked me up, we got your dinner into the container, and it's stayed hot while I got ready. Pretty neat don't you think?"

"Definitely," I beam.

"Here." Tristan hands me my knife and fork – they feel heavy, or I feel weak – I'm not sure which?

"Yummy," I exclaim with delight.

"Let it cool a while, these things really work, and I don't want you burning yourself," he says.

"What am I, five?" I retort sarcastically.

"No, I just' – "Tristan, don't treat me like a child," I warn.

"I wasn't – Christ!" He runs a hand through his hair in frustration and closes his eyes for a moment.

"Did you manage to get much sleep?" I ask.

"Yes, I slept with you last night, remember?"

"How could I remember? I was out of it, so please, just

answer my question, because you don't look like you've slept much," I say smartly, watching him.

"I can't sleep," he barks at me, then starts to pace the room.

"Tristan, what's wrong?" I instantly start to worry.

"Nothing, I'm just..." He keeps pacing, looking up at the ceiling.

"Tell me?" I plead. He stops pacing, puts his hands on his hips and stares back at me. I see the broken man again; he looks like he did when I left him. I wince at the memory. "Baby, what's wrong?" I ask and lift my arm, stretching my hand out to him.

"I won't have an argument about this Coral, there's no discussion. It's happening," he snaps, the tension now evident around his eyes.

I drop my arm and frown back at him. "Go on," I say, hoping I'm not going to freak out.

"Stuart's moving in with us," he says.

I cock one eyebrow up. "Why?" I question.

"Coral!" He warns.

"I'm only asking, not disagreeing," I say with my hands in the air.

Jeez, keep your pants on!

"Fine! I won't take the risk of anything like that ever happening again. I want security in the house, and I want it to be Stuart, I trust him, I already asked him, he said yes. End of discussion," he snaps.

"Actually that wasn't a discussion, I was being dictated to," I snap back. "It's not like anything like that *is* ever going to happen again, I think you're being over the top."

"Coral!" He closes his eyes and pinches his nose in frustration. "You nearly fucking died!" he growls menacingly – *Ok Mr Snappy Pants is cranky when he's tired!*

But as I really study him, as I really take him in, I start to notice something else...something he's hiding from me maybe, I don't know? Either way, he looks tense, really tense – *Yep, tense and tired, not a good combination, better not push his buttons.*

"I know I did," I say. "I don't need reminding. But fine, you want Stuart with us, you got it." I say and start tucking into my meal.

Tristan sags with relief, walks back over to me and sits on the edge of the bed. "Thank you," he softly says, then leans down and kisses my temple.

"What's really wrong Tristan?" I ask between mouthfuls.

"Eat!" He snaps.

"I am. What's wrong?" I argue. *Really could do with a glass of vino!*

"Coral' – "Tristan!" I mock tone his voice. "I think we've both learned a valuable lesson here don't you?" I question.

Tristan shakes his head in frustration. "And what lesson is that may I ask?"

"The lesson is that we shouldn't keep anything from each other. If I'd have told you about Susannah from the start, maybe it wouldn't have got into this mess, and it might have been solved some other way?" Tristan's eyes darken with the mention of her name. "Point is, we have to be honest and open with one another. I know something's on your mind, you look tense, I can see it in your face, and I can read you just as well as you can read me," I say feeling quite proud of myself, and to my great surprise, Tristan nods in agreement.

"You're right," he says.

"So?" I push.

"Eat, then I'll talk," he says gazing at the wall.

"I'm done," I say. Tristan cocks his head to the side. "No really baby, I'm done, I think my stomach's shrunk, and that was a huge portion, did Gladys portion it out by any chance?" I see the smile starting to creep around the edges of his eyes.

"Yes, she did," he says losing the grin and pushing the table down the bottom of the bed. "Are you tired?" he asks.

"Tristan..." My bottom lips starts to wobble, giving me away. I suddenly feel very emotional, very tired, and extremely overwhelmed. – *Why? Why do I feel like this?*

Tristan is up on the bed and has me in his arms in a split second.

"Sorry," I sniff. "Why do I keep feeling like this?" I say, weeping into his t-shirt.

"Darling, you've been through a traumatic event, you were shot, your heart stopped, you had major surgery. I'm sure it's very natural to feel overwhelmed by it all," he says kissing my hair.

"It is?"

"Yes."

"Tell me what's worrying you?" I croak.

Tristan sighs heavily. "I don't want to," he answers.

"Why?" I lift my head and look into his wide, worried, beautiful chocolate eyes.

"Because you have enough on your plate," he says.

"Hey, what worries you, worries me too you know.

Everything that affects you affects me. We're supposed to be a team, aren't we? Isn't that what couples are? They share everything?"

Tristan doesn't say anything he just stares down at me.

I shake my head feeling stupid for saying that. "I can't help feeling like that Tristan," I sniff. Suddenly he's wrapping his arms around me as best he can, and pulling me against his chest as he kisses the top of my head.

"Oh Coral," he croaks. "I feel like that too baby," he adds, sounding so exhausted.

"So tell me," I push.

He sits back up and looks down at me. "I can't sleep because...I keep..." he breaks off and looks away from me.

"Tristan," I whisper. "I told you my deepest darkest fears, stuff I've never told anyone. Can't you trust me like that?" I question, softly turning his face, so he has to look at me.

"Yes, of course, I can, it's just..." He takes a deep breath. "I keep having the same nightmare, and it doesn't matter what I do, I can't save you. And every time I dream it, I try to wake up because I know what's going to happen..." He breaks off running a hand through his hair.

"What happens?" I whisper – although I think I know.

"You die," he croaks, his eyes glistening over. *Oh, baby!*

"Tristan!" I pull him into my arms and squeeze him tight.

I get a flashback of my nightmare, the one that had Susannah in it, the nightmare where she stabbed Tristan, and he died, right in front of me. *I wonder if I was having another premonition?* A premonition of what Susannah was prepared to do, kill Tristan or me whether it be a knife, a gun…or some other way?

"Tristan, I'm not going anywhere baby, I give you my word I'll never die on you."

Tristan lays his head on my chest, right under my chin, it hurts, but I'll take the pain to comfort my man. I cradle him in my arms and try to soothe him as he soothes me, by rhythmically running my fingers through his hair, I try to think of a way to help him, but nothing comes to mind.

"Baby," Tristan says, lifting his head to look up at me.

"Yeah?" He looks so lost. I want to take his pain away for him, but I don't know how?

"I forgot to say, we're going home tomorrow." I close my eyes with relief. *Thank god we can get out of here.* "That's awesome baby, thank you," I say, opening my eyes and kissing his full soft lips.

"Yeah, it'll be nice to get back home," he says.

"Yes, it will," I answer agreeing wholeheartedly. "Am I getting a Nurse?"

"Yes, just for a week," he says.

"Ok," I acquiesce. "Did you get a chance to speak to Edith?" I ask, remembering our conversation last Sunday.

"You remembered?" he says sounding a little brighter.

"Yes, did you speak to her?"

Tristan looks up at me with those big brown, soulful eyes of his. "She's already with us baby," he says, looking a little worried.

"She is?" I squeak.

"Yeah...I didn't plan it that way, but after what happened to you..." Tristan shakes his head. "To cut a long story short, I called Edith last Tuesday, and asked her to stay for the short term, so she could see how she likes it. I told her what had happened to you and that I wanted someone I could trust to help me look after you and make sure you're behaving yourself if I have to go to any meetings..." Tristan trails off.

"You know Gladys would have done that," I say.

"I know, but with them leaving' – "Tristan, they're not going now," I say.

"They're not?" he questions.

"No, dividing their time, long story....oh and we have a wedding to go to."

Tristan frowns at me. "Who's?"

"Ours of course," I say teasing him. His mouth pops open in shock. "Joking," I say, laughing at myself then wincing.

"Does it hurt?" he softly asks. I pout and nod. Tristan smirks at me. "Serves you right," he taunts. "I nearly had heart failure," he adds.

"I thought you weren't worried about marrying me?" I squeak out.

"I'm not, at all... I just didn't know what you could have got planned in such a short space of time?"

"Oh!" I say, feeling relieved.

"Yeah, oh!" he mocks. "So who is getting married?"

"Gladys and Malcolm," I say. "The managed to get a cancellation date."

"Oh, ok." He smiles and places his head back on my chest.

As we lay there quietly holding one another, I realise I don't feel sleepy, I feel wide awake, too many thoughts racing through my head. I can't help thinking of what the future holds for us, for me. Life has changed rapidly, and I'm just starting to realise how much of an effect it's going to have on me.

For a start, I have no job. I know I have the money from Gladys and Malcolm, but that's not the point – *What am I going to do?* I can't *not* work that will drive me crazy! Maybe I should just go back to Chester House? Well, when I'm better. *Hmm, something to consider!*

And Tristan – I can't believe I'm going to be living with him! How weird is that? But it's not like I can go back to my studio, not at the moment anyway. I need looking after, and it's either with Tristan or Gladys, and I choose Tristan.

I wonder if Tristan knows what's happened to my studio? I ponder that thought for a moment, which brings up another question. If I decide to stay with Tristan – *Coral, what are you talking about?* I stop myself and think about what I just said... *If I decide to stay with Tristan?...*I already know I'm going to stay with Tristan, in-fact since Susannah shot me, all the fears I had about living with him, marrying him, committing to him, seem to have disappeared.

I'd marry him tomorrow if I could – the sooner, the better. *Whoa! Where did that come from?* I frown at my own thoughts, then shaking them off I try to get back to my studio. What am I going to do with it? Sell it? Keep it and rent it out? *I just don't know.* Which makes me think about Bob. Tristan said he was happy for him to live with us, I hope he says yes, I can't stand the thought of him down there...all on his own, it's just not right!

So if he does say yes, there will be Edith, Bob and Stuart living with us full time – *I don't even want to begin to think about how weird that's going to be!*

Which makes me think of Susannah, who's in a nuthouse, like my mom – *I have to speak to Tristan about it, as soon as we're home.*

I quickly shake off those thoughts and try to think of what else has changed.

Gladys and Malcolm are staying...well sort off – *I'm so happy about that!* And we have their wedding to go to. Then I wonder if Debs is still moving to Spain? I'm not sure I want her to, which makes me think of little Lily. I sigh inwardly. If they do decide to go, there's not much I can do about that...*I will miss them...badly.*

And lastly, My mother – *Oh mom, did you try to save me?*

I decide there, and then I want a grave for her. I want to

bury her properly. I hate her for what she did, falling apart on me like that, but I also love her...so much, she was my mother after all, and she didn't leave – my dad did.

I take a deep breath and clear my head of those thoughts, I could be here forever, which brings me back to Tristan. I think back to the night I told him about Susannah, he was so mad with me, I can't blame him, but I'm not too sure how I feel about him ending it, asking me to leave – *What if he does it again?*

What if I marry him and then do something really stupid and he leaves me? Where will that leave me? – Broken, totally and utterly broken, that's where!

I sigh inwardly...*I guess we have a lot to talk about.*

"Tristan, are you sleepy?" I ask, but I get no answer – *Jeez, that didn't take long!*

Poor Tristan, I hope he doesn't have another bad dream tonight. I've had enough experience to know how awful and how real they can seem. I squeeze him closer to me and revel in the feel of his solid, manly body against mine. I may be in the hospital, a place I would not send my worst enemy for any length of time, but I feel so happy, so content, that I wouldn't change a thing, except to take away Tristan's nightmares. *Hmm... Maybe the answer will come to me?*

With a full belly, and my beautiful man lying next to me, I begin to relax. I concentrate on the sound of Tristan's breathing, and it doesn't take long before I'm drifting off into a peaceful sleep...

CHAPTER SIX

I AM GOING HOME TODAY, which I am delighted about, and I'm in the en-suite bathroom, getting ready. I have cleaned my teeth and washed my face, and I feel so much better for it. Tristan is in the bathroom with me, waiting patiently as usual. I can't believe he's in here with me while I'm peeing! *This is so embarrassing!*

Once I'm done, I place my hand in his, and he helps me to my feet, I shuffle around, press the flush and wash my hands at the sink. *Ugh, look at my hair, greasy mop!*

"Looking forward to going home?" he asks.

"Like you wouldn't believe," I answer dryly.

I've said my goodbyes to Nurse Jenny, who's been great, and Dr Green came around this morning, and after a thorough examination, she reluctantly signed me out – *I will get it out of Tristan why they are so frosty towards one another!*

I have strict instructions to come back in a week and get a checkup with her. I guess that's not so bad. What is bad is that Tristan really has organised a nurse to come and check up on me for the next seven days, *I thought he was joking!* I am not looking forward to that; she might say I have to go back to the hospital.

"How are you feeling?" he asks. He's very serious today, whereas I'm giddy with excitement. *I'm getting out of here!*

"Great," I beam and involuntarily yawn. "And tired," I add knowing I can't hide it from him.

Tristan hands me the towel so I can dry my hands, and stares down at me, his eyes tight and his jaw tense.

"Don't," I say.

"Don't what?"

"Look at me like that," I say. "You don't want me to leave yet, I can see it in your eyes."

Tristan closes his eyes and gently pulls me into his embrace, wrapping his arms around me. "I just want to know you're ok," he says.

"I'll be fine baby," I say, wrapping my arms around his strong, muscular back. "Thank you for your help," I add, trying to pull him out of his brooding.

"You're very welcome," he says, kissing the top of my head. "Come on, let's get you dressed."

Placing my hand in his, I let him lead me back into the room.

I'M SITTING ON the edge of the bed in my horrid, hospital nightgown. Tristan has helped me into my new sweats, and is down on his knees, tying up the laces to my new trainers. He slowly walks around the bed and starts to untie the straps of my nightgown, his hand stills at the top tie, right where my shoulder blade is; and the massive gauze I have strapped across me.

"I'm ok," I say, trying to reassure him.

He says nothing and walks back to the bed, and then he slowly peels off the nightgown. "Ok?" he asks, as he helps me pull my new support vest over my head.

"Yes." I grit my teeth and smile up at him to hide the pain.

"Arms out," he says and pulls the zip-up hoody out of the bag of new clothes that Stuart purchased for me, and carefully helps me into it.

Everything is new, sweats, hoody and trainers. I could give Stu a big kiss for doing this. Although, when he turned up this morning and handed the bag of clothes to Tristan, I did panic for a second. I don't like the thought of him going through my clothes, but I instantly relaxed when I realised it was all new – *I wonder what happened to the clothes I was wearing when I was brought in here?*

Tristan leans forward and zips me up, then takes a step back. "You'll do," he says. He still looks so tired.

"Did you sleep last night?" I softly ask.

His eyes instantly go darker, hooded, trying to hide the truth. "Baby, I don't want you worrying about me," he says.

"Tough!" I bark, frowning back at him. *How can I not worry?*

He leans down and kisses me softly, his tongue gently teasing mine, my brain instantly goes foggy, and my legs go to jelly. *Will his kiss always have this effect on me?*

"What was that for?" I say trying to catch my breath.

Tristan doesn't answer me, he just gazes down at me with

his jaw tense, and his eyes strained. He softly strokes my cheek, and it's at that moment I have an epiphany.

"Tristan, I've got it," I say hoping this could be the solution.

"Got what?" he questions.

"Hypnotherapy," I say smiling up at him. "It might help you with the dream," I add.

Tristan's eyes widen with surprise, he runs his hand across his new beard and slowly starts to nod in agreement. "It's worth a try," he says.

"Do you have my mobile? I could call George and see if he can get you an appointment with Cindy?"

"It's at home baby," he answers numbly.

"Well don't let me forget to call as soon as we get in, ok?"

"Ok." He leans in and kisses me again. "Ready?" he asks.

"I'm more than ready to get out of here," I answer dryly, trying to hide how anxious I'm really feeling. I'm dying to get out of here, and I haven't told Tristan this because he looks tired and stressed enough as it is, but I'm really nervous about going back to the house. I'm afraid I'm going to freak out when I step in the house, or worse still, I won't want to live there anymore – which sucks – because I love that house.

"Arms up," Tristan says pulling me from my reverie.

"What?" I frown up at him.

"Coral, you can barely walk a few steps without being in pain, so please don't be difficult." Without another word, he leans forward and effortlessly lifts me into his arms.

"You are not carrying me out of here!" I scold.

"Yes I am, or we're not leaving," he argues.

"Tristan, please, just let me walk a little, if I get tired or I'm in pain, you can take over. I feel so stiff from lying still for so long, please let me loosen my legs up a little," I plead, he stares down at me with narrowed eyes.

"God you're frustrating," he huffs and carefully, reluctantly, stands me upright, keeping hold of both of my arms.

"Thank you, baby," I whisper. Then taking a deep breath in I stare at the door. *Ok, you can do this!*

I take a step forward, then another and smile up at Tristan trying my best to hide the pain. He's frowning down at me, he doesn't like it, I can tell, but it's tough.

I need to do this!

I keep shuffling forward until we reach the door, Tristan pulls it open for me, and I slowly walk through – *Boy this is going to take a while!*

"Feeling ok?" he asks, closing the door behind him.

I look back and say goodbye to my hospital bed. "Yeah, I'm good," I say, feeling drained already. Tristan readjusts my bag on his shoulder, and we slowly head down the stark white corridors. He doesn't moan about how long it's taking, he's so good and so patient with me.

"How far is it to the car park?" I ask a little breathlessly. My legs are shaking so badly it's really pissing me off – *I hate feeling like this!*

"At this rate, we'll get there by tomorrow morning," he answers dryly.

I stop and look up at him. "Very funny!" I sarcastically say. Tristan smirks at me –Ok, he's finding this funny, so I decide to wind him up about the surprise.

"What shall we do when we get home?" I ask, keeping my eyes straight ahead as we carry on walking.

Tristan instantly stiffens next to me. "What do you want to do?" he tries to answer casually.

"Snuggle up to you," I say turning to look up at him. "Peace and quiet, just me and you. Let's just veg out, get a pizza and watch a movie. What do you think?" I ask trying to hide my smile.

"Um...yeah that sounds good," he says trying to act nonchalant.

"Is that what you want to do?" I ask. *Oh dear, he doesn't know what to say or do.*

"Um...sure," he says, but his cheeks are starting to flush red.

I turn away from him trying to hide my smile, and accidentally catch my foot on a food trolley; it sends a thousand shock waves of pain up my body. *Holy crap!* I instantly freeze and wince in pain, squeezing my eyes shut while I try to control it – *Ouch! Damn it that hurt!*

Tristan wraps his arms around my waist and gently pulls me up against his body. "Enough," he whispers in my ear, and I crumble, all I want is to be in his arms.

I open my eyes and nod at him, I feel knackered, and I only walked a few steps. This is going to drive me crazy, I know it is – I start to cry in frustration.

"Oh, baby!" Tristan lifts me as carefully as he can into his arms. I wrap my arms around his neck, close my eyes and bury my head under his chin, I hate feeling this helpless.

Tristan starts walking, keeping his steps steady. I try to calm myself down and take a deep breath in, his scent invades my senses, knocking me for six – *I wish I could bottle it and carry it around with me.*

"You smell so good," I whisper, softly pecking his neck.

"You do to baby," he says planting a soft kiss on my hair.

"Tristan, I haven't showered in twelve days, so I don't know how you can say that," I grumble.

"You still smell good to me," he says.

I grip him closer to me and try to relax, suddenly Tristan stops walking. I open my eyes, look up and see we have reached the hospital reception – *Wow! It's so bright outside!*

I squint at the sunlight as Tristan walks through the electric doors – *I'm free!* – I glance at Tristan with the biggest grin spread across my face.

"Happy?" he asks, his smile reflecting mine.

"Yes, very," I say and peck him on the lips.

Stuart pulls up in the Jag, hops out, runs around the car and opens the back door for Tristan. "Thanks, Stu," we both say, he smiles and nods at us both.

Tristan slides inside, and gently moves me off his lap and then leaning across me, he clips my seatbelt into place. Stuart gets back in the car, starts the engine, and we head out of the hospital car park. I'm instantly drawn to the song playing on the radio – *Ah, music...how I have missed it!* Maria Callas is singing O Mio Babbino Caro – I love this piece. Gladys has her album; it's so beautiful, I close my eyes and let her amazing voice soothe me.

"You like this piece?" Tristan interrupts.

I open my eyes and look across at him. "Yes, now be quiet," I tease.

He smiles, takes hold of my hand, and we both sit silently until the piece has finished. Stuart must have it on Classic FM because another classical piece I don't know begins, it's good!

"You know, I thought everyone would be here today, to see me leaving," I say, pouting sorrowfully at him.

"Well, Gladys did say she was popping around at some point today," he says, his cheeks flushing.

"Oh!" I purposely put on a sad face.

Tristan squeezes my hand, but as I look out the window and see we are almost home, the fun of winding him up about the surprise instantly dissipates.

"Ok?" he asks, I turn to look at him, trying my best to hide my nerves, but when I smile at Tristan, I see he's just as nervous as me and trying his best to hide it too.

"You're nervous," I whisper. He swallows hard and turns away from me, I squeeze his hand. "Me too," I add.

As Stuart takes the left turn onto The Cliff, I get an instant flashback of hurtling towards the house in Rob's car, not knowing what I would find. I quickly hide my hands from Tristan and clench them into fists. As we reach the open gates, and Stuart gently glides down the driveway, my heart starts to hammer against my chest – *Why am I freaking out about this?* Susannah is gone. Tristan's ok, and so am I.

Stuart pulls to a stop outside the house, switching off the engine he nods to Tristan and exits the car. I decide I am over-reacting, I just need to be brave and get on with it, but as I picture myself going back inside the house, my mouth instantly goes dry, and I start to feel a little nauseous. Gritting my teeth at myself, I take a deep, steadying breath and try to think logically about it all – *Susannah is gone, the house is safe!*

Ok, I just need to get this over with. Taking another deep breath, I unclip my seatbelt and go to open the door, but Tristan's hand stops me.

"Tristan," I grumble – I know what he wants.

"Don't argue, it's happening," he says.

I huff in my seat and cross my arms – *This is ridiculous!*

Tristan quickly exits the car, walks around the back and opens the car door for me. I try to use it as my opportunity to duck under his arm so this isn't about to happen, but Tristan's too fast for me.

He leans down to me with both arms held out, effectively blocking me. "We can do this the easy way, or the hard way. Which will it be Coral?" He says with his head cocked to the side.

I narrow my eyes at him. "This is ridiculous," I huff. "I can walk you know, I'm not an invalid," I add.

"I wouldn't be doing this if you walked out the hospital by yourself, but you didn't, so stop arguing," he says, his voice low. I roll my eyes at him in annoyance, but somewhere, deep down inside, I love that he is this protective and careful with me.

Tristan slides in next to me and takes hold of my hand.

"Coral, I know you want to walk through that door, to prove something to yourself maybe, I don't know, but that's not going to happen, not in a million years. I really had to fight to get you discharged this soon, and it's on the proviso that you get plenty of rest, which means no exertions and no walking about. You heard what the doctor said, take it nice and easy. So, am I driving you back to the hospital, or are we going in?" Tristan's one eyebrow rises as he waits for my answer.

"Fine!" I grumble knowing he's right.

Tristan tries to hide the smirk that appears on his face and holds his arms out again. I wrap my hands around his neck, and he gently lifts me into his lap, then with absolute ease, he exits the car with me in his arms.

"What?" I question, he's lost his grin, and his broody look is back.

"You've lost a lot of weight," he says. I roll my eyes at him. *What does he expect?*

"That's because I was comatose for ten days, what's your excuse?" I question because he's lost weight too.

"My fiancé nearly died," he answers morosely. "Kind of lost my appetite," he adds.

I swallow hard and gaze at him – *Jeez, he really has lost weight. His face looks really thin.*

Tristan stops outside the front door. "Ready?" he asks, I nod and look up at the house.

I get an instant flashback, seeing Tristan tied up and bleeding, I clench my hands into fists, close my eyes and try to push the memory away –*Focus Coral!*

I take a deep breath and pull on my memory of Tristan making love to me in front of the fire, the night he proposed, I'm instantly flooded with a warm homely feeling – *Good, better, keep thinking like that!*

"Hey, ok?" Tristan asks. As I look up at the house again, I have to admit, it does feel strange being back here. I try to smile.

"I need to know you're ok about living here Coral, after what happened' – "Stop," I say placing my finger against his lips. "I love this house, it's beautiful. This is where I want to be Tristan, it already feels like this is *our* home, I don't want to move," I tell him.

"You don't?" he questions, I shake my head at him. "Ok, we stay," he says.

Tristan nods to Stuart, who has been patiently waiting for us and opens the front door.

"Thanks, Stu," Tristan says and walks into the entrance hallway.

I expect to hear the voices of my family and friends shouting surprise, as per Rob's info, but the house is empty, there's not a soul in sight? Tristan walks us into the kitchen and sits me down on the breakfast bar. I turn and see Stuart close the door, then walk over to us with my bag.

"Sir, shall I take this up for you?"

"No, that's fine Stuart, thanks," Tristan answers.

Stuart nods to Tristan and disappears up the stairs. I guess he's gone to his room. *I better remember not to walk around the house naked!*

I look around the huge expanse again, where is everybody? – *Was Rob winding me up?*

"What?' Tristan chuckles, 'you look disappointed," he adds.

"Do I?" I breathe, trying not to give it away that I know.

"Thirsty?" Tristan asks.

"Yeah..." I say.

"Coffee, orange juice or water? What would you like?" he asks.

"Wine would be nice," I answer dryly.

Tristan chuckles at me. "It's ten in the morning Coral!"

"So?" I whine, feeling antsy.

Tristan shakes his head at me. "No, no way. No alcohol until you're off your painkillers," he tells me.

"Fine," I mumble. I look around the kitchen and wrap my arms around myself, this feels so strange. I get another flashback of running around the house trying to find Tristan. I take a deep breath and slowly blow it out. Tristan walks over to me with two Champagne flutes, a bottle of bubbly, and some orange juice.

"I thought you said' – "It's alcohol-free," he beams interrupting me.

"Oh..." I watch him pop the cork with ease and pour a little into each glass, then he tops them both up with a little orange juice. He hands one to me and clinks his glass against mine.

"Welcome home baby," he leans down and gently presses his lips against mine. Desire explodes within me – I grip his hair at the nape with my free hand and kiss him, hard.

"Whoa, whoa!" He puts his glass down and takes a step back, holding his hands up in the air.

I instantly feel rejected, and I hate feeling like that. "How long are you going to keep denying me?" I hiss.

"Not until your better," he snaps, clenching his jaw. But my kiss must have affected him; he's breathing heavier than he was a moment ago and his eyes have dilated.

"Tristan, if we just take it easy' – "No!" he snaps.

I feel tearful and angry again, shaking my head at him, I

glug the drink back in one go, ease myself off the breakfast bar and hobble towards the stairs.

"Baby don't' – "Don't what?" I snap, stopping by the stairs.

Tristan clenches his jaw, walks over to me and grasps my face between his hands. His eyes are wide and dilated; his look intense. *Oh!* – I swallow hard.

"You think I don't want to, well you're wrong. I want you more now than I ever have," he closes his eyes and leans his forehead against mine. "Can't you see that?" he asks.

"No," I sniff.

"Baby, you're in no state to be doing this, what if I unintentionally hurt you?" he says.

"I don't care, I'll take the pain. I just want to feel you, be with you, and you're making me feel like a criminal. If I get it out of my system, I'm more likely to relax...." I swallow hard at the lump that's formed and try to continue. "Tristan the last time I saw you, you asked me to leave, you ended it. Then I find you half dead...tied up...bleeding..." I break off unable to continue.

"I know..." he sighs. "There hasn't been a single day that has passed without me thinking about that, I was stupid and angry and..." He breaks off and looks down at me with a painful, sorrowful look. "If I'd have lost you," he trembles.

"Why did you do that?" I whisper.

"Do what?" He questions, his brows pulling together.

"Tell me to go after we argued about Susannah?" I whisper.

"I will tell you," he says. "I give you my word I will, but not now. Can I show you my surprise first?" He questions.

"Surprise?" I question, frowning up at him.

"Yes." He smiles, his eyes crinkling sweetly at the corners, his dimples deepening. I really want answers, but I guess we have loads of time.

"Ok, fine," I answer mulishly.

He leans down and kisses me softly on the lips. "Don't move," he says. I watch Tristan walk over to his glass, drink it down in one go, and then he makes his way back over to me – *Boy he's sexy!* Even the way he walks, he just does things to me.

"You're so sexy baby," I whisper as he reaches me. He smiles his sweet, shy smile, his cheeks flushing slightly – A plan suddenly forms.

"Tristan, I need a shower, will you wash my hair? I think it will hurt too much if I try?" I say, batting my lashes at him, even though I know I look terrible.

Tristan cocks his head to the side. "Anything for you," he says, running his thumb across my bottom lip – It sends shivers to all the right places. *Maybe my plan will work?*

"But not now baby," he adds lifting me up into his arms. *Damn it!*

"Where are we going?" I ask.

"You'll see," he says and starts heading up the stairs. My heart starts slamming against my chest again, all I can see and remember are my own footsteps running up towards our room... trying to find him – *Fuck!*

"Tristan, please stop!" I squeak in panic.

Tristan stops midway on the stairs to our room. "What is it?" he asks.

"J-just...f-flashbacks," I stutter. I take one look up the stairs to the bedroom door and swallow hard. Last time I was here... Susannah was behind that door...I start to shake all over – *What is this?*

"Tristan, I'm scared," I croak, gripping him more tightly.

"Hey." He tilts me slightly, so I have to look up at him. "You have nothing to be afraid of, I will never, ever let anything like that happen again," he tells me firmly. "Baby, it's going to take some time for us both to get over this, I know that but I'll be right here, I'm not going anywhere," he softly says.

But the fear that rippled through me when I thought I might lose him pumps through my veins again. "I thought she'd k-killed you," I choke out, gripping his neck. "When I walked in the room...and you were so still...." I cut off and softly cry into his neck.

"I know baby," he says, rocking me gently. "But I really want to show you something," he says, adjusting me in his arms.

"I thought I was light?" I tease, sniffing loudly.

Tristan chuckles at me. "You are," he says, kissing my cheek with a soft, chaste kiss. "Far too slender," he adds.

I look up at the bedroom door again. "Ok, let's get this over with," I say gritting my teeth.

"You're so brave," he whispers, kissing my temple and then slowly and steadily, he takes the couple of steps needed and opens the bedroom door. *Oh my god!*

CHAPTER SEVEN

I GASP ALOUD AT what lies before me, the bedroom, our bedroom, has been completely re-designed. I hardly recognise it! All memories of Susannah and what happened that night immediately disappear. I turn to Tristan, my mouth gaping open, as he smiles his boyish shy smile at me.

"When did you?...How did you...?" I stop as I'm choking on my own words.

"Do you like it?" he softly asks.

I look around the room again. Everything has changed. The furniture, the bed, the colours on the wall – I feel like I've just walked into my studio, it's so bright and airy. Gone is the dark wood we'd chosen, there's now white cracked wooden furniture. The chocolate, mocha and cream colour scheme is now bright white and sky-blue, including the new bed covers. Our boat paintings from Hastings are up on the walls with several new items that have been artfully placed around the room, a small white sailing boat, a lighthouse, and a large wooden sailing wheel that's a clock – it looks really great.

There are several bouquets of flowers, making the room smell divine, and lots of balloons saying welcome home, and get well soon, and then I notice several grey fluffy teddy bears from the 'Me To You' range, which I love. Tristan walks us over to the bed and sits us down, right in the middle of the bed is the biggest teddy of all. It's looking very sorry for itself, but that's probably because it has a pink bandage wrapped around its head and written on the little pink cardigan are the words **I Love You, Get Well Soon.** Keeping me tight in his arms, Tristan leans across the bed, picks up the teddy and hands it to me. I hug it to me for a moment and then gaze around the room in awe.

"Do you like it?" Tristan asks again.

"The teddy?" I question hugging it to me again; it's so soft.

Tristan smiles. "Yes...well that and everything else," he adds gesturing around the room.

"I love it," I say. "From you?" I ask turning the teddy towards him.

Tristan nods his shy smile at me. "Yeah..." he chuckles.

"This is beautiful Tristan, the flowers, the balloons...all of it. It's a beautiful welcome home." I lean forward and kiss him, trying not to get too passionate about it, but I can't help myself, we haven't for what feels like so long, and I want him.

"Hey," Tristan says softly, pulling his lips away from mine. "Not until you're feeling better baby," he adds, running a cool soft finger down my cheek. "Please...be good."

"Ok." I relent and look around the room again. "Who did all of this?" I ask in wonder.

"I did, well, I knew what I wanted. Rob did the re-design, I did the flowers, banners, teddy bears and balloons," he says, gazing down at me with his warm, sweet, soulful eyes.

"That's so sweet baby," I say tears pricking my eyes. "But I have to ask why?" I add. Tristan lifts me from his lap, places me on the bed, stands and picks up the box of tissues.

"Why?" he questions, I nod back at him. "Because I didn't want it to look the same as before," he says; walking over to me, and sitting down on the edge of the bed, he hands me the box of tissues. "I didn't want the reminder, and I figured you didn't either. What do you really think?" he asks gazing down at me.

"I...I really, really like it," I squeak, dabbing my eyes with tissues – *God damn tears!*

"Good, I'm glad," he says standing to his feet. "Now, let's get you cleaned up," he adds holding his hand out to me.

"Ok," I squeak, I place my hand in his and slowly stand to my feet.

How I'm supposed to have sex with him considering I can hardly walk, I don't know? But I'm damn well going to give it a good try. We slowly make our way to the bathroom. Tristan closes the door and turns to me with wide, hungry eyes, he wants to too, I can see it – *Good, this might not be so hard after all.* The room suddenly charges with electricity, I can feel the pull from him, but my heart sinks when he starts to shake his head at me.

"It's not going to happen so you may as well give it up," he says in a firm voice. *Damn it!*

I pout back at him, turn around and un-zip my hoody. In my haste to get naked, I pull a little too harshly on the right arm, it sends shooting pains across my shoulder blade and through my right lung – *Holy fuck that hurt!*

My knees hit the floor as I gasp aloud in pain.

"God damn it Coral!" Tristan is instantly at my side, holding me to him. "What can I do?" he asks.

I shake my head at him and wait for the throbbing to ease; when it does, I look up at him feeling guilty. "I think I need your help," I whimper.

"Yes, you do. Now keep still," he snaps.

"I will," I tremble. *There's no way I want that to happen again!*

Without a word, he slowly undresses me. First my hoody, followed by my vest. Then he kneels down and unties my trainers, and gently pulls them off my feet, followed swiftly by my socks. Then he slowly peels my sweats down my legs, using his shoulders for support, I lift my one leg, then the other so Tristan can pull the sweats over my ankles; leaving all my clothes on the floor.

"You should know," he says, standing up straight. "I took the liberty of telling the detective in charge of the case everything that you told me. He has the P.I report your keys and your photograph. He'll be coming to see you tomorrow, I told him you were being discharged then – I figured you wouldn't want to see him today," he adds.

"Ok," I whisper, I'm in too much pain to argue about this.

I suddenly get a flashback.

"Tristan, the CCTV," I say remembering having it installed; it should all be on camera what Susannah did.

"CCTV?" He questions, his eyes darkening.

I nod, feeling guilty. This is something else he doesn't know about, I look down at the tiled floor. "I had it installed in the studio...in-case she entered my property again, there's one in the bedroom and one downstairs. When Susannah broke in..." I take a breath. "It'll be recorded on my laptop." I guiltily look up at him.

Tristan takes in a deep breath and closes his eyes – *Shit!* – I think he's really, really mad.

"Maybe the detective should have it?" I add.

"Yes, he should." He bites – I don't think he's very happy with me.

"I'm sorry Tristan," I whimper, staring down at the floor.

He lifts my chin to look at him. "I can't believe..." He stops for a moment, closes his eyes and takes a deep breath – *Yep, he's definitely angry with me.* When he opens his eyes and looks down at me, I can see his anger has dissipated, fractionally, his eyes a lighter brown. "He should know. I'll call him when we've finished," he adds.

"Is my studio ok?" I ask.

"Coral, right now' – "Tristan, I need to know my stuff isn't being pilfered. Has it been locked up?" Tristan presses his forefinger against my lips to silence me.

"I don't want you worrying about anything like that," he says.

"Well, I am," I muffle.

"Well don't, I have sorted it," he says. I go to ask him why, to question him, but he closes his eyes again. He looks so tired and exhausted; which is exactly how I feel.

"Ok, no more worrying," I say as another sharp pain shoots through me. I hiss and grab hold of his hand; he lets me squeeze him until the pain dies down.

"Ok?" He asks.

"Yeah..." I breathe.

"Stay there." He warns, and I watch him quickly strip out of his t-shirt, jeans, underwear, socks and trainers. *Tristan, what happened to you?*

My mouth unintentionally pops open, I start to shake my head. Standing before me in all his naked glory, I suddenly see how much weight he's really lost – I can see his ribs.

"Jesus Tristan," I whisper in shock. Tears pool in my eyes. I take the couple of steps needed and gently run my fingers across his torso.

"What?" He snaps. *Oh, Tristan!*

I swallow hard. "You...I can see your ribs?" I croak. "Didn't you eat – *at all?*" I question.

He solemnly shakes his head at me. "No. I didn't have any appetite, but I'm sure we'll both put it back on," he says, his eyes hooded again.

"We?" I question. Tristan gently turns me around, so I'm facing the huge mirror above the sinks – *Holy crap!*

I didn't take much notice in the hospital, but my face is sunken, my eyes look hollow, and they have dark rings underneath them; and I look fucking skinny – too skinny, even my boobs look smaller.

"See baby, not just me." He says running his hand across my collarbone, down to my ribs, then sliding over my pelvic bones that are jutting out – *Crap! I look anorexic!*

My bottom lip starts to tremble as I stare at our reflections.

Forever With Him

Catching my eye, Tristan turns me around and softly enfolds me in his arms. He's being so careful, so tender with me; it makes my love for him grow tenfold.

"Don't cry baby, you're safe," he soothes.

"I know, I just hate seeing us like this," I croak.

"We'll get better," he says gently rocking me. "Or look at it this way, we can eat as much junk food as we want over the next week," he chuckles once. I feel it vibrate through me, I really love his laugh.

"True," I chuckle back, still sniffling.

"Come on baby, let's get showered so we can get some food inside you," he says.

"And you," I sniff.

"Yes, and me," he says bending down to kiss me sweetly. "Turn around baby, we can't get this wet," he softly says.

"Ok." I turn my back to Tristan's front. He slowly peels the gauze off that's tightly taped across my shoulder, protecting the stitches. It feels good to get some fresh air on it; it's been itching so badly.

His eyes close for a fraction of a second as he stares down at my shoulder.

"You are one very lucky woman," he whispers darkly, trailing his finger lightly over the wound. "No nerve damage, a small splinter of bone which they managed to remove, she mainly hit muscle, which is why you're so sore..." He closes his eyes and takes a deep, ragged breath, then slowly opens them. "You're going to need physiotherapy," he adds, leaning down to place a soft tender kiss, right where she shot me.

"I know, Dr Green told me," I whisper, staring up at his reflection, trying to get him to make eye contact with me, but he's mesmerised. "Tristan," I whisper. "I'm ok."

"Does it hurt?" He asks, gently running his hand over my shoulder, kissing me there again.

"Not particularly, I just feel bruised, like I've been in a fight," I say.

He sighs heavily and finally looks up at me, then holds out his hand for me to take it. I place my hand in his and slowly turn around, and as I do, I catch my reflection and see my shoulder. There's a small, round mark with several stitches across it, it's red, raised and looks very sore, and several blue bruises are surrounding it, and it's at that moment that I realise, I'm going to be scarred, forever – *Great!*

Tristan slowly leads me over to the shower, opening the

door and stepping inside, he turns the water on, then takes my hand and helps me inside. Closing the door behind us, he checks the temperature, then he takes my hand and places it under the water.

"How's that feel?" He questions.

"Wonderful," I whisper.

Tristan takes hold of each of my hands and wraps them around his waist. Then wrapping his arms around me, he lifts me up, takes a step to the side and places us under the cascade of water. The moment my head is underneath it; I sigh with relief – What is it about showers that makes you miss them so much when you can't have one?

"Nice?" Tristan asks.

"Yeah...really nice," I whisper.

"Is it stinging?" he asks.

"What?"

"Your scar?"

"No Tristan, it's not," I say, even though it is, but I need this, I need to feel clean.

"Jesus!" He hisses, his arms enfolding me closer to him. I rest my head under the crook of his neck and place my cheek against his firm chest. I have missed this, missed us, missed the feel of his arms around me, and the smell of his skin. Then all of a sudden, and to my complete horror, Tristan starts to cry, strange, hoarse sounding manly sobs.

Holy Crap, he's really crying!

I can tell he's trying to fight it; to stop...It breaks my heart all over again. *My baby no!*

"Tristan!" I gasp.

"Don't move," he croaks. "Please baby, just stay here," he says his voice low and hoarse as his body racks with more strange, manly cries.

"Tristan, don't cry for me. I can't stand it, please..." I beg.

"Please baby...just stay here," he manages to choke out.

I relent and squeeze him tighter, even though it's making my shoulder throb with pain. I don't know how long we stay like that, but I hold him tight and let him cry it out, just like I did when he cried about missing his folks. I sigh inwardly. I have to try and look at it from his perspective, how I would feel if it was Tristan coming home after surviving being shot? I know I would cry in relief too – But it hurts, hurts so badly to hear him in pain, suffering, I want to take it away for him.

"I'm sorry," he finally chokes out.

I look up at him, his eyes are red and bloodshot, but he seems to have gotten it out of his system. He looks relieved – almost. He takes my face in his hands, leans down and tenderly kisses me.

"Why Coral? Why did you do that? You should have let her shoot *me*." He says, his eyes searching mine for an explanation.

"Oh Tristan...I love you...so much, and I'm so sorry, sorry for putting us through this, but I couldn't just stand by and watch her hurt you, not you...you're too much of a good man to have anything like that happen to you...I can't lose you, not now, not ever. If Susannah had shot you, you might not have survived...and I don't think you realise that for me, that would have been it, game over...there's no point being alive if you're not here with me' – "Stop," he says, his voice hoarse, his eyes are dark and blazing with fury. "Don't you ever say anything like that again," he growls.

"It's true," I croak, tears pooling in my eyes again. "I can't go on, not without you."

Tristan closes his eyes for a moment when he opens them they are round, wide, and full of fear. It's unnerving. I can see his fear, it's reflected in my eyes, my fear, his fear, the fear of us losing one another. "Let's just make sure nothing like this ever happens again," he says hoarsely. "Honesty, always...we have to talk to one another Coral, no secrets."

"No secrets," I agree.

"Oh, baby...I have missed you," he says, pulling me into his embrace.

"And I you Tristan," I sniff.

He takes in a deep breath, moving my cheek against his chest as he does, and slowly blows it out, then kissing the top of my head he says, "Come on baby, let's get finished up in here so we can eat."

"You're hungry," I mumble into his chest.

"Yes," he sighs. "I think my appetite has come back with a vengeance," he adds. I look up into his dark, weary, fearful eyes and slowly nod. "Turn around baby," he softly says. "Let's get these beautiful locks washed."

I smile and turn my back to him. I hear him pick up the shampoo, squirt some into his hands and begin his slow, meticulous massage...

I AM SAT CROSSED legged in the middle of the bed as Tristan sits behind me, slowly drying my hair. He's very meticulous about it, one strand at a time...*Jeez we'll be here all day at this rate!* But I can't do it myself, so I guess I just have to be patient. I feel warm and cosy, and I'm dressed in another new pair of dark blue sweats, and a light blue long-sleeved t-shirt to go with it – *I am being spoiled!*

Finally, he switches off the hairdryer.

I'm instantly drawn to the song that's playing, Sade's By Your Side, and I wonder for a moment if Tristan is playing it on purpose. If he's trying to tell me this is how he feels – It's certainly how I feel. I already know I'll never leave him now, no matter how hard it gets. I am his, forever.

"All done," he softly says, kissing the back of my head.

"Thank you, baby," I say and turn to kiss him – *Pain!* I wince and turn back around.

"The nurse will be here at twelve," he says, wrapping his arms around me and pulling me back against his chest.

"Good, I'm starting to hurt," I say, relishing the feeling of his arms wrapped around me. In fact, now I've showered and feel lovely and clean; I feel sleepy again.

"Come on sleepyhead, food and back to bed," he says kissing my temple.

"Food and then talking," I tell him.

"Talking?" He questions.

"Yes, we have a lot to talk about Tristan."

"Yes," he agrees. "We do, but food first." I groan and sit forward, Tristan moves, but I stop him by placing my hand on his shoulder. "What?" he says.

"Come here baby," I say.

He cocks his head to the side and scoots towards me, so his one leg is behind me, the other in front then looks up at me with those puppy dog eyes.

"Have I done something wrong?" he questions.

Tristan must have his player on shuffle because the track changes to Biffy Clyro's Many Of Horror. I feel myself choking up again, I swallow hard against the lump that's formed, and then I lean forward and take his face in my hands.

"I want to look at you," I say, swallowing hard again. I start examining the gash on his forehead. I probe softly with my fingers and trace the cut all the way into his hairline – I suddenly feel overwhelmed with rage...*Maybe Susannah can just rot in hell for this!*

"Hey," Tristan says. "Less of that."

"Of what?" I say between gritted teeth, staring at the nasty gash, the few stitches I can see.

"Anger," he softly says, stroking my cheek. "Your breathing has kicked up, and I can see it in your eyes Coral."

I close my eyes in frustration. "I'm sorry," I whisper. "I just...I hate seeing you like this," I add.

"Know the feeling," he retorts lightheartedly.

I open my eyes and stare at his wide eyes, they are sparkling with humour, but it has no effect on me. I feel moody and glum now I've seen his battle wound. I guess a lot's gone on lately, and I just need some time – Time to sit and be still, so I can try and get my head around it all.

"Come on," Tristan says jumping up off the bed. "I want to introduce you to Edith." I watch him walk over to his player, unplug it, and walk back over to me with his hand held out. Reluctantly, I gently scoot off the bed and place my hands in his...

CHAPTER EIGHT

TRISTAN GENTLY PLACES me down on one of the breakfast stools after carrying me down the stairs again – I guess I'm just going to have to put up with being an invalid for a while. Then he walks over to the stereo and reconnects his player. Stereophonics's It Means Nothing starts paying, I bite my lip and hide my smile – I really love this song. *It's freaky how similar our tastes are!*

Tristan walks back over to me. "Back in a sec," he says pecking my lips, then turns and walks down the entrance hall, towards the utility room. "Don't you dare move," he admonishes, as he looks back at me over his shoulder, then he winks and smiles at me.

I can't help the goofy grin that spreads across my face, his answering grin is breathtaking...*Oh Boy!* I place my hand on my chest in an effort to calm my racing heart, moments later, he returns with a woman following him, I take a good look at her.

She's short like me, quite plump, has curly black hair and piercing green eyes, her face is soft and round, and as she walks past Tristan into the bespoke kitchen; I see she looks naturally at home.

"Edith," Tristan says; his grin is infectious. Edith smiles warmly at him as he comes and stands beside me, wrapping his arm around my waist. "I'd like you to meet my future wife, Miss Coral Stevens. Coral, meet Edith."

"Well hello lass," she says. I'm surprised, she has a strong Scottish accent, and I love it. "I won't shake your hand, I don't want to hurt you," she adds. I wonder for a second if that's true, or Tristan's told her about me?

I smile back at her. "Hello Edith, it's really nice to meet you," I say.

"Ah, same here, glad to see you back home," she says

grinning widely at me – I'm already warming to her, she's so nice and cuddly; just like Gladys.

"Thanks," I whisper shyly and look up at Tristan; he's grinning like a fool.

"Now, what would you like to eat?" She asks looking directly at me. "This one looks like skin and bone," she says pointing to Tristan, "So it's a proper man's breakfast for him' – Tristan chuckles at her – 'How about you lass?"

I giggle along with them. "Um...breakfast sound good," I say, not wanting her to go out of her way.

"Now, if you want something lighter, you only have to say," she adds with a school teacher air about her, her hands placed firmly on her hips.

"Ok, but a breakfast sounds good," I say.

"Right you are, go on...off you go, the two of you. I'll bring you a drink...well actually I know Tristan has coffee. What would you like?" she asks.

I like her, she's funny, dominating, like a mother figure who will tell you off, I can see why Tristan hired her straight away.

"Coffee would be great," I say, smiling broadly at her.

"Alright, off you go now and relax; both of you," she says waving her hand at us.

Tristan lifts me up off the breakfast stool, still chortling to himself, takes hold of my hand, and we walk over to the large sofa.

"She's great," I whisper as we both sink down in the corner. Tristan picks up his controller and turns the music down a little just as the track changes to Snow Patrol's Chasing Cars.

"Yeah," he smiles. "She is."

"Kind of like a mother figure who'll scold you if you backchat her," I whisper, still chuckling.

"Yeah...she's done that with me enough times!" He laughs.

"She has?" I say, surprised.

"Yes, well jokingly of course, but she says that kind of thing because she cares," he says, his eyes warm with memories.

"What did she say?" I whisper, not wanting her to overhear us.

"Well, she mainly tells me off about working too hard, and if I don't eat regularly and well... she was the one that got me out and about again after Gran died…" Tristan trails off his cheeks flushing again.

I quickly squeeze his hand. "Hey, don't talk about it baby, I can see it upsets you." I softly say.

"It does but...I want you to know me Coral, inside out," he says, his knuckles skimming my cheek.

"Ok," I whisper, and wait for him to continue.

"Edith was...a tower of strength for me. Maybe there is a little of that mothering instinct that I gravitate towards...I mean I loved my folks, of course, I did, but I don't think it's the same as having your real parents, your biological mother and father raise you, as you well know. I guess what I'm trying to say is she felt like another mother to me. I was in pretty bad shape, not working...moping around the house, grieving of course, but also feeling sorry for myself. Edith kicked my arse into gear, and told me I needed to get up off my backside and out into the world again, no matter how painful it was." Tristan smiles at me and then drifts off for a moment. He's never talked about anything like this before, not how he truly felt, or what he was doing with his life and what he was going through.

He continues. "So I started socialising again, you know charity events, functions...I guess I realised how down I'd become, everything seemed monotonous. Always the same people, the same conversations. I knew then, I needed to take a good look at my life. I guess I hadn't realised how bored and how dreary my life had become. I started looking at going abroad for a while...travelling maybe, but I quickly brushed off the idea. I had responsibilities, companies to run, so I started going back into the office...and then one day I heard through the grapevine that John had died.

"I'd met both John and Joyce on several occasions, they always came across as a happy, respected couple, and they still looked at each other like...I don't know," Tristan laughs at himself, runs his hand through his hair, then continues.

"I can remember being at a function, it was a couple of years ago now, and as I stood there watching them from across the room, I could see how happy they both were. They still looked so into each other and it suddenly became clear to me, that what they had was what was missing in my life, Gran had been saying it for years..." Tristan breaks off again, and takes a few deep breaths.

"So I sent Joyce some flowers, as she did to me when my folks passed on, and then I get a call from her. We talked for quite a while, who better to understand what she was going through. Then a couple of weeks later she invited me down to see her, so I came down to Brighton, and we talked all night." Tristan stops as Edith is coming over to us, tray in hand, she places the tray on the coffee table, smiles at us both and wobbles back into the kitchen.

"Tristan, I didn't know you knew Joyce before...well buying the company?" I whisper, feeling shocked.

He turns and smiles at me. "Yes, we knew each other. I didn't want to tell you though, well not at the time. I was afraid you would think that it was all set up, you know, what happened between us..." I nod my head in agreement. He's right. I would have freaked out about it – *It's spooky how well he knows me!*

Tristan smiles at me, his dimples deep, then continues.

"Joyce told me of the difficult decision she had to make, to stay or leave as John had asked her to do, I offered to help her in any way I could, and it was left like that. A month later I get a call from her asking if I'm interested in branching out...and well, history tells the rest.

"But what I didn't expect for a single second was for you to come walking into my life, with your crazy talk, bad temper and hypnotic eyes. That day we met, I felt like you could see straight through me, right to the heart of me, I was instantly under your spell. That's why I pursued you, I had to know what it was about you that made me feel so good like there was a fire ignited in me and only you could tether the flame. Suddenly, my life became crystal clear, I knew what I wanted, what I needed, and it was you. I think I knew I loved you the moment I met you Coral. You're my lifeline baby, always will be."

"Oh Tristan," I start sniffling again and rest my head on his shoulder, I wrap my arm around his waist to comfort him.

"That's why I keep getting this nagging feeling like I...I just wish I could bring my folks back, just for one moment so they could see how happy you make me." He says, resting his head on mine.

"Tristan," I croak. "Me too, I would have loved to have met them," I add, looking up at him.

He leans forward and softly kisses me. "I know baby. Now, how about a coffee?"

"Yes please," I grin like a fool. Did I ever have a chance at avoiding him? I don't think I did, and I'm glad, look at us now... so happy. Pretty messed up, but very happy.

"Here baby," Tristan passes me a mug, and I take a welcome sip.

"So can I ask you something?" I whisper.

"Anything," he says.

"When I looked you up online and found images of you,

well this is two questions really," I say biting my lip, wondering which to ask first.

"Go on baby, don't be shy," he softly says, stirring his coffee.

"Ok, well, why so many blondes?" I ask, biting my bottom lip again with nerves.

"Blondes?" He questions, his one eyebrow quirking up.

"Yeah, you always seemed to have a Blonde on your arm?" I whisper.

"Did I?"

"Yes."

Tristan shrugs. "Couldn't say, maybe there are more blondes than brunettes working in law?"

"Maybe," I whisper.

"And your other question?" he asks.

"Well...you've kind of answered it actually," I say, feeling shy for some reason.

"I have?"

"Yes."

"And are you going to tell me?" he asks, smiling at me, teasing me. *Oh, screw it!*

"Ok...well I can remember thinking you looked...well I thought you looked miserable and moody – but now I know why" I add dryly.

"Miserable and moody?" He titters, his head cocked to the side.

"Well, you weren't smiling in any of the photos, you looked..." I stop and take a sip of coffee. *Are we really having this conversation?*

"Go on," he chuckles.

I sigh inwardly. "Unhappy...you looked like you wanted to be anywhere but where you were when the photos were taken." I blurt out.

"That's a keen observation, Miss Stevens," he teases. I smile shyly at him. "But you're right, I wasn't a happy chap," he says, taking a sip of his coffee and staring out at the view.

"And what about having a P.A in every office? It's pretty unusual Tristan, most bosses only have one?"

"True, but my P.A's aren't just my P.A's," he says.

I frown at him, my heart sinking to the pit of my stomach. "What do you *mean*?" I say a little breathlessly.

Tristan turns the full glare of his unhappy face on me. "Coral, when are you going to get it into your head that I don't sleep around, and even if I did, it would never be with a member of staff," he barks. I start to grin. He rolls his eyes at me. "Yes... well, except you," he says in frustration.

"So what *do* you mean?" I ask tentatively.

"My P.A's are my eyes and ears of the company. They tell me when cases are won, lost, who's performing and who isn't. They are not interested in anything but the company, no office gossip, no late night partying, they are serving as me when I'm not there, and their wage reflects that. You see, if you had stayed my darling, technically it would have been you running the company – if I was out of office," he adds. *Holy Crap!*

"Well, I'm glad it's not me," I scoff.

"Why not?" He asks lightly.

I laugh sarcastically at him. "Isn't it obvious?"

Tristan frowns at me. "Not to me, but I'm sure whatever ludicrous thing you're about to say will prove me wrong," he says, sighing heavily.

"Well, no one likes me, Tristan. I don't talk to anyone. I avoid the male solicitors like the plague, and as for the other secretaries...well, I know they bitch about me behind my back... but I can't blame them. I'm weird...a freaky fuck up."

"Will you please stop referring to yourself that way!" He snaps, glaring at me.

"Ok!" I squeak. *Jeez, keep your pants on!*

"Seriously Coral, you have got to stop it," he adds, running his hand through his hair. "So you're not very sociable, so what? There are a lot of other people are like that, but I doubt they walk around calling themselves a freak!" He spits.

"Ok, Tristan. I get your point, calm down." I reply.

He shakes his head several times and takes a sip of coffee, right at that moment Edith comes over to us. "Come on you two, brunch is ready. Where would you like to sit?"

"Coral?" Tristan asks, still frowning at me.

"I don't mind," I mumble.

"The table please Edith," Tristan says, taking another sip of his coffee. I watch as Edith sets up the table for us, then walks over to the stairs.

"Stuart!" She shouts at the top of her voice. "Breakfast!" I hear his footsteps come barrelling down the stairs. "You're over there dear," Edith says pointing to the breakfast bar. Stuart pats his taut stomach in appreciation, winks at me and takes a seat.

Tristan helps me to my feet, and I hobble over to the table. He helps me into the seat and brings our coffee's over. My stomach grumbles in appreciation, the smell of bacon and eggs are making me feel ravenous.

"There you go," Edith says placing our meals down. *Oh my god!*

"Wow, thank you, Edith," I say looking up at her in total appreciation, Tristan kisses her on the cheek before taking his seat, she smiles warmly at him.

"You're very welcome, now tuck in...I don't want to see a scrap left on those plates!" I swallow hard. *Is she serious? I can't eat all this!*

I look down at my plate. I have two sausages, two bacon, an egg fried in bread with an extra egg on the side, beans, tomatoes, mushrooms, black pudding, (yuck!) and what I think is bubble and squeak. Edith then comes over with a rack of toast and places some butter and jam beside it, then walks back into the kitchen.

Ok, I think I'm going to burst just looking at it!

"Is she serious?" I whisper to Tristan with wide eyes. He's already eating, typical!

"Just eat what you can," he firmly tells me – *He's still mad about what I said, great!*

I sigh heavily. "Ok," I whisper and pick up my knife and fork.

About ten minutes into the meal, I take my final bite. I'm done, I can't eat anymore. Tristan is still sat next to me, patiently waiting for me. I feel so sleepy now, I can barely keep my eyes open.

"Had enough?" Tristan asks.

I nod sleepily to him.

"Ok baby." He stands, lifts me into his arms and carries me over to the sofa. Then he sits down, with me on his lap, and I instantly fall asleep, cradled in the safety of his warm arms...

TRISTAN GENTLY WAKES me from my snooze. But I still feel so sleepy, so I keep my eyes closed. I can hear his music is still playing, I recognise the song. David Gray's This Years Love – Such a melancholy track, I wonder if this is how Tristan feels?

"Hey," Tristan says, stroking my cheek. "The nurse is here baby."

I force my eyes open. A young woman, maybe my age is standing in front of me in a pale blue uniform. "Hi Coral, I'm Theresa, but everyone calls me Terry," she says, smiling at me.

"Hi." I close my eyes again. "Just do what you need to do," I softly add.

"Alright Coral." Taking my right hand, she taps it several times. "This will sting a little. We're not going to give you an I.V drip, we're just going to place this catheter in your hand and every four hours you'll be given an injection for the pain. We will start weaning you off it though, so it should be out in a week's time," she says.

"Ok," I whisper, barely feeling the needle, but I do feel the pain relief.

"Coral?" She says sounding worried, I feel Tristan stiffen beneath me. She taps my cheek, so I open my eyes. She starts checking me, my eyes and my glands.

"I'm ok," I whisper. "Just really tired," I manage to add.

"I know you are, but I just want to make sure. You've gone very pale." Nurse Terry replies.

"Have I?" I murmur.

"Have you had much to drink today?" she asks shining a light in my eyes.

"Yes," I whisper. "She's had plenty," Tristan adds.

"Good, you need to keep your fluid intake up. Lots of water, ok?"

"Ok," I answer groggily.

"Alright then, I'll be back in a few hours," she says.

"Ok. Bye Terry." And I drift...

I WAKE UP IN our bed. Tristan is lying beside me, fully dressed and softly sleeping. *I wonder what time it is?* Tristan still has his music on, but for once it's a song I don't recognise. I hear a soft tap on the door, and then it's opened slightly.

"Hello?" Edith calls in a soft voice.

"It's ok," I whisper. "Come in." Edith carefully opens the door and tip-toes over to me with a tray in her hand – *Please don't be food!*

"Here you are lass," she whispers, placing the tray on the bedside table next to me. There's two large glasses of water, a pot of tea with milk and sugar and a plate of chocolate biscuits - *I think they're hobnobs?*

"Thank you, Edith, that's very kind of you," I whisper.

"Nonsense," she says patting my hand. "It's what I do." I smile up at her, pick up a glass of water and take several glugs. *Mmm so refreshing!*

Tristan stirs next to me, Edith smiles at me and tip-toes

back out of the room, giving me a cheery wave as she does. I really, really like her; and boy I could get used to this!

"Thirsty!" I hear Tristan croak. I go to lean across so I can pass him some water. "Coral, stop!"

I instantly freeze. "What?" I gasp, looking across at him.

"I'll get it," he says, leaning over me – *Honestly!*

"Tristan, you can't do that. I thought my stitches had split or something!" I scold.

"Oh," he says, looking a little guilty. "Sorry baby, but stretching like that and your stitches *will* split." He sighs heavily. "Coral, imagine you are strapped to that hospital bed, you wouldn't be able to move much would you?"

"Well no, but' – "Ah ah," he says, wagging his finger at me. "You need to act like that baby, you're still healing on the inside. One sudden movement could rip everything open again, which means another operation and more time in the hospital."

"Oh." I frown. "I hadn't thought of it like that."

"Well, will you now, for me?" he asks. His puppy dog eyes are back – *How can I resist?*

I lean down slowly and peck him softly on the lips. "For you, baby I'll do anything," I say. Tristan smiles his shy smile. "Who's this?" I ask.

"The music?" I nod. "Hoobastank, The Reason." He answers.

"It's good," I say as I nod away to the beat.

"Yes, it is," he says finishing off his water, and then he looks across at the tray. "Is that tea and biscuits?" He asks his eyes wide with glee.

"Um...yeah?" I chuckle.

"Brilliant!" He says, sliding over me so he can stuff a chocolate biscuit in his mouth. He rolls his eyes in ecstasy.

"Nice?" I giggle.

"Mmm," he chews, laughing as he does. "So good," he says picking another up. "Want one baby?"

"No," I chuckle. "I'm still stuffed from that breakfast." Tristan smiles and starts to pour us both teas. "Why are you so happy you've got biscuits?" I ask. His face falls – *Shit!*

He finishes pouring the tea, then sits next to me. "I told you, baby, my folks were poor, really poor. I never got any treats, certainly not biscuits...and I love chocolate hobnobs," he adds, taking another bite. *Ah, so they are hobnobs!*

"Did you get...you know, regular meals?" I whisper.

"Christ Coral, they weren't starving me!" He barks.

"I'm sorry, I'm just trying to understand," I say, staring at the water in my glass.

Tristan sighs. "Coral, I had three square meals a day, and always a small supper before bedtime – which is more than you ever had." He adds, softly stroking my cheek.

"I know," I say.

His mood shifts again, his eyes going dark. "Finish your water baby. Would you like some tea?" he asks in a low, demanding voice. *What is his problem?* – I look down at my half empty glass of water, glug the rest back and then pass it to him.

"No, no thanks," I say and turn on my side, facing away from him.

Tristan's been really snappy since we got back, and I'm trying to work out why. I know what I did could have got me killed, but how many times do I need to explain that I would do anything for him, anything to save him.

"Coral, please drink your tea." He softly asks.

"No," I murmur.

"Coral, what's wrong?" He sighs.

"You...being grumpy with me and I don't know why?" I croak.

"Actually, I'm *fucking furious* with you but now is not the time," he says.

"What?" I tremble, slowly sitting up to face him. "Why?" I breathe.

"Coral!" He warns.

"No now Tristan!" I snap.

"Fine!"

"Fine!"

We glare at one another, two angry fools, neither one of us backing down.

"Trust!" He growls, his jaw clenching together.

"Trust?" I bark back.

"Yes, if you had one-inkling of trust for me you would have told me what was going on while I was away." He shouts and then continues. "You would have told me about your late night stalker, about Susannah's behaviour, about her threatening you and her crazy, warped idea about me – Christ Coral we could have avoided all of this, all of it!" He shouts, bouncing to his feet. He starts pacing the room, running his hands through his hair in frustration and then he stops and glares down at me.

"I could have taken you away. We could have gone somewhere... anywhere! And I would have known you were safe and out of harm's way. But you didn't trust me. You didn't even try to tell me any of it. I keep trying to rationalise your reasons for dealing with it the way you did but…" Tristan shakes his head, clenches his jaw, crosses his arms and stares out the window.

Holy crap! I'm gobsmacked, speechless!

"We don't have a chance in hell if you don't tell me what's going on, regardless of my reaction," he adds, his voice low, monotonous.

"Tristan," I squeak, my eyes glistening over.

He glances down at me. "Don't turn on the waterworks," he hisses.

"Do you want me to go?" I sniff.

"No!" He bellows and runs his hands through his hair.

"So you're just mad at me because I didn't tell you what was going on?" I question because my instinct is telling me there's more to this.

"Christ Coral, what do you need, a big neon fucking sign?" He shouts, his arms splayed out to emphasise his point. He's far angrier than I have ever seen him, and I have no idea how to deal with it. I want to run away from him, as would be my usual response to any kind of confrontation, but I doubt I'll even get to the door before he stops me.

"Go away!" I shout.

"What?" He bellows, shocked and puzzled.

"Go away, get out! You're upsetting me, and I don't want to be around you when you're like this – Go, Tristan! Get the fuck out!" I shout.

He glares down at me. His fists clenched at his side, his cheeks flushed and his eyes dark.

"Go downstairs and kick the shit out of your punch bag!" I spit.

"Are you seriously kicking me out?" He hisses.

"Yes, what do you need Tristan, a big neon fucking sign?" I bellow, my eyes wild, my temper getting the best of me. It stings like buggery to shout his words back at him, but I don't need this right now!

"Coral," he says, his hand held out, his face full of apology.

"No." I turn away from him. "I'm serious Tristan, get out. I need to be on my own right now."

"For the love of God!" He hisses and marches out of the room, mumbling to himself as he does. *Well, that's just fucking marvellous!*

I lie back down on the bed and wince in pain – *Shit! I can't lie on my back.* I turn on my side and stare out at the view. I'm so mad I feel like I have steam coming out of my ears, but then the dam breaks and I weep uncontrollably into my pillow...

CHAPTER NINE

AFTER HALF AN hour of constant tears, I decide enough is enough. I get up slowly, my shoulder throbbing painfully, and head to the bathroom to clean up my face. I think I need to do something. Hanging around feeling sorry for myself is not helping. I stare back at myself in the mirror – *Christ, what a mess!*

My eyes are red and puffy, my cheeks shallow, and I realise it's still there, that inner-hate – my reflection still bothers me. I quickly look away and grit my teeth. I gently wash and dry my face, and then I take a deep, steadying breath, take one quick glance at myself, thankfully I look a little better, and head out of the bathroom.

As I stand in the bedroom wondering what to do, I think about going to find Tristan so I can tell him I'm sorry. I didn't mean to shout at him or to speak to him like that, but I can't stand loud voices, arguing, shouting – I had enough of that in my early years.

I realise at that moment that Gladys was the complete opposite. I mean, sure she'd shout at me if I'd done something that upset her, and I did a lot of that in my teens, but in general, she was always calm, and always spoke softly to me, and so has Tristan, well up until this point. *Go find him Coral!* I nod in agreement with myself.

As I head out of the bedroom, I pick up my e-reader just in-case he doesn't want to talk to me, and very slowly head down the stairs, literally one step at a time. The moment I reach the bottom stair I hear it – Eminem's Love The Way You Lie. Firstly, I didn't know Tristan liked Eminem, and secondly, he has it playing downstairs, and it is so loud up here, god knows how loud it is down there.

Jeez! He'll be deaf if he keeps playing it that loud!

As I walk over to the breakfast table and place my e-reader down, I realise someone's in the kitchen and spin around – Edith. I guess it's going to take some getting used to, living with other people. I make my lips smile, but it's off. Edith smiles sorrowfully at me, then quickly looks away and busies herself in the kitchen. *That was awkward!*

I take a deep breath and hobble along the hallway. When I reach the stairs taking me down to Tristan in the Gym, I hesitate. Maybe he wants to be alone? Maybe I shouldn't be the one apologising? After all, he was the one that shouted first. Why couldn't he have just told me that he was feeling that way? I shake my head in anger and stare up at the ceiling, hoping I'll get some divine guidance – *Go down there Coral!*

Ok, ok! I take the first step, and then slowly make my way down the stars. It takes some time in my invalid state, but finally, I reach the bottom, and I tentatively walk along the hallway until I reach the Gym. The door is cracked open, so I peek inside and see Tristan at his punch bag – Boy he looks mad and powerful, and sexy. I'm mesmerised. He has his vest and jogging bottoms on, he even has his boxing gloves on, and he's hitting the bag repeatedly, his jaw clenched as sweat pours off him. *Man, he's fast!*

I wouldn't like to be behind one of those punches, not that he would ever do that to me. I instantly think of him rescuing me from my attackers, the night he proposed. I remember how they both crumpled to the floor when he hit them – I shudder and wrap my arms around myself.

The song changes to 30 Seconds to Mars, The Kill. He stops punching, grabs hold of the bag and rests his forehead on it for a while, I guess he's catching his breath, and then he lifts his head, shaking it slightly, and mimes the words. I know it well, it's what I constantly listened to when Justin and I split. I close my eyes for a moment, hoping and praying Tristan isn't thinking about finishing it with me, that he's just listening to this track because he likes it, that it has nothing to do with me.

I open my eyes and watch him again. He takes a deep breath, steps back and starts kicking the bag, over and over – *God he's fast!* – I suddenly feel like I'm intruding, this is a private moment of his. I take one last lingering look at him and slowly hobble away.

Back in the living room, I pick up my e-reader. I decide to chill out on the sofa but then I think no because Edith is in the open-plan kitchen – *Christ! I just want to be on my own.* I head over to the library, open the door and find Stuart reading a book. *God damn it!*

"Coral." He says looking up at me. "Everything ok?" I frown at him and nod, quickly shutting the door as I do. I sigh inwardly. I guess I'm heading back up the stairs. It feels like it takes forever to get back up to our room, so when I finally make it, I feel exhausted. The moment I reach our bed, I collapse onto it and instantly fall asleep...

"CORAL," TRISTAN'S VOICE rouses me from my slumber. I look up at him with weary eyes. His vest is dripping with sweat, and he has a towel wrapped around his neck. He kneels down next to the bed and smiles apologetically at me. I don't smile back. I'm still hurt by what he said, and as childish as it sounds, even though I went to speak to him, I'm not sure if I should be the one apologising first.

I just don't know. *I feel so confused!*

"Coral' – "Go and shower Tristan," I say, staring down at the bed. His body just looks too good, and it's making me want him, here, now, despite how I feel.

He quickly stands and silently runs a hot, sweaty finger down my cheek. "I'm really sorry I shouted at you," he whispers, then leans down and softly kisses my cheek. "Just so you know, I've called the detective, he'll be here at nine o'clock tomorrow."

"Fine." I must be strong – I must not crumble. Even though all I want to do is wrap my arms around him and kiss him over and over again, and tell him everything's going to be ok. He turns, and slowly walks away with his head held low; reaching the bathroom, he softly closes the door behind him without looking at me. *God damn it!*

HALF AN HOUR later, Tristan finds me curled up in the recliner in the library. Thankfully, Stuart wasn't in here when I decided to try again, which pleased me. It's given me some time to think logically about what I want to say to Tristan. I have the fire on even though it's hot outside, it's warming a cold I feel right in my bones.

"Hey." He says kneeling down next to me.

He smells divine, shower gel, aftershave, and Tristan's potent scent all mixed into one. And for some odd reason he's dressed in a pair of light grey suit trousers, and a cream work shirt, he has the sleeves rolled up to his elbows and the top two buttons open – *He looks gorgeous!*

I put down my e-reader and look across at him. "Are you still mad at me?"

"Yes and no." He says with his brows pulled together.

Ok, here we go, be strong Coral!

I turn away from him and stare at the fire. "Tristan we hardly know each other, not really. So I want you to know, I did what I did because of what you told me about Olivia, and when I found out from her that it was Susannah that split..." I grit my teeth, trying to calm myself and continue. "The point is, you believed Susannah, not Olivia. I was so scared of you doing the same to me, I knew I had to wait, to bide my time...I couldn't risk losing you," I say. "I'm sorry if you think it was about trust because it wasn't, it was about you choosing to believe Susannah over me, and how my fragile self-esteem wouldn't have been able to handle that." I stare back at him with wide eyes.

Tristan stands and then sits in the chair opposite me. "I'm sorry," he says. "I didn't look at it that way, and now I understand why you didn't tell me. And I really am so sorry for shouting at you Coral. Can you forgive me for behaving so badly?"

"Yes Tristan, that's what people do when they love each other, they fight, forgive and make-up. But I have more questions, I want to talk." I demand.

"I know you do baby, but not now," he softly says.

"Why not now?" I huff.

"Because...well let me show you," he says, standing to his feet and offering me his hand.

"No," I say looking away from him. "I want to talk. I don't want to go anywhere."

"But baby' – "I'm mad at you too you know, but I haven't gone off at the deep end," I say tears pooling in my eyes – *Shit! Don't crumble!*

Tristan kneels down next to me and entwines his fingers with mine. "What are you mad about baby?" He softly asks.

"You...you told me you'd tell me and you haven't!" I squeak.

"Tell you what?" He softly asks.

"When I was last here, telling you about Susannah, you were going to walk out on me..." I stop and close my eyes, remembering his words when I begged him not to walk out on me like my Dad did. I remember what he said to me, *'You're already waiting for that to happen anyway.'*

"Why did you do that? Why did you *want* to walk out?

Why didn't you stop me leaving? Why did you tell me to go? What did you do when I left? I was devastated, my fears had come true. I opened up to you, told you everything and you… you just ended it! So don't you dare act all high and mighty and rave on at me about trust, you didn't trust me either!" I bite.

"That's a lot of questions," he says, his lips twitching at the corners.

He finds this funny?

"Jesus Tristan! You're laughing at me?" I bite.

He frowns, instantly losing the grin. "I wouldn't dare," he says, staring down at our fingers. "Everything you have asked me, I will answer but' – "But what Tristan?" I interrupt, feeling frustrated.

"You have guests arriving," he says. "It was supposed to be a surprise." He shakes his head then looks up at me with his puppy dog eyes. "Shall I tell them you're tired and we can do this tomorrow?" he asks.

He's still tense, I hadn't noticed that.

"Tristan, what's really wrong?" I ask, finally relenting and gently stroking his cheek. He stares back at me, judging whether or not to tell me. "Please…tell me," I add.

Tristan subtly shakes his head at me. "Not now," he whispers, swallowing hard.

So there is something else?

"Fine." I sigh inwardly and stare back at him for what feels like a very long time. And as I do, I come to the surprising conclusion, that even though I'm still mad at him, that even though he shouted at me, and has been snappy with me, and that he's basically revealed that he's holding something back from me, I still want him.

I cannot and will not live without this man. So I have to ask the question – What am I waiting for? It's at that very moment that I realise what it is that I want. So I guess I better let him know, but not yet.

"So this surprise," I say my frown deep.

"Yes," he says. "A late birthday celebration coupled with the fact that you are home, so it's a welcome home party too." He softly says.

"Oh," I whisper.

"Shall I ask them to come tomorrow instead?" He asks again.

"No Tristan, let's just get this over with so we can talk."

"Hey, I will answer all of your questions, but I'd rather you be in a better mood for this."

"Well, you shouldn't have shouted at me," I say still feeling sore.

Such conflicting feelings!

"I know, and I'm very sorry about that baby, I didn't handle it very well. But I want you to enjoy this evening which you won't do if you're still pissed at me." *He's right – again!*

I won't enjoy it if I stay mad, and right now I hate that I am still mad, the damn breaks again – *What the hell is wrong with me?*

"Hey," Tristan says wrapping his arms around me. I weep quietly into his neck.

"Why am I feeling like this?" I sniff.

"Baby, you've been through a traumatic event, it's normal to feel up and down."

"It is?" I squeak. I don't get it…I've had worse experiences than this and I was not a blubbering wreck then.

"Yes," he states. "Now come on, I'll take you upstairs so you can get cleaned up."

"Ok." Tristan lifts me up into his arms again, and despite how I feel, I relish the feel of his strong arms encasing me, protecting me.

"You promise we'll talk later?" I ask.

Tristan stops midway on the stairs. "Promise?" He questions. I nod twice. "You don't like that word," he says.

"I know, but it's nicer than 'your word'. And maybe you won't break your promises to me like my Dad did." I quietly say. Tristan leans down and kisses me, my lips part for his tongue, his taste…*Are we about to?* I moan slightly and deepen the kiss.

He stops kissing me, shakes his head slightly and leans his forehead against mine. "No!" he whispers, answering my unspoken question. "And yes, I promise we'll talk later. I won't ever break my promises to you Coral." He swiftly kisses me on the lips and continues up the stairs.

"Oh, and while you're at it, you can tell me why you were so frosty with Dr Green." He stops walking, and goes deathly white – *He looks like he's just seen a ghost!*

"Tristan!" I have stopped breathing. "What is it?" His jaw clenches several times as he glares at the wall. *Why won't he make eye contact with me?*

"Tristan' – "Coral stop!" He barks, marching into the bedroom and setting me down on the bed, he takes a deep breath and crouches down in front of me. "Baby, just for a few hours, can we just forget everything, all the questions we both have and just try to have a good time?" He says, his big eyes pleading – *God damn it!*

"Fine...Ok," I say my hands in the air, then a plan forms. "I promise to be good, enjoy tonight and not ask you any questions, on one condition."

"No!" He snaps, instantly reading my mind.

"But I want you," I say, trying to make my eyes go all puppy dog like Tristan's.

"And I want you, but no!" He is not to be argued with.

"Ok, how about a kiss?" I say as innocently as I can.

Tristan looks up at me, his eyes are wide and bleak. "Oh what you do to me," he says, leaning forward, his hands entwining in my hair, his lips gently meeting mine, a soft moan coming from his throat.

My lips part and our tongues gently and softly tease one another...*oh I have missed this*... I run my fingers through his hair, then take his face in my hands and kiss him more firmly. Tristan pulls away, but I take hold of his shoulders to stop him from moving.

"Kiss me again, like that," I whisper.

He takes my face in his hands, staring intensely at me and we begin all over again...

I HAVE CHANGED into a pair of jeans and a t-shirt, brushed my hair, and put on a little make-up. I could make more of an effort, but in all honesty, I'm bone tired again. Besides, if I get dressed up, I'll spoil the surprise for everyone. Since our very sexy kissing – Tristan really is an excellent kisser – I seem to have calmed down. I feel more balanced, and I don't feel angry anymore, any negativity seems to have magically disappeared.

So, while I was getting ready, I went over what I was thinking about earlier. Firstly, before everyone arrives, I need to tell Tristan that I told Gladys that he proposed to me. *I wonder if he'll be mad about that?*

Secondly, I haven't told him Carlos and Rob's news.

Thirdly, and most importantly, I need to tell Tristan I want to marry him sooner rather than later; so I'm going to need my engagement ring back. I look down at my hands, suddenly realising what's missing...*Shit!* Where's my watch? And more importantly, where's my bracelet that Tristan bought me? *Have I lost it?*

My heart starts hammering against my chest…*No!*

"Ready?" Tristan asks as he walks towards me with his arms open wide. I stare up at him from my seated position on the bed. He instantly registers the panic on my face and bends down in front of me. "What is it?" he softly asks.

"M-my bracelet…I think I've lost it," I whimper.

"No baby, it's in the safe with your watch. We can get them when we go downstairs."

I sag with relief. "Thank god," I whisper.

"You would have been upset if you'd lost it?" He questions.

"Mortified," I answer.

Tristan smiles shyly at me. "You really liked it that much?"

"I love it, and it would have killed me to lose it. Tristan, you picked that particular one for me, and I know you put a lot of thought into it, that's what makes it so special. I will always cherish it," I say, feeling the weight of my words.

"Baby, that is so sweet," he says. I smile shyly at him. "Shall we go?" he asks.

"Before we go down I need to tell you something," I say, patting the bed next to me.

"Ok." Tristan sits next to me on the bed and takes my hand in his.

"Ok, well firstly, when Gladys came to see me, she…" I shake my head and stare out of the window. I feel nervous, so I take a deep breath and continue. "I told her you proposed Tristan." He is silent, so I turn and stare at him. "And I know Rob knows too," I add, cocking one eyebrow up.

His cheeks flush red. "Ah, he told you," he says.

"That you two argued, yes."

"Are you mad I fought with him?"

"No. Surprised though…"

"He really cares about you."

"I know."

"Well, I guess the cats out of the bag…" He muses quietly.

"Are you mad?" I whisper, staring at the floor.

"No, why would I be?" He softly says. *Because we're arguing all the time, and because you've turned into Mr Snappy Pants!*

"Because you seem to be…" I stop and stare up at him, changing my mind on questioning him about it. "When Gladys took me back to hers after the news about my mother, Rob was there when I woke up. I finally found out why they disappeared," I say.

"And?" Tristan prompts.

"Carlos found a lump, they had a biopsy done and went away to wait for the results."

Tristan clutches my hand tighter. "Is he ok?" He softly asks.

"Yes, thank god…he is. Rob told me it was benign. Oh… and they're adopting a baby from China – Carlos has always wanted a family," I add.

Tristan frowns at the last part. "That's good baby," he says, but he seems miles away.

"Yeah…I haven't really seen him since Rob told me." I add.

Tristan smiles at me, but it doesn't reach his eyes; he's being very quiet again.

"And there's one more thing…" I say feeling really nervous. "I know we have a lot to talk about, and we seem to be arguing…a lot, but my feelings haven't changed Tristan. I love you, more now than ever before, it feels stronger for some reason…" I take a deep breath and slowly blow it out. "Did you hire the Wedding Planner?" I ask.

"No, I didn't really have the time as all hell broke loose," he answers dryly.

I nod and stare at my twisted fingers. *Come on Coral, be brave!*

"What is it?" he asks.

"I want to marry you, Tristan, like today if I could," I say, laughing nervously.

"Really?" He says, his eyebrows raised in surprise.

"Yes."

"Why?"

"I don't know," I whisper, shrugging, then wincing in pain – *Shouldn't have done that!*

"You don't know?" He questions.

"I just want my life to start with you. I want to be your wife, and I want to call you my husband."

Tristan stares down at the floor for a moment. "And the honeymoon?" He asks.

Honeymoon? I hadn't thought of that.

"We can do that when I'm better," I say, Tristan looks a little shocked and confused. "Ok, I'll be honest," I say cringing slightly.

Tristan instantly tenses up beside me. "Honest?" He whispers.

"Yes," I murmur.

"Ok," he says, shifting slightly.

"When you left to go back up north…and I had a whole

week to think about things…" I run my hand through my hair. "Tristan, I was bricking it, I mean really, really, bricking it. I just couldn't see how two people, who hardly know each other, could seem so right for each other…so quickly. I was going to talk to you about it when you got back, hold off the wedding for a while, move in together, get to know one another more… but then…" I take a deep breath. "When Susannah shot me, all I could think was that I saved you and that you would live. I wanted that more than anything else, I couldn't let her harm you, you're too good a person, and you do so much good," I say.

Tristan frowns at me. "I do good?" He questions.

I nod once. "Joyce told Gladys, Gladys told me," I explain.

"Told you what?" He asks.

"Well, I already knew you like to help others with affordable housing, but I didn't know how many other charities you contribute to, so how could I, a person who hasn't done anything good for anyone else, how can my life be saved and yours ended? It just didn't seem right." I take another deep breath. *This is hard to say!*

"That's why I did what I did, why you had to come first. But since being back here, in this house, with so many happy memories of us…of all we've been through so far…I guess it's my way of saying I'm ready and I don't want to look back. Plus, my over-active imagination will start giving me all the reasons why I shouldn't, when deep down inside I really want to." I take another deep breath.

"Tristan, I want you…I'll always want you, forever. Will you marry me in two weeks?"

"Two weeks?" He repeats, blinking rapidly at me.

"Yes." I firmly state. "I've thought about it a lot, you know, what kind of wedding I want, and I've realised I don't want anything big, in fact, this house is perfect for the occasion."

"Here?" He gasps and then swallows hard.

"Yes, and I want to ask Rob to be the Wedding Planner," I add.

His mouth pops open several times as he tries to find his words. It feels like I wait an eternity for him to say something. "You think your life is more important than mine?" He questions fiercely. *Oh, of all the things to say!*

"Yes!" I sigh. "Jesus Tristan is that the only thing you want to say, after everything I just told you?"

He shakes his head in horror. "How can you think that?" He gripes, disgusted.

I grit my teeth and try to reign in my escalating temper. "Tristan…please…" I whisper.

"Please what?" He asks, collapsing onto the bed, so he's staring up at the ceiling. "I don't know what else you want me to say Coral. You've just admitted to wanting to call the wedding off, to believing that your life is more important than mine and that now you want to get the wedding done and out of the way before you change your mind." *Shit! No, that's not how I meant it.*

I carefully move and kneel next to him. "That's not how I meant it," I say looking down at him.

"Then how did you mean it?" He questions.

I take a deep breath and place my hand over his heart.

"Tristan, I don't think you quite understand. I have spent my whole life believing that my destiny was set in stone and that I would die a lonely old lady. I knew I would never be able to have what other people have; it just wasn't possible for me. Never, in a million years, did I think anyone could change that for me, but *you* have. So I've had to do a lot of re-adjusting on my part, in my head and in my heart, re-examining my beliefs…" I take a breath. "I'm sorry Tristan, but we both agreed on being open and honest with one another, I've just done that, and you're pissed off about it?" I add.

"I'm not pissed that you've been honest," he retorts.

"You're not?" I question.

He shakes his head from side to side. *Oh, fuck this!*

Gently straddling him, I lean forward, place my head on his chest and try to hold him. "I am sorry that I had doubts and I didn't tell you, but please believe me when I tell you they are gone. I've never believed or wanted anything or anyone so badly before, not even my wish for a family when I was a kid. This… you and me…beats that hands down."

He slowly snakes his arms around me. "I still can't believe you think your life is more important than mine," he says kissing the top of my head.

"Well, I do, so tough!" I tease.

"That's ridiculous!" He scolds.

"Not to me," I say, squeezing him tighter.

He sighs heavily, and I silently wait for him to say something. "So…you wanted to wait to marry me, but now you don't?" He clarifies.

"Yes," I whisper.

"You're very confusing sometimes," he says.

"I know," I say, frowning at his accuracy.

Forever With Him

"You really want to be my wife?" He asks.

"More than ever," I whisper closing my eyes. "So I'll be needing my engagement ring back please," I add.

Tristan sighs heavily. "You really thought you wouldn't ever find anyone?" He asks.

"Never," I whisper. "I thought I was too fucked up."

"Coral," He takes my face in his hands, staring intensely at me. "You are not fucked up," he breathes and gently kisses me. Then carefully, he turns on his side, so we are face to face. "Why are you doing this? Are you scared you'll change your mind?" He softly asks.

"No. I want you Tristan, only you. I…I want to give you my whole heart. I want to have a life with you and build lots of happy memories and fill up photo albums. I want to tie myself to you in every way a person can, starting with a wedding."

"Don't you want to wait until you're better?"

"Tristan, I've been waiting my whole life for you, I just want it to start."

He gasps, briefly closes his eyes then leans down and softly kisses me. "Then marry you I shall in two-weeks-time in this house," he says, running a cool, soft finger down my cheek.

"Oh Tristan…I'm sorry," I choke. "I made a mess trying to figure everything out, but I know now, I'm just as sure about us as you were from the beginning, and I can't wait to marry you, lover."

"Lover?" He grins.

"Yeah…" I frown. "Just because we will be married doesn't mean we can't be lovers," I say feeling shy. "I know how lucky I am to be with you like I've said already, you're a real catch. You're smart, kind, funny and spontaneous, handsome and sexy…need I go on?" I question.

A grin starts to form across his beautiful face. I can't help grinning back like a fool.

"But we still have a lot to talk about," I add.

"I know," he breathes, and I can see it again in his eyes, something painful that he's holding back, but I decide not to push. For the moment, we both seem happier, so I'll keep my mouth shut.

"Shall we?" I say giving him my hand, he gently kisses it then stands and holds his arms out again. I roll my eyes at him, get to my feet and place my hands around his neck. Tristan lifts me into his arms, kisses me swiftly on the cheek, and we head down the stairs.

"You look nice," I whisper.

"Yeah?" He smiles his boyish smile, his dimples are soft.

"Yes, very sexy and you smell divine," I add, pecking his neck.

"Why thank you," he beams. Reaching the bottom stair, Tristan grins and places me down on the floor. "Look," he says pointing at the great room.

I turn my head and stop breathing. *Holy crap!*

The kitchen and living area have been decorated for the occasion. Hanging up are banners are saying 'Happy Birthday' and 'Get Well Soon' and there's balloons, party poppers, twinkly lights, and lots of soft glowing Chinese lanterns. Coldplay's Paradise is playing in the background – *Excellent choice Tristan!*

As I look into the kitchen, I see Edith is busy cooking up a storm, and Stuart is busy setting up champagne flutes on the breakfast bar; he turns and smiles at me then continues.

"Happy?" Tristan asks beaming at my shocked expression.

"Did you do all this?" I squeak.

"We all did," he says.

"But I thought this was supposed to be a surprise?"

"Changed my mind," he says, gazing down at me.

"Tristan!" I suddenly feel really guilty. We've been fighting with each other, yet he's done all of this…for me. Tears pool in my eyes again – *Crap! My makeup!*

"Hey." He pulls me into his arms. I rest my head against his chest.

"Sorry," I sniff. "I'm just so overwhelmed, thank you, Tristan." I lean up onto my tiptoes and kiss his cheek.

"Come on," he says taking me by the hand and leading me over to the sofa. "Take a seat baby." I carefully do so. "Would you like a drink?"

"Alcohol?" I tease.

"No baby," he softly says, kneeling in front of me. "Please, just until you're off your painkillers?"

"Ok," I relent.

"Back in a second," he says.

I watch him walk over to the kitchen, and pour two more bucks fizz with the alcohol-free champagne from earlier.

CHAPTER TEN

AS TRISTAN REACHES me, he hands me a glass, leans down, and softly kisses me. "Happy belated birthday," he says as he clinks his glass against mine.

"Thanks," I whisper. We both take a welcome sip. *Hmm, not bad considering there's no alcohol!* – "Aren't you drinking?" I add.

"If you can't drink, then I'm not drinking either," he says, sitting next to me.

"Oh." My heart swells with love for him again.

"Cheers," he says holding up his glass.

"Cheers." We clink glasses again, and both take a drink. "What's Edith cooking?" I ask; she seems very busy in the kitchen.

"I think its spicy buffalo wings – for the party," he adds.

"Smells divine," I say. "Do you think she needs some help?"

"No," he snaps, I turn and frown at him. "You're not going in there," he says.

"Fine!" I grumble. I'm sure moving around is better than getting stiff from being still so much.

"Coral, do you have any idea of my feelings for you?" He softly says, his voice trembling slightly.

I look up at him with wide eyes. "Yes, because it's exactly how I feel for you," I answer petulantly.

Tristan closes his eyes in frustration. "I'm sorry I'm snapping all the time, I just…" He runs a hand through his hair. "I don't want you in the kitchen, *hell* I don't want you doing anything at the moment. I want you to heal and get better…" He trails off and takes a big swig of bucks fizz.

"I know," I whisper, feeling guilty. *Why can't I just be happy with other people looking after me?*

Tristan turns and gazes at me. "Forgive me?" he whispers, I

nod feeling tearful again. "I'm sorry baby, I care about you more than you will ever know, and I know your character Coral. You're a stubborn, headstrong girl, and I feel that unless I'm firm with you, you'll do something daft like cooking, or cleaning or…" he shakes his head slightly, then continues. 'You shouldn't even be here, you should be in the hospital," he ends in a whisper and stares down at the floor. I think he's regretting getting me out of there.

"I'm sorry too," I manage to squeak out. "I'll be more careful, I promise. The last thing I want is to go back in there," I add.

Tristan turns and smiles at me, but I can tell it's forced. He reaches up and gently strokes my cheek. "I want to give you your birthday present now before everyone arrives. Is that ok?" He asks.

"Are you kidding me?" I squeak, my mouth popping open.

"What?" He softly asks, registering the look of shock on my face.

"When the hell did you manage to get me a present Tristan? With everything that's gone on…." I shake my head. "Are you secretly a super-hero or something?" I add, smirking at him.

Tristan smiles at me. "Actually, I got it a couple of weeks ago," he says smugly.

"Oh!" My face falls. "Sorry," I smile shyly at him.

"Don't be," he chuckles. "Back in a second," he says and strolls off to his office.

I can't believe I have a birthday present from him. I shake my head in wonder. Tristan quickly re-appears with a small flat box in his hand. My heart starts rapidly beating against my chest – *Ok, deep breaths Coral!*

Sitting next to me, he takes my hand in his, and in his most sexy, croaky voice he whispers, "Happy birthday darling." Then he leans forward and kisses me so softly and so sweetly, that I feel my bones liquefy.

I stop breathing. I want him, so badly. *Breathe Coral, breathe!*

"Coral?" His lips freeze against mine then he slowly pulls back, assessing me. "Are you alright?" he asks, his eyes searching mine for an answer.

I take a ragged breath, as a nervous giggle burst from within me. "I told you, Tristan, you have no idea of the effect you have on me," I manage to say.

He smiles his most dazzling smile, and carefully places the small box in my hand. It's deep red and brushed velvet, so I'm guessing a jewellery box – but I could be wrong. I swallow hard, my mouth going dry and run my hand over the top of it.

"Thank you," I whisper.

"You haven't even seen it yet," he says smiling broadly. "Open it," he adds excitedly.

"Ok," I say, laughing nervously. I slowly lift the lid, and there staring back at me is the most beautiful heart shaped antique silver locket necklace. *Oh wow!*

"Tristan," I choke. "It's beautiful…" I stop, unable to articulate anymore.

Tristan smiles and then lifts the locket out of the box. It's small, a perfect size, and has a beautiful filigree pattern on it. "Look," he says excitedly and opens the clasp.

And there staring back at me is one of the photos we had taken in Hastings of the two of us, but it's minuscule in size, it fits perfectly inside the locket. Closing the locket, he turns it over in my hand, there's an inscription engraved on the back. It's small though, so I have to bring it closer to read it…

You have my heart, keep it safe.
Tristan x

I choke back more tears. "Oh, Tristan…" I sniff. "It's so beautiful…and so sweet." I wrap my arms around him and squeeze as tightly as I can manage without pain. *What did I ever do to deserve such a thoughtful, loving man?*

"Hey now," he soothes, rocking me gently.

"I'm sorry," I croak.

"Don't be," he softly says, kissing the top of my head. "I take it you like it," he chuckles.

"Yes," I whisper craning my head back to look up at him. "It's magical." I lean up and softly kiss him.

"Magical?" He questions. I nod once, smiling shyly at him. "Ok, it's magical," he says. Then taking the necklace, he unclips the clasp and places it around my neck. "There, a perfect fit," he says proudly.

I look down at the locket laying on my t-shirt and start to laugh.

"What?" he chuckles.

"Doesn't exactly go with a t-shirt," I titter.

"Does it matter?" he asks.

"No," I shake my head. "It doesn't." I place the locket in my hand, bring it up to my lips and kiss it. *Wow, I'm still gobsmacked!*

"Here baby." Taking my right wrist, he clips my bracelet into place, then my watch on my left wrist.

"Thank you." We grin like fools in love at one another, I lean forward to kiss him, but I'm halted by a loud ping-pong echoing through the hallway. *There's a doorbell?*

"I guess they're here," Tristan says, grinning widely.

Stuart is straight up, walking the length of the hallway and opening the door to the first of our guests. Rob and Carlos bound in, their hands ladled with presents, balloons, and flowers; and to my great surprise, George and Phil are following them. Tristan and I stand ready to greet everyone, I notice Stuart shuts the door and stays there, scanning?

Rob comes bounding over to me with a ridiculous grin on his face. "Surprise!" He screeches and bursts out laughing, which starts me off.

Tristan walks over to him, halting him he shakes his hand, then shakes Carlos's, and they exchange a brief conversation. Then Tristan makes a beeline for George; they shake hands and start what looks like a deep, serious discussion. *I hope it's not about me.*

"Rob!" I beam, walking too quickly towards him and gasping because it hurts.

"Whoa!" Rob quickly makes up the distance and grabs my upper arms. "Take it easy," he says.

"Missed you," I whisper. I hug him, he carefully hugs me back then chuckles some more.

"How are you feeling?" He asks, pulling out of the embrace.

"Good, sore," I say. "Listen, while I've got you I need to tell you something."

"Ooh, gossip!" Rob laughs.

I roll my eyes at him. "I want you to be my Wedding Planner," I whisper.

"I thought we'd already established that?" He whispers back. "And why are we whispering?" *We did, I don't remember that?*

"You have two weeks." I challenge.

"Two weeks for what?" He asks and then his face falls as the penny drops. "No way!" He hisses. "That is not enough time, and you'll never get a venue booked in that timescale," he adds.

"Rob, I want it here. Tristan agrees. Look I don't want anything fancy, just something sweet and intimate. Do you think we'll get a priest person, you know…what are they called, Ministers or something?" I say, waving my hand in the air.

"So we are looking at a civil ceremony here?" he says. I nod once. "Well we better get a move on," he adds.

"Why?" I ask, frowning.

"Because you can't get married somewhere that isn't registered as a licensed venue." *How does he know this?*

"Oh!" My face falls, my heart sinking.

"Relax, I can get it sorted. But we also need to see if we can get a registrar that's available too."

My heart sinks even further, this may not happen as quickly as I thought. "Ok," I mumble.

Rob carefully wraps his arm around me. "Hey, don't sweat it, I'll get right on it, ok?"

I look up into the dark eyes of my very best friend and smile, feeling relieved. "Alright, it's now in your capable hands. I'm going to talk to Carlos now, but keep it under wraps what I said ok?"

Rob rolls his eyes at me, kisses my cheek and walks towards Tristan and George. "Where's the booze, Tristan?" He shouts.

Laughing and shaking my head at him, I turn and see Carlos placing presents on the kitchen table. I haven't really seen him properly, talked to him…since the news that Rob gave me. I dash over to him and wrap my arms around him, even though it hurts.

"Carlos!" I gush. "I haven't had a chance to talk to you," I whisper, choking up again.

"Hey now sunshine," he says, gently hugging me. "I'm so glad you're ok," he whispers.

"With you too," I say, and then I pull back, place my hands around his shoulders, and look him square in the eyes. "Are they really sure, you have the all clear?"

"Yes," he beams. I can see the relief in his eyes.

I take a deep breath. "Oh Carlos, you both had me so worried," I whisper.

"I know, Rob told me and knowing what you're like, in hindsight, we should have just told you," he says.

"Yes, you should have. But I guess it's in the past. I'm just so happy you're ok," I beam.

"Same here…with you," he says, his eyes glistening over, we hug fiercely and kiss each other on the cheek.

Rob appears with two champagne flutes and goes to hand one to me.

"Can't," I say.

"I know," he chuckles. "They're for us," he teases, handing my one to Carlos.

I laugh at his teasing ways. "Git!" I really want to playfully punch his arm, but I know that will hurt.

Rob chuckles at me, waltzes over to my glass and hands it to me and then he holds his glass up in the air. "To new beginnings," he says.

Carlos and I clink his glass. "To new beginnings," we both say then giggle. "I better go say hello to George and Phil," I add.

"It's good to see you," Carlos says.

"You too Carlos," I smile.

"Hey, what about me?" Rob jokes, Carlos and I chuckle at him.

"Take a look around you guys, this place is huge," I offer.

"I've already seen it," Rob jokes.

Oh yeah, he helped Tristan with the re-design of the bedroom! I turn back around and walk over to him and taking his hand in mine, I look up at him. "Thank you, Rob, for the re-design…in the bedroom…I really appreciate it," I say, trying not to cry.

Rob rolls his eyes at me. "Coral, you don't need to thank me. Now stop blubbering and go say hello to everyone!" He orders.

"Ok!" I say, laughing and choking back tears, and as I turn to walk over to George and Phil, I notice Tristan has already poured them both drinks, and he's still deep in discussion with George.

I kiss and awkwardly hug Phil. "Happy belated birthday," he says.

"Thanks," I squeak. *This is overwhelming.*

"How are you feeling?" he asks.

"Good, you know, a bit bruised, how are you?"

"Oh fine, I bought you some Moules Mariniere," he says, tapping a large Tupperware container.

"Really?" I beam.

"Yes," he smiles. "I figured you wouldn't be in any state to cook, so I made it for you." He cocks his head towards Edith. "Not that I needed to," he adds whispering.

"She's Tristan's housekeeper," I whisper back. "Edith's been with him forever, she's really nice." I quickly add.

"It's alright for some," he scoffs. "Better go put your present with the others," he adds.

Presents? *Crap, I hope I don't have to open them in front of everyone!*

"Phil, you didn't have to' – "Nonsense," he says interrupting me. "I'll see you in a bit ok, and we can talk men," he beams.

I chuckle as I watch him walk over to Rob and Carlos. Then taking a deep breath, I turn to face George. Tristan glances up and places his hand on George's shoulder. "Another time," he says.

George nods his head. "Yes, I think so. It's been a pleasure to meet you, Tristan."

"You too," Tristan says, they shake hands. Tristan walks over to me, gently plants a kiss on my forehead and then heads over to our other guests.

"Dear girl," George says with his arms open wide, his soft, wistful smile makes me crumble again.

"Oh, George!" I croak. I haven't seen him in so long, and he's talked to Tristan about my past, and so much has happened…so much I need to talk to him about. Tears spill down my cheeks – *Maybe this party wasn't such a good idea?*

"There now," George says gently folding me in his arms. "We'll talk soon," he whispers in my ear.

"Oh, George!" I croak again.

"I know, it's a lot to take in," he says, pulling back to assess me. "Now, let me take a good look at you." Tristan appears with some tissues in his hand. *How does he get so much right? How does he always seem to know what I need?*

I gaze adoringly at him. "Thanks," I take them from him and blow my nose.

"You look good," George surmises.

I laugh dryly at him. "Blubbering all over the place and unable to move, I don't think so George," I answer dryly.

"There's nothing wrong with tears," he says.

"I know," I whisper. *But seriously, I wish they would stop now!*

"Happy belated birthday," he says.

"Thanks," I answer shyly.

"We've got you a little gift, something to cheer you up," he says.

I cock one eyebrow up at him. "Cheer me up?"

George nods, grinning widely at me.

"Aunty Coral!" I hear Lily's voice screech, we both turn around. Lily is running flat out towards me – *Uh-oh! This is going to hurt!*

"Lily!" Debs shouts from the front door. Lily jerks to a stop with a guilty look on her face. "Come back here!" Debs orders. With a worried look on her face, she turns and walks somberly back towards Debs and Scott; they both kneel down and start talking to her.

"Catch up with you soon?" George questions.

"Yes please," I smile. "It's really good to see you, George."

"You too darling," he leans across and gently kisses my cheek and then walks over to Phil.

"Coral," Tristan appears, gently placing his arm around my waist. "Happy?" I nod unable to articulate anything. I finish my drink and place it on the side. "Hungry?" Tristan asks.

"Not yet thank you," I whisper and look down the hallway because Gladys and Malcolm have arrived, and are marching towards us.

"Darling!" Gladys wails with her hands in the air as she dashes over to me, she's so over-dramatic sometimes. Reaching me, she crushes me to her, making me gasp in pain. "Oh no!" She says standing back, patting me all over. "I'm so sorry darling."

"It's…ok," I say, trying to get my breath back. I feel a little light-headed from the pain.

"Tristan!" Gladys opens her arms wide and crushes him instead. "Oh darling boy!" she says her voice wobbling. Tristan seems bemused by her behaviour but enfolds her in his arms. Malcolm shakes his head at Gladys and smiles, then leans down and pecks my cheek.

"Happy birthday Coral."

"Thanks," I beam.

"Where shall I put these?" He asks, his hands full of presents. *This is going to be so embarrassing!*

"Um…just over there thanks," I point to the table.

"Right oh!" Malcolm says a quick hello to Tristan, shaking his hand, then makes his way over to the table. Tristan hands two Champagne flutes to Gladys who wonders over to Malcolm. As I look up, I notice Stuart is stood awkwardly with the front door open, although I don't understand why. I watch Debs, Scott & Lily walk over to us, Lily looks really upset. I grit my teeth in frustration – *Why did they have to make her cry?*

Debs pulls me into a bear hug. "You had me so worried," she scolds.

"I know," I whisper, wincing in pain. "Talk later?" I ask.

She nods once at me and then I awkwardly hug Scott. "Good to see you back on your feet," he says.

"Thanks," I smile tentatively at him.

"Aunty Coral?" Lily whimpers.

I look down at her flushed, tear-stained cheeks – *Poor kid!*

"Take my hand Lily," I say. Lily beams at me, places her tiny hand in mine, and we walk outside onto the patio. I carefully sit on one of the loungers and pat my lap. Lily carefully climbs up and rests her head against my chest.

"So, Mommy and Daddy told you off?" I question.

"Yes," she whimpers.

"Why?"

"Because Mommy said I wasn't allowed to run and hug you too hard because you're still poorly, but when I saw you I forgot." She sniffs.

"Well, I wouldn't have minded if you had hugged me hard," I say.

"You wouldn't?" She squeaks.

"No kiddo." I squeeze her tightly and kiss her hair.

"I'm so glad you're ok Aunty Coral, Mommy said you were really sick, she was crying a lot."

"Was she?" Lily nods. "Well, that's because we love each other and well…I was poorly, but I'm getting better now." She sniffs again.

Debs must have really told her off. *I need to cheer her up!*

"I'm really happy you came today. I simply couldn't celebrate my birthday without my beautiful little niece," I hug her to me and kiss her again.

"Oh yes!" She beams. "I forgot, happy birthday Aunty Coral, I got you a present," she says, bouncing up and down excitedly on my lap – *Ouch that hurts!*

"Can I open it?" I ask, gritting my teeth and trying to smile.

"Yes!" She squeals excitedly, jumps down from my lap, and runs back into the house. Moments later, she re-appears with a small square box, wrapped with shiny red paper, and it has a cute bow on the top – *How sweet!*

"Happy birthday," she beams holding the present out.

"Thank you, Lily." I take it from her and try to unwrap it, but there's so much sellotape! "Did you wrap this up yourself Lily?" I ask.

"Yes," she squeals excitedly. It's no good, I can't open it – *I have no strength!*

"Can you help me, Lily?" I say handing her the gift, her eyes widen as she takes the present off me, and only as a child can, she demolishes the paper in seconds.

I look down and sat in her hands is a clear plastic box, and inside the box is a small photo-frame in the shape of a red heart. Inside is a picture of me and Lily that was taken a couple of years ago, and on the frame are the words –**Always in My Heart**

"Lily it's beautiful," I say, tears pooling my eyes again. "Thank you."

"It's for when we leave," she whimpers.

"When you go to Spain?" I ask.

She nods once. "It's so you won't forget me," she says, tears spilling down her cheeks. *Crap!*

"Lily!" I open my arms, and she sinks into my lap. "I could never forget you." I let her cry it out, gently rocking her. "It's ok," I soothe, but she just doesn't stop crying. I feel like I need to probe, dig deeper as to why this little girl is so upset, so that's what I do.

"Don't you want to go to Spain Lily? You'll make lots of new friends."

She shakes her head and cries even harder – *Double Crap, this is not good!*

When she finally stops crying so much, she looks up at me. "I want to stay," she whimpers.

My heart sinks. "Yeah…I can see that Lily. Have you told Mommy?"

She shakes her head at me. I sigh inwardly. This is a difficult one. I really don't want to meddle in Scott and Debs life, but this child is unhappy, and that's just not right.

"Well, maybe you should tell Mommy," I say. "Be a big brave girl?"

Her bottom lip starts to wobble again, and she shakes her head at me.

"Maybe you want me to talk to Mommy?" I offer, and she nods at me. "Ok kiddo." I hug her to me for a while longer; this feels nice, really nice…

"Oh, there you are!" Joyce's voice booms. I look up and smile, then immediately frown. Joyce is mad at me, I can tell – *Great!*

"Hey Joyce, Lily and I were just talking, she got me this," I say showing Joyce my present, she slaps her hand to her mouth, trying to stop the tears – *What is it about everyone crying?*

"Oh Lily, that's so thoughtful sweetheart." Lily smiles up at Joyce. Then looking down at me, Joyce discreetly gestures for me to follow her, she wants to talk – *Crap!*

I swallow hard – I really don't want another bollocking!

"Hey Lily, guess what this house has?" I say.

"What?" She beams excitedly.

"A swimming pool," I say, my eyes widening, teasing her.

"Really?" She squeaks excitedly.

"Yes, and I bet if you ask Tristan nicely, he'll show you," I say smiling down at her.

"Ok," she beams. I kiss her forehead and release her from my arms. "See you later Aunty Coral," she says dashing off to find Tristan.

I look up at Joyce and frown. I'm seeing her in a completely different light now I know she and Tristan were already acquaintances before she sold. Shaking her head several times, she sighs heavily then places her hands on her hips – *Here we go!*

"Coral." She closes her eyes for a moment when she opens them she is glaring down at me. "Why on earth didn't you tell me what was going on, what *that* woman was doing?" she asks, her lips tightly pressed together.

I sigh inwardly. "You know..." I whisper.

"Of course I know," she hisses. "Tristan told me everything!" Ok, she is really pissed at me. *Damn you, Tristan Freeman!*

"Oh..." I wrap my arms around myself. I want to hide away. I don't want to talk about it anymore, but Joyce needs an explanation, I can see that, and in fairness, she deserves one, she's been so good to me.

"I'm sorry Joyce, to everyone...for not sharing, especially you...but I..." I break off. "If it makes you feel any better Tristan is really pissed at me!" I stare out at the view – I really love the light nights that summer brings.

Joyce sighs heavily, then comes and sits next to me. "Coral," she says grabbing hold of my hand and squeezing it tight. I turn and see she has her eyes closed. "I just don't understand why you didn't confide in me? I thought we had a good relationship?"

"We do Joyce...I just..." I stop and shake my head. "I nearly told you, so many times...but I knew it was Tristan I really needed to speak to about it. And I didn't want to worry you," I add.

"Worry me?" She says incredulously.

"Well, yeah..." I say. "You...you have enough going on," I add, thinking about John.

"Of all the things...." She says, then closes her eyes and takes a deep breath.

"Joyce, please...I don't think I can take anyone else being pissed off at me," I say, closing my eyes as I do, hoping she'll get the message. I feel her pat my hand. I open my eyes and smile tentatively at her.

"So he's mad at you?" Joyce says.

"Yes, very," I balk.

"Well, he has every right to be," she scolds.

"I know," I whisper.

"Oh, my dear girl!" Joyce carefully wraps her arm around my shoulder and presses her head against mine. "If I'd have lost you too…" She chokes out.

"I'm sorry," I say again and wrap my arms around her waist trying to soothe her, and we stay like that for a while. Honestly, I think it's Joyce that needs this more than me.

"Well…" She says, pulling back and sitting up straight. She takes a handkerchief out of her purse and dabs her eyes. "All is well now I suppose. Are you going back to the company?" she asks.

I frown up at her. "I don't know…maybe. Depends what happens I suppose…" I say, Joyce nods. Then I really think about it, by the time I'm better, Tristan might have hired someone else.

"I'm going to miss you so much," she says.

"Me too," I say. "When are you leaving?" I add.

"Oh not for another six weeks," she says despondently.

"Joyce, is that really where you want to be – In Florida?" I ask. Joyce smiles awkwardly at me, which pretty much answers my question. "Joyce, if you don't want to' – "I don't really have a choice," she interrupts. "I can't stay here," she adds, her eyes filling with unshed tears. I nod. I can understand that if I had lost Tristan…

"Come on," Joyce says brightly. "Let's go and open some presents!" *Crap!*

I plaster a fake smile on my face. Joyce helps me to my feet, and we slowly make our way back inside. As I scan the room, I instantly freeze – Malcolm's daughters, Erin and Ellie are here?

They both come rushing over to me. "Oh Coral, we're so happy to see you up and about," Ellie says. "Yes, Dad told us what happened, we were so shocked," Erin adds.

"I'm shocked you're here," I say, feeling bemused. "But thank you for coming," I quickly add.

"The kids have gone to watch a pantomime, we left the Dad's in charge," Ellie says, giggling. "Yeah, god knows what chaos we'll return to," Erin adds.

We all laugh, then I notice in my peripheral vision, a small balding man sitting uncomfortably on the sofa – *Bob!*

"Can we catch up in a while?" I ask.

"Sure." They say together, and I hobble as quickly as I can towards Bob.

He looks up as I slowly approach him. "Coral," he croaks, smiling widely at me. I sink to my knees in front of him and take his hands in mine.

"Hey, Bob." I softly say, tears threatening again.

"Hello sweetheart," he says, I can tell he's choking back the tears too.

"Bob!" I choke, as the memory of him lying on my studio floor; bleeding and hurting flood my mind. His head still looks sore from where Susannah attacked him. I reach up, and carefully hug him, he looks so frail. "How are you feeling?" I softly ask.

"You're worried about me?" he asks incredulously, pulling me back to look at me.

"Well yes…of course I am," I say.

Bob shakes his head at me. "You survived," he says, gently squeezing my shoulders.

"You too," I whisper, swallowing against the lump that's formed.

"Hell of a place he's got here," Bob says, changing the subject.

"Fancy living here?" I ask, taking the bull by the horns. Bob stares at me in disbelief. "I'm not kidding," I say. "Tristan's asked me to move in with him. I've said yes, so I won't be there to look after you and be close to you, which is how I would like it to be. So I want you to seriously consider this offer. We would like you to move in with us."

"We?" He questions.

"Yes. Tristan completely agrees. We both want you here, and it won't just be you, Bob, Edith is now living with us," I say pointing to her in the kitchen. "She's Tristan's housekeeper from London, and Stuart' – "I've met him," he interrupts.

"Well, he'll be here too so there will be five of us," I add, smiling broadly at him.

"You want me to move in here? With you?" he clarifies. I nod, grinning widely. "Well, I don't know Coral…" He says staring out at the summer evening.

"Great view huh?" I say.

"It ain't bad," he agrees, turning to smile at me. "Let me think about it," he says.

"Sure, take all the time you need. Are you back in your studio?" I ask.

"I want to be, but Gladys is insisting I stay with her a while longer."

"That's good," I say patting his frail hand. "Are you having a roast with her tomorrow?"

"I'm not sure," he says.

"Well, I'd like to catch up with you. Want to come here tomorrow?"

"For dinner?"

"Yes," I smile.

"Ok," he smiles back.

"Good," I say, then lean up and kiss his cheek. As usual, his cheeks flame and his shy smile appears. "I better go find Debs," I say. "It's great to see you, Bob."

"You too darling," he says gently patting my hand. I squeeze his hand once more and make my way over to Debs.

"We need to talk," I say and gesture for her to follow me. I walk over to the utility room and open the door, I wait for Debs then shut the door behind her.

"What's up?" She asks.

"Lily doesn't want to leave," I say.

"What?" Debs laughs.

"Debs, I'm serious." Her face falls. "She just told me she doesn't want to go, and she doesn't want to tell you that. I'm letting you know so you can speak to Scott. It's none of my business what happens, but she is one upset little girl, who wants to stay here, at home."

Debs' mouth pops open in shock. "She really said that to you?" I nod in reply. "Ok, thanks…I guess Scott and I have some talking to do," she muses.

"I'm really sorry Debs," I say. "I don't want to seem like I'm interfering, but I thought you would want to know." She nods distractedly at me. "I really am sorry," I add.

"Don't say that Coral. I'm really glad that you've told me," she says.

"Sure?" I ask.

"Yeah, it's just that we asked Lily about this? We sat her down and talked about it for ages, she said she was happy to go, excited even. I wonder why she hasn't been truthful?" She says, staring at the floor.

"I don't know? Maybe she's just saying it because of what happened to me, maybe she's just upset at the moment, she is only five after all." I wince at the thought, remembering so clearly what happened to me at that age.

Debs nods again deep in thought, then taking me by surprise she hugs me. "I love you Coral, thank you."

"I love you too Debs," I whisper.

Taking hold of my hand, she squeezes it once, then we both walk out of the room, and I go searching for my Hubby....*well hubby to be!*

CHAPTER ELEVEN

WE ARE ALL SITTING on the large u-shaped sofa. Everyone has eaten Edith's mammoth spread, and the party is in full swing. Tristan, Scott and Malcolm are having some deep discussion. Gladys is busy getting giggly with Rob, Phil and Carlos, I think they are getting a little tipsy – *I'm jealous!* George, Bob and Joyce are quietly chatting away, while Erin and Ellie are playing with Lily. Debs is sat next to me at the very end of the sofa, but she seems miles away; I hope I haven't upset her.

"Debs," I whisper. "You ok?"

She shakes her head at me. *Uh-oh!*

"What's wrong?" I ask.

"If Lily doesn't want to go to Spain, I don't know what we're going to do?" she whispers, but she looks really worried about something, and I don't think its Lily.

"Are you worried about money?" I ask. Not that she should be; she's got two hundred and fifty grand too, just like me.

Debs looks down at the floor. "No, not really,' – "Time for presents!" Rob bellows, jumping to his feet, effectively putting a stop to that conversation, everyone cheers and starts shuffling around.

I shake my head at Rob. "Come and see me?" I whisper to Debs.

"I will." She smiles, squeezing my hand.

Rob marches over to me, helps me to my feet and walks me over to the centre of the sofa. "Well, sit down then," he says, rolling his eyes at me.

"Rob!' – "Do it woman!" he warns.

I want to huff at him, but I don't. Instead, I carefully sit down. All eyes are on me, and the conversations have died down to a quiet hush. *Oh god! This is not happening!* Tristan must be reading my discomfort, because within seconds he's sat next to me, squeezing my hand.

"Right, who's first?" Rob asks.

"Ooh me, me!" Phil says, jumping to his feet. Walking over to the table, he picks up their present then walks over to me, grinning widely at George as he does. "From George and I, happy birthday!" He says, handing me a small flat box.

"Thank you," I say, smiling up at him. Reluctantly, I take the present off him and quickly demolish the wrapping paper. I need to get this over with, it's too embarrassing. Lifting the lid, I frown when I see a small white envelope. Taking it out of the box, I pull open the seal and take out the contents. *Oh, George!* – I have two tickets to see the Lion King!

"No way!" I gasp, smiling broadly. It's not until next year, but who cares. I've been dying to see it since it came out, but the tickets kept selling out on me. Feeling completely overwhelmed, I swallow hard and look up at George. "I…I don't know what to say…Thank you, so much." I manage to squeak out.

"I know you've always wanted to see it," George says, smiling fondly at me, then he walks over to me, and we hug, I do the same with Phil – *Wow! Maybe this won't be so bad after all!*

Rob proceeds to organise who goes next, he's so bossy sometimes! Erin and Ellie have bought me two bottles of wine, not that I expected anything from them – I'm still shocked they're here.

Bob – bless his cotton socks – has bought me a box of chocolates and another bottle of wine. Debs and Scott have bought me The Hairy Bikers Cookbook. Gladys and Malcolm, bath bubbles, a box set of make-up and a bottle of my favourite perfume. *I am being spoiled rotten!*

"Come on Joyce!" Rob says excitedly.

Joyce sits next to me, then opening her handbag, she takes out a small white envelope. "Happy birthday Coral," she says handing me the envelope and kissing my cheek.

"Thank you," I whisper. I look down at the gift, lift the seal and pull out the contents. Two return tickets to Florida – *Ok, I feel faint!*

"Joyce!" I gasp. "You shouldn't have!"

"Too late!" She smiles. *I'm speechless!*

Tears start to pool in my eyes. Without a word, I turn and pull Joyce into my arms. My shoulder is throbbing painfully, but I don't care. I hold her to me for the longest time.

"What is it?" Rob asks.

"Two tickets to Florida," Tristan says.

I finally release Joyce. "Thank you," I say trying not to choke up.

"You are more than welcome," she says, tears pooling in her eyes. I can't help the tears that start flowing down my cheeks, Joyce smiles at me, pulls her handkerchief out and dabs my cheeks dry.

"Thanks," I squeak, smiling and sniffing loudly, we both start laughing at each other, then we hug again.

"Our turn!" Rob pipes up excitedly.

I pull out of Joyce's arms and look up at Rob. Carlos stands, and walks over to the table, picking up a big shiny purple bag he walks over to me, then leans down and kisses my cheek.

"Happy birthday," he says smiling warmly at me.

"Thanks," I say, feeling embarrassed again. Opening the bag, I see two big presents wrapped in shiny purple paper, and what looks like a birthday card.

"Open the card first!" Rob demands.

"Ok," I laugh. Pulling the card out, I open it up and pull out the contents. *Whoa!* I have a voucher for Spa Tara. I know the place, it's right on the Marina, but I've never been.

"It's a full package," Rob explains, budging Joyce out of the way and sitting next to me. "Whatever you want, you can go on your own, or we can make a day of it," he adds cheerfully.

I look across at my awesome best friend. "Thanks you guys, it's brilliant!" I add, kissing Rob on the cheek.

"Come on!" he says. "Open the next one." He pulls out one of the boxes and passes it to me. I think he's more excited than I am. I rip the paper off and smile up at him.

"Friends?" I have never seen any of the series, how cool is that.

"It's the complete box set," he says. "Something funny to watch while you're recovering, or being miserable," he adds teasingly.

"Hey!" I smile up at him and bump his shoulder – *Shouldn't have done that, it hurt!* – "That's so cool," I gasp, trying to control the pain. "Thanks you two!"

Breathe Coral, breathe!

Carlos winks and smiles at me, while Rob passes me the next present, grinning excitedly at me. I cock one eyebrow up at him, it feels heavy. I smile and rip off the paper – *Whoa!*

I have a set of three Global Chef's knives. I have wanted a set of these for ages, but they're really expensive. These must have cost at least three hundred pounds, if not more. My face falls. I turn and gaze at Rob who's grinning widely at me.

"Tristan told us," he says. "About the cooking classes, you're going to take."

I turn and gape at Tristan, he grins widely at me.

I shake my head; I am in awe of all of this. "Rob!" I choke, pulling him into my arms. "Thank you."

"You're welcome!" He chuckles. Pulling out of his arms, I turn and blow a kiss to Carlos, who blows one back. Rob then jumps to his feet. "Your turn Tristan!"

"I've already had my present from Tristan," I say.

"You have?" He questions, all eyes are on me.

I reach down inside my t-shirt and carefully pull out my necklace. "Antique locket," I say.

"Oh Coral!" Joyce gasps, budging Rob out of the way and taking it between her manicured fingernails. "It's beautiful," she says, turning it over and inspecting it.

"I know." I choke up again.

"Actually," Tristan says turning to face me, his chocolate eyes capturing me. "That's one of your presents," he adds, leaning into me. I think he's about to kiss me, but instead, he whispers right in my ear. "And there's many more." *What!*

My mouth drops open as I stare back at him. He looks so intense, so sexy. The room is silent as we sit staring at one another, and begins to charge with that familiar electricity that flows between the two of us. Someone clears their throat, pulling me out of the little bubble that surrounds us, and several of our guests start chattering away with one another. I think we are making them feel uncomfortable.

Tristan breaks eye contact with a nervous chuckle, leans in, and kisses me lightly on the cheek. Then he stands, smiles his breathtaking smile at me and wanders off into his office. The moment he's gone Gladys, Debs, Erin and Ellie are straight over to me, each taking a turn to inspect my locket, each agreeing how beautiful it is. Tristan swiftly returns and sits next to me. I cannot take my eyes off him.

The conversation in the room quiets to a low rumble.

"More presents?" I whisper to him.

"Yes." He smiles, handing me a small white envelope.

I tentatively take it from him and ripping it open, I pull out the contents. I swallow hard and fight the tears again. I have a £1000 gift voucher for Ashdown Manna Cookery School. *Wow!*

"What is it?" Rob pipes up excitedly.

"Um…" I clear my throat. "Cooking classes," I whisper. Everyone oohs and ahhs!

"You can choose,' Tristan says, 'whatever you want to do. There's Italian, Spanish, Indian, Thai, Fish & Seafood, Middle Eastern, Bread and Baking, and if they don't do the course you want, just let me know, and we can book you in somewhere else."

"Thank you, Tristan, I love it," I say.

"I have another present for you," he whispers, his lips brushing against my ear. It makes my heart pound and my breathing stop when he's that close to me.

"Another?" I squeak breathlessly, I turn and stare wide-eyed at him.

"Yes." He smiles his enigmatic smile at me.

"Tristan' – "You can't have it yet, so don't worry. When you're better, and you've taken the cookery courses you want, then you can have it," he says grinning from ear to ear.

"Another surprise?" I question.

"Yes." His grin widens.

"You are over the top!" I lightly scold.

"Suck it up!" He teases. I can't help shaking my head and smiling at him. *I wonder what he has in store for me?*

"Oh…and you might not like this," he whispers.

"Like what?" I whisper back, frowning at him.

Tristan suddenly stands and turns the music down a little – which kind of annoys me because Rihanna just started singing You Da One, and I really love that song. I frown up at Tristan who nods to Edith. She wobbles over to us with a large Champagne bottle in her hand and tops up everyone's glasses; then Tristan walks to the centre of the room.

"Ladies and Gentleman," he says, gaining everyone's attention. "Coral," he softly says, his hand held out. "Please join me."

Oh Crap! Haven't I been embarrassed enough?

Joyce helps me to my feet. I walk over to Tristan and take his outstretched hand. He pulls me gently to his side and wraps his arm around my waist, so we are facing everyone.

"A toast. Coral, happy birthday darling!" He says raising his glass in the air.

Everyone follows suit, shouting happy birthday, Rob whoops and cheers with Phil, I can't help giggling at them both.

Tristan, to my horror, continues. "Also, I think I can speak freely for everyone in this room, when I say how lucky we all feel to have you home, safe and sound."

I hear Gladys stifle back a sob. *Mom! Don't cry!*

"To coming home safely," Tristan says raising his glass in the air again.

"Here, here!" Rob pipes up as everyone else echoes Tristan sentiments, and raises their glasses one more time. *I am dying here!*

Tristan smiles down at me, his shy boyish smile, then leans in and softly kisses me. I can tell he looks nervous, but I can't work out why.

"What's wrong?" I whisper.

He shakes his head slightly, smiles nervously, then he takes a deep breath and raises his glass again – *Huh?*

"Ladies and Gentleman, I have something else I would like to share with everyone here…and my parents," he says, nodding to the picture of them that's up on the wall. "As some of you may know, I lost both my parents last year…it's been…difficult to say the least and I would have loved…" He stops and swallows hard. *Oh no, Tristan!*

Turning to look at me he takes a deep breath and slowly blows it out. I suddenly realise he needs reassurance. "It's ok Tristan," I whisper. "I'm right here," I add, wrapping my arms around him, he leans down and pecks my forehead, then continues.

"I wish my parents could be here today, to share our happy news, but sadly it wasn't meant to be. As you all know, Coral and I have only known each other a short while, but I love her, and I will spend the rest of my life cherishing her." I cannot take my eyes off him. "So I would like you all to be the first to know that Miss Coral Stevens, the beautiful, captivating soul that she is, has consented to be my wife," he proudly says.

My mouth pops open – *Oh…he did not just say that… without telling me?*

Edith drops something in the kitchen, making a loud banging noise, and apart from Debs spitting her drink all over Scott, the room is completely silent. *Uh-oh!*

"And we would like to get married here, in this house, in two-weeks-time and you're all invited." Tristan then turns, places his glass down and takes my engagement ring out of his pocket. He takes my left hand, and slowly slides my engagement ring down my finger.

"You could have told me you were going to say that!" I

whisper to him. "But I do," I add, trying to take the sting out of my words because what he just did was sweet, and brave.

His face almost splits in two. I can't help grinning back at him. He leans down, and we give each other a peck on the lips – I want to French kiss him, but I don't think my family and friends would appreciate that.

I turn and look around the room. Gladys and Malcolm are quietly smiling up at us both. Joyce and Phil, who of course didn't know, look like they're going to expire. Rob and Carlos beam at one another, George blows me a kiss and Erin and Ellie are quietly smiling up at me, holding each other's hand. Bob is smiling, but he looks a little upset.

Lily startles us all by jumping up from her seat. "Yay!" She screams, jumping up and down. "Can I be a bridesmaid?" she asks running over to me.

"Yes," I whisper, she screams in delight.

"I knew you loved Aunty Coral," she says jumping up and down in front of Tristan.

We both look at each other and burst out laughing.

"Married?" Debs chokes standing to her feet then whips her head round to Gladys. "You knew!" she says.

"We only found out yesterday," Gladys says all innocently. *Guess the tables have turned!*

"Oh!" Debs seems to calm a little. "Seriously, you're getting married?" She adds in disbelief.

"Um…yeah," I say. "Whatever you do Deb's, don't congratulate us," I add sarcastically.

"Shit, sorry!" She gasps, then runs over to me and pulls me into a bear hug. "My little sister," she chokes, "finally getting hitched!"

"Yeah…" I gasp. "Debs, you're crushing me!"

"Oh sorry," she sniffs, stepping back. She smiles warmly at me, her cheeks red and tear-stained, but I can also see the apprehension behind her smile – she's worried.

"When you come over, I'll tell you everything," I whisper to her.

Her mouth pops open in surprise. "Oh…ok." She nods once at me her eyebrows still pulled together then turns to Tristan. "Congratulations!" she says reaching up to hug him.

Tristan and I are then passed from person to person for more hugs and congratulations. Gladys, Debs, Joyce, Erin and Ellie all admire my ring and agree it's a beautiful piece. Yep,

Tristan did very well, I think to myself. Until finally, I am back in Tristan's arms, and everyone is chatting again.

"Coral," Rob says marching over to us. "We have so much to do. Have you two really thought about this?" He adds, crossing his arms.

We both grin at Rob. "Rob, we haven't just decided to do this on a whim!"

He shakes his head in frustration. "Ok, ok. But there's so much to do," he frantically says. "But first things first, you guys need to get your wedding rings sorted," he orders.

"Coral and I will take a look online tomorrow," Tristan tells him.

"Oh…ok good," Rob says. "I'll get onto the registrar, and Coral, you need to take a look at wedding dresses – like *today!* If you like what I picked out we need to order it Pronto!"

"Ok, Rob, calm down…" I say, but Rob seems frantic. "Rob, if this is going to stress you out…?"

"No, it won't," he says. "But we need to get organised!"

"Ok, ok, come by tomorrow, and we can spend all afternoon *getting organised*," I giggle.

He seems to relax a little. "Ok, tomorrow," he says…

TWO HOURS LATER we finally have the house to ourselves. Nurse Terry has been and given me another shot, Edith and Stuart have both retired for the evening, and after a wonderful spread of food, and plenty of champagne, my family and friends have gone home; a little worse for wear I might add. *It's weird not drinking when other people do!*

I am stood in the bedroom, gazing out at the stars as it's a really clear night tonight. Tristan wraps his arms around me, his front to my back and kisses the top of my head.

"Hey beautiful," he says, kissing my hair.

"I've been spoiled," I say.

"You think so?" He says.

"Yes, so many presents. It's…overwhelming."

"Coral, sometimes I don't think you realise how much everyone loves you."

"I do…I just…" I trail off, turn around and wrap my arms around his back. "Thank you, Tristan, for my presents, for today…for everything."

He chuckles slightly. I feel it vibrate through me. "You are most welcome," he says. Hmm, feels so nice, wrapped up in his warm arms, I could stay here forever. "Come on, let's get ready for bed." He says, kissing the top of my head again.

"Ok." Reluctantly, I release my arms from his waist.

Tristan helps me undress until I'm practically naked; well apart from my knickers. "Tired?" he asks as he slips one of his t-shirts over my head.

"No," I say. "Why are you putting this on me?" I ask.

"So I can't see that gorgeous naked body of yours," he says, grinning widely at me. "Come on, into bed." Tristan pulls the covers back, and I gently slide myself in.

"I'm not tired," I say, in fact, I feel wired. "I spoke to Bob."

"Yeah?" Tristan unbuttons his shirt, and pulls it off, revealing his very sexy torso. I immediately lose my train of thought. Every muscle down below instantly clenches in delight, *I want him now!* He slowly saunters over to the chair in the room, throws his shirt over it and strips off his trousers, so he's just stood there, naked in the room; well apart from his boxers.

"Tristan, can you please stop parading around the room half naked and put on some clothes!" I scold.

He stops, slowly turns to me and smiles that enigmatic smile of his. *Holy Crap!*

"I'm not kidding!" I squeak, wanting to throw a pillow at him. "You have the same effect on me you know," I grumble.

"Ah, then I'm not being fair," he says and quickly covers himself up with a t-shirt.

I shake my head at his teasing ways.

"So," he says climbing into bed. "What did Bob have to say?"

We both scoot down, so we are lying on our pillows, facing one another.

"What were you talking to George about?" I question.

"You first." He grins – *Git!*

"Fine! I gave him our offer of moving in with us," I say.

"And?" Tristan prompts.

"He said he'll think about it. Oh and he's coming over tomorrow for a roast dinner."

"Did you tell Edith?"

"I *asked* Edith, and she said yes. Oh, and I invited Rob and Carlos, if they're coming over they should eat too," I say.

"Good idea." Tristan grins.

"Now, I don't want you to moan at me because it will only take about ten minutes, but I will be in the kitchen tomorrow.

I'm going to show Edith how to make West Indian Roast Chicken."

"Are you now?" Tristan teases.

"Yes, I am," I say a little petulantly.

"As you wish," he teases some more. I laugh and shake my head at him, then my face falls remembering what's going on tomorrow. *Ugh!*

"Nine o'clock," I grumble.

"For the Detective?" Tristan guesses.

"Yeah…I'm looking forward to that like a hole in the head," I grumble.

"Baby, if this is too much…?" He says.

"No, I think I'd rather get it done, out of the way," I muse.

"Ok." He says.

"So…" I say tucking my good hand under my pillow.

"So…" Tristan says doing the same. I can't help giggling, Tristan starts chuckling too. *Why am I finding this funny?*

"Why are you laughing?" I laugh.

"I have no idea!" He chuckles.

"We need to talk," I titter.

"I know," Tristan sighs.

"Do you want to go first?" I ask.

"Do you want me to answer all the questions you fired at me earlier?" He teases.

"You remember?" I ask, quite astonished.

"Yes baby, I do."

"Ok," I whisper.

Tristan shakes his head. "I've changed my mind, ladies, before gentleman."

I frown back at him. "Ok. Why were you frosty with Dr Green?"

"Next question," Tristan says, his jaw clenching, his pupils dilating. *Grrrrr!*

"Why?" I question, frowning at him.

"Next question," he warns. *Ok, maybe leave that one for last!*

"Ok," I sigh. "Why did you want to walk out on me, after I told you about Susannah?"

Tristan sighs. "I am so very sorry that I reacted that way Coral. I pride myself on being able to read people very well, and I got it so wrong with Susannah; and I was so mad, about so many things' – "What things?" I interrupt.

"Well, when you showed me that report, I realised I had got it completely wrong with Olivia.' – My heart sinks – 'You were right Coral, I should have believed her, not Susannah. But then again I'm glad it ended because if it hadn't, I wouldn't be here now with you." *Ok, feeling better!*

"Ok, but it still doesn't explain why you picked up your jacket and went to walk out on me? It really hurt me when you said 'I have to get away from you' I never thought you would ever say anything like that to me."

Tristan closes his eyes for a moment. "I know. I was mad with you for not telling me sooner, mad with you for investigating it all, mad that it was you stood in front of me with information that was making my whole world shift on its axis, and I was mad with myself because I had put you in harm's way. If you were right and Susannah was unstable, I'd not seen it, and she could have done anything to you..." Tristan trails off.

"So you just wanted some space?" I question.

"Yes, I was never going to leave you Coral. I was just so frustrated. I can remember thinking, 'why couldn't it have been Joyce or Stu that was handing me this information?' But oh no, it had to be you. I was also worried, I didn't want you involved, especially if it was true, which it turned out to be." He says, his cheeks flushing, his eyes darkening.

I can't help frowning. It still doesn't answer the question.

"What?" he asks gently stroking my cheek.

"When I grabbed my bag, and I asked you if it was over' – His lips press against mine, instantly silencing me. "I never answered you," he says.

"I know, but you know me, I think the worst, I can't help it."

"Coral, never in a million years...I just needed some time alone."

"Then why didn't you just say that at the time, like 'no we're not over I just want some space' that wouldn't have been hard to say, and I'd at least have known where we stood. But instead, you tell me to go?"

"I know...I know it was stupid and wrong and..." Tristan shakes his head. "I think it's fair to say that I've learned a hell of a lot. About myself, about you, about relationships...I want to put this right Coral. The last thing in the world I want is for us to be fighting and you're secretly wondering when I'm going to walk out, because I'm not, and I won't, ever. I promise you that."

"I promise I won't either," I say. "No matter how mad I am with you."

"Good." Tristan leans in and softly kisses me. *Oh boy! Here we go again, my libido is wide awake and ready to rock.*

"Stop," I mumble against his lips. "No more kissing," I breathe.

"Why?" Tristan smiles.

"Because I can't take it any further, and right now I want to."

"Me too," he says, smirking at me.

I shake my head and laugh. "Stop it, it's not funny!"

"No, it's not!" He says, still chuckling.

"What did you do when I left?" I ask.

Tristan instantly stops laughing. "I told you, I called Susannah, we talked, and she denied it all. Then I went for a swim to clear my head, I was about to head out to find you when Susannah knocked on my door."

"You…you were going to come and find me?" I squeak.

"Yes. I figured you were at Rob's, but I didn't know where that was, so I was about to call Joyce see if she knew." *He was going to come and get me, just like before!*

"Oh!" I swallow hard.

"Any more questions?" He asks.

"Yes," I whisper, closing my eyes. "Did you speak to Olivia?"

"No, I didn't get the chance."

I open my eyes and gaze at him. "Do you want to call Olivia?" I ask, biting my bottom lip.

Tristan leans forward and releases my lip from my teeth. "Coral are you asking out of curiosity, or because you think I still have feelings for her?" *I snort, caught out!*

"Both…I think?" I say frowning.

Tristan frowns back at me. "Coral, there are no feelings there' – "So if you had to choose?" I interrupt.

"It would be you," he tells me firmly.

"Ok, good." I breathe, feeling satisfied.

Tristan chuckles again. "Green-eyed monster!"

"I know, it's not nice, it's just…if you do still like her, I'd rather know now. I just want you to be sure this is really what you want, not what you think you want. I want reassurance that if Olivia were suddenly back on the market, you wouldn't go running to her."

"No way," Tristan says shaking his head. "Is that ever going to happen. What you and I have is so much stronger than what I had with Olivia. It's you I want," he reiterates.

Ok, feeling loads better about what happened, and Tristan's feelings for Olivia.

"Would it bother you if I did call her?" he asks. "I'd like to apologise to her, maybe she'll forgive me?" He muses.

"I don't mind," I say. "But it's doubtful she'll forgive you. She sounded angry and upset on the phone."

"Oh…" His face pales.

"Hey, we all make mistakes. No one's perfect," I add.

"I guess," he says, staring down at the bedding.

"Tristan." He looks up at me. "I want to organise a grave for my mom tomorrow?"

He frowns, looking worried. "We already have enough going on tomorrow. I don't want you overexerting yourself. Besides, after speaking to Gladys, I called the Psychiatric Facility. They kept your mother's belongings along with her ashes for you to collect, and I have located a plot at Hove Cemetery, or you could go for an alternative," he says.

"An alternative?" I question.

"Yes, when I did some research, I found there's a place called Woodland Burial. It's a non-traditional, eco-friendly way of burying someone. Instead of a gravestone, you plant a tree."

"A tree?" I squeak.

"You don't like the idea?" He asks.

"Tristan, I love it…and I think we should go with that option, but when did you sort of all this?" I ask incredulously.

He shrugs. "While you were recovering in hospital." *Wow, he's done so much!*

He's talked to the detective, re-designed this bedroom, got Edith and Stu living here, organised the party, sorted out my mother's burial; and bought me two beautiful birthday presents.

"Tristan," I whisper, tears pooling in my eyes. "Thank you, you've done so much, you've been wonderful baby," I sniff.

"Oh baby, don't cry." He says, as he gently strokes my cheek.

"Sorry," I sniff again. Tristan gently pulls me to him, wrapping his arm carefully around me. I snuggle closer to him, feeling safe and protected.

"Know this, my beautiful girl. It's not that I don't want you to cry, I'd rather you do it in front of me than hide it. It just… hurts, a lot, to see you upset. I want to see you happy, not sad." He kisses my head again. *Oh, Tristan!*

I look up at him. "Ok. You can always cry in front of me too, you know that, right?"

Tristan chuckles, but I notice his cheeks flush red. "Yeah baby, I know."

"Can we go see my studio tomorrow?" I say, feeling weird about going out.

Tristan frowns deeply. "No baby, how many times do I have to say it? I don't want you overexerting yourself. What are you worried about?" he asks.

I feign innocence. "I don't know… I just want to see it I guess." I say, looking away.

Tristan scoots down and takes my face in his hands. "Coral, be honest with me," he says. "You looked a little frightened then, what is it?"

I sigh inwardly. "Ok…ok…I'm freaking out about going outside again, and I don't know why?" I say, feeling stupid.

"That's normal baby," he says.

"It is?" I squeak.

"Yes, victims of traumatic events often take several weeks to process what happened, and even then, it can take a while to get back to normality." He softly says.

"Normality?" I snort. "Tristan, you should know I've never been normal," I tease.

"Hey!" He warns. "Stop making a joke of it."

I frown again. "Maybe I need to see Cindy?" I muse.

"That's a good idea. George said you've spoken to him and he's coming here on Tuesday afternoon. Maybe he can bring Cindy with him?" He strokes my cheek again, calming me.

"Ok, I'll call him. But I still need to sort my studio," I say.

His puppy dog eyes are back. "Darling, I had your studio packed up. It's all in boxes downstairs." He says, looking a little guilty.

"It is?" I gasp, staring back at him with wide eyes.

"Yes, in the big reception room." He says, smouldering me.

I swallow hard. My studio all packed up. *How weird is that?*

"Why did you do that?" I ask.

"Well, when the detectives had finished…Edith and I boxed everything up for you. I didn't think you'd want to go back there, and I knew you wouldn't be in any state to pack it all up. I threw away the clothes Susannah shredded though, I hope you don't mind?" He softly says.

"No, I don't mind. So my studio is empty and locked up?" I say, blinking rapidly. I'll never live there again – *That is weird!*

"Yes, apart from the furniture." He says, smiling softly at me.

"Ok," I say. I'm not really sure how I feel about that.

"You just need to decide what to do with it, when you're ready that is," Tristan adds.

Then it hits me, my bills and my mortgage! *Holy crap!* – I go to scoot out of bed so I can fire my laptop up and transfer some money, but Tristan stops me.

"Coral, what are you doing?" He asks, his arm stretched across me.

"I need to put my laptop on Tristan!" I squeak in a panic.

"Why? Why do you look panicked?" He asks, his jaw clenching.

"I'm not panicking Tristan, I just don't want to get charged," I say a little breathlessly.

He frowns deeply. "Charged? For what?" He asks.

"For being late on my mortgage and my bills, I need to transfer some money across to- " I stop talking because Tristan is looking very sheepish right now. "What have you done?" I huff. I already know this is going to have something to do with money.

"You had your monthly wage go into your account from Garland's, so you have no need to worry." He says, his eyes cast down, his face serious, but I can see his lips trying to twitch up into a smile – He's definitely done something!

"And?" I prompt. He's still not looking at me. "Look at me, Tristan." He knows I'm not going to like this.

He sighs, then trying to fight his smile, he looks up at me. "I transferred some money across to your account. I wasn't sure if your wages covered everything, so I thought better to be safe than sorry." He says, smiling widely at me now.

I cock one eyebrow up at him. "When you say 'some money'?"

Tristan loses the grin. "Does it matter how much?" He looks wary now, and so he damn well should be.

"Yes, it does! How much Tristan?" I balk.

He sighs again and looks down at the bed. "Twenty-five thousand." *Holy fuck!*

I nod my head several times. I know what to do, but I'm not going to tell him. I'll simply transfer the money back into his account tomorrow. I can't help the chuckle that escapes.

"Coral, I want you to have it. I don't want it back!" He says. How the hell does he read my mind like that? *It's spooky!*

I completely ignore him.

"I mean it!" He states.

"Fine!" I say. *I'm still transferring it back!*

He looks angry for a second, then shakes his head and smiles his wide smile at me. "God you know how to wind me up," he says. "But I'm so happy you're here."

I smile back at him. "So I guess I've officially moved in with you?"

"Yep," he says, grinning widely.

"Happy?" I ask, remembering Tristan teasing me when he told me he'd bought this place, and how happy he would be when I'd moved in.

"Yes, very," he says. "You?"

"I remember you teasing me about moving in," I say. "And yes, I am over the moon to be here, because you're here."

Tristan smiles then quickly frowns. "Are you really happy about having house guests living with us? Would you rather it be just the two of us?"

"I'm happy," I say. "Don't change anything."

"Ok." He grins. "Any other questions?"

"Yes, I have no job, Tristan. What am I going to do?" I ask feeling worried.

"Coral, you really shouldn't be worrying about that at the moment, your main priority is to heal, and when you're ready, we'll sort it."

I look up at him, feeling apprehensive about what he's saying, I mean I know I need to rest and recover, but there are only so many days I can do that for, then I need something, a project, anything to keep my mind busy.

"Tristan, I can't hang around not doing anything' – "Well you could always come back to Chester House?" He reluctantly suggests. "When you're better," he quickly adds.

"Maybe…I don't know," I muse. "But if I'm not there and Susannah is…locked away, who's working there?"

"Actually Karen is here at the moment, and Joyce is there too, just finishing off until I get back."

"Oh, ok." *I wanted to meet Karen, I wonder if I will?*

"Any other questions?" He asks again.

"Why?" I question curiously.

"Because I have questions, but I want you to finish first." He gazes down at me, patiently waiting.

"Um…well there is one more thing. But promise me you won't get mad?" I quietly say.

"Why would I get mad?" he says. I cock one eyebrow up at him. "Ok, I won't get mad." He laughs.

"Well, it's about Susannah," I say.

Tristan's face falls, and his eyes slowly darken. "What about Susannah?" He says through gritted teeth.

"Hey, you promised!" I squeak.

He closes his eyes briefly and takes a deep breath trying to reign in his temper when he opens them I can see his chocolate colour is coming back. "I'm sorry," he whispers. "Please continue."

"I don't want her rotting away in a Mental Institution Tristan, look what happened to my mother. Susannah is imbalanced, I know that, but only because of what happened. I'm sure with the right care and attention, she'll get back on her feet. And have the chance of a happy, full life, maybe even fall in love again, have a family…" I drift off, thinking about her rotting away in that horrid place.

"Coral, you're a complete conundrum to me," Tristan says, shaking his head. Then he turns over onto his back and stares up at the ceiling. "She almost killed you…she could have killed me, and you want to help her?" He says incredulously.

"Yes," I whisper.

"Why?" He balks.

"I've just told you why," I say.

"But…I just don't understand…" He says, running his hand through his hair.

"Tristan, if I remember rightly, you really liked Susannah before all this happened. You praised her and said she was the best member of staff you ever had, you trusted her, was fond of her even. Yet, you're happy for her to rot away in some awful place that makes a person worse, not better? She was let down by the system Tristan, just like my mom was, I just…" I stop and take a breath.

"Yes I did trust her," he spits. "But that was before I found out she was a complete lunatic."

"She is not a lunatic," I argue. "She's a very frightened, lost person. Tristan, she lost her husband who she evidently loved, god knows how I would have felt had I lost you…and then to lose your unborn child…" I break off shivering slightly, but I notice Tristan tense up beside me.

"What?" I question, sitting up so I can see his eyes.

"Nothing," he says closing his eyes so I can't see them.

"Tristan!" I scold. "Remember what we promised. We have to be honest and to talk to one another. I know you're keeping something back from me."

Tristan sighs heavily and runs his hand through his hair again. "What do you want me to do about Susannah?" He questions, trying to throw me off the scent.

"I don't know, can't we send her to the Priory or something?" I question.

"The Priory?" He snorts.

"You know what I mean," I say. "Will she be charged with attempted murder?"

"Probably, but her solicitor will no doubt plead insanity," he says.

"And if we drop the charges, she won't have to go to an Institution?" I question.

"Coral, why are you really doing this baby, because I'm trying really hard to understand?" He says.

"Because I'm guessing she was a happy, stable person before…" I drift off, imagining Susannah bouncing her baby on her knee, her husband beside her.

Tristan leans up on his elbow and stares down at me, then he softly strokes my cheek. "You want her to have a second chance?" he softly says. I nod my head. "Ok, we drop the charges as long as she goes where I want her to go, and right now, it's on a completely different continent. I don't want her anywhere near you or me," he snaps.

"Thank you," I muse. "I want to see her too," I add.

"No!" he barks.

"Tristan, you're not telling me what I can and can't do, let's just get that straight right now, before we're married. I want to see her, I will see her, and you can either come with me or not, it's your choice." *There, that told him!*

"Why on earth would you want to see her?" He challenges.

"I want to ask her something," I whisper.

"And what might that be?" He questions.

"It's a girl thing," I say.

"A girl thing?" He snorts sarcastically.

"Yep, anyway I'm done, well apart from my original question." Tristan tenses again. "You know…" I ponder on purpose, "the one about Dr Green?"

Tristan sighs and closes his eyes. "I was just pissed at her because she wanted to…" He stops for a moment then continues. "I'm not married to you, and I'm not next of kin, so we argued about who should tell you what had happened if you didn't remember. I got George in to see her, explain your past, and how it's best, knowing what you're like, for me to explain

125

everything to you. I knew it had to be someone that you trusted, not a complete stranger." Ok, I got that wrong. Why did I think there was more, that Tristan was hiding something from me?

"Why didn't you just say that to me earlier?" I question, but he doesn't answer me. "Tristan!" I prompt.

"What happened in the hospital Coral?" He questions, ignoring me.

"In the hospital?" I ask completely thrown.

"Yes, you had a dream…I think, a nightmare maybe, I don't know. But you said you would tell me," he says, finally looking at me.

I swallow hard. "Oh, that…" I whisper, frowning at his chest.

"Tell me, baby," he says, gently cupping my chin, so I have to look at him.

"I…I think I remember dying," I whisper.

Tristan inhales sharply. "You do?"

I nod again. "Yeah…it was really weird, I was outside my studio. I remember it was really foggy and I couldn't feel my feet hitting the ground, it was like…like I was floating. Anyway, I saw this bright white light, so I went to investigate. It was my mom Tristan, she was there talking to me, only she didn't look like my mom, but I knew it was her. She said that she was sorry, and that she'd been watching me, and that I had to leave her to come back here to you, she said that you needed me, then all I remember is pain, horrific pain and someone shouting 'she's back'." I swallow hard and look up at him.

"She's back?" He questions.

I nod solemnly at him.

"Are you scared about it?" He asks, his eyes wide.

"No, just a little freaked out. Do you think it's true, that is was my mom?"

"I couldn't say Coral," he says shaking his head. "But when Gran…right before she died she held her hand up in the air and said hello to my Gramps." He says swallowing hard.

I gasp. "She did?"

"Yeah, …it was a very bitter-sweet moment. I didn't want her to go, but I also thought if that's really true, and we meet the ones that we loved when we die, then I should feel happy for her, relieved even. But it doesn't matter what I think, what do you believe Coral? Do you think it was your mother?"

"Yes, I do," I whisper, my heart constricting for him again.

"Did she bring you comfort?" He softly asks.

"Yeah, …it was weird. It felt like it did before things got bad when we were all happy. I remember arguing with her that I wanted to stay, I think it's because wherever I was, there was no pain, no hate, no anger or rage, just peace and tranquillity."

He smiles softly at me then runs his finger under my eye. "You look exhausted," he says, which makes me realise how tired I am. "It's late, come on baby, let's sleep," he adds, sliding down the bed and carefully wrapping me in his arms.

"Yeah, it is," I say, feeling sleepy again.

"I have some more questions Coral, but this one can wait until tomorrow," he says.

"Ok…" I mumble.

"Sleep now gorgeous." Tristan starts humming Some Enchanted Evening to me as he gently strokes my back.

"Hmm, goodnight baby," I manage to say, and with a contented sigh, I drift off into a peaceful sleep…

CHAPTER TWELVE

I WAKE WITH THE most horrendous stabbing pain in my chest. *Holy Fuck!* Am I having a heart attack? I draw in as much breath as I can and shout for Tristan, he comes bounding out of the bathroom, completely naked, dripping soap suds all over the place.

"Shit Coral, what's wrong?" He shouts dashing over to me.

"I don't know," I pant, "I can't…breathe!"

"Fuck!" Picking up his mobile, he presses a button and puts it to his ear. "Ambulance," he shouts, then there's a knock on the door. Tristan grabs his t-shirt from the chair, covers up his man-bits, and opens the door. I see his face fall with relief. "Terry, thank God you're here…I've called for an ambulance. Do I need one?"

Nurse Terry steps hurriedly into the room, takes one look in my direction and dashes over to me. Within seconds, I feel the painkillers flooding my system, I sag with relief.

"No, all is well," Nurse Terry replies to Tristan once she's quickly checked me over.

"Oh thank God!" I hear Tristan say, and then he quietly talks into his mobile and ends the call.

"Coral, what happened?" Terry asks.

"I woke up with a sharp stabbing pain in my chest, I couldn't breathe." She nods and looks up at Tristan. "I think she'll be fine," she says. "You've probably slept in an awkward position and it's pulled at your scar tissue."

"You're sure?" Tristan questions.

"Yes, but if you disagree,' – "I'm not going back to the hospital. I feel fine now." I interrupt.

"I'll call Dr Green and see if she can come here. I apologise for the way I'm dressed…or not dressed," he adds to Nurse Terry, his cheeks flaming as he walks backwards into the bathroom.

I can't help chuckling at him. "Looking good there Tristan," I tease, winking at him.

He stops at the door, cocks his head to the side then shakes his head in exasperation at me, which makes me laugh even more. Terry stifles a couple of giggles as Tristan quickly closes the door, but when she turns to me, I see her cheeks are flushed, her eyes dilated, and she seems to be all fingers and thumbs.

"Feeling better?" She squeaks a little high pitched.

"Yeah, the pain's gone," I say, trying not to smirk at her. "So you think I was sleeping funny or something?" I question.

"Yes, that's my guess," she ponders. "Have you done any physical exercise?"

"No," I answer dryly.

"Good. Have you been having sex?" She asks.

"No, unfortunately not," I mumble.

"Not that then," she says. "Although I have to ask; how can you resist him?" she blurts, then slaps her hand to her mouth. I don't think she meant to say that.

"I can't," I laugh. "He's denying me!"

"Ah, well probably best," she says standing up to leave. I think she feels a little embarrassed. "Well I certainly feel awake now," she adds. "That was an eye-opener."

"I think Tristan was very embarrassed," I chuckle.

"Yes, I think he was too," she says. "Well, I'll be off, see you later."

"Bye Terry." She smiles at me as she heads out the door, with very red cheeks.

I look up at the new clock on the wall, 7.30am. *Great!* It's not going to be long until the detective is here. I suddenly feel wide awake, no point lying in bed trying to get back to sleep; besides I'm starving.

The door knocks again, and Edith enters with another tray. "Good morning Coral." She says handing me a glass of what I think is my veggie juice, and placing one on the side for Tristan.

"Wow, thanks, Edith," I say and glug half the glass down.

"How on earth can you drink that?" She says shaking her head.

"It's good for you," I say, smiling up at her.

"Do you have one every morning?" She asks.

"Yeah…pretty much," I say.

"Right you are." She says heading out of the room.

"Edith!" I call.

"Yes, dear?" She turns and smiles at me.

"Um…well' – "What do you need Coral?" she says impatiently, she must be busy. *Ok, now I'm a little intimidated!* She really is a straight-talking kind of woman, which is making me want to just make my own breakfast, but I know if I go down there and try to make myself something, Tristan will go bonkers – *It's ridiculous!*

"I'm hungry," I whisper.

She smiles warmly at me. "What would you like to eat?" She asks.

I think about it for a second. It's something I haven't had in a while, and I feel like I'm craving it; which is weird? – *Yep! Decision made!*

"Boiled eggs?" I ask.

"With tea and toast?" Edith asks.

"Marmite soldiers?" I ask, feeling like a child with Gladys.

Edith chuckles. "A fan of Marmite eh?" I nod vigorously then drink more juice. "As is Tristan," she says. *Huh! I never knew that?*

"Come down when you're ready lass," she says.

"Ok." I smile. "Oh…and Edith?"

"Yes, dear?" She adds.

"Thank you…for everything," I say.

"Everything?" She says, tittering at my serious expression.

"Yes, for being there for Tristan when he lost his folks…and looking after us both now. Just thank you, ok." I want her to know how much I appreciate everything she's done.

Edith comes storming over to me, her big boobs and bottom wobbling as she does, then she stops, and clasps her hands together in front of her. "I know it's not my place to say, but sometimes these things need to be said!" She takes a deep breath and continues. "You're a fine young lass Coral. I knew I'd like you because you've changed him." She says gesturing to the bathroom. "For the first time in a very long time, he's happy again. I knew whoever it was that was putting such a smile on his face must be a real gem, and you are. It's made me very happy to see him like this, he's been on his own for far too long, it's not natural," she says shaking her head in disapproval.

Then her face softens, and she takes my hand in hers. "You're a real sweetheart Coral…and so brave to save Tristan like that…" She adds, tears welling in her eyes.

"Well I think you're amazing too," I say, squeezing her hand back.

130

"Oh...come now, you're going to have this silly old bird crying at this rate." She titters.

"Sorry," I say, and pull the covers back to get out of bed.

"Do you want some help getting down the stairs?" She questions.

"No, I'm ok thanks," I say, my feet touching the floor.

"Alright, shall I put your eggs straight on?" She asks.

"Yes please...I'm starving." Edith pats my hand and heads out of the room.

I put on my new, white fluffy robe that Tristan bought for me, pick up my mobile and my mp3 player because I feel like some music, and carefully head down the stairs. Reaching the kitchen, I walk straight over to the sound system, plug my mp3 player in and choose Enya. I want some calming music. I hit shuffle and walk back over to the kitchen as the wonderful, mellow notes of Sumiregusa start filling the room – *Ah, so nice...*

EDITH AND I stop what we are doing and stare at each other because Tristan is frantically calling for me as he runs down the stairs.

"In the kitchen!" I shout back. I crack my second egg open and start dipping another soldier, then take a bite. *Mmm delicious and well cooked!*

"Christ Coral!" Tristan says entering the kitchen, running his hand through his hair. "I didn't know where you'd gone?"

"I was hungry," I say between mouthfuls.

He takes a deep breath in relief, I think, then smiles leans down and kisses my temple. He smells good, and he's dressed smartly too, suit trousers and a shirt, he looks so sexy. *I guess that's for the Detective?* I quickly push that thought away. I don't want to think too much about that.

"Who's this?" He asks as he takes a seat next to me. Enya is now singing On Your Shore, it's a very moving, soulful tune.

"You don't know?" I say, surprised.

"No...should I?" He laughs.

"Ok, if I said Caribbean Blue' – "Like your eyes," he interrupts.

I swallow hard and chuckle nervously. "Or Book of Days?" I ask.

"Ah, I remember that one coming out," he says. "This is Enya?"

"Yes." I giggle and carry on with my breakfast.

"Breakfast dear?" Edith asks Tristan.

"Please…" Tristan says looking down at my plate. "Is that marmite soldiers?" He asks, grinning widely, I nod as I'm busy eating.

"Would you like the same dear?" Edith asks, tittering to herself.

"Yes, I would thank you," Tristan says, his cheeks flaming. "I called Dr Green, she wants to see you at ten-thirty," he adds. *God damn it!*

I decide not to let it spoil my good mood. "Ok." I feel very happy today. Relaxed and content, I guess that's because I'm in love. "Do you have any idea how much I love you?" I ask.

His cup of tea stops at his lips, and I hear Edith make a strange squeaky sound. "I'm betting I love you more," he retorts taking a sip.

"I very much doubt that," I banter, eating more soldiers.

Edith places Tristan's breakfast in front of him just as I'm finished. I decide I want a bath. Sliding off the breakfast stool, I pick up my mobile.

"Where are you going?" Tristan asks, stopping me by placing his hand on my arm.

"Upstairs to take a bath," I say, entwining my fingers with his.

"Don't go," he pleads, his eyes wide and round.

"You want me to stay while you have breakfast?" I ask. He nods, smiling shyly at me. I simply cannot resist him, besides we have plenty of time.

"Ok." I kiss his cheek and sit back up on the breakfast stool.

Tristan may have asked me to stay, and he hasn't let go of my hand, but he seems very quiet and distant again. So I decide to go through my mobile. I haven't looked at it since what happened with Susannah. I smile widely as I see I have several text messages from Rob. The first one is asking me about dancing. Rob wants us to go out and shake some moves when I'm better. I haven't done that in a while, and I think with everything they have gone through, and Tristan and I, we all deserve it. I instantly picture Tristan and I dancing in a dark, nightclub; getting all hot and sweaty as our bodies grind against one another – *Ok stop!*

I blow out a deep breath. I can't think about that because it's just making me want to strip him and shag him senseless. So, to try and take my mind of those thoughts, I text Rob back letting him know how much of a sexy dancer Tristan is, and that we're

Forever With Him

in, as soon as I'm better we'll go dancing. I can't help smiling. I'm really looking forward to that.

Then I open the second text. Rob is asking me about the house, and how I want it decorated for the wedding? I roll my eyes and text him back. Letting him know that we'll discuss that when he gets here – I think he's stressing, which makes me feel bad. I don't want him to be stressed, not with everything he and Carlos have been through.

I will make it my mission to reassure him that is doesn't have to be a perfect day, that even if things go wrong, it won't matter – Marrying Tristan is my only concern, as long as the right person turns up to do that, I'll be happy.

Then I open the third text, and my heart sinks. Rob wants us to spend some time alone, just the two of us – he wants to catch up, like old times. I can't help worrying. I hope he and Carlos really are ok, and he wasn't just saying that. I text back, letting him know he just has to say when – It's not like I have a job anymore! I suddenly feel really glum. I'm really going to have to give it some serious thinking, I can't hang around not doing anything; it's going to drive me crazy.

"Secret admirer?" Tristan says. I look up, he's grinning widely at me.

"Yes," I tease.

His face falls. "Who?"

"Joking Tristan, there never will be anyone else for me," I say.

"Me neither...so?" He prompts.

"Rob," I giggle.

Tristan rolls his eyes. "You're seeing him this lunchtime?"

I shrug. "I know, he just..."

"He just what?" he asks.

"Are you jealous?" I ask.

"No. But I am worried," he retorts.

"Worried?" I half-laugh.

He turns and glares at me. "Is he a bad influence on you?"

"No," I answer my voice low.

"Well, he let you get really drunk that night you were out' – "Stop right there." I interrupt. "I am a grown woman Tristan, and if I want to get drunk, I'll get drunk. Besides, Rob would never let anything happen to me, he and Carlos are very protective of me."

"Ok." He submits mulishly, as he returns to his breakfast.

I try to work out why Tristan is acting like this. It's not like

Rob, and I would hit the town, get pissed and party till four in the morning, not with the state I'm in. I frown down at my mobile and ponder a little more…*Shit! No way!*

I think I've worked it out.

"Tristan, Rob is my very best friend, and he was the one I would always confide in. You know it's you now, don't you?" I softly say.

Tristan turns and smiles at me, I can see the relief in his eyes. "I do now."

"He's still my friend though, I know he's a guy, but try and think of him as a girl…you know, he's my girlfriend, I can talk to him about…well, girly stuff."

"Like what?" He asks, bemused.

"Periods, hairstyles, clothing, hormones…shall I go on?"

Tristan sniggers and shakes his head. "No, I get it." He grins.

"Good, so long as you know that," I say. "Because I will spend time with him, I'm not going to dump my friend because I now have a boyfriend…well fiancé…husband to be…" I splutter. "I hate people like that," I add, staring down at my hands.

"Me too," he says. I suddenly feel really sorry for Tristan; he has no friends of his own. "Hey," he says lifting my chin. "Don't feel sorry for me." *How does he do that?*

"Well I do," I retort.

"Well you shouldn't," he says. "I have everything I have ever wanted in the palm of my hands."

I swallow hard – He says the sweetest things. "Me too Tristan."

"Good, now let's get you in that bath."

"Tristan," I chuckle. "I don't think I need help' – "Coral, what if you accidentally slipped?" He asks. His serious face is back, he's not to be argued with. I want to roll my eyes at him and laugh, but I don't think he's in the mood for that. Besides, he has a point.

"You're right," I say and head over to unplug my player…

I LEAN MY head back and close my eyes. Then I sink further down into the bath. Hmm, I'm surrounded by bubbles, and Enya's music – *Perfect!* Tristan is in the bedroom, looking through the video footage on my laptop from the CCTV. He said he would make a copy of what's recorded so we can give it to the Detective. I feel my stomach flutter nervously, making me feel nauseous – *Don't think about that Coral!* I take a deep breath and slowly blow it out, trying my best to keep myself calm….

"READY?" TRISTAN ASKS as he helps me into my long sleeved jumper. I feel the colour drain out of my cheeks. I shake my head, I feel sick. I don't want to see the detective. I don't want to talk about what happened anymore. I just want to forget it all and move on.

"We have to do this, you know that right?" He says.

"But if we're dropping the charges…?" I whisper.

"I don't think we should do that," he says.

"Why not?" I frown.

"You know why," he says. "Besides, seeing Susannah wrecking your studio and attacking Bob…" He growls, his jaw clenching several times. He's right. But I can't work out why I want to save her because part of me doesn't. She should be punished for what she did, to Tristan, to Bob and to me – *God I'm so confused!*

"Coral," Tristan tilts my chin round to look at him. "You can change your mind baby, you know that, right?" I nod and try to fight against the stupid lump in my throat. I'm getting really pissed off with this feeling tearful crap. This is not me, I am strong, not weak; and I have never been like this before…I just don't understand.

"Hey," he says gently wrapping his arm around me. "You're ok now baby, you're safe."

"I know," I tremble.

"Then why are you so afraid?" He softly asks.

"I just…" I sniff loudly. "I'm just feeling so emotionally raw at the moment Tristan, and it's really annoying. I don't like feeling like this, I…I've never been this tearful before, it's like…I don't know, I've been through much worse, and I didn't cry then," I say, sighing heavily.

"Worse than getting shot?" He asks incredulously.

Ok, he has a point!

"No…I guess not," I sniff. Tristan lets me go, stands, picks up the box of tissues and hands them to me. "Thanks," I whimper and blow my nose. "I'm worried, Tristan."

"About what?" He softly asks.

"That you'll…well…get fed up with me…" I stop and shake my head at myself. "I just don't want you to think I'm like this all the time because I'm not!" I say, feeling angry.

"Hey." He smiles. "I know that Coral, so please baby don't worry. It's wasted energy."

"Ok," I mumble.

"We better get down there," he says holding his hand out to me.

Reluctantly, I place my hand in his and get to my feet. I turn to walk towards the bedroom door, but Tristan stops me by gently tugging on my hand.

"What?" I whisper.

Without a word, he pulls me into him and starts slowly dancing us around the bedroom, humming Some Enchanted Evening to me as he does. My mind floods with all the memories I have of us so far, especially the first night he hummed me to sleep with that tune.

"I want to tell you something," he whispers, pulling me from my reverie.

"Ok." I smile up at him.

"When I first met you, apart from thinking you were the most attractive woman I have ever met, I…well, I didn't quite know where to look. Your beautiful eyes had captured me, the colour, the shape. I swear to god I knew then I could stare at your face all day, but then I found myself drawn to your very sexy lips. I had to stop myself from leaning down and kissing them, they looked so…so' – "Kissable?" I interrupt.

Tristan chuckles. "How did you know?"

"Because it's how I feel about your lips," I say, feeling shy again.

"Is it now," he teases gently twirling me around.

"Yes," I giggle.

"And when I followed you up to the boardroom, I couldn't help looking at that fine figure of yours…" He laughs a little nervously, his cheeks flushing.

"And you were wondering what I would look like naked?" I ask, feeling brave.

He smiles wryly at me, then shrugs. "Well, I am a man!" He chuckles.

"Well, you weren't the only one thinking that," I say.

His mouth pops open. "Really?" I smile and nod shyly at him. "Well, well, Miss Stevens, surprising me again!" I giggle then rest my head against Tristan's chest, as we continue to dance around the bedroom. "Feeling better?" Tristan asks as he carefully twirls me around once more.

"Yes," I say smiling up at him because it's true.

"Good." He smiles, then leans down and kisses me. "Arms up," he softly says.

I know it's making him feel like he has a purpose, that he's looking after me. So I place my hands around his neck, he lifts me into his arms, and we head out the bedroom…

DETECTIVE MARSH IS a woman. She's tall, maybe five feet seven, slim, well looks very fit actually; has strawberry blonde hair that's tied back into a neat ponytail, and has very little make-up on, but is strikingly pretty. She's got to be in her late thirties, or early forties, I'm not sure. She's dressed in black fitted trousers, black boots, and a short-sleeved cream shirt, she looks smart, intelligent and has an air about her that says *'don't fuck with me'* – I like her.

"I thought you said the Detective was a man?" I whisper to Tristan as we walk over to her.

"It was?" He says, gripping my hand.

"Good morning Miss Stevens. Mr Freeman." She nods to us both, then smiles at me.

"Detective," Tristan nods to her.

"Hi." I manage to squeak out. *I'm so nervous!*

"I'm Detective Annie Marsh." I feel all the blood drain out of my face. *Annie. That was my mother's name.*

"Are you alright?" She asks me.

I nod and frown back at her.

She reaches out and shakes Tristan's hand. "Mr Freeman. Detective Ward has unfortunately been put on sick leave so I'll be heading the investigation from now on." She says very formally.

"Please, take a seat," Tristan says.

We all sit around the kitchen table. Edith comes over and asks if we would like drinks. Tristan and Detective Marsh ask for coffee, I don't have anything, I don't think I can stomach it. Tristan takes hold of my hand and gives it a gentle, supportive squeeze.

"Coral, I can tell you're nervous. So we're going to get through this as quickly as possible so you can get back to recovering, peacefully." She smiles. *Good, feeling better!*

"Ok." I breathe.

"Detective I have the recordings," Tristan says handing over a small USB drive.

"Thank you, Mr Freeman." She takes the drive and places it in her black briefcase. "I have something for you Coral," she says and produces a brown A4 Envelope. She slides it across the table to me. I open it up and hesitantly look inside. I can see my family photo, the A4 photo of Tristan and I, plus the key to my studio that Susannah copied.

"Thank you," I whisper, sealing the envelope. If I really look at the photo of my old family, I know it will make me cry.

"Mr Freeman, you should know our investigation has thrown some interesting light on the events leading up to Miss Johnson's attack."

"Oh?" Tristan's head cocks to the side. "How so?"

Detective Marsh's eyes flit from Tristan's to mine, then back to his again, she looks a little uncomfortable.

"Detective, whatever you have to say to me, you can say in front of Coral. She's my fiancé, we'll be getting married shortly. There are no secrets between us." He clarifies.

Detective Marsh nods once, takes out a pen and pad, then some paperwork and flicks through it until she finds what she's looking for. "Because of the nature of the attack, and the fact that it all stems from…" She flicks more notes. "Ah yes, from the fact that Ms Johnson has being diagnosed with Obsessive Compulsive Disorder, we had to find out if this was, well a one-off incident." She takes a sip of coffee then continues.

"With your approval, of course, we interviewed several members of your staff. It seems they all had taken a disliking to her and that she has upset them in one way or another, but unfortunately they knew you….liked her," she says, looking uncomfortable again.

Tristan shifts in his chair.

"And from the P.I report you handed to us, we also took the liberty of interviewing your ex-partner; Mrs Olivia Logan."

"Oh?" Tristan's face falls, the colour draining from his cheeks.

"Yes, it seems…well, I should ask really. Is it true that you were given information regarding Mrs Logan fidelity that led to the demise of your relationship?"

"Yes." His tone is flat, uninterested, but above all polite.

"This information was given to you by Ms Johnson?" she clarifies.

"Yes." Tristan states.

"And I take it you were not aware, suspicious even of any wrongdoing on Ms Johnson's part?"

"Of course not," he scoffs. "She wouldn't have still been working for me had I known that," he answers dryly.

Detective Marsh's eyebrows shoot up. "Mrs Logan also gave us some of your other ex-partners names, so we could interview them too."

"Who?" Tristan questions, his brow furrowing, his hand tightening around mine.

"Cathy Holmes. Rebecca Braithwaite and Sarah Clarence," Detective Marsh takes another sip of coffee. "Mr Freeman, I'm sorry to have to tell you this. But I have to say, I made it very clear to each of these women that you and Miss Stevens could actually sue them all, and that each of them could be held for criminal neglect' – "I'm sorry Detective Marsh, but why would we want to sue them?" He interrupts.

"Each of them has admitted to being harassed by Ms Johnson, in-fact Rebecca was attacked by Ms Johnson only days before she stopped dating you." *Holy crap!*

"What?" Tristan bellows launching to his feet. He's radiating anger and tension.

"Tristan," I look up at him with my empty hand. He takes a deep breath, places his hand back in mine and slowly sinks back into the chair.

"I don't believe this," he hisses staring down at the table then he looks up at the Detective. "I apologise," he says. "Please... continue." His jaw clenches several times as he stares back at her.

Detective Marsh shifts in her chair, and I notice for one tiny tenth of a second, her eyes linger on his chest. She shifts again, clears her throat and continues. "I take it you weren't aware?" She asks.

"No." Tristan glares at her, his eyes going dark.

I squeeze his hand trying to calm him.

"Am I correct that you dated each of these women?" She questions.

"Yes." Another one worded answer. She frowns back at him, trying to work something out.

"Why don't you just say what's on your mind Detective." I pipe up.

"Yes, please do," Tristan adds.

She looks at me, then Tristan then looks down at her notes for a moment, pondering. Squaring her shoulders, she looks up and stares Tristan directly in the eyes. I think she likes him and is trying not to show it.

"Alright, I'm finding it hard to believe that a well-rounded, and successful bachelor like yourself, would accept that these

139

women would suddenly want nothing more to do with you, after dating successfully for several months?"

"People change their minds." Tristan balks.

Detective Marsh narrows her eyes at him. I don't think she believes him. "Mr Freeman. I've been told you're a private man, and that even though you dated these women, it was low key. Not even your parents knew, is that true?"

"Yes." He barks. I can tell he's getting frustrated.

"And you never thought to question why each of them just suddenly dropped off the grid?" She asks, frowning inquisitively at him.

"Are you trying to accuse him of something?" I say.

"No Miss Stevens. I'm just trying to get the facts straight." She sternly answers her look telling me to shut the hell up. *Oops!*

"No," Tristan says. "I never thought to question it."

Detective Marsh frowns again. "Am I correct that they all gave you the same reason for the relationship ending?"

Tristan inhales sharply. "They told you that?" He breathes.

"Yes. Mr Freeman this is a police investigation, most people hear that, and they quake in their boots. These women were only too pleased to get it all out, everything that happened, everything that was said."

"I see," Tristan says, staring at our fingers tightly wrapped around one another.

"I'm still finding it hard to believe that you believed them." She says.

Is she flirting with him?

"I wasn't in a position to question it," Tristan says.

Ok, this is killing me. Question what? What do Tristan and the Detective know that I don't? I decide to ask. "What did Susannah do and say to them?" I question, looking from Tristan to Detective Marsh.

Detective Marsh turns to me. "Well, from what we have been told, each one was pretty much the same. Once Ms Johnson was aware of their relationship, she became involved. If they called, she would tell them Mr Freeman wasn't available, and she wasn't passing messages on. When each of them questioned Ms Johnson as to why Mr Freeman hadn't called them back, she lied."

"How?" Tristan questions.

"Ms Johnson was very manipulative. She made herself out to be the one in the middle, she promised them that she had passed messages on and they believed her, but she also lied to them and told them you were dating several women behind their backs. Now, this is where it gets interesting. They all said exactly the same thing that they were suspicious of Ms Johnson, yet they continued to date you. Did either of them approach you about her, ask you anything about her?" Detective Marsh asks.

"No." Tristan answers.

"Well, when Ms Johnson became aware that these women were still dating you, after trying to get them to finish with you, she took things to another level."

"Another level?" Tristan questions.

Detective Marsh looks uncomfortable again. "None of them had any evidence of course, but each of them believes that somehow, she had entered their properties, and each one admitted that Susannah had stalked them, then threatened them outside their homes. They were so intimidated by her that they did as she asked, apart from Rebecca."

"Rebecca?" Tristan whispers, his eyes wide.

"Do you remember what happened to her?" Detective Marsh asks, her eyes narrowing.

Tristan nods. "She just…disappeared. When I finally got hold of her, she told me she'd gone to stay with her mother in France for a while…" Tristan trails off, deep in thought.

"Yes, well Rebecca was the final straw for Susannah. When she realised you were still dating her, she attacked her outside her home, so brutally in-fact that she was hospitalised. She told the officer that interviewed her that it was a stranger that attacked her, so no charges and no investigation. That's why Rebecca went to France, to recover from her ordeal."

Tristan hangs his head in horror.

My mouth has gone so dry, I can't swallow – *Poor Rebecca!*

Detective Marsh continues. "According to Rebecca, after attacking her, Susannah threatened her that if she continued to see you, she would find her and kill her." *Oh my God!*

Tristan gasps, he looks horrified. "Detective…I very much doubt Rebecca would want to speak to me but please…pass on my sincerest apologies. Had I any reason to suspect any of this was going on…" Tristan hangs his head in his hands. "I would have protected her." I wrap my arm around his shoulder and tightly squeeze – *Holy fuck! Susannah really is crazy!*

"Of course Mr Freeman, I will pass that message on. I also think you should know that the reasons these women gave for ending the relationship, was in no way true. It was all Ms

Johnson's doing. Putting two and two together, I think it was to break you down, to knock your confidence so if you confided in her, she would be the one to comfort you and manipulate you into believing her, but that didn't work out for her, did it." Detective Marsh smiles, a little smugly for my liking.

"Christ!" Tristan looks up at her in complete bewilderment.

Detective Marsh suddenly frowns deeply. "The only part I don't understand is why she didn't make her move sooner? She evidently wanted you for herself." She muses.

"Susannah did approach me, but I said no, that I wasn't interested," Tristan says.

"Ah, I see. How long ago was that?" She questions.

"Years ago," Tristan says. "Before I dated any of these women."

Detective Marsh looks surprised. "You rejected her, yet she continued to work with you?"

Tristan shrugs. "Yes."

Detective Marsh brings the pen to her mouth and starts tapping it repeatedly against her bottom lip. "Hmm, maybe it was more along the lines of if she can't have you, then neither can anybody else?" She ponders to herself.

Tristan suddenly looks really irritated. "Detective Marsh, this is all very interesting, but Coral is still in pain, she should still be in the hospital, in-fact we have an appointment this morning." He runs his hand through his hair. "You came here to question Coral. I'd like that over and done with so she can get back to recovering." He orders.

He is not a happy man. *Fuck!*

Detective Marsh nods. "Of course Mr Freeman, we can continue this some other time."

Tristan nods in approval. *No! I want to know what was said!*

Detective Marsh takes another sip of coffee and looks directly at me. "So, I know this is going to be difficult Miss Stevens, but I'd like you to run through the events leading up to Ms Johnson's attack." I swallow hard and nod once. "Take your time," she adds.

I take a deep breath and start at the very beginning....

FOURTY FIVE MINUTES later and Detective Marsh is still questioning me, she's being very thorough, but I don't see what else I can tell her, and I feel exhausted. I just want her to go.

"Detective," Tristan interrupts. "We have a hospital appointment at 10.30am."

Crap! I forgot about that!
"I see…" She doesn't look too pleased.
"Do you have everything you need?" Tristan asks.
"I do have more questions," she says. "I don't want to leave any stone unturned, Mr Freeman." She explains.
"Yes, well maybe another time," he says.
"Alright." She stands, places her pen, pad, and notes in her briefcase then shakes Tristan's hand. "I'll call you," she says. Tristan nods once and then she nods at me. "I hope you feel better soon Miss Stevens," she adds.
"Thanks," I murmur. She smiles softly at me. Tristan walks around the table and sees Detective Marsh to the front door. *I'm so glad that's over!*
"Stuart?" Tristan calls as he marches back over to me. "Come on baby, let's go," he says holding his hand out.
"Go?" I question.
"Yes, to the hospital," he says.
"I'm not going back." I pout, crossing my arms.
"Coral, Dr Green wants to examine you and, make sure everything is as it should be," he explains softly as though he's speaking to a child. "And if we don't get a move on we're going to be late." *He's not to be argued with, and I'm too tired to bother.*
I sigh inwardly, pick up the envelope, stand and walk over to Edith in the kitchen. "Edith, would you mind putting this in our bedroom for me?"
"Of course," she smiles. "Pop it on the counter I'm going up in a moment with some clean washing."
"Ok…Oh and Rob, Carlos and Bob will be here at 12, if we're not back' – "Not to worry lass," she says placing her hand on my good shoulder. "You go and get checked out, I'll make them feel welcome," she says.
I nod numbly at her and walk over to Tristan. "I'm sorry Coral," he says taking my hand. "But I want to be sure."
"I know," I murmur. "Tristan, what was the Detective talking about? What did they all say to you when they ended it?" I ask as we head towards the front door.
"Later," he whispers, leaning down to kiss me. *God damn it!*
As we silently head out to the car, I try to push the sickening feeling away. Talking to the Detective has bought it all back, and I don't like reliving frightening events, and that night with Susannah, is one I know I'll never forget…

CHAPTER THIRTEEN

ARRIVING BACK AT the house after our little trip to the hospital, Tristan picks me up into his arms again and carries me into the house. Dr Green was great, her examination of me was very thorough, and I was pleased to be given the all clear. No more hospital stays, Tristan looked relieved too. And now I'm exhausted, I just want to sleep for the rest of the day – but I hate letting people down, so I guess I've just got to suck it up.

"Ok?" Tristan asks placing me down on the sofa.

"Yeah, better now I'm home," I say. "They should all be here soon, Rob said he was picking Bob up," I add as the wonderful smell of a roast dinner wafts towards me

The doorbell rings. *I guess they are here!*

"Are you sure you want to do this now?" Tristan asks, looking concerned.

"Yes," I say, throwing a fake smile in for good measure. "Tristan I'm ok, don't worry."

"Hard not to," he says, cocking one eyebrow up at me, then leaning towards me he gently pecks me on the lips.

"What were you talking to Dr Green about?" I ask. They seemed to be having another heated debate.

"Nothing," he says lightly. Then he leans in and kisses me again, his tongue gently lapping against mine – All thoughts disappear.

"Get a room!" I hear Rob bellow.

Tristan and I both turn and smile awkwardly at Rob. He comes bounding over to us, with an ear to ear grin. I notice Carlos is slowly following with Bob.

"Ready to get this show on the road?" Rob asks.

"Yes." I sigh inwardly. *Why do I feel like crying again?*

"Marvelous!" He says and sags into the sofa next to me.

"I'll just say hi to Bob and Carlos first," I tell him. Tristan helps me to my feet, and moments later I hobble back over to the sofa with Tristan's help and sit next to Rob.

"Right, here's the magazines," he says placing several in my lap. "The ones with the coloured tabs are the dresses I've chosen, the red tab is the one I think is the perfect one for you, so you need to go through them and pick which one you like."

"And if I don't like any of the ones you picked?" I question.

"Then we'll have to find something else, but you're not going to have much choice considering the timeline!" he scoffs.

"I know," I murmur.

"Have you two sorted your rings out yet?" Rob says looking from me to Tristan.

"No," I answer feeling guilty.

"What!?" Rob screeches.

"Rob! Coral is still healing you know. She woke up in severe pain this morning, hence the trip to the hospital for a check-up, and she's had to sit through forty-five minutes of intense questioning from the Detective in charge of the case!" Tristan informs him in a not so nice manner.

"Oh…" Rob looks crestfallen. "Sorry," he adds looking up at Tristan, who narrows his eyes at him, then storms off into the kitchen. "I think I've upset him," Rob whispers.

"Don't worry about it, it's me he's mad at," I whisper back.

"Oh?" Rob says, frowning down at me. "Is he being a bastard to you Coral, because you don't have to stand for any shit you know' – "Hey," I place my hand on his arm. "Tristan's been wonderful with me Rob, very sweet and very caring…" I break off and stare at the floor.

"Then why am I not convinced?" he softly says.

He looks worried. I sigh heavily. And in a moment of pure clarity, I decide to tell Rob everything, and I mean *everything*. If he knows then maybe, he'll take it easier on Tristan. I couldn't stand it if those two hate each other. But we need some alone time for that, an idea forms.

"Just go with me on this," I whisper to Rob.

"Huh?" Rob looks confused.

Taking the magazines off my lap, and getting to my feet, I begin. "Edith, how long will it be until dinner?"

"Oh…about thirty minutes," she says with a big smile.

I smile back at her. "Ok, thanks." I walk over to the table where Carlos and Bob are seated, playing checkers. "Hey, do you guys mind if Rob and I disappear for a while, wedding stuff…

you know?" Carlos beams at me, but Bob looks a little upset. "Bob, we'll chat after dinner. Is that ok?"

He smiles up at me. "Go on then," he says.

"Thanks." I lean down and kiss his cheek. Then I walk over to Tristan who is busy pouring wine for everyone.

He turns and frowns at me. "You should be resting," he tells me in a firm tone.

I purposely roll my eyes at him. "Will you carry me downstairs? Rob wants to take a look at the gardens, it might be where we have the wedding, you know outside instead of inside?" I say casually.

"Of course I will gorgeous," Tristan smiles broadly at me.

I turn and wink at Rob who is still looking confused – *Honestly, get with the programme!* Tristan lifts me into his arms and carries me down the stairs. I can hear Rob following, and once we are in the garden, Tristan releases me. "See you in a while," he says, softly stroking my cheek.

"I'll miss you," I whisper back. I watch him walk back inside then I turn to Rob, feeling totally anxious about what I'm going to tell him.

"What was all that about?" Rob says.

"I wanted some privacy," I whisper.

"Ok." Rob frowns. I walk over to him, link my arm in his, and we start walking steadily through the garden. "Coral, I know you've fallen in love with him, but he is…you know… treating you right?" Rob asks.

"Yes," I whisper – although he has been very snappy lately. "He's just stressed, Rob. I nearly died, and I don't think he's quite recovered from that yet. It's like he's been hit by a truck. He's doing his very best, trying to handle all of this, but he's worried. He just wants me to get better, and I haven't exactly made this easy on him. You know what I'm like Rob, I always feel like I have to handle everything on my own."

"So why does he look so serious all the time? I couldn't really see you hooking up with a serious dude; you're too funny for that Coral." Rob rightly points out.

I laugh at Rob. "He's not serious all the time, and you're right, I wouldn't get together with someone who had had their funny bone removed. Tristan is funny, he makes me laugh, and I make him laugh. You'll see, when this all blows over and were both more relaxed, you'll see how great he is."

Rob still doesn't look convinced. "You're not just saying that are you?" He whispers.

I shake my head at him. "Rob, there's so many things you don't know about me. I'm a very lucky woman to have him." I tell him.

"Why would you say that?" He asks his eyes wide with worry.

I stop walking, look up at Rob, and then I take a deep breathe and tell him everything. All the things that happened when I was a kid, why I'm the way I am, why I act the way I do. Of course, he already knows I see George, but now he knows the reasons why.

I tell him about being raped, and how freaked out I am about men. Then I tell him everything that happened with Tristan. How we met, our conversations, why I feel so lucky to have him. I explain why I felt so lost when he and Carlos left without a word, and how awful I felt when I found out Debs and Gladys' news, and all the weird stuff that happened with Susannah – *Now I really do feel drained!*

"Ok, I think I need to sit down," he says, looking around him. There are no chairs close by, so Rob just sinks down onto the grass with his head between his knees.

I carefully sit next to him and patiently wait for him to say something.

"Coral, why didn't you tell me?" I go to answer him, but he pipes up again. "I can't believe that happened..." he adds, shaking his head in disbelief. "I'm so sorry Coral," he softly adds, in-fact, he looks a little sick.

"Hey, I didn't say it to upset you!" I half-laugh.

"No wonder you think he's an angel, and no wonder you freaked out so much when you met him," Rob says.

"I know. Not many men would put up with me Rob. He's so patient with me, I...I still feel like I'm dreaming and any minute now I'm going to wake up," I say, shaking my head.

"Coral, I...I don't know what to say?" Rob chokes.

"Hey, you don't have to say anything – But I didn't think you'd have this reaction," I add.

"Sorry babes, but that was a real shocker!" Rob whispers.

"Sorry," I say again. Rob lies back on the grass and stares up at the sky. "Rob, you and Carlos really are ok aren't you?" I hesitantly ask.

Rob looks across at me. "Of course we are. We're better than we've ever been sunshine, don't worry about us." He says, smiling up at me.

"Ok, if you say you're good, then I won't worry. Will you go easy on him now?" I ask.

"Who?" He laughs.

I smile and roll my eyes at him. "Tristan of course! Rob, I love you, you're my best friend, but I love Tristan too, so much. So can you just try to get along with him, for me?"

"I do get along with him, well…sort of. I just want him to treat you right!" Rob retorts.

"Oh Rob, he does. He really, really does," I gush.

"Really? You're really that happy with him? I mean, yeah what's not to like right? He's successful, minted, handsome… well actually a very sexy hunk of a man, but all that means fuck all if you don't have mutual respect, admiration and love for one another. Do you guys have that?"

I grin like a fool and nod my head. "Yes," I whisper, swallowing hard against the lump in my throat.

"Hey, there's no need for tears," Rob softly says.

"Rob, have you ever seen me cry?" I question.

He frowns up at me. "Um…no actually, I don't think I have – that's weird?" He adds.

"Freaky fuck up!" I laugh, tapping my head.

He snorts and rolls his eyes at me. "Oh yeah, you're a real freak show Coral, what with your perfectly pretty face, figure to die for and you're awesome personality!"

My mouth pops open. "Did you…did you really just say that?" I choke out.

"Coral, you may feel like a freak, but I don't think you are. I've never thought you're weird or freaky, got issues, yes, but most people have. I think you're beautiful, inside and out. You are one of the nicest, funniest, warm-hearted people I have ever met, and I choose my friends carefully – but you already know that," he adds, smiling up at me.

"Rob!" I squeak, as silent tears begin cascading down my cheeks. *What a sweet thing to say!* "Sorry, Tristan's turned me into a blubberer," I add, sniffing loudly.

Rob gets up from the grass, chuckling away to himself, and wraps his arm around my waist. "That's right, you let it all out sunshine," he teases, making me giggle-sob. "Howl the whole neighbourhood down if you want to," he sniggers, which makes me howl with laughter instead.

This is what I love about Rob, he always knows the right thing to say to cheer me up. As I bounce from laughter to tears and back again, I have a sudden epiphany. Maybe Rob is right, and Tristan is generally a serious kind of guy? He's certainly not a joker like Rob, but maybe that's what attracted me to him in the first place, his intensity – it really kind of turns me on.

"There, there sunshine," Rob says, rolling his eyes at me.

"Hey!" I scold, looking up at him. "Enough with the sarcasm," I bite.

His face falls. "Gotcha!" I tease and howl with laughter at his shocked expression.

"Coral!" Rob gasps in disbelief and playfully slaps my leg.

I try to stop laughing, but I haven't felt this light in days, so I let it take over. Rob soon joins in, and we both fall back onto the grass in a fit of giggles. In fact, I'm laughing so hard that my belly is starting to hurt, but I'm loving it. I don't know how long we are there for, but it feels like a very long time.

"Coral?" I look up and see Tristan walking across the grass to us.

"Rob, you asked if we could hang out, just us?" I quickly say.

"Yes," Rob whispers back.

"How's tomorrow?" I giggle.

"Carlos is out for the afternoon, we'll have the place to ourselves. Come over!"

"Done. I'll be there," I quickly whisper back.

Rob helps me sit up, wraps his arm around my waist and gently squeezes. "You do want this don't you Coral?"

"I want Tristan Rob, forever. Now, let's get back upstairs so you can show me the dress you found." I say smiling fondly at my wonderful best friend.

TRISTAN HAS BEEN very quiet today. I can't help wondering why as I wave goodbye to Rob, Carlos and Bob. Shutting the front door, I wander over to him. He's sat on the sofa, deep in thought as he reads through some sort of paperwork. Reaching him, I hold my hand out to him, he takes hold of it, and I sink down next to him.

"Are you going to tell me what's wrong?" I ask.

"I have a function to go to this Friday, I wanted you to come with me, but I don't think it's a good idea at the moment," he says, his brow furrowed.

"A function?" I question.

"Yes, an associate. It's his 90th birthday. His wife's organised a surprise birthday party for him." He says, his tone firm.

"That sounds nice, I'd love to go with you," I say.

His lips press into a hard line. "Coral, how many times do I have to say, I don't want you overdoing it."

"I don't think sitting at a table, eating food, and drinking wine is overdoing it," I argue.

"You want to go?" He asks.

"Of course I want to go," I tell him. "I want to do all those things with you, Tristan." He frowns at me again. "Are you going to tell me what's really wrong?" I huff.

Tristan stares at me for the longest time – *Shit!* – Something really is wrong, but I don't think I'm going to get it out of him, so I decide on a different tactic.

"I found my wedding dress," I say. It's a perfectly simple design, medieval, a-lined, short sleeved and it covers my battle scar–I fell in love with it the moment I saw it! Plus, it will be here on Friday, unlike so many others where there was at least a four-week wait. Rob wanted me to really glam it up, he wasn't too impressed with my choice, but as I reminded him, I want this to be an intimate, simple, relaxed day –*No big deal!*

Tristan smiles at me, but it's off. *Ok, now I'm getting pissed off!*

"I know you're holding something back," I grate. "It's written all over your face," I add, trying to hold my temper in.

"No," he says, shaking his head. "There's nothing."

"Tristan, you made me a promise, no secrets. So please… just tell me." I beg with closed lids.

"No! You've been through enough!" he snaps.

My eyes dart open. "And what you have to tell me is really bad? What are you afraid of? You think I'll finally crack' – "Coral, for once in your life, just do as I ask!" He shouts – *He really doesn't want me to know.*

"Fine!" I snap back.

"Fine!" He grumbles.

"Well…for now anyway," I huff.

"I have some work to do." Without looking at me, Tristan stands and stalks towards his office, mumbling to himself as he does – *Well that's just marvellous!*

"Coral," Edith says as she reaches me. "Can I get you anything?" I shake my head, fighting back the tears again. "Can I say something?" she whispers. I nod, so she sits down next to me. "He's just worried," she softly tells me.

"I know, but that's no reason to keep snapping at me." I squeak.

"He's only doing that because he cares." I shake my head

and stare out the window. "He was never like this with *her*," she says.

I turn and look at Edith. Her chest is pushed out, her nose in the air. If she were a dragon, I swear she'd be breathing fire through her nostrils right now.

"Who?" I ask, bewildered.

"Olivia." I blink back at Edith while my brain catches up. *Oh shit!* Of course, Edith was living with Tristan when Olivia came on the scene.

"Why do you say that?" I whisper.

Edith shakes her head in disapproval. "I always thought he could do better. She always seemed...well, indifferent to him – cold. I never liked her, I know I shouldn't be saying this to you, it's not my place. I'm just trying to make you understand, to let you know that he never acted like this with her. I've known Tristan longer than you, and well, I've never seen him so in love, so protective. You are his true match, his mirror image." I frown back at Edith. I don't think that's true.

"You are the same," she says. "That's why you fight so much, both stubborn and both capable of very deep love, whereas Olivia...." Edith shakes her head and purses her lips. "Take, take, take that's all she ever did, she never deserved him; not a good man like Tristan. I just want you to know this, so you don't worry. He's hard on you because he cares so much and because he loves you so very much."

"I guess," I grumble.

"Oh, no guessing needed lass, you are perfectly matched. I'm so glad she's out of his life, I dread to think what would have become of him if he'd married her." Edith whispers.

"Edith," I giggle. "You're making her sound like the wicked witch of the west."

"That's a perfect example of how I used to think of her," Edith says with pursed lips.

I gasp. "She was that bad? I don't understand? Why would Tristan be with somebody like that?"

"Oh she was all sweetness and light to his face, but people always slip up, and eventually their true character is revealed." She says with a smug smile.

"How do you mean?" I whisper, totally intrigued.

"Well, years ago, Tristan had this really big case on. It was the last day in court, and he was always exhausted when it was all over. Happy of course, because he would always win, but it was long hours, not much sleep and by the time he got home, all he wanted to do was relax with a glass of wine. But she, she always got her way, she always got what she wanted; she never took his feelings into account. I don't know how she did it, but she would always convince him, somehow, that she was right – manipulative little b-' Edith abruptly stops and looks across at me. "Sorry lass, I shouldn't be telling you any of this."

"Yes, you should," I firmly tell her. "Edith I don't think of you as Tristan's housekeeper. You are so much more than that, and I'd like to think that as we get to know one another, we'll become great friends. So whatever you do, don't worry about speaking your mind, ok?"

Edith nods and continues. "Well, she organised a party for him. It wasn't for him, of course, it was to advance his career. Everything she did was to get him more money, more status. So instead of coming home to a quiet house, he came home to a house full of guests, a big party going on. Oh, I remember, he was so mad at her, but somehow she managed to turn the tables on him and make him feel guilty. I remember feeling so mad at her because they'd had a conversation not two weeks before in which she'd mentioned the party. Tristan made it very clear to her that he didn't want that, but she went on ahead and did it anyway. Horrible woman!" She adds. *Whoa!*

My head is spinning. I still don't get why he would be with someone like that, but then again, Justin was a bastard compared to Tristan's sweet nature.

"Coral, you must not let Tristan know I divulged this information to you," Edith says her face a worrying picture.

"Of course not Edith, it'll be our little secret," I smile.

"Alright then," she says, patting my hand. "Well, I better get on. You look, tired lass, why don't you go and take a nap?" She suggests.

"Yeah...I think I will," I say. Nurse Terry has already been this afternoon, so at least I won't be disturbed.

"Is there anything, in particular, you would like for tea?" she asks as I get to my feet.

My appetite has disappeared again. I'm tired, drained, pissed off and fed up – Tristan is holding something back from me, and it's killing me that he won't tell me. But worst of all, I hate that we are fighting like this.

"No, I don't mind...whatever," I say frowning at the floor. "Ask Tristan," I add despondently as I walk towards the stairs.

"Coral," Edith calls. I turn and look back at her. "He will come around sweetheart."

I try to smile at her, but it's a weak ass attempt. I quickly turn away before I start crying again and head up the stairs. When I reach our bedroom, I spy the envelope Detective Marsh gave me sitting on the bed. I walk over, pick it up, carefully lie down and rip open the envelope. The key falls out first, I pick it up and twist it round in my fingers. *I'll never live in my studio again!*

I shake my head at that thought and then place it on the bedside cabinet. Then I take out the A4 photo of Tristan and me, hold it up in front of me, and stare at the two of us.

"Why won't you tell me?" I say to Tristan's image, of course, I get no answer. *I'm talking to a piece of paper!*

Shaking my head at myself, I place it next to me on the bed. Then with trembling fingers, I pull out the picture of my family.

"Mom," I whisper, tracing her smiling face with my fingertips. Tears pool in my eyes again. *Please, no more crying!*

I hug the photo to me, keeping it close to my heart, and close my eyes; hoping sleep will come quickly.

I AM DREAMING I am in the forest again, the darkness of the deep green trees surrounding me. I feel lost like something is missing. I start searching on foot, weaving in and out of the trees. Then suddenly, out of the corner of my eye, I see my mother next to one of the smallest trees, it looks like the tree is glowing bright white, not my mom. I stagger towards it, only when I get there, she's gone and then the tree disappears.

"Mom?" I call out for her, but I get no reply. I look around me, searching for her, trying to understand why the tree has gone.

"Look." Her voice whispers from behind me. I spin around and see she looks like she did in my last dream of her. I know it's her, but she's just a strange white light, floating in front of me. "See..." She says pointing down at the ground.

I turn and look down at the damp, muddy ground, there's a big hole from where the tree and its roots were. I hesitantly take a step closer to the hole and peek inside. *No!*

There, lying inside the hole is a baby, a naked newborn baby...

MY FACE IS being stroked, someone is trying to wake me. I try to push the hand away...*No, I want to stay in the dream!* "Coral..." Tristan's voice softly calls. I make no move even though I'm half awake. "Come on darling, wake up. It's time for tea." *No, no more food!*

I groan and go to turn over, but a dull ache in my bladder is waking me – *Damn it!*

"Ugh..." I open my eyes and see Tristan sitting on the edge of the bed, staring down at me. His broody look is still there. "I'm not hungry Tristan," I tell him as I get to my feet.

"Coral, you need to' – "Are you going to tell me what you're keeping from me?" I say staring back at him. I can tell he's not going to so I walk towards the bathroom.

"Coral, I think it's best that' – I shut the bathroom door on him, effectively blocking him out. If he does not tell me what is going on, *like tonight*, I am going to stay with Rob and Carlos. He won't tell me what Detective Marsh meant either, even though I hounded him in the car. Maybe I need to give him an ultimatum? *Yeah, an ultimatum, that's what I'll do he's sure to tell me then!*

When I'm done, I look up at my reflection as I wash my hands and nod in agreement with myself. Then the dream comes back to me, I stop washing and turn the water off. What the hell was that all about? I try to figure it out, but nothing comes to mind that makes any sense, so I shrug it off and get back to Tristan. Right, so I'm going to Rob's if he doesn't tell me what's going on. Then I remember I can't do that, I can't walk out on him, we promised each other we would never do that. *Damn it!*

I dry my hands, lean forward and stare at my reflection. I look different...I feel different. Shaking my head at myself, I try to think of what other weapons I have in my arsenal, there must be something I can do or say that will get him to tell me? Sex?–*Yes!* He's always talkative after sex, maybe this is the way? *Right then!*

I take my time removing my jumper and jeans, being careful with my shoulder. Then I stare at myself in the mirror; all I'm wearing is a set of my new bra and knickers. Dark blue lacy thong and the bra is the same colour, only it has pretty, light blue stitching across each cup. I wonder for a moment if I should try this completely naked?

No, this is more enticing...*I think?*

Taking a deep breath and summoning up some courage from somewhere, I head back into the bedroom, only when I do, I find Tristan sat on the edge of the bed with my old family photo in his hand, completely mesmerised.

"You look like your mother," he says, transfixed. "But then again, I can see your dad too," he adds, frowning thoughtfully.

I completely ignore him, walk over and stand in front of

him with my hands on my hips, but he doesn't look up at me. *Look at me, Tristan! I'm half naked in front of you for Christ's sake, look up!*

"Edith has made us a bread and butter pudding," he absently says, still staring at the photo. My stomach grumbles in appreciation – *No! Be quiet!*

"Are you purposely ignoring me?" he asks, keeping his eyes fixed on the photo. I stay silent. *Tell me what you know!* I say over, and over in my head, willing him to tell me.

"I take it you are," he says. "That's very immature of you," he adds, his brows creasing together. *Hmm, this isn't working!*

"Actually, I'm trying to coax you into having sex with me," I huff, my foot starts tapping.

"I'm well aware of that," he says, finally looking up at me with those big, round chocolate eyes of his – *Damn it, this isn't working!*

Plan B - In a vain attempt to seduce him, I run my fingers through his hair. "Do you have any idea how much I missed having you to myself today?" I question – *Because I have missed him, big time, even though I'm mad at him!* He slowly shakes his head. His eyes are dark and dilated; his look heated.

I lean down and gently kiss him. "I missed you so badly it hurt," I whisper against his lips.

"That badly?" He teases. I nod once. Then being brave, I straddle him and grind myself against his growing erection. I want him badly. I have missed the feel of him buried deep inside me.

"Coral, No."

"Yes."

"No."

"Yes."

"We could argue about this all day, but it's not happening," he tells me firmly.

"Why not?" I frown.

He stays silent, so I reach down and cup his erection in my hand. *Oh, it's been so long...* Tristan steadies my hand, looks up at me and stares back at me for the longest time. I am mesmerised, frozen in place – *What is that look in his eyes?* Taking me by complete surprise, his hand splays out across my belly, and he just leaves it there and stares down at it. I frown and stare down too, then rest my hand on the top of his.

"I'm not made of glass," I grumble.

"No!" He firmly tells me, keeping his eyes fixed on my belly, his jaw tensing a couple of times.

"I want you buried deep within me," I whisper. "I want to lose myself in you all evening," I add hoping it's too good an opportunity for him to miss.

Keeping his hand on my belly, he takes a deep breath and closes his eyes for a moment, when he opens them they are gazing at my belly again. "As tempting as that is," he whispers then swallows hard. "We have something we need to talk about." He adds.

His eyes meet mine, and I see they are swimming with emotion.

I take his face in my hands. "What is it? Why do you look so sad?"

His head drops again, his eyes gazing at my belly for a moment, then he lifts his head, takes my face in his hands and kisses me softly. Pulling back, he gazes at me again, and I can see it in his eyes, whatever this is, it's serious – *Crap!*

"What's wrong?" I whisper, his thumbs skate softly across my cheeks. "This is hard for you to say?" I quickly surmise.

He nods solemnly at me. *Fuck! What do I do?*

I close my eyes for a moment, trying to work out what to do when I open them and look at him, his eyes are blazing and dark. "It's ok Tristan," I gently say, stroking his cheeks as I do. "Take your time," I add, even though the suspense is killing me.

His head drops again, his eyes gazing at my belly for a moment, then he lifts his head, takes my face in his hands and kisses me softly again. "Coral..." he croaks.

"What?" I push because it seems like he just can't get his words out. He briefly closes his eyes then places his hand back on my belly. I place my hand over his. "Please Tristan...tell me," I beg.

"You were pregnant," he breathes, his eyes are almost black now, his jaw strained.

"What?" I half-laugh shaking my head at him, then it slowly starts to sink in what he just said, *'You were pregnant'* I swallow hard against the lump in my throat.

"Were?" I whisper, staring down at his hand still splayed across my belly.

"They think it was the stress, the trauma of what happened," he quietly says.

"I was pregnant?" I whisper disbelievingly, slowly shaking my head.

"Yes, very early stages. One week, maybe a few more days...?" He replies, his jaw tensing again.

"But...but we used protection?" I squeak.

"Coral, don't you remember? After you told me about your past and the test you had done...we spent all that weekend having unprotected sex."

Shit! - He's right, we did!

I stare disbelievingly at him.

I was pregnant?
That means...?
This means...?
I was pregnant!

I start rapidly shaking my head in horror – *This can't be true, can it?*

"But I can't get pregnant," I whisper in defiance. *He's got it wrong, he must have done.*

"Wrong diagnoses, you can conceive," Tristan says, watching me carefully.

"But...how do you know that?" I whisper, staring at Tristan with wide eyes.

"When you were brought in, and they managed to resuscitate you. They started doing the usual checks before you went down to theatre..." Tristan stops and runs a hand through his hair. "One of the nurses noticed you were bleeding...down there...at first, they thought it was internal haemorrhaging, they did all sorts of tests, but your blood was showing high levels of human chorionic gonadotrophin. Apparently, it's what your body produces in the early stages of pregnancy..." He swallows hard.

"I...I miscarried?" I whisper in horror.

Tristan nods, unable to say anymore. His eyes are bleak, his cheeks flushed. I stare down at my belly again. I was pregnant, and I didn't even know it. I didn't feel anything. *What does that say about me?*

"I didn't know...I couldn't feel anything..." I breathe staring down at our hands. "How could I not know?" I ask.

"Dr Green is...well she said once I'd told you, that you could go and speak to her about it, she said anytime, just call. That's if you want to," he quietly says.

So that's what they were arguing about!

A tsunami size wave of guilt washes over me. "This is my fault," I whisper. "If I had told you what was going on with

Susannah if she hadn't tried to...maybe the baby....?" I stop, unable to continue.

"Coral don't," Tristan says, running his thumb across my lips. "You have nothing to feel guilty about – Nothing!" He firmly adds.

"I lost our baby Tristan, so don't try and tell me I shouldn't feel guilty." I bite.

We stare at one another again, two stubborn fools.

"Do they know…?" I squeeze my eyes shut unable to finish.

"Know what baby?" He whispers, stroking my cheek.

"What is was…boy or girl?" My voice is barely audible. Suddenly the dream I was just having makes perfect sense...the baby...the newborn baby! Maybe my subconscious was trying to tell me?

"No Coral, they don't know." I nod my head. "How do you feel?" He asks.

"Confused, worried, shocked..." I stare out into space. "Sad…" I add wistfully.

"I am so sorry baby," he softly says.

"Me too," I whisper. I detangle myself from him, walk over to the ceiling height windows and stare out at the view, trying to assimilate some rational thinking, but my head is swimming. I was pregnant with Tristan's child. I look back at him. He's being patient as usual, but his head is hung low as he stares down at the floor. In fact, I'd say he looks lost, and just as cut up about the news as I am – *Oh Tristan!*

I walk back over to him, and carefully straddle him again.

He looks up at me. "I...I don't know how to make this better Coral, tell me what to do?"

I shake my head at him. "I don't even know where to start… there's a whole myriad of emotions," I choke.

"Do you want me to ask George to come around?" He softly asks.

I shake my head at him. "No, I want you, Tristan. I want you to be my first port of call, always, not George."

"Really?" He looks confused and surprised.

"Yes. Isn't that how it's supposed to be?" I whisper.

"Yes, but' – "Tristan…when Susannah attacked you, and I found you lying on the bed…" I close my eyes remembering, there was so much blood. "There was a split second when I thought you were dead, that I'd lost you forever," I swallow hard. "I vowed to myself that I would never shut you out again and that I would let you in, despite how scared it makes me, only when I thought that there was no more fear. Almost losing you made me realise I want to be open with you, always. I want to tell you all the things I'm feeling right now, even if you don't like what you hear…" I end in a whisper.

"You do?" He says, surprised.

"Yes," I answer firmly.

"Oh, baby." He pulls me into his chest and wraps his arms around me. "That's like hearing you say you loved me for the first time." He softly adds.

"Want to know my first question?" I say.

"Yes." He whispers.

"How are *you* feeling?" I question.

"What?" He pulls back, gripping my upper arms and frowns at me.

"Hearing that I was pregnant…then losing it. How has it made you feel?" Tristan is quiet for a really long time, but I bide my time and try to be patient with him.

"I…I've thought about a lot of things," he finally says, staring at my belly again.

"And the first thing is…?" I prompt.

"That you *can* have children, you have that honour back, it wasn't taken away from you," he softly says. It suddenly hits me – *This is why he's been so reluctant to have sex with me!*

"Are they really sure?" I question. "I was definitely pregnant?" *How can I feel sad about losing something I didn't even know I had?*

"Yes, that's probably why you're so up and down. The nurse said that you'll be fine one minute, crying the next, because your hormones are all out of whack." *That explains the crying!*

"Oh…" I stare down at the bed. "We were going to be parents?" I say, trying to get my head around it.

"Yes," he breathes.

"And how do you feel about that?" I question.

"Over the moon," he admits.

My heart sinks. "You *did* want children," I tremble, remembering our conversation in the kitchen.

"Hey." He pulls on my chin. "Less of that, when we discussed it I was completely honest with you. Then when I was told in the hospital that you had fallen pregnant…I…I thought it was the most wonderful news, second to you saying you love me and you want to marry me…" Tristan takes a deep breath. "Then when they told me you had miscarried, I was so angry. Why did that have to happen to you? Hadn't you been through enough? Then, after a while I started to feel a little more positive, you could conceive, and I thought that...over time, after me giving you the news, that you might want to try again...maybe." He looks up at me with dark, sad eyes.

"Oh, Tristan!" I wrap my arms around his neck and cradle his head under my chin. "Tristan, I'm not ready for a baby yet," I croak. "I just want you all to myself for a while."

"Hey." He leans back and takes my face in his hands. "Whenever...whatever you want Coral, however, you want this to work, it's all up to you." He says, gazing up at me.

"Don't you get a say?" I question.

Tristan smiles enigmatically at me. "I want whatever you want." I shake my head at him. "What?" He questions.

"Is that why you've denied me?" I whisper, staring at his full lips.

Tristan sighs heavily. "Partly, if we started...we would have had to use protection, and I know you would have questioned that, but mainly I want you better first, I'm worried about hurting you."

"Thought so," I say.

"Baby." He snakes his thumb across my bottom lip. "You're taking this all too well."

"Am I?" I gaze down at my belly again. "I don't think I am Tristan. I think I'm in shock. This crying thing is new to me, and I seem to be doing an awful lot of it lately, and I *hate* it!" I hiss. "I hate feeling up and down."

"I know," he whispers.

We sit in silence for a while, just holding one another, both deep in thought.

"Hey," Tristan lifts my head to look at him. "What do you want Coral, some food, a bath, a shower?" He softly asks.

"I want you to make love to me then shower with me. I need help washing my hair." *There I've said it, he likes it or he doesn't.*

He sighs heavily and briefly shuts his lids. "Baby...your still in pain," he says gazing at me with wide, worried eyes.

"I don't care," I bark. "I'll take the pain. I just want to feel you."

"Can't you feel this?" He questions, wrapping his arms around me and squeezing me gently.

"It's not the same," I scold. "And you know it."

Pulling back to assess me, he smiles wryly at me then shakes his head in frustration. *He's saying no!*

"Please," I beg. "We'll go slow…please, Tristan. I need to do this with you."

"Why?" He questions, searching my face.

"Because it's my way of being closest to you like I'm part of you, connected to you…I've missed you like that, I've missed us like that, I just…" I take a moment trying to think of the right words to explain how I feel. "It's like, being with you like that, after what happened to me when I was young, it's like….like I kind of completely lose myself in you. It's the only way I feel I can express myself, express my love for you. When we make love, all I feel is pure love flowing through me, it's magical," I say.

"Oh baby," he breathes and gently takes me in his arms, kissing me sweetly.

"Is that a yes," I murmur against his lips, teasing his tongue with mine.

"Yes," he whispers. He's breathing hard, and his eyes are dilated.

"I guess we're going to need that box of condoms after all," I whisper, smiling coyly at him.

His face falls to his broody look. "If this hurts you," he warns. "I'm stopping," he adds in a tone that's not to be argued with.

"Ok." I quickly submit, not wanting to rock the boat.

He cocks one eyebrow up at me then laughs with sarcasm. "Well now I know what to do when *I* want you to do something," he muses.

"You do?" I whisper, running my hands through his soft hair.

"Yes, deny you sex. You'll do anything for it," he laughs.

"Anything for you," I tell him.

"Yes, for me," he smiles, making me melt.

"I'm all yours baby," I giggle, holding my good arm out. "You better take me before I internally combust."

"Coral," Tristan stills me. "I know you're strong, much stronger than I originally thought, but' – I place my fingers on his lips. "I need time," I tell him. "Time to process it, but right now I just want to forget about everything and be with you." I gaze back at him, mentally pleading with him not to change his mind.

"You're sure?" he questions.

"Yes, I'm absolutely positive," I say and leaning forward

I softly kiss him. Desire unfolds deep within me, I pull back panting. "Take me," I whisper.

Tristan wraps his arms around me and carefully lays me down on the bed. The full length of his body is lying on top of me, his elbows supporting his weight. I can feel his erection digging into my belly...*Oh God, I want him...so badly.*

"I really do love you, Coral Stevens," he softly says.

CHAPTER FOURTEEN

HIS LIPS SWOOP DOWN, crushing hard against mine and making me moan aloud with pleasure. Passion unfurls thick and heavy in my body as our tongues tease and tantalise each other. I wrap my legs around him, pushing his erection into my groin, grinding against him.

"You're a hungry little thing," he growls.

"Yes," I pant. "For you, always."

Standing to his feet, Tristan bends down and takes off his shoes, then in double quick time, he strips off his clothing. *My sexy man!* I watch him walk over to his bedside cabinet, open the drawer, pull out the box of condoms and throw it on the bed. In my haste to feel him inside me, I rip open the box, pull out a condom, rip open the foil and take out the horrid thing. *Maybe I should go on the pill?*

I look up at Tristan with hungry eyes and see his eyes reflecting the same thing. *Wow, he really is a sight to behold. So gorgeous, so fit...my beautiful man.* Tristan slowly and seductively crawls up the bed to me, kissing every inch of me as he does.

My head cranes back as I moan in delight. *God, I need this!*

"God you're sexy," he breathes. Reaching my bra, he pulls the material aside on each cup, so my nipples are exposed, they are already hard and aching for his touch. Slowly, he leans down and gently sucks my right nipple.

"Ahh...Tristan!" I feel it right down below. Then he moves and does the same with my left nipple. "Tristan," I mewl my eyes involuntarily closing.

"We're going to take this real slow baby," he says as he starts to nip, kiss and suck his way down my torso, stopping when he reaches the material of my lacy thongs. Jesus, I want him in me now, I don't want to take it slow! Peeling the material of my knickers to the side, his mouth swoops down, and his tongue starts to gently flick my clitoris, over and over, round and round, then up and down. It builds so fast inside me that I don't have any time to think about it – and I come, hard, my body bowing as the waves ripple through me.

"Coral," he chuckles. "You're so responsive to me, you turn me on so much baby," he adds. Reluctantly, I open my eyes and smile up at him. He holds his hand out to me, I know what he wants, but I want to taste him, I want him in my mouth.

"But I want to' – "No!" he softly scolds, freakily reading my mind. "Not until you're better," he says, so I place the condom in his hand.

Kneeling up, he carefully places the condom on his fine manly parts, smiling wickedly at me as he does, and then he is on top of me again, his elbows supporting his weight, the head of his erection teasing my sex.

I push my hips up and grind against him.

"Slow baby," he whispers staring down at me.

"Ok," I relent. *I'll behave!*

"Good." He smiles wickedly at me again, and slowly starts to enter me, inch by inch, until he's completely filled me – *Yes!*

I close my eyes, my head craning back, wanting friction. I need to feel him moving inside me.

"Oh baby," he breathes, and starts to slowly move – in and out, in and out. I want to move, to grind against him, work with his rhythm, but he wants me to be careful, and I know if I push it he'll stop. "Coral," he softly mewls.

I open my eyes and gaze up at him. "Oh, Tristan...I have missed this," I pant as we keep up the slow, sexy rhythm. "Ah..." Tristan suddenly moves hitting the right spot inside me. I feel myself tighten around him – *Oh no! Not yet...please...*

"Jesus," he hisses, moving a little quicker.

And the build-up just doesn't stop. The more he moves, the heavier and thicker it seems to build within me. I feel like I haven't done this before, it's all happening so fast.

"Tristan," I moan trying to hold onto the sensation as I tightly grip his biceps.

His mouth swoops down on mine, and we can barely kiss each other for panting so hard. Tristan moans a deep sexy sound and closes his eyes. He's hovering above me, his lips inches from mine as he moves in and out of me, he smells so good...tastes so good...*Oh, Tristan!*

"Come with me, baby." He says, staring down at me with wide eyes.

"No!" *I don't want this to stop.*

"Yes," he hisses. "Now!" And he climaxes, just as I explode around him – *No!*

Tristan wraps his arms around me and turns onto his back, so I'm lying on top of him. I can't help smiling as I watch him slowly come down from his orgasm. He really does have a lovely face. Opening his eyes, he grins like a fool in love, leans up and gently kisses the tip of my nose.

"How are you feeling?" He asks.

"Oh, you know..." I tease.

"Actually I don't," he says dryly. "Was that not to your satisfaction Miss Stevens?"

"Yes," I giggle. I can still feel him inside me, so I wriggle in playfulness, but it sends shooting pains across my shoulder. "Shit!" I wince in pain and squeeze my eyes shut trying to block it out.

"Coral!" Tristan balks.

"I'm ok," I whimper.

"Right that's it," he snaps. "No more sex until you're better."

"No!" I argue. "I didn't feel any pain having sex. You can't use that one against me, Tristan, so stop it!" He frowns back at me. "I mean it!" I say.

"Fine!" He pouts. It makes me giggle. "I'm funny too?" he balks.

"Hey." I pull on his chin, so he has to look at me. "That was amazing Tristan, I don't think I'm ever going to get enough of you like that."

"Round two?" he asks mischievously. *Huh?* One minute he's saying no, the next he wants more?

"Wait!" I say. "What were you and Detective Marsh talking about?"

Tristan sighs gently pulls out of me and then moves me, so I'm lying next to him. Then he lies flat on his back and looks up at the ceiling.

"Tristan?" I prompt.

He sighs again and closes his eyes. "You remember when we first talked after your accident with Lily and I told you my cxes didn't..." He trails off, running a hand through his hair, and just stares up at the ceiling. I scoot closer, so I'm half lying across him, then lean down and kiss his big, beautiful shoulder.

He shakes his head and smiles wryly at me. "I can't believe I actually believed them, but when you hear it several times, you start to believe it's true I guess..." he ponders to himself.

"Hear what? What did they say, Tristan? I'm climbing the walls here!"

He swallows hard, then smiles shyly at me. "They all said the same thing Coral, that I'm boring and predictable, they all said that I make myself out to be a charming guy, but I'm a fake, shallow, cold-hearted man, who's..." He swallows hard again and runs his hand through his hair. "They said I'm the worst sex they've ever had, and believe me, baby, to a man, that's the biggest blow a woman can make. Male egos can't take that, and it made me feel so unworthy of them." He looks hurt, betrayed and heartbroken.

"Susannah!" I hiss, my teeth grinding together because this is all her fault. "Your nothing like that Tristan, nothing! I know I haven't had lots of lovers, but you make just being with you feel like magic, and as for the sex..." I shake my head. "You take me so high I don't ever want to come back down." I smile shyly at him.

"Thank you, baby," he smiles, then his face falls; he's got his serious head-on again.

"Tristan, what is it?" I ask, running my fingers through his hair.

He closes his eyes for a moment. "That feels so good," he smiles, his eyes still closed. I keep running my fingers through his hair, then lean down and kiss his forehead, then his eyelid, then his nose, his cheek and finally his very soft and very kissable lips.

He opens his eyes and gazes up at me, he looks apprehensive.

"Tell me," I push, suddenly realising we seem to have to do that a lot with each other. Maybe Edith is right, and we are mirror images of each other?

"My question, from last night," he softly says.

I smile down at him. "You can ask me, baby, you know that right?"

He smiles his shy smile at me, then frowns and nods his head. "It's not really a question, more like I need answers I guess...but I'm reluctant to ask you because I don't want you reliving it, but I'm also desperate to know. George won't tell me without your permission and...I keep getting these awful scenarios running through my mind, I think if I knew...how it happened, I can relax a little," Tristan breaks off, staring up at the ceiling again.

I frown hard trying to work out what it is. "Ask me, baby?" I say caressing his cheek, still running my fingers through his hair.

Tristan briefly looks at me, then closes his eyes and sighs. "How were you raped," he gushes, and then his words start coming out at rapid fire speed. "Was it on the beach, in a dark alley? Did someone see and not help you' – I silence him by placing my finger against his lips.

I feel the blood drain out of my face. "Tristan, have you really been worrying about how and when?" I ask, completely mortified.

"Yeah…every now and then it comes up and…I…I just think if I knew…" He stops and gazes back at me. I swallow hard. I really don't feel like going through this now, but I can't have him thinking the worst.

"Ok," I breathe. "It was at a hotel." I blurt.

Tristan frowns back at me. "A hotel?"

"I'm not like that Tristan, you know that right?" I squeak in panic.

"Like what?" he asks, he seems baffled.

"Well…you know. I don't sleep around." I whisper.

Tristan sighs with relief. "Of course I know that, but how did you' – "How did I end up in a hotel room with a man I didn't know?" I say.

He nods solemnly at me.

"I told you I made a stupid mistake, and I did. Long story short, I got on with him really well, so much so that I didn't want the evening to end. We'd been sat at the bar in the hotel drinking for hours, and when the bar closed, he asked me if I wanted a night-cap. I said no that I'm not that kind of girl, he said he wasn't thinking of that he just wanted to stay in my company - he was very convincing." I add.

"Oh, I bet he was," Tristan growls.

"Well, that's it. I'm sure you can figure out the rest…" I murmur.

"Didn't anyone hear you?" he asks.

"Hear me?"

"Didn't you scream?"

I slowly shake my head. "Tristan, he hit me when I tried to fight him off, then he tied me up, I was pretty out of it. And I know it sounds really, really bad, but compared to what happened to me as a kid, it was…mild." I shake my head and swallow hard. "Once I got my mind around the fact that it was going to happen, I just went away, blanked it out as though I wasn't there like I used to as a kid." I take a deep breath. "Honestly, I thought that was it. I thought he was one of those psychos who rape and torture women then kill them, so I was... preparing more for the pain of being killed." I close my eyes and wince, remembering it all too clearly.

"Baby stop' – "No, you should know. He was so rough with me that I was more worried about him killing me than what it felt like when he was raping me. I can remember thinking, this hurts really badly, how much pain am I going to feel if he kills me? But I guess I must have passed out at some point."

"Oh, baby." Tristan pulls me to him, I lay my head on his chest. He wraps his arms around me, and we lay quietly for a while, both deep in thought. I can't believe he's been thinking about the how and where...*My poor baby!*

"If he tied you up, how did you escape Coral?" Tristan asks, pulling me from my musing.

I look up at him. "Escape?" Tristan swallows hard and nods again. "When I came to, I realised my hands and ankles were free. Then he stirred next to me and went off to the bathroom. The moment he locked the door, I grabbed my jeans, my t-shirt and my bag, then I ran."

"You ran out of there completely naked?" He balks, his eyes wide.

"Yes, it was chance to escape, I was going to take it. I ran to the stairwell yanked my clothing on and ran all the way back to Gladys's." I say, remembering how wrecked my feet were.

Tristan clenches his jaw. "But if he hit you, didn't Gladys question it?"

I lean up on my elbow and stroke his cheek. "Gladys had been away the weekend. It happened on a Saturday night, by Sunday afternoon she was back and I...well, I lied. I told her I'd been attacked by some drunken idiot when I went to pick up my pizza, and that he'd hit me and fled with my dinner." I can't help the smile that starts to spread across my face.

"Are you laughing?" Tristan chokes, a look of shock plastered across his face.

"Yes, I'm sorry. I just got an image of some random drunken dude running down the high street with my pizza box in his hand. He's pretty drunk, so in my head, he falls over a lot. I find things like that funny, as long as no-one gets hurt." I say, trying to hide the smile.

Tristan grins back at me. "You're the type of person to laugh at people who fall over in the snow, aren't you?" *Oops! Guilty as charged!*

"Yes, as long as they're not hurt," I reiterate.

"Ok, your drunken pizza guy is funny. I can see him in my head too!" Tristan laughs.

The laughter in me quickly fades. "Why didn't you tell me this earlier Tristan? I could have put your mind at rest."

His face falls. "I know," he sighs. "I just didn't want you having to you know...go through it all again."

I nod, and then I remember him talking to George at my party. "Tristan, what were you talking to George about at the party? Does he know I was pregnant?"

"No, he doesn't know baby. I wouldn't dream of telling anyone until you knew. And we were talking about you." He adds.

"Me?"

"Yes."

"What about me?" I ask.

Tristan shakes his head at me.

"I thought we agreed. No secrets?"

"It's not a secret. It's a surprise." Oh, another present? *A girl could get used to this!*

"Ok," I smile and lean forward to kiss him. "You know, Rob's gonna kill me if we don't get these wedding rings organised."

Tristan grins widely. "Why don't we take a look after dinner? I thought we could have an early night in bed together, watch a film on my laptop, what do you think?" *Hmm, more time in bed, more chance of more sex, I'm in!*

"Good idea," I beam, leaning in to kiss him again, and then I remember. "Oh...just so you know, I'm going over to Rob's tomorrow afternoon. Carlos is going out, so we're having a girlie afternoon."

"You are?" He says surprised.

"Yes, I am." *Does he expect me to ask for his permission or something?*

"Coral, you're doing too much' – "No I'm not. Tristan, I miss Rob, and I haven't really talked to him since he got back. I'm his friend, and he needs me. I think he wants to tell me about Carlos, about what happened, and I want to catch up with him too." I tell him.

"Are you going to stay in?" He asks, his brow furrowed.

"Yes, I told you we are. I'll only be a few hours." Tristan half smiles at me, but I can see the worry in his eyes. "I'm not going to drink," I say smirking at him.

He still doesn't look too happy.

"What's wrong?" I question, trying to keep my cool.

"I'm going to miss you," he whispers, completely throwing me. "And I can't help it Coral, I'll worry, I know I will. You're not healed yet and if something happened' – "Hey," I lean down and press my lips against his. "Nothing is going to happen to me, I know it seems like Rob and I are a little crazy when we're together, but it's not always like that. We've had plenty of non-drunken nights in where we just talk...and laugh..." I trail off, not really knowing what else to say.

"Just promise me, you'll be good. That you'll come home if you're in pain, or you're tired, or' – "I will, I promise I'll be good." I say pressing my lips against his again – He seems placated. "Now, I don't know about you, but I'm ready for round two," I tease.

"Why don't we make it three rounds," he teases back.

I giggle in delight, and we start all over again...

WE ARE SAT at the breakfast bar, eating Edith's delicious Bread and Butter Pudding; she even made her own custard. I must ask her to teach me how to do that. After our lovemaking, Tristan took me into the shower and gently washed my hair, just like before. Only this time I did the same to him, but I couldn't help kissing the scar and stitches on his head, trying to soothe it better as he bent his head down for me to wash his hair; it was a very sweet, intimate moment. I never knew being with someone, someone you love so much could feel like this; so close, so connected and together.

But the more we sit here, both quietly contemplating, the more I can feel myself getting pissed off with Tristan. I've spent three days questioning why I have felt so tearful, god knows how many times I have said this to him, that I don't understand it, yet all this could have been avoided if he'd told me that I had fallen pregnant and then miscarried...I shake my head, I can't even believe it's true, but the point is, if he'd have told me, I would have understood all this crazy crying.

I'm trying to understand his reasons for holding back. I keep trying to put myself in his shoes, thinking what I would do, and it's making me mad to know, that even though we have promised each other to be honest and have no secrets, he has kept this from me from the very moment I woke up in hospital.

My appetite suddenly plummets – I feel sick.

I place my spoon down and stare out the window at the evening sun. I don't want to fight with Tristan about this, I think we've done enough of that, but I'm angry, and I don't know what to do with it. Normally, I'd go and train with Will so I can get rid of the pent-up frustration, but I can't even do that.

"What's wrong?" Tristan asks.

I grit my teeth and stare straight ahead.

"Coral, we have to talk to one another," he says. *Ha! He's got a cheek saying that.*

I turn and glare at him. "Yes, you *should* have talked to me," I quietly hiss so Edith can't hear me.

"Baby," he breathes, staring back at me with wide, guilty, heart melting chocolate brown eyes – *No!*

"Edith," I call.

She turns and smiles at me. "Yes, Coral?"

"Can you give us some privacy please," I say.

Her face falls, but she nods reading my expression. "I'll be downstairs if you need me," she says, quickly wobbling away.

The moment she turns the corner, and she's out of view, I turn to Tristan.

"I know what you're going to say," he mumbles, reading me easily again.

"Well, I'm gonna say it anyway!" I snap. "You should have told me in hospital Tristan. I've been walking around thinking I'm falling apart at the seams, but I'm not…it's just fucking hormones!" I shout.

He puts down his spoon and closes his eyes for a moment. When he re-opens them, he doesn't look at me he simply takes my hand in his and gently squeezes it. "I know I was wrong," he says staring down at the floor. "I realise that now, I should have told you straight away. And I'm so sorry for not doing so, I thought – Christ!" He runs his free hand through his hair and then meets my eyes. I can't help glaring at him. "Dr Green' –

"Dr Green?" I interrupt.

It suddenly hits me again, that this was the reason they were arguing.

"She wanted to tell me," I snap, I feel myself getting tearful again – *I want to scream!*

"Yes," he quietly says, staring at the floor again.

I swipe my hand over my cheeks, dashing the silent tears away. "I'm so fucking mad at you right now," I hiss, scowling at him.

"I know," he says, taking me by surprise. "I'm mad at me too," he adds in the most sorrowful voice – *No! Don't do this, don't be nice, fight back!*

"Ugh..." I dash his hand away and slide off the breakfast stool.

"Where are you going, baby?" He softly asks.

"To see if I can speak to Dr Green!" I storm off into his office, slamming the door behind me.

I REPLACE THE handset and lay my head against Tristan's large, leather chair. Now I really do feel sick. Dr Green has told me that we need to be really careful because it's very easy to fall pregnant after a miscarriage, and that she advises – as I don't want children yet – to go onto another form of contraception and that using condoms is not the safest way. But I really don't like the thought of having to take a pill every day, and I don't like the thought of some implant in my body – that's a bit X-Files for my liking – and the thought of having a coil fitted – *Ugh!* When she mentioned that one I automatically crossed my legs, no definitely not going for that one. I sigh inwardly and close my eyes. What am I going to do? I'm still really pissed at Tristan, and to be honest I want to run. I want to get away from this place. Then it hits me, there's only one place I want to be right now – the beach.

I know we promised we wouldn't walk out on one another, but I need to get out of here, which makes me suddenly see things from Tristan's perspective. How he must have felt when he went to walk out on me after I told him about Susannah. He wasn't leaving me he just wanted to get away from me, just like I need to do now – *Right!*

Launching myself out of the chair, my shoulder throbbing painfully at me, I yank his office door open. I'm surprised to see Tristan is still sitting at the breakfast bar, with a wounded look on his face. *Tough!* – I need to do this, for my own sanity!

I march over to him. "Where's Stuart?" I snap.

"In the library," he softly says.

"Right!" I march over, yank the door open and find Stuart sitting in one of the chairs, reading a book; he looks up at me in surprise.

"Coral? Is everything ok?"

"I'd like to go down to the beach. Will you take me?" I ask, my voice firm and hard.

"O-of course," he stutters, his eyebrows pinching together.

"Good, I'll be down in a minute," I say, closing the door and heading back past the kitchen.

"Coral, what are you doing?" Tristan softly asks.

I stop, gripping my hands into fists and turn to glare at him. "I need some space Tristan, I'm going down to the beach to watch the sunset, and to try and calm down!" I bite.

"Ok," he says. Standing awkwardly, and placing his hands in his jean pockets, he stares down at the floor. "Stuart's taking you?" he asks. I know he's checking.

"Yes." I turn away from him and head upstairs so I can get changed into my jeans.

WHEN I GET back I notice it's gone ten o'clock, I didn't realise I'd been out for so long, but I wanted to watch the sky change from sunset to black night with sparkly stars, and I feel better for it. I'm not angry anymore; in fact, I'm not anything – I have come back feeling numb. Maybe, it's another hormone that's out of whack or something? Or maybe the truth about the fact that I can have children, that I was with child…and lost it, has finally caught up with me? Tristan is nowhere to be seen when I head down the hallway. The house is quiet and dark, except for the low lights that are on in the kitchen.

"Coral?" Stuart says, walking in behind me.

"Thanks, Stuart," I say. I'm sure he got bored standing around guarding me.

"You're welcome," he says, hovering from one foot to the other. *What is he waiting for?*

"You can retire if you want to," I say.

He looks relieved. "Thank you. Goodnight Coral."

I plaster a fake smile on my face. "Night Stuart."

He nods at me and heads upstairs to his room.

I really feel like a glass of wine, but I know I shouldn't, then I spy a bottle the bottle of red that was opened by Rob, it's still sitting on the breakfast table. I walk over to it and pick it up and as I do I catch my reflection in the ceiling height windows. Placing the wine back down, I shuffle over to the window, stand right in front of it, and take a deep breath. I slowly pull up my long-sleeved t-shirt and run my hand over my flat stomach, trying to imagine what it would feel like to see my belly grow and protrude, wondering what it would feel like to have life growing inside me. I look up at myself, keeping my hand on my belly, and the enormity of it hits me again.

I had Tristan's child inside me, my child, our child, my flesh, his flesh…I close my eyes and try to imagine what the child would have looked like. Would he have had brown hair like his parents? Would he have had beautiful big brown eyes like his father, or cool, aqua blue eyes like me? Would his cheeks have flushed like Tristan's, or been plain like mine? And his temperament – Would he have been firey like me, or cool, calm and kind like Tristan, or maybe a mixture of us both?

Cool fingers splay out over my hand that is still resting on my belly. *Tristan!*

I can smell his scent, and feel the warmth of his body behind me. I take a step back so I can feel the length of his body against mine, and rest the back of my head against his chest. I feel warm, safe, cherished.

"I missed you," he whispers. I take a deep breath in, his scent overpowers me again.

"And I you," I whisper back, keeping my eyes closed.

"What are you thinking?" he asks, his breath warm against my cheek.

"I was thinking about what Junior would be like, what he would look like, more you or me, or a mixture of us both?" I whisper.

"Junior?" He croaks sexily.

"Uh-huh..." I swallow hard and try not to cry.

"A boy?" he softly says, his hand pressing firmer against my belly.

"Yeah...I just...I don't know why, I just thought – him," I softly say.

"Him?" Tristan reiterates.

"Yeah..." I sigh.

"Baby, I'm so sorry." I open my eyes and stare at our reflections, meeting Tristan's gaze.

"Don't Tristan, it's done, and it's in the past. I'm not mad at you anymore," I say.

"You're not?" I shake my head. "I'm glad you're home," he softly adds, kissing my cheek, and then he goes to move.

"Don't move," I beg, staring up at him with wide eyes.

Because I like this image, I like seeing us reflected like this, his hand on my belly. It's making me realise how much of a wonderful father he will make, and how much of a wonderful man he is, and that he'll make an exceptional husband, one that will truly care if we have a child. I imagine him being very doting and caring throughout the pregnancy, and just as involved afterwards. And it's at that moment that I realise how completely and utterly in love I am with him, and that losing our baby, even though I didn't know I was pregnant, has made me realise I do want that.

I want to have a child with him one day. I want to give that to him. I want him to feel safe, secure, loved and cherished. I want him to have a family again...he deserves that, more than anything else.

"I am completely and utterly in love with you, do you know that?" I say.

He smiles his shy smile at me. "Even though I screwed up, big time?" he asks.

"Even more when you screw up," I say. "I know why you didn't tell me earlier," I add.

"You do?" he says, looking guilty again.

"Yes. It's because you love me so much, you didn't want to pile that on top of everything else that's gone on, I understand your reasons." I whisper.

He nods once and closes his eyes as he slowly wraps his other arm around my chest, pulling me tighter against him, neither one of us have moved our hands from my belly.

"One day Tristan, I'm going to give you what I think you truly need, and what I think I need, a family. I promise you that. I just want you to myself for a while first."

"Coral," he breathes, squeezing me tighter. He sounds like he's fighting tears again.

"Are you happy with that? I ask.

"Very," he whispers, his voice hoarse.

"Good, I'm exhausted, baby. Let's go to bed."

"Do you want anything?" he asks.

"Just some water please." Tristan kisses the top of my head, slowly turns me around, gets to his knees and gently kisses my belly several times. Then he looks up at me with those, big, round eyes of his.

"One day," he says, gently kissing me there once more.

Oh! My heart melts!

Getting to his feet, he leans in, softly kisses me on the lips then heads off to the kitchen to get us some water. My, my, he always seems to surprise me with how sweet he is, how loving and caring. As I look up, he winks at me as he pours two large glasses of water, making my heart jump into my throat... *Yeah...my sexy man*...Desire spikes hot and heavy in my belly. I suddenly feel wide-awake as blood pounds through my veins, heating my skin and making my heart pound a frantic tattoo against my chest. I can feel my lips swelling as I stare at Tristan, I'm aching for his kiss.

I hadn't noticed before, but he's dressed casually in a pair of dark blue jeans, and a light blue baggy shirt with the top three buttons open, tantalising me with his sexy chest, and his feet are bare...*He looks so fucking sexy right now!*

I dash over to the kitchen, slam him up against the fridge door, and kiss him hard. Tristan instantly reciprocates as my tongue does a sexy salsa with his. I push the full length of my body against his, as my fingers frantically try to undo the buttons on his shirt. Tristan's hands are everywhere, all over my body and then I hear him moan a low sexy sound, making my sex feel like it's on fire.

"I want you," I pant, pulling back to tackle the button and zip on his jeans.

"The feelings mutual," He growls as a low, sexy moan reverberates from deep in his throat. As he continues to kiss me, his hands skim over my backside, squeezing tight. It turns me on so much to know he wants me like this. He's just as hungry for me as I am for him...despite our...disagreements.

Tristan moans again. "I want to take you so badly," he grunts, kissing me hard again.

"Here, now!" I pant, kissing him back.

Tristan pulls back, my face in his hands. "You missed Nurse Terry," he says. "Aren't you in pain?" *Yes, but I don't care!*

"No." I kiss him again, a low moan resonating from deep within me.

"Wait," he says pulling back again. I frown up at him. "I'm not saying no." He quickly placates, seeing the look on my face. "I just want you to take the painkillers she left, and I want to take you upstairs so I can lay you down, where you'll be comfortable, where I can make love to you."

"I don't want to make love Tristan. I want to fuck – now!"

He smiles a slow, sexy smile. "Do you now," he says, his thumb skimming over my swollen lips, my lips part, then taking myself by surprise, I take his thumb in my mouth and suck, hard.

Tristan's eyes widen in response as I gently bite down on the pad, his lips part and his breathing kicks up a few more notches.

"Turn around," he says, and there's a sexy, sensual, promise in the way he's said it. I slowly turn, and he gently picks me up by the waist and moves us, so we're stood in front of the breakfast bar; our reflections clear in the windows in front of us, then he places both of my hands down, so they rest on the breakfast bar.

"Don't move those hands," he warns.

My body tingles from head to toe with sexual promise. He moves my hair out of the way and starts to plant soft, wet kisses from my earlobe, all the way down my neck, and across my shoulder.

"You want me to fuck you?" he whispers in my ear, making me gasp. *Jeez!* – His voice is so low and sexy. I feel a strange tingling sensation start at the top of my head and work its way right down to my toes.

"Answer me," he says in his husky voice.

"Yes," I whisper. He starts to skim his hands across my stomach and up and over my breasts, my nipples are straining against the material of my bra.

"Tristan," I moan; my eyes closing automatically, my head craning back.

"This is going to be quick," he whispers huskily in my ear. "Just as you want, then I'm going to take you upstairs and make love to you," he adds, breathing hard in my ear.

I want to touch him, to feel him.

His hands disappear, and taking me by surprise, he cups my sex and starts rubbing between my legs, the material of my jeans hitting the exact right spot.

"Ahh..." I moan loudly, the feeling is exquisite. Then he pops the button open on my jeans and slowly slides the zip down. Then his hands are inside the material, skimming across my backside, squeezing gently. "Tristan...please," I beg. In one swift movement, he has my jeans and knickers down at my knees, I gasp, and my eyes burst open.

"Don't move," he warns again as I hear his zip being pulled down on his jeans.

Placing a condom on the breakfast bar, he shoves his jeans and boxers down, rips open the condom, sheaths himself, then he presses his body hard against mine. I can feel his erection pressing hard against my backside, his strong chest against my back, the heat of his body searing my skin.

"Yes," I moan; my body trembling for his touch.

His hands skim across my breasts again. Then his one hand heads north, skimming across my collarbone, gently pulling my neck to the side, giving his lips access. He leans down, and trails kisses up and down my neck, his teeth skimming my skin – *Fuck, I'm going to come!* His other hand heads south, softly moving across my torso down to my belly, then finally reaching my sex. The moment his fingers find my clitoris, my breath catches, and I quiver from head to toe.

"Do you have any idea how utterly breathtaking you are?" he says in his husky, sexy voice.

"Tristan...." I whisper. I want to feel him in me – now!

His lips, tongue, and teeth brush against my neck reflecting what his fingers are doing down below. Touching, rubbing, so many sensations...then I feel two of his fingers gently slide inside me.

"Ah...Tristan," I moan; my head craned back. *I can't take it anymore.*

"I want to make sure you're ready," he whispers, gently biting my earlobe.

"I am," I pant.

My lips part, as he continues his sensual assault. His fingers moving in and out, his thumb teasing my clitoris.

"Please..." I beg. *Fuck me, Tristan!*

And just as though he can read my mind, he pulls his fingers from inside me, leans back, centres his erection at my opening and in one smooth jolt, he's inside me. Filling me right up, all of him...*oh I feel so full...*His one hand grips my hip, the other returns to my clitoris gently teasing.

"Yes!" I hiss.

"I don't want to hurt you," he says, gently pulling out and pushing into me again.

"You won't," I moan. "Let go, Tristan," I say, my eyes squeezed shut.

I need this, after all our fighting, everything that's happened...I just want him, always. He growls a low, sexy sound then really starts to pound into me – *Holy fuck!* Pain shoots across my shoulder blade and through my right lung, while everything south of my naval contracts in ecstasy, what a strange sensation, pleasure and pain all rolled into one.

"Ahh..." I cry out. Tristan stills. "Don't stop," I pant. "Please..." He starts to move again, cautiously pounding into me. Everything quickens, and I tighten up around his erection. *Yes...oh it's so good this way, so deep...*

"Jesus," he hisses, gaining speed.

"Come with me," I cry out. *Oh, I'm so close...*

"Coral," he moans, his breathing ragged.

I feel so tight, he feels so big inside me. I can feel him... everywhere. He moves slightly again, hitting that sweet spot inside me, just as his fingers circle faster, bringing my clitoris to a sweet crescendo, and all in one I come, climaxing hard, a double whammy, the most explosive orgasm that I've had so far.

"Coral!" he cries out and then stills as we collapse onto the breakfast bar...

CHAPTER FIFTEEN

I AM LYING IN post-coital bliss, spread out across Tristan's chest, feeling replete, happy, on top of the world. After our sexy fucking in the kitchen, we headed upstairs, and I reluctantly took the tablets Nurse Terry left, then Tristan made sweet, slow love to me. I shiver slightly and huddle closer to him. Tristan instantly picks up on it.

"You're cold, and that's because you didn't eat much for tea tonight." He scolds. "I'm going to run you a bath," he adds, and before I can stop him, he's up on his feet and stalking into the bathroom.

I curl up, pulling the covers over me and start to drift...

"Coral?" Tristan calls. *Hmm, too tired to move...* The next thing I know the cover is pulled off me and I'm up in his arms again. "Come on sleepy, bath, then bed."

Tristan gently lowers my feet into the bath and holds both my hands while I carefully sink down into the water. Ben Howard is singing in the background, I know the song, Only Love. It makes me smile that Tristan has this playing. He sinks in opposite me, then takes my right foot and starts to massage. Hmm, so nice...I close my eyes and softly sing along with Ben.

"What are we going to do tomorrow morning?" Tristan asks, interrupting my warbling.

I sigh inwardly. "I guess I should unpack my stuff," I say, thinking about my studio and all my belongings downstairs – It still feels weird that it's happened, that I'll never live there again, it all seems to have happened so fast.

"No overexerting yourself," Tristan softly scolds.

I roll my eyes and smile, then frown. "Tristan, I want to collect my mother's ashes so we can organise her grave, will you call them for me?"

"Of course I will darling." He softly says.

"Thanks." I'm so glad he's doing that for me, I don't think I could have handled it right now. I try to think of something else to get my mind off it. "We didn't choose any rings today. I guess we should do that tomorrow?" I say.

"Yes, we should, or Rob will be barking his orders at us," Tristan sniggers.

"I know," I giggle.

"Can I ask you something?" He says.

"Anything," I whisper.

"Earlier, when the detective told you her name, you looked…upset?"

He doesn't miss a thing!

"Annie was my mom's name," I tell him, trying not to think about it.

"Oh…" He says then frowns.

"It's a nice name," I add.

"Yeah, it is," he softly says. "Can I ask you another question?"

"Yes," I giggle.

Tristan leans down and kisses the pad on each of my toes. "You took Bob outside today, what did you talk to him about?"

"Oh…um, well…I told him about Susannah, what had happened to her, and that I might be dropping the charges."

"Might be? Have you changed your mind?" He questions with his head cocked to the side.

"No…I won't make my decision until I've seen her." Tristan sighs heavily. "Bob said he doesn't mind what I do, and that he doesn't really want to be dragged into court, he just wants to move on," I add.

"Hmm, well I guess that's his decision to make," Tristan says.

"Yes, it is." I know Tristan doesn't like this, but there's not much he can do about it.

"And what about Rob? You were both gone a long time." He cautiously asks.

I sigh inwardly. *Do I tell Tristan the truth, or do I lie?*

I take a deep breath and look directly at him. "I was talking to him about you."

"Me?" His fingers still on my feet.

"Yes and please don't stop, it's so nice, here, I'll show you." I pick up his right foot and start to massage.

He smiles at me and nods. "You're right, that is nice." His fingers kneed deeper into my foot. "So, what about me Coral? I know he doesn't like me," he adds.

"You're wrong!" I tell him firmly. "Look, I know you and Rob didn't get off to a good start, but he's just worried that's all."

"Worried about what?" Tristan questions, his cheeks flaming slightly.

"That you're treating me right." I softly say.

Tristan's head cocks to the side. "Am I treating you right?" he asks.

"Of course you are!" I gasp. "Tristan, how could you think that? Rob's just worried because you come across as a pretty serious guy, you know – Intense. He just wants to know that, well his words were, 'we should have mutual respect, admiration and love for one another'. I told him we do have that and that you are wonderful to me. He didn't look convinced...so I told him all about me." I end in a whisper – I can't quite believe Rob knows.

Tristan gasps. "Everything?" he breathes.

I nod once. "I wanted him to understand Tristan, and to not be so hard on you. I told him that you're worried about me and that I don't really think you've got over the shock of what happened to me, and well, long story short, Rob now thinks you're an angel too."

Tristan's one eyebrow cocks up. "An angel?"

I blow him a kiss. "My angel."

He laughs and shakes his head at me. "Well, I guess that explains the change in his behaviour when you both came back up."

"Tristan, isn't it good that he was protective like that? I mean, what if I'd got together with a guy that I thought was nice, but he turned out to be a complete ogre? Rob and Carlos would have got me out of there, I know they would. I don't think any person can ask for better friends than that!"

"No, I agree completely. And now I see things from his point of view too, so it makes sense."

"Will you try harder with him for me? Try to be more friendly?"

Tristan laughs again, gives my big toe another kiss then picks up my other foot. "Of course I will baby."

"Thank you," I whisper. "I really want you two to get along. Rob's really funny Tristan, and I have a lot to thank him for, he's kept my head above water for a long time now."

Tristan frowns down at the water. "Yes, I'm starting to realise how much of a great friend he has been to you. I promise I'll really try with him."

"Well, Rob's asked us to go dancing, so that's a way to get to know one another," I say sweetly.

"Dancing?" Tristan chuckles.

"Yeah...well, when I'm better that is. What's funny?" I add as he's really chuckling now.

"I just pictured you expecting me to dance with Rob, that's all." He chortles.

I burst out laughing. "Yeah right, like you would!"

"No," he laughs, shaking his head. "I would not."

I chuckle some more, then swap his feet over. Ben is still singing in the background, Tristan must have put his album on, and it's pretty good. It's official, Tristan has good taste in music.

WE ARE HUDDLED in bed, wrapped up in each other's arms. Now I feel exhausted. Tristan is gently tracing his fingers up and down on my back. *Mmm, it's so nice.*

"Joe's been asking after you," Tristan says.

"She has?" I say, feeling surprised. Then I have a sudden wave of guilt, I haven't always been nice to her.

"Yeah...I think she's quite fond of you," he adds.

"Joe's sweet," I say. Wondering how she's doing, and how long she's got until her kids are back.

"She asked Joyce if she could come and see you, she knows about your mother passing away and..." He stops, his hands stilling on my back.

"About Susannah?" I guess.

"Yes, she visited you in hospital, but you were still unconscious." He adds, his tone firm.

"Well, what about popping into the office tomorrow? I wanted to meet Karen too," I add.

"No. They can come here," he says. "I'll speak to Joyce tomorrow, organise for them to come over at lunchtime." He says, his voice still firm.

I lean my chin on his chest and gaze up at him. "Tristan, I really want to go see my studio. Maybe we could take a walk on the beach, pop into the office briefly to see everyone and then eat out for lunch? We'd only be out a couple of hours." I say, batting my lashes at him.

"Coral' – "Tristan, I'll be horizontal on Rob's sofa for the rest of the day, I promise. So you don't need to worry." I tell him.

"Argh! You are so frustrating!" He balks. *I've won!*

"So that's a yes, you'll come out with me?" I say, trying not to smile.

"Yes." He reluctantly answers and then his lips set into a hard line. I want to giggle at him, but I stop myself, I don't want to rock the boat.

"I love you, Tristan. Sleep, tight baby." I kiss his mighty fine pecks, then rest my head on his chest and listen to the soft, slow sound of his heart gently beating.

THE FOLLOWING MORNING, I wake to a flood of bright, yellow sunshine filling the bedroom. I smile a lazy, happy smile and turn to reach out for Tristan, but he's not there.

"Tristan?" I call out for him, but I get no answer. Just as I'm about to climb out of bed, there's a knock on the door. "Come in," I shout and carefully swing my legs out, so my feet hit the floor.

"Good morning Coral." Edith comes wobbling in with my veggie juice, followed by Nurse Terry.

"Morning," I say to one and all.

"You're looking much brighter this morning," Edith tells me.

"I feel it," I say, quickly looking away from her, because I just got a flash image of Tristan and I having hot, sexy sex – *That's the reason I feel so good!*

"Well, something's certainly put a sparkle in your eyes?" Nurse Terry says as she gives me a hit of painkillers. I smile coyly and wink at her. "Oh!" She goes bright red and tries to hide her smile. "Yes, that would do it," she whispers.

Edith picks up some washing and smiles at me. "See you downstairs for breakfast," she says, heading out of the bedroom.

"Edith, do you know where Tristan is?" I ask.

"Yes, he's swimming lass," she says as she wobbles out of sight. *Hmph!*

"How are you generally feeling Coral?" Nurse Terry asks.

"Oh fine," I say, feeling a little deflated. I want to go swimming too! I have missed it so much. "Can I go swimming?" I ask.

She shakes her head at me. "Not a good idea," she says. "And neither is sex, if Dr Green found out, she'd have you carted back to the hospital," she adds, softly scolding me.

"I'm not going without sex," I say crossing my arms defiantly.

Nurse Terry laughs. "That's fine, I won't tell her, but just be careful, take it easy. Ok?" She says as she checks my stitches.

"Sure..." I mumble.

"Alright, I'll be back at 12," Terry says.

"Um...actually I won't be here, I should be back by 1pm though?" I say lightly.

Terry sighs and shakes her head at me. "Coral' – "I'm just going to spend some time with my sister. I'll be sitting in the garden, relaxing." I lie, feeling utterly guilty.

"Hmm, well just make sure you do. You're meant to be having bed rest. You're not supposed to be leaving the house you know." She adds in a very stern voice.

"Don't worry, I'll take it easy," I add to reassure her.

"Alright then, I'll see you back here at 1pm, no later!" She warns.

"I'll be here," I say.

"Ok. See you later," she adds as she disappears through the bedroom door. Then I hear a kerfuffle going on, Terry mumbling something and Tristan apologising.

"Hey," I beam as Tristan walks through the door in a pair of wet swimming trunks, his sexy torso all on show for me. "What a delightful site to wake up to," I add as he walks over to me.

He shakes his head in laughter and smiles that gorgeous shy smile of his.

"Good morning beautiful." He bends down, dripping water all over me and kisses me, hard. "How are you feeling this morning?" He asks, smiling widely against my lips.

"Good, really good. How about you?" I say a little breathlessly.

"Never better," he says, leaning in to kiss me again.

"Want some help in the shower?" I tease, brushing my lips against his. Tristan can't help laughing against my lips. "What?" I say, trying to feign innocence.

"You're such a sexy tease," he croakily adds. Then making me squeal with delight, he swiftly lifts me into his arms and carries me into the bathroom...

AN HOUR LATER and we are sat in the kitchen eating our omelettes. Mmm, spinach and mushroom omelette. Edith can really cook! The radio is playing in the kitchen, the Lumineers are busy singing Ho Hey. I can't help tapping my feet as I listen to the song, then I notice Tristan is doing the same, we both glance at one another at the same time and both smile, ridiculous ear to ear grins.

"I like this song," he says. "Are you my sweetheart baby?" He asks, referencing to the song.

"Of course I am," I chuckle.

He grins widely at me. "How are you feeling?" He asks.

"Fine, why?" I ask fluttering my lashes at him.

"I didn't overdo it earlier did I?" he whispers. Hmm, when Tristan carried me into the bathroom earlier, he gently washed my hair and my whole body, taking his sweet time in a *very* particular area. Then once I'd done the same to him, he took me back into the bedroom, lay me down on the bed and we had hot, sexy sex again.

"No," I whisper back, pecking him on the cheek.

He smiles from ear to ear again. "You seem to be healing quickly," he says.

"I generally do," I nod.

"You said you would when you got out of the hospital." He adds.

I nod and stare down at my omelette. "I hate hospitals Tristan, they scare me," I whisper, swallowing hard.

"Scare you?" He questions, eyes wide, his fork in mid-air. I nod again. "Why?" He whispers.

I take a deep breath. "Just...really bad memories..." I trail off. I really don't want to think about them, not today.

"Will you tell me, one day?" He asks, softly reaching out and squeezing my hand.

I nod and turn to smile at him. Then we both finish our omelettes at the same time, which I'm amazed at. I guess Tristan really has listened to me because he eats much slower nowadays.

Tristan leans forward and pecks me on the lips. "You look gorgeous today," he adds, looking down at my bare legs. I'm in my jean shorts and a t-shirt. It's supposed to be baking out there today, so I didn't want to be in jeans.

"Thanks," I squeak, even though I'm feeling self-conscious about my legs.

"What?" He questions, picking up on it.

"Isn't there anything I can keep to myself?" I whisper feeling embarrassed. I quickly glance across at Edith who's busy cleaning up the kitchen, I do not want her to hear this.

Tristan opens his mouth to question me, but his mobile rings in his pocket, effectively putting a stop to that conversation – thank god! Pulling it out and pressing answer, he puts the phone to his ear. "Tristan Freeman?" He smiles down at me and mouths 'later' *Hmph!*

I narrow my eyes at him. I guess I haven't got away with it.

"Ok…send it over Mark, I'll go and take a look....yep, and

Claire?...Good, no that'll be fine." Tristan hangs up. "Sorry baby, I've got to take a look at one thing, and then we can go," he says, smiling broadly at me.

"Ok," I squeak, my grin reflecting his.

He seems in a much better mood, as am I – *Must be the sex!* Tristan heads off towards his office, and I sit back, relax, and enjoy my cappuccino.

"HE DID WHAT!?" I hear Tristan bellow from his office. Edith and I both stop and stare at one another. I wonder what that's about? Moments later, Tristan comes marching out of his office shaking his head in anger and disgust.

"Un-fucking-believable," he hisses to himself. "Complete incompetence!"

"What's wrong?" I ask.

Tristan halts and looks up at me. I don't think he expected to see me still sitting here.

"N-nothing!" He says frowning deeply.

"Tristan, haven't you worked it out yet?" I laugh.

"Worked what out?" He asks, frowning at me.

"That you always say 'nothing' when it's got something to do with me, so I instantly know you're holding something back. What happened to talking to one another, to trust, to honesty, to not having any secrets?" I say with one eyebrow cocked up.

Tristan clenches his jaw several times as he stares back at me. I stand, walk over to him, take both his hands in mine and smile up at him. "When are you going to learn that I'm a lot stronger than I look?"

"I know you're strong," he says.

"Then have a little faith," I softly say.

"It's not that baby," he says, gently stroking my cheek.

"Tristan," I close my eyes and take a deep breath. "You have to stop doing this."

He sighs heavily, nods once and stares at the floor. "I thought, as I was in the office, I'd call the Psychiatric establishment your mother was in, so we could arrange the collection. I wanted to know if Stuart could do it." He suddenly stops, his face winces as though he's in pain.

"And?" I prompt.

"You...your," He runs a hand through his hair. "Your father collected her belongings. If you want to bury her ashes, we'll need to contact him to get them back! They won't give me his number as I'm not related; you'll have to ask for it." He adds, bristling with tension. *Am I dreaming? Did he really just say that?*

I release Tristan's hand, reach up and pinch myself. Nope, not dreaming! I stare, wide-eyed at Tristan, I have no words.

"Coral?" He asks gently. "Talk to me, baby."

My mouth opens to say something, but nothing comes out. *Why would he...?*

Tristan places his hands on my upper arms and gently squeezes. "Coral, come back to me baby," he softly says, his eyes searching mine.

I suddenly feel enraged. "How would he know she was dead, he hasn't' – "Apparently they never divorced." Tristan interrupts, shaking his head in wonder.

"What?" I tremble.

Tristan shakes his head in disbelief again. "I know, hard to believe, but the fact is, he was informed of her death the same day as you, and when you didn't immediately come forward for her belongings' – "I thought you had spoken to them?" I balk.

"I had," Tristan growls in annoyance. "They assured me her belongings were there for you, which they were, but your father turned up on Friday morning and took them with him."

My world starts to tilt and sway. "I...I don't understand, why would he do that?" I whisper.

"I don't know baby," Tristan says his voice a soft tune against the ringing going on in my ears.

"Tristan," I whisper. "I think I'm gonna' – The moment I say it, I am up in his arms, and he's carrying me over to the sofa.

"Deep breaths baby," he soothes.

"Ok," I murmur trying to do so.

"Would you like some water?" He asks gently placing me down.

I shake my head at him. "You have to get them back Tristan," I whimper.

"Oh I will," he assures me in a forceful tone.

"Thank you," I breathe.

"Coral, do you want to talk to your father' – "Never!" I spit. "He left me, Tristan *and* my mom. I guess he has his reasons for splitting with her, but where did that leave me? He left, and he never came back, he abandoned me. He didn't give a fuck about me, and I don't give a fuck about him. I just want my mom's stuff back!" I rant, feeling really pissed at my father, but secretly hurt too. Why has he done this?

"I'll sort it," Tristan says in his authoritative tone.

"I know," I say because I believe him, he will.

"So you're sure if he asks about you?' – "Tell him I told him to go fuck himself!" I hiss.

We both sit quietly for a while. Why can't something just be easy and simple for once? I can't believe my father's done that, I am so mad at him. I just wanted to get my mom's stuff back, lay her to rest, and get on with my life – *Right!*

"Can I have the number please?" I ask.

"You want to do this now?" Tristan asks, looking slightly alarmed.

"Yes. I just want to get it sorted Tristan. I want to lay my mom to rest and get on with my life. I'm so tired of the past hanging over my head like a big black cloud."

Tristan nods. "I understand baby." He leans forward and kisses my forehead. "I'll go and get the number." A few moments later, Tristan returns and kneels down in front of me. "I have them on the line, you just have to confirm who you are and they will give you *his* details," he says his voice low.

I hold my hand out, Tristan places his mobile in my hand, and a pen and writing pad in the other – *Ok, here goes!*

"This is Coral Stevens." I snap. The woman on the line asks me a few security questions, apologises several times then gives me *his* number. I scratch it down in a hurry, my writing is so scrawny from shaking so much. I hang up, and in a moment of pure clarity, I realise I do want to speak to my father. I want him to know how pissed I am at him for doing this.

I start punching the number into Tristan's mobile.

"Coral, what are you' – "I changed my mind," I growl, feeling utterly incensed that he would do this. Tristan briefly closes his eyes. I put his mobile to my ear, and wait for the line to be answered. It's a home line, so I don't know *who's* going to answer, which is making me more nervous.

My leg is in full jigging mode, and I'm biting my bottom lip.

"Hello?" A woman answers.

"Put Gavin Foster on the phone," I spit.

"Who is this?" She asks, her voice sharp.

"His long-lost daughter Coral," I drawl sarcastically.

"Oh..." I hear her calling for him. *Oh shit! What am I doing?* My heart is trying to jump out of my chest, and I can feel a cold sweat coming on.

"Coral?" Oh...hearing his voice. I remember it, I recognise it – *The bastard!*

Forever With Him

"Why have you taken my mother's belongings and her ashes?" I snap.

"I...I didn't think you would have' – "I want them back!" I shout.

"Oh..." I can hear the sadness in his voice. "It's a bit late for that baby girl' – "Don't you dare call me that!" I growl.

He sighs heavily down the line. "I buried your mother's ashes at the local cemetery, you're too late darling," he softly says.

"You what!?" I bellow, my heart really thrumming now, literally trying to claw it's way up my throat.

"I'm so sorry Coral' – "Fuck you and your god damn apologies!" I bark. Tristan's eyes briefly close again then he takes my free hand and grips it tightly. "Where have you buried her?" I ask, sniffing slightly.

"In Wells Cemetary in Somerset, do you want the plot number?" He softly asks.

"Yes." I snap.

"It's 512. Coral I'm still in Shepton Mallet if you want to see me' – "See you?" I choke out. "The man that abandoned me? Are you joking?" I laugh sarcastically – *What is this guy on?*

"No. I'd love to see you, make it up to you, tell you how' – I pass the phone to Tristan. "I can't talk to him, can you tell him to send her belonging's to me...Oh, but I don't want him to know where I live' – "Don't worry darling I'll sort it," he says.

I stand and start pacing the room, but stop when I turn around and look up at the two framed photos of Tristan and his folks that are hanging up on the wall behind the sofa. I soften a little seeing their smiling faces and sit back down.

"Mr Foster?...Tristan Freeman speaking, Coral's husband....yes she's married. She is extremely upset right now, and has asked me to speak on her behalf......I'm afraid that won't be possible. I'm presuming from the conversation I've just heard that you have already buried her mother's ashes?....I see, well Coral would like her mother's personal items sent to her, I'm presuming you have no need for them?" He asks, a little dryly. "Yes...I see, no you haven't got a prayer...Mr Foster if she doesn't want to see you then that's it, I respect my wife's wishes. Now, this is the address I'd like you to send them to." Tristan gives him his company address in Birmingham. "Address it to Claire James she's my P.A....no....as soon as possible. I will pass that on, but I doubt it will make any difference. Goodbye Mr Foster." Tristan hangs up then makes another call.

189

"Good morning Claire......Fine, thank you. Claire, a package will be arriving from Somerset, I don't have time to explain right now, but as soon as you receive it I want it couriered same day to my home address in Brighton....yes please.....thank you, Claire...She's getting there, thank you for asking.....I will." Tristan hangs up. "Claire says hi, and she hopes you're feeling better soon."

I nod despondently at Tristan. "What did he say?" I ask squeezing my eyes shut.

"You really want to know?" Tristan softly asks.

"Yes," I whisper, although I'm not sure I do.

"He wants to see you." I nod once. I thought that's what Tristan would say.

"I don't want to see him," I say, my voice trembling on me. I open my eyes and look up at my wonderful husband to be.

"I know baby." He softly says, kneeling in front of me again.

"Thank you for doing that," I say, reaching up and stroking his cheek.

"You don't need to thank me Coral, it's not something I can really say 'you're welcome' for?"

"You can," I whisper. "If you weren't here, I'm not sure if I would have got that sorted so...so calmly....and efficiently."

"Then you are welcome my love." He says, smiling sorrowfully at me.

I look up at Tristan and smile. "Good idea saying you're my husband and having it sent to Birmingham, at least that will throw him off the scent if he tries to find me."

"That's what I thought," he says, smiling sorrowfully at me. "Is this the address for the cemetery?" I nod once. "We can still plant a tree for her baby," he adds.

"I know," I whisper, staring down at the floor.

I feel his fingertips lift my chin. "Coral, did you want to stay in today?"

"No, I don't want this day ruined because of him." I take a deep breath, close my eyes and try to get back to how I was feeling ten minutes ago – Happy, playful...in love.

I push all thoughts of my asshole father to the back of my mind. I am not happy he has buried her so far away, but maybe if I bury something that was just mine and my moms, like the photograph, and then plant the tree, it will be like...well like it's our tree, a place just for us. Although, there is still a part of me that doesn't understand why I am doing this, why I feel so compelled to bury her and to have her near me. After all, she failed me so badly, and I have spent most of my adult life despising her and wishing she were dead, and now she is...I swallow hard and fight against the tears – *No, not today! No tears today!*

I open my eyes, smile at Tristan then yank him by the shirt and crush his lips to mine. "Let's go and have some fun," I say.

"You're sure?" he murmurs against my lips, taking both my hands in his.

"Yes," I whisper. He groans and kisses me back forcefully. We are all tongues and touch and low moans – *Ok maybe I should take him back upstairs?*

"If you carry on kissing me like that, I'm taking you upstairs," I whisper against his lips.

He smiles against my lips. "Right, yes..." he says still a little sidetracked. I can't help smiling goofily at him. He leans down once more, and pecks me sweetly on the lips, then holds his hand out for me. "Let's go then." He says.

I place my hand in his, pick up my over the shoulder bag, and place it over my head.

"Should you be wearing that?" He asks standing beside me.

"It's on my good shoulder, it doesn't hurt, and besides, I feel weird without a bag..." I muse as I slip my feet into my open wedges.

"Ok," he smiles and leans down to peck me on the lips. "You're sure you're ok?" he asks again.

I nod, place my hand in his, and Tristan leads us towards the front door. I glance up at the framed painting of the E-type that's been hung in the entrance hallway. Hmm, I want to buy something for Tristan to say thank you. He's been so good to me, so sweet. I lift my locket from my neck and squeeze the heart in my hand...*Yes, very sweet!* Hopefully, I'll find some inspiration while we are out.

Tristan opens the door to the big Jaguar and helps me inside, for some unknown reason Tristan didn't want to drive today. Either way, I can't help feeling buoyant despite what's happened. Tristan and I seem to be really getting along again, both happier, more relaxed, plus it's a beautiful, hot sunny day today. *Hmm blue skies and sunshine, I wish England was like this all the time.*

Tristan looks across at me, smiles sweetly, and squeezes my hand. Boy, he looks so good today. He's dressed in a short-sleeved cream linen shirt with the top three buttons open. I'm sure it's to tease me. His dark blue knee-length shorts and his manly flip flops. For some reason, I'm reminded of the first time I travelled in this car with him, just those few short weeks ago. *God, I had it so bad for him, even back then!* I can't help smiling to myself. Look how far we've come, and how much has happened.

"What are you thinking about?" He asks, looking intrigued.

"I'm thinking about the first time I was in this car with you."

"Yeah?" I nod, smiling broadly. "Elaborate, please..." He says squeezing my hand again.

"No way!" I scoff, smiling up at him.

"Why not?" He laughs.

"Some things just shouldn't be said," I giggle.

"Oh really?" He teases.

"Yes, so stop it!" I titter.

"Oh...I'll get it out of you," he banters.

"You think so, do you?" I tease, batting my lashes at him – *Thank god I put some make-up on!*

"Oh yes, I certainly do." He says with full confidence.

I shake my head, laughing at his teasing ways.

Stuart pulls up at the gym and parks in a bay.

"Ready?" Tristan beams.

"Yep!" I reply perkily.

Tristan jumps out, runs around the car and opens my door for me, bowing grandly as he does. "My lady," he says, holding both his hands out to me. I giggle at his sweet, playful gesture, we really do seem to be back on track! Taking his hands, he gently pulls me to my feet, brings me into his chest and leans down to kiss me.

"Tell me," he pleads against my lips.

"No!" I banter.

"Oh...you infuriating woman!" He teases.

"Ok, maybe I will if you're good?" I tease.

"Good?"

"Uh-huh."

"Good, how?"

"Well...let me think? Hmm...no moaning about how long we are out, and no broodiness! I want this to be a relaxed, nice day out, ok?"

He instantly puts on his broody face. *I think he's teasing me?*

"Seriously?" I pout.

His face splits into an ear to ear grin. *Bastard!*

"You know...I really love it when you're playful like this Tristan."

"Oh you do, do you?"

"Yes."

"Just playful?" I shake my head and bite my bottom lip.

"What else do you like?" He questions, running a finger down my cheek.

"I'm not saying," I tease.

This time Tristan pouts. I have to giggle.

"Ok, maybe I will if you act like you are incandescently happy?"

His purposely puts on a big, happy, smiling face, then says, "I already am incandescently happy. I'm with you." *Oh, bugger me!*

I melt, again and gaze up at Tristan, no ogle is probably the appropriate word, then quickly pull out of it – *Jeez! He really knows how to knock me for six sometimes.*

Tristan cocks his head to the side and chuckles at me. "You ok?"

"Yes," I chuckle. "Come on. Let's get this over with so we can take a walk."

"As you wish," he says and taking my hand in his, we start strolling across the car park.

"Coral!" A male voice shouts. Tristan instantly stiffens beside me and then we both turn to see who it is. I instantly relax when I see Will jogging across the car park towards us.

"It's Will," I whisper, Tristan instantly relaxes. "Will!" I beam as he reaches me and carefully hugs me.

"What the hell are you doing out of the hospital?" He asks.

I glance across at Tristan; he has an I-told-you-so look on his face.

"I hate hospitals Will. I had to get out of there!"

"Surely you shouldn't be walking about though?" *Not him too!* So I decide to ignore that and introduce him to Tristan instead.

"Will, meet my fiancé, Tristan Freeman. Tristan this is my personal trainer Will Richards."

They shake hands. "You're engaged?" Will says a little shocked.

"Yep." I nod twice. "Oh, you and Natalie should come to the wedding! It's in two weeks up at the house on The Cliff." I gesture behind me with my head. Will seems surprised by my invitation. "That's if you want to," I add.

"We'd love to. I'll check with Nat, make sure she hasn't already arranged something."

"Cool, I'll call you at the gym tomorrow?"

"Great. I'd better get back. It's good to see you up and about Coral."

"Thanks, Will."

"Nice to meet you, Tristan," he says, shaking Tristan's hand again.

"You too," Tristan says, and with that Will nods to us both, and heads back towards the gym.

"Another admirer," Tristan says with one eyebrow cocked up.

"Ugh! Will's married," I groan.

"So?" Tristan smirks.

"Seriously?" I choke. "Are you gonna go broody on me?" I say frowning at him.

"No, but I think you should change trainers." He adds, still smirking at me.

I laugh loudly at that one. "Oh Tristan, Will does not like me like that."

"Ok..." he says. "Have it your own way." *Shit!* Is he right?

Is Will attracted to me? He's never given me any reason to believe that he is, and he's never made me feel uncomfortable either. I shake my head and shrug it off. No, no, it's just Tristan being Tristan. We take each other's hands again and continue walking across the car park, just as we reach the steps leading down to the concourse, I look up and see a tall, slim male standing outside the studios; and from my guesstimate, he's right outside my place. Who is that? I keep my eyes focused on him as we head down the steps. I watch as he takes a step forward and knocks on my patio door and then he puts his face up against the window, his hands either side, looking for me I guess. Just as we reach the bottom step, the man suddenly turns, so he's directly facing us and freezes.

I instantly do the same – *Holy fuck!*

194

CHAPTER SIXTEEN

TRISTAN ARCHES AN eyebrow and looks down at me. I grip his hand tighter and stare straight ahead. He cocks his head to the side, and then his gaze follows mine, down to my studio. "Coral. Who is that?" He asks, his voice low. I can't speak, my heart is hammering against my chest, and my mouth has gone dry – *What the hell is he doing here?*

"Coral!" I turn and look up at Tristan with wide eyes. "Who is it?"

"My ex...Justin," I whisper. Tristan's face instantly hardens. "Don't cause a scene!" I add.

"What do you want me to do, shake his hand?" He spits sarcastically.

"No." I take a few deep breaths trying to calm myself. I never, ever thought I would see him again. I was told that he'd moved...gone to Manchester or somewhere up north?

"Then what do you want me to do?" Tristan questions, he lets go of my hand and runs both hands through his hair, he's practically bristling with tension.

"Nothing, you don't have to do anything Tristan," I say, staring down at Justin again. He raises his hand and waves at me, I do not wave back. He looks so different. Gone is the skinny boy that I knew, now he looks like a man, all bulked up, grown up. His hair is still the same messy, sandy blonde, his eyes ice blue. His cheekbones are more defined, his jaw more chiselled, and his lips...I swallow hard – He looks good...really good. Then I remember the heartbreak I endured over this man, the pain, the sleepless nights, the anger, the hate – I suddenly feel really pissed at him – I mean really, *really,* pissed. How dare he turn up here!

"Give me one minute!" I say to Tristan through gritted teeth, and without waiting for his reply, I start marching down the concourse. I know Tristan is following me, but that's good, I want him to – It doesn't take long for me to reach Justin.

"What are you doing here?" I snap, my foot tapping, my hands on my hips. I'm on a roll today! *Anyone else wanna come out the woodwork, bring it on!*

"Hello Coral, it's nice to see you too?" He says, a little sarcastically.

"Answer my question!" I bellow – *Keep your cool Coral!*

"See you haven't changed," he says dryly. "Still the same bad temper."

"Fuck you!" I hiss.

"Oh, nice..." He says, nodding his head. "Really nice!"

"Well, what did you expect Justin? A loving embrace, a kiss; or one last fuck for old times sake?" I spit.

"Jesus Coral, what's your problem?" He says looking all wounded and shocked.

I almost choke vomit on him. "My problem?" I choke.

"Yeah...you don't have to be so antagonistic towards me," he says, looking bruised.

"Are you fucking kidding me?" I say, totally incensed, my hands clenching into fists.

"Coral," Tristan says, I turn and see he's stood a couple of feet away from me. "Come, let's go. I don't want you getting upset like this." He says his eyes dark and worried.

"No!" I stamp my foot, instantly wishing I hadn't – It sends shooting pains up my body, across my shoulder and through my lung. I hiss and try to hide it, but Tristan can see right through me.

"Right that's it, we're done here!" Tristan says stepping towards me.

"Er...I don't think so," Justin says stepping in front of me. *Oh, fuck a duck!*

"Move, now!" Tristan warns taking a step closer to Justin, they are almost nose to nose.

"Ok stop!" I shout, stepping in-between them and holding both hands out towards their chests. *The last thing I want is these two fighting!*

"Tristan here's the key, why don't you get the air-con on and I'll be inside in a second."

"No!" He growls – He and Justin seem to be having some sort of pissing contest.

They are both stood there like frozen statues, eyeballing one another, sizing each other up. Tristan is radiating tension, his jaw clenching every couple of seconds. Justin has his fists clenched at his sides, just waiting for Tristan to pounce – Justin was never afraid of confrontation.

"Ok fine!" I snap. "You!" I poke Justin in the arm. He stops trying to stare Tristan down, rubs his arm and looks down at me. "What are you doing here Justin?" I say shaking my head at him.

"Well now you're asking nicely' – "You've got a fucking cheek, you expect me to be nice to you when you did the dirty behind my back with my *best* friend?" I squeak.

Justin's mouth pops open, then he closes it, changing his mind on whatever he was going to say, then he does the same again. Lost for words, I guess.

"You know what I don't actually care why you're here. Just go...please...and don't come back." I tell him.

"I'm back in Brighton," he says.

I'm stumped, shocked, it's my turn to be speechless. Then I finally find my voice. "Why?" I question breathlessly.

"I got a great job offer," he says. *Hmph!* "And Harriet and I split." *Oh!* My heart sinks into my stomach. I shrug it off as though it doesn't bother me, but it does. "Coral..." He reaches his hand out to me, his eyes pleading with me – *Damn those baby blues!*

"No!" I take a step back from him. "I'll ask you one last time then I'm going inside. Why are you here?"

"For you." *Fuck!*

"Me?" I squeak. Justin nods once. *Damn it, I know that look.* "You want me back?" I quickly surmise.

"Yes, if you would have me back..." Justin shakes his head. "Look I'm sorry to just turn up like this, but my mom said you were in the paper and when I read...when I read that you'd got shot, I had to come and see you. I had to see for myself that you were ok."

"Well, I am," I retort, feeling shocked by his words.

"Yes, I can see that," he says a ghost of a smile on his lips.

"Look, Justin' – "I am sorry Coral, for everything, for doing what I did, for hurting you...I guess you could say I've grown up, seen the light...and in all that time we've been apart, there hasn't been a day that's gone by where I haven't thought of you." *No fucking way!*

"Justin..." I swallow hard, then look across at Tristan, he looks like he's about to expire. "You need to go, now," I say, and turn to unlock the patio door.

"That's it?" He says, his voice trembling. "I tell you all of that, and that's all you have to say?"

I take a deep breath and turn to face him. "Justin I'm engaged. This is my fiancé Tristan Freeman." His mouth pops open, his eyes darting back and forth between the two of us. I don't think he believes me. I lift up my left hand and wiggle the ring under his nose, he stares down at the ring on my finger for a moment. Putting my hand down, I take a step closer to him, we are only inches apart, and I'm thrown back in time for a moment – *Whoa! I always did like his smell!*

I look up at him looking down at me, his baby blue eyes scorching me. He's tall, but not as tall as Tristan, but his body has changed so much, he's bulked up like Tristan, but not as big, and this t-shirt he's wearing…it looks really, really good on him – *Coral, what are you doing?* – I shake my head to get myself together then I take a deep breath and say my piece.

"Look J, it doesn't matter that your back in Brighton. It doesn't matter that you've missed me, or that you want me back. It's never going to happen, ever. I love Tristan' – "He doesn't know you like I know you." He interrupts, his voice giving away his feelings – *He's hurt!*

"No J that's where you've got it wrong. You remember how you were always trying to get me to talk to you, to tell you things about myself, why I'm the way I am?" I softly say.

He slowly nods once. "You wanted so much from me that I couldn't give you, that's because it wasn't meant to be with you, it was meant to be with him," I say glancing over to Tristan. I can see the relief in his eyes. "Tristan knows everything about me, you don't."

"But that's not fair Coral, how can I compete with that…if you won't let me in…?" He says, shaking his head in disagreement.

"Justin. You and me, it's never going to happen. I'm getting married in two weeks time." Justin looks completely devastated.

"Please…" he begs, swallowing hard. "Don't do this Coral, give me another chance. Just…let's meet up, try again. I've missed you treacle, so badly."

*Oh!...*I used to love it when he called me that – *Get a grip Coral!*

I take a deep breath, pull my shoulders back and look him square in the eye. "Justin, you ripped my heart out and stamped all over it. I don't care what your excuses are for your actions back then, the point is I would never, ever have done that to you, no matter how unhappy I was. That's a huge difference in values don't you think? And well, Tristan and I, we share the same values. I know that without a shadow of a doubt he would never, ever do that to me' – "Damn right!" Tristan pipes up, interrupting me. It makes me want to smile, but I don't and continue.

"And you did Justin! It's something I can forgive, and I *do* forgive you, and part of me will always love you, but it was over the moment I caught you two at it!" I spit.

"Please..." He begs again, his eyes closed for a second. "I can make you happy, you know I can, let me make it up to you." I suddenly start to feel faint. I'm not sure if it's the relentless sun beating down on me, or Justin's words, or both, but either way, I need to sit down before my legs give way.

"Tristan." I reach my hand out to him, and he's instantly over to me.

"What is it?" He softly asks, gripping me by the waist.

"I feel faint," I whisper, closing my eyes and leaning against him.

"Keys?" I drop them into his hands. He walks us the couple of steps to the door, unlocks it, yanks it open, lifts me into his arms and carries me over to the sofa. Releasing me, he dashes over to the sink, fills a glass with water and comes back over to me. Kneeling in front of me, he hands me the glass. "Here, take a sip, it's nice and cold." He adds.

I put the glass to my lips and take a welcome sip. I'm instantly reminded of the first time he was attentive like this, the day of my hangover, the day he was at the office and caught me scoffing that muffin. And then my reaction when he told me Joyce had sold, he dashed off to get me water back then – I shake my head and almost laugh at the crazy situation.

"Coral?" Justin goes to take a step inside the studio.

Tristan is instantly to his feet. "You need to leave. Now." He threatens in a cold, hard voice – He is radiating tension.

"No," Justin argues, crossing his arms.

"Do you want me to help you leave?" Tristan threatens. *Oh crap!*

Justin holds his arms out wide, a slight smile on his face – *Oh, you really don't want to upset Tristan like that!*

"Bring it on!" He sneers at Tristan.

Tristan's hands bunch into fists. I can tell he's itching to chuck Justin out. "If you actually *did* give a fuck about her, you'd see she's in no state to be dealing with this!" Tristan hisses through gritted teeth.

"Justin!" I shout. "Go now, I mean it!"

Justin puts his hands in his pockets and stays where he is, he hasn't taken his eyes off me. "Do you want me to leave?" He asks me.

"Yes! I've already asked you to!" I snap, glaring at him.

Finally, after what seems like an eternity, he nods once looking down at the floor then looks up at me. "I'll see you soon Coral," he says with a determined look on his face.

I shake my head at him and look away. *He always was a cocky son-of-a-bitch!* Tristan walks over to the air-con, switches it onto full, then heads over and pulls the patio door shut, and then locks it.

"Is he gone?" I ask.

"Yes." He hisses.

"Thank you," I whisper, taking another sip.

"What for?" Tristan asks, his hands fisting at his side as he stares out at Justin's retreating figure.

"For not trying to take over, for letting me say my piece." I watch him walk back over to me, kneel down and gently stroke my cheek and then he leans in for a kiss. I pucker my lips playfully and press them hard against his. *Hmm, he tastes so good.*

"I'm very proud of you," he says pulling back.

"You are?" I squeak, surprised.

"Yes, I thought you were going to punch him in the face, but you did really well. You were mad, I could see that, and you handled it." He says I think with pride.

"I don't feel like I handled it," I choke out.

"You did Coral." I can't help laughing at that one. "Now, tell me, how are you feeling? Are you still faint?"

"No, I'm good now," I say.

"Well I think we should go home, you've had enough excitement for one day." He firmly tells me.

"I thought we had a deal?" I say, purposely pouting.

"A deal?" He questions.

"Yes! No moaning about going home and no broodiness?" I firmly say. *Hmph!*

"Yes...well, that was before' – "Tristan, I'll say it again. When are you going to learn that I'm stronger than I look?" He smiles and then frowns as he stares down at my hand with the catheter in it. "Look, I will admit, if you weren't in my life and Justin had turned up, I would be a mess, and I'd be running to Rob to help me assimilate it all, all the feelings that I know would have come up. But you are in my life, and I couldn't give a damn about what just happened. It's no big deal, and I don't want it to affect our day together – capiche?" I add in an Al Capone accent.

"That was really good," Tristan chuckles.

"I know, I can do accents quite well," I say, chuckling along with him.

"So it would seem." He teases in an equally impressive Al Capone voice.

"Wow! So are you," I say, chuckling some more.

Tristan suddenly stops laughing, his expression turning serious. "So really, you're ok?" he asks. I lean forward and squeeze his cheeks, so it makes his lips pucker up and kiss him.

"Yes," I say, realising his cheeks.

"Ow!" He says, flexing his jaw. I giggle again. "Right, well I'll be back in a second," he says heading off to the bathroom. The moment he shuts the door, my head falls into my hands – *What the fuck just happened?*

I look up and stare at my almost empty studio. I mean everything I just said to Tristan is true, I don't care that Justin's back, or that...he wants me back...or that...I drift off, my mind flooding with memories of Justin and me, because we were, at a certain point in our relationship, so in love with one another – *No!*

I grip my hair in my hands and try to push the images away. It's Tristan I want, it's Tristan I love, I can't live without him. Right on cue, I hear Tristan washing his hands, any second now he's going to come through that door – *Right, game face on Coral!*

I take a deep breath, push all thoughts of Justin away, get to my feet and walk over to the kitchenette. Opening one of the cupboards, I see my plates, cups, and glasses are still here. I can't really see the point in packing them up and taking them back with us, Tristan and I have already picked a set that we are using – *Hmm...what to do?*

"Uh-oh," Tristan teases as he reaches me. "Should I have packed those?"

"No..." I shake my head and close the cupboard. "I was just thinking about what I should do with them?"

"Oh." He says lightly.

"Actually I was thinking about all the furniture...If I rent this place out, it will need all this stuff anyway, won't it?" I say gesturing to the general area.

"Yes, it will. But you might want to change the sofa." He suggests.

"Why?" I frown up at him.

"Most people who rent these out have a futon or sofa-bed instead." He simply says.

"Why?" I ask, incredulously, those things, as far as I know, are really uncomfortable.

Tristan shrugs his shoulders. "Get more money if it can sleep, four people." He tells me.

"Seriously?" I scoff. "Even though it has an open gallery bedroom? I mean…it's not like…you know…either couple would be able to'" – "Have sex without being seen or heard?" Tristan says, finishing my sentence for me with a wicked grin.

"Yes!" I giggle, feeling a little nervous that he can read me *that* easily. "You did a good job," I add, looking around the baron room. I suddenly realise there's no blood stain on the floor from where Bob was lying – I quickly squash that line of thinking.

"Shall we go up?" Tristan asks.

"Up?" I question.

"Yes. Don't you want to check if I got everything from your bedroom?" He asks, with raised eyebrows.

"Oh…well I suppose so," I say trying to work out Tristan's odd expression.

Taking his hand, I follow him up the creaking stairs. *What is that sweet smell?* The moment we reach the bedroom, Tristan takes a step back and gestures to the room – *Oh wow!* There are twinkly lights, lots of electric candles, and wildflowers everywhere making the room smell divine. *Why has he done this?*

"When did you do this?" I squeak, my mouth hanging open as I scan the bedroom.

"I didn't, well I wanted to do this, but I didn't want to leave you either, so I asked Edith, she came down early this morning with Stuart." He smiles. "Do you like it?" *Is he kidding?*

"Like it?" I scoff. "Tristan, it looks magical," I say, beaming from ear to ear. "But why have you'" – "Why have I done this?" I nod, unable to say anymore.

Tristan takes my hand, leads me over to my bed and sits me down, then kneeling down in front of me he looks up at me with those puppy dog eyes of his. "What's the last memory you have of this place?"

I swallow hard. "Seeing Bob on the floor…" I whisper, unable to say anymore.

"Thought so, well I wanted to change that." He softly says.

"You do?" I squeak.

"Yes." I stare around the room again. "Plus, I've never made love to you here," he adds.

My mouth pops open. I stare down at him, a little shocked. "You...you want to make love – now?" I manage to squeak out.

Tristan smiles shyly at me. "I thought it would be a nice way to replace the old memory," he says a little nervously, looking down at my hand again.

"Make love – now?" I choke, almost laughing.

"If you don't want to..." He says, looking a little hurt.

"Yes." I smile down at him. "I do." What a wonderful thing to have done. *Justin would never have done something like this!*

"But can you tell me something first?" I ask.

"Anything." He smiles his dazzling smile at me.

I swoon for a second then snap out of it. "Are you ok?"

"Me?" He questions, his brows knitting together.

"Um...yeah," I shake my head. "Tristan, my ex just turned up on my doorstep confessing his love for me – aren't you upset about that?"

"Should I be?" He questions. *Huh?*

"You mean...me?" I quickly surmise.

"Do you still have feelings for him Coral?" He asks his brows pulled together.

"Tristan, what I said to him was true. There will always be a part of me that will love him, but it's over. It's you I love, you I want, and I want to spend the rest of my life with."

He smiles shyly at me. "Then I have nothing to fear, and no, I'm not upset. I'm not going to say it didn't kill me to see you standing so close to him though..." He trails off.

I smile shyly at him, lean down, take his face in my hands and softly kiss him...

TRISTAN IS HELPING me pull my t-shirt over my head. I can't help giggling as I look up at him. That was fun, very sweet and will, without a shadow of a doubt be the best memory I will ever take away from this place.

"Thank you," I whisper, smiling shyly at him.

"Oh Coral...it is indeed my pleasure." He teases, his eyes glinting wickedly, I can't help laughing. "So what now my beautiful, darling girl?" He asks, leaning down to kiss me. *Oh!*

My heart melts, he really is on top form today. "Um..." I try to get my brain firing again. "How about some ice-cream?" I say.

"Ice-cream?" He asks frowning down at my odd reaction – *Get a grip Coral!*

"Uh-huh! Ice-cream and a walk on the beach," I manage to squeak out.

"Your wish is my command." He says leaning down to kiss me again. I watch Tristan walk over to the candles and switch them off, he does the same with the twinkly lights. "Shall I get Stuart to take the flowers back to the house?" He asks. I don't answer him because something's really bothering me...niggling away in the back of my mind. I try to work out what it is?

"Coral?" He stops what he's doing and stares down at me.

Then I remember – *Holy fuck!* Bile rises in my throat. I whip my head round to look at Tristan, my eyes wide with fear.

"What's wrong?" He whispers, frozen just like me.

"The CCTV," I mouth, my voice unable to get the words out, my mouth completely dry. I squeeze my eyes shut. It will have recorded us...having sex...just like...just like when I was a kid – *Oh god, I feel sick...No, no, no...*I sink onto the bed feeling completely horrified.

"Coral?" Tristan is straight over to me, his one hand on my forehead, his other hand holding my good hand. "Baby, what's wrong, you've gone as white as a ghost."

"The CCTV," I whisper, my voice barely audible.

"Gone," he says, frowning up at me. I instantly relax, but now I feel a cold, damp sweat layering my body, the after-effects of the shock. "Coral, you didn't really think I'd' – "No," I interrupt, "Not intentionally, of course not."

Tristan sags with relief. "Good, you ok?"

"Getting there," I breathe.

Tristan leans forward and kisses my forehead. "You're sweating!"

I look down and see my hands are shaking – *Fuck!* Not now...please....we're having such a wonderful day.

"Back in a sec!" Tristan dashes off, moments later he returns with a tea towel in his hands. "Here baby," he kneels down again and places the cold, wet towel against my forehead – *Oh that's so nice!*

I close my eyes as it soothes and cools me. "Thank you," I whisper.

"Coral, this is my fault. I'm so sorry baby. I should have told you I had it removed when we packed this place up – Shit!" I open my eyes and see Tristan run his hand through his hair in frustration.

"It's ok," I whisper. "Don't be mad at yourself."

"Well, I am." He snaps.

"Please...don't be. This has been such a great day so far, well apart from the crappy parts. We both seem so much happier, more relaxed. I want the whole day to be like this, so please...I'm begging you, don't spoil it." I croak.

Tristan takes a deep breath in and slowly blows it out. "Ok baby." He smiles up at me. "Feeling better?" He adds.

I smile down at him. That was not a nice feeling! *I need to get out of here!*

"Yeah, let's go," I say, slowly getting to my feet.

Tristan nods takes the tea towel off my forehead, and we slowly head down the stairs...

WE'VE HAD THE most wonderful morning. We ate ice-cream, which was another surprise as my favourite is rum & raisin, the same as Tristan, as we strolled hand in hand along the beach. Popped into the office, much to Joyce's surprise and I met Karen, she's really cool, and I think, possibly, is going to become a new friend – who's actually a girl. And Joe, ah sweet Joe, is getting her kids back on Friday, she is beyond excited – I'm so pleased for her. I said I'd pop over to her place on Sunday to meet her kids and say hello. And now we are sat inside a cute little bistro on North Laine as Tristan was too hot to sit outside, and we've just tucked into a really delicious salad.

"Nice?" Tristan asks.

"Very nice," I say beaming back at him.

"Shall we?" He says, gesturing for us to leave.

"Yes." I stand, take his hand, and we head over to pay the bill.

I quickly whip my purse out without Tristan seeing and hand the male waiter my card. Tristan turns his head just in time to see me do it.

"No!" He shouts to the waiter who instantly freezes with my card in one hand, and the wireless payment machine in the other.

"Put that card through right now!" I laugh.

He smiles a little awkwardly, looking from me to Tristan.

"Please..." I beg. "He won't let me pay for anything." The waiter hesitates as he looks across at Tristan's stern expression, his hand held out with *his* card.

Oh, fuck it! – Yanking the machine and my card out of his hands, I push my card into the slot and give the machine back to him.

"Too late!" I say smiling sweetly at Tristan who's teeth clamp together in annoyance. In my peripheral vision, I can see the waiter is trying really hard not to laugh. I chuckle away to myself, feeling triumphant. Tristan is as stiff as a board as he stands next to me, which makes me want to laugh even harder.

"Thank you, have a good day." The waiter brings my attention back to him. I take my card and receipt – Wow! A whopping £22.75, that's what Tristan's arguing about?

"Why did you just do that?" Tristan snaps as we head outside.

I curl my hand around his toned bicep and look up at him. "What? I can't treat you?" I question. His lips press into a hard line. "Tristan' – "I don't want you spending your money," he says a little harshly.

I stop walking, Tristan follows suit. "Ok, just hold on a minute," I say my hand held up. "Are you saying I can't spend *my* money on you, I can't treat *you*, but it's ok for *you* to treat *me*?"

Tristan shrugs. "I'm a man Coral, it's what I do."

"What?" I say laughing a little.

Tristan sighs then places his hands on my cheeks. "It's my job, my responsibility to take care of you and provide for you. It makes me feel like I'm doing what I should be doing as your partner when you take that away from me..." He shakes his head and starts to smile. "It's emasculating."

My mouth pops open. "Are you kidding me?" I squeak, half laughing as I do.

Tristan's brows knit together. "No." *Holy fuck, he's serious!*

"I...I don't really know what to say to that?" I say, totally mind blown.

"Speechless? That's a first," he teases.

I cock one eyebrow up at him. "Tristan...I...I'm sorry, I didn't mean to make you feel like that...but'– "You want to treat me too?" He says finishing my sentence for me.

I nod up at him. "Ok, well in the future, when you do, just let me know in advance ok?"

"Why?" I frown. Tristan laughs and shakes his head at me. "Oh, I get it," I say. "If it's not too expensive, you'll go along with it, but if it is, you won't let me pay?"

Horror registers on his face as he realises I've worked it out.

"That's crazy," I say. "But if it makes you happy..." I lean up and kiss him.

"Thank you," he whispers, leaning his forehead against mine.

"Well I suppose, in a way, you just paid for lunch anyway!"

I bark, remembering the money he's put into my account. *I must remember to transfer it back to him!*

"Yes, I suppose I have," he says, smiling triumphantly at me, which makes me shake my head at him and laugh.

We start strolling down North Laine, hand in hand, both happy and relaxed, despite what's gone on today, and then I see it, that little bit of inspiration I was looking for. I quickly look around me trying to find a shop I can send Tristan into so I can buy him the present – *Yes, I love those!*

"Tristan," I stop and look up at him. "I'm tired. I want to get home, but I really want to pop into that shop, there's a new album out that I want. But you see that chocolate shop behind you?"

Tristan gazes quizzically at me for a moment, then turns and looks at the shop. "Yes," he says, almost laughing as he turns back to me.

"Well, I have a thing for the dark chocolate rum balls that they sell, they're absolutely delicious," I say, batting my lashes for optimal effect.

"You want me to go get you some baby?" *Oh, Tristan, you've fallen for it so easily, that's so cute!*

"Do you mind?" I ask, trying to make my eyes big and round like his.

"Of course I don't." He says, smiling sweetly at me.

"Ok, I'll be back in a sec," I say, I lean up and peck his lips. "I'll meet you back here in a couple of minutes, ok."

Without waiting for him to say anything, I scuttle into the music shop and go straight to the counter, there's no time for looking, and ask the sales clerk if they have what I want. He smiles at me, I think he's trying to flirt, punches some details into his computer then nods once at me.

I almost jump up and down with glee. "Great!"

"Um...it's in the back," he says. "I'll have to go find it." *Crap!*

"Ok," I squeak. "But quick as you can, it's for a present, and I don't want him to see," I say gesturing to Tristan walking out the chocolate shop opposite us.

He looks out the window, his face instantly falling – *Yeah, he's a pretty big guy!* He sighs, looking a little glum, but heads off to the back of the store. I watch Tristan through the window, waiting patiently for me. *Come on hurry up!*

The sales clerk makes me jump as he returns. "Here you go." He scans the DVD and goes to place it in a bag.

"No, it's ok," I say taking it off him and stuffing it into my bag, luckily it just about fits. "I'll be wrapping it up when I get home anyway." I hand him my card, punch my pin into the machine and wait impatiently for the payment to go through.

Finally, he hands me back my card and receipt, I stuff them into my bag. "Thanks," I say as I fly out the shop. "Hey," I say bounding over to Tristan.

"Hey yourself!" He pulls me into his arms and softly kisses me on the cheek. "Get your album?" He adds. *Oh crap, I should have just picked a random one up!*

"Um...no, they'd sold out. I can get one online." I say. *Phew, nice save Coral!* I try not to smirk at myself.

"Are you sure, we can find another store?" He says.

"No, really Tristan, I just want to get home," I say, faking tiredness.

"Ok, look." He holds up a big bag beaming broadly at me. *Holy crap!*

"Jeez Tristan, how many did you buy?" I say scanning the bag. I only buy a few at a time as they are very more-ish and I'll eat far too many!

His face falls. "Um...all of them."

"All of them?" I squeak.

"Well, I've never tried them before so..." He trails off registering my shocked expression. These little babies are not cheap; he must have spent so much – just on chocolate. "Ask, and ye shall receive," he says, smiling again.

"Wow!" I titter then I wrap my arms around his waist and squeeze him tight. "Thank you, baby." He really is the sweetest – his folks did such a fine job with him.

We start walking again, strolling along in the sunshine without a care in the world, but now I've got the present, I want to buy him a big card too. Plus, I need to get some wrapping paper. *Hmm, what to do?* – Right at that moment, his mobile starts ringing. Pulling it out of his pocket, he answers it and is quickly drawn into a deep conversation. I scan up and down the lane, thankfully, a few doors up I see a card shop. *Yes!*

I gesture to Tristan that I'm going in. He nods and continues with his conversation. Entering the shop, I quickly dash over to the big cards and start scanning; knowing I need to do this quickly.

"Can I help you?" I spin around, and a lady in her fifties with a kind smile is waiting for me to answer her. I quickly reel off what I'm looking for and that I've got to be quick. "No problem dear, here are the large cards, have a look through. Do you know what colour wrapping paper you would like, I can find it for you," she suggests.

I quickly tell her, and just as I pick the card that I like, she comes over with some gunmetal grey wrapping paper – perfect, very manly.

"Brilliant," I say and pick up the card. It's big, about double the size of A4 and has a beautiful picture of a tropical sunset on it, and written on the front are the words - *Anywhere is Paradise when I'm with you* – Perfect! I open the card and quickly read the inscription.

> Tropical sunsets are beautiful
> Walks on the beach are romantic, it's true
> But I don't need any of that because I'm
> Already in paradise with you
> That's how much I love you baby

I almost start crying, almost. This is perfect and says exactly how I feel about Tristan. I really don't care where I am, as long as I'm with him. Dashing over to the counter I give the lady the card so she can scan it, along with the wrapping paper. I take one more glance around the store, and I notice, sat on a dusty clear shelf is a big teddy from the 'Me to You' range – I have to have it.

"That teddy," I say a little breathlessly, pointing up to it.

"Oh, he's been there a while. I can knock you some of the price if you like, people tend to buy the little ones."

"I'll take him, whatever the price," I state.

"Alright then," She smiles at me and asks her assistant, a young girl who looks fresh out of school to fetch it for me, moments later, she brings it over. He's a bit dusty, but now I see him up close, he's even more perfect. There's a big patch on his head as though he's been injured – just like Tristan's gash on his head. He's a shaggy plush grey teddy, with a cute blue nose and he's holding a big blue and light pink heart that says 'I love you this much' It really is perfect.

"Tatty teddy that one's called," she tells me. "He's really soft, don't you think?" And boy is he, he's so squidgy.

"Yeah," I giggle. "He's lovely." But how am I going to get him back to the house without Tristan seeing, and what am I going to say? "Do you have any of those big bags?"

"Yes, over here. What colour would you like?" she asks.

Hmm, Tristan seems to like silver and greys, and it matches

the teddy bear and the wrapping paper. I pick the bag, she scans it, I hand her my card to pay for everything and stuff the teddy and the wrapping paper inside the bag, just as Tristan casually waltzes inside.

"Hey," I say, thanking the heavens I don't blush and give myself away.

"What are you doing in here?" He smiles.

"Oh..." *Quick Coral, say anything!* "Um...I just thought I'd um...get a gift for Joyce, you know a little leaving present." I turn away from him and swallow hard. The lady hands me my card and receipt with a conspiratorial wink. I smile back at her and head out the shop with Tristan.

"Everything ok with the phone call?" I ask, hoping he doesn't question me any further.

"Yes, just work you know..." He says waving his hand and shrugging.

I smile up at him. "Great, ready to go?"

Tristan pulls me into his arms. "Darling, if you want to do something for Joyce, organise anything, you only have to say you know that right?" *Sweet!*

"Yes, I do' – My mobile buzzes in my bag interrupting us. Tristan releases me so I can answer it. "Debs?"

"Hi." She sounds so down, it's not like her.

"What's wrong?" I ask. I'm immediately worried.

"Can I come over?" She whispers.

"Debs, what's wrong?" I ask again.

"I...Oh, Coral!" She bursts into tears – *Shit!*

"Debs come round, we should be back shortly," I say, feeling frantic.

"You're out?" She croaks.

"Yeah, I wanted to stretch my legs." I muse.

"Oh..." She's still sniffling down the line.

"Do you want me to come to you?" I ask looking up at Tristan.

"No, no...it's ok. Um...Lily's staying over at a friend's for the night." She sounds so despondent.

"Deb's it's no problem, you want me to come to you just say so?" I tell her sternly.

"No...I want...I have to get out of this house," she whispers.

"Then do it," I say, wondering what the hell is going on. "Come and stay with me for the night?" I look up at Tristan. He's frowning at my worried expression and nodding in approval.

"Deb's it's no problem. Tristan will leave us to it, he won't mind at all you know."

"He won't?" She croaks.

"Deb's even if he did, do you really think I'm the type of person to let anyone dictate to me who I will and won't spend my time with?" I say sounding exasperated, Tristan starts smirking at me. I hear her whisper a laugh. "Debs come over!" I order. "Stay the night."

"You're sure?" She asks.

"Yes," I answer firmly.

"Ok," she whispers. "I'll go pack a bag...um...see you in a while." She manages to squeak the last bit out.

"Debs, you're worrying me, are you ok to drive?" I ask. 'Stuart' Tristan mouths at me. I nod in approval. "I can send Stuart to pick you up?" I get no response. "Debs?"

"No...it's a nice idea' – "I'm sending Stuart," I say and cover the phone. "How long?" I ask Tristan.

"He could be there in say...an hour?" He says looking at his watch.

"He'll be there in forty minutes," I say to Debs. "Be ready!" *She's always late!*

"I will," she mumbles, sniffing loudly.

"Bye Debs, be safe," I whisper.

"See you." She hangs up.

I put my mobile back in my bag, wondering what that's all about.

"Forty minutes?" Tristan questions, his head cocked to the side.

"Debs is always late," I explain. Tristan nods takes his mobile out of his pocket and calls Stuart. He tells him where to pick us up, and we head in that direction...

CHAPTER SEVENTEEN

AS SOON WE GET back in the car, I call Rob and let him know what's going on, and that I'm really worried about Debs, but he tells me that I should see her this afternoon and we can hang out tomorrow. I hate letting him down, but he told me not to worry, and we'll have just as much fun tomorrow; reluctantly I agreed. Ten minutes later, Stuart drops us off at the house and heads back out to pick Debs up.

"Do you mind if I head out?" Tristan says.

"Tristan, you don't need my permission to go out!" I bite unintentionally.

"I wasn't asking for your permission. If you want me here for any reason, then I'd stay." He softly says. I immediately feel guilty.

I walk over to him and wrap my arms around his waist. "I'm sorry, that was uncalled for."

Tristan wraps his arms around me and gently rocks us. "You're stressed?" He says.

"Yes, I'm worried about Debs. I've never heard her like that, ever!" I swallow hard.

"Really?" He asks, surprised.

"Yeah...she's always been really up and perky, like Gladys," I say, still feeling bemused. "She's never called on me for anything."

"Well, whatever it is, I'm sure you'll soon hear about it." Tristan kisses the top of my head.

"Yeah..." I sigh. "Just because I'm curious, where are you off to?" I ask.

"Thought I'd call Joyce and see if she wants a game of golf." He casually says.

"You can play golf?" I squeak, looking up at him.

"Yeah?" He smiles down at me then pecks my lips.

"Will you teach me?" I ask.

212

"You want to learn how to play golf?" He chuckles.

I narrow my eyes at him. "What's funny about that?"

"Nothing," he chuckles releasing me. "I'll go and call her."

"Ok." I watch him walk into his office. Damn, he hasn't even left, and I'm already missing him. Shaking my head at myself, I head outside onto the patio, and carefully lie down on one of the sun loungers, trying my best to stay still and soak up some rays. A couple of minutes later Tristan re-appears and sits on my lounger, he lifts my legs and places them on his lap.

"You have such sexy legs," he says, running both hands up and down my stumpy, chunky legs. I involuntarily snort then look away from him, and I know he's going to do it.

Reaching up, he pulls on my chin, so I have to look at him. "Ah yes, earlier...in the kitchen." I know exactly what he's talking about. "Come on, out with it," he says, his hands skimming up and down my legs again – *He's turning me on, big time!*

"Ok, well for starters can you please stop doing that?" His face falls, his eyes darkening. "Oh...I didn't mean...bollocks!" I hiss, feeling totally deflated and guilty. "Tristan, I just asked you to stop because you were turning me on – big time!" I quickly add.

He instantly looks relieved and relaxes. "Ok," he smirks, leaning down to kiss my one knee, then the other. *Whoa! His lips on my legs!*

I take a deep calming breath. "Ok, not helping!" I breathe. He cocks his head to the side, grinning broadly at me. "You are such a tease!" I softly scold, laughing at him.

"I'm sorry," he says then his face falls as he stares down at my legs again. "You don't like them, do you?" I bite my lip and frown. *How has he worked that out?*

"Tristan, you know...I'm still working on...well, liking myself...you know being ok being me, feeling ok about being in my own skin. I know I've still got a long, long way to go." I say, feeling shy that I shared that with him. Tristan nods several times, his eyes still on my legs and then he leans down once more, and kisses my knees again. It sends tingles, everywhere.

"I've going to kiss every inch of these beautiful legs tonight. Maybe my kisses will help to heal you," he says leaning in to kiss my lips. *Oh my god!* I think my heart just exploded with love.

"Oh, Tristan!" I mewl, kissing him back and crying at the same time. Then I reach up and wrap my arms around his neck, trying my best to crush him to me. "I love you...so much." I choke, gripping him tighter then wincing in pain.

"Careful baby," he says, gently rubbing my back. Then he takes my arms from around his neck and skims my cheeks with his knuckles again. "Are you in pain?"

"Yes," I say, trying to catch my breath.

"Nurse Terry will be here soon." He says, wrapping his arm around my waist and pulling me closer to him, I wrap my arms around his torso and rest my head on his shoulder. "Joyce is out, with Gladys," he adds.

"Oh, I'm sorry baby." I lean up and run my hands through his hair; he looks a little upset about it. "Oh!" *Brainwave!* "Tristan, call Malcolm. I know he plays and Gladys told me in the hospital that he really likes you and thinks you're a fine man!" I say.

Tristan gazes adoringly at me. "You...are so sweet," he says brushing his knuckles down my cheek. I laugh and smile shyly at him. "It's a great idea baby, I'll call him." He adds, leaning down to peck me on the lips and then he stands and walks back into the house...

I AM STOOD on the doorstep kissing Tristan goodbye. Apparently, Malcolm jumped at his offer, and also suggested they eat out too, so I know I won't see Tristan for hours. It's already killing me knowing that fact. I hear the Jag rumbling down the driveway, so I pull back and gaze up at Tristan.

"Have a good time baby," I say, leaning up to peck him on the lips once more.

"Please, for me, be careful," he says, kissing me back with a worried expression.

"I will, I promise." Tristan pulls me into his arms and hugs me tightly. Nurse Terry has been and given me another shot, so it doesn't hurt too much. Stuart pulls to a stop and Tristan, the gentleman that he is, walks over and opens the back door for Debs. She jumps out without even thanking him and runs towards me, arms open wide, and I can see she's been crying, a lot –*Oh no, Debs!* Reaching me, she hugs me a little too hard.

"Oh Debs, what's wrong?" I gasp, wincing in pain.

"Oh crap! Did I hurt you?" she says pulling back and checking me over.

"It's ok," I gasp again.

Tristan returns to us and leans down to kiss me goodbye again.

"See you soon baby," he says, we gaze at one another for a couple of seconds.

"Bye," I whisper, my heart cracking in two.

He takes my good hand, squeezes it once then turns to Debs. "Debbie, whatever is wrong, I hope you get it sorted," he says, his cheeks flaming.

"Thanks." She sniffs.

Tristan smiles softly at me once more, before heading over to the car. Opening the door, he looks back at me again and holds my gaze for a couple of seconds then he smiles to himself, gets into the car and shuts the door. With a goofy grin on my face, I wave at Tristan as Stuart pulls away.

"Come on," I say, linking my arm in Debs. "Let's get you a drink; you look like you could use one!" Debs smiles at me, but it doesn't reach her eyes.

We wander back into the house and head straight into the kitchen.

"What do you fancy?" I ask. Debs shakes her head at me then bursts into tears she puts her face in her hands and sobs, uncontrollably!

"Debs!" I dash around the breakfast bar and pull her into my arms, then I shuffle us over to the sofa, and we sit, silently, with Debs cradled in my arms while she cries it out. I don't know how long we stay like that for, but finally, she stops crying, turns her head, so we are face to face and swallows hard.

"Scott's having an affair," she whimpers, blinking rapidly as fresh tears silently stream down her face.

"What!?" I bellow, jumping to my feet, my hands automatically bunching into fists.

"Calm down Coral," she sighs, blowing her nose.

"Calm....do...." I can't even get the words out, I am that livid!

"Coral, I can't take it if you're going to be like this. I know you love me, and that's why you're so mad, but I need you to be calm for me, please..." she begs, drying her tears with fresh tissues. *Oh!* I take a deep breath and slowly blow it out. *Ok, ok, calm Coral...calm...*I nod at Debs and sit next to her. I take her hand in mine, linking our fingers together, she feels cold.

"Debs, your hand is cold, when was the last time you ate?" I softly ask.

"I...I don't know," she whispers.

"Debs...you should eat," I softly tell her. *Jeez, I sound like Tristan!*

"I don't have any appetite," she sniffs.

I nod understanding that completely. "Do...do you want to

215

talk about it?" I tentatively ask, knowing she has never confided in me.

Debs sighs heavily and seems to regain some of her composure. "It was a year ago..." She drifts off again. *Huh?*

"A year ago?" I say, frowning in confusion.

"Yeah...a new girl that started at Scott's place...it had been going on for three months when..." Debs stops again and squeezes her eyes shut.

"Oh Debs, I'm so sorry," I offer not knowing what else to say.

"Scott just came home one night, he'd organised for Lily to stay with her friends, he said we needed some quality time together, then he sat me down and told me."

"He...he told you?" I squeak. Debs nods several times. *Whoa!* I try to think of something logical to ask. "Um... well is it still going on?" I ask she shakes her head at me. "And you know this, for certain?" I ask, and she nods again. "That bastard!" I spit, I can't help it – He is the father of my niece and my sister's husband. How dare he!

"Sorry," I immediately say. "I'm calm now," I add, although I feel anything but calm – I need a drink. "Debs, let me get you a drink?" I offer.

"Please," she sniffs.

"What would you like?" I ask, searching her face.

"I don't know," she says, sniffing again with a little laugh.

"Wine?" She shakes her head – *Hmm?* "Vodka and orange?"

"Sounds good," she sniffs.

"Be right back," I say and head over to the kitchen. Edith appears with some clean washing in her hand.

"Hello Coral, would you like me to – Oh!" Edith stops as she sees Debs, sitting on the sofa, still blubbering.

"Edith, you remember my sister, Debbie?" I whisper.

"Yes," she whispers back, her eyes wide. "Is she alright?" she asks, as I add ice to Debs' drink.

"No, she not," I say frowning deeply.

"Oh dear...Is there anything I can do?" she asks sweetly.

I turn and place my hand on her arm. "No, but thank you, Edith, it's very kind of you to ask."

"Well..." She looks around the kitchen, not knowing what to do with herself. "I'll...I'll just be downstairs then, in the garden. If you need me just shout," she says heading off in that direction – I can almost see the comedy side of it, almost.

I head back over to Debs. "Here you go," I say sighing

deeply and sitting next to her. "Debs, I don't quite understand, if it happened a year ago' – "Spain." She interrupts, taking several gulps of her drink.

"Spain?" *Ok, now I'm really confused.*

"I knew there was a part of me that had to forgive him, we hadn't exactly been getting along that well' – "It's no excuse!" I spit. "Sorry, I won't interrupt again," I quickly add.

Debs nods and continues. "Coral, take it from me, it's not easy married life. You have to work at it, you have to make the time for one another, you have to keep letting each other know that that person is still so special to you, no matter how long you've been together. But Scott and I...I don't know we just kind of...unintentionally drifted apart." She takes another drink.

"We love each other, make no mistake about that, but...I don't know, I think when you both work, you have a house and a child to care for, life just kind of gets in the way and sometimes you forget about each other, in that way I mean."

"What are you trying to say Debs; you guys weren't...having sex anymore?" I say, trying not to cringe.

"No of course not, we were...it's just..." Debs stops and shakes her head. "You know if there's one thing I've learned is that men are more insecure than women, they just don't show it or talk about it like women do. And believe it or not, what makes them feel secure is knowing that that can still satisfy you like no other man can," she tells me.

Ew! Not sure if I want to hear this!

"Debs' – "Fact of life Coral, you'd be wise to heed this information. Don't make the same mistakes I did." She firmly adds.

"What do you mean?" I whisper.

Debs sighs takes another drink then laughs at herself. "Fantasies," she says, draining her glass – *Ok, I definitely don't want to hear this.*

"Another?" I say taking her glass of her and walking into the kitchen. Unfortunately, Debs follows me.

"You don't want me to tell you, do you?" she says.

I swallow hard. "No, it's not that, I just..." I shake my head, make her another drink, pour myself an orange juice, and turn to stare at her. "Debs, sex isn't exactly something I can... comfortably talk about." *There, I said it!*

"What do you mean?" she asks, taking her drink from me. "I know you've always been shy...but that's not what you meant, is it?" I slowly shake my head at her. "Then what *do* you mean Coral?" she asks in her big sister tone.

"Come on, let's sit," I say heading back over to the sofa. We both sit, and Debs waits patiently for me to continue. I take a deep breath, steel myself and say it. "Before I came to live with you and Gladys, I was sexually abused by a paedophile ring."

"What!?" She screeches launching to her feet, her vodka and orange juice sloshing everywhere.

"Debs, this is going to sound ironic, but I need *you* to be calm right now." I look up at her, my eyes pleading.

"Oh!" She stares down at me for a moment, blinking rapidly, then she knocks her drink back in one go, grabs a load of tissues, gets to her knees and cleans up the sloshes of liquid. When she's done, she silently takes a seat next to me and takes hold of my hand.

"Why didn't you tell me Coral?" she whispers, staring at the floor – I think she's in shock.

"It's not easy to tell someone something like that," I say, taking a sip of juice. "Anyway, this isn't about me, this is about you. I did plan on telling you everything, but in all honesty, it's not important. It was in the past, and this is the present – and right now, we should be talking about you. So, fantasies?"

Debs turns and looks at me, her blue eyes wide. "You can't tell me something like that and just expect me to let it go," she whispers.

I sigh inwardly, maybe I shouldn't have told her yet. "Look, Debs, you *can* ask me about it, but not now, some other time ok? What's going on with you and Scott is much more important, so I'll say again, fantasies?"

Debs swallows hard, frowning deeply and nods once. "Ok. Well, we weren't honest with each other; well actually, more like Scott wasn't being honest with me. I thought we satisfied each other in that area, but apparently not!" she scoffs. "So with that going on and us not really having the time for each other...well... Scott said he doesn't feel anything for her, that he loves me, it's just she was giving him his kicks, making him feel good about himself, and I wasn't."

Talk about a kick in the teeth – *Keep it zipped Stevens!*

"Ok," I mumble, trying to understand.

"Coral, you can never blame one person when either partner has an affair, both people are to blame," Debs tells me.

"Um...I guess," I say, remembering Justin, remembering how he wanted to experiment and try different things, but I wouldn't. I suddenly see things in a different light and from Justin's perspective. Still, I wouldn't have shagged around, I'd

Forever With Him

have talked and then left if the relationship wasn't making me happy, not done the dirty like he did, but I guess everyone is different, and that no-one is perfect.

"Debs, I'm confused...this happened a year ago, but you guys are still together? I'm presuming you forgave him?" I question.

"Not at first, in fact, he moved out." Her face falls, and she looks paler than I've ever seen her.

"He did?" I squeak.

"Yes. I told him to go and stay in a hotel, which he did; we told Lily he had to go away for work. When he first told me, I thought about a lot of things...and the last thing I wanted was for us to split, for Lily to grow up without her daddy there. I don't know about you Coral, but as a teenager, I used to hate it when my friends used to talk about their dad's, I didn't have one, and I really felt like I missed out. Maybe that's why I married so young?" She muses, staring at the floor for a moment.

"Anyway, he's at the hotel, and I don't speak to him for a month. Then he calls me and says he's missing Lily and me. By then I'd calmed down enough to actually have a conversation, so I met him at the hotel, we had a meal, and we talked all night. And I realised it felt like it did when we were dating, just fresh you know..." Debs stares down at the floor for a second. "So he moved back in, and we started...well dating again. We took it in turns each week, booking a different hotel for the Saturday night – you know Gina?" I nod, her friend at work.

"Well, she knew what was going on and said she would have Lily stay over at hers, so that's what we did. We dated, stayed in hotels and well, got back to us being good again. I'm not going to say the hurt is gone, and I'm still working on trusting him again...but I don't want to lose him Coral, I love him." Debs turns to me, her baby blue eyes filling with tears again.

"I know," I whisper. "You could have asked me to have Lily," I add, feeling sore that she didn't.

"I didn't want you or mom finding out. I needed to do this on my own, Gina understood, she'd been through the same thing with her husband." Debs tells me.

Ok, I actually feel sick now. What if Tristan does that to me? What if we get bored with one another? My heart starts palpitating, my breathing hitching up. I feel a panic attack coming on. I quickly get to my feet and throw a fake smile at Debs.

"Loo break," I offer and scuttle off to the downstairs bathroom.

219

Ok, I am definitely freaking out here. What the hell am I doing marrying a man I hardly know? What if Tristan has all these fantasies going round in his head and he won't tell me, and the same thing happens to us, some girl comes along and plays out those fantasies with him? *Oh god! Oh no!* I fall to the floor, my bottom hitting the hard linoleum surface. I put my head in my hands and start a mantra...*That won't happen to us...That won't happen to us...That won't hap* – "Coral?" Debs calls outside the bathroom door, interrupting me.

I lift my head and call out to her. "It's open," I tremble. Debs pushes the door open and gasps when she sees me.

"Coral!" She breathes and sinks down next to me. "What's wrong?"

"I'm freaking out!" I choke. "That's what's wrong!"

She looks relieved. "Bloody hell Coral, I'd thought your stitches had split." She shakes her head at me. "What are you freaking out about?" she softly asks.

"Tristan!" I squeak.

Debs smiles at me. "You have no worries there Coral, he can't take his eyes off you."

"And Scott couldn't with you either, you two used to be so lovey-dovey it was almost sickening! Why do you think I said no so many times when you offered for me to stay over with you?" I blurt then take a deep breath.

"Oh!" Her cheeks flame. "Yeah, that can be uncomfortable," she adds.

"You don't say!" I retort dryly.

"Sorry, didn't realise that's why you kept saying no," she giggles.

"Debs, it doesn't matter," I say trying to calm my racing heart. "Fuck!" I hiss and squeeze my eyes shut. "I can't lose him, Debs, not ever, not to anyone!" I balk, my hands bunching into fists.

"I know, but you're really worrying me now, please calm down little sis!" Debs softly says. Following several deep breaths, I start to feel a little better, but either way, it's made me realise Tristan, and I need to lay everything out on the table. I need to know if I'm not fulfilling him, giving him his kicks as Debs put it – I can't have the same thing happen as it did with Justin.

"Feeling better?" Debs softly asks, reaching out and tucking my hair behind my ear.

"Yeah...I think so," I mumble. "My ass hurts, let's get out of here," I add.

Debs stands and helps me to my feet. "I do mean it Coral. I don't think you need to worry about Tristan at all, but I am surprised you're marrying him," she says as we head back to the sofa.

"Why?" I say, frowning at her.

"Well, and don't take this the wrong way, but it's not like you've played the field, seen all your options before making a choice' – "Neither did you, you married the first guy you met in college!" I retort.

"Oh I dated, I dated loads of guys had lots of guy friends, and Scott was one of them, but I soon realised he was the one I had the most fun with, the one I missed. The one, even though we weren't dating, that was my best friend. He was always there for me to talk to. I chose Scott over all the others, but I didn't know I was going to marry him. I just realised I loved him and I wanted him in my life."

"Well that's how I feel about Tristan, I don't need or want to play the field, I don't need to see what my other options are, I'm not stupid Debs, I know I can pretty much choose any guy I want, and I choose Tristan, end of story. Did you want another drink?" I ask, trying to get off the subject.

"I'll get it," Debs smiles wryly at me and then heads off to the kitchen. As she's getting her drink, I think about what she's told me, and I can't help wondering why she's upset *now*, especially as this happened a year ago? Debs returns and sits next to me.

I turn and frown at her. "Debs, if this all happened a year ago, then why are you upset now? I don't get it?"

"Yeah...kind of didn't explain myself very well there did I?" she laughs.

"You're laughing?" I choke, then I glug the rest of my orange juice back.

Debs frowns then takes a sip of her drink. "When Scott told me, I asked him to quit the company. There was no way I could even begin to try and see clearly if he was seeing her every day, and give him his dues, he walked into work and quit the very next day. But they told him he couldn't leave without giving his notice, so he had no choice but to come clean to his boss – who's a woman!" Debs giggles then sighs. "Anyway, she told him to work from the hotel until he'd worked his notice, then he went and worked for Malcolm on the building sites, and he loved it, I mean really loved it. So to cut a long story short we were moving to Spain because Scott got offered a job over there, still building work, but shorter hours, more time for us. It's so cheap living in Spain that I could go part-time too; which means we'd have loads of time for Lily and each other," Debs sighs heavily.

"So what's the problem?" I say, still not understanding.

"Lily doesn't want to go, remember?" She whispers.

"Oh!" *Shit!* My face falls. "Have I fucked it all up for you Debs?" I whisper, feeling mortified.

"No Coral," she says, grabbing my good hand. "I would never have forgiven myself if we'd have dragged her away and she was just going along with what we wanted."

"So you talked to her?" I tentatively ask.

"Yes, yesterday. Scott and I sat her down and told her she was in trouble if she didn't tell us the truth about moving, and well, the floodgates opened, and she told us everything."

"Everything?" I question.

Debs nods looking a little ghostly. "She'd been talking to her friend at school, who told her that mommy's and daddies pretend that everything's ok, then they divorce and go and live somewhere else, and that's what Lily thought was going to happen."

"You're kidding?" I choke. *Poor Lily!*

"Nope, I had very strong words with his mother last night. Anyway, Scott and I talked and talked about what to do, and then we argued about it for ages. He wants to go, said it would be good for Lily and for us, but I said it was wrong, that if she doesn't want to go, we shouldn't drag her away..." Debs shakes her head at me. "And well...he left last night...and he's gone to *her*, I know he has!" She adds, wailing loudly into her hands again.

I frown down at her. That doesn't make any sense – at all?

"Er...Debs, did he say that was where he was going?" I calmly ask.

"No, but I know he has!" She bawls, throwing her body onto the sofa and curling up into a ball – She is now crying hysterically!

"How can you *know* without really knowing?" I ask. *This is bizarre!*

"I just do," she says, her bottom lip wobbling as she stares up at me. *No, you don't!*

"Give me a sec," I say, patting her hip. I think I know a way to sort this. I get to my feet and head over to my handbag on the kitchen table. Taking my mobile out without Debs seeing, I step out onto the patio and call Scott's number.

He quickly answers. "Hello?" *Ooh, he sounds glum!*

"Scott," I whisper. "It's Coral."

"Oh...H-hi?" He says sounding surprised.

"Scott, I'm going to ask you a question," I tell him firmly.

"Ok," he answers hesitantly.

"Are you with the woman you had an affair with?" The line is silent for a long time. "Well, are you?" I snap.

"You know about that?" He whispers.

"Er...yeah, kind of by accident," I say and then continue, trying to make up a story on the fly. "I called Debs today to see if she wanted to meet up, she sounded upset and well, she told me what happened. The point is, she's here with me at Trist-our place, crying her heart out because she thinks you've run into that woman's arms' – "I haven't!" he interrupts. He certainly sounds genuine.

"I didn't think you had," I say. "So, can you do me a favour and tell her that?"

"I'm still in Brighton Coral, at the Metropole. I'll come straight over' – "No, please, talk to her first, I...well I wanted to spend some time with Debs tonight."

Scott laughs. "Ok, let me speak to her, I can always come and pick her up in a while. Oh and Coral, I really am sorry, for hurting her, please don't be mad at me."

"Well half an hour ago, I'd have strung you up by your balls, but I guess you can say I've calmed down now!" I tell him sternly.

"Oh...er...thanks, I guess," Scott says.

"Hmm. Hold on a sec, and I'll pass you over." I walk back into the house, go straight over to Debs and tap her on the hip, she stops her wailing and looks up at me. "I have Scott for you," I say shoving my mobile in her hand and walking back outside to give them some privacy, but I can still hear.

"Hello?" Debs trembles, she listens for a while then bursts into fresh tears. *Jeez Scott, cheer her up, don't make her cry!* "Oh Scott," she blubbers. "I love you too, I miss you baby...yes...more than you..." Debs is doing a giggle-sob. I guess that's good. "No you don't...really? Ok, sweetcheeks....later," she whispers. *Sweetcheeks?*

Five seconds later she's tapping me on the shoulder, making me jump a mile. "Jesus!" I hiss. "Don't do that Debs!"

"Oh sorry," she says wrapping her arms around me. "Thank you," she adds, crushing me again.

"Can't...breathe!" I choke.

Debs instantly releases me. "Oh Coral, he's at the Metropole, and he's not with her!" She says, her whole face radiating joy.

"I know," I say, smiling along with her. "But what are you guys going to do? Stay or go to Spain?"

Debs shrugs. "Not sure, I guess we'll figure it out."

"So you might not leave?" I beam.

"You don't want us to?" she says, frowning at me.

"No, I don't." *There I said it!*

"But...we've haven't hung out in ages?" she says.

"I know," I whisper. "I...I find it hard to..." I stop, shaking my head. "Look, I'm sorry Debs, I know I haven't been that great these past few years, and I guess what I'm trying to say is things are different now. I feel...stable, secure, and it would make me so happy if you guys stayed, and if you do, I promise you we'll spend more time together like we used to. And I'd love to have Lily stay over, which would give you and Scott more time together-" I stop talking because Debs is crying silent tears. "Debs, stop crying!" I scold.

"Oh Coral!" She pulls me into her arms, hugging me tightly. "I've missed you."

"Missed you too sis," I whisper.

Pulling back from me, her eyebrows knit together. "You really want to marry Tristan? I mean don't get me wrong, he is absolutely friggin' gorgeous, and he certainly seems genuine, but it's just so soon," Debs says, looking worried.

"I know," I whisper. "But I couldn't imagine spending the rest of my life with anyone but him," I take a deep breath. "He knows Debs' – she gasps – 'about everything and yet, for some unknown reason he still loves me," I say frowning at the floor.

"Not for an unknown reason," she says shaking her head and tucking my hair behind my ear again. "You're amazing Coral, he's lucky to have you." I snort at that one. Debs rolls her eyes at me. "Well, I'm going to get drunk! How about you?" she says, her eyes twinkling.

Linking her arm in mine, we walk back into the house.

"I can't drink Debs because of the painkillers, but I can always laugh my ass off at you getting drunk." I giggle. Debs stops, puts her hands on her hips and stares down at me. *Uh-oh!*

"Well I feel like I need a good drink after what you've revealed to me today," she says in a very serious voice.

"Oh," I swallow hard and look away from her.

"Don't think you're getting away with not talking this

through' – "Debs briefly, ok? It's not something I like to talk about," I quickly interrupt.

"Ok, ok," she softly says. "Just let me get the vodka; then we can talk."

"Oh! I just remembered. You'll never guess what happened today?" I say, following her into the kitchen. I launch into the story of Justin turning up, and the conversation that followed, and what happened afterwards. By the time I'm almost finished we are on the sofa, and Debs has the vodka, orange and ice-cubes on the coffee table.

"...And I get up the stairs, and my whole bedroom is decorated with lights and flowers and...Oh, Debs, it scares me how much I love Tristan. It's happened so fast, but it feels so...so indelible already." I tell her.

"Love can feel like that Coral." She says smiling widely.

"I guess," I shrug.

"What are you going to do about Justin?"

"Nothing," I squeak. "He did look good though," I muse.

"I'll bet he did," she teases. "He was a right looker back then, sounds like a proper hunk now though!"

I roll my eyes at her teasing, flirting ways. "Yeah well, too much, too little, too late I'm afraid. It's Tristan I want, always."

"Still, nice to know you've always got someone on the back burner if it goes wrong with Tristan." Debs slaps her hand over her mouth.

I glare back at her. "I think that vodka is making you brave!" I growl. "So you don't think Tristan, and I will make it?" I bite.

"Coral, I didn't mean it like that. Honestly, I'm sorry." I take a deep breath and stare out the window. I'm mad Debs has said that, but I don't really want to be angry with her. "Really, I didn't mean it like that!" she adds.

"Don't worry about it," I say, half smiling at her.

Debs takes a deep breath then smiles wearily at me. "So," she says, pouring herself another vodka. I wish I could get drunk with her! "Can I ask you some questions about...you know?"

I sigh inwardly. "If you must, but Debs, I swear I will know if you gossip about this to your friends' – "I would never' – I hold my hand up to stop her. "You are one of the worst gossips I have ever met, it doesn't mean I love you any less, but I swear Debs, cross me on this, and you'll wish you hadn't! This is private, never to be shared with anyone, not even Scott." I glare at her, trying to get her to understand how serious I am. "If I hear about this I know it will have come from you, and that will be it for us just so you know, I'll never speak to you again. Am I making myself clear?"

"Crystal," she whispers, swallowing hard.

Her cheeks are red, her eyes wide and dilated – *Yeah, she gets it!*

"Ok," I nod. "Ask away," I say gesturing with my hand...

TWO HOURS LATER and Debs is still knocking the vodka's back. Thankfully her questions about my past didn't last too long, she was more interested in Tristan and how it all got started. And now, well now she's busy telling me off for skimping on the wedding. I think, like Rob, she wants me to have a big occasion, all the bells and whistles, but that's just not me.

"Come on Coral!" Debs slurs, putting her arm around my waist and pulling me to my feet. "Let's dance!" *I wonder if I sound this bad when I'm drunk?*

"Debs," I giggle. "There's no music?"

"Isn't there?" she slurs, trying to focus on one of the small speakers in the room. "Well...I can hear music," she says.

"Yeah, who's singing?" I chuckle, trying to hold her upright, keep her steady.

"Feel the love," she shouts, punching her hand in the air and trying to dance, but she's way too drunk for that.

"Rudimental?" I question.

"Yeah!" she says, singing the tune and sloshing vodka and orange down her top. *Oops!*

Now I know she's really *is* drunk, because she doubles over laughing at herself. I'm just in time to take the glass from her before she falls onto the floor in a fit of giggles – but I can't help laughing along with her.

Edith appears in the hallway, smiling at me. I roll my eyes at her as Debs continues to kill herself laughing. The doorbell suddenly pings – Oh, I hope that isn't Scott, I don't want Debs to go, we are having such a good time together. I turn and see Edith wobbling towards the door, then I turn back to watch Debs still giggling on the floor.

"Debs," I giggle. "You ok?"

"No!" Edith shouts. "You can't come in here!" I immediately put the vodka down and hobble as quickly as I can towards Edith, pulling the front door open wide to see who it is.

Holy fuck, Olivia!

CHAPTER EIGHTEEN

THIS IS THE FOURTH surprise today, and I'm not sure if I can take anymore. First, my asshole father burying my mother's ashes, then Justin turning up out of the blue and confessing his love for me, then Debs with her news about Scott and now *her*.

"You must be Coral?" Her smooth, sultry voice says.

I swallow hard, trying to find my voice. "Hello Olivia," I whisper back.

"Coral," Edith says looking across at me. "Tristan will not be happy if you let Olivia in, not without Stuart being here," she says as politely as she can. But I can tell she has steam coming out of her ears – she really doesn't like this woman.

"What's going on?" Deb slurs from behind me – *Oh crap!* "Who are you?" she asks narrowing her eyes at Olivia, while she leans on Edith and me.

"Look, Olivia, this is not a good time," I say wincing in pain because Debs is getting heavier and heavier. I turn away from Olivia so I can attempt to lean Debs against the wall but I'm too late, she slides down my body and passes out in a drunken heap on the floor.

"Oh!" *Shit!* "Debs!"

"Oh no!" Edith says. "What should we do?"

"Grab my mobile Edith; it's on the coffee table." Edith wobbles off as I attempt to lift Debs up, but she's a dead weight in my arms.

"No Coral," Edith says as she reaches me. "You could rip your stitches open."

"True," I say. Taking my mobile from her, I call Scott. "Scott, your wife, has passed out on the floor," I chuckle because partly it is funny, but on a whole other level – it really isn't.

"Tristan and Stuart are out, Edith and I can't move her' – "I'm on my way," he drawls and hangs up.

I turn to Olivia, who's smiling at the whole situation. God, she is so pretty, prettier than her driving licence made her out to be. Her makeup is perfect, her nails, dark long and shiny. Shoulder length, straight and silky, almost black hair, wide green eyes, tanned skin, tall and slim. She's dressed in a black fitted pencil skirt to the knee, with a deep green, short-sleeved silk blouse; and killer black stilettos – she looks amazing, especially considering she's had, two kids. *Jeez, my self-esteem is taking a heavy knock right now.*

"She can't hold her liquor very well, can she?" Olivia says, laughing a little sarcastically.

It immediately gets my back up. "Why are you here Olivia?" I snap.

"I wanted to see Tristan," she says. "He called me yesterday, but I couldn't talk at the time." She adds, casually flicking her hair. *Ugh! He called her, and he didn't tell me?* Now I'm pissed at Tristan!

"So you just thought you'd turn up here, unannounced and uninvited?" I say as calmly and politely as I can.

"Yes." She looks from me to Edith then crosses her arms defiantly.

"Well, I agree with Edith. You can't come in without Tristan or Stuart being here." I tell her firmly.

"How silly," she says, smiling coyly.

"Silly?" I laugh. "Not really, considering Susannah tried to kill Tristan *and* me," I say, trying to hide the quiver in my voice.

"Yes, I heard about that," she says, looking me up and down.

"You should go," I say, my voice trembling, giving me away. Thankfully, I see Scott's car turn into the driveway. He quickly pulls up, gets out the car and dashes over to us.

"Oh, Debs!" He says, laughing a little. Then he reaches down and attempts to lift her into his arms. I bend down and help as much as I can. 'Stay' I mouth to him without Olivia seeing, Scott frowns and nods once at me, then I purposely say it aloud.

"Why don't you stay Scott? Take Debs over to the sofa and let me get you a drink." I follow him over to the sofa, hoping Olivia will just go home, but unfortunately, I look back and see Olivia barge straight past Edith, walk through the front door and saunter down the hallway, her heels clicking against the hard flooring, perusing the place as she does.

"Olivia!" Edith shouts. "You can't come in here," she says marching after her, leaving the door wide open. Right at that moment, I hear the rumble of the Jag in the driveway. *Tristan's back early, thank god!*

Seconds later, I hear Tristan shout my name from outside, which is quickly followed by Tristan and Stuart running into the house, and seeing everyone they both come to an abrupt halt. Tristan's gaze finds me first, then he looks at Scott with Debs in his arms, then Edith, then the look of horror on his face as he registers Olivia, standing here in our house is priceless – He looks outraged!

"Hello Tristan," she says, but I can't see her face as she has her back to me.

He completely ignores her and marches over to me. When he reaches me, he takes my face in his hands, his eyes searching mine. "Are you ok?" He asks, concern written all over his face. He starts checking me over, not waiting for an answer.

"Hey," I whisper, taking hold of both his hands. "I'm fine. Edith answered the door because we thought it was Scott coming to collect Debs." I turn back to Edith and smile. I don't want her to think I'm blaming her then I look up at Tristan again.

"Debs passed out," I say rolling my eyes and smiling. "Olivia told us that she couldn't talk to you when you called her yesterday, so she decided to turn up, unannounced. Edith said she couldn't come in, but she just barged past her." I narrow my eyes at Olivia, who has turned to look at us both – *There stick that in your pipe and smoke it!*

I turn away and look up at Tristan. He looks a little relieved, his face softening a little, then surprising me he enfolds me into his arms and gently rocks me. "I missed you," he whispers in my ear, kissing my hair a couple of times.

"I thought you were eating out?" I say as I hear Stuart shut the front door.

"No, I wanted to get back to you," he says, pulling back to assess me once more.

Then taking no prisoners, he leans down and kisses me, forcefully. Honestly, I think this is for Olivia's benefit, and as childish as it seems, I revel in it and kiss him back with as much passion as I can muster, when he pulls back, we are both breathless. I smile up at him, and almost laugh, but decided it's probably best to hide it. Tristan silently runs his knuckles down my cheek, kisses the tip of my nose then looks up at Scott.

"Scott, good to see you, would you like a drink?" He asks.

"Nah, I'm good mate, I've gotta get Debs home."

"You're more than welcome to stay?" Tristan suggests. I can see Scott thinking about it, weighing up his options. "It's quite a drive back to Worthing, I don't think you'll get her up the stairs on your own, and it's a little late to send Stuart with you," Tristan adds.

"True," Scott laughs. "Alright then, well stay."

"Have you eaten?" Tristan asks. Scott shakes his head. "Edith," Tristan says. "Can you rustle something up for us all?"

"Of course Tristan, anything in particular?" she asks.

"Coral?" Tristan says looking down at me. I'm about to answer him when Debs suddenly comes to, and I know, I can tell by her face – *Shit!*

"She gonna be sick!" I shout rushing over to her and grabbing the wastepaper basket as I do, luckily I get there just in time as she starts hurling into it. "Ugh! Debs." Thankfully Scott takes over, but I notice he looks a little green himself. Back at Tristan's side, I wrap my arms around his waist. "Edith, I don't mind what we have," I answer, "Whatever's easy, it's quite late," I say, looking up at the clock on the wall, it's 8.15pm – very late for a married woman with kids to be out. I don't understand why she's here?

She wants Tristan! I bite my lip at that thought, not again.

Edith smiles at me and wobbles into the kitchen, just as Stuart wonders over and helps Scott get Debs to her feet, at least she's stopped hurling. I watch them walk her past us and into the downstairs bathroom.

Finally, Tristan turns his arctic glare on Olivia. "What are you doing here?" He says very slowly, articulating each word with a hiss, his voice low and menacing.

"That's a dazzling display of affection you're putting on their Tristan," she says, ignoring his rising temper.

"Tristan," I whisper, he looks down at me. "Would you like to speak to Olivia alone?" I ask sweetly, purposely widening my eyes.

"No baby, stay." He says pecking my forehead.

"Ok," I whisper smiling up at him. Then I turn and narrow my eyes at Olivia – See, he's mine! – *Jeez, I sound like Susannah!* I frown at that thought.

"Get out!" Tristan growls at Olivia, gripping my upper arms. I think it's so he doesn't march her out himself.

"Darling," she softly says. "You called me remember?"

"Yes I did," he says. "But never, for a moment...did I expect you to turn up here, uninvited, at our home and harass my fiancé. You have no idea what's she's been through, none at all. And now…now I regret calling you, I wish I hadn't." He's livid. His voice is almost shaking with anger, so he takes a deep calming breath. "Get the fuck out of *our* house Olivia." He says, slowly enunciating each word, so he's making himself perfectly clear to her, and to me.

Olivia's face pales. "Tristan darling, come along now. There's no need for that kind of language," she says, smiling back at him, she doesn't seem to be affected by his mood at all.

"Stuart!" Tristan shouts.

Stuart appears from the utility room – I guess he was still helping Scott with Debs.

"Your choice Olivia, leave, or Stuart helps you leave?" Stuart tries to hide his smile; he seems to be enjoying this. He walks over to Olivia, so he's stood right next to her, and politely gestures for her to walk with him.

"No!" She snaps. "I came here to speak to you." She adds keeping her eyes locked on Tristan. And I know – I just know!

"Olivia, why are you really here?" I ask. She looks down at me in the most disgusting way, as though I shouldn't be addressing her directly. "Well?" I prompt, my teeth grinding together.

"As I said, it's Tristan I want to speak to." She snaps at me.

"Anything you have to say to me, you can say in front of Coral." He snaps back.

She narrows her eyes at him. Then she crosses her arms and sticks her nose in the air. "I'm leaving Jeremy," she says in the most casual way.

I stop breathing – She's here for Tristan, I know she is.

"Why?" Tristan snaps.

"You know why," she says, her eyes darkening as she and Tristan stare at one another.

"And now you're back on the market, you want to see if Tristan is free, right?" I say sarcastically. Olivia looks down at me again, as though I'm a street rat, and just stares at me with the most insulting look in her eyes. A slight smile twitches her lips and then she looks away from me, trying her best to hide the filthy look she wants to give me. *What a bitch!*

Edith was so right about her. Tristan, you better say the right thing to this woman! I turn and look up at him, and I'm shocked to see he looks entranced by her. His cheeks have flushed, and his eyes have darkened. The atmosphere suddenly plummets…it's so dense.

"That's right Tristan," she smiles seductively at him. "It's still there," she adds.

I take a step back out of Tristan's arms. *This is not happening!*

"You…you want her?" I manage to squeak out, blinking rapidly at him.

Tristan turns and glares down at me. Then without a word, he marches over to Olivia, grabs her by the arm and starts marching her out of the house. I guess he's answering my question without words.

"Tristan!" She shouts, yanking her arm out of his grasp.

They both stop and stare at one another, only inches apart.

"Olivia…" Tristan takes a moment and stares down at the floor. He's still livid. "Please leave…before I do something I'll really regret." He warns.

"Darling, you know I've never stopped thinking about you, about what we had. How you used to take control' - her eyes flash to me for a brief second – 'how you used to give me what I need, Jeremy won't do that with me. I know you're still attracted to me." She says reaching up to touch his face, but he grabs her hand and twists her around, so her back is to his front.

"You have no idea what I like, who I am, or what I need. Coral, who you seem to think so little off, is more woman than you could ever be. She is everything I have ever wanted, and that's because she's everything you're not," he barks.

"Tristan," she gasps, her head tipping back – It's almost as though she's enjoying this. Tristan twists her around, yanks her by the arm and starts dragging her out again. "Tristan, you are hurting me!" she shouts as I hobble behind Tristan, trying to keep up.

"Go home Olivia," he snaps as he yanks the front door open.

"But, you're message sounded so wounded, I thought you needed me?" She says, all sorrowfully.

Tristan shoves her out of the house, so she's stood on the front porch. "What the fuck did you ever do for me?" he asks. "Nothing, that's what! You're a selfish, stuck-up, snobby bitch. And I'll tell you something else, I'm glad Susannah lied, I'm glad she told me-" Tristan suddenly stops, registering something on Olivia's face.

"No!" he gasps in horror, taking a step back. He shakes his head several times, running both hands through his hair.

Then he steps forward and grabs hold of her upper arms. "It was Jeremy, wasn't it?" he growls, shaking her.

The sickening smile that spreads across her face is shocking. "Finally worked it out," she laughs.

"How could you?" He growls.

"Well, you were never going to ask me, were you?" she questions, gazing up at him.

"Ask you what?" He snaps.

"To marry you," she softly says.

"That's beside the point, Olivia!" Tristan snaps.

"No Tristan, it's precisely the point!" she snaps back. "What did you expect me to do, wait around for you to make up your mind?" She glares back at him. "I had to have a backup darling," she adds.

Tristan looks shocked and hurt as he blinks back at her. "Money!" He shouts he's seething. "It's all you were ever interested in. You were never concerned about me. You just wanted to be with someone who could continue the lavish lifestyle that you are so accustomed to." He bawls.

"Really Tristan, you don't want to try again?" she asks, batting her lashes at him. And she's smirking at him, evidently finding his pain, his suffering amusing – I want to beat her to a pulp, maybe she'll learn some respect – God, she's worse than Susannah!

I want to look away, but I can't. I wish Tristan would let go of her. I don't like him touching her. The moment I think that he pushes her backwards, making her stumble in her heels. "If you were the last woman on earth I wouldn't go anywhere near you. You're nothing but an empty hollow shell." He says his voice low and void of emotion.

"Just words again Tristan. And you seem so angry, so tense... and we both know how to sort that," Olivia smiles coyly at me. *What! What the fuck does that mean?*

Tristan sighs heavily. "Olivia, why don't you fuck off, and go sink your teeth into some other poor, unsuspecting fool, I'm done here!"

"Well, I'm not," she states, crossing her arms then glaring at me.

Tristan sighs heavily, he looks so tired and fed up. He closes his eyes in frustration and pinches the bridge of his nose. I take a deep breath, hobble over to him and wrap my arms around his waist.

Tristan reciprocates and wraps his arms tightly around me.

"Go home, Olivia!" I snap, squeezing Tristan.

"Olivia, I will slap a restraining order on you if I see you anywhere near this house – Christ, anywhere near Brighton!" he adds. Olivia is still smiling at him. "In fact, you've just convinced me to do it anyway. You'll be hearing from my solicitor." Tristan adds.

She instantly loses the grin. "I was the best thing that ever happened to you," she snarls, pointing her shiny manicured fingernail at him. "Or ever will have," she adds looking me up and down – *Cheeky bitch!*

I want to slap her down, I go to move, but Tristan grips my upper arms, keeping me close to his body.

"Leave-now!" Tristan threatens.

With one last look at Tristan, Olivia sticks her nose up in the air and stomps over to her sporty Mercedes. Tristan turns us around so I can't see her anymore. Stuart follows Olivia outside, I guess he's making sure she leaves, moments later he returns.

"Sir, may I suggest locking the gates tonight?"

"Yes, good idea," Tristan says. *Oh great, just great! Another crazy stalker woman after Tristan!* I shake my head and sigh inwardly. Then I feel it building inside me, I try to fight against it because I don't want it to happen.

Don't fall apart Coral! – But I'm too late, I've had enough today. Both of our exes, my father, Debs' news, and the fact that I was pregnant, and Susannah shot me...almost killed me – It's all just too much.

The floodgates burst wide open.

"Baby!" Tristan gasps and lifts me into his arms. He carries me into the library, away from everyone, and shuts the door behind him. "Oh Coral, I'm so sorry she turned up, so sorry," he softly says, sitting down in the recliner with me in his lap.

"Why didn't you tell me?" I mewl, weeping into his neck.

"That I'd called her?" I silently nod, then look up at him. "Well, you said you didn't mind baby, I wasn't keeping it a secret; it just wasn't a big deal to me. I thought I wanted...*needed* her forgiveness for what I did." He says, shaking his head in disgust.

"She wants you back." I whimper. Tristan shrugs. "Should I be worried? Do you still have feelings for her?" I tentatively ask.

"No baby, I don't," he firmly tells me.

"What did she mean when she said 'you seemed angry and tense and we both know how to sort that'?" I tentatively ask.

"She was just saying that to wind you up Coral," he says, but his eyes are telling a different story.

"Liar," I whisper, pleading with him to tell me.

"Coral, I..." Tristan breaks off, shaking his head. *Ok, I'll leave that one – for now!*

"What happened on the porch, you realised something?" I ask.

"She *was* seeing him when she was supposed to be with me." He says, his face going pale.

"What?" I choke.

"I knew the moment I said it that she had been concealing the truth from me. She was always a very good actress," he adds.

"Susannah was right?" I gasp.

"I couldn't say if Susannah had actually caught her...maybe she knew something was going on?" He says, frowning thoughtfully. I wonder if Susannah did know if she had actually caught them kissing? I must remember to ask her that when I finally see her.

"Then I'm glad Susannah got her out of your life," I say. "And she cheated on you with Jeremy, her husband, who she is now divorcing?" Tristan solemnly nods. "And you're really not going to see her again?" I ask.

"Coral, after that little stunt she's just pulled, she can stick my apology – that is evidently no longer needed – where the sun doesn't shine." He barks, I have to snigger at that one.

"She's so pretty," I say, my tears slowing down.

"Not as pretty as you baby." I look up at Tristan, his dreamy chocolate eyes instantly melting me. "You blow her out of the water," he says, wiping my tears away with his thumbs.

"Oh Tristan, don't be silly, she's stunning."

"Not as stunning as you," he reiterates. I need to get off this subject. I think about what Debs told me, how it made me feel, which makes me panic again, my earlier fears coming back to me.

"Tristan," I say gripping him tighter. "I have so much to tell you and to ask you," I sniff.

"You do?" He says picking up a box of tissues and handing them to me. I take them off him, blow my nose and dry my tears.

"Yes." I finally say.

"Ask away," he says – But now he's here, I can't find the right words to say, so I ask him something else.

"Did you have a nice time with Malcolm?" I ask a little high pitched.

"That's what you wanted to ask me?" He laughs, looking a little puzzled.

"No," I chuckle.

"Ok. Yes, I had a good time, Malcolm's a great player, I learned quite a lot. But I'm much more intrigued with what you have to ask me," he says, cupping my chin to look up at him.

I sigh inwardly – *There's no time like the present Coral!*

"Fine," I mumble, I look down at my hands and start blurting it all out at top speed. "Long story short, Scott had an affair last year. Debs told me…she…well she told me it happened because they stopped spending quality time together, but more importantly that he…" I cringe and close my eyes for a second when I re-open them I decide to be brave and look Tristan square in the eyes.

"Debs said that Scott said that he wasn't feeling fulfilled by Debs…in the bedroom I mean and that he had…fantasies that he…" I stop and shake my head. "Debs didn't realise, and I guess he did those things, whatever they were with this other woman. Debs said he got his kicks from her, that this other woman was making him feel good about himself, not Debs, and that it was partly her fault for not recognising that." I take a deep breath and continue. "Debs said that men are more insecure than women and they get most of their security by knowing they are, well – satisfying their woman in the bedroom. Is that true?" I ask. Tristan nods – *Holy Crap, we are doomed!*

"What are you looking so frightened about?" He softly asks.

"I'm freaking out Tristan! What if that happens to us? What if I can't satisfy you and you go play out your fantasies with another woman? I mean, you hear about it all the time, and I already know of one affair going on at Chester House, there's bound to be more. We have to talk Tristan, I can't lose you because of this, tell me your fantasies please, please…and I'll play them out with you, I'll do whatever it takes' – His lips reach mine, silencing me.

When he's finished kissing me, I am breathless, my bones feel like jelly, and I have lost my train of thought – I guess that was his plan.

"Miss Coral Stevens, soon to be, Mrs Coral Freeman – stop worrying. I want to live a long and happy life with you, not have you die at a young age because your heart couldn't take any more anxiety. You have got to learn to relax darling and not think the worst, please, for me, try to relax?" I nod mutely. "Ok good. And I hear you, baby, we will talk, but not now. Later?"

I nod once more. "Good, but you should know. You already satisfy me in the bedroom baby, in more ways than you will ever know."

"I do?" I squeak.

"Yes." He answers firmly.

I frown down at our entwined fingers. "Tristan, what are you doing with me? What are you doing with someone so insecure, when you're so...so confident? Don't you want to be with someone more like you?"

"I think you are confident, I think you're brave, and you hold your own Coral, it's so refreshing. Those other women I dated, they never challenged me, not like you do, but I'm guessing your confidence has taken a knock because of Olivia. Am I right?"

I nod again, feeling stupid.

"Yes, she is confident Coral, but there's healthy confidence and downright cocky confidence, and Olivia was the latter. Believe me when I say that can be really off-putting," he says.

I frown up at him. "What do you mean?"

Tristan's eyebrows knit together. "I want to do something," he says, standing us both up. "Stay here and don't move," he adds, giving me a quick, chaste kiss before he leaves. Moments later, he walks back in with his portable speakers, his MP3 player, and locks the door behind him.

"Tristan, what are you doing?" Ignoring me, he switches on the speaker and fires up his player. Phil Collins' True Colours starts drifting sweetly through the speaker. I can't help thinking how ironic, considering what I've bought him.

My eyes involuntarily fill with tears – *It's such a beautiful song.*

Tristan takes the couple of steps needed to reach me, helps me to my feet, and pulls me into him. I can feel the length of his solid, muscled body against mine, the heat of his skin, his breath on my cheek, his potent scent – I cannot take my eyes away from his.

The next thing I know, we are slowly dancing around the library as Tristan softly sings the words to me, I have to fight so hard to stop the tears from falling. I don't want to cry, even though I feel completely overwhelmed by this beautiful, sweet gesture. *How is it that he always seems to know what to do to make me feel better?*

The words to this song and Tristan singing them to me are exactly what I need to hear. Because the world does make me feel crazy sometimes, and I'm pretty sure there are times when I have really sad eyes and I know, I know Tristan will always be there for me, and that he loves me just the way I am.

"She would never dance with me," he says as Phil moves onto Groovy Kind of Love, yet another classic.

"Olivia?" I whisper as we continue to slowly sway in each other's arms.

Tristan nods solemnly at me, carefully lifts his hand and twirls me around.

"Why? You're a wonderful dancer?" I say, frowning up at him.

"She um…well, how can I put it? She was cold Coral, an ice-block compared to you." He softly says.

I raise my eyebrows surprised by his words and his honesty. "She…she was cold?" I squeak, but seeing her today and after what Edith told me, I have to agree with him.

"I never realised it," he says, his eyes boring into mine. "My Gran never liked her that much, said that she was just after a man with money and status, but I was blinded by her, looking through rose coloured spectacles. I thought that what we had was love, but she never did anything for me, certainly nothing sweet like you've done my darling."

"Me?" I breathe.

Tristan nods again. "The painting of the Jag, the photos of my folks. Cooking a nice meal for me. Do you realise how much it all meant to me?" He asks. He's intense again.

I smile up at him. "I guess I do now," I say. *I must do more things like that for him!*

Then I frown up at him. "Are you saying she never like…you know, cooked you a nice dinner for when you got home from work or' – "She never did anything like that Coral. She was spoilt and expected everything to be done for her, but like I said, I wasn't seeing clearly, and she was selfish. I thought what we had was a strong, a deep connection; but it pales in significance compared to the connection we have. I don't think you realise how good you make me feel. I have never counted the notches on my bedpost, but I have had more partners than you, and I'll tell you now baby, you make me feel like none of the others did. You make me so happy." *Whoa!*

I swallow hard and smile up at him.

Tristan continues. "When I went back to London after meeting you for the first time, I couldn't stop thinking about you, and every time I did, I couldn't wipe the smile off my face.

I think Edith thought my face was going to split in two." He smiles as if he remembers back then.

"Oh." I swallow hard again. *What a declaration!*

His broody look appears. "Don't ever change," he whispers, then leans down and softly kisses me, his tongue gently lapping against mine – *I want him, now!*

"Coral?" I hear Debs shout in a croaky voice.

I sigh inwardly. "I better go to her," I whisper against his lips.

"Yes, let's go see your sister," he says, releasing me and switching off his player and the speaker.

"Don't say I told you about' – "I won't mention a thing," he interrupts. "But you should already know that." *Trust Coral, trust him!*

"I'm sorry," I whisper. "I trust you, Tristan," I add.

"You're getting there." He smiles warmly at me, leans down and quickly kisses me before taking my hand and leading me out of the library.

"Debs," I say, pulling her into me. "You ok?" I ask.

"My head feels like it's being crushed in a vice," she says, swaying a little.

"We're going home Coral." Scott pipes up.

"Are you sure? Don't you want to eat something first?" I ask.

"I want to go home," Debs whimpers. "I want my bed."

"Ok." I can't help giggling at her face, she looks so sorry for herself. Scott pulls his keys out of his pocket and reaches his hand out to Tristan. "Thanks all the same, maybe we can stay over some other time?"

"We'd love that," Tristan says shaking his hand then releasing it. "Here, let me get the door for you," he adds as Scott and Stuart shuffle Debs towards it, trying to keep her upright.

"Are you sure you'll be ok getting her in the house?" I ask Scott as they sit Debs in his car.

"Yeah...I've seen her in worse states," he says, smiling broadly.

I smile back at him; he's right I've seen Debs worse than this. I lean inside the car and kiss Debs on the cheek. "Make sure you eat, please?"

"Yes mom," she answers dryly. I chuckle at her and shut the door, and then I turn to Scott and reluctantly hug him. "You ever do that to my sister again, and I *will* have your balls on a platter," I whisper, and then I pull out of the hug and glare up at him.

239

He quickly clears his throat. "Um...yes. I'm sure you will," he says not knowing where to look. I nod once and walk over to Tristan, we watch Scott get in the car, and I wave to them both as Scott drives steadily out of the driveway. As soon as we are back in the house, Tristan double locks the door and presses the button for the gates. I watch him, mesmerised again as he watches the gates slowly come to a close.

"So," he says turning to smile at me. "It's been quite a day," he says pulling me into his arms.

"That's putting it mildly," I answer dryly, resting my chin on his chest so I can look up at him.

"Nurse Terry will be here soon. Let's eat and then we can get you to bed," he says, his eyebrows pinched.

"Bed?" I question.

Tristan traces his fingertip under my one eye. "You look exhausted," he says, his worried look is back. And now he's said that it makes me realise how tired I really do feel.

"You're right," I yawn. "I am."

"Just as I thought," he says, taking my hand and leading me over to the kitchen table.

"Oh!" I suddenly remember the gifts I bought for him. "Baby, come with me for a moment please," I say, taking his hand. He looks completely mystified but gets to his feet. I lead us into the library, shut the door and take him over to one of the recliners.

"Sit please," I ask nicely. Tristan gazes quizzically at me for a moment then gracefully sits. "Now, you know how this works as we've done this before' – "Coral, no. You're exhausted, please baby let's just eat and go to bed." He says with worried eyes.

I can't help chuckling at him. *Sex? Tristan thinks I want to have sex?* – Well, I do but..."Tristan, this isn't about sex, so please just close your eyes," I giggle.

"Oh...ok." Reluctantly, he closes his eyes, but I notice his hands subconsciously move towards his groin, protecting himself or stopping me, I'm not sure? Either way, it makes me laugh again. I pick up the bag that I hid behind the sofa and carefully place it in his lap.

"Open sesame," I tease.

His eyes dart open. "What's this?"

"A gift," I smile.

"You brought me a present?" he says, his eyebrows pinched together.

"Two," I whisper, smiling and widening my eyes. His eyes narrow. "Don't you want it?" I squeak.

"Of course I do baby, I just..." He trails off, staring down at the gift.

"Tristan, are you purposely trying to wound me?" I huff.

"No, of course not," he sighs.

"For the love of God Tristan, will you just please accept these presents graciously, and accept that if I want to buy you a present, I will buy you a present, whenever I want, no matter what time of year and no matter how much it costs!" I say my hands on my hips, my mouth pressed into a hard line.

"Point taken, thank you, baby," he says looking a little guilty.

Now I feel guilty. "Tristan," I place my hand over his to stop him from opening the bag. "You've been amazing Tristan, really sweet, so attentive and I...I just wanted you to know how much I appreciate everything you've done for me. And I know what you're going to say, that I don't need to thank you, that it's what you do, what you want to do for me, but this," I point at the bag. "This is my way of telling you that I appreciate it and that I love you." I lean in and quickly peck his lips. "Will you do something for me though?"

"Anything." He breathes, staring up at me with big, wide eyes.

"Open the card first?"

"I have a card?" He beams.

"Uh-huh." Tristan opens the bag, pulls out the big white envelope and opens it up. He reads the front, swallows hard then opens it up. I wait, impatiently while he reads the verse.

"Tristan this is true. The money, the house, the cars, the gifts, they don't mean anything without you. Your loving fiancé, Coral."

Jeez, I didn't know he was going to read it out loud.

"Come here, baby." He puts the bag to the side and pulls me onto his lap. "You see what I mean. Olivia would never have done something like that for me. I mean, sure she'd buy me a birthday and Christmas present, but that was it, nothing else, and she was loaded. You don't have any money – well you do now – yet, you've done this, for me?"

I nod and smile shyly at him. "I just want you to know I love, admire, and appreciate you, and I'm grateful you're in my life, Tristan."

"I'm grateful for you too baby." He softly says.

"Even though we fight?" I tease.

"Even more so when we fight." He grins.

"Me too," I giggle. "Well come on then, open them up. I'm dying to see your face...Oh, it's not expensive...nothing radical...I just' – His lips silence me.

"I know whatever it is, I'm going to love it," he murmurs against my lips. I beam at him, he grins back for a second then dives in the bag. He pulls the DVD out first, thank god, I'm not sure if men even like teddy bears. Ripping the paper off, he stares down at the cover.

"Phil Collins. Finally, the first farewell tour?" He swallows hard.

"Ah crap! You've already got it haven't you?" It's very hard buying something for someone who's rich.

"No," he whispers, still staring down at it.

"Really?" I beam, feeling triumphant. "You do like it, don't you? You said you never had anyone to go to his concert with, so I thought I'd bring the concert to you?"

Without a word, he places the DVD on the table next to him and pulls me gently down to meet his lips and kisses me, slowly, enticingly, then stops and leans me back, so he's gazing down at me. "You really are the most beautiful soul I have ever met Coral Stevens. I swear to you, I'm going to do everything within my power to make you happy baby, every day, for the rest of my life."

"Oh Tristan, me too," I whisper, reaching out to stroke his stubbly beard. "So you like it?" I giggle.

Tristan shakes his head at me and laughs. "That's a ludicrous thing to ask," he says, grinning from ear to ear. "I love it. Thank you, baby," he finally says.

"You are more than welcome," I tease.

"Shall I open the next one?" He says. I frown, feeling a little uneasy. "What?" He questions.

"I just...I don't know if men like that kind of thing, so don't worry if you don't...or if you think it's really girly..." I stop and titter at the look on Tristan's face. "Just open it," I say, rolling my eyes. He picks it up, pulls off the paper and reads the teddy bears logo on the heart.

"Now that is cute baby, you picked this for me?"

"Yeah...I just saw it and thought of you. Too girlie?"

"No, totally sweet and adorable, and I love you this much too," he says, grinning from ear to ear. "Thank you," he adds, pulling me into him and holding me tight.

Forever With Him

Then totally spoiling the moment, I involuntarily yawn. "Sorry," I whisper, smiling up at him.

"Thank you, baby, you spoil me. But you're tired, so come on, up you get, let's eat and get you to bed." Tristan lifts me off his lap, takes my hand and we head out the library and back over to the kitchen table.

Edith comes over to us, looking very guilty. "Tristan, I am so sorry about Oli' – "Edith, it wasn't your fault, don't feel guilty. Olivia shouldn't have done that." He tells her firmly.

She smiles down at me, pats Tristan on the shoulder then heads back into the kitchen. Moments later she re-appears with two plates of poached salmon salad, with new potatoes. As she places them down, I realise how famished I am.

"Thank you," Tristan says as I smile up at her.

"Well, Stuart ate out while you had your round of golf, so he's retired for the evening," she says. "Can I get you anything else?" She asks.

"Coral?" Tristan asks. I shake my head as I'm already eating. "No thanks Edith, we're good." The intercom buzzes for the gates. "That'll be Nurse Terry," Tristan says, rising to let her in.

"Let me," Edith says and wobbles over to the door. I listen as she asks who it is, then buzzes Nurse Terry in. Moments later, Edith opens the front door, and Nurse Terry heads straight over to us.

"Oh, you're eating, I'm sorry to disturb you," she says.

"No worries," I say giving her my right hand.

"You look tired," she says. "I think bed rest tomorrow."

"I agree," Tristan says. I frown at them both. "Rob can come here," Tristan adds in a tone that's not to be argued with. "Don't worry, I'll disappear."

My face pales hearing him say that I swallow hard. "Don't say that," I whisper, trying to admonish him, but coming off sounding frightened.

"Hey." He reaches out and takes my free hand, squeezing it gently.

"All done Coral," Terry says. "And I do mean it," she says looking at both of us. "Bed rest tomorrow or I'll have no choice but to tell Dr Green and I know you won't want that," she adds looking down at me. I nod, reluctantly. "Good, see you tomorrow." Edith follows her to the door and waits a couple of minutes then she presses the button to shut the gates. Reaching us, she bids us both goodnight and heads up the stairs, and we continue with our meal.

"I guess I better text Rob," I mumble. Then I remember – *Shit!* "I have George and Cindy tomorrow!" I say in a panic.

"I'll call George," Tristan says.

"I don't want to let him down," I say, feeling guilty.

"He won't mind a bit Coral, he'll understand. You are still healing darling."

"What about Cindy? I still need to pay her for her time," I say sounding a little frantic.

Tristan snorts. "Of all the things to worry about Coral," he says, shaking his head. "Do you really think you need to worry about money?"

"No, I guess not," I mumble. "I just hate letting people down."

"I know," he whispers, reaching up to stroke my cheek. "That's one of the many things I love about you." *Oh…I have missed him today.*

"I missed you today," I whisper, yawning again.

"I missed you too baby, that's why I came home early."

"It's a good job that you did," I say.

"Yes it was, wasn't it – well done by the way," he adds, sounding proud.

"For what?" I squeak.

"Not drinking." *Huh?*

I frown at him, not understanding.

"Coral, I think you know this yourself…or maybe you don't, but sometimes you use alcohol as a coping mechanism, things get too rough, and you reach for a drink. Yet, after all, you've been through today, speaking to your father and finding out what he'd done, Justin, Debbie and then Olivia turning up, you haven't touched a drop. I am very proud of you for that."

"I'm not an alcoholic Tristan." I snap.

"I never said you were." He retorts.

I frown down at my half eaten plate of food, my appetite has vanished again. I sigh inwardly. He didn't mean it like that, I know he didn't – I guess I'm more tired and cranky than I realised. Tristan has his forearm resting on the table, so I lean down and rest my head on it, facing away from him, and softly stroke his hand.

"I'm sorry. I'm tired and grumpy. I know you didn't mean it like that, and you're right, I do use it to help me cope. When Debs told me about Scott, and I panicked about us, about you, I really wanted a hit, but I didn't. I know it's not wise to do at the moment, but now I'm really, really glad I didn't because I don't think I would have handled Olivia turning up like that."

Tristan softly strokes my hair. "Baby, please finish your meal."

"I think I'm too tired Tristan, besides I've lost my appetite."

I feel him kiss my hair. "Because so much has happened today?" He asks.

"I guess," I mumble, sitting back up because that was not comfortable. My shoulder hurts, my lungs feel like there on fire, hell my whole body hurts. I feel like I did when I first came out of the hospital.

"I think I need to go to bed now," I say, my eyes involuntarily closing on me. I manage to get to my feet, and I'm about to kiss Tristan goodnight, but he quickly stands and lifts me up into his arms.

"Tristan," I mumble, trying to tell him off. "Stay, finish your dinner."

He kisses my hair and grips me closer to his body. "I will, but I'm putting you to bed first, my sweet girl."

"Oh...ok," I whisper, my head lolling against his shoulder. And as hard as I try to fight it, sleep finally takes me, and I drift off in Tristan's arms...

CHAPTER NINETEEN

I AM HAVING ANOTHER nightmare from which I cannot wake. Olivia is in the house, stalking us. Its night time and all the lights are off, I can see the sky outside is black. And it's like I'm her, and I'm seeing things from her perspective – through her eyes – just like the time I dreamt of Susannah. Olivia sneaks up the stairs, creeps past Stuart and Edith's bedrooms, and slowly walks up the last flight of stairs. Reaching our bedroom door, she carefully twists the door handle and gently pushes it open. She walks forward, into our bedroom, and stares down at Tristan and me wrapped up in each other's arms as we sleep soundly in our bed.

Get out! I screech at myself, or her – *It's so confusing!*

The dream suddenly shifts. I'm in the green forest, and I'm looking down at the newborn baby in the hole, only he's not moving this time, he's not looking up at me. And I'm choked with horror *-No!*

Suddenly, I'm outside my studio, and I'm kissing Justin – *No! No...please stop!*

The dream shifts again. I'm in a cemetery, trying to find my mom. My dad is there, he tries to grab hold of my hand, wanting to take me with him – *No!* I pull my hand out of his and start running...and he's chasing me, nearly catching me... *No, leave me alone*!

Then I'm on the boat, the one where I first dreamt of Tristan and I'm dashing around trying to find him, screaming out for him because I'm afraid and I don't know why, but he's not answering me.

I run up the stairs and search the deck, and I suddenly realise I am alone – Tristan is not here. I look around and see I am not moored in a beautiful little cove, I am out at sea, and there's a storm brewing, a big one – I am so scared. My legs start to shake with fear. The sky darkens, blackening at an incredible rate. The sea is swelling, almost throwing me overboard as the white waves start crashing over the deck. I scream out for Tristan again, but he doesn't come to me. I grab hold of the mainsail, hanging on, praying I survive.

The boat starts to make strange noises, groaning in response to the battering it's getting. I want to cover my ears, but if I let go; surely I'll die. I hear the most frightening, thunderous noise, it literally terrifies me. I know I have no choice but to turn around and see what it is, and just as I do the most enormous wave crashes over me, taking me and the boat down into the icy, black depths of the Atlantic.

I thrash around, swimming as much as I can, trying to get back to the surface, but there's just blackness in front of me, I can't see anything. I'm so disorientated, so cold, I can't get my bearings, and my whole body feels like millions of needles are puncturing me at the same time. I keep kicking, trying to reach the surface. I have no more air in my lungs, and I know this is it, I am going to drown, I am going to die – Just as I think that the dream shifts again, and I'm lying soaking wet on the beach – I think I'm home?

I sit up, shivering from head to toe and look around me. I'm not sure if its sunrise or sunset, but the warm sun is welcoming on my frozen skin. I wrap my arms around myself trying to generate some heat. The storm has gone, the sea is calm, the sky a light hazy blue.

I stagger to my feet and search the beach, but the world is eerily silent. No cars, no trains, no people, I can't even hear any birds singing – I have to get back to the house, I have to find Tristan!

As I take a step forward, my mother appears in her ghost-like way, her light blinding me.

"See..." She says as she did before, and points up to a building. I instantly recognise it. It's the hotel where *he* raped me. I quickly look away – *No! I don't want to see...*

I'm suddenly catapulted to a place I don't know. There's music playing, I think it's Frank Sinatra? The room is big and grand with a huge chandelier hanging from the ceiling, the lights are low and soft. There are so many people around, dressed up to the nines. Men in dinner suits, women in beautiful flowing gowns, some people are dancing, some are chatting. I look down and see I'm in a long black dress, and I have a glass of champagne in my hand. I see her in my peripheral vision again, I spin around and face her; my mother is still with me.

"See..." My mother whispers in my ear and points across the room. I look up and see Tristan in a black dinner suit, smiling at me as he walks towards me.

"No, not him, see..." My mother says, pointing what looks like a hot, white stick out in front of her. I look back in the direction she is pointing, and I see *him*...the guy who raped me. He's walking right behind Tristan, across the dance floor. He's also dressed in a dinner suit and has a glass of champagne in his hand.

"He knows you..." My mother whispers. Right on cue he stops, turns to me, raises his glass at me and takes a sip; then smiles an evil, twisted smile – *No!*

MY EYES DART OPEN – *Fuck!* I dash out of bed, my body protesting in pain and reach the toilet just in time for me to violently vomit, over and over again. I hear Tristan approach, and feel him gently pull as much of my hair as he can out of the firing line; his other hand is gently rubbing my back, trying to soothe me – *Oh Tristan!*

I squeeze my eyes shut, trying to block out the horrifying images, the overwhelming feelings, the fear, the helplessness... My body finally gives in. I stop dry retching, and now I feel totally exhausted. *Why is being sick, so tiring?*

"Baby?" Tristan softly says. I lean up and press the flush. I can't talk to him, I don't think I can even look at him right now because I know I'll just crumble, and I need to work it all out in my own head first, what that was all about.

I stagger to my feet. Tristan helps me over to the sinks. Reaching forward I pick up my electric toothbrush, add some toothpaste and start brushing my teeth.

"Did you want some Gaviscon?" He asks.

I nod without looking at him. He walks over to the bathroom cupboard and pulls a new bottle out. Walking over to me, he picks up one of the glasses we use for rinsing our mouths out, pours a little into it and waits for me to finish.

When I'm done, I put my toothbrush back and keeping my eyes on the floor, I turn my body to face Tristan's. Tentatively, he reaches out and passes me the glass. I turn to the sinks, gripping them for balance, close my eyes and slowly drink down the thick, pink liquid.

"Coral," Tristan says, his voice trembling. "You're never this quiet, you're worrying me. What's wrong?"

I put the glass down, and stare down at the sink. "Just a bad dream Tristan, a nightmare," I say keeping my eyes down, my voice not sounding like my own.

"Want to talk about it?" He softly asks. I shake my head at him, unable to get any words out. "Why won't you look at me?" He adds.

I stare despondently at the floor. I feel utterly guilty for ignoring him.

Tristan sighs heavily. "What can I do Coral?" I shake my head again. He sighs heavily. "I'm calling George," he says, and with that, he walks out of the bathroom – *Fuck!*

I AM SAT IN the cinema room, waiting impatiently for George to turn up. He wasn't due here for another hour. Tristan said this was probably the best place for us to talk, to have some peace and quiet. Terry has been and given me my morning shot, so I'm not in as much pain, but I still hurt all over. Earlier, I took a long, hot shower trying to wash away the feelings, the guilt – I have avoided Tristan this last hour – and to try and warm my body back up. I still feel so cold.

I also feel racked with guilt. I told Tristan he would always be my first port of call from now on, but I guess I was wrong – I'm still freaky Coral. *Ugh! I can't even talk to my own husband to be!* I grit my teeth at myself in anger. My leg won't stop jigging up and down, and I'm biting my fingernails. *Argh! I hate feeling like this!*

I hear muffled voices coming down the hallway, I can tell its Tristan and George. They stop right outside the door, whispering to one another. Maybe they don't realise it's open or that I can hear them?

"George, give me your honest opinion, please. She's been almost catatonic since she woke, she's avoiding me, hell she hasn't even looked at me," Tristan stops and takes a deep breath. "Look, if she needs hospitalising then just say so, and I'll make it happen...I...I don't know what to do? I've never seen her like this before." He says, sounding frantic.

"Tristan, please try not to worry. I have seen Coral like this, many times before. Once she talks it through and releases whatever it is that has upset her, I'm sure she'll be back in your arms in no time at all. So much has gone on for her these last few weeks, and from what you've told me, it's bound to have some effect, on both of you – eventually, something has to give."

"Ok...ok. I just..." Tristan sighs, he sounds so downhearted.

"You want her happy and healthy?" George questions.

"Yes," Tristan breathes. "Of course I do."

"Time Tristan, she just needs time, be patient, and she will come back to you."

"Ok, thank you, George. Would you like a drink of some sort?"

"Please," George says.

"Hot, cold...?"

"A pot of tea for us both I think. Coral always seems to like that when she's having a session."

"I'll get Edith to bring it down," he says.

"Thank you, Tristan - and try not worry," George says.

"Easier said than done," Tristan retorts then I hear his footsteps climbing the stairs.

George taps lightly on the door, then pops his head inside, I don't look up at him.

"Coral, I need to know you're ok with me coming in. Can you nod your head once for yes?" I nod once, keeping my eyes on the floor. "Good, well done." George enters and sits diagonally to me. I'm on the big couch, and he's on one of the squidgy chairs.

I decide that whatever I do, I can't look at him. This needs to be done without eye-contact. If I break it, I feel like I will break, like my brain will just explode on me.

"Tristan is very worried about you Coral' – "What do you think about death George?"

"Death?"

"Yes."

"In what context are you referring?"

I sigh inwardly. "When people die, do you think they just shut down or do you think there's another side to it like our spirit or soul lives on?"

"Many believe' – "What do you believe George?"

"It's not really relevant what I believe Coral, but what you believe is."

I swallow hard. "My mother keeps visiting me in my dreams, only it doesn't look like her, but I know it's her, she's just this bright white light that floats in the air, and I can hear her, she whispers things to me."

"Many people have had the same sort of image of their loved ones when they have passed on." George softly says.

"Am I crazy George? Am I turning psychotic like my mother? Is Tristan really going to hospitalise me?"

"Not in the way you're thinking of. Tristan wants you to be in the best hands if you are sick Coral' – "Am I sick?" I interrupt, still biting my nails.

"No. In my professional opinion, you are not, and you are not psychotic or crazy as you put it. You have been through one hell of a journey in such a small amount of time. Even someone with no prior history like yourself would be having difficulties, I guarantee you that." *Ok, feeling a little better about turning into a nutcase!*

"She told me about my baby," I whisper.

"You baby?" George says, sounding worried.

"I was pregnant, only a week or so' – I hear George gasp –'the Doctors told Tristan, he told me. I miscarried my baby, and she showed me before he told me, only at the time, what she showed me didn't make any sense, and the baby was still alive, looking up at me."

"I'm so sorry to hear that news Coral." George softly says.

I nod, despondently.

"What did your mother show you about the baby Coral?"

"The baby in the hole, he's so still...not moving... and not looking at me." I hear George frantically scribbling something onto his writing pad.

"Where was the baby Coral?"

"In the hole."

"What hole?"

"The hole in the forest where the tree was, then it disappeared, and the baby was in there."

"The tree disappeared?"

"Yes, one minute it was there, then it was gone, and then she showed me the baby in the hole."

"Your mother?"

"Yes. She said 'see', and I looked down and there was the baby."

"I see. Can you think of any reason why the tree would disappear? Have you been out to the woods lately?"

"I dreamt of the woods before. Tristan was there, and he disappeared, like smoke. I didn't want him to go, and I tried to get to him, but something invisible was holding me back."

"I see, has it been just that one other dream of Tristan in the woods?" *Right on the mark Gorge!*

"No."

"There have been others?"

"Yes. Just one."

"Can you tell me Coral?" I cringe inwardly. "Coral?"

"Do you know Twilight?"

"Twilight?" George questions.

"Yes, you know…the films that have been out about the girl who falls in love with a vampire."

"I've never seen them Coral," George replies.

"Ok, well in the first dream I had, Tristan was Edward the vampire, then he changed into Tristan and bought a red apple to my lips. I couldn't move again, I wanted to reach out to him. Then he said 'take a bite' then the dream ended."

"I see, and had you been to the woods at all?"

"No."

"Can you think of anything that might be the reason for the tree disappearing?"

"To make room for the baby?" I guess, shrugging my shoulders.

"Possibly," George says. I search the recesses of my mind, trying to work out – then it hits me, Tristan said about planting a tree.

"This could be relevant though? I want to bury my mother's ashes, I want to give her a gravestone, but Tristan found a place nearby and instead of a plot with a gravestone, you plant a tree."

"Ah…" George is scribbling again. "Yes, that may be what this is about Coral, putting your mother to rest."

"You think so?" I whisper, feeling like the freak that I am.

"Yes, and you're also dealing with the fact that you lost your child."

"I didn't know I was pregnant." I tremble.

"Sometimes, that can make it even more traumatic."

"Why?" I croak. *Don't cry!*

"Often, women feel guilty for not knowing they were pregnant, and they tend to question it over and over again, 'what did I do wrong?' Or, 'what didn't I do that I should have done?'. Also, other women have shared with me that they felt somewhat betrayed by their bodies, let down as they weren't given any signs or indications that they were pregnant."

"Oh." I swallow hard.

"Have you felt any of those feelings Coral?"

It takes a long time for me to answer. "I...I don't know. I suppose at the time when Tristan told me, I felt guilty because if I hadn't gone to his place, and Susannah hadn't shot me, we might still be pregnant. But the guilt didn't last that long because no matter what way I look at it, I still would have gone to Tristan, even if I knew she had a gun. So, in a way, I lost, and I gained. I lost our baby, but I gained Tristan, he is alive."

"I see, and how do you feel when you see the baby in the hole?"

"The first time I didn't understand, but I wanted to help it, it looked so tiny and fragile."

"And the second time?" My teeth clamp together. "Coral?"

"I didn't want to see. The baby wasn't moving. I'm glad it only lasted a split second then the dream changed." I snap.

"I see, how are you feeling Coral, in general? Happy, sad, angry?"

"Happy."

"Elaborate please."

"I am in love. Tristan is a wonderful man, who I clearly do not deserve, but he wants me so I will spend the rest of my life trying to make him happy."

"I see, so can you tell me what made you so sick this morning?"

"All of it," I barely whisper.

"All of what Coral?"

"The dream."

"Can you share that with me?"

I take a deep breath and begin. "Olivia was here in the house' – "I do apologise Coral, but who is Olivia?"

"Tristan's ex-girlfriend, she came here yesterday, and Tristan told her to leave."

"Alright, please continue."

"It was night time, and Olivia was in the house, only I was Olivia, like before when I dreamed of Susannah. Olivia walked up into our bedroom and watched Tristan and I sleeping. Then the dream changed to the baby in the hole in the woods and then...Justin," I end in a whisper.

"Justin was in your dream?"

We both halt our conversation as we hear Edith coming down the stairs, she tentatively knocks on the door, then walks in and places the tray down; without a word she hurries out of the room, closing the door behind her.

"Please continue Coral. You said Justin was in your dream? George says.

"Yes. Tristan and I went to my studio yesterday, I wanted to see it, only Justin was there trying to find me. He's back in Brighton and has split with Harriet, he told me he has missed me, that he wants me back, he wants to try again."

"I see, so what happened with Justin in the dream?" I close my eyes and grit my teeth. "Coral," George whispers. "Whatever you tell me; stays with me."

"I know," I whisper and take a deep breath. "I...I was kissing Justin." I say, squeezing my eyes shut. "I don't love him, I love Tristan," I shout.

"I know Coral, that much is plainly clear for all to see."

"Then why did I kiss Justin?" I squeak.

"Sometimes, seeing someone from our past ignites old feelings, triggers emotions. I'm sure it was nothing more than you remembering what it was like being with him."

"I feel..." I stop, I can't say it.

"What Coral, what do you feel?"

"Guilty," I whisper.

"For kissing Justin?"

"Yes, for betraying Tristan."

"You haven't betrayed Tristan, it was just a dream." George softly placates.

I hang my head in my hands. "I don't understand that George, why would I even want to do that? Even if it was a dream, I meant what I said when I told him I would never have him back, and that it's Tristan I want and who I love. I even purposely told Justin I'm marrying Tristan."

"Again Coral, I will reiterate. Dreams are a way of our subconscious deciphering the events of the day, and sometimes those details can be confusing and a little muddled up."

"Maybe," I whisper.

"Coral, do you think you can spend the rest of your life never finding another man attractive?"

"Yes. I don't want to be attracted to anyone else but Tristan." I balk.

"But as human beings, we don't work like that. You can take any male or female who is deeply in love with their mate, yet, they can still find others attractive, they may never do anything about that attraction, but it doesn't mean the attraction isn't there."

"Oh!"

"So can you answer my next question honestly?"

"I'll try," I whisper.

"When you saw Justin, did you feel attracted to him, like you were before?"

It takes a long time for me to pluck up the courage to answer, because deep down inside, I don't want to admit it to myself.

I sigh heavily, it's no good. "Yes."

"Coral, that is perfectly natural and nothing to feel ashamed about, or guilty." George softly placates.

"I bet Tristan didn't dream of kissing Olivia last night," I shout.

"But Tristan isn't you Coral. Justin was the first person you allowed yourself to be close to, well as close as you could be. As I've explained before, the relationships we have with our partners are very different emotionally, to the ones we have with our parents, siblings, family members."

"I know," I whisper, still feeling guilty.

"Would you like a cup of tea?" My stomach can't take it – *No way!*

"No, I'm ok thanks. But help yourself, George, I don't mind." I wait while George makes his drink and takes a sip. "The dream didn't end there George," I whisper, feeling terrified. I wrap my arms around myself, I'm still so cold.

"It didn't?" George says. I shake my head and finally look up at him. "Welcome back," he smiles. I shake my head and stare down at the floor, silent tears start flowing down my cheeks – *Pissing me right off!*

"Here darling," George says passing me the tissues. I take them from him and swipe angrily at my cheeks. "When you're ready," George prompts.

"Did Tristan tell you that I spoke to my dad?"

"Yes," he says. "He buried your mother's ashes I believe?"

"Yes. In the dream…the part after Justin. I was at a cemetery trying to find my mom, and my dad turned up. He wanted to take me away, he wouldn't let go of me, but then I escaped, and I ran, but I was scared because he was running after me, trying to catch up with me."

"Tristan told me he wants to communicate with you?"

"Yes."

"And you don't want to?"

"No."

"Well, again Coral, dreams are our way of processing these

things. The fact that he was holding onto you signifies that he wants the connection. The fact that you ran away signifies you don't want the connection." *Ok, feeling a little better about that part!*

I take a deep breath. "You remember the dream I told you about, the one on the boat with Tristan?"

"Yes."

"Well after running from my dad, I was on the boat again, and I couldn't find Tristan. I was so scared, and I didn't understand why? I cried out for him, ran all over the boat, only to realise, in the end – that I was alone....and then..." I stop and squeeze my eyes shut.

"Take your time Coral." George gently prompts.

I take another deep breath. "I ran up on deck to see if he was up there, but he wasn't. And we weren't in the cove like before. I was out at sea and..." I swallow hard, I don't want to remember.

"What happened Coral?" George whispers.

"A storm; a dark black storm came over. This huge wave capsized the boat, I went down...I was so cold, so scared...it was so dark, so black. I couldn't even see my hands in front of my face, and I knew I was drowning, that I was going to die alone in those icy depths."

"And that's where the dream ended?" George asks. I shake my head. "When you're ready," George softly says.

I close my eyes, this is the part I'm most scared of, the part I'm frightened off. "I...I was on the beach here, in Brighton. I was soaking wet and freezing cold. My mother appeared to me again, she pointed up at a building and said 'see' so I looked and it was the hotel I was raped in." *Breathe Coral, Breathe...*I take another lung full of air. "Then it changed again, and I was somewhere I haven't been before, it was like a posh party or something? There were so many people all dressed up, there was music playing, and people were dancing. When I looked down at myself, I saw that I was dressed up too, and I had champagne in my hand. Then my mother whispered to me again, she pointed across the room and said 'see' I looked up and Tristan was walking towards me. Then she pointed again..." I clench my hands into fists.

"Take your time Coral, there's no rush darling."

I take another deep cleansing breath. "When she said 'see' again, I recognised who she was pointing at, it wasn't Tristan she wanted me to see it was...*him.*"

"Who is *he* Coral?"

"The man who raped me," I gasp, trying to choke back the tears.

"He was at the party?" George asks, as he frantically scribbles more notes.

I nod. "He was walking across the dance floor all dressed up, then she...she whispered, 'he knows you', and he stopped and looked right at me, raising his glass to me and smiling at me and...Oh, George! What if she's right? What if he did know me, or does know me...?" I suddenly start to feel really woozy – *Oh ok, I think I'm going to faint.*

"Coral?" George reaches across to me. "Are you feeling unwell?"

"I feel faint," I whisper.

"Come on sweetheart let's get you some fresh air." Taking my hand and putting his arm around my waist, he leads me out of the room. "Which way Coral?"

"Right," I whisper, and we head down the hallway, through the bi-folding doors and out into the bright sunny day.

"Better?" George asks as I try my best to fill my lungs with lots of clean, fresh air.

"I think so?" I whisper.

We take a seat, side by side on the outdoor lounger; although it's more like a big comfy sofa. George keeps hold of my hand, squeezing every now and then. "Feeling better?"

"Yes," I whisper, staring at the grass. The world is no longer spinning.

"Good, now; I'd like to go through each part of the dream. Is that ok?" I nod despondently. "Ok. Olivia' – "George, she is so pretty." I interrupt.

"Completely irrelevant," George snaps in exasperation. I look up at him and frown. "Coral, don't you realise? It doesn't matter how pretty a woman is, or how good looking a man is, we are all looking for connection above anything else; a very deep, loving connection. So you see your fear of Olivia is just that; a silly fear, a misguided belief. You need to break that belief down. Tristan is with you because he feels that level of connection with you and wants to make it permanent by committing to you and by marrying you."

I nod, understanding what he means. "It's my own insecurities?" I whisper.

"Yes."

"Ok."

"Good, now the baby. How do you really feel about it Coral? You were led to believe you couldn't conceive and now you know you can."

"I'm scared. I've told Tristan we will have a family one day, but not yet. I want him to myself for a while, but I think the real reason for holding it off is that I don't think I'll be a very good mother. I mean, what child is going to want someone with issues like I have? How am I supposed to make a child feel secure when I struggle with that myself?" I stop and shake my head.

"Well, from what I've learned over the years, motherhood changes that. A protective instinct kicks in, to provide, to love, to cherish. Again Coral, these are just your fears talking, I think you'll make an exceptional mother."

"You do?" I squeak.

"Yes." I frown and hug myself – *Hmm, me a good mother...* George continues. "Justin, well we discussed him, so please try to put it out of your mind."

"Ok," I whisper.

"Your father, well I think you were very brave to speak to him Coral, that can't have been easy?"

I shake my head. "I wasn't very nice to him."

"Well, he doesn't exactly deserve your love, patience and respect, he needs to earn it."

"You think I should let him back into my life?" I squeak in horror.

"That is completely up to you. And as far as your mother goes, I think the sooner you lay her to rest, physically, emotionally and mentally, the better. You need to get it done, say your goodbyes and move on."

"I know," I whisper. "I've been thinking the same thing."

"Good. Now, the storm at sea has a water aspect to it. Many believe large waves, storms and tsunamis often represent unresolved emotions. The fact that you were alone on the boat and the wave hit you is not saying that you are alone Coral, it's saying that you didn't deal with whatever issues that came up at the time, so subconsciously you were feeling alone. You repressed them instead of talking through them. For instance, did you speak to Tristan about how you really felt when Justin turned up, were you truthful with him?"

"No."

"And what about when you spoke to your father?"

I shake my head.

"And Olivia?"

"I don't want Tristan to know I'm worried about her like I was with Susannah. He already knows I'm insecure' – "Coral, stop hiding and be honest with him, tell him your fears, your real fears. I guarantee you if you do, these dreams will stop, your subconscious won't need to do the work because you've dealt with it at the time. Do you understand?"

"Yes George, I do. I know what you're saying, stop bottling it all up. But what about what my mom showed me at the end?"

"Irrelevant."

My mouth pops open. "How can you say that?"

"It was just a dream Coral."

"So what...I should just forget it?" I squeak, my throat tightening up on me.

"Fear, that's what this is. Do you really think Tristan would let anything happen to you?"

"I don't think its fear George," I say, shaking my head.

"You don't?" He cocks his head to the side.

"No, I think it's a missing piece of the puzzle."

"What puzzle?"

I shrug. "I don't know..." I say, feeling panicky again. I wish I could just hide away somewhere, from everyone, everything – well apart from Tristan. I let go of George's hand, bring my legs up, wrap my arms around them, then bury my head between my knees so I can't see anymore.

"Would you like a glass of water?" George softly asks.

"Please," I squeak, starting to rock myself. I feel George stand – *He's going to go!*

"Don't leave me!" I gasp, grabbing his arm.

In that very moment, I feel like I'm coming out of my shell, my hiding place, and all I want is Tristan.

"Tristan," I whisper. "George, I want Tristan."

"Ok," he softly says, then takes his mobile out of his pocket and makes a call. "Hello Tristan, we are outside, could you bring Coral a glass of water? Thank you." George hangs up. "He'll be here in a moment darling, deep breaths."

I do as he says and breathe deeply, in and out. A couple of minutes later, Tristan appears. *Oh...what have I done, he looks frantic...*He quickly reaches us, bends down in front of me and hands me the water, I take a tiny sip, give George the glass and launch myself into Tristan's open arms, gripping my arms so tightly around his neck he has to tell me.

"Coral, you're choking me." He gently pulls on my arms, so I'm not hurting him.

"Oh Tristan, I'm sorry...so sorry. I didn't mean to worry you." I say, squeezing him tightly.

"I know baby," he says wrapping his arms around me. Then he lifts me up into his arms, and sits next to George, with me sitting on his lap, safely cocooned in his arms. I grip onto him never wanting to let go.

"Hey, it's ok baby. I'm here, I'm not going anywhere," he soothes.

"Would you like me to give you both a moment?" George says.

I shake my head. "George, do you think it's true? That I do know him?"

"I couldn't say Coral," he says, looking mystified.

"But she showed me the baby, and that came true?" I feel Tristan stiffen beneath me.

"She did, yes," George says frowning deeply, then he looks up at me. "Coral, I can't really give you any answers with regards to the last part of the dream. But as far as the rest is concerned, it's just your mind trying to assimilate everything's that's happened into something tangible, something you can make sense of so that you can deal with it. But now you know what you need to do?" he says, looking sternly at me.

"Yes," I whisper. "Talk it through." George smiles and pats my hand. "George, I'm so sorry. I didn't...I didn't want to drag you over here like this. You are not at my beck and call. I apologise, profusely." Tristan squeezes me around my waist and gently kisses my temple.

"Nonsense," George says, smiling warmly at me. "I was due here anyway. Anytime you need me, you just call. If I'm around, I will come to you."

"Well let's go for this not happening again!" I snort.

"You look drained," he quickly assesses. "And as Tristan has pointed out, you are still recovering. Would you like me to stay and we can continue, or would you like me to come over tomorrow, or another day this week?"

"Can I call you?" I say, feeling guilty.

"Don't look so guilty Coral, and yes you can." George stands, I go to stand too, but George stops me. "Don't get up, I'll see myself out. Stay out here for a while, get some fresh air - and talk to Tristan." He adds, scolding me again.

"I will," I whisper.

"Alright then," George leans down and takes my hand, we both squeeze at the same time, then smile at one another.

"George...really, thank you," I gush.

George rolls his eyes at Tristan, who chuckles in return – *Great I'm funny now?*

"Say hi to Phil for me?" I add.

"I will." George shakes Tristan's hand, then gently places his hand on the top of my head for a moment. "No more worrying."

"Ok," I squeak and watch him walk away.

"Baby," Tristan says. I turn to look at him. "I've called Rob and cancelled today." I nod. I think that's a good idea. "I said I'd get you to call him to re-arrange," he adds.

"Ok, I will," I whisper.

"And Coral," he breathes.

"Yeah?" I gaze into his wide eyes.

"Don't ever do that to me again," he says, his tone clipped.

I bite my lip, feeling utterly guilty and nod solemnly at him. Tristan pulls me closer to him and we just silently sit there, wrapped in each other's arms. Letting the morning sun warm us, listening to the bird's twitter and the bees buzz by us. I don't know how long we actually sit there for, but I start to feel like I need to give Tristan some sort of explanation for my behaviour, and then I think not, and decide, instead, on honesty.

If he thinks I'm crazy at the end of it, there's not much I can do about it. So, I take a deep breath, summon up some courage and tell him the dream, from beginning to end.

"No wonder you looked like you did." He says, frowning deeply.

"How did I look?" I whisper.

"Shellshocked." He says, staring straight ahead.

"Oh," I frown down at my twisted hands. "I'm sorry I kissed Justin." I feel sick again.

Tristan chuckles at me. "Of all the things to worry about," he says, shaking his head.

"It doesn't bother you?" I whisper.

"Baby, George is right. It was just a dream. I know it's me you love, that's all the reassurance I'll ever need. I know you'd never do anything behind my back."

"Ok," I whisper, and peck his cheek.

"Why didn't you tell me that you've been seeing your mother?" He softly asks.

"I was scared," I say, feeling embarrassed.

"Of me?" He says incredulously.

"No, not *of* you, of what you thought *of* me, I'm not normal. I don't behave like other people do, and to turn around and say I see and hear dead people in my dreams isn't exactly a good sign, is it? Although..." I trail off – *I wonder?*

"What?" I shake my head trying to work it out. "Tell me Coral." Tristan sternly adds.

"I used to have premonitions as a teenager," I whisper.

"You did?" Tristan says, surprised.

"Yeah..." I trail off, still thinking the possibilities through.

"What kind of premonitions?" Tristan prompts.

"Um...like I would know who was calling when the phone rang...you know stuff like that." I look up at Tristan, his mouth is open, his eyes wide.

"It's not just 'stuff like that' Coral. What else could you do?" He says, amazed I think.

"Um...I would know what people were going to say before they said it, and I would always kind of know in advance if I was going to have a good or bad day at school."

"How would you know that?" Tristan whispers, I think it's his turn to be in shock.

I shrug. "Just...I'd wake up, and I'd just get this feeling and then like...a blurry flash image of the future."

"You're kidding?" He says, totally wowed by what I'm telling him.

"No, but the most profound one was when I saved Gladys."

"You...you saved Gladys?" Tristan chokes.

"Yeah...I'd had this weird dream, and I woke up feeling terrified. Over the next hour this voice kept whispering 'don't let her go' anyway, long story short I begged Gladys not to go' –

"Go where?" He interrupts.

I launch into the story. "...Anyway, after that, she swore she would always believe me if I said not to go."

"I'm sure she did," he says dryly.

"Tristan, I am sorry. I didn't mean to panic you. It's just that last part really, really freaked me out. I didn't know how to handle it, or how to handle telling you."

"You know if that was a premonition and he did turn up, he wouldn't get anywhere near you. You know that right? I would protect you," he whispers, his hand gently stroking my back.

"I know," I whisper back. "I just have this weird feeling, like she's right, that I do know him."

"Well if you do, and you meet the bastard again, we can do something about what he did' – "Hey, I know you're mad about what he did, but' – "Mad?" He chokes incredulously.

I sigh inwardly. I need to get off this subject. "I'm hungry," I whisper, going to move.

"Coral wait, while you were down here with George, I was thinking an idea over, I even mentioned it to Rob, he thought I was 'bang on' and that we should just do it."

"Do what?" I question, my eyes wide.

"Go away for a break, just me and you, somewhere quiet and tranquil. Just for a few days so you can get away from all of this, to rest up and recuperate. What do you think?" Tristan asks.

I smile and then titter. *Freaky, that's what I think!*

"What?" Tristan says, his lips twitching.

I shake my head. "I was just thinking the same, that I just want to get away...from everything. I seriously felt like my head was going to explode earlier, too much in one go I guess, and Tristan' – "Yes?"

"I'm still in so much pain. I've been hiding it from you because I hate feeling helpless. It's who I am and how I handle things. But my body is telling me off, telling me I need to just stop fighting it and let go."

His eyes close and he pinches the bridge of his nose in frustration. "I knew you shouldn't have come out of the hospital yet," he hisses.

"Oh, no, no, no! You're wrong there and right. Tristan, I was right to come out, hospitals freak me out, but I should have just had bed rest when we got back. I'm sorry, acting like I'm ok is something I'm very good at," I sheepishly admit.

He nods once, his jaw tense. "Yes, I'm starting to realise that, how good you really are at it. You were not ok yesterday were you?" He asks, almost shouting.

I guiltily shake my head at him.

He sighs heavily. "Coral, why' – "I just wanted us to have a nice day! We both seemed so much happier, more relaxed. I didn't want anything to spoil it, I'm sorry ok!" I squeak in a high pitched tone.

Tristan sighs heavily again, his eyes closing for a moment.

"I really like the sound of going away," I add, trying to placate him.

"You do?" He whispers.

"Yes, I really do."

"Then that's what we'll do."

"Where are we going to go?" I say excitedly.

"Devon, Cornwall, somewhere remote. I'll see if we can

get somewhere that looks out on a beach so we can watch the sunsets. I'll cook so you can just relax' – "But' – "Coral, I want to look after you baby – don't interrupt me," he scolds, seeing me about to then continues, "I don't feel as though I'm doing a very good job of it so far. So just let me do what I want to do!" He tells me in his authoritative voice.

"Ok." I squeak.

Tristan finally smiles. "I think it sounds great, just us. What say you?"

"Really?" I squeak. "Just us?"

Tristan laughs at my happy, excited face. "Yes, baby, just us."

"Won't you get bored?"

"Bored?" He chokes. "Why on earth would you think I'll get bored? I'm never bored when I'm with you."

"Never a dull moment with me around," I mumble dryly.

"That's not how I meant it," he scolds.

"Oh...I know you didn't, I meant it for me, you know taking the piss out of myself," I say half smiling. Hmm, just me and Tristan – *Holy crap! Just me and Tristan, the possibilities are endless!*

I can't help giggling with excitement. "I'm so excited," I say, almost bouncing in his lap. Then I remember something. "What about the function this Friday?"

"It's not important baby." He tells me firmly.

"But I think we should go!" I argue.

"Coral' – "Where is it, Tristan?" I interrupt.

He sighs heavily. "London."

"That wouldn't be so bad, we could' – "Coral. Please don't argue with me about this," he says, sounding weary.

"You're sure you don't want to go?" I ask.

"Yes, positive," Tristan says; he still looks worried. So I'll keep it on the back burner for now. If I feel well enough by Friday, I think we should definitely go.

"Do you think we'll get somewhere? It's still holiday season; I bet most of the places will be booked up by now," I say, trying to change the subject.

"O ye of little faith," Tristan whispers, leaning down to kiss me.

"You think we'll get somewhere?" I question.

"Baby, I know we'll get somewhere." He says in a thoroughly determined voice. Then Tristan smiles at me, takes my hand with the catheter in it and stares at it; his beautiful smile quickly turns into another frown.

"I'm ok," I whisper.

He cocks one eyebrow up at me. I look away feeling guilty. "If you lie to me again about how you're feeling, I swear to god Coral – I will not be responsible for my actions!" He snaps, almost shouting.

I nod once at him, biting my lip.

"Right, let's get upstairs then. We need to pack, and I need to call Terry; we're going to need a good amount of painkillers to take with us." *Ugh...tablets!*

Tristan smiles at my pouting face and keeping me in his arms he walks us back into the house.

CHAPTER TWENTY

I'M SAT OUTSIDE ON the sun lounger, waiting for Tristan to come out of his office. We are all packed up and ready to go. It feels very surreal. I can't believe that in only a few hours I'll be on holiday, away from Brighton, I never been away from Brighton before. I want to call myself a freak, but for the first time ever, I stop myself.

Tristan has called Dr Green to let her know I won't be there on Friday for my check-up, she has sent Nurse Terry over with a big bag of painkillers – *Yuck!* But at least the catheter is now out of my hand, it feels sore and is bruised slightly, but I'm sure it will heal quickly. He also called George and Gladys, who promised to tell Debs. I don't want her worrying about me, with everything she has going on – I can't help wondering if they've come to a decision yet, whether they are staying or leaving?

And earlier, I spoke to Rob. Who is panicking because of the wedding coming up, but agreed it's what I need, to get away. I feel guilty leaving my best friend on such short notice, but I need this, I know I really do, and Rob did tell me not to worry, that I haven't upset him, or let him down – He knows me so well. There's still a lot to sort out here, my mother's burial, speaking to Susannah; and I need to find a job – but for now, I am not going to worry about any of that. I am going to relax; give my body and my mind what it needs; what it's desperate for – some serious r-n-r!

"Hey baby," Tristan says bounding over to me. "Do you have a passport?"

"A passport?" I laugh.

"Yep."

"I thought you said, Devon or Cornwall?"

"I did." He smiles, shrugging his shoulders.

"We're flying?" I balk.

"Yes." Tristan cocks his head to the side. "You've never been on a plane before?"

I swallow hard and shake my head at him.

"Ah baby," he coos, kneeling down in front of me. "Look, this is what I've found. They had a cancellation." Tristan passes me several sheets of A4 paper. "I've booked it and booked the flights; Heathrow to Newquay. It would have taken us five hours plus to get there by car, but flying will only take a couple of hours."

I look down at the paperwork. At the top it says 'Porth Beach Villa Retreat' He's rented a villa? *Of course, he has!* I want to roll my eyes, we couldn't have just rented a cottage, of course not, this is Tristan we are talking about. I giggle at my own sarcasm and look at the images. *Hmm, it looks fabulous.* Very modern, two bedroom villa, set back, so it looks directly over the sea and a beautiful white sandy beach, and it's surrounded by Cornwall's rocky coast. It's breathtaking. I look down and read the description.

'Porth is a quiet, stunning bay perfectly situated between livelier Newquay and up-market Watergate Bay; with Jamie Oliver's restaurant Fifteen, and numerous other sandy beaches close by. The villa is located in a quiet location and is furnished in a contemporary, but comfortable style; offering modern facilities all within a stones' throw of the beach. Porth beach is a quiet and sheltered beach with rock pools and a freshwater stream at low tide. Enjoy a stroll to Lusty Glaze beach with its adventure sports, just 500m away, or stroll along the coastal path to Watergate Bay or Newquay. Only 3 miles from Newquay Airport, and less than a mile to Newquay Train station.'

I look up at Tristan and smile. "Wow!" Is all I can say. I'm giddy with excitement, it's so beautiful. In fact, it's making me re-think this place – I miss being so close to the water.

"Do you like it?" He asks his smile wide.

"I love it, Tristan," I say, gushing inside.

"Good. Well, we better get going, or we're going to miss our flights."

"But I don't have a passport ?" I squeak.

"You don't need one baby, not to fly inland; you just need some I.D. Have you got a driving licence?" He asks, smirking at me.

"Yes." I narrow my eyes at him – *What is he laughing at?*

"That will do." He chuckles to himself.

"What?" I can't help smiling back.

Tristan laughs, shaking his head slightly. "Just remembering you having a tantrum when you realised I was going to buy you a car, that's all." *Hmm, two can play that game!*

I cross my arms and pout. "Well, I have to say I was a little disappointed I didn't get an F-Type for my birthday," I gripe petulantly.

Tristan's mouth pops open. "You...you wanted one?" He gasps in disbelief – I want to laugh, and I feel guilty for winding him up, but it's just too good an opportunity to miss, so I slowly nod my head, looking forlorn. "You're serious?" He chokes.

I look up at him and make my bottom lip quiver.

"I knew I should have got you one!" He says, castigating himself; he looks really mad.

Trying not to laugh, I hold my hands out to him; he gently pulls me to my feet. "So you thought I was funny when I said no to you buying me a car?" I ask making Tristan sigh. I can't stand it anymore – A smile starts to creep across my face, then I start to giggle, making Tristan frown even harder at me.

"What?" He asks.

"Just getting you back..." I chuckle. "You know...for thinking it was funny...I didn't really want a car for my birthday, Tristan." I say, trying so hard to stop the laughter.

He lets out a long breath and narrows his eyes at me; they darken fractionally, and suddenly, he's looking really intense as he stares back at me – *Oh shit!*

"I should put you over my knee for that." He bites.

I inhale sharply, all humour gone. "Excuse me?" I whisper, my eyes wide.

As we stand staring at one another, something...something passes between us that I can't quite put my finger on.

"Let's get going." He says, ignoring me. "Or we'll miss our flight." He opens his hand out to me, in a daze, I place my hand in his, and we head out to the car...

STUART HAS DRIVEN us to Heathrow Airport. It has only taken an hour and a half to get here. I am so excited to be flying, and I'm confident I'll enjoy it because I have Tristan by my side. We have checked our luggage; so we locate a bar while we wait for our flight. Tristan is hungry again – I have butterflies racing around my stomach, so I don't want to eat anything, just-in-case. As Tristan peruses the menu, I sit back, watching the people around me. Some look stressed and are dashing about, other's look relaxed, like I feel; and I wonder if they are flying off on holiday too?

I turn and beam at Tristan. "Baby, aren't you going to eat something?" He asks.

"No." Tristan pulls a face. "I don't want to just-in-case I get sick on the flight. I'll eat when we land, ok?" I tell him softly.

Tristan smiles at me. "Ok," he says taking my hand in his – the one that had the catheter in it – and he gently kisses me where the needle was. *He is so sweet!*

A male waiter comes over and asks us if we want to order. Tristan asks for a Chicken salad sandwich and half a lager, then stops and frowns at me. "I don't mind Tristan. If you want a beer then have one, you deserve it." He smiles his enigmatic smile at me and nods to the waiter, who quickly scurries off.

"You really don't mind?" He says, squeezing my hand.

"No, I don't; not at all. Tristan, I've not exactly made this easy on you, and if I could, I would join you. But I can't because I'm being good." I say, smiling sweetly at him.

"Yes, you are," he says.

"Tristan, why didn't we just drive?" I ask because I'm curious.

"Five hours of bumping up and down in a car?" He says, shaking his head at me. "I didn't want you to go through that baby. I'm more worried about you than I'm letting on. At least this way, we'll be there in no time at all, which means we can both start relaxing."

I swallow hard. *He really does care!*

"How often do they fly from here to Newquay?" I ask.

"It changes." Tristan answers then narrows his eyes at me. "Why?" *Damn it!* I hate being this easy to read.

"Ok, just hear me out," I say, staring back at his wide eyes. "Please?" I add in a whiny voice.

Tristan sighs. "Alright, fire away!" he says, waving his hand at me.

"If, I feel better by Friday, and because it will be easy to do, I think we should go to your function,' Tristan goes to interrupt, so I hold my finger up at him. "Only if I'm better, I won't lie to you Tristan, if I don't feel well enough we won't go, but if I do because we've relaxed for a few days, then I think we should."

"Why are you so eager to go?" He questions.

"Because when you told me about it, you had this look in your eye. You like this old guy, whoever he is. I know you want to go." I say with one eyebrow arched.

He cocks his head to the side, his eyes still narrowed. "You caught that huh?"

"Yep, which makes me think that even if I don't feel well enough, you should go anyway," I say.

His eyes darken, his face going pale. "Absolutely not! I am not leaving you alone. And don't even think about arguing that point, it's not happening Coral!"

Well, that told me!

"Ok, you're not going on your own, but if I feel well enough' – "We'll fly that evening, stay in a hotel and fly back Saturday morning," he says, not looking too pleased.

"Why a hotel? Can't we stay at your place in London?"

"No." He says, shaking his head.

I frown back at him. "You don't want me to see it?" I question.

Tristan sighs leans forward and takes my hand in his. "Coral...I've already rented it out. Besides, there are too many memories there, my folks...Olivia, it's part of my past, and I want to move on," he says, swallowing hard.

"Ok," I say, leaning forward to kiss him and run my hands through his hair. The waiter arrives with his food and beer, Tristan thanks him and starts munching his sandwich. And even though I won't get to see his old place, I can't help smiling.

"What are you smiling about?" He asks between mouthfuls.

"I just...I think it'll be fun to go to the function that's all!" I say, feeling triumphant. Tristan's lips twitch, I know he's trying not to smile. "Go on," I tease.

"Go on what?" He growls.

"Smile," I say grinning broadly at him.

He sighs heavily, puts down his sandwich, and looks up at me, his face is still serious. His lips twitch as he continues to stare broodingly at me as I continue to giggle. He shakes his head at me and then grins a wide, happy smile. 'Frustrating woman' he mouths at me, then returns to his food...

HALF AN HOUR later our flight is called. The butterflies in my stomach multiply a thousandfold. I swallow hard and try not to get too nervous.

"Hey, flying is cool baby," Tristan says, beaming widely at me. "You have nothing to worry about, ok?"

"Ok," I squeak. I take his outstretched hand, and we walk over to the terminal. Only I'm surprised when we don't go down one of those tunnels; like I've seen them do in films. Instead, we are ushered outside onto the tarmac where there's a small plane waiting. It's not a big jet like I was expecting, and says Flybe across the side of it – I try not to panic.

"Hey," Tristan turns me to face him and softly runs his knuckle against my cheek. "You know these are the safest kind of planes to fly in, right?"

"They are?" I squeak, looking back at it – *It has propellers for god's sake!*

"Yes," Tristan chuckles. "This is a Bombardier Dash 8 Q400 Propeller Plane." *How does he know that?*

"And how does that make it safer than other planes?" I breathe.

"Because it has propellers," he says, smiling sweetly at me.

"And that makes a difference because....?" I question.

"When the engines fail in a jet, it's a dead stick in the sky. With propellers, the pilot can guide the plane down and safely land."

"Oh!" I whisper and swallow hard – *Don't panic!*

"And this has both, so we'll be safe," he adds, really smiling at me now. I can't help laughing nervously. "Come on, the sooner we are on, the sooner you will see that there's nothing to fear." Tristan claps my hand in his, and we follow the crowd of people.

I hesitate slightly when it's our turn to take the small steps leading up to the plane. Tristan squeezes my hand, making me feel safe, then gestures for me to go first. I take a deep breath and walk up the steps, stopping when I step inside and see the air-hostess.

"Good afternoon. Welcome to flight 462 heading to Newquay." A very pretty brunette says, then she gets an eye full of Tristan walking in behind me, she instantly looks flustered – *Great!*

Tristan passes our tickets to her. "Good afternoon...Mr Freeman, Miss Stevens. You're right down the end, seats 15a and 15b." She rips off the stubs and hands our tickets back to Tristan.

"Thank you." He smiles politely at her, and I see her blush. *God damn it!*

"Come on baby," Tristan says tugging on my hand. I try not to pout and follow him down the aisle to our seats. "Window seat?" He asks, looking amused. *Hmph!*

"She likes you," I whisper.

"Who?" He asks, bemused.

"The air hostess," I whisper.

Tristan rolls his eyes at me. "Coral, do you want the window seat or not because we'll be taking off in the next five minutes?" He sharply asks. *Oh!*

I quickly scramble into the window seat. Tristan places my handbag in the overhead compartment, while I clip my seatbelt into place. My right leg is already jigging up and down, my left foot is doing a dance all of its own, and I'm biting down so hard on my bottom lip, that it's becoming painful. Tristan turns my head, pulls my lip from between my teeth and settles his hand on my knee; it instantly stops bouncing up and down. The other air-hostess gains everyone's attention and begins the pre-flight safety speech, but it's just white noise to me, then she takes her seat, and a voice comes out over the tanner.

"Ladies and gentleman, welcome to flight 462 to Newquay. We hope you enjoy the flight today. Once we have taken off, our air hostesses Julie and Cindy will be handing out refreshments. We estimate our arrival to be on time, due to the beautiful weather we are having today. Thank you for flying with Flybe."

I take a deep breath, the fear seems to have faded, and now I'm feeling excited again. I look across at Tristan, he smiles widely at me. The plane starts to turn. I can hear the propellers, feel the slight bump from the wheels as it taxis to the runway. Then we really start to move, we are racing down the runway; holy hell that's fast– I squeeze Tristan's hand tighter. The next thing I know, the inertia is gone and we are lifting up into the air...*Holy Fuck!* – I want to scream, it's so exhilarating! *This is so cool!* I look out the window and see the ground getting smaller, more minuscule as the second's tick by – *Oh wow!*.

Five minutes into the flight, and I'm still staring out the window in amazement. England is so beautiful from up here; so green. *Who knew!*

"Coral." I turn and look at Tristan, he is grinning so widely, literally from ear to ear. "Are you ok?" I smile widely at him and frantically nod my head, unable to articulate anything yet. "Can I have my hand back then?" He asks. *Oops!*

"Sorry," I whisper, feeling shy and release his hand from my grip. He opens and closes his hand a few times, laughing as he does – *Jeez, I must have really squeezed it!*

"Tristan...that was...wow!" I breathlessly say.

"See, nothing to worry about," he coos.

The same air hostess that greeted us appears, asking if we want refreshments. I can tell she's trying really hard to be professional, and not ogle at Tristan. I turn away and look out the window so she can't see my smug smile, because he's mine, and he is hard to resist, and I find it very hard not to stare at him too. He really is very handsome...

WE HAVE ARRIVED at Newquay Cornwall Airport. It's very smart and clean compared to Heathrow. However, I was quite annoyed to have arrived as it only felt like we'd been on the plane twenty minutes; in-fact I didn't want to get off. I even enjoyed the landing. Actually, I was quite fascinated by it all, much to Tristan's amusement.

And right now, Tristan has our bags in one of those strollers. He locates a rental car desk and starts casually walking over to it, keeping my hand in his. I quickly pull out my mobile and send a text to Rob, Malcolm (Gladys has lost another mobile) and Debs, letting them know we have arrived safely. But as I do that I notice the number for the gym, Will!

Crap! I said I was going to call him. Feeling guilty, I call the gym, give them my number and ask them to get Will to call me back, or let Rob know if he and his wife are coming to the wedding. Tristan has one eyebrow cocked up when I look up at him.

"What?" I whisper.

"Calling your admirer," he teases.

I roll my eyes at him and stuff my mobile back in my bag. "Tristan, do we really need a car?" I ask, as we stop and wait in line.

"Of course we need a car!" He scoffs.

"Why? Do you plan on driving us around for the next ten days?" I ask sarcastically.

"No, but' – "You do know the place we are staying at is only three miles away?" I say.

"What, you want to walk?" He chuckles sarcastically.

"No, I just don't get why you would want to waste money on paying for a car all week, just for it to be sat in the driveway?"

"Coral' – "Why don't we just get a taxi? The place we are staying at...what was it? – Porth Beach, I'm sure there are lots of places to eat and drink, so we don't need to visit a supermarket." Tristan doesn't look convinced, so I roll my eyes at him. "Look if we want to go to Watergate Bay for a meal, for instance, I'm sure you're not going to want to drive. What if you want a glass of wine?" He's not having any of it, I can tell. "Ok, get a car," I say waving my hand in the air.

He pulls me into him. I can feel the full length of his body pressed against mine. "I want a car, so if anything..." He frowns and then seems to shake it off and smiles. "If I need to get you somewhere, I have access to a vehicle to be able to do that, ok?"

"Ok," I say nodding several times. He's right, again! Cornwall is remote, and if we did need a car for any reason – I stop those thoughts in their tracks. We are on holiday! And I am on holiday for the first time ever. I will endeavour to smile the whole time we are here.

LANA DEL RAY is singing about Video Games. I like this song, so I sing along to it, but as I glance across at Tristan, I can't help smiling at the disgusted look on his face – It's comical. We are sat in a Nissan Juke, it's a bright red, 4x4 thing, not the prettiest car in the world, but does the job. Earlier, at the rental car desk, I thought Tristan was going to expire when they said all they had left was this or a Kia Picanto – Now that would have been funny to see, Tristan squashed into the driver's seat of one of those. The car isn't sounding too healthy right now though, its engine screaming as it struggles up one of Cornwall's many winding, steep roads.

Tristan looks so funny as he sits in the driver seat though, rolling his eyes at its lack of power. *We should have bought his Jag!* Then I shake off that thought, if we had, I wouldn't have experienced my first flight – It was so cool! Although, there is a part of me that doesn't understand why Tristan didn't order some kind of posh, executive car? I mean, I know it was short notice, but still, it's not like he can't afford it.

"Do you think we'll ever get there?" He questions sarcastically. I can't help giggling. Tristan eventually joins in, and chuckles along with me, finally seeing the funny side of it... *Honestly, men and fast cars!!*

"Tristan, can I ask you something?" I say.

"Anything," he answers.

"Why didn't you...well hire a better car in advance...you know something posh like the Jag?" I question.

He grins widely. "Posh like the Jag?"

"Well, I think it's a posh car!" I say cocking an eyebrow up at him.

He chuckles at my response and then shrugs his shoulders. "I just...I don't want you feeling overwhelmed by my wealth and....well, I want you to want me for me, not what I can offer you." He quietly says.

I swallow hard. "Tristan, I do want you for you. Not your money." I softly reply.

He smiles at me and clasps my hand in his. "I know Coral, it's just hard getting used to being with someone who thinks like that. You're so different to anyone I've ever dated."

I lean across and kiss his flushed cheek. "Same here baby."

Finally, we see the villa Tristan has rented. Tristan parks the car, and we both step out. A guy is waiting for us. He's all surfer dude with bleached blonde hair, a wicked tan, no top on, surfer board shorts, and bare feet. I think he's a teenager, or maybe a guy in his twenties that still looks young? I hear seagulls, I can smell and see the sea, and there is sand along the edges of the roads – *It's so cool!* You don't get that in Brighton, but I guess that's because it's a pebbled beach.

I can't believe I'm on holiday! I feel like jumping up and down.

"Mr Freeman?" The boy says in a strong Cornish accent – I love it.

"Yes." Tristan walks over, and they shake hands.

"Yeah...I'm Jake." He says in the most laid-back way. "My mom said to tell you that the downstairs shower is on the brink, people before you busted it, but she's gonna send someone over to fix it, so just use the one upstairs." He says, smiling broadly.

"Ok," Tristan chuckles as Jake hands him the keys to the property. He continues to smile at Tristan, and as I take a step closer, I notice his eyes look really blurry. *Is he stoned?*

Jake continues. "Yeah...but the barbeque is awesome dude... want me to show you where everything is?" he asks.

"No, that's fine thanks," Tristan says, I can tell he's trying not to laugh.

"Cool. How long are you here for?" Jake asks, smiling cheekily at me.

He seems harmless, and his grin is really cute, for a boy, and I feel so happy right now, that I can't help smiling back at him.

"Ten days," Tristan says, looking from me to Jake with a frown.

I stop smiling – *What's his problem?*

"Cool, the weather is supposed to be awesome...you guys surf?" He really is a chatty young man.

"No," Tristan says, getting our luggage out of the boot.

"You?" Jake asks me directly.

"No Jake, no surfing. I was in an accident, we're just here to relax and unwind."

"Oh..." It seems to take a while for his brain to register this. "Well...if you feel like it, my best friend is having a party on Saturday, it's his birthday," he explains nodding his head at the same time then continues. "You guys should come along...it'll be cool."

"We'll bear that in mind Jake, but right now I want to get inside and get something to eat – No offence," Tristan adds, I grit my teeth at him.

"None taken dude!" Jake smiles at us both. "Catch you later...." He says, putting his hand in the air as he turns and walks down the hill.

I cross my arms and put on my stern face.

"What?" Tristan says. His hands and arms are full of our luggage.

"Why were you like that with him?" I say, scowling at him.

"Isn't it obvious?" He scoffs, climbing the steps to the house.

I follow him up and stop when we reach the front door. "No. Well, it wasn't to me?" I say.

"Coral." Tristan awkwardly hands me the key. "Can you unlock the door please?"

I do so, push the door open, and gesture for Tristan to go first. He walks into the kitchen, which is very modern and spotlessly clean and dumps our bags down on the floor.

"Well?" I say, still scowling.

"Coral, are you blind?" He says, casually strolling over to me, stripping his t-shirt off as he does and throwing it on the floor. *Damn, he looks hot!* Now all he's dressed in are a pair of dark blue combat shorts and a pair of flip-flops.

I swallow hard. "Blind?" I whisper as he reaches me, and pulls me against his body. I can feel his erection digging into my belly. I put my hands on his arms, his strong arms. I'm swooning at him again.

"Yes, he was flirting with you," Tristan adds.

"No, he wasn't," I laugh. "He was more chatty with you. Besides, I thought he was a nice kid, the harmless type, and I don't think that very often about men, or boys which he evidently was." I say.

"Hmm. I still think he wanted you," he says.

"Tristan Freeman, are you jealous?" I titter.

"No," he growls, kissing me hungrily.

I pull back feeling breathless. "If you think for one second that I'd be interested in a young boy like that, you've got another

Forever With Him

thing coming – besides he was a complete stoner! Did you see the state of his eyes?" I chuckle.

"Yes, I did," Tristan says, gazing down at me with such a seductive look.

"So...what now?" I ask, revelling in the fact that I am not in Brighton.

"Food," Tristan says in his stern voice.

"Really?" I squeak. "You're hungry again?"

"Not me, you. Remember what you said to me at the airport?" *Ah yes, I do remember.*

"Just let me get changed and we can head out for something, ok?" I say.

Tristan growls and kisses me hard again. "Wrap your legs around me," he says as he lifts me up. I do exactly that and kiss him back. "We're going to find the bedrooms first," he croaks in that sexy, husky voice of his. I smile against his lips, as he heads through the apartment in search of a bed...

DAMN! THAT WAS sexy, sex! I love that about us, that we just can't get seem to get enough of each other, that Tristan feels the same way about me as I do about him.

"So much for relaxing!" I giggle, trying to catch my breath.

"Sorry, I couldn't help it. I wanted you, badly," Tristan says, turning on his side to look at me. "How are you feeling darling, in any pain?"

His serious face is back. He's worried about me, I know that.

"No baby, no pain," I say, reaching up and tenderly touching his cheek.

His look changes, playful Tristan is back. He leans up and rests his head on his hand. I am flat on back, staring up at him. Then he places his forefinger at the hollow base of my throat, then slowly, he runs his finger down my chest, between my breasts, all the way down my sternum, down my abdomen, until finally, he reaches my sex.

My breath catches with the contact. I cannot take my eyes off his. He slowly circles his forefinger down there, then shocking me again, he reaches up and places his finger in his mouth and sucks.

"Hmm, delicious," he says, his eyes glinting wickedly.

"Tristan Freeman, you are a dirty boy!" I playfully scold.

"So, is dirty Tristan another part of me that you love?" He

questions, suddenly going serious. There's a double meaning there – I'm sure there is.

"Yes," I whisper shyly. My heart is racing against my chest.

He nods once, then reaching up he places his free hand against my cheek. "Coral, there's something' – My stomach grumbles, very loudly, stopping him in his tracks. "I'm going to go and get us something to eat." He says scrambling up from the bed.

"Wait, Tristan..." I take hold of his arm, stopping him. "What were you about to say?"

"Not now Coral. You're hungry, and so am I." He dashes off to the en-suite.

When he returns, he yanks his shorts on, commando style, and stuffs his feet into his flip-flops. I can't help frowning up at him, he has something to tell me, something important – I know he does.

"Baby..." He slides onto the bed. "I don't know about you, but I feel like having something to eat, then going down to spend the afternoon on the beach; and I thought, if I pick something up now, we could just eat in tonight. What do you think?"

"Sounds great!" I beam. *Maybe he'll tell me later?*

He smiles that sexy, slow smile at me. "Ok," he chuckles. "What do you fancy for lunch?"

I think about it for a second. "A Cornish pasty," I say.

"A Cornish pasty?" He questions quizzically.

"Um...yeah, I've never been to Cornwall Tristan. It's one of Gladys's favourite places, she tried to bring me here once, for a holiday. I was young..." I shake my head, remembering. "I had a meltdown in the car...she had to turn back. I stayed with John and Joyce while she and Debs came down here; they did that every year while we were kids." I stop feeling guilty that I put Gladys through that.

"What are you trying to tell me Coral?" He says, looking worried.

I laugh nervously. "I...I've never had a holiday," I whisper, feeling embarrassed.

His mouth pops open. "You've never had a holiday?" Tristan balks, looking slightly alarmed. I turn on my side, so I'm facing him, look down at the bed and shake my head. Tristan gasps. "This is your first holiday – ever?"

"Actually my first holiday was going to Hastings with you," I whisper.

Tristan's eyes are wide, and he's blinking rapidly at me.

Forever With Him

"Coral, I knew you'd never been abroad but...are you saying you've never left Brighton?" He asks, swallowing hard.

"Well no, I go to Worthing and Peacehaven, but that's not the same." I shake my head again – I want to say 'I'm a freaky fuck up remember' but I don't because I know he won't like that.

"You've never had a holiday?" He repeats, incredulously.

"Well...yeah. Joyce would insist I did, but I'd just hang out at the beach in Brighton. Rob's tried to get me to go abroad with him, plenty of times; but I always said no. It felt safer like that. I think as a child, I freaked out because I still didn't trust Gladys, I thought she was taking me away and making me live somewhere else." I say, staring up at him.

Tristan looks a little sick, then he seems to regain his composure. "So, why do you want a pasty?" He says, trying to shake it off.

"Gladys used to bring one back for me." I smile, remembering her doing that. "You know a real bona fide Cornish Pasty."

"She did?" He says, stroking my cheek, smiling warmly at me.

"We don't have to have that if you want something else, Tristan."

"No, pasty sounds good." He says.

"When in Rome," I giggle.

"What shall I bring back for tea?" He smiles.

"I don't know, surprise me," I say.

"Ok, gorgeous. I won't be long." He gets up off the bed and walks out the bedroom. *Damn, he has a cute butt.*

He stops halfway down the hallway and retracts his steps. "Coral Stevens, I'm warning you now, if you do anything daft while I'm gone' – "Like what?" I challenge, trying not to laugh because he looks so serious.

He cocks one eyebrow up at me, and crosses his arms – *Oh fuck it!* Picking up a pillow, I throw it with accurate precision, and it hits him right in the face, making me giggle.

"Did you just throw a pillow at me?" He cocks his head to the side.

"Yes!" I tease. "What are you going to do about it?"

"Oh...there are many, many things I could do about it," he says, his dark eyes burning with some unnamed emotion, pinning me to the bed. I cannot look away, and I can't move.

I don't want to move - *Holy crap! What is that look?*

He continues to stare down at me, then his eyes slowly work

their way down my naked body; it's like he's drinking me in. My lips part automatically, my breathing hitches up, and my heart is going like the clappers –*Holy crap!* How can he turn me on so much by just looking at me? He's not even touching me for Christ sake!

'Stay,' I mouth as I sit up – because I want him again, now.

"As tempting as that is Miss Stevens, we need to eat!" Tristan smiles his sexy smile at me the steps forward, arms still crossed, leans down without touching me and pecks me on the lips. Then he stands and walks out of the bedroom, but just as he reaches the door, he turns and mouths 'later' to me – *Bastard!* I laugh and shake my head at his teasing ways, then in a dreamy loved-up state I lie back down on the bed.

I HAVE HAD THE most wonderful four days of my entire life. I feel so relaxed, so content, I am blissfully happy. This morning, after waking up and feeling so good, Tristan agreed that we will go to the function tonight. Our flights are booked, so we are heading over to the airport this afternoon – I'm quite excited, and nervous. I want to make a good impression tonight. I want Tristan to be proud of me. Then I realise that tomorrow is Saturday, and in one week, I'll be married...*Hmm, Mrs Coral Freeman* – I like the sound of that, it has a lovely ring to it – I snort with laughter at my own words. Then I remember - *Shit! The rings!* – We haven't done that yet. We'd better get that sorted tomorrow!

With a contented sigh, I sit up from my horizontal position. Tristan and I are on the beach, soaking up some rays. Baby, I Love Your Way by Big Mountain is blasting in my ears, reminding me of Tristan, and how I feel about him. I quietly sing along as I take in my surroundings. The waves are calm today, not many surfers out. But there are so many little kids out with their parents, splashing about in the sea, playing in the rock pools, building sand castles – And I'm surprised at myself, I don't feel angry like I used to when I'd see happy families. Instead, I feel happy for them.

I watch a man throw his toddler up in the air, the kids face is a picture as his father catches him, they both look so happy. Then I'm drawn to a woman spraying her kid with sunscreen, she's wriggling about, I guess she doesn't like it, but her mother soon finishes, and I watch the little girl take an older boys hand, they both dash down the beach and dive into the sea. The only emotion I feel coming to the surface is that well, it's pretty cute.

All these happy families – it's kind of making me think that it is possible after all.

I sigh contentedly, it's so beautiful here. In fact, I think I could quite happily live here, forever. I frown at that thought, I never thought I would want to leave Brighton, yet here I am, seriously thinking about it. *How odd!*

I look up at the sky. It is yet another blue-skied, sunshiny day. How lucky we are to be having such lovely weather. I pick up the bottle of water and take several glugs, then I look down at my watch – nearly lunchtime – no wonder I'm hungry. *Honestly!* I shake my head at myself. I don't know how doing so little can give a person such an appetite? *Maybe it's all the sex?* – I nod in agreement with myself and look across at Tristan, my sexy man. I can tell by his face he is sleeping. I don't want to wake him. He needs his rest as much as I do; but I need food, which gives me an idea. Pulling my little notepad out of the new beach bag that Tristan bought for me, I scribble a note for him.

> My sexy husband to be, I am hungry, so I've gone to get lunch.
> I didn't want to wake you.
> So please, don't worry, I'll be back soon.
> But if you do worry, I have my mobile, call me.
> Your loving wife to be, Coral xXx

Then I stand, throw my bag over my shoulder, place the note on my lounger and put the bottle of sun lotion on top of it – so it doesn't blow away in the breeze. Then I blow Tristan a kiss and head off to the local shops.

I CANNOT WAIT to tell Tristan my news. As I reach the beach and I search for him, I can't help panicking – Tristan isn't on his lounger. I wonder if he's gone back up to the villa? I'm sure he would have called me if he'd done that. I shake it off and continue walking down the beach, loving the feeling of the sand between my toes – I don't know why, but at that very moment, I look up and instantly freeze. *Whoa!*

Tristan has popped up out of the sea – I guess he went for a swim. As he wades, very gracefully out of the water, I notice several mothers stop what they are doing with their children and stare at Tristan – I can't blame them, I'm mesmerised too.

I'm instantly reminded of an old diet coke advert where all the women stop what they are doing and stare at the sexy guy – Yep, Tristan is doing his own advert right now, and he doesn't even know it! The song from the advert starts playing in head as I continue to watch him walk up the beach, I Just Want To Make Love To You by Etta James – *How fitting!* Just as I think that Tristan runs both his hands through his soaking wet hair, his stomach muscles rippling as he does. He looks so hot. My sexy husband to be.

"Oh my God!" I hear a young woman say. I turn and see I have stopped a couple of feet away from two young girls lying on their towels; they look like they are in their early twenties.

"Cassie!" The one slaps her friend's thigh; waking her from her snooze.

"What?" She sleepily grumbles.

"Look." The other says, pointing down the beach to Tristan.

"Blimey!" Cassie says, sitting up and putting her shades on. "Bloody hell! Who is he?"

I have to stifle a giggle. Their mouths are gaping open as they watch my perfect specimen of a man walk up the beach.

"Come on Lara!" Cassie says, standing to her feet. "Let's go chat him up!"

What? No! They can't do that!

Lara has stood up too, and they are both adjusting their bikinis, checking each other over so they look their best – *Holy crap!* They really *are* going to walk over to him – *You have to say something Coral!*

"I don't think he'll talk to you," I say.

They turn in unison and stare at me. "Oh...?" Cassie says. "Why? Do you know him?" she asks in a firm tone.

I nod my head and try to hide my coy smile. "Um...yeah I do."

Lara's face falls. "Is he your boyfriend?" She asks, placing her hands on her hips.

"Fiancé," I smile. "We're getting married on Saturday," I add.

Cassie makes an exaggerated huff, gives me a funny look then lies back down, but Lara smiles at me. "Lucky you," she giggles then says. "Going for a swim Cas, I need cooling down!" She turns and winks at me. I think I know what she means, what she's referring to, Tristan is enough to make any woman feel hot and bothered, Lara smiles at me, then she heads down the beach.

As I look back down the beach, I see Tristan has reached our loungers, just as he bends down he happens to look up. He stops dead in his tracks as he sees me, and the sexiest, lazy smile spreads across his face, his dimples on full wattage – and I swoon, again.

In my peripheral vision, I see Cassie shake her head and turn on her side, so she can't see anymore. I want to walk over to Tristan, but yet again, I'm frozen in place staring at him like a friggin' statue. He cocks his head to the side, still smiling at me. I smile back at him and slightly shake my head at myself. My, my, the things he does to me. I can tell he's chuckling to himself as he picks up his aviators and slides them on and then he casually starts walking over to me.

"Hi baby," he says as he reaches me.

"Hi," I squeak. Tristan leans down and kisses me, softly, sexily. A soft moan escapes me, making Tristan chuckle.

"Missed me?" He whispers; softly stroking my cheek.

"Yes," I squeak. "You?"

"I always miss you when I'm not with you," he says, making my heart pound. "Need some help?" He asks looking down at my arms that are full to the brim with our lunch, well, mainly Tristan's lunch, the man eats like a horse.

"Yeah...I think I do," I laugh, and like the gentleman that he is, Tristan takes the food out of my arms, takes hold of my hand and we casually stroll back over to our loungers.

"You were about to get chatted up," I say as I tuck into my delicious tuna salad.

Tristan has just taken a bite of his tuna baguette, so he quickly chews, swallows then frowns, I think in discomfort. "I was?" He says.

I nod. "Don't look now, but there are two girls not far from us who were admiring the view as much as I was. Then they both got up and said they were going to come over and chat you up!"

"They were?" He says, sounding surprised.

"Seriously?" I scoff, cocking my head to the side. "Tristan, why do you sound so surprised? I think every woman on this beach was watching you walk out of the sea." Etta James is still singing in my head...*I just want to make love to you...dadum dadum...*Tristan looks around, catching several women staring at him, they quickly look away – and if I'm not mistaken, are a little embarrassed to be caught staring at him.

Shaking his head, Tristan turns back to me and shrugs. "It's just a body Coral."

I shake my head at him. "No Tristan, it's not!"

"Yes," he argues. "It is."

"No, it's not!" I reiterate. "It's you, baby. I don't think you realise it, but I'm betting every woman that was watching you had all sort of naughty thoughts flying around their heads, you're every woman's fantasy!" I add.

His cheeks flush as he shakes his head at me. "Don't forget, we have the function in London tonight," he tells me and obviously not wanting to carry on the previous conversation, he continues with his lunch.

CHAPTER TWENTY-ONE

WE HAVE ARRIVED at the Millennium Hotel in Kensington. We are not staying here tonight though, as they were fully booked when Tristan enquired. So instead we are staying at the Hilton in Kensington, just a short drive past Holland Park. Earlier, Stuart picked us up from Heathrow and got us across town to the hotel and then he picked us up and drove us over to The Millennium Hotel. London is oozing with money. I never knew it was like this. Every car that we passed as Stuart drove us here in the Jag was a Bentley, Rolls Royce or a sporty choice like a Ferrari or Lamborghini – so much wealth!

I'm nervous and excited about tonight's function, but I'm managing to hold it together. Tristan is dressed in a very snazzy dinner suit, and I am in a full-length black dress. It's fitted, with a slit up the right leg, and covers my shoulders (I didn't want my scar or bruising on show) is slightly scooped at the neck and comes down just past my elbows. It's elegant, and I feel good wearing it, so that's a huge bonus. As we walk into the hotel, we are quickly guided to the correct function room for the party. At the double doors, a waiter in a finely dressed suit holds a tray out to us, it has several glasses of champagne balanced on it – *How do they do that?*

Tristan shakes his head at him. "Can I get you a drink from the bar, Sir?" He asks his face deadpan.

"Coral?" Tristan asks, looking down at me. I really want a glass of wine, but I know I shouldn't be mixing alcohol with the tablets.

"A glass of still water with lemon please," I say politely to the waiter.

"And for you Sir?" He asks Tristan.

"Tristan, have a glass of bubbly," I whisper up to him.

"You don't mind?" He whispers back. I shake my head and smile. "Ok baby." Tristan nods to the waiter and takes a glass off the tray. The waiter holds up two fingers and gestures to one of the young waiters who is standing with their backs against the wall, ready to help.

"A glass of still water with lemon for this lady," he tells the young boy.

"Yes, sir." He quickly scuttles off as Tristan guides us into one of the hotel's spacious wood and mahogany panelled suites. There's a dance floor in the middle of the room, with at least a hundred round tables surrounding it, which are all set up ready for the meal. There are so many different glasses, bottles of wine, and goblets of water on each table and everything is shining brightly, even the cutlery. There's a live band over in the far right-hand corner of the room who are busy playing a Frank Sinatra tune, Strangers in the Night. As I look above me I see the ceiling is twinkling sweetly with tiny little lights, making them look like stars above us, and in the centre of the ceiling is a large chandelier, sparkling so brightly it's hard to look at – This room is so elegant, so beautiful.

The waiter arrives with my glass of water, and I graciously accept it then take a gulp. Tristan and I are waiting in line to greet the birthday boy. I am so nervous. I keep glancing across at Tristan, and each time I have, he has given my waist a supportive squeeze. The people here are dripping with money, which is making me feel even more uncomfortable. Tristan's had years to get used to this, whereas I've never been to anything remotely this glamorous.

Several associates have greeted Tristan, shaking his hand and asking why he hasn't been around so much. I want to tell them to back off and stop questioning him. I mean, isn't it obvious? His parents both died for Christ's sake, don't they realise that? A man in his fifties approaches us, with a woman on his arm, maybe his wife? He has very rosy cheeks, huge jowls and a massive belly, whereas she looks like a stick insect next to him and the amount of jewellery she has on is enough to sink the Titanic. I have to stifle the giggle that wants to burst out of me.

"Tristan!" He bellows.

Tristan smiles back at him and releases his hand from my waist so they can shake hands. "Phillip, good to see you," Tristan says.

"Good god man, I didn't think you were going to make it tonight!" He says in a very loud, posh accent.

Forever With Him

"Change of plans," Tristan says, leaning forward to kiss the woman on both cheeks. "Isabelle, it's lovely to see you. How are you?" He asks.

"Much better, thank you for asking darling," she says, smiling warmly at him. "It's so good to see you. And who is this delightful young lady at your side?"

"Forgive me, may I introduce Miss Coral Stevens, my fiancé."

The woman's mouth gapes open. "Well, Congratulations!" The man bellows, making several people turn to see what he's shouting about. *Oh God! Ground open up!*

"Tristan, that's wonderful news," the woman adds, she seems genuine.

"Thank you." Tristan turns to me, beaming brightly. "Coral, may I introduce Mr and Mrs Phillip Stanford." Stanford & Co – I know the name.

"Hello, it's a pleasure to meet you both," I say, smiling and nodding and feeling utterly grateful that I don't have a free hand, not with my clutch bag in one and my drink in the other – I would not want to shake his hand.

The woman pipes up. "Come along Phillip, we promised Brandon we would say hello. Nice to have met you Coral, what an unusual name," she muses to herself. "Tristan darling, we'll catch up in a while," she adds.

Tristan nods, then Phillip shakes Tristan's hand once more, and I watch them turn and walk away when I turn back around I see we're next in line. The couple we are here to see are still talking to the people in front of us, so it gives me an opportunity to study them both.

The old woman is impeccably dressed. Her makeup is perfect, her short silver hair is perfectly styled and her shiny silver, floor length dress looks like it cost a fortune too; she is oozing old money. The man standing next to her is short in comparison, but that's probably because he is hunched over, he looks like he's one hundred and twenty, not ninety. He's dressed in a dinner suit and has a posh looking walking stick in one hand. The couple in front of us turn to walk away.

It's finally our turn. I'm so nervous. Tristan's cheeks flame as he steps forward, his hand squeezing my waist. I look up at him, and I can tell he's nervous too, although I don't know why. We take the couple of steps needed and stand in front of the elderly couple who've been greeting all of their guests. The woman gasps as she turns around and sees Tristan standing before her.

"Tristan!" she exclaims in delight.

"Hello, Sophia." Tristan smiles warmly at her, then leans in and gently embraces her.

"Oh, darling! We didn't think you could make it tonight, not with everything that has happened," she says, squeezing him tight. "It's so lovely to see you," she adds.

Tristan chuckles pulls back and kisses both her cheeks. "It's lovely to see you too Sophia, you look well."

"As do you, have you been away darling?" she asks, keeping her hands on his upper arms.

"Yes, a short break down in Cornwall. Sophia, may I introduce to you Miss Coral Stevens, my fiancé. Coral, this is Sophia Leveson-Gower."

Her mouth pops open in shock as she takes me in. Then she looks up at Tristan, he smiles shyly at her and nods once, her shocked expression suddenly turns to warmth, and she smiles lovingly at him.

"How wonderful darling," she softly says to him. Turning back to me, she surprises me by placing her hand on my left shoulder and kissing both my cheeks. "How lovely to meet you Coral."

"It's nice to meet you too," I say, smiling shyly.

"Oh, how lovely," she gushes. "Harry darling," she says interrupting the man next to her, who's still talking to the guests that were before us. "Harry darling, look who's here," Sophia says.

"Tristan!" He grins widely and stretches his hand out to Tristan, they shake. "Sorry about that, got caught up with whats-his-face," he adds, smiling broadly at me.

"Harry, you're looking well," Tristan says, chuckling slightly.

"Honestly," Sophia says shaking her head at him. "Who is what's-his-face?" she asks, placing her hands on her hips.

"Never mind," he says. "Who's this?" he says, waving his hand at me. "Such beauty as yours should be put on canvas," he adds.

My mouth pops open in shock, Tristan chuckles in response.

"Harry!" Sophia scolds. "Stop flirting."

"You know this young lady?" He asks Tristan.

"I should hope so," Tristan says, placing his arm around my waist. "Harry Leveson-Gower I am pleased to present to you my fiancé, Miss Coral Stevens."

"You're getting married?" He croaks. Tristan laughs and

nods. "Finally!" He throws his hand up as he says this, gesturing to Sophia.

"Oh Harry," she scolds. "Where are your manners?"

"You know, if I were a hundred years younger, you'd have some competition," he tells Tristan. *Ok, he sounds like Bob!* Nevertheless, I'm shocked again, and embarrassed. This is this his wife next to him, and he's trying to flirt with me? *This is funny!*

"You'd have to fight me for her," Tristan cajoles. He and Tristan obviously know each other very well.

"Where have you been?" Harry asks Tristan.

Tristan smiles a little awkwardly at him. "I know. I haven't been around much since..." He trails off, his cheeks flaming.

"We heard darling, and we are both so sorry," Sophia says, clutching his hand. "Did you get our flowers?"

"Yes, I did thank you," Tristan says.

"That's good darling." Sophia nods.

"Well, we'll come and see you both in a little while," Tristan says, glancing back at the queue of people behind us.

"Yes darling, please do," Sophia replies.

Tristan smiles at them both, and we graciously glide out of the way of the other guests, patiently waiting in line.

TRISTAN HAS BEEN amazing this evening, so gentlemanly and thoughtful. I was so nervous about coming here, but he's made the whole evening feel effortless. *How does he do that?*

"Happy?" He asks for the tenth time tonight. I smile a ridiculous smile at him, his answering grin is breathtaking. "Want to go?" I nod shyly. I want my man. I want to get him back to the hotel, and I want to get him very naked. "Ok," he chuckles.

"What are you laughing at?" I ask, feigning innocence.

"That wicked look in your eyes, I can tell what you're thinking, and I couldn't think of a better way to end the evening – But can I leave you alone for one moment?" He adds.

"Alone?" I question.

"Yes, there's an associate I need to talk to, and I'd rather do that alone."

"Why?" I laugh.

"Because he's not going to like what I say to him," he says.

"Stirring up trouble Mr Freeman, you should be ashamed of yourself," I tease.

Tristan smiles, then leans in and softly pecks my cheek. "Back in a moment," he whispers in my ear, just as he runs a cool soft finger delicately down my neck. Everything south of my navel clenches in delight. *Is the room spinning?*

"Don't tempt me," I growl. I really would pounce on him, not giving a damn what others think.

"Ok, I'm going!" He chuckles, and I watch in appreciation as my man strides across the room.

"He's a catch alright." A woman's voice says.

I spin around and see Sophia standing behind me. "Hello Sophia," I smile shyly at her.

"It's Coral isn't it?" She asks.

"Yes." I smile again and hold out my hand, she places her hand in mine, and we shake. I'm surprised as her handshake is firm for an older lady. I suddenly panic as realisation dawns. She could be the competition. *Shit! Should I be talking to her?*

"It's nice to be able to finally talk to you alone Coral, I've been watching you all evening," she says. I swallow hard – *Why would she be doing that?*

"Oh...ok," I say, trying not to frown.

"It's so refreshing to see a couple who actually like each other, as you and Tristan are clearly displaying." *What do I say to that?*

"Maybe it's because we are still new to one another," I joke.

"Oh no, I've been around a long time, you two seem complete with one another and genuinely happy."

I smile at her. "Yes, we are," I say feeling shy and taking a sip of water.

"It's very refreshing to see," she continues. "This is a cutthroat business. I've seen so many couples pass through here, only to be ripping each other's heads off with divorce proceedings a year later."

"Really?" I squeak.

She laughs at my surprised reaction. "Yes, unfortunately, but tell me Coral, how did you meet Tristan?" *Crap, how do I explain this one?*

"Have you heard of Garland & Associates in Brighton?"

"John and Joyce," she nods. "So sad, he was a lovely man," she muses.

"Yes, he was," I say, swallowing hard. *I miss you, John...*

"You knew him?" she questions.

"Joyce is my mother's best friend, so yes. John and Joyce were like an Aunt and Uncle to me."

"Oh, I see...I'm so sorry dear, I didn't mean to bring it up." I can see she means it.

"No please...it's ok, I don't mind talking about it. But in answer to your question, I used to work for Joyce, that's how I met Tristan. He took over the company."

"Ah yes he did, I remember hearing about that."

"Sophia..." A croaky male voice calls.

We both turn in unison and see Harry standing behind us. I feel Tristan approaching, so it doesn't make me jump when he slides his arm around my waist.

"Tristan, I was just saying to Coral how happy you both look," Sophia says.

Tristan gazes adoringly at me, making me feel shy. "She makes me very happy," he tells her.

"Yes, darling I can see that, and I'm so pleased for you. Well, it's late. Come, Harry, we should get you home." Sophia says.

I look at the clock on the wall, it's only 9pm. *Maybe he goes to bed early?*

"Nonsense," he argues. "I haven't seen this young whippersnapper in a long time," he says pointing to Tristan. "We need to catch up, and I need to get to know this beautiful young lady a little more too," he adds.

Sophia rolls her eyes at him. Tristan and I grin at one another. *This old guy is a scream!*

"Shall we?" Tristan gestures, he's waiting to see if I'm happy with this which I am, so I nod and place my hand in the crook of his arm.

"Oh no you don't," Harry says, holding his arm out to me.

Tristan laughs, takes my hand and places it on Harry's arm. "I'm watching you," he teases Harry.

"You need to," Harry jokes, and we head over to his table...

I AM STOOD at the bar waiting for Tristan to finish talking to an associate. I feel exhausted. After speaking to so many people this evening and dancing the night away with Tristan, and Harry, to Tristan and Sophia's amused expressions. I am definitely ready to leave. I actually feel quite proud of myself. I haven't freaked out or felt uncomfortable once, but that probably has something to do with Tristan's constant presence. I sigh blissfully and turn around to place my empty glass on the bar. I'm instantly aware of a man's body that's stood a little too closely for my liking. I glance up at him and almost faint.

No! Not you...this is not happening!

I feel paralysed with fear. My heart has jumped into my mouth, I can't breathe, and I can't look away either. His evil black eyes stare down at me as a sickening smile spreads across his face. I didn't think I would ever see those eyes again – Not in this lifetime.

"I remember you," he whispers. My whole body shudders as I hear his words. I want to scream at the top of my lungs, but I can't – not here. I squeeze my eyes shut for a moment, trying to block him out. *Tristan, please hurry back!*

He moves closer to me, I take a step to the side, trying to put some distance between us, but he discreetly grabs hold of my elbow stopping me. *No!* I'm instantly transported back in time – I'm five years old again – My heart is palpitating, my hands are sweating, and my legs are uncontrollably shaking, I feel like I'm going to pass out.

Tristan…where are you?

"Let go of me," I growl.

He laughs, an evil twisted laugh, my stomach twists and rolls in response. *Oh god! I think I'm going to be sick!* Bile rises in my throat. I swallow hard and try to stay focused.

I feel his hand touch the top of my shoulder. "You're still so shy," he whispers. "And your skin…still so soft," he adds, tracing his finger down my forearm.

"Don't touch me," I snap, pulling my arm out of his reach.

His smile widens. He takes a step to the side, so he's stood right in front of me. I take a step to the right, I need to get away from him, but he mimics my movement, effectively blocking me from running away from him.

"Come on Coral," he cajoles.

I snap my head up and glare at him – *He remembers my name?*

"Stay away from me." I threaten, tears pooling in my eyes.

He laughs again and takes a step to the side. "Vodka on the rocks." He snaps at the barman.

I want to run, but I feel like my feet are encased in cement. *Come on Coral, you can do this, get away from him!* My eyes frantically dart around the room, hoping and praying that I can catch Tristan's eye and he can save me and get me away from this evil, twisted man, but the fear quickly turns to anger. I can feel the adrenalin pumping through my veins, getting ready for fight or flight. I grit my teeth and try to control the rage building within me. I swear if I had a gun I would shoot this man, kill him dead, right here in front of all these people. I close my eyes and take a deep rasping breath…*Tristan, help me!*

In an attempt to get away from him, I take a step to the

side, then I shakily take a step forward, but my leg trembles, and I almost fall flat on my face.

He reaches out and takes hold of my elbow. "Leaving so soon?" He smirks.

"Let go of me." I yank my arm out of his hold. I try to take another step forward, but my legs feel like jelly – *Fuck! Come on legs, work!*

He starts laughing, evidently finding my suffering amusing. I look up and see Tristan in the corner of the room. I mentally beg him to look my way, and almost as though he can telepathically hear me, he turns his head, and our eyes meet. He smiles his enigmatic smile at me and winks. Then his face falls as he takes in my expression. He says something to the man he's talking to, then begins quickly striding over to me, locking eyes with me the whole time – *Thank god!*

"Who's that?" The evil bastard asks.

"My fiancé," I snap.

"Tristan Freeman is your fiancé?" He says, sounding surprised and I have to say a little worried.

"Yes." I snap, keeping my eyes fixed on Tristan – And he's going to fucking kill you when I tell him who you are – I turn and look up at him. "You're a dead man," I threaten.

He instantly loses the grin, and I can see the fear in his black eyes.

"Coral?" Tristan says as he reaches me. "You ok?" He cocks his head to the side, trying to read my expression. "Simon," Tristan says, nodding to the man. *So that's his name!*

"Tristan." Simon reaches his hand out, and they shake. I think I'm going to be sick. I need to get us both out of here now, but I seem to have lost the power of speech! *Fuck!* The room is spinning, my ears are ringing, and my stomach is doing summersaults.

"Tristan, it's been a while," he says. "Sorry to hear about your folks," he adds.

"Thanks." Tristan turns and frowns down at me.

"Heard you branched out," Simon says.

"Yes, down' – "Tristan" I interrupt, finally finding my voice. I do not want him to tell this fucker where we live. "Escort me to the ladies?" I whimper.

"Of course," he says. Holding his arm out for me, I wrap my hand around his strong forearm and grip tightly. Tristan places his other hand over mine and squeezes it once, then he starts to walk us forward, but my legs still aren't working properly, so I stumble slightly.

"Coral?" Tristan stops, wraps his arm around my waist to steady me, and guides us out of the great room. We silently head down the hallway until we reach the restrooms. "Baby, what's wrong?" He asks, gently stroking my cheek.

I take a deep breath in, trying to work out what to do. This function is important to Tristan, I know that on the one hand, I want to be here to support him, I don't want to let him down, but on the other hand, I want to run screaming from the building. I stare ahead, trying to think of the right thing to do – I could feign sickness?

Tristan can stay, I can go back to the hotel room and tell him when he gets back? But I know, deep down inside that I don't want to be alone, and if I tell him the truth like right now, he won't be able to help himself, I know he won't. He'll charge in there without thinking of the consequences and beat that fucker to a pulp, I know he will. And where will that get us? Tristan would be charged with GBH, and possibly have a prison sentence, he could lose everything he's built, his businesses, his homes.

No, I shake my head at myself– I can't tell him here, it will have to be later when we are back in Cornwall, and Tristan can't get near him. He'll have time to calm down, think about things logically. But then again, I think I need to be away from Tristan, he's going to know something's wrong, I know he will, and he can read me like a book. I swallow hard.

How do I tell him that the man he just shook hands with, is in fact, the man that sexually abused me all those years ago?

"Coral, come back to me baby," He says with wide, worried eyes.

"Tristan," I whisper. "I'm so sorry, but I think I need to go back to the hotel."

"Are you sick?" He asks, looking extremely worried.

"Not feeling a hundred percent," I murmur, my stomach twisting into knots.

"Do we need to head over to A&E?" He asks, a little frantically.

"No baby, I think I just need to lie down, I feel a little dizzy that's all. Lots of talking and dancing, it's kind of taken it out of me. It's nothing to worry about." I manager to say.

He pulls me to him and kisses my forehead. "Let's go back to the hotel," he says.

Forever With Him

"No, you stay. I know how important this is to you, I'm just sorry I can't stay," I argue.

"No Coral' – "Tristan, for once in your life will you just do as I ask. I want you to stay, I'll be fine, Stuart can take me back to the hotel," I plead. Tristan doesn't look convinced. "Please baby, stay. Harry and Sophia have been waiting to speak to you again. I can ask Stuart to stay in the room with me if that puts your mind at rest," I add.

Tristan sighs heavily as he rubs his hands up and down my arms. "No. I don't like leaving you," he says. "I'll make my excuses to Sophia and Harry."

"Tristan stay," I say again, trying my best to give him my warmest, most convincing smile.

"There are a few more associates I need to catch up with," he ponders aloud.

I reach up onto my tip-toes and plant a soft kiss on his cheek. "Take as long as you need baby, I'll wait up for you." I manage to smile again. "Oh, and if you like, invite Harry and Sophia to the wedding," I add.

"You wouldn't mind?" He asks.

"Of course not, they're a lovely couple," I say.

"Alright." He gazes down at me, strokes my cheek and then frowns deeply at me. "Are you being honest with me? You would tell me if there was something more?" He asks.

My stomach flips over, I don't want to lie to him, but I don't want him to see I'm hiding something either. "Tristan, let's not rehash that argument. I should have told you what was going on over the last few days, I know that. I'm just tired." I say, cringing inside because I'm lying to him again. But it's for his own good and mine. I don't want to spend the next ten years visiting my fiancé in prison.

"Sorry," he says. "I can't help worrying about you," he adds smiling down at me with his deep dimpled smile.

"Don't be, it's one of the many things I love about you," I say, softly stroking his cheek.

His enigmatic smile broadens, flashing his perfect teeth. "So you'll wait up for me?" He croaks in his ultra sexy voice.

"Yes," I whisper as seductively as I can and plant a soft kiss on the side of his neck, right at the spot that drives him wild. A deep, husky growl reverberates from deep within his throat. It has never failed to instantly turn me on. So I'm shocked, but not surprised when I feel no reaction. Right now, I just feel totally numb, head to toe – numb.

"Get back to the function baby, I'll call Stuart," I say.

"No." Tristan pulls his mobile out from his pocket and calls Stuart, when he's finished he slips his mobile back into his trouser pocket. "He'll be here in five," he adds and leans down to kiss me. As his lips softly meet mine, I hear his breath catch, I usually have the same reaction, but again, there's just nothing – Now I'm actually starting to freak out about us. *Are we ok? Am I ok?* I part my lips, giving his tongue access to my mouth, hoping it will stir some kind of reaction within me, but when his tongue touches mine, I feel myself tense up – I can't do this. *Shit! What if there is something wrong with me and I don't feel the way I used to feel?*

"Hey." Tristan stops kissing me, tilts my head back and gazes down at me with dark, worried eyes. "You must be feeling rough," he says. "Normally I kiss you, and you pounce on me like a wild woman," he jokingly adds, but I can tell it's a mask, hiding his fear.

"Tristan, I still feel the same about you, I just feel...." I close my eyes and try to think of something to placate him. "Woozy," I add.

Tristan frowns then places his hand on my forehead. "You do feel a little warm," he says.

"I'll be fine" I reiterate. He frowns and shakes his head slightly, then Tristan suddenly looks up over my head, I turn around and see Stuart waiting for us.

"Hey Stu," Tristan says. I smile weakly at him. Stuart nods to us both. He is the most reticent man I have ever met.

"Let's go," Tristan says wrapping his arm around my shoulders.

We walk outside into the cool night air, and over to the waiting Jag. Stuart opens the back door, and I slip inside the sumptuous leather seats. Kneeling down, Tristan leans into me and kisses me softly.

"I'll be as quick as I can. I can't stand being away from you for too long," he says kissing me again. "Did I tell you how beautiful you look tonight?" he adds, shattering my heart into a million pieces.

"Yes," I whisper. "Did I tell you how handsome *you* look tonight, and how safe and protected you make me feel?" Tristan smiles his shy, bashful smile at me; we silently gaze at one another for a moment, then he leans down once more, and softly kisses me.

"See you soon beautiful," he whispers in my ear, planting a soft, wet kiss under my earlobe.

"I'll miss you," I whisper back. Tristan takes my hand squeezes it once, then slowly stands. "Oh hey, Tristan don't..." I stop, I can't say it.

He leans down to me. "What baby?"

"I just...stay away from that guy, Simon," I say.

His eyes narrow. "Did he say something to you Coral?" He asks, his voice low, his whole body tensing up.

"No...I just have a funny feeling about him..." I drift off.

"Well, I've never done business with him, but I'll stay away from him, for you. Ok?" He says, smiling sweetly at me.

"Ok, I love you." I murmur.

"Love you too baby, see you soon." He holds up his hand as he slowly closes the door, I lift up my hand and wave back at him, smiling as broadly as I can, but Tristan doesn't smile back at me, he looks as though he's in pain, actual physical pain. *Tristan, what's wrong?*

As the car pulls out into traffic, I watch Tristan blow out a deep breath; his gazing following the car the whole time, until, eventually, I can no longer see him.

The enormity of the situation finally hits me. I start shaking from head to toe. I feel the tears bubble up to the surface and an angry scream building within me. I grip my hair with both hands, trying to hold onto my sanity.

Suddenly Stu pipes up, bringing me out of my stupor. "Coral?" He questions, his voice laced with worry. "Shall I turn around?" He asks.

"No!" I squeak. "Please Stu, just get me to the hotel as quickly as you can," I manage to choke out.

"Right." Stu slams his foot down and starts to race through traffic, and what seems like moments later we pull up outside the hotel.

"Stu, will you walk me up to the room?" I ask, he turns in his seat and frowns back at me. I can see what he's thinking – Going into the boss' girlfriends hotel room, just the two of us, but there's no way in hell anything like that would ever happen.

"Tristan did say to come up if you asked, it's just' – "Please Stu, I don't think I'll make it up there, and I don't want to be on my own. I just want you to stay in the suite until Tristan returns. I'll be in the bedroom anyway, please..." I plead.

"If it makes you feel...more secure," he says, frowning deeply.

"It will," I tremble.

"Alright." Stu drives forward and finds a parking bay. He exits the car and opens my door for me. Offering his hand out, I gladly take it and stumble as I get to my feet, Stuart quickly catches me, I can tell he feels uncomfortable touching me like he's feeling up his boss's wife.

"Stu, nothing untoward is happening here, I give you my word. I don't want to make you feel uncomfortable, but I'm feeling quite faint. Can I take your arm?" I ask.

Stu looks a little taken aback at first then he smiles a little awkwardly at me. "By all means," he says, offering me his arm.

"Thanks." I grip his arm tightly, and we walk in into the hotel.

In no time at all, we have taken the lift to the top floor, and Stuart is gently guiding me into the sumptuous suite. Reaching the main room, I slowly sink into sofa next to the fire and stare blankly at it.

"Can I get you anything?" Stuart asks.

"A Brandy?" I whisper.

"Coming right up." I hear Stuart clonking around at the bar, moments later he's handing me a glass.

"Thanks, Stuart," I say and neck the whole thing back. I know I shouldn't, but I need the instant hit.

"Did you want another?" He asks, frowning down at me.

"No, no thanks," I say. "I'm going to bed now, but you'll stay in here?" I ask.

Stuart shuffles from one foot to the other. "If it makes you feel more comfortable."

"It will. Thank you, Stuart." I get to my feet and slowly make my way into the bedroom.

Shutting the door behind me, I stare numbly around the room. I feel the tears building, but I can't cry. Tristan will know something is wrong and I don't want to tell him until we're out of London and away from that fucker.

I feel cold, so cold. I throw my clutch onto the bed and wrap my arms around myself, trying to generate some heat. I need a shower. I feel so dirty and disgusting. Stripping my dress off me as carefully as I can so I don't rip my stitches open, I rid myself of the rest of my clothing and head into the en-suite.

THE FOLLOWING MORNING we arrive back at the villa in Cornwall. Tristan picks up our bags from the boot, and I slowly follow him up the stairs, he unlocks the front door and gestures for me to go first. I have been trying since Tristan came back last night to act normal, but I'm not sure if I'm very convincing. I walk into the villa and just stand there, gazing out at the view. The sky is a perfect blue, the sun is shining, making everything seem brighter and more beautiful. How anyone can have a problem on a day like this is beyond me – Except I do, and I know that today, I'm going to have to face it.

"Alright," Tristan says, sighing heavily. I turn to see he has shut the door, placed our bags down and is stood a few feet away from me with his arms crossed. "I know something's bothering you. Ever since I got back last night, you've hardly spoken a word. Have I done something wrong?" I shake my head at him. "Then what is it Coral?"

It's taken such a humungous effort on my part to keep this to myself. Having to wait until we are far enough away from the fucker so Tristan can't do anything stupid – like kill him, has really taken its toll on me. My legs start shaking, actually physically shaking, making my knees knock together, I look down at them willing them to stop but the rest of my body soon joins in, and I'm literally shaking from head to toe.

"Tristan," I whimper and burst into uncontrollable, hoarse sounding sobs. He's straight over to me, wrapping his arms around me, squeezing me tight and making me feel safe.

"Christ Coral, what's wrong?" He asks, holding me tight, trying to stop me from shaking out of his hold. He holds me for the longest time, letting me cry it out. When I stop shaking so much, and I feel calm enough to tell him, I get a flash image of what he used to do to me as a child. *No!*

Then I feel it, the swish of saliva before you're sick. "Gonna be sick!" I shout.

Tristan releases me, I run down the hallway, into the bedroom, fling the en-suite door open and manage to reach the toilet in time – and it hurts, it hurts so much. The heaving is making my right lung really burn, and my shoulder is painfully throbbing. I feel Tristan kneel down next to me, and take as much of my hair out of the firing line as he can, his other hand is softly stroking my back. When the dry heaving stops, I flush the toilet, and Tristan helps me to my feet.

"Need to clean my teeth," I manage to croak.

"Coral, do we need to go back to A&E? – Tell me?" I look up at our reflections, Tristan looks worried and out of his depth.

"This isn't about that Tristan. Something happened last night, but I couldn't tell you until we were back here," I croak.

"Why?" He asks, looking quite perplexed now.

"Trust me," I say, staring at his reflection. "Please Tristan, just trust me on this. I'm going to clean my teeth and then I'm going to come and find you in the living room. But I'm going to need a Brandy for this, and so will you." I say.

"Coral' – "Tristan, I'm begging you. Trust me." I stare back at him, my eyes pleading with his. He nods once, leans forward, kisses the back of my hair and then walks out of the bathroom. Taking a deep rasping breath, I start cleaning my teeth. When I'm done, I find my Gaviscon and take two big mouthfuls of it, and then I take another deep breath, square my shoulders and head out the bathroom.

TRISTAN IS SAT on the sofa with a glass of Brandy in each hand. I silently take a seat next to him. He glances across at me and hands me a glass. I take a tentative sip, then I glug the whole thing back. *Ouch!* It burns as it goes down, then seconds later I feel it flood through my body, warming up a cold I can't seem to shake off. I see my hand is shaking as I place the glass down on the coffee table, so I clench my hands into fists trying to hide it.

"Coral, what's wrong baby?" Tristan asks, his voice soft.

"Please promise me something," I plead, my voice trembling.

"Anything," he breathes.

I reach out with my free hand and entwine our fingers together. "I promised you the other day that I would talk to you, tell you if something was wrong, or bothering me, and you said that we would work things out together?" Tristan nods once. "Ok, I'm about to tell you something that you're not going to like. So please, promise me that you won't go off at the deep end. That you'll keep your head and think logically about this?"

"I'll try," he softly says, lifting my chin, so I have to look at him. "Tell me," he adds in his authoritative voice.

I swallow hard and begin. "Last night...that guy...Simon' –
"I knew he'd upset you!" He barks.

"Tristan!" I scold then the tears start again, making my vision blurry, spilling down my cheeks. "I really need you to be calm Tristan...please..." I sniff, trying to fight the tears, but I choke out another hoarse sounding sob.

"Christ..." He puts his Brandy down and pulls me into his arms.

I curl up on his lap. I feel safer like that.

"I'm sorry Coral...I'm sorry," he says, gently rubbing his hand up and down my back, soothing me. I listen to the sound of his heart gently beating; we stay like that for a while with Tristan gently rocking me.

"Coral, I promise you. I won't say another word," he suddenly pipes up. Somehow, I doubt that. But I need to tell him – I have to get it out.

I take a deep, steadying breath. "He's the one Tristan."

"The one who what baby?" He asks, his voice deep, low, icy.

"Who abused me when I was..," I stop, I can't say any more.

Tristan's body has frozen beneath me. His hand has stopped in the middle of my back. His heart has gone into overdrive, and his breathing has stopped. The silent tears continue to fall, one after the other down my cheeks. I wrap my arms around his neck and bury my head under his chin, I feel like a child again, a frightened child. I grip him even tighter as the tears continue to flow. A part of me doesn't want to see his reaction, I'm afraid of what he might do. Not to me, to Simon, and then I think that I probably should have had Stuart come with us, so he could physically try to stop Tristan if he decided to drive up to London and confront Simon. Then I think no, I don't want him involved, not in this. I decide my best plan of action is to do nothing and just wait until Tristan's ready to ask any questions.

I still can't believe I've met my abuser again, another shudder runs through my body. What are the chances of him turning up like that? It's almost as though Tristan is the key, and that he has been all along.

Finally, he speaks. "Are you sure?" His voice is lower, colder than I have ever heard before.

"Yes," I answer firmly. "I'll never forget those eyes... even though I've tried..so hard to forget." I squeeze my eyes shut.

His arms squeeze tighter around me, almost too tight. "One hundred percent positive?" He asks, kissing the top of my head.

"Yes. And he knew too. The fucker teased me about it, Tristan, that's what he was doing last night ..." I break off, I can't continue.

Tristan gasps then growls. "He teased you? How did he tease you Coral? What did he say?" He sneers. He's fuming and trying to hold it in.

I take a deep breath. "That he remembered me, then he touched me' – Tristan stiffens again – 'twice, and...he said...my skin was," I stop again, I feel sick. I take another deep breath. "That my skin was still soft, he knew my name, Tristan!" I sit up and look at him. "He didn't think he was such a big man when he saw you walking towards me though. When he asked if I knew you, I told him you were my fiancé, he seemed worried' – "He should be," Tristan growls interrupting me. It sends a shiver down my spine.

"I threatened him," I sniff.

"You did?" Tristan says, surprised.

"Yeah...I...I told him he's a dead man." I shake my head. "That was a stupid thing to have done. I shouldn't have, I know that now. But I was so' – Tristan's lips find mine, gently silencing me with a sweet, soft, chaste kiss.

"Whatever you do," he chokes out. "Do not apologise for what you said to him Coral."

I swallow hard. "I'm scared, Tristan."

"Hey." He reaches up and places his hands on my cheeks. "I will never let anything happen to you," he says, his voice firm, his eyes searching mine.

"It's not me I'm worried about," I squeak.

"Then what are you worried about?" He asks, searching my face.

"You! I'm worried you'll do something to him...that's why I didn't tell you yesterday. I don't fancy visiting you in prison," I choke out. He briefly closes his eyes, and he takes a very deep breath, then releasing his hands from my cheeks, Tristan picks up his glass and knocks back his Brandy. He stares ahead, clenches his jaw several times and then slowly shakes his head.

"No wonder the fucker disappeared when I walked back in. I thought it was odd," he says.

"Do you know who he works for? Maybe we can tell his employer?" I say.

"He runs his own company Coral." He says, his eyes narrowed as he stares straight ahead, his mind elsewhere.

"Do you know the name of the company?" I ask.

"What are you thinking Coral?"

I shrug. "I don't know, I just..." I drift off.

"I thought you didn't want retribution," he states.

"I wasn't thinking that," I say.

"Then what were you thinking?" Tristan asks, still staring ahead, contemplating.

I shrug again. I'm not sure what I'm thinking or saying. I have no idea what to do now. I never thought I would ever see him again, and now I have...I shake my head and grit my teeth. "You understand why I had to leave last night, don't you?" I squeak out.

"Of course I do, but I'm mad at myself. My gut instinct

was telling me there was something wrong, but..." Tristan drifts off for a moment. "You were right baby," he finally turns and looks at me. "If you'd have told me last night, I'd have killed the fucker." With that, he gets to his feet, picks up his mobile and heads for the door. "You haven't eaten today, so I'm going to get us some breakfast." He yanks the door open, and without looking back at me he storms through the door, slamming it shut behind him.

I sigh inwardly. I don't think he's gone to get food at all, I think he's gone so he can calm down, which is fair enough, I can understand that. I shiver again and wrap my arms around myself. I feel so tired, exhausted now I've got it out. I wander off to the bedroom, climb under the quilt, pull it over my head, and curl up into a ball.

CHAPTER TWENTY-TWO

I HAVE DRESSED IN MY warm sweats and hoody, hoping they would warm me up, but I still feel cold. I look up at the clock on the wall, it's twelve noon, I must have drifted off for a while. I'm amazed I didn't have any nightmares, but then again, I didn't sleep a wink last night. I even pretended to be asleep when Tristan got back so he couldn't see my eyes, it seems they give me away too easily. I look out at the view, there are so many people out on the beach, but I don't feel like going outside today, I just want to hide away and forget the world. I hate that the fucker has made me feel like this.

As I walk into the living room I'm startled by a presence in the room, I immediately realise its Tristan and relax. It's strange I didn't hear him come back though. He's sat on the sofa with his laptop on his thighs, his legs stretched out in front of him, his feet resting on the coffee table. He looks up at me, his big brown eyes are wide and worried. "Hey, baby." He reaches his hand out to me.

I take his hand and sink down onto the sofa next to him. "Why are you looking at me like that?" I ask.

Tristan sighs. "Because I shouldn't have left you last night at the function, and I shouldn't have walked out on you today' – I silence him with my finger. "Stop it. You did what you needed to do Tristan. I'm not upset you went out today, so don't *you* be. I was fine, I slept for a while, and then I did some thinking." I tell him firmly.

He reaches up and cups my cheek with his hand. He looks like he could cry. "What were you thinking baby?" he softly asks.

"That I am not having my first ever holiday ruined because of that fucker!" I spit.

Tristan smiles, but it doesn't reach his eyes. "You want us to forget it?" He says.

"I think so," I say.

Tristan moves his laptop to the side and pats his legs. I climb up, so I'm sitting sideways on his lap. "Are you sure?" He questions, squeezing me tight.

"Positive," I say. Tristan glances down at his laptop and bends forward to close the lid. "Whoa! Wait!" I shout. "You know something?" I ask.

"No, I was just looking at his company website." He says, frowning at me, but I can tell he's hiding something.

"Let me see," I say, intrigued all of a sudden and pull the laptop onto my legs.

"Conundrum!" Tristan mutters, and I know he means me.

I reach forward and lift the screen back up. At the top of the page, it says Smith, Miller & Associates. I click on the button that says 'Meet Our Team' I see his face, the fucker, Simon Smith, CEO – *Ugh!* Part of me wants to slam the laptop shut, but I'm still intrigued to know more, so I continue to scroll. There are lots of faces coming up with snazzy job titles, but nothing comes up that's of any interest to me, so I stop scrolling. I'm about to push the laptop away when I notice there are two more tabs open at the top of the screen. I move the cursor over to the first one and hover over it.

"What's this?" I ask.

"Coral, baby...I just," Tristan sighs heavily and runs his hand through his hair. "You were sleeping so I thought I'd do a little research and see if I can find anything out," he says, he looks worried. "I really don't want you seeing this," he adds.

"What is it?" I ask.

"Information on his family and his businesses," He says frowning at me.

I look back at the screen. "He has a family?" I squeak.

"It would seem so," Tristan says.

I stare back at the tab. What kind of sicko does that to kids and yet, he has a family?

"Coral, can we just leave this for now?" Tristan asks.

I argue with myself for a moment. Do I really want to know, or do I want to forget it? Curiosity gets the better of me.

"Coral please don't!" Tristan shouts - *Too late!*

Tristan has found an old newspaper report. At the top of the screen, it says The Guardian, March 14th 1992. I scroll a little more. My hand freezes when I see the face of a woman, a redhead that I recognise.

"His wife?" I whisper.

Tristan nods once.

I look back at the screen and begin reading the report...

'Following the suspicious disappearance of Mrs Erica Smith in the Cote d'Azure, Scotland Yard have arrested her husband, Mr Simon Smith. He has been charged with her homicide and will remain in custody until bail is set. Mr Smith has repeatedly denied any charges and has ample alibis for the night of her disappearance. Holidaying with friends on their luxury motor yacht in the south of France, Mrs Smith had, according to Mr Smith, stayed on board whilst the remaining party dined in St Tropez. When they returned, Mrs Smith had disappeared. Police were called to the scene, and within hours blood and hair samples were taken from the rear of the yacht. Police divers were called to the scene, yet no body was recovered. It has been reported that Mrs Smith was filing for divorce from Mr Smith and had been in talks with the journalist, Brian Evans. Mr Evans has mysteriously disappeared. Mr Evans colleagues have been called in by Scotland Yard to give testimony, following rumours that Mrs Smith was about to blow the whistle on her husband's corrupt businesses. According to reports, she admitted that her husband had several off-shore accounts and was guilty of fraud and embezzlement. She claimed that 'Smith's & Millers Solicitors' was being used as a front for his apparent dealings with the drugs and human trafficking black market, and most disturbingly, child pornography. However, with no substantial evidence linking Mr Smith to the crime, the judge ruled for a dismissal, and all charges were dropped.'

I feel sick. He's a fucking psycho, a psycho that I threatened. *Fuck!* My heart starts manically beating against my chest. "He bumped her off!" I manage to squeak.

"Baby' – "I threatened him, Tristan, I threatened him!" I shout out. What if he comes after us? What if he hurts Tristan? *Oh God! Oh no...*

"Hey, stop it," Tristan says, taking hold of my shoulders and softly shaking me. "There's no need to be afraid. Nothing is going to happen to us," he tells me firmly.

"But' – "Coral, don't worry, please." I squeeze my eyes shut. Tristan takes my face in his hands. "Look at me, baby." I open my eyes and see that his eyes have a cool, steely determination.

He doesn't seem worried at all. "This was a long time ago Coral. For all we know, he's squeaky clean now." *I very much doubt that!*

I blink rapidly at him, trying my best not to freak out. "But what if he took my threat seriously…If he…if he hurt you," I break off and take a deep breath. "Promise me, Tristan, promise me you won't do anything about this, I don't care what he did to me…I don't care!" I shout out. The thought of losing Tristan overtakes me, and it's like the steel hand is there again, gripping my heart.

"Hey." Tristan pulls me against his chest, holding me tight, rocking me gently. "You always think the worst Coral, everything is going to be fine. I promise you."

"You don't think he'll do anything?" I question.

"No. As far as I know, he's a legitimate businessman. I'm sure he's more worried about you spilling the beans than you should be about what you said to him."

"You really think that?" I ask, looking up at him.

"Yes. I'm positive." He says, soothing me.

I stare back at him, I see only truth. "Ok," I sniff. "What's on the other tab?" I ask this time, I don't need another shock like that.

"Just random family photos," Tristan says.

I look down at the screen again, for some unknown reason I'm intrigued again. Maybe it's because I can't understand how a man that did that sort of thing to kids would have a family of his own. I pick up the laptop and start scrolling again. There's a photo of him, and then underneath that there's another photo in which he has his arm around a small boy, he looks afraid and so unhappy. I read the information on the photo. 'Dillon Smith with his father, Simon'. I stare at the boy again, and I suddenly realise why I recognise him. I swallow hard. It can't be true – can it? Bile rises in my throat. I start shaking my head in disbelief.

"What?" Tristan stiffens beneath me.

"Him," I whisper, shakily pointing at the boy.

"What about him?" Tristan softly pushes.

"He…" I turn and stare wide-eyed at Tristan. "He's the boy," I add, my voice barely audible.

"What boy baby?" He asks, his voice still soft.

"The boy that…." I shake my head. "I was made to…" I frown down at the screen – He made his own son do it? What a sick bastard!

"Baby, you're worrying me, take a deep breath and tell me," he says.

As I continue to stare wide-eyed at the boy, I do exactly that, breathing in and out several times. *Ugh!* I feel sick again. Then all of a sudden a strange calm washes over me. Dillon looks so sad in the photo and a little older than how I remember him. But I do remember how scared he was – terrified actually. I can't believe his own father made him do this. I shake my head, poor kid. I take another deep breath and turn to Tristan.

"Tristan, this is the boy I was made to have sex with." Tristan stares back at me for a moment and then looks down at the photo of the scruffy, dark-haired boy with the sad look in his eyes.

"You're sure?" He whispers.

"Yes, I would never forget his face." Just like I've never forget his father's face – *Ugh!*

"So the boy you were made to…it's his son?" He says incredulously.

I silently nod and look back at Dillon. He looks ill, he has dark rings under his eyes, and he's pale and skinny.

"But…that…?" Tristan seems as shocked as I am. "His own son?" He gasps, slowly shaking his head.

I start scrolling again. There are several more photos of Dillon, and he's not smiling in any of them. "Do you think we can find him?" I ask.

"Do you want to?" He gasps.

"Yes, I think I do."

"Why?" He breathes.

"I don't know," I whisper. I stare back at all the photos of him. I stop when I see one that reminds me of a photo Gladys once took. I was six or seven, standing up like Dillon is. I remember she wanted a photo of me with John and Joyce. They both came and knelt behind me, John had reached up and put his arm around my shoulder, in the photograph I am grimacing, my eyes wide with fear – I hated the fact that he was touching me.

In this photo, Dillon has a man crouched down behind him too, he has his hands on Dillon's hips. Dillon's jaw is clenched, and his hands are balled up into fists, his eyes wide with fear. *Why do I get the feeling that he doesn't like to be touched? Just like me?*

"Baby, I don't think that's a good idea," Tristan says.

I sigh inwardly, probably not. "He doesn't look very happy, does he?" I whimper.

"No baby, he doesn't," Tristan replies.

"Poor Dillon," I shake my head. "God knows how long it went on for him." I shudder and look away from the screen for a moment, but I can't seem to stop. I want to see more of the boy that went through the same horror like me, so I continue scrolling. Then I change my mind, it's just more photos of Dillon and his sicko father. Just as I'm about to stop, I see half a photo at the bottom of the screen. Two boys this time, one is Dillon. I cock my head to the side, there's something familiar, something about the shape of the other boy's forehead. I read the line above the photo – Dillon Smith with his big brother Kane.

I scroll down and see that the boy Kane is stood next to Dillon, his arm around him. Dillon is grimacing again, his brother Kane is smiling widely at the camera, a defiant glint in his eye. I drift off, remembering something from my past. He was there when it was all happening. I mean several kids were brought along, but I remember, Kane was always there, in the background. I remember the strange look in his eyes like he was enjoying it. But my instinct is telling me there's more to this, more to the boy with the crazy look in his eyes, but what exactly.

"Coral, I really think you should stop this now," Tristan says.

I shake my head at him. I'm mesmerised by what I'm seeing. "His brother, I remember, he...he was always there...in the background..." I whisper.

Tristan groans as though he's in pain.

As I continue to scan the photos, I suddenly freeze. I can only see the man's hair and his forehead, but I recognise that forehead, the style of his hair. I shake my head slightly. *It can't be, surely?* That would just be too freaky to be a coincidence.

"What?" Tristan asks, but I don't answer him. "Coral, what is it baby, what have you seen?"

I shakily press the button so the screen scrolls down, my heart is in my mouth, my ears are ringing, and I can feel the blood pumping through my veins. And there he is, Kane Smith, the man who raped me is staring back at me. Almost black hair, bright blue eyes, chiselled features. He's smiling in the photograph, but I can see the evil behind those eyes, the malicious intent – just like his father. A rush of adrenaline floods my system. He told me his name was Sam. I don't believe this! I start shaking my head in denial. This is some kind of sick fucking joke!

"Coral, what's wrong?" Tristan says, shaking me gently, trying to pull me out of it.

I close my eyes for a moment, my hands gripping into fists. *No, no, no...This can't be happening!* I open my eyes and with careful, controlled movements, I put the laptop to the side, get to my feet and start pacing, my hands gripping my hair, my breath coming in sharp gusts. *This is...unbelievable!* I'm sexually abused by a man as a child and then when I'm all grown up his adult son rapes me?

I want to scream!

"Coral?" Tristan softly says. "Please tell me what's going on." His voice is strained, I can tell he's hurting, and I don't want to cause him any further pain, he's been through enough.

I take several deep calming breaths, and when I feel ready, I open my eyes, climb onto his lap and wrap my arms tightly around his neck. "You promise?" I whisper, inches from his face, my eyes pleading with his.

"Yes. I promise." Tristan says, slightly bemused.

Keeping my eyes firmly locked on his I say the words. "He's the guy that raped me."

Tristan instantly stiffens beneath me, it's like every muscle in his body has reacted. It feels like I'm sitting on hard rock, not a human body. His eyes instantly turn dark. His cheeks have flushed, and his breathing has kicked up, his jaw is tensing too, but he keeps his eyes locked on mine. We stay like that for a while, just staring at one another. I'm glad Tristan hasn't freaked out. It wouldn't do either of us any good if he did.

He swallows hard, then reaches up and tenderly places his hand on my cheek. "You're sure?" he says, his voice wavering.

"Tristan, I would never forget his face." I whimper, then I realise something, something I hadn't pieced together before. I gasp again. "He did know me! The fucker knew me when he raped me, he recognised me – He knew!" I screech – I feel outraged.

I get up from Tristan's lap and start pacing again. I grip my hair in my fists while I try to work it out. He must have seen me, recognised me, and decided to pursue me, knowing all along what he was going to do. Something is recalled from deep within my psyche, something I thought I heard him say when I was half-conscious and he was raping me...*I always wondered what it would be like with you...*

I fall to the floor, my knees giving way on me. Then I feel it, the rage flooding my veins, I bring my fists up and slam them down onto the floor, over and over again in anger. Tristan is instantly over to me, he crouches behind me, takes hold of my arms and pulls them against my chest.

"Stop it Coral, stop!" He wraps his arms around me, squeezing me tight.

I suddenly remember the dream of my mother, the one where she said he knows you, and I cry out again. "My mom was right Tristan," I croak. "I remembered something he said to me when he was raping me, he said, '*I always wondered what it would be like with you*' He knew Tristan, he knew!" I scream out in rage.

"Jesus..." Tristan breathes, squeezing me tighter.

I feel angry, sick and violated all over again – *Mother Fucker!*

The anger quickly turns to tears. The floodgates open and I cry angry, wretched tears, howling out loud as the realisation keeps hitting me over and over again. I don't think I'm going to be able to stop. Tristan doesn't move an inch, he just stays on the floor with me, his arms tightly wrapped around me. It takes a while for me to calm down, but once the crying has ceased, Tristan helps me to my feet so I can take another bathroom break.

When I'm done, I head back into the living room. Tristan is stood up, waiting for my return, I'm trying not to, but I feel angry again, and vulnerable and stupid and most of all, ashamed. *How could I have not seen it?*

Tristan has poured us both another Brandy. He takes my hand and sits me down on the sofa. "Here baby, drink this." He says, handing me a glass.

"I shouldn't," I say.

"Baby, one more isn't going to mess with your painkillers, besides I think you need it. Take it, baby, drink it." I take the glass from Tristan and take a sip. Tristan gestures for me to sit on his lap again, so I clumsily climb onto him. "How are you feeling baby?" He softly asks.

"Angry and stupid, and ashamed," I spit. "I can't believe..." I break off and shake my head.

"That you knew him?" He questions.

I look up at him and nod. Tristan tenses his jaw several times. I can see it in his eyes, he wants to kill him, to kill both of them – I'm instantly worried.

"Tristan, promise me you won't do anything stupid, if it got back to you, linked to you..." I take a deep breath. "If anything happened to you..." I trail off not wanting to think about it. Tristan takes a deep breath and slowly blows it out. He still hasn't looked at his laptop. I think he's trying very hard not to lose it like if he does look at the screen, at Kane's photo, he'll punch it to the floor in anger.

"Promise me," I prompt.

"I won't do anything, I promise." He states, his voice firm, sharp.

I smile tentatively at him. "Ok." I take another sip at the same time as Tristan, for some reason it makes me smile.

"I'm glad you told me what happened last night. I'm glad you didn't keep this to yourself or try to handle it on your own," he says, but he's miles away, I can tell.

"I did contemplate not telling you. I was going to get another P.I report." Tristan stiffens once more beneath me. "But then I thought no, you'll handle it. Like you are now, I should give you more credit." I croak.

"I don't feel like I'm handling it," he says through gritted teeth. "Inside I'm screaming!"

I wrap my free arm around his neck and bury my head under his chin, he starts stroking my back, making me feel safe and warm.

We sit silently for a while, both sipping our Brandy's, deep in thought...

"What do you want to do Coral?" I look up at Tristan and see he's glaring at Kane's photograph, his eyes wild with hate and fury.

"I don't know," I say, frowning deeply. "Well as in so much as I don't know what to do about it, now that I know who they are. I don't want to go to court, but I don't want them to get away with it either." I swallow hard. Why do I want retribution? I've never wanted that, but I guess that was before I knew who either of them was. I guess knowing changes things.

"Maybe that's what we should do?" I emphasise the *'we'*. "You know, have him investigated? They might find some incriminating evidence that Kane's done this before, which I'm sure he has, and as for his father...." I suggest.

Tristan is still glaring at Kane but nods once in agreement. We've got to get the fucker back, somehow. He can't get away with this! *Ugh!* The sheer audacity of Simon last night, and then Kane...raping me because he just wondering what it would be like? Sick fucks!

Ugh! I hope they both rot in hell when they die! I gulp back the last of my Brandy and place the glass on the coffee table, I feel drained now.

Forever With Him

"You look tired," Tristan says, spookily reading me again. He glances at me and then locks eyes with Kane, but his look has changed, the pure rage has gone, something else has replaced it, but I don't know what. Is it revenge?

I lean forward and slam the laptop shut. "No need to look at his ugly mug anymore," I croak.

Tristan sighs, as though it's in relief. "Baby, do you want me to come and lie down with you?"

"I need you more than sleep Tristan." I take a deep breath. "I need you to comfort me. I don't want to be on my own," I say, my voice trembling again.

"Oh, baby!" He pulls me closer to his body, squeezing me tight. "Has it bought it all back?" He questions darkly.

"Yes..." I grip him closer to me. "Make it go away, wash it all away for me Tristan," I whimper.

"I will baby, I will." Tristan kisses the top of my head several times. "What do you want, a shower or a bath?"

I shiver again. "A bath I think," I say.

Tristan kisses the top of my head once more. "Do you feel like eating anything yet?" He asks. I still feel nauseous, so I shake my head at him. "Ok." Tristan drains the Brandy out of his glass. "I'll go and get the bath ready." *I do not want to be on my own!*

"I'm coming with you," I say jumping off his lap, but I haven't had this much to drink in a while, not on an empty stomach, so I sway slightly. "Whoa!" It makes me giggle.

Tristan catches me by the elbows. "Drunken bum," He teases.

"Oh ha ha ha!" I titter.

Tristan turns his back to me and crouches down. "Wanna hitch a ride?" He asks. He's trying to be playful, to lighten the moment, and I so love him for it.

"Yes," I chuckle and climb onto his back.

He slowly stands as I wrap my legs around his waist, and hug his mighty fine shoulders and chest with my arms. I kiss his neck over and over as he walks us steadily into the en-suite. Reaching the built-in sinks, he sits me down, then turns and gently pecks me on the lips. Then he takes my face in his hands, gently strokes my hair out of my face and kisses me, hard.

"You're so brave Coral." I smile up at him, blinking back more tears.

With another kiss on my forehead, Tristan swiftly turns around, and I watch him turn on the taps, get the water to the right temperature, and then add some bath bubbles. *Smells like cinnamon!*

"Tristan, I don't feel like going out today. Will you stay in with me?" I whisper.

"Of course I'll stay in with you," he snorts. "What did you think I was going to do, swan off to the beach as though nothing's happened?" He says, shaking his head at me.

I roll my eyes at him. "You know what I meant," I retort dryly.

He walks back over to me and places his hands either side of my face. "Why don't we have one of your chill out days? We can get back out on the beach tomorrow, that's if you feel like it?" He says and gives me a soft, chaste kiss.

"Ok," I say, feeling lighter.

Tristan freezes, he looks like he's just had a light bulb moment. "I bought the Phil Collins DVD with me. We could watch that if you like?" He says, beaming brightly at me.

"Good idea," I say.

"We could draw the blinds, curl up in bed, and watch it on my laptop," he adds, his cheeks flushing red.

"That's twice you've mentioned that," I say. "Does it have some kind of significance for you?" I question.

His brow furrows, then he smiles shyly at me and shrugs. "I've never done that before," he murmurs, then swiftly turns away from me and switches off the taps. "Bath's ready," he quietly says, but he doesn't turn around to look at me, which I find strange.

I scoot down off the sinks and reaching him, I try to turn him around so I can see his face, but he won't budge, he doesn't want to look at me – Why? I reach my hand around, so it's resting on his cheek, and try to coax him to look at me. He finally relents and turns to gaze down at me, his cheeks are still blushed, his eyes dark, and he looks like he's hurting.

I crane my neck back and look up at him. He's so tall when I have nothing on my feet. "What's wrong Tristan? Please tell me…" I say, stroking his cheek.

He sighs heavily. "Coral, I…" He stops and runs his hand through his hair. "Olivia had…it doesn't matter," he sighs. His broody look is back.

"Ok," I say, pretending like I'm letting this go, but I'm not. "Help me get my hoody off?" I lightly ask.

Tristan helps me undress. When I'm naked, I pin my hair up then Tristan helps me into the bath. I scoot into the middle and curl my arms around my legs. I watch him silently undress, wondering how I'm going to approach this. Then I think maybe I shouldn't. Maybe I should just wait and see if Tristan says something.

"Front or back?" He asks before he climbs in.

"Back please, if that's ok?" I ask, looking up at him – He's still brooding.

I lift up my left hand, it's my good shoulder, and offer it to him. Tristan gently places his hand on mine. I feel no pressure on my hand as he nimbly steps into the water. Releasing me, he slowly sinks down behind me with his legs either side of mine and gently pulls me back, so I'm resting against his chest.

He silently picks up one of our new Sea Sponges. It's mustard yellow, delicately soft, but looks like fungus spores to me. Tristan thought it was hilarious when I said that aloud in the shop. But I have to admit, it is a great sponge, it feels really, really nice. Tristan dunks it in the water, then slowly massages it across my shoulders, down my arms, across my breasts and my stomach. And I suddenly realise, he's washing me clean, like he said he would – *God I love this man.*

I close my eyes and savour the moment. After everything that happened last night and today, it feels absolutely wonderful, like Tristan actually *is* washing it all away. With each stroke, I feel cleaner, less angry, and more myself. I take a deep cleansing breath and slowly blow it out. I am melting like chocolate, my troubles drifting away.

"Olivia had very singular tastes," he says, pulling me out of my relaxing moment. I feel him kiss my temple and then he continues washing me.

"I don't understand?" I whisper, not really sure if I should push, or if I actually want to know.

Tristan sighs again. I think this is painful for him to say. "As far as she was concerned' – he kisses my temple again – 'beds were for fucking and sleeping in."

My eyes are wide open now, and I feel very alert.

"But you said you'd had breakfast in bed' – "Not with her Coral, a couple of other women I dated. It only happened a few times." I swallow hard. I'm not sure if I want to hear this. It seems very odd to me that you can live with someone, yet never do anything sweet like that together. I mean, Justin was no angel, but we did that plenty of times. In fact, most Sundays were spent nursing our hangovers, eating junk food and watching our favourite films in bed.

"So,...so you never...I mean, she never wanted to do nice things like that?" I tentatively ask.

"Nice wasn't in Olivia's vocabulary," he says, kissing my hair this time.

I try to work it out. Edith hated her, that's obvious. And Tristan's made it very clear to me that he was wrapped up in her web, blinded by her, walking around with rose coloured spectacles on – god knows I'm guilty of that, I thought Justin walked on water when I met him. Yet, he's said that she was cold and that she never did anything nice for him, not cook him something, or spontaneously buy him something, or just treat him well, and now this. I don't understand how he could have been with such a cold stone, heartless bitch when he's so sweet and gentlemanly and charismatic and – "What are you thinking Coral?" He sounds worried.

"I'm just trying to get my head around it, Tristan," I mumble.

"Get your head around what?" He softly says, still washing me and planting a soft kiss on my cheek.

"Why you were with her," I whisper. "She sounds' – *Shut up Coral!*

"Go on baby, speak your mind," he pushes.

"No, I don't want to," I murmur.

"Why?" He asks, kissing my cheek again.

"Because it's disrespectful, I didn't know you back then, and I don't know Olivia, so who am I to judge?" I say.

"Good point, but I'd still like to know what you think," he says, adding another kiss to my cheek, and moves the sponge to my legs, gently washing my troubles away.

"I just...I guess I just don't see what you would have had in common. Like, well, did you ever do this? Take a bath together? Or take a walk, or watch a movie together?" I ask.

"No," he scoffs. "Definitely not."

"But, didn't you want to?" I ask, completely confounded by this conversation.

"It never crossed my mind." He says. "Did you?" He asks.

"I never showered or bathed with Justin, no. But we had lazy days in bed," I say.

"What's it like?" He asks his voice soft and croaky by my ear.

"Nice Tristan, it's really nice." I frown down at the water. All I'm doing is getting frustrated, and I just want to relax.

"Hey, what's wrong?" He says, his hand stilling on my leg.

"I just...what the hell did the two of you do together?" I ask, feeling really irritated, but I don't give him time to answer and start rambling at top speed. "I mean, Justin and I had some things in common, one of those was partying, hard. We'd get dressed up, go out on the town, his mates would join us and Harriet's other friends would too, and we'd all have a blast. We'd do a pub crawl then end up in a nightclub and then the chipy or pizza place on the way home. When we were sober, it was the cinema, or bowling, or renting a film and staying in, or just hanging out on the beach." I take a deep breath. "Sorry. That was uncalled for." I say, shaking my head at myself.

"No baby, it wasn't. You're right, and to answer your question, what we had in common was success' – "You mean money!" I snap.

"No, well, yes for her," Tristan chuckles, then his tone is serious again. "I was consumed with success, she was addicted to wealth. She came from old money and had very high standards. She liked things done...a certain way, her way." He says, as though it's a painful reminder. "When I did well, she would congratulate and encourage me' – "You mean boost your ego!" I say with sarcasm. *Shut up Coral!* "I'm sorry, I won't interrupt again," I add.

"That's ok baby." Tristan plants another sweet kiss on my cheek. "But yes, you're right. She was very good at making me feel even more...obsessively inspired let's say. And as you know, being successful and having all the things I didn't get in my formative years was extremely important to me. She wanted more power, more money. I wanted more…of everything I suppose. Once I got a taste of the good life, what's it's like to be wealthy, to have whatever you want, whenever you want it, I just wanted more." Tristan sighs heavily. "I think, looking back on it, I really was quite obsessed and blinded by it all. I think it went to my head a little bit," he adds with a dry titter.

"Sounds like it did," I snort dryly. "I don't think we'd have got on if we'd have met when you were younger," I add.

"No, I don't think we would have either. I was accused of being rather arrogant in my late twenties, and I suppose into my early thirties too. Strange really, I think I started to mellow out once Olivia was gone. I guess I didn't realise how much of an effect she was having on me, on who I was, and what I really wanted to achieve. I started doing the charity and affordable housing projects about six months after we split."

"You became a better man, the man you are now. But maybe

she was supposed to be with you, you know, to take you to your extremes, so when she'd gone, you could come back down to earth with a big bump and reassess your life." I say.

Tristan chuckles wraps his arms around me and kisses my temple. "I think you might be right Coral. You know, I think you know me better than I know myself."

"Ditto," I snort, trying not to laugh.

"I think you are the brightest, sweetest woman I have ever met," he whispers, making my heart expand with love.

"And I think you're a pain in the arse sometimes, but I love you very much Tristan Freeman, with all of my heart." I retort dryly.

"Ditto," he teases.

"Hey!" I playfully slap his hand making him chuckle. "Do you think you ever really loved her Tristan?" I wistfully ask.

"Maybe...I don't know...I think looking back on it, I was afraid," he says.

"Afraid?" I gasp. I couldn't imagine Tristan being scared of anything.

"Yes." He squeezes me tighter.

"Of what Tristan?" I turn and look up at him.

"of being alone," he answers, his eyes boring into mine.

I reach up and softly caress his cheek. "You never have to be afraid of that again," I softly tell him.

"I know, I have you," He says, reaching down to kiss me.

Desire – full-on heavy in my belly, hits me like a sledgehammer – Desire.

I'm glad it's there, and I haven't lost what I have with Tristan, but for the first time, I don't want it; not right now anyway. I'm tired, hungry, and I'm still feeling a little odd.

"Hungry," I murmur against his lips.

"Are you?" He croaks, his lips brushing softly down my neck.

"Not like that Tristan," I whisper.

"I know," he says, still kissing my neck. "Shall I go and get some lunch ready?"

"No!" I freeze. "Don't leave me alone Tristan, please..." I say, my voice trembling again.

"Hey, I won't. I'm right here baby," He wraps his arms around me again and kisses my temple. "Want to help me with lunch?" He asks.

"Yes, I do, but can we just stay here a little longer?" I ask, holding him tight.

"Baby, we can do whatever you want," he says, kissing my temple once more.

That was a very odd conversation. I'm sure there's more to it, to what Tristan was actually trying to say, I try to shake it off, she was one weird woman. I take a deep breath and slowly blow it out. I close my eyes and try to focus – focus on Tristan, the wedding, our future together – as I keep breathing and concentrating on the future, I finally start to relax…

THE FOLLOWING DAY, I wake so early that it's still dark outside. I guess that's because I dozed off so many times yesterday, but what a great day we had. Tristan seemed to be in his element, just chilling out on the bed with me. It was quite a funny day, despite what happened that morning. We watched my favourite films, Twilight, with a lot of eye-rolling from Tristan, and The Matrix, which he enjoyed. Then we watched his favourite films, Fast & Furious, with a lot of eye-rolling from me, and Alien, which was awesome. Sigourney Weaver really kicks ass in the movie, but I did hide under the covers at the scary bits, much to Tristan's amusement. We laughed a lot, ate a lot, talked a lot and ended the evening with soul expanding, mind-blowing sex, and eventually, we fell asleep in each other's arms.

I turn on my side and watch him softly sleeping. His long eyelashes are gently resting on his cheeks, his mouth is slightly open, his perfect lips pouting at me, and his hair is all messed up, he looks too cute and adorable. Right at that moment his lips twitch into a smile, I can't help smiling to myself, wondering what he's dreaming about – I hope it's me.

I turn onto my back and stare up at the ceiling. I still can't believe what's happened over the past couple of days. If we hadn't gone to Harry's birthday function, I never would have met Simon, and found out he was my abuser, which led to finding out his son Kane was responsible for raping me. I shudder slightly – I need some fresh air, so I decide to get up. What I really want to do, because it helps me think and gives me a clear head, is to get my sweats and trainers on and go pound it out on the beach. But I can't, still healing. *So annoying!*

I carefully step out of bed, so I don't wake Tristan, pull on my sweats, my support vest and hoody, then slip my feet into my flip-flops. I quietly pad along the hallway and into the kitchen. I look up at the clock – 5.40am. I'll be just in time for sunrise if I hurry. I scribble a note for Tristan, letting him know I'm down at the beach and head out of the house. The air is cool on my face, and as I make my way down the steps to the beach, I take a deep breath in, I love the smell of the sea. Kicking off my flip-flops, I leave them on the bottom step. I really like the feeling of sand beneath my feet and between my toes.

The sun is about to break over the horizon, and the sea is calm today, just a few soft waves lapping to the shore. I take my time walking down to the water's edge, thinking over everything that's happened. I think about how I now know who the bad men are that did those terrible things to me. And that yesterday, I wanted so badly to have revenge and for them to suffer. But where does it end? We do something to them, and they could retaliate and do something to us. So I have to ask myself the question. Is it really worth it? Do I really want all that shit swirling around in my head, always worrying if something's going to happen, or, do I want to continue with moving on, letting it go and getting on with my life as I did when I didn't know who they were?

I decide, like I have so many times before, that it happened, that it's in the past and there's nothing I can do about it. No-one has invented time travel yet, so I can't go back and change any of it. Then I think to myself, would I really want to? It's a ridiculous question to ask, of course, it is, but if I wasn't the way I am, and Tristan wasn't the way he is, I have to ask – Would we have ever met? Would this amazing relationship have blossomed into what it is now? And the answer is no, I don't think it would have. We would be different people, living different lives.

The sun is about to break out over the horizon, so I quiet my mind and simply be. I soak it up in silence, watching the most beautiful scene unfold before me. It's breathtaking, truly breathtaking. Gold's, pinks, aquamarines and sky blue all mixing together, creating the most awe-inspiring, picture-perfect scene.

And I know, in that very instance, I know – I'm done.

I don't want any part of my past hanging over me anymore. George has always told me that I have a choice. I know that I can choose to pursue this and get revenge, or I can choose to stick to my beliefs, that Karma will make it happen, not me. That someday, hopefully, it will bite them both on the ass, and that's good enough for me; so in that very moment, that's what I choose, to move on.

I close my eyes and imagine I have an open box in front of me. I place my mother, my father, my sister, Simon and Kane inside that box. I imagine having a key in my hand, and I lock the box. Then I open my eyes, and still pretending I have the key in my hand, I take a couple of steps closer to the water's edge. I feel the waves spread over my toes, I really like the way it makes my feet tingle, then I take a deep breath, reach back, and with as much force as I can, I throw the invisible key into the ocean.

I feel free like a huge weight has been lifted from my shoulders. I finally feel like I can move on. All I want from now on is the here and now, and my future with Tristan. I smile at the ocean, and at the sun that is gradually creeping up into the sky, and sigh with relief.

I feel him before he calls out to me. I guess he's doing that, so he doesn't make me jump, it makes me grin even wider because he's so thoughtful like that. Tristan comes and stands next to me, his arm brushing against my shoulder, and he just stares straight ahead. I don't look up at him, I just keep focusing in front of me, that's the only place I want to keep looking from now on.

Tristan's fingers reach out for my hand. I silently enclose my hand in his, and he gives me a gentle squeeze. Neither of us says anything, the moment is already so beautiful it doesn't need any words. We stay like that for a long time, just watching and appreciating what's before us, but soon enough, the early morning bathers start to arrive, spoiling the blissful silence, so I turn to Tristan and look up at him.

"Ok?" He simply asks.

"Ok," I say nodding once and squeezing his hand because I do feel ok. He leans down, gives me a quick sweet kiss and then we silently make our way back to the villa.

As we eat breakfast, I tell Tristan all about my moment out on the beach, my epiphany if you like. And he says that he agrees with my decision, but I have a tiny suspicion he's not entirely happy about it, but if he isn't, he's certainly hiding it well.

After breakfast, we head out for a long walk along the coastal path. We visit touristy places, have clotted cream scones with cups of tea, then take a really long stroll along Watergate Bay's huge beach, eating ice-cream of course, so by the time we get back to the villa, it's just past lunchtime. I am shattered, but feeling on top of the world. I am blissfully happy again, in-love and ready for my future with Tristan.

We decide to spend the afternoon at the beach on our loungers, just being plain lazy. About an hour into soaking up some rays, I suddenly remember what I found on Friday.

"Oh my God Tristan!" I gasp, jumping up from my horizontal position.

"What, what's wrong?" He says, mimicking me and sitting straight up.

"Sorry," I giggle. "I didn't mean to startle you, nothing's wrong," I add.

"Coral!" He scolds.

"Sorry." I chuckle at him, I sit next to him on his lounger, kiss his cheek in apology, then reel of my story…

IT'S 5PM, AND we are stood in the jewellery shop that I found on my search for some food on Friday. I'm so happy I found it. Wearns is a traditional Cornish Jewellers that's been going since 1890. The pieces of jewellery are actually quite simple in design, which is what I actually want for a wedding band – but I think my mind was made up when the jeweller told me about their history; their story. I knew it there and then that this is the place we will get our wedding rings from.

"Are you looking for anything in particular?" The shop owner asked me, as I browsed the store.

"Yes. Wedding bands?" I said.

She smiled at me and then led me over to the right section.

"Wow, they look really nice, so shiny! If we try them on and they fit, can we take them straight away?" I asked.

"Of course," she said. "Unless you want an engraving?"

"Oh…" I hadn't thought of that. "How quickly can you do that?" I asked.

"Within a couple of weeks," she said.

"Ah, we're getting married on Saturday." She looked quite shocked when I told her this. *Yeah, I know; we are very late in sorting out the rings.*

"Well, if you like what you see, you can always come back once you're married and have them engraved?" She suggested. *Hmm…I wonder?*

Then she proceeded to tell me about the jewellers, the history.

"We use shipwrecked Cornish tin in our Gold and Silver alloys. The ship had been at the bottom of the sea since 1863. The steamer, SS Liverpool, had left London after calling at Plymouth and Penzance, it was carrying Cornish tin ingots when it sank after colliding with the barque Laplata, which had just left Liverpool and was on its way to Lima, in Peru. The wreck lies just off the north coast of Anglesey. The tin salvaged was in the form of ingots, which bear the Bolitho's of Penzance

Forever With Him

smelters mark." Her story of the shipwrecked steamer, the sea and the Cornish tradition had me thinking how romantic it was.

She continued. "You know, jewellery made from our unique and very special alloy offers an everlasting memory of Cornwall. Not only for those who want a reminder of their Cornish heritage, but also for those with a love for Cornwall." I immediately agreed. Cornwall has captured me, in so many ways; I really have fallen in love with the place.

"Also, many people find our jewellery nostalgic, those that have a nautical connection or an interest in shipwrecks..." I nodded my head in agreement, remembering the story that goes with my engagement ring. He was a sailor, lost at sea, and she waited for her long lost love to come home, this just seems so fitting, so perfect.

I immediately placed a deposit down, asked her to hold both the rings I had chosen, and hurried back to tell Tristan – Only, that day, when I got back to the beach, I kind of got sidetracked with Tristan doing his diet coke thing.

"So what do you think?" I say to Tristan. Both our rings are plain, white gold, made with Cornish tin, and they are both so shiny, except Tristan's is a little wider.

"I don't know Coral," he says as he stares down at the ring on his wedding finger.

"Don't you like it?" I ask.

"Yes, of course, I do." He looks over my head at the saleswoman. "Can you give us a moment?" he asks, very politely. I turn around and see her blush and smile at Tristan, I want to roll my eyes at her, she walks over to the other counter and pretends to be busy, I guess that's so she can't hear us.

"Baby," Tristan says, bringing me back to him.

"Yeah?" I look up at him.

"Don't you want...you know something more...well, upmarket, expensive?" He whispers.

I snort with laughter. "Expensive? You think spending over £500 pounds on each ring is in-expensive?" Tristan shrugs.

I have to remember he is rich, but that's not what this is about. It's nostalgic and romantic, and these aren't the kind of rings you see every day, not in the big, well-known jewellers anyway.

Tristan cocks his head to the side. "It's the story you told me, isn't it?"

I nod my head, and look down at the shiny ring on my wedding finger for a moment, then look up at him again. He frowns down at me then looks at his ring again. I shake my head at myself, and look down at the floor – I don't think he likes them, which is fair enough, and if he doesn't, we'll just have to find something else.

"Coral," Tristan lifts my chin, so I have to look up at him. "What's on your mind? I want to know baby. I want to know everything, how you think, how you feel – Tell me." He pleads.

I swallow hard – *You can do this Coral!*

"Ok," I take a breath. "It just seems right Tristan, like I said to you on the beach, my engagement ring had a background story to it, and so do these rings – Ok, not so romantic, but at the same time I think it *is* romantic, because we are here, in Cornwall. I've never had a holiday before, yet here I am, with you, and..." I break off.

"Keep going," he prompts – *He knows me so well, it's freaky!*

"I just...I've really fallen in love Tristan, with Cornwall...I..." I swallow hard. *Do I tell him, or don't I?*

I take another deep breath. "I think I want to live here," I say, staring up at his wide eyes. I shake my head and laugh at myself. "I know that sounds stupid...But I really feel like this place has got into my soul...like, like it's, well...the first *place* that I feel l can call home."

Tristan gasps; I can see he is totally taken back by what I'm saying.

"And then I found this place, and the history, and the fact that they not only have wedding bands but the two I have chosen fit us both perfectly, it just feels right – like it was meant to be. Like we were meant to come here on holiday, that I was meant to find this place, it's like it's all happened for a reason." *There, I'm done – I've said it!*

"You want to live here?" He asks his eyes boring into me.

"I think so. Yes," I whisper.

"Leave your family, your friends, your comfort zone?" He questions.

"Tristan, I don't think you quite understand. I don't need a comfort zone anymore, because, well to put it simply, I'm not afraid anymore because I have you. If you had a business opportunity somewhere else in the world, I would go with you to that place, I would follow you anywhere Tristan, you know that, right?"

He still looks shocked, but silently nods his head.

"Look, I...I don't quite understand why I feel this way, I just know I do. From the moment we got here, I just felt so at ease, even though I'm in a strange place. Each day has just got better and better, I even spoke to a woman on Friday while I was waiting for your baguette to be made, she was a complete stranger!" Tristan's inhales sharply. "I was telling her how much I love this place, she said the same, that she had moved here years ago and that it was the best decision she had ever made. She said her kids are so happy here, that it's a great place for them to grow up in, and I agree..." I stare out the window for a moment. "I think Cornwall would be the most fantastic place to raise a family." I smile shyly at Tristan knowing I have mentioned kids again. "Well, one day!" I quickly add.

"We have a lot to talk about," he finally says. I nod my head feeling guilty. "Don't do that," he adds, slowly shaking his head.

"Do what?" I whisper.

"Look so guilty!" He leans down and softly places his lips against mine. "I am so happy you just told me that," he murmurs against my lips.

"Why?" I whisper back.

"Because I want you to tell me how you feel, I want you to be honest with me," he says, his proximity and his scent, making me catch my breath. I stare down at his lips, which look so deliciously kissable right now, that I cannot pull my gaze away from them, which is a monumental tribute to his eyes.

Eventually, I find my voice. "And the rings?" I croak my mouth dry.

"I love these rings, I just wanted to be sure this was what you want baby." I finally succumb and look up at his eyes; they are soft milk chocolate, warm and glowing with love.

"Oh, Tristan!" I wrap my arms around his back and hug him tightly, my head against his chest. He wraps his arms tightly around me then I feel him kiss the top of my head a couple of times.

"Baby," he says, rocking me gently. "Shall we eat out tonight and celebrate?"

"Yes," I whisper.

"Do you feel up to it?" he asks. I look up at him and nod, smiling like a fool. He grins back at me. "Good. Let's get these paid for so we can get back and shower." My heart starts pumping against my chest – *Hmm, showering with my sexy hubby to be...*

CHAPTER TWENTY-THREE

IT'S WEDNESDAY EVENING, and it's the last day of our almost perfect holiday in Cornwall. We have spent nine, bar that glitch, magical days here. I am trying my very best not to feel glum about going home, and I don't think I would be if what's happening tomorrow wasn't happening – because as per my wishes, I am laying my mother to rest tomorrow morning.

Last week, when Edith called Tristan to let him know my mother's belongings had arrived at the house, I asked him to organise for us to plant the tree before the wedding. I didn't want it hanging over my head when I said I do, and the only time they could fit us in at short notice, was at ten o'clock tomorrow morning. Hence the reason we are flying back so early, and the reason we are heading straight over to Woodland Burial once we get back to Brighton. I swallow hard. It's going to be weird, really, really weird.

And to make matters worse, Tristan is going back to work tomorrow. Joyce is officially leaving the company Friday, so he's got a lot of work to do. Tristan is not happy about this, as he doesn't want to leave me, but as I pointed out to him, I won't be alone. The moment Tristan told me when the burial would happen, and that he reluctantly had no choice but to go back to work, I called Gladys. I wanted to spend some time with her – my real mother – but she's going to be out for the day with Malcolm.

However, she did inform me that Bob is back in his studio, and I know I shouldn't be, but I'm worried about him being down there on his own. So I'm going to take him out for lunch tomorrow and get some food shopping in for him. And after speaking to Gladys, I called Rob to see if he and Carlos wanted to come with me, which they said yes to, it will be nice to catch up with everyone. I also need to speak to Susannah, and I need to do it before a court date is issued, which is something else I'm not looking forward to – *Snap out of it Coral!*

I sigh inwardly and look out at our beautiful surroundings. We are sat outside on a decked terrace at Watergate Bay Hotel. The Beach Hut is one of the hotel's many restaurants and looks directly out to sea, it's simply breathtaking. When we came here on Sunday, we both agreed it would be the perfect place to spend our last evening, and we were right, it is perfect.

The restaurant is busy, which is always a good sign, and there are still lots of people out on the beach, soaking up the last few hours of daylight before the sun sets. Outside on the terrace, I can hear the waves gently breaking, feel the wind in my hair, and I swear I have seen a seal bob his head up to say hello, but I haven't seen him since, so maybe not.

Earlier, after our very lazy day on the beach, Tristan made love to me – twice – then we took a long, lazy shower together. And as he did before, he gently washed my hair then slowly dried it for me – God knows what state it would be in if he hadn't been doing that for me. Major plus point is that I am healing so quickly – apart from all the sex, which I am not complaining about – I have done nothing but eat, sleep and sunbathe. I feel really, really, good. As each day has passed, the pain I was suffering has become less severe, and I know Tristan can tell, because he seems really relaxed and content, like me.

I look across at him. Hmm…Tristan looks very handsome this evening. He's sitting adjacent to me, relaxing and soaking up the views, so I stare at his profile. He's really caught the sun, his skin has bronzed so sexily, and his hair is a little lighter, the copper tints shining brightly in the evening sun. He's wearing a pair of light beige suit trousers, a cream shirt with the sleeves rolled up on his forearms, and the top three buttons are open, giving me an eye full of his bronzed chest. He looks tanned, healthy, happy, and very sexy!

I am wearing my new olive green, halter-neck dress, with matching stilettos that Tristan bought for me yesterday. I feel sexy. I'm still dumbstruck that Tristan bought it for me. He was only meant to be getting our lunch, but he'd seen it in a shop window and thought it would suit me – I can't say if it does, but I love it – He is so sweet.

The waiter has been over to us and given us our menus and some bread and olives to nibble on. Tristan has had a glass of wine, and so have I, just the one – I must be good.

"So," Tristan says, bringing my attention to him. "I think

it's time for your other birthday presents." He says, smiling widely at me.

"What?" I chuckle nervously. *Did he just say presents?*

With his most sexy smile, he pulls a small white envelope out of his jacket pocket and hands it to me. "Happy belated birthday darling. Open it, baby." He smiles.

"Ok," I say a little nervously. I tentatively rip open the envelope, and carefully pull out the contents. *Whoa!*

Two return tickets to Hawaii – he remembered! And it's for a whole month in January.

"Tristan!" I gasp. "You remembered," I warble, tears pooling in my eyes. He smiles widely at my shocked expression.

"Of course I did." He takes my free hand and gently kisses it. "I know it seems strange, giving you this now instead of at the party," he smiles, his eyes downcast for a moment, then looks up at me again. "I didn't want to overwhelm you," he adds.

He's right - this would have had me blubbering like a fool!

"I don't know what to say…" I choke. I cannot believe I am finally going to Hawaii. "For a whole month?" I question.

"Yes. When I had a look online, I wasn't sure which surfing competition you wanted to see – there are lots of them," he adds, then continues. "So, I figured if I booked a long stay, I've covered all the competitions. Besides, I want you to be able to explore all the islands, really soak it up. I want to make up for all the holidays you've never had." He says, gazing adoringly at me. *Oh, Tristan!*

I swallow hard against the lump that's formed. I just keep on falling deeper in love with him, much deeper than I had ever imagined I could feel for someone – I really could not ask for more.

"Tristan, you are so sweet." I lean forward, caressing his cheek and softly kiss him. "Thank you, baby." *Wow! Hawaii!* I carefully stow the tickets in my clutch.

His grin widens. "I'm not done," he says.

"You're not?" I squeak, my eyes wide.

His grin deepens, his dimples making me swoon. "Do you remember that I had a surprise organised for the Saturday after your birthday?" He asks, totally throwing me.

"Um…yeah…?" *Breathe Coral, breathe…*

"Happy belated birthday darling," he says, handing me another envelope. *Another present?*

"What's this?" I ask feeling shocked, my heart strumming loudly in my ears.

"Open it, and you'll see," he teases. I smile and shake my head at him. Opening the seal and pulling out several pieces of paperwork, I read the first paragraph....*Holy Crap! A full course of sailing lessons!*

"Tristan!" I gasp.

"Obviously, I had to cancel the first lesson, we'll re-arrange it when you're better," he says. I suddenly remember our conversation that occurred after dining at The Hilton with Gladys and Malcolm. He *had* organised something for the Saturday after my birthday, I remember him teasing me about it. *Wow, it seems so long ago.*

"You did this...ages ago?" I whisper in disbelief. "When you asked about my birthday?"

"Yes." He smiles triumphantly at me.

I swallow hard. "Tristan, I can't believe you remembered that..." I croak. Then I think about actually going out there and learning to sail...Panic suddenly grips me, I don't want to do that on my own. *What if I get it wrong and fall overboard?*

"Hey," Tristan says tugging on my chin, so I have to look up at him. "I'll be with you," he says, reading my anxiety. My fears instantly fade, and I start to feel a little calmer.

"I can't believe you did this," I whisper staring at the paperwork. "You really are a wonderful man," I say. *This is too much!*

"And you are a wonderful woman," he says, melting my heart.

I swallow hard. "Thank you, Tristan, this is...overwhelming." I look up at him smiling back at me and shake my head at him, tears pooling in my eyes. "You're spoiling me," I sniff.

"No, I'm not." He states in his authoritative voice. It makes me chuckle at him. "Coral, are you sure you don't want to try sailing on your own? I don't want you to feel like I'm suffocating you."

"Suffocating me?" I squeak.

"I don't have any friends or many hobbies that would take me away from you, but I don't want that to influence you. I don't want you feeling like you have to do everything with me, I want you to have the choice." He says, gazing intensely at me.

"I want you to come with me," I whisper, gazing back at him.

"You do?" He clarifies.

"Definitely," I scoff. "Who will save me if I do something daft like fall overboard?" I add, my tone dry.

Tristan chuckles at me. "Ok," he says, squeezing my hand – *Oh, I'm so in love with him.*

"Now, on a more serious note, I want to talk to you about what you told me the other day." He adds.

"The other day?" I whisper, folding the paperwork and popping it into my clutch.

"Yes, in the jewellers. I don't want to sound pessimistic Coral, but lots of people get that holiday feeling when away from home. A feeling of never wanting to leave, imagining themselves living at the place they've come to visit – It's very common," he adds, popping an olive into his mouth.

"It is?" I say, feeling morose.

"Hey." Tristan pulls his chair closer to me. "Why don't you tell me why you are feeling this way?" I stare back at his wide eyes and slowly nod.

I take a deep breath and begin. "Ok. I love the house that you've bought for us, so much so that if we could, I would say let's bring it with us, but we can't do that. It's just...I guess, I bought my studio because it was right on the water, it calms me, and I guess being here has made me realise how much I miss that, that it's more important to me than I thought it was. I know it sounds crazy, but even though that little villa we are staying in is only two bedrooms, I'd gladly swap it for Brighton. I think it's...you know, just waking up every morning to that view, and I know we have amazing views in Brighton, but it's the other aspects too."

"Like what Coral?" Tristan asks. He's very serious again, soaking up every word I am saying, but I love that he is. I have overheard so many women at work moaning about the fact that their boyfriend, or husband, doesn't listen to them – So right now, I feel like one very lucky woman.

"Being able to hear the water for one, the gentle lapping of the sea when she's calm, the roar of the waves when it's windy, and the smell of the sea – it's so potent, don't you think?"

Tristan nods once, still listening intently.

"It's always been my dream to live in a house on a beach, like literally *on a beach* – but I never thought I would be in the position to be able to have that. Maybe that's why I subconsciously went for my studio, even though it's so tiny. It's used to drive me mad sometimes..." I laugh, shaking off the memory.

"Coral, why didn't you tell me this when I made it perfectly clear to you that I was buying a house for us?" he says.

My face falls. "You know why," I whisper, remembering

how I felt back then – *Like a different person compared to how I feel now!*

Tristan shakes his head in frustration.

"I knew I shouldn't have told you," I add, looking down at the weather-worn, sun-bleached wooden table.

"Hey, that's not why I'm frustrated," he says, so I look up at him. "You didn't say anything to me because you couldn't see yourself in a relationship, right?" I nod once. "But you thought the house was magical?" he questions. He's still serious.

I smile and nod again. "Tristan, I'd never seen inside a million pound house before, at the time, I was so in awe of it all. I can remember feeling like I was a princess at the top of a castle that overlooked the sea, and well...then there was you," I stop right there.

Tristan smiles his shy smile. "So, if we had dated and I say... had stayed in hotels while we did, then we decided to move in together, that wouldn't have been the house you would have chosen?" He concludes.

I shake my head. "No, I don't think it would have been. But please understand me, Tristan, because I don't want to sound unappreciative of what you did, I really do love that house, and I really do think it's magical, I just know it would have been a different house I'd have fallen in love with."

"A house right on the beach, or at least overlooking it?" He asks, deep in thought.

"Yes." I swallow hard and take a sip of my wine.

"Well, I guess that changes things," he says.

"Changes what?" I whisper, slightly panicked.

"My plans," he says, with wide teasing eyes.

I smile back at him, feeling calmer. "What plans?"

"Well, I had every intention of buying more properties now the houses in Birmingham and Leeds have sold. I suppose those plans don't necessarily have to change, but where we live will change the other plans I had set in motion."

"What other plans Tristan?" I ask, giddy with excitement.

"Oh no," he says, shaking his head at me. "For my eyes only," he adds teasingly.

"You are such a tease!" I say pouting at him.

"As are you," He laughs.

I take a deep breath and ask the question. "So you wouldn't mind living here?" I ask.

"No Coral, I wouldn't. It's fairly easy to commute nowadays, and if this really is where you want to be, then we shall be here," he says.

"Really?" I squeak.

"Under one condition," Tristan says. My face falls. "You don't make any hard and fast decisions, just yet."

"Why?" I soberly ask.

"I've already told you, baby, it's very common to think like this when on holiday. Look, if we get back to Brighton and everything is back to normal, and you say 'I still want Cornwall', then we'll do it, deal?"

"You want me to wait, to think it over?" I ask.

"Yes, I do." He softly says.

"Ok. It's a deal." I acquiesce.

Tristan smiles warmly at me, leans forward and softly pecks me on the lips. Hmm, he tastes so good. He suddenly pulls back, I look up and realise the waiter has arrived to take our order.

IT'S LATE, 10PM to be exact. Tristan and I have enjoyed the magnificent sunset and are quietly sipping our coffees. The meal we ate this evening was delicious, I've never had Lobster Thermidor before, much to Tristan's amusement, but it was absolutely mouthwatering. The restaurant has taken on a very romantic feel not that the sun has set and the stars are out. Soft lighting, soulful plinky-plonky music quietly playing in the background, and the moment the sun went down, a waiter came along placing candles in glass jars on each table.

I look across at Tristan, he's been staring out to sea for the past ten minutes, come to think of it he's been pretty pre-occupied all evening. Maybe he's wondering about his plans? Well, whatever they are, they are taking his attention away from me. *How to get him back?* Hmm...I put my cup down, and stare at his beautiful profile. I want to do something sexy for Tristan tonight, but I don't know what. I sit for a moment thinking it through when I have a sudden epiphany - Maybe a little lap dance? I can do that, I'm a good dancer, and if I slip into something sexy, he might really enjoy it. Feeling good about that idea, I sit back, cross my legs and hitch my dress up a little, making sure the top of my lacy-hold up is on show.

Tristan turns to look at me, his eyes immediately resting on my legs. Then his eyes reach mine, I can see they have darkened, in-fact his whole demeanour has changed. I smile teasingly at him, pick up my long mint chocolate stick that came with the coffee's and gently place it in my mouth, then slowly suck. I hope I'm making myself very clear to him.

He shifts in his seat as he watches me slowly suck the chocolate, his lips part, and he swallows hard. *Oh yeah! I'm definitely affecting him, brilliant!*

I cock my head to the side, and smirk, then look directly at his crotch. Then I lean forward so no-one can hear me. "Mr Freeman," I whisper, gazing back at his heated look. "Am I turning you on?"

Tristan's jaw clenches. "Coral," he warns.

"What?" I feign innocence.

"Don't give me that innocent look," he says his voice deep and husky.

It makes me want him, here, now. "You better take me back then," I challenge.

Tristan shakes his head at me, places his hand at the top of my leg and pulls my dress back down to my knee. "Coral, you already have enough admirers this evening," he says scanning the restaurant. "Please don't show them what's mine," he adds then looks back out to sea. *Hmph, what's up with him? I was only teasing!*

I rack my brains for an explanation, but nothing comes to me. "Hey," I touch his forearm. "You ok?" He turns and stares at me, and it's as though he's debating whether or not to tell me something. He smiles, but it quickly turns into a frown. He reaches over, squeezes my leg once more and then turns away.

"Have I done something wrong?" I ask, feeling totally deflated – and rejected – and I don't like feeling like that.

"Let's get back," he says, gesturing to the waiter, completely ignoring my question.

"Why?" I grumble.

"Because we need to talk," he says, his tone clipped.

Fuck! I don't like the sound of that.

"About what?" I gripe.

Tristan turns in his seat, giving me his full attention. He crosses his one leg over the other, leans back in his chair, cocks his head to the side and just sits their appraising me, his forefinger running back and forth across his bottom lip. I swallow hard. His eyes darken, and his whole persona seems to have shifted, playful Tristan has definitely left the building. I'm sure he's doing it on purpose though, trying to distract me and its bloody well working!

Jeez! Why does he always have to look so intense? It makes me feel nervous, bashful, shy even. 'Fantasies.' He finally mouths. My heart leaps into my mouth. Why can't I look away from him? It's like he's pinning me to the chair. And why am I feeling so breathless?

"Why can't we talk about that here?" I whisper breathlessly. I don't want to leave yet.

"Coral, I really don't think this is the appropriate place to have that kind of conversation," he says, glancing at the other diners and then locking eyes with me. "Do you want to go back Coral?" he asks, in an even deeper voice, his forefinger now tapping his bottom lip.

My sex starts throbbing – *Crap!* – I quickly look away because I am not going to get this out if I look at him.

"Oh...well yeah, I guess...I'll um...I'll just pop to the ladies then," I say, feeling completely perplexed. The moment I push my chair back, Tristan stands and gives me his hand to help me up. "Thanks," I whisper, but I'm already a million miles away.

I walk through the restaurant in a complete daze, trying my best to calm my racing thoughts. Once I'm done, and I'm washing my hands, I take a deep breath and stare up at myself in the mirror. I look good, healthy, tanned – I was relaxed, but now...? Now I just feel on edge, and nervous as hell.

Shaking my head at myself, I look up at my reflection again. *You wanted this conversation Stevens! Don't go all weak at the knees because it's about to happen.* I nod in agreement with myself. I am about to marry this man if we can't openly talk about this sort of stuff – we're fucked! But what if I don't like what he says? What if he wants to do things I can't or won't do? What if – *Stop it Coral! You are being ridiculous!*

I look up at myself again. "This is Tristan we are talking about, the kindest, sweetest, most loving man you've ever met!" I whisper to my reflection. Then, agreeing wholeheartedly with myself, I pick up my clutch and make my way back to the restaurant. Tristan is standing next to our table with his suit jacket on, waiting for me to return, and there's an odd expression on his face – *What is that?*

Ok, now I'm really worrying.

"Bills paid and I've ordered the taxi," he tells me as I reach him. "Shall we?"

I frown up at him. "Why are you acting...weird?" I mutter, feeling a little annoyed now.

"Coral," he quietly says, leaning down to whisper right in my ear. "People are watching us, and I don't want a scene, please be good and just come with me." I look around the restaurant and see that Tristan is right. Several diners have stopped what they are doing and are silently watching us. *Ugh! Don't they have anything better to do?*

"Fine!" I grumble and place my hand in his. We head out of the restaurant, and silently stand next to one another, not touching at all – *Hurry up Taxi!*

The wind has kicked up, so of course, I start to shiver. "Where's your wrap?" Tristan asks.

"I didn't bring it," I say, purposely not looking at him. In my peripheral vision, I see Tristan shrug out of his jacket, stand behind me, and gently place it over my shoulders, then I feel him kiss the back of my hair. "Thanks," I mumble, my good manners taking over.

The taxi arrives, thank god, and Tristan opens the door for me, I slide across the seat. Tristan climbs in next to me, and we head back to the villa – in total silence. I study his profile for a moment. He's staring out of the window deep in thought – *Don't think the worst, don't think the worst...*

I turn away from him and stare out of my window, nervously biting my lip – *Jesus age Christ!* I was blissfully happy ten minutes ago. Why does it now feel so serious? Tears pool in my eyes, fucking hormones. Five minutes in and the taxi drops us outside the villa. Tristan pays him, clasps my hand in his and gently pulls me across the seat. We step out the taxi, and Tristan shuts the door.

"Tristan," I croak, but I can't look up at him.

"Inside," he says, leading me up the steps.

My legs are shaking so badly – Why do I feel like this is such a humungous deal? Like it could make or break us? I swallow hard and try to control the panic attack I feel coming on. Tristan opens the front door, steps aside to let me in, shuts the door behind him and walks over to me. Taking his jacket from my shoulders, he hangs it on the back of the breakfast stool, then returning to me, he clasps my hand in his and walks us over to the sofa – *I need a drink!*

I manage to find my voice. "Tristan, you're really scaring me," I tremble.

"I'm sorry, but I'm scared too," he replies, his voice equally shaky.

"You're scared?" I squeak, finally looking at him.

He nods once. "I think I need a drink for this, you?"

My mouth pops open in shock. *This is not good, not good at all!*

"Sure," I murmur. My heart sinks to the pit of my stomach. I don't think I'm going to like this. What's wrong with Tristan? He looks so, so...sad? Worried maybe, I'm not sure?

I watch him walk over to the mini-bar and pour us both a Brandy. Then sitting next to me, he hands one to me and takes a sip of his. "Can you forgive me Coral for my despicable behaviour at the restaurant, and in the taxi?" He asks, staring at the amber liquid in his glass. *Why does he seem so melancholy?*

"Tristan, I don't think you're behaviour was despicable? Weird yes, but not bad," I say, trying to calm my racing heart.

"Ok," he says, still staring into his glass.

"You know, when you act like this, you have me thinking you're more fucked up than me," I scoff. The corner of his lips turn up as he stares into his glass – Now I know something is really wrong because he would be telling me off for saying I'm fucked up – which I am – kind of.

"Tristan, is this about what you want to talk about, you know...fantasies?" I say swallowing hard. He nods once. "Ok, this is hard for you to say?" I surmise.

He nods again. *Shit!*

"Want some help?" I ask lightly, even though I feel like I'm about to explode.

He turns and gazes at me, and I can see he's worried. "I'm really worried about scaring you away. I can't lose you Coral." He says, echoing my thoughts.

"You're not going to lose me, Tristan," I tell him firmly. He turns away, shaking his head slightly and gulps back the rest of his Brandy. I watch him walk over to the mini bar.

"Tristan, will you please just tell me what's going on. I'm really freaking out over here!"

He sighs heavily, his eyes closing as he does. "Ok...when I was with Olivia, we had...we did..." He breaks off, running his hand through his hair, and pours the brandy into his glass.

"What Tristan?" I push. "Just say it!" I add feeling frustrated.

"She liked things...a certain way. And well, it turned out I liked it too," he says, stopping to gaze down at me. "I was trying to tell you the other day when we took a bath."

I swallow hard. I knew there was more to that conversation. What was it he said? *'Olivia had very singular tastes'* I get a sour taste in mouth, so I take a big gulp of Brandy. What else did he say? I rack my brains, trying to think back on it...Then I remember.

'She liked things done a certain way.'

'As far as she was concerned beds were for fucking and sleeping in.'

I take another gulp of Brandy, I don't like where this is going.

Tristan continues. "I always knew with how you are, it would be an extremely sensitive subject to broach. Like I said, I don't want to scare you away from me, and I don't want you to think that if we don't do what I like, I won't be happy, or satisfied, because I am." He gazes down at me for a moment and then takes three quick strides over to me.

He sinks down to his knees in front of me, then taking my hand in his he squeezes tight. "You have to know Coral, I really am very, very happy," he says, his eyes wide with fear. I can feel the intensity rolling off him like waves.

I reach out and stroke his cheek. "I know that baby," I whisper. "Tristan, it doesn't matter what you tell me, I'm not going anywhere. You can't frighten me away, I know there's not a single bad bone in your body, so why don't you just say it, and we can talk about it," I add.

I stare back at him, he looks so anxious right now, and it's stressing me out. "Baby, just say it!" I snap, exasperated.

"Olivia liked to be dominated in the bedroom." He blurts it out so fast it takes a second for my brain to catch up. *Dominated?* I frown back at him, not understanding what he's trying to say. "We had a sub-dom relationship?" He slowly adds, as though he's speaking to a child. It takes a moment for my brain to register what he just said. I blink rapidly at him, trying to work out how I feel about it.

"Coral, please say something," he begs, he looks like he's in pain.

I feel slightly nauseous like I've just been punched in the gut. "That's what she meant," I whisper, my eyes wide with fear. "When Olivia was in the house, she said something about knowing what you need to de-stress."

"Yes." He says.

Oh!...Oh!...Oh! *This is not happening!*

I try to think of the first logical thing to ask. Finally, after what feels like forever, it comes to me. "Do you need it, Tristan?" I ask my heart in my mouth.

"No, I don't." He firmly tells me.

I slowly blow the breath out I'd been holding in relief. "Then why would she say that?" I query.

"Because back then, I did need it," he admits.

I frown back at him. "I...I don't understand?"

Tristan stands and sits next to me on the sofa. "You're still here," he says, looking down at our entwined fingers.

"Why wouldn't I be?" I say incredulously.

"With your past, and with everything you've been through, your associations with men, sex..." He trails off. "I thought you might walk out on me, end the relationship," he adds.

"Tristan, I told you before, and I'll tell you again. I'm a lot stronger than I look." He turns and gazes at me like I'm the air that he breathes; it makes my heart swell with love for him. "So why don't you tell me all about it," I softly add, even though I feel like I'm in a state of panic.

"You're not worried?" He asks. *Deep breathes...deep breathes...*

I swallow hard. "No, not worried. If you say you don't need it then I have no need to be worried, but I am curious," I whisper, staring back at him with wide eyes.

Tristan nods once then begins. "My life was very stressful when I knew Olivia, in all honesty, looking back on it, she was probably the one stressing me out," he laughs sardonically then sighs.

"I was still practising law, and I always had high profile cases, so to win or lose was a huge deal, not just for me but for the company too. Quite honestly, I think I'd taken on too much, I should have pulled out of taking the cases on and concentrated on the business, but I enjoyed being in court, I wasn't ready to give it up. So, with trying to grow the business, building a property portfolio, looking after my folks, working ridiculous hours, and dealing with Olivia, I was...overloaded. Olivia was the one that introduced it to me, I'd never done anything like that before, she had, and I found it very....de-stressing." Tristan stops and gazes at me. *Fuck!*

"Any questions so far?" He asks.

I shake my head at him. *Yes, millions!*

"I'm not a dominant by nature Coral, I don't crave control like most dominants do, and I've never had that kind of relationship with anyone else, just Olivia. Yes, I'm an alpha-male, I know that about myself, but it was more..." Tristan sighs and runs his hand through his hair. "Coral, I never realised it before, but Olivia pulled the strings in our relationship, outside the bedroom I mean, she was the dominant one, whatever she wanted, she got like I said to you, I was blind. That's why I love our relationship so much, we're balanced, and we are equals. I don't try to control you because I don't want or need to, and you don't try to control me either, and I love it, I feel very settled with you and very secure." Tristan smiles warmly at me, and gently strokes my cheek. "Coral, all that kinky shit means nothing if you don't feel like you have a connection with that person." He tells me firmly.

"You didn't feel connected to Olivia?" I say, trying to keep my voice steady.

"Sometimes...rarely," He laughs, then gently scoots forward and takes my face in his hands. "I have never felt as connected to a woman as I do with you."

"Oh..." I swallow hard. "Do you want to do that with me?" I have stopped breathing.

"I don't need to do that with you if that's what you're asking. What I had with them, all of the other women I ever dated pales in comparison to what we have."

My mind is whizzing. I get a sudden flashback. We had just arrived here, we'd made love, and he was about to tell me something important, but he stopped because my belly groaned – I must admit, I was hungry – I haven't pushed him to tell me since, which I normally would have done. I wonder if this is what he wanted to tell me? Then I remember something else, something, quite frankly, I'm shocked I've forgotten about.

It shocked me when he said it, but I guess I've been having such a good time, it hasn't crossed my mind. *'I should put you over my knee for that.'*

I swallow hard. "Is this what you were going to tell me when we arrived here?"

"Yes. Coral, when you said you wanted to talk about fantasies..." Tristan shakes his head a couple of times. "It shocked me, but it also pleased me too, but I..." He breaks off again.

"So when you said 'I should put you over my knee for that' – "Yeah...I'm sorry about that, it kind of slipped out," he says, frowning deeply. "I could see the shock on your face, and I was furious with myself for letting it happen, but then I felt all those old feelings come back, what it feels like to...well, to do that kind of thing and it turns me on Coral. And I couldn't help visualising and thinking how I would feel if I did do those things with you."

"Oh..." Is all I can manage.

Tristan swallows hard. "I want you to know me Coral,

inside out, all of me. I've been battling with it since I met you, whether or not to tell you. Please tell me I've done the right thing here and that I'm not going to lose you?"

I stare back at Tristan, seeing him in a completely different light.

Holy Fuck!

Tristan Freeman, my future husband, likes to dominate women. And I have no idea how I feel about that…

CHAPTER TWENTY-FOUR

HOW IN THE HELL did I not see this, or work it out? *Holy mother of God!* I suddenly get it. Everything falls into place. I've seen dominant Tristan before, it was staring me in the face when I first met him in reception that day. And the day after I met him and we went to Munchies, then at that restaurant for lunch, he had a certain look in his eyes then, a certain aura. I remember it made me squirm in my seat I was that uncomfortable. It was like he could see right through me like he was thinking about what I looked like naked, how I would be as a lover, and what he would do to me as my lover, and it's kind of sexy, to be honest. Admittedly, I just thought he was an intense kind of guy, with a very intense look, but obviously not.

That's why Olivia said what she said, because of what they used to do. Then I remember what I said to him earlier on the beach while we were having lunch, that he was every woman's fantasy, and that he was about to be chatted up. I thought he was just feeling shy, but he wasn't, he was avoiding the conversation.

Then I get another flashback. When we arrived here and we were teasing one another, and I threw that pillow at him, he had the same look in his eyes then – *Holy crap!*

Another memory fills my mind. It was ages ago when we were taking a bath together. Tristan was questioning me about my sex life, what I had and hadn't done and he'd mentioned domination then – *Fuck!*

How could I have not seen this? How could I have been so blind? I swallow hard, then knock back the rest of the brandy in one go, but I think I need another.

"Coral?" Tristan takes my hand and squeezes it tight. "You're killing me over here, what are you thinking?" He says, throwing my words back at me.

I swallow hard again. "I just..." I shake my head. "Ok, this is going to sound stupid, but I thought men that like domination are...you know, fuck ups with major issues. You don't seem like that to me?" Tristan starts smiling at me. "You're laughing at me?" I choke, he instantly loses the grin. "You know I'm not too impressed you've kept this from me!" I bark, my temper rising.

"If I'd have told you when we met, you never would have seen me again," he softly says.

"Entrapment!" I blurt, getting to my feet.

"Is that how you feel?" He asks. "Like I've trapped you?"

"Well, I'm not going to leave you," I squeak. "It's too late for that, I'm too in-love with you to leave!" With shaking legs, I walk over to the mini-bar and pour another brandy, almost missing the glass because my hands are shaking so badly, I take a big gulp. "So what exactly does this mean Tristan? You want to do all kinds of weird, horrible things to me?" I ask, my voice shaking, giving me away.

"No baby, no weird horrible things." Tristan is instantly to his feet, he takes the brandy off me and wraps his big strong arms around me, squeezing me so tight, it's almost painful. "I'm still the same man," he says, his voice shaking slightly.

I wrap my arms around his back and squeeze him tight – *Fuck!* Is he? Is he still the same man to me? I don't know. "Tristan, I think I'm in shock. I just need some time to process this, and get my head around it," I tremble.

He squeezes me even tighter. "You said you wanted to talk about fantasies Coral, would you have preferred it if I had lied to you and kept this to myself? To not be honest about what I like and don't like?" He asks.

"No, it's just...I'm so inexperienced Tristan, and I'm scared," I tremble.

"Don't be frightened baby. I'll say it again, this does not have to happen, any of it." He squeezes me even tighter. "Sweet Jesus, I'm so sorry Coral. I've been so worried about telling you. But when you did what you did with that chocolate stick..." He breaks off and takes a deep breath. "It turned me on so much I couldn't think straight, I just wanted to get you back here. I knew I had no choice anymore, that I had to tell you, I couldn't avoid it any longer. A part of me wanted to just let it go and never bring up the subject, but you are one determined woman. I knew that one day you would ask me about it and that you'd see straight through me if I tried to hide the truth, what a fool I am," he adds, his tone sombre.

"You stupid bugger," I blurt. "You scared me, Tristan! I thought....well I didn't know what to think? You just went weird on me. Don't ever do that to me again Tristan Freeman!"

"I won't. I promise. Have I frightened you away Coral? Do you want some time, we can hold back the wedding' – I reach up and silence him with my lips. Then I pull back and gaze up at him for the longest time. I can see the trepidation in his eyes, it would kill him to lose me, but as I continue to gaze up at his wide, worried eyes, I feel like I'm gazing right into his very soul, and I can only see love. Yes, he's still the same man, my man, who's looking desperately worried right now.

"Stop it," I scold. "We are not holding anything back. Despite what you've told me, I still want you, Tristan. I still want to marry you. I still want to spend the rest of my life with you. And you're right, I wouldn't have let the subject go because after Debs told me about Scott, I realised for the first time I was just as much to blame for Justin running off with Harriet as he was. I know they shouldn't have done it the way they did, but the point is, he never would have gone if I'd opened up to him if we'd have expressed ourselves sexually. I guess, I just didn't feel secure enough with him to do that, but with you I do. I'm afraid Tristan, afraid of losing you because I'm not satisfying you." I take a deep cleansing breath, surprised I just said all of that. "We just need to sit down and talk it through it all," I add.

Tristan looks so relieved, I think he may cry. He crushes me to him again. "I'm sorry," he whispers.

"Stop saying you're sorry," I croak. "I understand you're apprehension and what you must have been feeling."

Tristan kisses the top of my head several times. "So we're ok, for now?" he asks, still afraid, still hesitant.

"Yes," I whisper, although I still feel apprehensive.

"Thank god," he breathes, gently rocking me. "Oh baby, you're so strong, so beautiful and sweet."

"Don't forget supportive and sexy," I tease, trying to lighten the mood. *Must be the booze!*

Tristan chuckles, but we stay like that for a while, just holding one another. I really should be in shock and frightened stupid, I have no idea what this means for our sex life.

"Hey," I pull back and look up at him. "We're going to talk about this, and you're going to be completely honest with me. But first, I'm going to the bathroom, and when I get back I expect a brandy waiting for me – and a kiss," I add, smiling up at him.

"Your wish is my command baby." He says.

I reach up, peck him on the lips then head to the en-suite. I stand in front of the mirror, staring back at myself, trying to wrap my head around it. I think Tristan thinks I'm a prude, and I'm not. Ok, I've only ever slept with one other guy before him, but I've read erotic novels. And I must admit, certain things turned me on, but I knew it would never happen because I wouldn't – no couldn't – allow a man to have control over me in the bedroom. It would be too much like my past, like what they did to me when I was a kid. But I'm an adult now, a woman with wants and needs of my own.

Admittedly, if he'd said to me when we met *'I like kinky sex'* I'd have run a mile, but I know him now. I know who he is, and he's a good man, a kind man, and I know he would never, ever hurt me.

My heart suddenly sinks to the pit of my stomach. Unless… unless he does want to hurt me? That's part of the whole dom-sub thing, I think? Pleasure-Pain – I shake my head, I don't think I can do that. I swallow hard. He's told me it makes no difference and that it's not something he needs, yet he's admitted that it really turns him on. I slap my hand to my mouth, trying to fight off the nausea – *Oh God…Is this the end of us?*

I blink back the tears, then stare at myself for the longest time, trying to find some courage from somewhere – but honestly, I'm bricking it. Tristan may want to do…things that… and if I can't, then how can I ever say I truly satisfy him? We would have to part ways, surely? I blink back more tears – *Come on Coral!*

I take a deep breath and narrow my eyes at myself. *The only way to find out is to go talk to him!* I take a deep rasping breath, pull back my shoulders, and head out the en-suite. When I return, Tristan is sitting on the sofa with two Brandy's in his hand. As I sit next to him, he leans forward, he's still hesitant and nervous, he kisses me sweetly and hands me my glass.

"So I've thought about it," I say, taking a good gulp. "And I guess I'm mostly worried about, well…the whole pleasure, pain thing?" I say, cringing inside.

Tristan's one eyebrow cocks up in surprise. "Er…I never did any of that," he says.

I frown. "But I thought that's what being a dominant is about?"

"No baby, it's about control," he softly says, reaching up and tucking my hair behind my ear.

"Oh? So you...well Olivia didn't' – "The only aspect Olivia liked was the parts we played. The roles if you like, she submitted, and I was the dominant."

"For your pleasure only?" I ask, taking a sip of my Brandy.

"No, hers too." I frown down at my glass. "She made a list for me," he continues. "She'd done this before, so she knew what she liked, it was just a case of putting that into practice, mixing it up, so she never knew what was coming. For the dominant, well for me, it was a huge turn on because I got to control her, well in the bedroom I was in control. As for the submissive, well Olivia said she liked it because it gave her a sense of freedom, a sense of release if you like, no decisions to be made, just doing what you're asked to do and getting rewarded for it – it really turned her on," he adds.

"So you never hurt her? Never bruised her?" I ask, keeping my eyes downcast.

"Christ no!" He says a little exasperated. "It wasn't like that Coral, it was all for pleasure. I would never do that to a woman, even if she wanted me to. That's too heavy for my liking."

"But you wanted to spank me?" I whisper, trying to be brave.

"Not to cause pain Coral. I meant it in a fun, sexual way. Look, spanking was part of it, yes, but only for pleasure baby." I frown again trying to understand it.

Then I remember that Justin slapped my ass once when we were having sex, and it freaked me out. I went mad at him – *Shit!*

"Lots of men like that baby," Tristan continues, echoing my thoughts. "But it doesn't have to be in a done in a dom-sub way, just two people finding out what they like, and what turns them on. And Olivia liked me being dominant in the bedroom."

"And...um...spanking her turned you on?" I whisper, my voice is barely audible.

"Yes." He tells me firmly.

I take a deep breath. "So no weird painful stuff going on?" I ask.

"No." Tristan sighs. "Coral, Olivia was used to it, so some things we did...well she'd like it rough..." Tristan sighs again. "I'm not explaining myself very well. Look, as a, for instance, Olivia liked to be blindfolded, tied up, spanked, denied orgasm then fucked – hard. She found good old regular sex to be...insignificant." He tells me, his eyes wide and dark.

"You two never made love?" I squeak, totally shocked and getting more of an idea of what their relationship was about.

Tristan slowly shakes his head at me. I can see the pain in his eyes and the regret. "But you're so good at it?" I say, still mystified.

Tristan smiles crookedly at me. "Thank you, baby," He reaches forward and softly strokes my cheek. "I guess, at the time I was ok with that, but I have to admit, not long before we split, she started asking me to be rougher with her, she wanted more pain, harder hits, and that was definitely not my scene." *Holy fuck – kinky bitch!*

I swallow hard. "What else did you do Tristan?"

"All sorts," he says, his cheeks flushing red.

"Spill!" I order. Tristan smiles a little awkwardly and then tells me a few more kinky things that they got up to. It's all stuff I would imagine any couple would do as they explore each other's wants and needs. Role-playing, toys, all that kind of stuff, nothing drastic, or painful, just a hell of a lot more than I've ever done, I start to relax a little.

Ok, so maybe this isn't such a big deal after all. What he's basically saying to me is that Olivia liked to be controlled in the bedroom. That's how she got her kicks, and as for Tristan, well if she was always a bossy cow with him, then I'm sure he did enjoy telling her what to do in the bedroom – dominating her probably gave him a huge high.

I can't help the giggle that bursts from within me. Tristan's head whips around, I glance across at him, still giggling, and see his mouth is open, his eyes wide.

"Coral!" He gasps.

"What?" I chuckle.

"You're laughing!" He chokes, his intensity fading, his eyes softening and the tension draining from his face.

"Oh Tristan," I giggle. "It's not that big a deal," I add.

"Not a..." He breaks off, looking quite shocked I have to say, then starts to shake his head. "You know, you never react the way I think you're going to," he adds, a smile starting to creep across his face, his dimples deepening.

"Sorry," I chuckle. "But when you told me you were a dominant, I had the most awful scenarios go racing around my head, but what you're basically saying to me, is the two of you experimented with what you liked." I take a deep breath and continue. "I may not have had much experience Tristan, but I have read some erotica, some of it turned me on, and some of it revolted me, but I know everyone is different and likes different things. Either way, I didn't really give it much thought because I never imagined I would be able to do anything like that with a guy because of my...issues," I say, the laughter fading. "But I'm willing to try, with you," I say. "Well depending on what you want to try that is," I add with sarcasm.

Tristan's eyes darken, his dominant look creeping in, weird really because I've always found it very sexy, I just didn't know it was dominance.

"What did you like in the books you read Coral?" He asks in his sexy, husky voice. He leans back against the sofa, his arm spread out behind me, and takes a sip while he waits for my answer.

I shake my head at him. "No way Mr Freeman, we are doing this my way!"

"Your way?" He questions, his head cocked to the side.

"Yes. I want you to tell me what you've done, and in return, I'll tell you if it's something that I've read and if it well...did things for me," I say, feeling shy. "Deal?" I add.

"Deal," Tristan throws his enigmatic smile at me, leans forward, and kisses me tenderly again...

TRISTAN AND I are quietly sipping more Brandy. It would seem, from the hour-long conversation we've just had, that the things that turn me on, which I've never tried, are pretty much the same things that turn Tristan on. Apart from the odd thing here or there, that we are both willing to try with one another. Hmm, a sexual spanking from Tristan – I wonder how I'm actually going to feel about that? But as Tristan has assured me, several times tonight *'You don't like it, baby, just say so, and we'll stop.'* This, as he again, has informed me several times, will not be a sub-dom thing, but a relationship, in which two people explore, and hopefully fulfil each other's wants and needs.

I feel kind of weird and excited at the same time. I have to remind myself that I did want this conversation, and now it's out there, what we both want, I really hope I don't fuck it up, and Tristan leaves me – I immediately stop that line of thinking. I know he won't leave me, he's crazy about me. Christ, he's deeply in love with me, any fool can see that, so it's about time I damn well accepted it too. But there's a part of me that feels like I'm not matched with him anymore, he's done so many different things, and he's so experienced compared to me.

I want to know what it's like, but I'm so nervous about it all. I sigh inwardly, the only way I'm going to know if this is something I can handle is to try it. I swallow hard and try to be brave.

"So what do you think now Coral?" Tristan asks.

I stare back at him, wondering what to say and feeling so shy again. "Um..." I laugh nervously and throw back the rest of my brandy. Then I stand, take my glass over to the mini-bar, and turn to gaze at him. "Why don't you show me," I say in a moment of bravery.

"What?" Tristan smirks then loses the grin as he stares back at my anxious face.

"Show me, I want to know what it's like and if this is something I can do for you."

"Coral, you don't need to do it for me, I've told you that," he replies.

"I know, but I want to know." I walk over and stand in front of him. "Show me," I say again, holding out my shaking hand to him.

"You want to try?" He asks, lowering his head and looking up at me through his long lashes. His eyes are so dark now, and his demeanour...is so hot!

I swallow hard. "Yes," I answer firmly.

Jeez! – I'm so nervous, yet so turned on. I stare back at him, wondering if I'm doing the right thing here. Tristan hasn't moved an inch, he's still staring up at me, his eyes narrowed as he does. Making a decision maybe, I don't know? So I decide to prompt him into action.

"Tristan," I close my eyes and take a deep calming breath. "You know all this talking about sex has got me really turned on' – His lips reach mine, instantly silencing me, and it's like no kiss I've had from him before. This is different, way, way different. This is dirty, sexy kissing.

I feel him bend down and his hands quickly skim up my legs as he grabs hold of my hips and lifts me up. I quickly wrap my legs around him as he moves forward and pushes me up against the living room wall. He gropes my ass, squeezes my hips, and he's pushing his erection hard against me as the kiss continues, commanding me, possessing me, taking not giving, but most of all it's really freaking hot!

Tristan is really turned on. I'm really turned on – *Holy fuck!*

I grip his hair hard and kiss him back with every inch of passion that's burning through my veins for this man, our moans and grunts filling the silence. And it just doesn't stop. It's like all the tension, all the passion, want and need is flooding out of him. It's like he's finally kissing me the way he probably wanted to kiss me the moment he met me.

I get a flashback of him saving me from falling outside Munchies, how he held me in his arms, his eyes burning into mine – *Whoa!* Yes, it was there too...I remember now.

After what seems like the longest, most passionate kiss in history, he pulls back panting hard and releases me. I slowly slide down his body. "Coral, you're still healing, we need to be careful." He commands in a deep, sexy voice, his lips inches from mine – *Whoa!* My lips feel so big and swollen.

I look up, and there it is, that look in his eyes. It's the exact same look he had when we first met, right there in reception at Chester House. No wonder it made me feel weird and freaked out. Maybe I was subconsciously picking up on it?

"Are you going to show me, or not?" I pant, although I think he's just given me a pretty good taster – And I want more.

He reaches out, his hand caressing my cheek for a moment, his eyes boring into mine, it's like he's debating whether or not to. Decision made, he takes a step back and silently holds his hand out to me. I place my hand in his, my heart a beat away from bursting out of my chest and I walk with him into the bedroom – *What's he going to do?*

We stop a few feet from the bed. Tristan releases my hand, picks up his MP3 player and selects a track. The sexiest, slow, soulful sound fills the speakers.

"Who's this?" I breathe.

Tristan turns to me. "Massive Attack, Teardrops," he says.

"Oh..." I swallow hard and just stare back at him – Frozen.

"Coral, do you really want to do this?" I nod in reply and reach up to unclip my halter-neck dress. "Allow me," he says in his sexy, husky voice.

I drop my arms and watch him casually stroll over to me. Just watching the way he walks is getting me all hot and bothered. Tristan stands right in front of me, we are both still breathing heavy. He reaches out and slowly skims his forefinger across my collarbone. I look up at him through my lashes – I'm so glad I put my makeup on tonight – and smile, he smiles back.

I think we are both relieved. I guess we both feel more secure in knowing what we want from each other. I'm so glad Debs came around and told me about Scott. At least now, I will hopefully, be giving Tristan his kicks, so fingers crossed, he won't fall into another woman's arms – *Stop it Coral! Tristan is right in front of you – concentrate!*

I look up at Tristan again, and without a word, he spins his forefinger in the air. *Oh!* He wants me to turn around. I smile coquettishly at him and slowly turn around. He pulls me back gently so I can feel his body against mine, his hard erection pressed against my backside.

"Mmm..." I close my eyes.

He keeps his one hand gently pressed on my belly, and then he slowly moves all of my hair to my left shoulder. Then I feel him gently place a kiss on my scar. Then his lips are on my right shoulder, planting more soft wet kisses as he works his way up my neck, right up to my ear. He gently bites my earlobe, making me groan with want.

"Hmm, you smell so good baby," he says in his deep, husky voice, his teeth grazing my earlobe once more.

"Tristan," I whisper, keeping my eyes closed. I want him, now. And I know he wants me because I can feel his erection harden against my backside, his breath coming in sharp gusts. He suddenly kneels down behind me. I feel his hands either side of my knees. His fingertips start to skim lightly up my legs, underneath the thin material of my dress, my head falls back, and my mouth is slack with want and need.

Tristan's breathe hitches when he reaches my lacy hold-ups. "So sexy," he slowly says, in his deepest voice. His hands continue to lightly skim up my legs until they reach the front of my lacy thong. "Mmm, I do approve Miss Stevens," he teases.

Then his one hand pushes against my belly again, pulling me against his erection, while his other hand reaches underneath the lacy material of my thong, and stops when he reaches my sex. I feel his lips kissing my neck and shoulder, driving me wild. Then he circles my clitoris a couple of times, and sinks two fingers inside me, his thumb still caressing.

"Ahh...Tristan," I moan.

"Oh baby," he whispers. "You're so ready." His fingers begin their torture, in and out. *Christ I'm going to come!* But I still want to try something different, I want to know what it's like, yet Tristan still hasn't agreed or disagreed?

"Tie me up," I whisper.

"No baby, not until you're healed," he whispers back, kissing my neck several times. *Jeez, my legs are going to give way.*

I want to roll my eyes, he's still so worried about me, even though I'm so much better. "Blindfold me then," I whisper, trying to be brave.

Tristan's hands still. "Coral," he whispers. "Not now."

I open my eyes, turn my head and meet his heated gaze. I reach up and softly caress his cheek. "I want to try," I whisper. "I thought you were going to show me?" I can see he's still hesitant about this. "I trust you," I tell him. He still looks torn. "Do it, Tristan," I challenge. "Show me what its like," I add, my heart racing.

Tristan takes hold of my wrist, registering my pulse then kisses the inside of my hand. "Ok," he reluctantly says, his eyes darkening. "Close your eyes baby," he softly demands, so I do. He gently pulls his fingers from inside me. I hear him opening a drawer, and then he's behind me again. I can feel the heat of his body, smell his potent scent. *Fuck! What's he going to do?*

All my senses are on high alert, yet I'm turned on big time.

"Are you sure?" he questions, still not touching me.

"Yes," I say as confidently as I can.

"This is one of my ties," Tristan whispers. "I'm going to place it over your eyes now," he adds, then slowly and carefully does so, and ties it at the back of my head. "Don't be afraid," he softly says.

"I'm not," I pant. I open my eyes, I can't see a thing. It's pitch black. *Whoa!*

His arms encase me, one around my chest, the other around my waist, squeezing me tight. "I'll never hurt you Coral," he whispers in my right ear.

"I know," I whisper back. *Boy, I love this guy!*

"Just tell me to stop ok," he softly adds.

"I will, I promise," I tell him.

"Ok baby. I'm going to undress you now," Tristan whispers.

His fingers begin slowly tracing across my shoulders, up towards my neck, I feel him unclip my dress. He slowly peels the dress down my body, until I feel it pool at my feet. I'm not wearing a bra, so now all I'm in are my knickers, hold-ups and stilettos.

"Wow!" Tristan exclaims in delight, I can tell he's moved, so he's in front of me. "You are such a sight to behold baby." I feel him gently kiss my lips. "I'm going to kiss you all over, my beautiful girl." Tristan lifts me into his arms and gently lays me down on the bed. *Oh my God!*

This is so hot, I have no idea where he'll touch or kiss me next, and that's what's driving me wild and turning me on so much.

"I want you to do something Coral," he demands.

"What?" I whisper.

"Lay your hands down each side of you, and keep them there." *What?*

"Why?" I whisper. He doesn't answer me, but I hear him stripping his clothing, it makes me smile. Then I feel his weight on the bed, crawling up to me? Tristan lifts my chin, the contact of his fingers making me gasp aloud.

"Because I said so," he says in his deepest, sexiest voice.

I almost climax – I swallow several times, I'm panting for Christ' sake!

"Answer me, baby," he says, a little softer.

"Ok," I whisper. I lay my arms down either side of me. My hands are pushing into the bed, my fingers gripping the covers. He plants his lips on mine for a moment, his tongue softly invading my mouth and then he starts trailing soft, wet kisses down the left side of my neck.

His lips are the only thing that's touching me. I cannot feel his hands or the weight of his body. Then he kisses my lips again and repeats the process down the right side of my neck. I'm squirming inside, and my breath is coming in sharp gusts – *Damn this is amazing!*

"Oh baby," Tristan says, planting another kiss on my lips. "You're so responsive, so beautiful." He begins again, kissing the hollow base of my throat, working his way down in between my breasts, and I know where he's heading. He stops abruptly, and then I feel his soft lips gently suck my already pert nipple into his mouth – *Holy Fuck! I'm going to come.*

"Tristan," I cry out. He moves and does the same with my left nipple. "Ahh..." I feel him shift his weight slightly as he trails kisses down the centre of my body. He stops again, and I feel his fingers softly stroke my torso. *Whoa! That feels so sensual, so sexy!*

His fingers work their way down towards my knickers, his lips following, with sweet kisses. He cups the material between his fingers and slowly peels them off.

I feel so...so exposed - I know what he's going to do, and I know the moment he touches my sex, that'll be it, I'll come. I know I will.

"Even better," I hear him say, I think he's smiling. "Oh Coral, you should see yourself now, wearing nothing but hold-ups and heels. You look so fucking sexy. I am so turned on right now."

"Tristan," I whisper, pushing my hips up – I want to feel him inside me, so badly.

I hear him chuckle. Then I feel his weight shift again. Taking me by surprise, he lifts my right leg and kisses my ankle, then works his way up, over my calf and then he's kissing my knee.

"Ah yes," he says. "These sexy legs of yours, if I remember

rightly, I was going to kiss every inch of them," he whispers. *He remembered, oh Tristan!*

He continues this way, heading north, kissing my legs all over until he reaches the apex of my thighs. *Oh god!* I am so hot, panting, wanting, needing him inside me now! My hands are pulling at the sheets, my body fit to burst – I'm being taken away on a sensual journey.

"Tristan...I want you, in me..." I manage to garble.

"All in good time," he teases. I feel him lift my left leg and begin the same process as he did with my right – *Jesus I'm going to internally combust!*

As he reaches the apex of my thighs again, he takes both my legs in his hands, bends my knees and pushes them up, then opens them wide – *Whoa!*

His hands are resting on my shins, pushing down, holding me still. Then I feel his lips, there on my sex – I stop breathing. His tongue slowly begins to tease, up and down, licking me, tasting me and then blowing on me – I hiss in response, trying so hard to control myself.

"Oh baby," he says in his most sexy, husky voice. "You have the prettiest pussy I have ever seen." *What?*

Did he really just say that? I am gasping, I can hardly contain myself as Tristan chuckles and continues his sensual torture, licking, sucking, twirling...and I know that's it, I cannot hold on.

"Tristan!" I scream as the most intense orgasm I have ever had rips through me, sending my senses into disarray. I think I have left planet earth.

Tristan continues, licking sucking, tasting my orgasm. *Christ, stop, I'm too sensitive!*

I feel the pressure building again – *No! No way, I can't, not again?* - My body has other ideas. Tristan releases his right hand from my leg, then I feel two fingers gently slide inside me, my muscles are still clenching, squeezing his fingers as they move in and out of me, his tongue continues to bring me to the brink – *Holy mother of God!*

And I come again, my back bowing and my head craning back as waves of ecstasy continue to pulse through me. *Whoa!*

"Baby," Tristan says, I can tell he's smiling as he lets go of my other leg. I feel his body cover mine, and then his hands are releasing the tie. I blink several times as light fills my irises. I look up, Tristan is hovering over me.

"You ok?" he asks, stroking my hair away from my face.

I can see he looks concerned. I hear the music change, something equally as sensual, a saxophone, it's a haunting melodic tune.

"Tristan," I moan. My eyes closing for a moment, I still feel like I'm floating.

"I'll take that as a yes," he titters. His lips swoop down, kissing me hard. I can taste my orgasm on his lips and his tongue.

"Mmm," I moan. I open my eyes and look up at the man I adore, the man that seems to know my body better than I do.

Tristan softly kisses me once more and gazes down at me. "Well done baby. Did you enjoy that?"

"Tristan that was..." Words fail me. His answering grin is breathtaking, but now I want to repay the favour. I go to move, but Tristan shakes his head at me. "But I want to," I moan.

"It's late baby, maybe tomorrow?" He says, his eyes glinting wickedly.

"I'll hold you to that," I tease.

"I'm sure you will," he says. He moves his position, so his legs are either side of me, then stretches across me to the bedside table and grabs a condom. I look up at his impressive length, looming large above me and lick my lips.

"Like what you see," he says, coming back to me and throwing the condom on the bed. Then taking his erection in his hand, he begins to stroke himself, slowly, up and down. I'm mesmerised.

"Let me," I say, reaching up.

He shakes his head at me. His dark, broody – sorry, dominant – look is there. I put my hand back down. Then taking me by surprise, Tristan moves forward, so his erection is almost at my lips. "Kiss it," he demands.

I smile up at him, lick my lips and gently kiss his tip.

"Ahh..." His eyes close in response, as he continues to stroke himself. So I lean up, take his tip into my mouth and gently suck, his eyes dart open.

"Jesus!" He hisses, but he doesn't move, so I continue to suck him, he's getting harder in my mouth, even though I only have his tip – God he tastes good.

"No more," he says, suddenly moving back. I watch him sheath himself with the condom, and then he leans down and plants a soft kiss on my lips.

"Turn over baby." *Oh!*

I carefully turn onto my stomach. Tristan shuffles back and starts to knead my buttocks. "Mmm..." It feels so good.

"Are you in pain?" he softly asks, his hands stroking up and down my back and then squeezing my butt cheeks.

"No." I smile. I'm still floating...

"Ok, then onto your knees baby," he tells me. *Oh!* I lean up then rest my weight on my forearms. "Good." His hands continue to caress my backside. I can feel his erection at the opening of my sex – *Come on Tristan, Fuck me!*

Suddenly his hands are gone, then his left one grips my hip, and he pushes the head of his erection into me and stops.

"Yes," I moan, my eyes closing to the sensation. Then he pulls out of me, and his right hand comes down with a light slap on my right butt cheek – *Fuck!* – Tristan forces his full length into me before I have time to assimilate it. *Whoa!*

He pushes his length in and out of me, causing friction. I realise my butt cheek is tingling, but it didn't hurt. "Tristan," I moan. This is exquisite.

He pulls out of me again. *No!* – Then he does the same, pushing into me as he brings his hand down for another light slap – *Damn!*

"Coral..." He moans. Tristan picks up the pace, gaining speed as he slams into me, making low grunting breathless sounds as he does. He brings his hand down once more onto my right cheek, and I come, instantly, again and again, squeezing hard against his length as he really starts to move, fucking me like he's never done before, and it is so erotic, so sexy. I have no words, so I moan a long drawn out sound – it's all I can manage.

"Fuck Coral," Tristan shouts through clenched teeth. Both his hands are gripping my thighs so hard, it's almost painful. My insides respond again, coming hard for the second time – *What the...* Tristan suddenly stills, finding his release. I am still pulsing around his length, the waves continuing one after the other.

"Christ Coral," Tristan gasps between gritted teeth. Then gently wrapping his arm around my waist, he takes me with him as we collapse onto the bed. I lie panting, facing Tristan, wrapped up in his warm arms. "Baby, are you ok?" Tristan asks.

I am unable to respond...I feel...so...so satisfied, satiated, how odd?

"Coral, please look at me," he whispers in a worried voice.

My eyes dart open and meet his.

"Tell me you're ok," he says, stroking my hair back away from my face again, searching my eyes for an answer.

"Tristan, that was...." Again, I'm lost for words. I close my eyes and grin from ear to ear.

"You enjoyed that?" He asks, sounding a little more relieved.

"Tristan," I pant. "That was amazing, you can do that to me again...anytime," I whisper.

"You're not just saying that are you Coral?" he asks, his concern evident.

I open my eyes, take his face in my hands and stare intently into his eyes. *How can I make him understand?*

"No, I'm not just saying that. Let me tell you something," I say, swallowing hard. "When I was with Justin, and we used to... well, you know, I would get flashbacks of what happened when I was a kid..." I shake my head, not wanting to remember.

"Coral, you don't have to' – "Explain myself?" I interrupt.

Tristan nods. "Yes, I do. I should have told you this already...but maybe things happen for a reason, so something as important as this is said at the right time," I ponder, then continue. "From the first time you made love to me, and every time since, I haven't had a single flashback. I will admit, I was apprehensive about trying what we just did, and I'll tell you now that would never, ever have happened with any other man, but that was mind-blowing Tristan. What we just did was only possible because you make me feel so safe, so loved and protected. This is the relationship I've secretly dreamed of having all my life, the intimacy, feeling connected, in-love." I look down feeling shy, and chuckle.

"I still think I'm going to wake up and it's all been a very long, wonderful dream. You make everything disappear when we make love. All I see, think and feel is you, Tristan, there's no fear at all."

"Oh, baby." Tristan pulls me into him and holds me close. His one arm wrapped around me, his other gently stroking my back. I have my head on his chest, my arms holding him tight, our legs are entwined together – I am in heaven. Hmm…heaven? Maybe that should be our wedding song? Which reminds me, the haunting track is still playing.

"Tristan, this music, who is it?" I sleepily mumble.

"Vangelis. It's the Love Theme from Bladerunner."

"Oh," I whisper.

"Do you like it?" He asks.

"Yeah..." I breathe. But there's something I need to know before sleep takes me. "Tristan, did *you* enjoy that?" I ask hesitantly.

He kisses the top of my head several times. "Very much so, that was hot baby," he says, I can tell he's smiling.

"Better than how it was with Olivia?" I squeak.

"Don't do that Coral," he says.

"Do what?" I whisper – although I think I know what he's about to say.

"Compare yourself to her. Look, I know you're insecure, well some of the time you are, but just don't do it ok. Look at it this way, if I asked you to compare me with Justin' – I snort before he's even had a chance to finish. "It's ridiculous right?" He says.

"Yes," I smile. "Point made. I will never say that again," I add, feeling like the luckiest woman on planet earth. "Can I ask you something else?" I whisper.

Tristan chuckles. "I was about to doze off..." And leaves the sentence hanging.

"Why did you take the blindfold off?" I whisper shyly.

"You didn't want me to?" He asks, a little shocked I think.

"No, it's not that, I just wondered?" I feign innocence.

"Baby steps," he says.

"What?" I chuckle.

"Bit by bit Coral. I had every intention of talking about this more thoroughly tomorrow. But now is as good a time as any I suppose. I could have gone the whole distance, but I just wanted you to get a taste of it first. But this is good baby, I want you to communicate with me. So next time, do you want to try it with the blindfold on until we're finished?"

"I surely do," I say teasingly.

Tristan chuckles and squeezes me tight again. "Always surprising me," he murmurs to himself, then starts humming to Bladerunner.

"Tristan, can I ask you something else?"

He really starts laughing now. "You have your talkative head on," he says, still laughing.

"Sorry," I mumble. "Another time."

"Hey, I want to know now so spill!"

"Ok, I'm only asking because you didn't mention it, and I think you have done this, but you haven't said because, well… because of my past." I swallow hard. "You've tried anal sex haven't you?"

He instantly stops breathing, and because I'm lying on his chest, I can hear how quickly his heart has picked up. "What makes you say that Coral?" He asks, his voice sounding worried.

"I…I just think with everything else you've tried. You know… it's common. More common than people think it is and...well, I guess..." I sigh heavily, lean up, prop my head on my hand and gaze down at him. His eyes are wide and dark, his body frozen as he stares up at me. "It's ok Tristan if you don't want to tell me. I just...well, Justin...he wanted..." I stop, look down, and shake my head feeling nervous.

"Hey," Tristan lifts my chin. "You don't have to prove anything to me Coral' – "I'm not trying to prove something..." I laugh nervously. "When Justin said he wanted to try it, I had no-one to ask. I couldn't talk to Harriet, or my mom or my sister, so I had a look online. The only reason I did that was because Justin kept going on and on about how 'pleasurable' it was supposed to be. Selfish bastard just wanted to try it, he didn't really give a damn about how it would affect me, but then, how could he when he didn't know' – "Coral, your waffling," Tristan says, grinning widely at me.

"Sorry," I laugh. "I guess I'm just curious," I add feeling shy again.

Tristan sighs heavily and reaches up to caress my cheek. "Yes." He simply says, answering my question.

I knew it. "And it's...?" I can't find the right words.

"Very pleasurable," he says. "But most people freak out about it, and I'm very surprised you're not."

"So am I," I laugh. "I guess, I just..." I laugh nervously again. "Tristan, I've...I've never felt so free as I do with you. It's like, I just feel like I want to try...you know, and I feel like I can with you. I know you won't hurt me or make me do anything I don't want to do. That's what always scared me about experimenting with Justin, I was afraid if I said stop, he wouldn't." I swallow hard then continue. "I trust you, and I love you, so maybe that's why I feel ok about it? I want to try everything with you, Tristan. I feel like I can go on a sexual journey with you and I won't get hurt. No pain, just pleasure, I'm...I'm not afraid Tristan."

"I can see that," he answers sarcastically, one eyebrow cocked up in amusement.

"Hey!" I slap his large shoulder playfully.

"Coral, whatever you want, and however, you want our intimate time to be spent is all up to you." He brings my face down to his and kisses me, hard. "But come now darling, get comfortable. It's very late, and we have an early flight, we'll talk more about this tomorrow, ok?"

"Ok," I breath, peck his lips once more, and snuggle against his chest, feeling safe, warm and yet again, even more in love than I was this morning.

"Love you, baby," Tristan says, squeezing me tight.

"Love doesn't even begin to cover it," I say, grinning widely. "Stars, moons, across universes, until the end of time, infinity.... forever."

Tristan chuckles. "Sleep now gorgeous."

"Night Tristan," I retort dryly.

He chuckles again. I close my eyes and listen to the sound of Tristan's slow breathing, his strong heart slowly beating, and before I know it I am drifting off.

CHAPTER TWENTY-FIVE

WE ARE SAT IN the VIP lounge at Newquay Cornwall Airport. Tristan is reading a paper, Financial Times, to be precise, while I have my nose stuck in a very erotic novel on my e-reader. In fact, it's actually turning me on, in here, with all these other people around me. I guess that because it's making me think of Tristan, of what he revealed to me last night, and then what we got up to afterwards. I still can't believe Tristan's a dominant, well he's not, but kind of is, and he's to be my husband in two days' time – *Whoa!*

Every time I have thought that my heart has fluttered madly against my chest. I still can't believe that I'm going to be married. I shake my head and try to get back to the novel, which is supposed to be taking my mind off what's going to happen when we get back to Brighton, but I can't concentrate.

I sigh inwardly. What the hell am I going to do with myself next week? I put my e-reader down and stare out of the window. Tristan will be back at work, I have a whole week without him. It's going to drive me mad, I know it is. I can't sit around not doing anything – "Coral." Tristan pulls me from my musing.

"Hmm," I turn and look at him. He's put his paper down, and he's looking at me with his head cocked to the side.

"Holiday blues?" He asks, clasping my hand in his.

"No." I frown and glance down at our hands.

"Then what is it darling?" He asks, looking concerned, his eyebrows scrunching together.

"Is Karen still at Chester House?" I ask.

His frown deepens. "Yes, for now." I nod once and stare out of the window. He's not going to like it, I know he's not. "Coral, will you please tell me what's wrong?" He pleads.

"I want to go back," I whisper.

"To Chester House?" He guesses his eyes wide.

"Yes," I reply nonchalantly.

"No - Absolutely not!" He barks.

"Tristan, if I want to go back to work, I will go back to work! I'm almost healed, and I am not going to sit around the house all day while you go off being commander and chief!"

His eyes close briefly. "I'll only be gone a few hours a day," he softly says.

"It doesn't make any difference how long you're out for Tristan, I need to do this." I squeak.

"Why?" He asks in defeat.

"Don't you know me at all?" I whisper.

A very lazy, sexy smile appears. "Oh I do," he says. "Intimately," he adds. *Oh!* I know his meaning and his game.

"Mr Freeman," I chide. "Behave!"

Tristan chuckles slightly then frowns. "I don't want you working' – "I thought you said we have no need to control one another?" I point out, remembering what he told me.

He narrows his eyes at me. "Ok, you got me there. But I still don't want' – "I'm going back to work!" I tell him firmly.

"What about taking the cookery courses instead?" He says.

"I'm not ready to do that yet Tristan, cooking requires a lot of moving about. I'm not healed enough for that, besides I don't see how I'm supposed to fit it in with two months of physiotherapy scheduled for three afternoons a week!" *That told him!*

His lips set into a hard line. He can't argue that one. His eyes close again, and he pinches the bridge of his nose in frustration. Then opening his paper back up, he continues reading, shaking his head and mumbling to himself as he does.

I stifle the giggle that wants to burst out of me – then I have an idea.

"Tristan." He looks up at me over his paper. He is not a happy man. Maybe this will change his mind. "Will you take me shopping?" I ask trying to sound girlie and sweet.

"Shopping?" He says his voice low.

"Uh-huh. I don't want to be in trousers all the time, so I was thinking, maybe you could help me chose some new work clothes, you know, like skirts and dresses?" I instantly picture it. Tristan's in his office, I'm at my desk, he calls me in to do something for him, but I'm in the mood, so I lock the door, hitch up my skirt and give him a glimpse of the sexy stockings and frilly knickers I have on...Hmm.

"Who knows what could happen?" I whisper seductively. I lean forward, peck his cheek, then sit back to look at him. His eyes are dark and tempting, his look heated. He swallows hard, shifts slightly in his seat, pulls his newspaper down, so it's hiding his hand, and readjusts his man bits. *Oh yeah! That worked.*

I innocently bat my lashes at him. "So will you take me?" I whisper shyly.

Tristan clears his throat, lifts his hand and places it behind my neck, and then he slowly pulls me down towards his face, stopping right before our lips meet. "You are one hell of a negotiator," he breathes, his eyes boring into me.

"Do we have a deal?" I whisper gazing at his wide, dark chocolate eyes.

"Oh baby, you know I'm going to say yes to that. Besides, I can keep an eye on you at work, but be warned, if I think you look tired I'm sending you home." He tells me firmly.

"Yes boss," I giggle.

He narrows his eyes at me. "Frustrating woman!" He hisses.

"Kiss me," I challenge. Tristan glances at the other passengers and then quickly pecks me on the lips. Releasing his hand from my neck, I sit back in my seat feeling triumphant.

"I'm presuming you won't go back until Monday?" He says petulantly.

"Monday sounds good. Shall we go shopping Sunday?"

"The day after the Wedding?" He says incredulously.

"Yes, I think it'll be fun. Just think what we could get up to in the changing rooms." I say, grinning broadly. *Just think of the possibilities!*

His mouth pops open. "I don't think so Coral," he retorts, knowing my meaning.

"Why not?" I moan.

He leans into me. "Because they have cameras – and besides, the last thing in the world I want is for anyone to see my wife in the throes of passion." I shiver internally, all humour gone – No, definitely not if they have cameras. Tristan grasps my hand in his. "You ok?" I nod once. He squeezes my hand again. "Let's go shopping tomorrow," he adds.

"Tomorrow?" I look up at him. "But you're working?"

"Yes, I am. I can spare a couple of hours at lunchtime though. Besides, I've made plans for us on Sunday," he says in his authoritative voice, trying to hide a smile.

"You have?" I squeak, wondering what it is.

"Yes." Tristan turns and grins widely at me. "My wedding present to you," he softly adds. *Oh...holy mother of God...Crap, crap, triple Crapiola!*

"What?" He asks, registering the look of horror on my face.

"You...you've got me a wedding present?" I squeak feeling mortified. I haven't got Tristan a wedding present? What kind of a fiancé does that make me?

Tristan throws his paper into the chair next to him, reaches over, lifts me up, and sits me on his lap. "What are you looking so upset about?" He asks, holding his hand against my cheek so I can't look away. *Crap!*

Tears pool in my eyes – I am a horrid person, who does not deserve him.

"Hey," Tristan softly says. "There's no need for tears." I sniff loudly and stare down at my twisted fingers. "Coral, please tell me what you're upset about," he says, his voice tender and full of love.

"I...I haven't got you a wedding present," I squeak, keeping my eyes downcast. "What does that say about me?" I croak, swiping at the stupid tears rolling down my cheeks. Tristan chuckles, my eyes dart up to meet his. "You think it's funny?" I sniff.

"Coral, it's the last thing in the world I was expecting – especially with what you've been through," he softly says, tenderly stroking my cheek again.

"But you've got me one!" I squeak a little high pitched.

Tristan chuckles again. "Yes, but I..." He stops and looks down at my hands that are anxiously pressed together. He brings them to his lips and kisses them several times. "I don't need a wedding present baby," he says.

"You don't?" I whisper.

"Coral, you're everything I've ever wanted, so you kind of are my wedding present."

My mouth gapes open. "Oh Tristan," I mewl, wrapping my arms around his neck and cradling my head under his chin, not giving a damn who's in the room with us.

"I can't wait to open you up," he adds in his sexy, husky voice.

I gasp and look up at him. "Tristan Freeman, you have a very dirty mind!" I retort, trying not to laugh, and failing badly. Tristan laughs too and pulls me forward so he can gently kiss my forehead.

WE ARE DRIVING back to the house in the big Jag. I take a deep breath in and slowly blow it out. It's done, I have said goodbye to my mother and laid her to rest. When Stuart collected us from the airport, he had her belongings sitting on the back seat for me, so as we drove back to Brighton, I looked through them and decided on the items to bury.

A photograph of me as a baby in her arms, my father beside her, they both looked so happy. And a photograph of Kelly too, she was older, a couple of years maybe, as she sat on my mother's lap, with her father I'm presuming stood behind them both. It was a very strange experience, but at least I feel as though I can move on now. I can focus on the future and on the life I am going to have with Tristan.

It still feels weird being back in Brighton and back to reality.

On the one hand, I am beyond excited to be marrying Tristan, and I'm looking forward to seeing my friends and family again, but on the other hand, I feel quite sombre. I still haven't decided what to do with my studio, which reminds me, I need to unpack all my stuff. And I still have no job, even though I'll be at Chester House while I search for a new one - All the problems that were here before we went away are still here.

There's a dark part of me, an old part of me that wants to run away, back to Cornwall, but I know I can't do that. But more than anything else, I'm feeling melancholy because I now have to share Tristan – our little bubble has been burst, and I want it back, so badly.

"Hey," Tristan says, squeezing my hand as Stuart pulls up outside the house. "Everything ok?" He softly asks.

I turn and put on my best fake smile. "Sure," I say. That did not sound convincing.

"Shall I take the bags inside sir?" Stuart asks.

Tristan nods to him but keeps his eyes firmly locked on mine. "You didn't cry," he says, softly stroking my cheek. To be fair, I'm surprised I didn't as I stood at my mother's would be grave and lay the photographs down, then planted the tree. Tristan held my hand as I said my silent goodbyes, he's been so good to me, so supportive – Maybe it just needs time to catch up with me?

"I think it's because I feel relieved more than anything else," I say.

"You're so brave," he says, squeezing my hand again.

I shake my head and stare out the window at the house.

Tristan sighs. "What is it Coral?" I shrug. "Holiday blues?" Tristan asks again.

"No Tristan it's not," I tell him firmly.

Tristan unclips his seatbelt. I feel him slide across the seat to me. Reaching up, he cups his fingers under my chin and turns my head to face him. "Tell me," he demands, his tone sharp.

I sigh heavily. "Just...back to reality I guess," I say trying not to frown. I really don't want to tell him how much I'm going to miss him today, how desperately empty I already feel, and he hasn't even left yet.

Tristan swallows hard. "Are you having second thoughts?" He says his voice almost a whisper.

I frown at him. "Second thoughts about what?"

"Marrying me," he says his voice solemn.

My eyes widen as I stare back at him. "No Tristan, no second thoughts. My feet are toasty warm, how about yours?" I ask.

"On fire. And no – no second thoughts. I've been waiting to marry you all of my life," he tells me, "I just hadn't found you yet." And I melt – He really does say the sweetest things.

I smile a genuine smile. "Sorry," I say reaching up to caress his beautiful face. "I just know how much I'm going to miss you today that's all."

Tristan sags with relief. "Me too," he says leaning in to kiss me. "Let's get inside, you look tired," he adds. *I feel tired!*

I've been taking a morning and afternoon nap every day for the past nine days, and I feel like I need one. I look down at my watch, it's 11.15am – Rob won't be here until twelve to collect me, I guess I have time.

"Ok," I smile sweetly at him and peck him on the lips.

Tristan jumps out the car and comes around to my side. Opening the door, he gives me his hand, I so love that about him. I place my hand in his and step out into the morning sunshine.

"Dr Green has called," he says. "She wants to see you on Monday."

"Ok," I sigh. Tristan squeezes my hand, and we head through the open door.

Edith is in the kitchen, ready to greet us both. I smile warmly at her as we walk over.

"Well hello you two," she says. "You both look so well, did you have a good time?" She asks, directing her question at us both.

"Edith, we had a fantastic time, thank you," Tristan says, grinning widely.

I smile up at Tristan and squeeze his hand. We had more than a fantastic time, we had a very eye-opening, sexy sex time, that's what we had. Tristan gazes down at me and winks. I swear he's reading my thoughts right now.

"Well it's good to have you both back," Edith says.

"Thanks, Edith," I say, smiling fondly at her.

"Can I get you anything?" She asks, looking from me to Tristan.

"Coral's tired, so she's going to take a nap, but I'm famished. Can you rustle me up a quick sandwich before I head into the office?" Tristan asks.

I smile and roll my eyes at him – *Where does he put it all?*

"Of course," Edith replies and busies herself in the kitchen.

"Tristan, stay and eat. I'll see you tonight," I tell him. I don't want a long goodbye. I think my heart may crack in two.

"I'll be back in a second," he tells Edith, and completely ignoring me, he tugs on my hand. We head up the stairs, hand in hand, and I realise this is the first time since I came out of the hospital that Tristan hasn't carried me up or down these stairs. Wow, what a difference, I really do feel so much better. Maybe we should have a honeymoon? Reaching our bedroom, Tristan opens the door and gestures for me to go first.

I walk in and spy our big bed. *Hmm...*

Taking me by surprise, Tristan lifts me up into his arms, lays me down on the bed, and snuggles up next to me. "Thank you my gorgeous, sexy girl for the best holiday I've ever had." He says, his eyes glowing with sincerity, his knuckles skimming my cheek as he hovers over me.

I grin broadly at him. "The best?" I tease.

He nods then smiles his shy smile.

"Wait until our honeymoon," I say, even though we haven't booked it.

His cheeks flush. "Looking forward to it Miss Stevens, but may I remind you we haven't booked anything yet?" He says, spookily reading me.

"I know, but now I've healed so much, I think we should," I say.

Tristan looks a little worried. "You want to go away next week?"

"No baby, I know you need to catch up with work. Maybe sometime after Gladys's wedding?" I suggest.

"Ok." He smiles. "Where would you like to go?" He asks.

I start giggling. "Tristan, I have no idea...why don't you surprise me," I suggest.

"You're sure?" He asks.

"Absolutely positive," I say, trying to stifle a yawn. Tristan suddenly looks serious again. He takes my face between his hands, staring intently at me, then leans down and softly meets my lips. "Mmm..." I murmur he tastes so good.

"I'm so in love with you Coral," he croaks in his low, sexy voice, kissing my lips, my cheek and finally my forehead. "I'm a very lucky man." I smile goofily at him. He kisses me once more on the lips. "I'll miss you today. It's going to feel very strange not being with you," he adds.

"I know," I whisper, trying not to think about it. "But you'll be back for tea, right?" I add, slightly panicked.

"Yes baby, I promise." I yawn again. "Come on, get some sleep." He strokes my hair, and begins humming our song, my song as his fingers stroke my forehead, and softly run through my hair. *Some Enchanted Evening* – And I drift.

I HAVE HAD the most wonderful afternoon. It's been great seeing Rob and Carlos again, and Bob is in great shape too, so I feel much more relaxed now. We ate lunch at Hotel Seattle, it has a wonderful decking area that looks right over the Marina. Then Carlos took Bob back to his studio so they could play another game of checkers, while Rob and I went off to the supermarket to get him some decent food.

However, it turns out that since Susannah's attack on Bob I'm not the only one who's concerned about him. I have found out that Bob's been back in his studio for four days now and that Carlos has been to see him every day and taken him out for lunch, and he's dined at Gladys's twice, and Joyce took him out for tea last night too. He seems in good spirits, and I'm grateful that my family and friends have been taking care of him while I've been away.

"Hey, Bob?" I say as Rob, and I put away his fresh groceries. "Have you thought any more about my offer?"

"What offer?" Rob pipes up.

"Nothing to do with you, Delgado!" I tease. Rob smirks at me then sticks his nose up in the air as though he's not bothered, it makes me giggle.

"Yes, I have," Bob says.

"And?" I prompt, as I join him on the sundeck – Looks like he's beaten Carlos at checkers, again.

"It's not for me darling, I like being here. And you kids need your space," he says, gazing out at the view – Yeah, I get that, it's pretty awesome. "Doesn't mean I don't appreciate the offer though," he adds.

I reach over and squeeze his hand. "You're sure?" I question.

"Positive," he tells me.

"Ok." I sigh inwardly, I hope he's telling the truth and not just saying that because he thinks he'll be a burden. I shall ask Tristan to talk to him, just to make sure.

"Well, we better get going," Rob says. He's got a client later, and he hates being late, plus, Tristan made him promise he'd get me home safely.

However, I have an ulterior motive, a plan. I know Tristan won't like it, but after saying my goodbyes to my mother, and feeling relieved because of it, I feel like I really need to get this over and done with too. I want a clean slate. I want to be able to marry Tristan without anything hanging over my head, my decision on the beach includes this too – I need a fresh start.

"I want to stay," I say, looking up at him. "You and Carlos go, I'll be fine."

"Coral!" Rob bites. "Do you want Tristan and I to get on?" he says, his hands on his hips.

"Of course I do," I choke.

"Then why are you doing this? He's going to bite my head off if he finds out I didn't get you home!" I roll my eyes at him, pull out my mobile and call Tristan.

It's answered on the second ring. "Hey, baby." He sounds busy.

"Just wanted to let you know Rob is leaving but I'm staying on with Bob for a while, I'll get a taxi back later," I tell him.

"Don't do that Coral, just call Stuart, and he'll come and pick you up." He replies.

"Ok." I walk away from everyone so they can't hear me. "I know you're busy, but want to tell you how much I'm missing you. I hope you haven't made any plans for tonight." I whisper.

"Why?" Tristan asks I can tell he's smiling.

"Because I plan on having my wicked way with you," I whisper.

"I'll hold you to that," he growls sexily. "Baby gotta go."

"Ok, bye!" I squeak and hang up. I don't want to be the girlfriend – no wife – that constantly bugs him at work. I walk back over to Rob and smile smugly at him. "See, there's no problem," I say.

"Evidently," Rob snorts – I bob my tongue out at him. He

chuckles at me then he and Carlos get up to leave. I hug them both, hard.

"See you both tomorrow then," I say. Pre-wedding checks apparently.

"Nervous?" Rob asks as he hugs me.

"No, not at all," I softly say.

He pulls back and assesses me. "Oh god! Look at the dreamy loved up look in her eyes Carlos, it's sickening!" He teases.

"Hey!" I scowl at Rob. Carlos pulls me in for a hug. "Ignore him, he's just jealous!" he sniggers, making me chuckle. Rob pouts at us. I wave to them both as they head down the concourse.

"Hey Bob," I say, sitting next to him. "I wanted to ask you something," I add, feeling nervous.

"You can ask me anything," Bob says sweetly.

I take a deep breath, I hope he says yes. "Well, I wanted to ask...will you give me away on Saturday?" I swallow hard and wait for his answer.

"Oh Coral," Bob chokes then grabbing my hand, he squeezes it tight. "Nothing would give me greater pleasure darling."

I blink back the tears that have pooled in my eyes. "Thanks," I croak.

"Coral, I'm sure it's not something you want to talk about, but I wanted to say, I'm so sorry about your mother. Carlos told me all about it while you were away."

"Oh," I whisper, feeling surprised.

"Can I ask *you* something?" Bob says.

"Of course," I whisper, my heart speeding up.

"Well, it's a bit delicate," he says, hesitant.

"It's ok Bob, you can ask me," I tell him, trying to ease his discomfort.

"You're adopted," he states, I nod once. "Is your father still alive?" I nod once more. "Are you in contact with him? I only ask because of what you've just asked of me," he says, his voice soft.

"No, I don't see him Bob...he...well he left when I was four. I haven't seen him since," I whisper, remembering the sound of his voice when I recently spoke to him, how it called to me on a such a deep level – I didn't think that would happen, it's been so long.

"I'm sorry Coral, but I'm sure if he knew you, he'd be very proud of who you are," he says, patting my hand. "I am," he adds. *Oh, Bob!*

"Thanks, Bob," I squeak, trying to keep the tears at bay. "How about another game?" I add, trying to get off the subject.

"Double or nothing?" Bob smiles.

"Yes," I giggle.

Bob sets up the game while I head back inside and get us some more lemonade.

MY HEART IS hammering as I walk down the stark white corridor. This place looks just like the hospital my mother was in, and just like before, I can hear the cries, screams and delusional mumbling's of the patients – I shiver internally, it gives me the creeps. The male nurse guides me through a set of doors and down another corridor. Susannah has been in solitary confinement since her attack on Tristan and me, and if I don't drop the charges, she'll go on trial for attempted murder – I wonder if she knows that?

Finally, the male nurse stops and points to a door. It has a tiny window with metal bars across it. I step forward and look through. The first thing I notice is that Susannah is sat on the wide window ledge, her arms wrapped tightly around her legs, as she stares despondently out of the window that has metal bars in front of it. It's a very bright room, which I wasn't expecting. The walls are white, as is the bedding on the small, single bed in the corner.

"Am I allowed in?" I ask, stepping away from the window.

"No. You can speak to her in the visitor's room," he says, looking me up and down.

"Ok." I frown at him. He doesn't seem very nice, not the kind of guy I would expect to be working here. He's short, with a belly that's bulging over his trousers, has small beady eyes that are framed with thick glasses, and thin lips. He's really creepy.

"I'll show you where it is," he says in a not so nice manner. He reaches out to take hold of my arm. I step out of his reach – *Ugh! Definitely a creep!*

"You carry on," I say, gesturing for him to go first. "I'll follow you."

He grimaces at me, sniffs as though he's displeased and walks ahead. I follow him down another corridor and into a small room, it's very bleak. Grey walls, grey desk and chair, with a large window dividing the room in half, in the centre is a circular grate – I guess that's so I can hear her.

"Take a seat, I'll bring her through," he says, smiling down at me. I shudder. Somehow, I get the feeling he likes this part of his job, manhandling the patients – *Don't think about him Coral, concentrate!*

Moments later, he shuffles Susannah into the room, and keeping a firm grip on her arm, he practically shoves her into the chair opposite me. This doesn't seem to bother her at all, she seems completely despondent, and she hasn't looked up at me, but I'm guessing that's because she's so knocked out from all the drugs swishing around her system. I feel a twinge of sadness, she looks a right mess. She's wearing a light grey baggy cotton top with matching bottoms, her hair is greasy and lank, and her face is pale and sunken with dark grey rings underneath her eyes. I should be feeling weird about this, I should be freaking out, after all, this woman tried to kill me, but the only emotion that's coming to the surface is sorrow – and I know, in that very moment – I was right to come here.

The male nurse nods to me then stand, waiting over in the corner, watching Susannah.

"Susannah?" I softly say.

Her eyes slowly come up to meet mine, and when they focus on me, they fill with tears, which quickly overflow, and begin spilling down her cheeks.

"Hello Coral," she whispers and then looks down at her twisted hands on the table. "I'm glad you have come," she adds.

"You are?" I say, surprised.

"Yes. I wanted to write a letter to you, but they won't let me," she says, her voice full of anguish. "I know what I did was unforgivable. Every morning when I wake, I thank god you did what you did and stopped me from harming Tristan, he's a good man." She says, her voice almost a whisper.

"He is," I agree.

"I wanted to tell you I'm glad you survived too, and I'm sorry, sorry for trying to hurt you." She looks up at me briefly, and I can see she means it.

I swallow hard, fighting the tears. "Are they treating you well Susannah?" I ask, glancing at the creepy nurse behind her.

Susannah shrugs and then sighs heavily. "Doesn't really matter," she whispers, her eyes meeting mine again.

I can't help frowning, wondering what she means by that. Has she been mistreated? Abused in some way? You hear about that kind of thing all the time – *Concentrate Coral!*

I take a deep breath. "Susannah, I came here to ask you a question," I softly say.

"Did you?" *Christ! It's like there's no life left in the woman!*

"Yes. Do you want another chance?" I ask.

"Another chance?" she asks her voice wistful.

"Yes, a chance to love again. Have a husband, a family, do you want that?"

"There's only one thing I want now," she answers morosely.

"And what is that?" I whisper.

"Peace." She blinks back more tears.

"Peace? Do you need forgiveness, Susannah?"

"You want to forgive me for what I did?" she questions impassively.

"If it helps you, then yes, you have my forgiveness." She winces at my words as though they have cut her. Does it hurt her to have my forgiveness? "Has that helped you?" I softly ask.

"I don't deserve your forgiveness," she says, her voice bleak.

"Well you have it," I tell her. "Susannah, please answer my question. Do you want to get better? Have a second chance?"

"I am resigned to my fate," she says, her head hung low.

"You don't want a second chance?" I ask.

She shakes her head at me, keeping her eyes downcast. "I miss them," she whimpers. "All the time. I can't stand the pain. I don't want it anymore," she adds, wiping her hand across her nose.

"Do...do you mean your husband and your baby Susannah?" I ask.

She winces again. "There's nothing more for me here now." My sharp intake of breath makes her look up. "Thank you for coming to see me Coral," she adds flatly and gets to her feet. The male nurse comes over and takes hold of her arm.

I quickly stand. "Susannah," I whisper, staring back at her with wide eyes. I think I know what she's trying to tell me.

As the nurse tugs on her arm, she suddenly turns back and looks at me. "I just want to see him them again," she whispers in such a sad, melancholy voice. The male nurse drags her away, I watch him walk her out of the room and close the door behind him.

I feel sick. I think Susannah was trying to tell me that she...I can't even say the word. She's already attempted it twice and failed. But that look in her eyes, and what she said, it wouldn't surprise me if she succeeds. I guess that's made my decision for me. I'm dropping the charges, there's no point putting someone on trial for attempted murder when they couldn't give a damn about their own life – *Ugh! I need to get out of here!*

Getting to my feet, I dash over to the door, yank it open

and start running down the corridor. It makes my shoulder throb painfully at me, but I don't care. I keep looking above me, following the exit signs, so I don't get lost. Reaching the door to reception, I knock loudly so the woman on the front desk can buzz me through. Just as I push the door open, a loud alarm starts pulsing through the building, and red lights begin flashing everywhere. Several men in white uniforms come dashing out of the door next to me and run in the direction I have just come from.

"Solitary!" I hear a man shout into his radio as he runs past me.

And I know, I just know – It's Susannah. *No!*

I have no idea why I do, why I feel so compelled and so concerned, but I start running down the corridor, my shoulder protesting painfully at me again and the jolting movement making my lung burn. I finally reach the solitary section, slow down to a walking pace, and follow one of the uniforms into the room. *No!*

I feel like I've walked into the set of a horror movie – only this is real, so real! *Oh my God!* I slap my hand to my mouth in shock. *What have you done?*

Susannah is lying on the floor in a pool of thick, dark red blood. The male nurse who brought me here is lying in the corner, seemingly knocked out. I shake my head in horror. I don't think I have ever seen so much blood before.

One of the nurses has his hand over her throat, trying to stop the blood from pouring out of her. Another nurse is trying to stop the blood pouring from her wrists, while another injects her with something. Susannah is still alive, but choking and gurgling on her own blood. I am frozen, completely horrified by what I am seeing.

'There's nothing here for me now.'
'I miss them.'
'I can't stand the pain, I don't want it anymore.'

I shake my head as her words from the conversation we just had rush through my mind. I watch, feeling helpless as the nurses try to save her. This is what Susannah wanted. This is her peace. *Oh, Susannah!*

As I take a step forward, someone shouts 'I shouldn't be in here', but I don't take any notice of them. I take another step forward, get to my knees and lock eyes with her. We stare at each other for a few seconds, an unspoken truth passing between us.

I nod in resignation, reach forward and place my hand on her forehead.

Susannah is going to die.

This is what she wanted. I can see she looks frightened and I don't want her to be afraid, or think she is alone because she's not – I'm here.

"It's ok," I whisper. "You can let go now."

Her lips twitch, trying to smile I think, and then, with one last blood-curdling breath, she is gone...

I PUT MY KEY in the lock and twist it. Everything feels surreal. I don't even feel like I'm in my own body. I push the door open, take out my key, step inside and shut the door behind me. I can't believe I just witnessed that – and I was there when it happened. Susannah must have been so...so sad. My heart breaks for her. *Oh, Susannah...*

I stare down at the floor, feeling numb with shock. I hear laughter. Tristan and Edith are in the kitchen. As my senses start to come back to me, I realise there's music playing, James Morrison's I Won't Let Go – That's probably why Tristan hasn't heard me come home. But the song, which I know so well, makes me think of Susannah and her desperate love for her husband that died and the baby she lost.

I bring my hand to my mouth and blink back tears. Is she with her husband and baby now? Is she at peace? Have they all found one another? *Oh, I hope so.* In my peripheral vision, I see Stuart coming up the stairs from the ground floor, he gasps in horror when he sees me.

"Jesus Christ – Tristan!" He bellows, dashing over to me. "Where are you hurt Coral?" He desperately says, completely panicked.

"Coral!" Tristan bellows as he runs over to me, his face completely horror-struck. "Coral! He gasps as he reaches me, taking me in his arms, checking me all over. "What's happened, where are you hurt? – Christ, call an ambulance Stu'!" Stuart pulls his mobile out of his pocket.

"Coral?" Tristan bellows, shaking me. "What's happened?"

I frown up at him, still feeling shocked by what I just witnessed.

"What?" I tremble, trying to work out why he and Stuart are acting so panicked, they don't know what's happened yet?

"The blood," Tristan shouts, his eyes wide with panic.

"What?" I say, bemused.

"Coral look," he says, gesturing to my body. I look down and see what he means – *No!*

I'm covered in Susannah's blood. It's on my wedges, and my white linen trousers have two deep red circles on the knees where I knelt down next to her. My green vest top has splatters all over it, there are blobs of blood on my arms and my right hand, the hand that I put on Susannah's forehead; is stained a deep red too.

I shake my head, revolted.

"Coral!" Tristan shouts, shaking me again.

"It's not my blood!" I manage to shout.

Tristan and Stuart freeze. "You're not hurt?" Tristan questions, his eyes searching my face.

I shake my head at him. "Then who Coral, who's hurt?" He asks, his voice lower, calmer. I look up at him; he looks desperately worried.

"Susannah," I manage to whimper.

His face falls, but I can see the relief in his eyes. "Susannah?" He questions. I shake my head, unable to give him any explanation. I have to get out of these clothes – now!

I pull out of Tristan's hold, and run full pelt down the hallway, past the kitchen, up the two flights of stairs and into our bedroom. Tristan is right behind me as I yank the en-suite door open, then the shower door. I step inside, turn the shower on, rip my vest top off, kick my one foot, then the other, my wedges flying into the air, and strip my linen trousers off me, taking my knickers with them too. Completely naked and feeling as though I want to throw up, I dive underneath the shower. I pick up my loafer, squirt some shower cream onto it and start frantically scrubbing, the water pooling at my feet becoming a red river, swirling around and around – *No!*

I close my eyes and choke back the horror as I continue to scrub my skin. I know Tristan is right beside me, I can feel his body heat, smell his potent scent.

"Coral, what happened?" he softly asks. I open my eyes and look up at him. I shake my head, still unable to articulate anything, still scrubbing hard.

Tristan's hand stills me. "Baby, please, tell me what happened?"

I take a deep breath and meet his worried gaze. "She...she killed herself Tristan...she's gone," I garble – then burst into tears.

"Oh my god!" Tristan looks horrified, but not caring that

he's fully dressed, he steps into the shower, wraps me in his arms and holds me for the longest time...

I'M SAT IN the middle of the bed with my hair wrapped up in a towel. The warm fluffy robe that Tristan bought for me is wrapped around me, keeping me warm. Tristan has gone downstairs to get me a Brandy, and I think he is getting one for himself too. He looks just as shocked as I feel. Tristan enters the bedroom with two large glasses of amber liquid. He sits next to me, hands me my drink then puts his arm around my waist, giving me a gentle squeeze.

We are both silent as we sip our drinks. I still can't believe that's just happened. Susannah must have been so desperately sad to do that, to resort to such drastic measures. I look down at my glass and glug the rest back. I can feel it hitting me; burning at first, then warming as it trickles down. Even though he hasn't asked yet, I know Tristan's going to need an explanation, and I'd rather get it done, out of the way now. I take a deep breath, and tell him what happened, from beginning to end.

"I wish you'd have told me you were going to see her," he says, his eyes closed, his fingers pinching the bridge of his nose.

"Why? What difference would it have made," I whimper.

"I'd have pulled you away, got you out of there, so you didn't see any of it," he says through gritted teeth. "That must have been...just...so horrific Coral," he adds, shaking his head in disbelief, his face pale.

"It was," I choke.

Tristan hands me the last drop of his Brandy. "I think you need it more than I do," he explains.

I half smile at him and glug it back. I'm starting to feel a little calmer now, less shocked, and more resigned. I don't know how Susannah did that, what she used to cause such damage, especially because she's in a mental institution where patients are consistently spot checked for weapons, but whatever it was, she was determined to get it right and to succeed. I shake my head not understanding it, what a waste of a life, and such a young life too. I mean, I didn't have an easy start, it was bloody horrendous actually, but never, at any point, have I thought about taking my own life. But I have to think about Susannah's situation, and how she evidently felt about her husband, losing him must have hit her so hard. I couldn't imagine Tristan not being in my life, and I know, deep down inside, if he died, I would not survive that.

"She must have been so sad," I whisper, my heart breaking for her again.

"Yes, much worse than..." Tristan breaks off. I look up at him. He looks like he's in pain. I'm reminded of what Susannah told me about the man that used to work for Tristan that committed suicide and how he felt bad that he didn't know what he was going through, and that it was too late to help him.

"You couldn't have done anything to help her Tristan. This isn't your fault, you know that right?" I softly say.

He sighs heavily and slowly nods, then he looks up at me. "Baby, let me dry your hair," he softly says.

"Can we have another Brandy first?" I ask.

"One condition," he tells me. He's frowning deeply, I want to reach up and stroke the v that forms between his eyebrows.

"What is it Tristan," I softly ask.

"You promise me you'll eat tonight. Edith has made a fish pie, she's keeping it warm until you're ready." My stomach grumbles in appreciation – I only had a small salad at lunch.

I nod once. "I just want to...I don't know, get over the shock a little first," I breathe.

"That's understandable baby," Tristan says, kissing my temple. "I'll be back in a moment." I watch him stand, and walk out of the room.

I have desperately missed him today. I think I was actually starting to piss Rob off. The number of times he had to snap me out of another daydream about Tristan was unbelievable – Embarrassing now I think of it. In a daze, I get to my feet, then head over to my walk-in closet so I can get dressed...

CHAPTER TWENTY-SIX

WE ARE SITTING at the kitchen table eating Edith's Fish Pie. It's really delicious, but not going down too well. I force myself to eat it though, I need to build my strength back up and put some weight back on. Tristan and I both look better, I can't see his ribs anymore, and I don't look so skinny, but I want to get back to how I was before. But there's trouble brewing, I can feel it. Tristan keeps glancing across at me every now and then. I think he's mad? – *Why oh why did that have to happen?* I was only going to see her so I could come to a decision, and then she – "You promised me," Tristan says, his voice raw, interrupting my inner musing.

"I know," I whisper, feeling guilty for not telling him, but if Susannah hadn't have done what she's done, I'm sure this would be a different conversation.

"Then why?" He asks, dropping his fork onto his half-eaten plate of food.

"I didn't want you to worry. I just thought...if I see her then I can make a decision. I hate it when I don't have the answer to something, and I didn't want it hanging over me before I married you. I wanted to know, one way or the other, what direction my life was going in once I'd committed myself to you." I state. "I didn't know she was going to do that Tristan..." I add in a whisper.

He squeezes his eyes shut for a moment. Ok, he's not mad, he's fuming. He silently picks up his fork and continues shoving food into his mouth.

The silence stretches between us.

I sigh inwardly and try to eat some more pie.

Thankfully, Tristan's mobile begins buzzing on the table in front of us.

With one furious glance at me, he picks it up and answers

it. "Freeman!" He snaps and listens for a moment. "Detective Marsh...yes' he looks across at me, glaring again, 'we've heard the news." Releasing me from his glare, he listens again, nodding his head several times. "No, I don't...Detective, I really think, considering the tragic circumstances that all charges are dropped.....No, let them be, I want them to get on with their lives as we will endeavour to do...Yes, thank you, Detective." Tristan hangs up.

"What was,' – "Should I tell you?" He questions, his voice low.

He *is* furious with me – *Great!*

"Yes, you,' – "Why should I tell you?" He shouts, his hand slamming down on the table, making me flinch. "Yet again Coral, you did something behind my back, instead of telling me you were going to do it!"

He is apoplectic with rage.

I look down at my plate. I will not cry. "I'm sorry Tristan," I whisper, twisting the fork round between my fingers.

"Sorry!" He chokes, almost bouncing off the chair.

"You're only this mad because of what Susannah did," I say.

"No, I'm not!" He shouts. I look up and meet his glare. "This has nothing to do with that!"

"Tristan..." I reach out to him.

"Don't!" He warns, recoiling from me – I hear Edith disappear into the Utility room. "Do I scare you so much that you don't feel you can be honest with me, that you can talk to me?" He questions, his voice shaking with adrenalin. I glance down at his body, he's bristling with tension, and his hands are balled up into fists. *Crap!*

"No!" I bark, glaring back at him. "You don't scare me," I tell him firmly.

"Then what?" He shouts. "You don't trust me?" *We're back to that?*

"I'm sorry!" I repeat, shaking my head and looking down at my plate.

"Not good enough!" He shouts again.

Ok, now I'm getting pissed!

"No-one is perfect Tristan, everyone makes mistakes!" I shout back.

"Mistakes yes, but purposely not telling me, is hiding the truth from me. I know you did that Coral, I just don't understand why? What, did you think I was going to stop you?" He asks, laughing sarcastically at me. I'm about to answer him, but he cuts in. "Because let's get something straight' – he's still being sarcastic – 'no-one tells you what to do, do they Coral!" He says, throwing my own words back at me.

I look up and grit my teeth at him. "No, they don't!" I snap.

"So what's the reason Coral?" He booms again. "What, cat got your tongue?"

I am no good at this, at confrontation – I want to run and hide.

"You are making me doubt us, doubt what we have!" He bellows.

I gasp aloud and look up at him. "What?" I tremble.

"You heard me!" He booms, launching to his feet and knocking his chair back in the process. "How am I supposed to build a trusting relationship with you? You tell me about that fucker who abused you, the slimeball that raped you, but you can't tell me something as simple as this? All you had to do is pick up the phone and say 'Hi Tristan, just to let you know I'm going to see Susannah' It's that fucking simple!" He scorns, his cheeks flaming.

He shakes his head at me. "Jesus Christ Coral, every time I think we've taken a step closer to one another, you do something or behave in a certain way that takes us ten steps back! It's like you're purposely self-destructing us." He stops shouting and starts pacing the room, looking up at the ceiling, while running his hands through his hair.

Then he stops pacing, and still staring up at the ceiling he starts laughing, hysterically. It's unnerving. Then he turns and glares at me, his hands on his hips, he's deciding something, I can tell. I watch his facial features change from anger to completely impassive like he's turned to stone, there's no emotion there at all.

I try to breathe, but no air will come. "Tristan...I," I break off, he looks like a complete stranger to me; his expression is so cold.

"I love you, and I wanted to marry you, but you decided this on your own, so I'm deciding this on my own. Until you can learn to communicate effectively with me, the wedding's off!" He tells me, his voice as emotionless as his face.

"What?" I breathe. I try to stand, but my legs are shaking so badly that it just doesn't happen. So I just stare up at him, mouth open, trying to think of something to say.

"Oh fuck this!" He snarls stomping away from me. I turn

and watch him pick up his jacket, and his keys, open the front door and slam it behind him. *Ok, that did not just happen!*

I stare numbly at the front door. He didn't mean what he said, surely? I swallow hard. He was just threatening because he was so mad, he must have been? Or maybe he wasn't? *Stupid, stupid, stupid Coral!* I should have told him I was going to see her. I turn back around and stare morosely out of the window, hoping and secretly praying he's going to come back through that door. I imagine him running over to me, and we fall into each other's arms, both forgiving, both loving one another. Then I see his face again, the unemotional, faceless expression he wore only moments ago before he walked out.

It was so cold. Not like my Tristan with his warm cheeks and eyes that crinkle sweetly at the corners when he smiles. Not my Tristan with eyes so warm and soulful, I could spend the rest of my life swimming in the depths of them. Not my Tristan with his cute freckles and dimples on his face, and a smile so beautiful that he must be straight from heaven, my own personal angel.

No, the man that walked out on me was not my Tristan.

A shiver runs right from the top of my head all the way down to my toes. I suddenly feel very, very cold. A hollow sob tries to escape me. I slap my hand to my mouth and choke it back, I will not cry. I take a deep, steadying breath, and it's in that moment of complete numbness that I realise that I need to prepare myself for the possibility that he was truthful and that he really does feel that way – I'm not even sure if he's coming back – *Oh God!*

His words start reverberating in my head, over and over...

'You're making me doubt us, doubt what we have.'

'How am I supposed to build a trusting relationship with you?'

'It's like your purposely self-destructing us.'

'I love you, and I wanted to marry you.'

'Until you can learn to communicate effectively with me, the wedding's off.'

I inhale sharply and grip my stomach, trying to stop it from turning over. I hear Edith coming out of the utility room, I guess she went to hide, or give us some privacy. Either way, I don't want any kind of conversation with her right now, so I get to my feet and make my way into the library, once inside I lock the door behind me.

I stare around the empty room. Feeling frightened by the prospect that I may lose Tristan, I curl up in the recliner, wrap my arms around my legs and stare numbly ahead, wondering if

I will see Tristan tonight, wondering if he'll ever come back? I can't even think about not seeing him, or what it would feel like not to have him in my life – But then something happens, a shift within me, and I actually start to feel really pissed off.

I mean, there's a part of me that understands his frustration that I didn't tell him, but that's no excuse to go bonkers at me – *Who the hell does he think he is?*

I get to my feet and start pacing the room, clenching my fists in anger. I just watched a woman die; she took her own life for god's sake. He should be comforting me, not shouting at me. Then the more I think about it, the more I just think screw you Tristan Freeman, you don't want to marry me, well the feeling is mutual. I don't want to marry a man who acts like that, in fact, what the hell am I doing marrying a man I hardly know anyway?

This is unbelievable! How dare he walk out on me, and how dare he threaten to call off the wedding. God, I'm so mad, furiously beyond pissed off. And I can't go and punch the crap out of the punch bag to relieve the tension. I squeeze my fists tighter trying to relieve some of the tension. Then I stop pacing and take a deep breath trying to calm myself. Getting this stressed is not good for me, I know that, but I'm still so mad and so hurt.

And then it hits me – George! I need to speak to George. Maybe he'll have some words of wisdom, something that will help calm me down. Because right now, Tristan is not the only one re-thinking our relationship – *Right!* Marching out of the library, I grab my mobile, stomp back into the library and make the call.

Half an hour later, I say goodbye to George. He has helped calm me down a little bit, and also explained that relationships can be like this, that they take work, patience and understanding. He understood my point of view, but he also understood Tristan's, although he didn't completely agree or disagree with him walking out on me. So once again, I feel lost, out of my depth and really confused. I still don't know what to do. Part of me wants to pack a bag and go stay with Rob, but the other half wants to stay. I can't keep running away from situations I find difficult or challenging – And I think, tonight, Tristan has been both of those.

At some point during my internal battle, I fall asleep in the chair...

I JERK AWAKE. Where am I? Oh yes, in the library. I hear a strange noise coming from the main room. I guess it's what woke me up – *Shit! What time is it?* Though the room is pitch-black, I stagger to my feet and look down at my watch – 3.35am? A shiver runs through me. I feel so cold. I'm guessing Tristan isn't home? Surely he'd come and find me if he was?

The sinking feeling washes over me again – What if he says we're through? Then I remember I'm mad at him too, well sort off, it's kind of faded a bit now. I shake my head and try to push those thoughts away, then I hear it again, the strange noise. *Has someone broken in?* My heart starts hammering against my chest. *What is that?* I hear it again, and it sounds like someone moving furniture around? Then I hear a loud bang, which makes me jump, but it's quickly followed by an epithet – *Tristan?*

I launch myself forward, unlock the door and take a cautious step into the living area. The room is eerily silent, the only light coming from the full moon, making strange patterns across the floor and the furniture. I look to my right and see the front door is wide-open – *Holy fuck!*

"Tristan?" I whisper. Stuart silently appears opposite me, at the foot of the stairs, which makes me jump. He lifts his finger to his mouth, telling me to be silent. Then he holds his hand up flat and beckons me to move away, back into the library, into safety. *Fuck!*

I nod once and take a step back. My mouth is dry, my fingers tingling – Both our heads whip round when we hear another bang. It's coming from the kitchen. Then we hear what sounds like hysterical laughter. Stuart warns me to stay and silently walks over to the kitchen. My heart feels like it's going to explode – *Who the hell is it?*

Smiling in relief, Stuart looks up at me. "Coral, there's no danger," he says.

I dash over to the kitchen and find Tristan in a crumpled heap on the floor, and I can smell what I think is pizza? Stuart flicks on the lights, and I gasp aloud at the state of him. There are pizza slices splattered all over the kitchen floor next to a large pizza box, and a broken plate – *Oh Tristan!*

"Hey baby," he slurs as he tries to focus on me. *Holy crap! Tristan is drunk!*

"Hi," I squeak, kneeling in front of him. "Tristan, look at me. Are you hurt?" I ask, holding his face in my hands.

"You...are in trouble," he slurs. I want to shout at him that he is too, but I don't. There's no point trying to put your point across to anyone when they are this pissed.

I sigh inwardly. "Where have you been?" I ask.

"Joyce," he slurs.

"You went drinking with Joyce?" I question, that's odd!

"Yes…she really loves you…" He looks up, barely able to focus on me. "And so do I."

I stare back at him feeling embarrassed because Stuart is right here, hearing all of this. "Coral, I'll get the door and reset the alarm," he says, he must have sensed my unease.

"Thanks, Stu." He nods once and walks away. I sit down on the cold tiled floor next to Tristan. "So I'm guessing you were hungry?" I say, sighing heavily.

"Yes…" he slurs. "I didn't eat much dinner…" He tries to look angry, but he just looks like he's pulling silly faces.

"Me neither," I whisper.

"Joyce said…you are challenging…" His eyes close, I think he's about to pass out.

"Tristan!" I shout, shaking him. "Open your eyes." I have to get him to the sofa. He can't sleep on the kitchen floor, although, the state he's in, he probably wouldn't be able to tell the difference.

"Tristan!" I shout again.

His one eye pops open. "Are we home?" *Ok, that's funny!*

"Yes." I can't help chuckling to myself.

"There are two of you…" He grins and lunges forward grabbing hold of me, but he's so drunk that he sinks down on top of me, his body weight crushing me – *Holy fuck!*

Edith appears in her pyjamas, gasping when she takes in what's happened to her spotlessly clean kitchen and seeing Tristan on top of me.

"A little help!" I gasp to Stuart and Edith. They pull Tristan off me, then all three of us, lift him to his feet, he's still awake and grinning like an idiot. I go to throw his arm over my shoulder, but Stuart stops me.

"There's an easier way," he says, smirking at me.

Making it look effortless, he takes hold of Tristan, bends down and lifts him up, so his torso is across his shoulders, his legs to the right, his arms to the left. Stuart steadies him and carefully carries him over to the sofa. As Stuart places him down, Edith flicks on the small reading lamp next to the sofa, while I sink down in front of Tristan.

"Will that be all?" Stuart asks.

I sigh inwardly. "Yes, thank you, Stuart."

"He's gonna have one helluva hangover tomorrow," he says, shaking his head as he walks away. *Yes, he certainly will!*

"Can I get you anything?" Edith asks, she still looks fast asleep.

"No, thanks, Edith," I whisper. "I'll get Tristan settled then clean up the kitchen. You get yourself back to bed."

"Are you sure?" She asks, yawning widely.

"Positive," I whisper, smiling up at her.

"Alright then, goodnight Coral," she says, smiling warmly at me.

"Night Edith," I watch her walk away and turn back to Tristan, he's still grinning like a fool. Then his head falls back, and his eyes close.

"Tristan, wake up!" I shout. "I need to undress you." His t-shirt and jeans are covered in pizza sauce.

I pull him forward so I can grab his t-shirt. I manage to yank it up over his back, and pull it over his head, before he flops back against the sofa – *Hmm even in his drunken state one look at his sexy body has me wanting him.* I shake my head at myself, throw his t-shirt to the floor, take his belt in my hand and unbuckle it.

I glance up at him; he has his sexy grin going on.

"Want some?" He slurs, trying to flex his hips towards me.

"I always want you like that Tristan, but not tonight!" I tell him.

He pouts at me. A brief smile flits across my lips.

"Come on, lift up," I tell him. He tries three times to push his hips up. Eventually, he makes it, and I manage to pull his jeans down to his feet. I pull his trainers and socks off, then slide his jeans off, leaving his clothes on the floor.

"I think I'm a little drunk," he says, the sweetest grin spreading across his face. *Ok, that's just too cute!*

"Yes." I smile. "I think you are."

"I love you Coral Stevens...my beautiful wife," he slurs, gazing lovingly at me.

"Not yet," I say.

"In here..." He says, trying to hold his hand against his heart. "You are..." My heart swells with love for this drunken man before me.

"Hungry?" I ask, trying not to get too overwhelmed. Honestly, one minute I'm mad as hell, the next I'm almost blubbering – *What are you doing to me, Tristan?*

"Hmm..." He lunges forward again.

"Hey!" I push him back. "Not that kind of hungry!"

"I want...you," he says, his stomach rumbling. *He needs food!*

"Later, let's eat first, ok?" I say, trying to placate him. "Don't you dare move!" I warn.

He grins a sweet I'm drunk but so in love with you smile.

Ignoring how cute he looks, I dash over to the kitchen. There are several slices of pizza on the floor, next to the broken plate, why he didn't just eat it out of the box, I don't know. Shaking my head, I pick up the pizza box from the floor, open the lid and find that half of the pizza is still intact.

I grab some kitchen towels and dash back over to him. I grab the throw off the sofa, lay it across his legs and place the pizza box on top, then opening the lid, I take a slice out and hand it to him.

"Here Tristan, eat this."

"Thanks..." He grins at me and then demolishes the slice.

I walk back over to the kitchen, fill a glass with water and find some Nurofen – he's definitely going to need it – and head back over to him.

Tristan picks up another pizza slice, although how he's managing it, I don't know. I watch it sway in the air as he tries to guide it towards his mouth, I almost reach out to help, but he finally manages it. He demolishes the second slice then smiles apologetically at me.

"You..." he whispers. "Always you...forever..." He breathes, his eyes barely open now.

"Tristan?" I tap his cheek, he sleepily opens one eye. "Take these," I say, he smiles goofily at me and tries to sit up, but it doesn't happen.

Wow, he really is drunk!

I climb onto the sofa and kneel next to him. "Tristan, open your mouth." He pops his mouth open then smiles drunkenly at me. *This is funny, but not working!*

"Tristan, push out your tongue," I say, trying not to laugh. He does so and I manage to pop the tablets on his tongue. "Here, take a sip." I put the glass to his lips, he takes a good couple of gulps, his head swaying, his eyes barely open. "Ok?" I ask, taking the glass from him.

"The room is spinning!" He says, trying to focus on me.

"I know baby its ok. I'm here, sleep now," I soothe, stroking his hair. And just like that, his head hits the back of the sofa, and he's out cold. *Oh boy!*

I get to my feet and silently tip-toe up the stairs. Grabbing the quilt from the spare bedroom, I carefully head back down the stairs, so I don't fall over, that would not help the situation. Reaching Tristan, I throw the quilt on the floor and step over to him. I lift up his legs, swinging him around as I do, and prop them up on the sofa. His upper body has moved in the process, but it doesn't look very comfortable, so I take his inner arm and pull so that he's lying in the recovery position. Placing a pillow under his head, I lean down, stroke his hair, softly kiss his temple, and place the quilt on top of him.

"You have a lot of explaining to do," I whisper to him. Then shaking my head at him, I head into the kitchen to clean up the mess...

IT'S EARLY, 8AM to be precise. Rob is going to be here in two hours with Carlos and his team of people. The house is being decorated today for the wedding – what Rob has in mind I do not know – but Tristan and I have strict instructions not to be here when it all starts this afternoon. Apparently, I am only allowed back in the house later on tonight as long as I'm downstairs on the ground floor, or up in our bedroom. The same applies to tomorrow morning. I have to stay upstairs all morning until it is time. If I want anything, I have to use my mobile and call down to Edith. *Ridiculous!*

Tristan is not staying with me tonight. Rob's one condition for doing this, he said '*break all other traditions, but the groom does not spend the night before with you, or see you until you walk down the aisle*'. I rolled my eyes at him but agreed.

Apparently, Tristan's staying at Joyce's, and Rob and Carlos are staying here with me, or at their place, whichever I decide. And as per Rob's instructions, this morning will be my pre-wedding tryout. Once I've tried the dress and shoes on, and Carlos has styled my hair, and done my make-up, Tristan and I are practically being frogmarched out of our own home. Rob has given his spare keys to his apartment though, so at least Tristan and I have somewhere to hang out today – *That's if he wants to see me?*

I sigh inwardly and take a sip of coffee. *Will he still be mad at me?* I'm mad at him. He has a lot of explaining to do. I just don't get why he blew up like that? Maybe he has wedding nerves? It's supposed to affect men more than women, or maybe not. I just don't know. I stare at his beautiful face and take another sip of coffee. He's going to have a very sore head today. I wonder if

Stuart can get him up to our room without waking him? I really don't want anyone to see him like this, and I know Rob will ask questions, which in all honesty, I won't have the answers to.

Is the wedding still on?
I have no idea.
Did Tristan stay out all night deciding our fate?
Again I have no idea.
Does he really feel as though I don't trust him?
Because I do with my life.
Is he really doubting us?
I truly hope not.

I take another sip of coffee. I know he said a lot of lovey-dovey things last night – and I'm pleased as punch that he's a happy drunk – but that doesn't mean he's changed his mind, people say all kinds of crap when they're drunk. I guess I'm not going to get any answers until he's awake, and if we both decide to end it, there's no point in any wedding preparations because there won't be any wedding to go to.

I feel really pissed with myself again. I should have just told him I was going to see Susannah. If I had, we wouldn't be in this mess. I shudder slightly remembering what she did. Then I sigh inwardly. If Rob thinks I'm having second thoughts, he'll call the whole thing off – I know he will. So whatever happens, he can't know about this. *Damn it!*

I walk over to Stuart. He's sat at the breakfast bar, quietly reading a newspaper and sipping his coffee. He turns and smiles at me.

"Stuart, would you be able to carry Tristan up to our bedroom?" I ask. "I don't want anyone seeing him like this," I add my eyes downcast, my fingers twisting against one another – I am so anxious.

"It's no problem," Stuart says. He gets to his feet, then taking me by surprise he squeezes my left arm. "You alright?" I glance up at him, nod once then look down at the floor, trying to hide how I'm really feeling. "Ok, let's get him upstairs."

I head up the stairs, Stuart following with Tristan. When I reach our bedroom, I yank the door open as wide as it will go so Stuart can get through. Walking over to the bed, he places Tristan down, nods once to me and then leaves the room. With a heavy heart, I place his glass of water on the side, along with some Nurofen, and my cup of coffee. Then I pull the curtains across, leaving just a small gap, so it's not pitch black, and then

I get Tristan into a comfortable position and scribble a simple note for him.

I'm sorry X

I leave it next to the water and stare down at his face while he sleeps, drinking him in. This may be the last time I ever get to do this. I want to kiss him, kiss his warm cheek, but that just feels like I'm prolonging the agony of what may come. No. I'm better to cut myself off now than to make it any worse by staying here with him. I take one last look at him, pick up my cup of coffee and then turn away.

I decide I can't let anyone know what's going on, I am going to have to be brave, suck it up and be like I used to be, act as though nothing bothers me, but the fear of us ending grips me again, and I choke back the tears. Someone taps on the bedroom door, making me jump. I quickly dash the tears away and quietly open the door, so as not to wake Tristan.

"Coral," Edith whispers. "Your mobile's been ringing," she adds, her tone soft as she takes in my pitiful expression.

"Thanks." I take it from her.

"Can I get you some breakfast lass?" I shake my head at her. "Ok." She reaches up, squeezes my arm then heads down the stairs.

I unlock my mobile and see I have two missed calls from Joyce, one from Malcolm and a text from Debs.

I open the text first – Are you ok?

Why would Deb's text me that? I send her one back.

Yes, I'm fine – It's all I can muster.

Then I take one more look at Tristan, feeling torn in two. Part of me is still pissed at him, but the other part is terrified that he may wake up and say that everything he said last night was true, and that he does feel that way. I know there's nothing I can do about it if that's his decision, but the thought of not having him in my life is making me feel that empty, hollow ache I used to have, only tripled a million times over – And I don't ever want to feel like that again. I take a deep, steadying breath and head out the bedroom, softly closing the door behind me.

Back downstairs, I head over to the kitchen and pour myself another coffee. I didn't sleep a wink last night, I literally watched the sunrise as I sat next to Tristan, wondering the whole time what today will bring – I choke back tears again.

Oh God, please don't leave me, Tristan!

Trying to get myself together I pick up my coffee, head

down the stairs and walk out into the garden. It is yet, another beautiful, blue-skied, sunshiny day. It is not reflecting my melancholy, slightly pissed mood at all. Sitting cross-legged, in the middle of the lawn, I put on my sunglasses and return Joyce's call first.

"Hello sweetheart," Joyce softly says.

"Hey Joyce," I go for upbeat but sound morose.

"I thought I would give you the heads up," Joyce says, sounding worried. My heart instantly plummets to the bottom of my stomach, my cup of coffee starts shaking so badly in my hand that I have to put it down.

"Coral?" Joyce prompts.

"Heads up?" I manage to croak.

"Gladys is on the warpath!" Joyce says.

Huh? I instantly feel brighter as this isn't about Tristan. "Sorry?" I ask, bemused.

"Darling, she knows about Susannah' – "How?" I gasp.

"It was in The Argus darling." *Jeez, bad news really does travel fast!*

"Oh crap!" I groan, holding my head in my hand. "What does it say?" I ask.

"That you were there when it happened. And Gladys, well you know what she's like sweetheart. She's on her way over to you," Joyce warns.

"What?" I screech. "No! Joyce, I can't...I can't handle this right now!" I stop, gritting my teeth and trying to choke back the stupid ass tears.

"Why Coral? Whatever's the matter?" Joyce asks her tone soft.

"I..." I can't speak. And I'm not even sure I want to share either.

"Darling would you like me to come over?" She softly adds.

"Please Joyce. That would be..." I stop again and take a deep breath.

"I'll see you in five," she says and hangs up.

God damn it! – I cannot have Gladys over here now. I need to call her, calm her down. Feeling beyond tired, I pick up my coffee and take a quick sip, then I call Malcolm's number, but I already know I'm too late, I can hear Gladys shouting upstairs.

"Hello Coral," he says. I swear he's rolling his eyes.

"I'm in the garden," I tell him. "And can you please ask Mom to keep her voice down! Tristan was working late, he's still sleeping," I hiss.

"No problem Coral." Malcolm hangs up, and the shouting quickly stops – *Thank god!*

I sigh, curl my hands around my coffee cup and sit sipping it. I see Gladys appear in my peripheral vision. I know it shouldn't, but she makes me laugh when she's mad; especially when she is walking fast, and her butt is wobbling from side to side.

Stopping in front of me, with a face like thunder and her hands on her hips, she opens her mouth to begin, but I quickly cut in. "Mom!" I shout, holding my hand up to stop her. "I know you're upset, but it was my choice to go and see Susannah and no-one else's. I am a grown woman who will do what she wants when she wants to do it. You gave me a chance at a good life, a wholesome life. Can't you understand that I wanted the same for Susannah? She lost her baby, and her husband died in Iraq; he was the love of her life, Gladys. Your husband only left you, but I'm guessing it still devastated you?" I question.

"Well, yes of course it did' – "Imagine he hadn't left, and like John, he suddenly died. Try to imagine what that would have felt like. Because I'm guessing it would have felt a trillion times worse. I wanted to help Susannah and give her a second chance. You taught me that people screw up and you have to forgive them and give them another chance."

Hmm, maybe that's what I should do with Tristan?

"Coral Stevens! That has nothing to do with this. Joyce hasn't gone postal because John died has she?" She screeches.

I shake my head in exasperation. *I don't need this right now!*

Gladys continues. "She was unstable Coral! Can't you understand that I didn't want you anywhere near her? What if she tried to...to do something to you when she killed herself, what if she attacked you? She tried it once before and almost killed you for goodness sake! And if she'd have succeeded, then no, absolutely not, I would not have given her a second chance. Do you think rapists and murderers deserve second chances?"

I wince at her words. "No!" I bite.

"Well then!" She huffs, puffing her cheeks out.

Malcolm appears with two cups in his hand. "Good morning Coral." He smiles apologetically at me as he passes Gladys her coffee.

I try to smile at him. "Mom, apart from coming over here to shout at me, is there anything else you are here for? Because I have a hell of a lot going on today," I say, trying not to shout.

"Oh well...no," she says, sipping her drink. "Well, apart

from wanting to see you, make sure you're alright." She says she's still pissed at me.

I grit my teeth and stare straight ahead.

"So are you alright?" She asks.

"Fine! Thanks for asking," I bite sarcastically.

"Oh Coral, I'm sorry," she says, softening a little. "Did she really...you know...in front of you?" Gladys asks wistfully.

God damn it!

"Darling, I don't think that's something Coral wishes to recall." Malcolm softly says.

I half smile at him – *Thank you, Malcolm!*

"No....well...I suppose not," Gladys says. "Are you alright though darling?" She asks again in her soft, mothering tone.

I almost crumble. "Yes Mom, I'm fine," I sigh. "And I'm sorry for snapping at you."

"Well, I'm sorry for shouting...." Gladys says. Malcolm seems to be guiding her. "And well, for not listening before judging," she adds, taking another sip. *Whoa!*

"It's ok, I understand your point of view," I tell her, trying not to sound too gloomy. Maybe I should just go and wake Tristan up. I hate not knowing what's going to happen between us.

We sit around for five minutes, Gladys and Malcolm both chatting away, I nod and smile in the right places, hoping I'm hiding what's going on.

"Darling, we must be going," Malcolm says, draining the last of his coffee. "Off to collect the family, I've put them up at the Hilton, didn't want them being late tomorrow," he explains, his eyes twinkling brightly.

Right – tomorrow!

"I'll see you out," I say getting to my feet – *I need more coffee!*

At the door, I say my goodbyes and leave it open as I see Joyce arriving in her car, they both beep their horns and wave as they pass one another. Joyce smiles warmly at me as she pulls up and steps out of her car, I try to smile back at her. As usual, she looks like she's just stepped out of the salon with her perfect nails, hair and make-up. She's wearing a fine, cream, silk trouser suit, that just makes her look, wow! *How does she do that?*

"Darling," she says walking towards me with her arms open wide. I fall into them and manage, somehow, to keep the tears at bay. Joyce goes to pull back, but I grip her tighter, not wanting to let go. I suddenly realise that between Joyce and Gladys

Forever With Him

leaving, although Gladys isn't now, it's Joyce who I'll miss the most, much more than Gladys.

I try to understand why that is? Gladys is my mother, Joyce, my aunty, and I love them both, unconditionally. Then it hits me, Joyce is my inspiration. She is a headstrong businesswoman; a woman I have always admired and I will always feel indebted to her. Joyce gave me a job, a vocation, and she may not realise it, but her no-nonsense attitude is one of the things that helped to keep me on the straight and narrow.

"Come along now, you're made of tougher stuff!" Joyce says, squeezing me one more time. Then she pulls back so she can assess me. "I see I was too late," she says, gesturing to Gladys and Malcolm.

I roll my eyes. "Yeah...but it's her way of showing she cares," I say.

"Yes, she does," Joyce smiles.

"Would you like a drink? I ask, trying for upbeat and failing miserably.

"Tea please, Coral," Joyce says. I smile widely as it feels like I'm back at work. Joyce follows me into the kitchen and sits on one of the breakfast stools. "Now," she says in a very business-like manner. "Let's talk." I quickly whip my head round to her and silently shake my head. I don't want anyone to overhear our conversation Then I mouth 'downstairs' to her. Joyce nods once, understanding. When I've made her pot of tea, and placed all the essentials onto a tray, I add my coffee cup, and we head out into the bright, sunlit day. We sit on the large outdoor sofa, the same one George and I sat on.

"So, I guess you know that Tristan and I had a fight last night?" I ask, taking a sip.

"Yes," Joyce says, sipping her tea.

I grit my teeth in frustration. "I think we're through," I say.

"Nonsense!" Joyce quips.

I turn and look at her, feeling surprised. "He said so, Joyce! And to be quite honest, I don't think I want to be with him either, not after the way he shouted at me," I say, wondering if I sound childish.

"Coral, we all say things we don't mean in the heat of the moment. Goodness, John and I...we had some terrible fights, but we always knew that the love would still be there. No matter how bad the fight was, or what we said, or how hurt we were; we always came back to one another." She tells me.

I frown at the floor. "So he told you what happened?"

"Briefly," Joyce says.

"I can't believe he stayed out so late – and got so drunk!" I add.

"Late?" Joyce questions.

"Um yeah...he didn't get back till gone three, and he was really drunk," I scoff.

"Three?" Joyce gasps.

"Wasn't he with you?" I ask my eyes wide with fear. *If he wasn't then who was he with?*

"Coral, you always think the worst!" Joyce says a little exasperated. "He came over at around eight-ish and left after midnight, but I'm sure he was alone for the rest of the night. Probably avoiding coming home to you because he'd walked out on you, he did say he wasn't feeling too good about doing that." Joyce tells me.

"Oh!" I look down at my cup again.

"Darling girl, you have to start learning to trust, and not worry so much. Yes, he was angry that you didn't tell him what your plans were, especially as it involved Susannah, but I think you'll find that he was much more upset with the fact that you were there, alone when she...did what she did," Joyce tells me.

"You think?" I squeak.

Joyce titters at me. "Coral, how on earth can you be thinking such silly thoughts, and have so much doubt when you're marrying him tomorrow?"

I shrug. I have no answer for that.

"You still think you're unworthy," Joyce says, and it's a statement.

How does she know this?

I stare ahead. I think I'll always feel like that.

"You're not," she says, leaning over and squeezing my hand.

"I'm an idiot!" I bite. "I don't deserve him."

"Yes you do," Joyce firmly retorts.

"Yeah well...maybe I do. But right now, I'm just...angry!" I shake my head and drink more coffee.

"You've changed," Joyce says, completely throwing me.

"I have?" I squeak.

"Yes Coral, in so many ways," Joyce sighs, an old memory ignited in her eyes. "It always made me so unhappy seeing you putting on such a brave face, even though I knew you were in turmoil. How I wished I could take whatever it was away for you, so when you smiled, I could see that you were genuinely happy. John and I wondered about it often, trying to work out what we could do, so that we could help you. But we both knew it had to come from you, and that hopefully someday, you would be free of whatever it was that made you so sad." Joyce softly says.

"You knew I was sad?" I say, feeling shocked.

"Coral, you're not that hard to read. For others yes, they probably wouldn't realise the difference between your fake smiles and your genuine ones, but I did, and I still do. Anyway, my point is, is that I think you have found what it was that you needed, in order to free yourself of whatever it was that was haunting you." I swallow hard. "Am I right darling?" I look up at her. Poor Joyce, all this time so worried about me. I decide as I did with Rob and Debs to tell Joyce why.

"Yes Joyce, you are right. I have found what I needed, and I found it in Tristan. The easiest way to explain it, and as simple as it may sound, is that he broke down my walls, my barriers if you like. He's set me free, but I would like to share with you why I used to feel like that if that's ok?" I say.

Joyce leans across and squeezes my hand again. "Only if you want to darling."

"I do," I tell her firmly then give Joyce a very brief story of my past. When I've finished, I look up at Joyce, expecting a telling off for not sharing with her sooner, but I'm gobsmacked to see she doesn't look surprised or shocked like Rob or Debs did.

"You knew?" I question.

"No, not knew, but had my own suspicions. I was hoping I was wrong." Joyce takes my hand again and stares ahead for a while.

"Tristan said that you said that I'm...challenging?" I whisper.

"Well, you are!" Joyce titters. "You're the most mercurial person I know," she adds, sipping more tea.

"What does that mean?" I laugh. I never took any notice in English lessons.

Joyce raises an eyebrow in surprise. "You don't know?"

"Joyce," I giggle. "You know I didn't pay attention in class!"

"Oh yes, well I suppose not no. Well, a mercurial person is someone who has sudden or unpredictable changes in mood." She tells me.

"Oh!" My face falls. I remember Tristan kind of saying that to me, only he said...*'you really do jump ship don't you'*...Hmm.

"I'm not proud Joyce," I say. "And I'm sorry if I was like that with you, especially at work. I really did try to stay balanced, guess I didn't always get it right." I mumble.

"Coral, don't you understand? If I didn't want you working there, no matter what your moods were like, I'd have let you go." *Whoa!*

"But you didn't?" I squeak.

"No darling I didn't. Now, why don't you tell me what's really on your mind?"

I sigh inwardly – There's no hiding from Joyce.

"I'm going to miss you so much," I croak.

"And I will miss you too, but you're avoiding the question."

I take another sip of coffee. "I just...I guess after last night...I can't help questioning if we're right for each other, all we seem to have done since I came out of the hospital is argue with one another. I just..." I shake my head, not knowing what else to say. And then I backtrack on my own words – we haven't just argued, we've loved one another too.

"Wedding jitters," Joyce says.

"What?" I half-laugh.

"You're about to get married Coral. I always hoped this would happen for you, that you'd find a good man to take care of you like I had with John. But it doesn't mean I wasn't really nervous the day of my wedding. I am from a working-class family, John was upper class, our upbringings were so very different, and at the time, I felt as though the only thing I was bringing to our marriage were my university loans. It took John a very long time to convince me that it didn't matter and that all he wanted was me. Are you feeling that way?"

"No. I know Tristan doesn't care about my financial status and I don't care about his either. I guess I'm just feeling..." I trail off. I don't want her to know everything that goes on between Tristan and me, what happened last night was private, and the only people who can sort it, or end it, are Tristan and me.

"Definitely wedding jitters," Joyce says rising to her feet. "But unfortunately, I have to get over to the office darling, and collect a few things," Joyce tells me – this must be hard for her.

"Did you want me to come with you? I ask.

"I'll be fine darling," Joyce replies, she is putting on a brave face.

"Ok," I whisper, deep in thought. Then I panic. "Isn't Tristan supposed to be in today?"

"No darling, we managed to get everything finalised yesterday. Didn't he tell you?"

"He didn't really get the chance," I mutter – No wonder he was laughing with Edith in the kitchen when I got back, he must have been so excited to tell me – *Oh I'm such a fuck up sometimes!*

I get to my feet and hug Joyce. "Everything will be fine sweetheart, you'll see," she says smiling warmly at me – But I'm still not convinced.

"I'll see you out," I say not bothering to put a fake smile on, not now she can see straight through them – *Great!*

"No, you stay here darling. I'll see you tomorrow," Joyce says, her eyes sparkling brightly.

"Ok," I breathe. "Tomorrow." I watch Joyce walk away then sit back down, letting my mind drift over the conversation we just had...

I AM SITTING in Edith's bathroom, waiting for Carlos to finish. I didn't want to disturb Tristan, so we are here, instead of our en-suite upstairs. I thought I would feel more relaxed after my little chat with Joyce, but I don't – at all. I just want Tristan to wake up, so I know either way, what's going on. *Concentrate Coral!* We have done my make-up trial, and Carlos is now doing my hair, and as promised, I have kept my eyes closed for half an hour now. Carlos knows what I'm like, and knows I would have been protesting every five minutes, instead of waiting to see the finished result, which would have driven him mad.

"Finished!" Carlos says excitedly.

I open my eyes and look at my 'wedding hair' as he calls it. *Wow!*

Carlos has curled my hair into big soft tendrils, loosely scooped the crown back and pinned it into place with what looks like a very old-fashioned hairpiece. It's a beautiful looking piece, silver, very shiny and has blue sapphires entwined within each delicate flower.

"It's antique," he says smiling at our reflections. "Our wedding present to you."

I gasp in shock. "Carlos, you..." I stop unable to articulate anymore.

Earlier, when I tried the dress on, I had to fight so hard not to break down and confess my fears to Carlos, and now this? I blink my eyes rapidly, trying to stop the tears from forming.

"Don't you like it sunshine?" He asks.

"Yes, of course, I do," I manage to choke out.

He kneels down next to the chair and takes my hand in his. "What's wrong?" he asks, gently squeezing my hand.

"Oh Carlos," I croak. "I think the wedding may be off," I sniff.

Carlos gasps. "Why?"

I shake my head. I don't want to tell him. Then I think, maybe he can give me some advice? He and Rob have been married for years now, I'm sure he can tell me something that will ease my fears.

"Don't tell Rob," I whisper.

"I won't, I promise. Now come on, let it all out sunshine." I take a deep breath and start at the beginning when I'm done, Carlos looks a little mystified.

"Is that it?" He says.

"Um...yeah?" I frown back at him.

"Coral, you're over analysing it. Look, I get his point of view, but I get yours too. And as for what he said, we all say things we don't mean when we're mad sunshine."

"Yeah, I know that Carlos, Joyce said the same thing. But I'm pissed at him, he really upset me last night, I'm not even sure if I should be doing this!" I squeak in a high pitched voice.

Carlos sighs sorrowfully at me. "You know he's right for you Coral. I know you know that." I shake my head and fight back more tears. "Look, if there wasn't any wedding and he just walked out, you wouldn't think the two of you are through, you'd just be pissed at him, and the two of you would sort it out when he woke up!"

"Maybe," I mumble.

"Coral, do you know how many times I have told Rob it's over and stormed out?"

"You have?" I gasp.

Carlos titters at my shocked expression. "Yep, loads of times, we are not as perfect as you think we are," he says.

"But' – "Hey, I'm not complaining, the make-up sex is really great!" He interrupts, his eyes glinting wickedly.

I think my chin actually hits the floor.

"Now, what you need to do is make him one of those fabulous hangover Smoothies of yours, take it up to him, make him drink it, and then shag his brains out!"

I burst out laughing. "Shag his brains out?"

"Yes. Now let me get this out of your hair so you can do exactly that!"

"Oh Carlos," I sigh. "I really do love you. And thank you for the gift, it's beautiful."

"Just like you." He blows me a kiss.

I smile back at him, feeling a little better. Then I watch Carlos taking his time as he carefully removes the hairpiece.

"Right, all done! Come on, this is defcon five! We need to execute this plan immediately. We can't have you worrying like this." Taking hold of my hand, he marches me out of Edith's bedroom...

TEN MINUTES LATER, I am stood in the kitchen, with my coffee in one hand and Tristan's Smoothie in the other. I look up at Carlos, feeling very apprehensive – *I'm not sure this is a good idea!*

"You'll be fine," he tells me. "Now go on, go and do what I told you!" He adds, his eyes glinting wickedly.

I sigh heavily and head back up the stairs. Reaching our bedroom door, I silently push it open. Then I tentatively walk across the large space and place both our drinks down on the bedside cabinet. Tristan is in exactly the same position I left him in earlier. I pick up the chair, place it next to the bed, and just stare at him while I drink my coffee. I wonder if Carlos is right and that I am over-reacting? Or maybe Joyce is right, and I've got wedding nerves? I sigh inwardly, pull my leg up and gently shake him with my foot.

"Tristan," I coo. "Wake up, it's time to drink your smoothie." I get nothing. *Hmph!*

I take another sip of my coffee, I'm about to shake him again when his one eye flutters open.

"Good morning," I say, trying to sound confident.

"No need to shout." He groans, his face contorted in pain.

It makes me want to laugh at him. There's no way any shagging is about to commence; besides I'm not sure I do want to shag him.

"Sorry," I bluntly say. I put my cup down, and pick up the Nurofen and his Smoothie. "Tristan, I promise you if you drink this and go back to sleep, when you wake, you won't even feel like you had a drink last night."

He looks so sorrowfully at me, I thaw a little. "Ok," he croaks. I hand him the glass.

"Want these too?" I ask, showing him the Nurofen in my open palm.

He nods once, his eyes half closed and drinks the rest of the Smoothie back with the tablets. His head hits the pillow the moment he's done, and he's out cold again.

I smirk at him. He reminds me of me when I'm hung-over. Taking the glass out of his hand, I pick up my coffee cup, and walk out of the bedroom, softly closing the door behind me...

CHAPTER TWENTY-SEVEN

AT TWELVE NOON, Edith calls everyone into the kitchen. She has made a wonderful spread of food for everyone. There's cold meats, pork pies, boiled eggs, lots of salad, bread rolls and my favourite, Jacket Potatoes that have been cut in half and have cheese melted on them. My stomach rumbles in appreciation. Carlos, Rob, and I are sitting at the breakfast bar, while the four chaps from Rob's team are sitting around the breakfast table. I've never met them before, but they all seem like a jovial bunch.

I wonder for a moment if I should take something up for Tristan, but quickly decide against it. I'm still mad at him and worried. I have no idea what he's going to say to me when he wakes up, or what my reaction will be to it, and that has my stomach fluttering with nerves, which is making eating food a daunting task. I put down my fork and stare into space. The radio is playing in the background. Edith must have it on some lovey-dovey station because they keep playing lovey-dovey songs, which is not helping.

"I knew you'd have wedding nerves!" Rob titters, eyeing my half eaten plate of food.

Carlos kicks his foot. "Leave her alone Rob!" I bob my tongue out at him and try to eat some more, but it's just not happening. Kodaline's All I Want starts playing. It's sad and haunting, so of course, I know it. I close my eyes and try not to listen, it's too poignant. It reminds me of Justin leaving, and the pain I felt back then. I try not to think about how I'll feel if this is over between Tristan and me, but all I can hear are the words...

'So you brought out the best of me.'
'A part of me I've never seen.'

Forever With Him

'You took my soul and wiped it clean.'
'Our love was made for movie screens'

I blink back tears as I try to block out the rest of the song out, but it's just not happening. I instantly feel like throwing up. I launch myself off the stool, dash down the hallway and run down the stairs, not stopping until I've reached the garden – *Holy fuck!* I take several deep breaths trying to calm myself down, and I suddenly realise that losing Tristan won't feel like it did when Justin and I split, it will be something else entirely. Something I can't even put into words, something that I think will feel like death like he's dead and I'm dead, only I'm not dead. I'm just this empty shell of a person, walking around in a body, not thinking or feeling anything anymore.

And at that moment, I realise I'm not angry with Tristan anymore, the fear of losing him, of really thinking what it would feel like to not have him in my life has overtaken that, I sink down onto one of the sun loungers, and hang my head in my hands.

I feel him before I see him. My breath catches in my throat, I slowly turn around and watch Tristan's tall figure walking over to me. I stop breathing and try to work out his demeanour. Is he mad, sad, happy? I have no idea. But I do notice that he's dressed only in a pair of baggy, light grey pyjama bottoms that are hanging low on his hips, his torso is bare and beautiful, and his hair is all messed up, he looks as sexy as hell.

I bet Rob enjoyed the show – *Coral!*

Then I notice it, the little note I left on the bedside cabinet is in his hand. Reaching me, he sinks to his knees in front of me and takes my hand in his and just stares down at it.

"I think it's me that should be sorry, not you." He sighs heavily and looks up at me with his wide chocolate eyes, then swallows hard. Then he stares down at the floor, his eyebrows pinched together. I stay silent. "Coral, if you want...some time... to rethink us, I can understand that. My behaviour last night was...unforgivable. I never should have said those things to you."

"Why did you Tristan, why did you react like that?" I ask in a not so nice manner.

He shakes his head and stares down at our entwined fingertips.

"Spit it out, Tristan!" I bite.

He looks up at me all wounded and broken. "I...I don't know why I said those things. I was angry at you and angry at myself for being angry with you. I was pissed as hell with Susannah for doing that…and mortified you'd seen it…" He breaks off for a moment. "I'm so sorry for reacting that way, for shouting at you, and for walking out on you. I wasn't very supportive. I should have been comforting you after what you'd seen, not shouting at you and walking out." He says with his head hung low.

"I don't believe this!" I hiss, my leg jigging up and down with anxiety. The hell this man has put me through over the past twenty-four hours. Tristan tentatively reaches up, takes my face in his hands and gazes up at me, his eyes are red and bloodshot – Has he been crying?

"Coral, I will spend the rest of my life making it up to you for my appalling behaviour last night. I am so, so sorry, but if it's any conciliation they're just words baby – You have my heart, it's yours, forever." I swallow hard. I seemed to have lost the power of speech.

Tristan squeezes his eyes shut for a moment, and then he glances up at me again. I can see the pain and the apprehension as he's not sure what my reaction is going to be.

"Can you ever forgive me?" He asks, swallowing hard again and staring at the floor.

I sigh heavily. "I don't know," I whisper.

His eyes dart up to mine, his face panic-stricken, his hands slide down from my face and rest on his thighs.

"You said some pretty harsh stuff Tristan' – "I didn't mean a word of it," he interrupts, his breath coming in sharp gusts.

"Tristan, you said the wedding was off, that I was making you doubt us, and that I'm self-destructing us!" I say, scowling at him.

"I know, I know," he says, his eyes wider than I've ever seen them. "I don't doubt us, and I know you're not self-destructing us, and I want to marry you, more than you will ever know," he sighs heavily. "I was an asshole for saying those things to you, I know that…I was really angry, and I didn't know what to do with it, and I took it out on you, and I shouldn't have. I'm so sorry." He says, his voice breaking on him.

I shake my head in anger. "You know I did a lot of thinking last night. And you're right if we can't talk to one another, be open and honest with one another without it turning into a fight, then we don't have a chance of working together Tristan." I take a deep breath. "I needed you last night, and you completely let me down! I know what I did was wrong and that I should have told you I was going to see…" I shake my head, I can't say her name. "But I would have thought that after she did…what she did, it would have made the fact that I didn't tell you about it insignificant. I watched her die, Tristan! And where were you?" I get to my feet and start pacing. I can't believe I'm angry again, but I am, and I know I'm right. He's got to learn, well we both have, but he's got to learn that he can't do that to me, no matter how mad he is.

"Coral…did you…do you want me…to leave?" He can barely speak, he's breathing like he's been running up a hill and looks completely beside himself.

I walk back over and sink down in front of him. "Tristan, I love you. But you have got to learn that you just can't say stuff like that to me, whether you mean it or not. And if you ever walk out on me again, we're through." I say my voice firm.

He inhales sharply and locks eyes with me. "I am serious," I say with one eyebrow arched.

"I know, I can see that," he says, swallowing hard again. "I promise you I won't," he adds, his eyes screaming sincerity.

"Good. Look…if you feel angry just…walk into another room! Don't walk out of the house and then come back at god knows what time, leaving me hanging without even so much as a call or a text." I say shaking my head at him.

"Coral, I won't' – I hold my hand up to silence him. "The worst part is that I thought you knew me, I thought you knew that…that you just," I take a deep breath. "That you can't say things like that and not expect me to believe you, Tristan! I thought that's at least one thing you really did know about me." I bite.

"I do know that," he whispers.

"Then why Tristan? I mean, I get you have this need to protect me, and I love that side of you. I just don't understand your reaction?" Tristan winces at my words. I swear there's something…something he's still keeping from me, something that's playing on his mind. Ever since we found out about Simon and Kane, he's been acting a little off, only slightly. Just every now and then I catch him drifting off.

"What?" I snap.

He frowns and shakes his head. "Nothing, I lost it, and I'm sorry. And you're right. Part of it is because I want to protect you, but not just physically. I want to protect you emotionally and mentally too. I think your heart and mind have been through enough. I will do anything to ease that burden. I just wish you'd have told me yesterday and I'd have gone with you, then if Susannah had still...taken her life, I would have been able to protect you from that, but I couldn't because you didn't tell me."

We both sigh heavily, which makes me want to smile. I have to try so hard not to show it. "You can't protect me from everything Tristan," I whisper.

"I know," he murmurs looking down at the grass. "Doesn't mean I'm not going to try," he adds sardonically – We are going around in circles.

"I guess...we still have a lot to learn," I say.

"Yes, we do," he says looking up at me with those big puppy dog eyes.

"You better be a good husband, to me Mr Freeman," I say. I am teasing, but he doesn't know that yet because I'm keeping my face deadpan.

He inhales sharply. "You...you still want to' – "Tristan, we had a fight, well not so much a fight as you shouting and walking out, but I think we've resolved some issues because of it. And even though I wavered, and really did think for a moment that you were not the man for me, I soon changed my mind." I look down at him.

"Coral, I'm so sorry I didn't call or text you. I did go to, loads of times, but each time I did, I changed my mind. I knew you'd be mad, really mad. So mad in fact that I didn't expect you to be here when I got back. I thought you'd head over to Rob's."

"I nearly did," I say.

"I'm so glad you didn't," he says, taking both my hands in his. "I really hope you can forgive me because the thought of not being with you...I can't even put into words."

We just gaze at one another. I'm not sure I can forgive him yet, I still feel pissed at him. Tristan breaks eye contact and stares down at the grass. Seeing him suffering like this makes me change my mind. I don't want to see him in pain, I want him happy and in love, which is exactly how I feel.

I love him, and he's forgiven, it really is that simple. "Ask me again," I say.

He looks up at me. "Am I forgiven?" He asks his eyes wide with trepidation.

"Kind of," I say, finally smiling at him.

Tristan smiles his shy smile. "I would really like to kiss you, Miss Stevens," he says. "May I?" He adds.

"Be my guest," I whisper.

He takes my face in his hands, and just hovers there for a moment, millimetres from my lips, and then he leans in and kisses me passionately, his tongue lapping against mine, turning me on big time. He moans and gasps, then grabs me by the waist and pulls me down off the lounger, so I'm straddling him. I kiss him back with every inch of passion, love and desire I have for this man, my hands gripping his hair, my breath coming in sharp gusts. Mmm...He tastes of toothpaste and Tristan, and the way he's kissing me is making me question...*Are we about to have sex outside?* We are rudely interrupted by whoops and cheers coming from the upstairs balcony, I bury my head in Tristan's neck, feeling embarrassed.

"Get back to work Rob!" Tristan shouts, but I can tell he's smiling.

Then he cups me under the chin, making me look up at him, takes my face in his hands again, and kisses me for what feels like an eternity. We get a bit overheated, our hands all over each other, the kiss intensifying, only this time there is no interruption. When he pulls back, we are both breathless, and I can feel his erection digging into me, he wants me – and the feeling is mutual.

"Thank you for looking after me last night, I didn't deserve it," he says, his face morose.

"Are you kidding!" I squeak. "Tristan, no matter how mad I was with you, I would never want to see any harm come to you. I think...well, people should always look after each other like that, you know…get the drunk one safely to bed." I smile shyly and laugh at myself.

"I agree baby, and I will always, always get your drunken ass safely to bed." He chuckles.

"Tristan Freeman, how dare you say such things!" I retort, laughing along with him.

He smiles up at me, then his serious expression returns. "How are you feeling today darling? You know...I mean what happened with…." He can't say it, and I don't want to talk about it either. It was a shockingly horrible thing to witness, and I can't do anything about it, so I need to put it behind me, like everything else.

"I'll tell you what. I'll make you a deal?" I say, feeling as though I've just hitched a ride to cloud nine – we are still together, so all is well in the world.

"A deal?" He smirks.

"Yes." I smile a ridiculously happy smile.

"I'm all ears." He teases as his hands playfully squeeze my butt cheeks.

"Well, I think we are both sorry?" I question Tristan nods. "So the deal is we don't talk about it, what happened I mean. We put it behind us as a lesson learned, and enjoy today after all this is our last day as singletons!" I giggle.

Tristan rolls his eyes at me. "We are not singletons!"

"We're not married yet either!" I snort. "So do we have a deal?" Then I remember. "Actually, before you say deal, and this isn't me thinking the worst, I'm just curious...where did you go when you left Joyce's?" I ask light heartedly – He was so drunk, I wonder if he's hung-over?

"How do you know I went to see her?" He asks, surprised.

"You told me," I giggle. "And she came by today," I add.

"Joyce was here?" He says, surprised again.

"Yeah..." I look down at his chest. "I was in a bit of a mess, I stayed up all night watching you sleep, running things over in my head. I'd missed her call telling me that Gladys was mad at me and on her way over' – "Gladys has been here too?" He interrupts.

"Yes," I say, not wanting to remember why.

"Why?" He questions.

God damn it! I don't want to think or talk about it. I sigh heavily. "It's already in The Argus Tristan," I say, frowning deeply.

"What is baby?" He softly asks, gently tucking my hair behind my ear.

"Susannah's..." I can't say it.

"Already?" He chokes eyes wide.

"Yeah...Gladys read it, she was pretty mad I was there. Anyway, long story short, Joyce came over, and we talked, she said you left hers after midnight."

"I did?" He says, gazing down at the grass. Trying to remember I guess?

"Do you even remember where you went?" I giggle.

"I seem to recollect some bar. I think there was a nightclub on the lower level?"

"You were so drunk!" I giggle.

"Yeah...I'm sorry about that," he says, looking a little embarrassed.

"Don't be," I laugh. "Tristan you were adorable! I'll take drunk Tristan over mad Tristan anytime, which reminds me – Are you hung-over? Does your head hurt baby?" I ask, stroking his cheek and his hair.

Forever With Him

He pushes his bottom lip out and nods his head.

"You are?" I squeak, feeling sorry for him. I mean, I know hangovers are self-inflicted, but still, I always want comforting when I feel like that, maybe Tristan does too.

"Ahh, poor baby." I pull him to me, cradling his head against my chest, and wrap my arms around him. "What can I do? Do you want a drink, something to eat, some more painkillers?" I ask sweetly.

"Oh Coral..." Tristan breathes, squeezing me tight.

"Tell me," I push.

He pulls back and looks up at me. "Well, as you're asking. I would like some food, and some painkillers, and some sex," he says in a sweet boyish voice.

"Very cute Mr Freeman," I giggle. "In that order?"

"No, not necessarily," His sexy grin is back, his dimples deep.

"Can I tell you a secret?" I whisper.

"Please do," he says his voice low and husky.

"I'm always really horny when I'm hung-over," I admit.

"Me too," Tristan says, leaning in and kissing my neck. I'm still wearing my baggy pyjama bottoms and vest top that I got changed into last night, just thin scraps of material that can easily be removed.

"Have you ever done it outside?" I ask.

"No, actually I haven't. Is that what you want to do Coral?" He mumbles against my skin.

I pull his head back and grip his hair. "Yes, now fiancé."

"We can't," he croaks, his wide eyes dark.

"Why not?" I moan. "That part of the garden is completely concealed," I add, gesturing to it with my chin.

"I haven't got any condoms with me," he explains.

"We don't need them," I chortle.

"You want to try for' – "You remember last Thursday, I went off for an hour...said I was getting a surprise organised for us?" I interrupt.

"Yeah...?" Tristan is hesitant and looks worried.

"Surprise!" I squeal, holding my arms out. "This is my kind of...well, a wedding present to you, that's not a gift because I am going to get you' – "You've lost me?" He interrupts.

"Oh right! Well, when I decided that I wanted to go on the pill, I called the family planning clinic in Newquay and spoke to a lovely nurse, she said she could only give me a month's supply and that we'd still have to use condoms for seven days. And well,

407

the seven days are up baby. So, are you going to have outdoor sex with me or not?" I challenge, staring at his very kissable lips.

"You've gone on the pill?" He questions.

"Yes." I smile.

"Why?" he breathes.

"Because I wanted to do that for you and for us, and I really don't like condoms, they kind of, take the spontaneity out of sex, don't you think?"

Tristan grins wickedly at me and pulls my lips down to meet his.

"Is that a yes," I mumble against his lips.

"Oh, baby...of course, it's a yes, wrap your legs around me," he softly says, so I do.

Tristan stands and keeping his hands firmly planted on my backside, we head over to the dark, secluded part of the garden...

CARLOS IS RIGHT! Making up sex is very gratifying. After our little bit of fun in the garden, we ate lunch, had sex again and then took a shower together – with a very sexy break in-between washing each other's hair – and then Tristan took me shopping. Of course, he didn't just by me a couple of skirts, he bought me ten skirts, all different styles and colours, and five fitted dresses, all work clothes. Then he took me into the lingerie department. *Boy, my man has kinky tastes!*

When we got back from shopping, Rob made us come down through the garage instead of the house as he didn't want the surprise ruined, I couldn't help laughing and rolling my eyes at him. And now its early evening and Tristan and I are curled up on the large outdoor sofa. Rob, Carlos and I are sipping Rum Daiquiri's, Rob's idea, and apparently, we are having a Chinese tonight, but I doubt I'll eat much, my stomach keeps flipping over every time I think about getting married tomorrow.

But I have decided to stay here tonight, I want to sleep in our bed, our bed that has Tristan's scent all over it, I know it will help calm me, but it's going to feel very strange not having him next to me. I'm hoping I'll be out for the count the moment my head hits the pillow as I feel so tired now I've sat still for a while, and I'm trying not to be melancholy about Tristan leaving tonight, but I can't help it – I don't want him to go.

Rob has informed me that Will and his wife Natalie, won't be coming to the wedding tomorrow, which I'm a little sad about – Tristan seemed pleased though – and neither will Harry and Sophia. Apparently, they have some family thing going on.

However, we did pop into the office before we came back, and Joe will be here tomorrow with her kids. It will be nice to finally meet them. I'm so glad they're all together again.

I look up at Tristan and sigh inwardly. Joyce will be here soon to collect him. I hate that he is leaving me, today of all days, after our fight last night, and our sexy making up, I just don't want to let him go.

"Come on Coral, another!" Rob chuckles. I think he's already drunk – *How did that happen?*

"No. I'm not getting pissed Rob!" I firmly tell him.

He pulls a face and I can tell Tristan isn't too pleased he's said that either, besides, the last thing I want on my wedding day is to be hungover.

"Suit yourself!" He teases, and I watch him pour two more for him and Carlos.

I finish mine off and curl myself around Tristan. He pulls me closer to him and kisses the top of my head. Hmm, he smells divine, freshly showered, aftershave and Tristan's potent scent all mixed into one – His mobile buzzes in his pocket, making my heart sink.

"Joyce is here," Tristan whispers. *No, you can't go!*

"Why don't you ask her if she would like to join us for a cocktail before you go?" I say.

"Good idea." Tristan kisses my head again and makes the call. I think he's just as reluctant to leave me as I am to see him leaving. "She's on her way down," he adds, squeezing me tight.

I sit up and pour a cocktail for Joyce. "Yay! I knew you'd come round!" Rob chuckles.

"It's for Joyce!" I tell him firmly. Then I put the glass down and walk over to Rob, grabbing him by the arm, I yank him out of hearing range. "Rob, are you purposely trying to wind Tristan up?" I hiss.

"No!" he titters. "But he is pretty easy to rile," he snorts and then really starts laughing. *Oh boy!* This is going to be a long night, I can tell, and all I want is to curl up in bed – with Tristan.

"Ok, look, Rob, I love that you and Carlos are here, and I promise you we will have a good time tonight, but I'm not getting drunk ok! It's my wedding day tomorrow, you know what I'm like when I'm hungover. Christ, I'll have to make the registrar marry us in bed!" I say dryly.

Rob snorts with laughter. "You're so right Coral, you cannot handle being hungover – Joyce!" he bellows, running over to hug her. *Yep, Rob is definitely pissed!*

Part of me wants to join him, but it's so not worth it. I will definitely need a clear head tomorrow. I take a deep breath and smile at Carlos, who rolls his eyes, then winks at me. I shake my head in laughter and head back over to Tristan.

THIRTY MINUTES LATER, Tristan and I are in the cinema room saying our goodbyes, well more like there's a lot of lip synchronisation going on.

"I hate this," I murmur against his lips, crushing his body closer to mine.

"So do I," he says, resting his forehead against mine. I open my eyes, stare at his perfect lips for a moment, then look up, only to find he has his eyes open, and he's gazing down at me as though he's the lucky one, not the other way around – *How ludicrous!*

"I miss you already," he murmurs, staring down at my lips.

"This sucks, big time! Why did I agree to this?" I say, gritting my teeth.

"I know you may not think it now, but try to imagine how you're going to feel tomorrow," he softly placates.

"Like I want to run down the aisle at a hundred miles an hour leaving Bob in a cloud of dust?" I answer dryly.

Tristan chuckles at my little rant. "I think it will make it feel more...powerful, more profound," he says.

"You do?" I look up at his wide eyes and see they are soft and glowing with love.

"Yes, I won't have touched you for so long. Not stroked your cheek, or held your hand, or kissed these very, very kissable lips." His lips swoop down, his tongue gently lapping against mine, but it quickly develops into something else.

My hand's fist in his hair, as his one hand crushes me against him, his other hand curling into the back of my hair. Tristan moans hungrily, it sends lightning bolts of electricity right to my sex, which makes me moan aloud with want and need. I'll never get enough of him, ever. Someone knocks the door, pulling us out of the concentrated, intense little bubble. *Damn it!*

I want to shout 'go away', but that's rude, especially if that was Joyce. Tristan smooths my hair back, trying to make me look presentable, I think? He's grinning widely as he does this, I seem to have lost all control and just want to take him to bed where we can stay, forever. Then I notice how messy I've made his hair too.

"Come here baby," I say, smiling up at him. Tristan bends

his head down so I can do the same to him. "You better go," I say. "Before Joyce tells us both off, besides I need to keep an eye on Rob. I think he's more nervous than me, and he's already drunk!" I add.

"Yes, he definitely is," Tristan chuckles. He leans down to kiss me once more, but I pull back and shake my head, biting my lip as I do.

"Not a good idea, I may not let you go," I say a little breathlessly.

Not taking any notice, he takes my face in his hands, kisses me passionately for a few seconds and then gently pecks me on the lips. He pulls back and smiles his most enigmatic smile, his eyes crinkling sweetly, his dimples on full wattage. It's the smile I fell for, the very first smile he gave me when he followed me down to my desk, on the first day I met him – And I swoon.

"See you at the altar," he says.

"Don't be late," I tease.

"I doubt Joyce would allow that," he retorts, grinning widely. *Argh! This is so hard!*

"Please go, Tristan, before I get upset. I do not want puffy eyes tomorrow ok?" I say, trying to fight the overwhelming feeling of heartache.

"Your wish is my command," he says.

I watch him lean down and pick up his overnight bag, and throw it over his shoulder. This is hurting so badly, like an actual physical ache, I swallow hard and try to focus on *not* crying.

"You'll call me?" he says. "If you need me for anything, if you get scared, have a bad dream...whatever it is, and I'll come straight over. Promise me you will?" He adds, gazing down at me.

I have lost the power of speech, so I just nod.

He smiles a little crookedly at me and opens the door, then he clasps my hand in his, and we walk through the garage and out onto the driveway. Joyce is waiting in her car, she smiles when she sees us both, and I give her a little wave. Tristan lets go of my hand, leaving me feeling bereft and walks over to the car. He winks at me as he throws his bag in the boot, then with one last lingering look – which makes my soul feel like it's losing half of itself – he steps into Joyce's car. They both wave as she pulls away, and I hold up my hand, trying my best not to fall apart...

AS I STAND in our bedroom staring out at the view, I suddenly realise how content I feel. I thought I would be nervous about today, scared shitless actually. Yet, as I stand in my wedding gown with my bouquet of sunflowers in my hand, I feel so calm and so ready to do this. In fact, I feel like I'm in a dream, floating up in the clouds. I chuckle to myself, I can't believe this is about to happen, that I'm going to marry the man of my dreams. But then again, the calmness may have something to do with the fact that I have Beyonce's Smash Into You on repeat, the words reflecting my feelings completely.

"It's time Aunty Coral!" Lily squeals excitedly as she runs into the room.

I turn and see her bounding over to me. She looks so sweet in her ivory sundress, her big blue eyes wide, her blonde curls bouncing around her face, and her tiny sunflower neatly pinned into her hair. Gladys, Joyce, Debs and Carlos have been up here with me all morning, and are now downstairs, waiting with our other guests.

Time to get this show on the road!

"Ok kiddo!" I grin widely at her and switch off my player.

"You look so pretty," she says.

"Not as pretty as you," I say, she smiles shyly at me.

"Coral, everyone's ready. Bob's waiting on the first landing," Debs says.

She looks so lovely in her pale lemon sundress. "Debs, you look gorgeous!" I tell her.

"And you look calm – too calm!" she adds.

"This is what I want Debs," I shrug. "I have no need to be nervous."

"Right!" Debs rolls her eyes at me, then leans forward and carefully hugs me. "Don't want to ruin the hair and make-up," she adds sarcastically, making me chuckle – Carlos nearly had a fit when Gladys tried to hug me. "Good luck, I'll see you down there," she says to me, then turns to Lily. "Now be a good girl Lily' – "Debs, she'll be fine. Go!" I tell her, she leans down, gives Lily a kiss on the cheek and then disappears.

James Lasts Cavalleria Rusticana starts drifting up the stairs. When I told Tristan last week that it was the first piece of music I imagined dancing to with him, he insisted we have it as the music I walk down the aisle to. And now it's playing it seems so fitting and so right.

"Guess it's just us Lily," I say grinning widely at her. "Shall we hold hands, so neither one of us falls down the stairs?" I add, making a funny face.

Forever With Him

Lily giggles. "You're funny Aunty Coral." I laugh along with her and take her tiny hand in mine.

We walk out of the bedroom, and I see Bob waiting for me – he looks very handsome in his black tuxedo and bow-tie. Lily and I manage to make it down the first flight of stairs without any catastrophes. Reaching Bob, he holds his arm out for me. I place my hand in the crook of his elbow then lean forward and kiss his cheek.

"Thank you for doing this Bob," I smile widely at him.

"You look...beautiful," Bob says, choking back the tears.

"Thanks, Bob," I say smiling widely. "Ok Lily, you're up. Hold onto the bannister as you go down the stairs ok?" Lily nods, then she places her hand on the bannister and carefully makes her way down the stairs, Bob, and I slowly follow. As we get further down, I start to see what Rob's done with the place. It looks magical, like something out of a fairy-tale! And the smell, it's so overpowering.

As we reach the bottom of the stairs, I'm completely blown away.

Rob has completely transformed this part of the house into a magical garden. I have never seen so many wildflowers in my entire life, and they are everywhere. Hanging from the ceilings, on the walls, scattered across the floors – Just everywhere – *Oh wow!*

All of the furniture has been removed to make way for our guests, who are sitting in neat rows of chairs, that are wrapped in some kind of floaty lemon material. And Rob has erected some sort of ivory canopy out on the balcony, protecting us from the blazing sun, and over on the far side of the room, where our guests are seated, I can see the doors out to the balcony are open wide, and there's an archway of flowers.

Everyone oohs and ahhs as Lily walks towards them, throwing petals into the air. Almost everyone has their cameras or mobile phones out, taking pictures of Lily and then Bob and I. As we continue to walk forward, I can't help searching for Tristan, it feels like I haven't seen him in forever, but no sign of him, not yet anyway. However I do see Rob & Malcolm who are also in black tuxedos with bow-ties, they both look very handsome.

I see all the faces of the people that I love and care about smiling back at me. Gladys bursts into tears as I glance at her, it makes me smile. I catch Rob's eye and wink at him, he's done an amazing job. As we walk further into the room, I finally see Tristan waiting for me under an altar of wildflowers, and green ivory. My breath instantly catches in my throat – how handsome, how debonair he looks in his matching Tuxedo, and the look on his face says it all. At first, he looks shocked and kind of awestruck. Then he places his hand on his heart and swallows hard, then his features change into his most dazzling smile, his dimples deep – and he's shaved his beard off.

I smile back at him feeling shy for the first time today and continue to walk towards him. Finally reaching Tristan, I pass my flowers to Lily, and then Bob places my hand in his. I turn and face Tristan as he clasps both my hands in his, and gives them a gentle squeeze.

"Hi," he whispers.

"Hi," I whisper back.

"You look breathtaking," he says, making me feel shy.

"So do you," I whisper back, he smiles shyly.

The registrar begins. "Ladies and Gentleman…" And I drift off...

As I stand before Tristan, gazing up at his eyes that are glowing with love, sincerity and awe, I feel my heart slowly and steadily thump against my chest. I thought I would be nervous once I got here, right at this moment, standing right before him, about to make my vows. But all I feel is a calm, contented blissful feeling, the same feeling I had when I first dreamt of Tristan and being on that boat with him.

I never thought I would hear myself say the words, but I can't wait to marry him, to become his wife and for him to be my husband. It's hard to describe how proud I feel to be with him, he really is a wonderful man – "Tristan Freeman, do you take this woman, Coral Stevens to be your wife?" The registrar says – *Oh shit where have I been? Concentrate Coral!*

"I do." Tristan's voice rings loud and clear.

"Do you promise to love, honour, cherish and protect her, forsaking all others and holding only unto her?"

"I do." He looks so earnest as he says this, so proud, his tone soft and full of love – I swoon up at him.

"Coral Stevens, do you take this man, Tristan Freeman to be your husband?" I swallow hard – my turn.

"I do," I say, a little too loudly, I almost laugh out loud at myself but manage to hold it in.

"Do you promise to love, honour, cherish and protect him, forsaking all others and holding only unto him?"

"I do," I say.

"Tristan, please take this ring and place it on your bride's finger and state your pledge to her."

I don't know about Tristan, but I have recited my vows so many times, so I don't screw it up, that I could say them backwards. Taking my ring and placing it at the tip of my finger Tristan gazes down at me and begins.

"I, Tristan Freeman, take you Coral Stevens to be my lawfully wedded wife. I give you this ring as a sign of my eternal love for you. Before these witnesses, I solemnly vow to love, honour, and protect you. To bring you comfort in times of need, to share your joy, and uphold your dreams. I will cherish and respect you, always, in good times and bad, for the rest of our lives, and I promise to love you faithfully, forsaking all others. To have and to hold from this day forward. For better, for worse, for richer, for poorer, in sickness and in health, until death do us part. This is my solemn vow to you." *Whoa!*

Tristan is so intense as he recites his vows to me, then he smiles crookedly and slowly slides the ring down my finger. I gaze up into his warm eyes, I can only see love. It literally feels like my heart is melting like chocolate, and all my old barriers are crumbling to the ground.

The registrar has to nudge me to snap me out of it–*Oops, my turn.*

I almost giggle aloud, but manage to hold it in.

"Coral, please take this ring and place it on your groom's finger and state your pledge to him."

I take the ring, and place it at the tip of Tristan's finger and look up at him.

"I, Coral Stevens, take you Tristan Freeman to be my lawfully wedded husband. I promise to love and adore you for as long as we both shall live. I vow to bring you comfort in times of need, to share your joy and to support you in all of your dreams and goals. I promise to love you faithfully, forsaking all others, and to trust and respect you. I give you my, hand, my heart and my undying love, forever. To have and to hold from this day forward. For better, for worse, for richer, for poorer, in sickness and in health, until death do us part."

It takes a monumental effort on my part to pull my eyes away from his so I can slide the ring down his finger. When I'm done I look up Tristan, his breathtaking smile is making me swoon again. I titter to myself and smile shyly at him.

"Coral and Tristan, in so much as the two of you have agreed to live together in Matrimony and have promised your love for each other by these vows. I now pronounce you Husband and Wife. Congratulations, you may kiss your bride." *Whoa! I'm married!*

How strange, I feel like my world that has felt so disjointed for so long, has settled solidly where it should be – I am home.

Tristan reaches up, places his hands either side of my face and then leans down, so he's inches from my lips. "I love you, wife," he whispers.

"I love you to husband," I softly say.

I pull on his lapels, so his lips meet mine. He kisses me tenderly, with absolute adoration. The explosion of love that erupts within me takes me by complete surprise, and I think Tristan's feeling it too. It's like we're alone, in an empty room. I pull him closer to me so I can feel the length of his warm body pressed tightly against mine and I really go to town, kissing him with every fibre of my being. I wrap my arms around his neck, and he reciprocates by wrapping his arms around my waist and crushing me to him.

I hear someone clear their throat, and someone else giggle, but I keep on going. I don't ever want to stop kissing him. Then I hear Rob whoop loudly, and the room erupts in thunderous applause. I pull back from Tristan's lips, he keeps me pressed tight against his body as I gaze up at him, we both laugh, then Tristan turns us around to face our guests.

I'm immediately blinded by several flashes going off at the same time. *Whoa!*

The next thing I know I am pulled out of his embrace and passed from person to person for hugs, kisses and congratulations. Gladys is crying, and so are Debs, Joyce, *and* Carlos!

Rob pulls me into a bear hug, swinging me around as he does.

"Oh Rob, this place looks amazing!" I screech as he continues to spin me around. "It's magical, thank you so much." I hug him fiercely, he finally lets me go, and I can tell he is fighting back the tears.

He clears his throat and blows out a deep breath. "I'm glad you like it. Oh Coral, I'm so happy for you," he says, hugging me tightly once more, then he makes a funny squeaky noise and dashes off. A few moments later I am back in Tristan's arms.

Once all the congratulations are over, a waiter from the caterers Rob hired hand Tristan and I some kind of bubbly drink, I would say it's champagne, but it's pink.

Rob comes bounding over to us and shakes Tristan's hand.

"Congrats you guys, you both look great!" He says he seems to have regained his composure.

"Rob, what is this?" I ask, holding my glass up.

"Champagne cocktail!" I frown at him.

He rolls his eyes at me. "I know you don't like champagne, but just try it. I guarantee you'll like it," he adds.

I take a tentative sip. "Wow, that's delicious! What's in it?"

"Raspberry liquor," he says, smiling smugly at me.

"Awesome!" I grin from ear to ear and clink glasses with him. Tristan chuckles at me, then nods to Stuart. I turn and watch him walk out the front door. "Where's Stuart going?" I ask.

"You'll see. Come on drink up," he says, and glugs back the rest of his glass.

"Why do I need to that?" I question playfully.

He grins from ear to ear. "Surprise!"

"Oh." I take the last swig, Rob takes my glass from me, and I can tell, he knows. "You know what this is about?" I gasp. He nods, grinning from ear to ear. Then I notice everyone else is doing the same. "Everyone knows!" I gasp, looking up at Tristan. Ok, he's smiling so broadly now that if he continues like this his face may actually split in two.

"Come on gorgeous." He tugs on my hand and leads me down the hallway. I turn to see all our guests are watching us, cocktails raised in their hands, all smiling.

"Tristan, we can't just leave our guests!" I balk.

He stops right at the front door and reaches up to tenderly stroke my cheek. "Of course we can, they all know this was planned Coral. We won't be long baby," he softly says.

"We're coming back?" I question, trying not to frown.

"Of course we are." His wide grin is back again, it's infectious. He looks like a bashful schoolboy. I grin back at him and then Tristan turns and gives a small wave to everyone. I do the same, even though I have no clue what's going on. They all cheer and wave back at us as we leave the house…

CHAPTER TWENTY-EIGHT

TRISTAN CLASPS MY hand in his, and we walk over to the big Jag where Stuart is waiting for us with the back door held open. "Congratulations to you both," he says.

"Thank you, Stuart." We both reply at the same time, I climb into the car, and as I slide across the seat, I playfully pull on Tristan's hand. He climbs in beside me, still grinning broadly and shuts the door, seconds later we are on the move.

"Where are we going?" I ask, unable to contain myself. My leg is nervously jigging up and down.

"Patience," he says, clasping his hand on my knee. "But while I have you here, I would like to take this opportunity to tell you how devastatingly beautiful you look, and how very proud I am to be able to call you my wife." A single tear pricks my right eye, which kind of annoys me, I haven't cried today. "Ah baby, no need for tears," Tristan coos.

I swallow hard against the lump that's formed and smile back at him.

"I promised myself I would not blubber today. Now, look what you've done!" I tease, laughing slightly. Tristan chuckles along with me. "And just so *you* know, I'm proud of you too Tristan. And may *I* just say how handsome and debonair you look today – my very own James Bond!" I wink then giggle at him.

"James Bond eh?" He says in a very impressive Sean Connery accent. It makes me laugh aloud, a carefree laugh. I can't believe how light I feel, I'm still floating, but higher now, I'm so happy!

Stuart pulls into the gym car-park and parks in a bay.

"Are we going swimming?" I tease dryly.

"Throw you into the sea if you carry on with that sarcasm!" Tristan retorts, grinning widely.

"You wouldn't dare!" I tease back.

"Oh Coral, don't you know me at all?" He laughs. *Shit! Would he?* He laughs even harder at my shocked expression. "Come on beautiful, we can't be too long. We don't want to miss our own wedding party." Tristan hops out the car and runs around my side to open my door for me. I can't believe I'm about to step onto this car-park that I have walked across so many times, in my wedding dress – *How odd!*

Tristan takes hold of both of my hands and pulls me into his solid, manly chest. "Twenty," he says to Stuart, then clasps my hand in his and we start walking towards my studio.

"Are you really not going to tell me what's going on?" I squeak, feeling so excited.

"Nope." Tristan remains tight-lipped as he lifts my dress and helps me down the steps to the concourse. We head straight past my studio, which is weird, take a right and start walking down one of the Jetties. I keep looking around me as we continue walking, hoping for some sort of clue as to what's about to happen, we take another right, and I realise we are heading deeper into the marina. Suddenly, Tristan holds his hand up in the air. I look down the Jetty and see a man dressed in shorts and t-shirt with a clipboard in his hand, he raises his hand back to Tristan.

"Who's he?" I ask.

"Oh Coral, I'm not going to tell you what the surprise is so stop asking!" He says grinning widely at me, then he leans down and gently pecks my cheek.

"Mr Freeman, good to see you again." The man says as we reach him, he warmly shakes Tristan's hand. He seems very jovial, and I notice that his face is very brown and weather-worn, like leather. "Congratulations to you both," he adds, smiling warmly at us.

"Thank you, Sam," Tristan says, slapping him on the shoulder. "May I introduce my wife, Mrs Coral Freeman." *Whoa!* - I feel my heart crash against my chest and begin beating wildly out of control. I have to take several deep breaths to try and calm it down – *What was that?*

"Mrs Freeman." Sam nods to me but doesn't reach out to shake my hand – I wonder if Tristan has said something to him?

"Hello Sam," I say, my voice shaking slightly – *Mrs Freeman! How weird is that?*

"Is everything ready?" Tristan asks.

"Yes. I just need you to sign here and here, and you can be on your way." Sam cheerfully says.

"Excellent!" Tristan takes the clipboard, quickly scribbles his signature and hands the clipboard back. "Thanks for getting everything organised so quickly Sam," Tristan says, shaking his hand again.

"It was my pleasure," Sam says, he seems like a nice guy. I am still baffled.

"Well, nice to meet you, Mrs Freeman," he says, nodding his head to me.

"You too," I smile back at him.

"Good luck to you both," Sam adds.

"Thank you, Sam, see you soon," Tristan says.

Sam smiles, nods once at Tristan and then walks away.

I still have no idea what's going on.

"Any idea?" Tristan asks with his one eyebrow cocked up as he grins widely at me, waiting for my answer.

"None whatsoever," I choke out dryly.

"Good, I'm glad." He takes a step back from me, then turns, with both arms open wide and gestures to the massive boat behind him. "Ta-da!"

I swallow hard and then begin blinking so rapidly I think I may lose some eyelashes. Eventually, I find my voice. "Why are you pointing at this boat Tristan?" I say breathlessly.

"It's not a boat," he scoffs in horror. "It's a luxury motor yacht!" *Of course, it is!*

"Well, why are you pointing at it?" I slowly repeat.

He drops his arms and smiles so sexily at me it actually takes my attention away from the *'luxury motor yacht'* then he pulls me into his embrace. His left arm is tightly wrapped around my waist, holding me close to him. He reaches up with his right hand and gently moves a stray hair away from my cheek.

"It's my wedding present to you." He softly says then continues. "I didn't buy you a house on the beach, so I thought I'd bring the sea to you, by buying you this."

My mouth gapes open, I am speechless.

"Do you like it?" He asks, looking a little worried.

I slowly shake my head as I stare up at the sparkling white yacht – she looks brand new! This is far too much, I burst into tears.

"Ah baby, don't cry." Tristan wraps his right arm around my shoulders, pulling me tight against him and gently rocks me. He's bought me a yacht as a wedding gift, and what have I got him? Sweet F.A, that's what! I am going to have to make up for

Forever With Him

this big-time! But how? What do you get for a man that already has everything? I will have to think really hard about this!

"Oh Tristan," I mewl, trying to stop myself from crying, so I don't ruin my wedding make-up. "This is too much," I croak, staring up into his wide chocolate eyes.

Tristan hands me his handkerchief, I carefully dab my tears away.

"No Coral, it's not," he softly says, reaching down to gently kiss my lips. "Would you like to see inside?" He adds excitedly.

It makes me giggle. "You know a nice bottle of perfume would have sufficed," I softly chide.

"I don't think so!" Tristan scoffs at me. "Shall we?" He adds he's grinning like a schoolboy again.

I look up the magnificent yacht before me, still completely stunned.

"Coral, do you want to have a quick tour because we need to get back?" he softly says.

I feel befuddled. "Ok," I squeak. I just... *Wow!*

Tristan clasps my hand, and we take the couple of steps to the rear of the Yacht, then lifting me up into his arms, he steps aboard her.

"First threshold to carry you over," he says, grinning widely as he puts me down.

I am still speechless.

"Matt!" Tristan shouts.

A man in his late fifties pops his head over the higher deck and looks down at us. "Tristan!" He says, holding his hand up and smiling down at us. I think they know each other.

"That's Matt, the captain," Tristan explains.

My mouth pops open again. "We have a captain?" I squeak, my eyes wide.

"And cabin crew." Tristan is really smiling again.

I shake my head at him – *So over the top!* – I gaze around at my surroundings. The decking is a very light beech colour, there are sumptuous light grey and beige leather seating, a dining table with four chairs, and set back behind the table are double, full height glass doors, but the windows are tinted so I can't see inside. Right in front of me are a set of white curved stairs leading to the upper deck. Matt comes bouncing down those stairs, followed by two young blonde boys who are smartly dressed in white uniforms.

"Hello Tristan," Matt says, warmly shaking his hand. "Have the plans changed?" He asks, glancing across at me.

"No, not at all. Is everything ready?" Tristan asks.

Matt nods once. "These are our crew, Harry and Peter," he says, gesturing to the two boys.

They both nod at Tristan and me in a very professional manner.

Tristan nods to them both. "May I introduce my wife, Mrs Coral Freeman." Here we go again. My heart slams against my chest, beating wildly, making me catch my breath.

"Hello," I say, a little breathlessly.

"Nice to meet you, Mrs Freeman," Matt says, noticing he doesn't reach for my hand either.

"We're just going to take a quick tour," Tristan explains.

"Then we shall leave you to it," Matt says, and the two boys follow him off the yacht.

"Right then my darling wife, this is the Princess 35M, she's a 115ft Diesel engine, and she can reach speeds of up to 27 knots," he says.

I cock an eyebrow up at him. He chuckles at me, then continues.

"She has air-conditioning, a fantastic generator, and as you can see we have ample space." He adds, gesturing to all of her, then he clasps my hand in his, and we take the steps up to the next deck, where there are several built-in sun loungers on the foredeck – and a Jacuzzi?

"We have full height windows to port and starboard, and it has a vast saloon. It also has hydraulic folding balconies with sliding doors either side, which really creates a sense of space and light – I thought you'd like that," he adds.

I blink up at him. *Still in shock Tristan!*

"Like it so far?" Tristan asks, trying not to smile at my bemused expression.

"Yes," I squeak, I don't really know what else to say – *What's not to like?*

Tristan tugs my hand and leads me toward a door, I notice a plaque above it has the word 'Helm' carved into it, and I have no idea what it means. I have a lot to learn.

"This is the Helm," Tristan tells me as we step inside.

I'm guessing it's where the captain will spend most of his time because right in front of me is a long desk with several computer screens and lots of other electrical bits and pieces. In the middle of this sits a large leather captain's chair, in front of that, a large steering wheel. The panoramic windows offer the most spectacular view across the Marina. Behind all of this, is the most luxurious seating area, all plush leather single seats, and two large sofas with a large table neatly nestled in the centre.

"Shall we move on?" Tristan asks.

"Ok," I choke.

We head through another door, down a set of curved stairs where we enter the galley. It's all dark woods, black shiny work surfaces and top of the range oven and hob. *Wow!* I shake my head in wonder, but we head through another door and walk down a small corridor.

"W.C to your left," Tristan says as we go steaming past it, then Tristan opens a set of double doors, and we walk into the most luxurious living area.

On my right, there's a large plasma screen T.V up on the wall. In the centre of the room there are several sofas in the same grey and beige colours, there's a mini-bar to my left, and directly in front of me are the full height doors that I first saw when we came aboard. I can see the dining table and chairs outside. *Whoa!*

Tristan tugs my hand again, and taking me off to the left we head down another set of stairs and walk along a narrow hallway. "Guest bedrooms," he says pointing to the doors as we pass them. "Guest bathroom," he points again and then stops when we reach the end of the hallway. "Our room," he says his eyes twinkly wickedly.

He opens the double doors and gestures for me to go first. I walk into the most luxurious bedroom. I'm surprised there's so much room, the bed is huge, yet it looks dwarfed by all the space. And again, everything is luxurious and has the same colour scheme, dark woods, grey and beige bedding, and the panoramic windows are making the space feel so light and breezy. I notice in the corner of the room are two glasses of pink bubbly waiting for us.

Tristan lets go of my hand, and as he walks over to the far end of the room, he points to another door. "Master bath," he says. "Take a look." I walk over to the door, open it up and gasp aloud. It has a frigging bath. I mean, I expected a decent bathroom with a nice shower and all the other bits and bobs, but not a bath too. I shake my head in awe. I hear music, and I instantly know the song – Etta James's At Last.

Oh no! Don't cry, don't cry!

"Coral," Tristan calls.

I swallow hard, and fighting back the tears, I walk out of the bathroom. Tristan is standing on the far side of the room, looking as handsome as ever, he holds his hand out to me. "Dance with me?"

I nod, because I have lost the power of speech again, and walk across the room to my beautiful husband. He pulls me close to him, takes my hand in his and we slowly dance around the bedroom to Etta's song. And I melt, again.

"How did I get this lucky?" I ask.

"It's just a yacht," he softly says.

"I wasn't talking about the yacht Tristan, I meant you."

"Oh!" He smiles shyly at me and spins me around. "Shouldn't it be I who is saying that to you?" He questions.

"Do you feel lucky?" I question, feeling brave.

"Oh, more than you will ever now," he says, the depth of his words and the sincerity in his eyes is making my heart expand again. I'm not sure how much more love I can fill it up with.

Unfortunately, the song comes to an end. "Thank you for the dance, my beautiful, captivating wife." Tristan spins me around once more, making me giggle. "Shall we have a quick drink before we go back?" He asks.

"Yes," I say, blinking up at him.

Tristan walks over and collects the champagne, I watch him walk back to me, wondering again, how I became so lucky. I smile up at him, and accept the glass he hands me.

"To us." He says, grinning from ear to ear.

"To us," I say. We clink glasses, and both take a sip. "Mmm, delicious," I say, taking another gulp. "Do we really have to go back so soon?" I ask.

"You don't want to go back?" He says, chortling at me.

"Well, I was thinking..." I turn and glance down at the large bed, then bat my lashes at him.

His very sexy smile appears. "Later," he chuckles. I pout at him which makes him laugh even harder, so I reach up to kiss him, but he takes a step back. "We both know what will happen if we kiss in here," he says, and even though I know he's right, I still feel rejected. "Come on, we'd better get back." Tristan drains his glass, so I knock the rest of mine back and place my hand in his open palm. "I'm not saying no," he tells me. "I fully intend to sneak off with you this afternoon and have my wicked way with you," he adds. The most wonderful, exhilarating, spine-tingling feeling spreads through my entire body.

"I hold you to that husband," I say smiling up at him.

When we reach the stairs, Tristan stops and gazes down at

me. "By the way, we are staying here tonight, and we're stretching her legs tomorrow, we'll be out for the whole day," he says.

"Really?" I squeak feeling thoroughly delighted.

"Yes, my darling wife." His lips swoop down to mine, his kiss is tender and intense all at the same time, but he pulls back quickly. "Ah, I want you!" He barks, frustrated.

I snort back at him. "The feelings mutual," I say dryly which makes Tristan laugh.

We head up on deck then make our way back towards the car.

I'm still in shock…I can't believe he bought a yacht for me.

The moment Stuart pulls up at the house, Tristan jumps out the car and comes around to my side. Opening the door, he helps me to my feet and then lifts me up into his arms, making me giggle in delight.

"Tristan, what are you doing?" I laugh.

"I have to carry you over the threshold baby," he says puckering his lips for a kiss, so I lean forward and plant my lips on his…

HALF AN HOUR later and we've both had another glass of champagne, and I'm about to have a chat with Joyce, but Tristan stops me. "Time for our wedding dance," he says.

"But we haven't picked a song?" I say my eyes wide with worry.

"I have," he says, shrugging and smiling lovingly at me.

"You have?" I squeak.

"Yes." He's laughing at me again. "Is that ok?" He adds.

I smile shyly and nod my head.

"Come on then, let's show them how it's done." Taking my hand, he nods to Rob and leads me into the centre of the room. The conversations die down to a quiet hush. For the first time today, I actually feel embarrassed. I look around at all our guests, they all have their mobiles out, so they are going to video us, or take photos. *Shit! What if I fall over?*

"I won't let you fall," Tristan says, reading my mind again.

"Ok," I breathe. "What song have you chosen?" I ask.

Tristan smiles widely at me and shakes his head. "Surprise," he whispers.

"You're going to make me cry!" I say.

"Hope not," Tristan chuckles.

Bryan Adams', I'll Always Be Right There starts playing – *Oh no! I am going to cry!*

"Keep your eyes on me," Tristan whispers and starts to twirl us around. I am having heart palpitations. *Ok, ok, breathe Coral, breathe!*

"You ok?" Tristan asks, bringing my hand up to his lips. I nod mutely. The words to this song are so beautiful, and perfect. He really does get some things so right.

"Forever," I whisper, smiling up at him.

"Forever," he whispers back.

The song comes to an end. Tristan stops and leans down to kiss me. The room erupts in applause again. Bryan Adams is swiftly followed by Aerosmith's Don't Wanna Miss A Thing.

"I love this song," I whisper to Tristan. "Dance with me husband?"

"With pleasure wife," I giggle with glee as Tristan spins me around, then pulls me back and captures me in his arms...

IT'S LATE IN the afternoon, and the party is in full swing. We have all eaten from the amazing buffet of food, and the cocktails are still flowing, and the dancing has continued. But I realise how exhausted I already feel, I have talked so much today. Having so many people to talk to is draining – or maybe that's because I'm still healing? Either way, I'm glad there's only a small bunch of us, god knows what it would be like if this had been a huge wedding – I snort at myself – Who am I kidding? I don't know any other people, so how can it be a big wedding?

I've spent time with Erin, Ellie and their partners, chatted with Joe for ages – her kids have joined Lilly, Erin and Ellie's kids outside. I think they're enjoying playing in the massive garden. I've chatted with George and Phil, and Cindy Crosby who came with her husband Josh, and Claire and Karen are both here, so it's been really cool to get to know them both a little more.

Of course, my family are all here, which makes me think of Tristan and the fact that his folks are no longer with us. I turn and gaze across the room at my gorgeous man who is chatting away with Rob, he doesn't seem sad about it, but I bet it's playing on his mind. Just as I think that I see…I shake my head – I did not just see that, surely? I blink twice, and they're gone – *Whoa!*

Tristan suddenly throws his head back in laughter, he's killing himself laughing. Rob must have said something really funny to him. I'm so glad those two are getting along now. I try to shake off the vision I just had and turn around so I can sit down. My feet are hurting from dancing so much. I've never danced with so many partners before. Rob, Carlos, Bob, George and Phil have twirled me around so many times, although Phil did squidge my toes three times. And of course, my wonderful husband has danced with me plenty of times, and he is, by far, the best dancer in this room.

Just when I thought I could give my feet a rest, Malcolm comes over to me and asks for a dance. I smile politely and agree. He takes my hand, and we start twirling around – He's very good at this, thank god!

"You look very happy Coral," he says as we softly turn in time to Rebecca Ferguson's Nothings Real But Love.

"I am," I beam.

Malcolm smiles down at me. "Coral, there's something I want to tell you," he says staring down at me with a serious expression.

"Ok," I say, wondering what this is going to be about.

"I love Gladys very much Coral, I want you to know directly from me that you have no need to worry. She's turned my life around, right when I'd got to the stage when I didn't think I would meet anyone to spend the next half of my life with, and I thank god every day that we met, I feel very blessed. I want you to know I will always take care of her. There isn't anything in this world I wouldn't do for her and I intend to spend the rest of my life making her days happy and full of love." He smiles down at my quite frankly shocked expression.

"But there's something else I want *you* to know." He stops and takes a deep breath. "I know about your past darling, that your father abandoned you, that you lost your sister and that your mother was institutionalised. I just want you to know I think you are one brave, courageous young woman, and I wanted to offer something to you..." He takes another breath hesitating. "I want to offer you me," he says, smiling down at me. "As your father," he adds.

My chin hits the floor, it takes a few moments for it to sink in, what he's just said.

Malcolm continues. "I know we haven't known each other very long, but believe me Coral, I will be there for you whenever you need me, to give you advice, as a shoulder to cry on, or if you just need someone to comfort you. I want to give to you all the love and affection you should have received from your father all those years ago." I blink back the tears as I stare up at him, totally dumbfounded.

Malcolm smiles apologetically. "I'm sorry darling, I didn't mean to upset you."

I shake my head, he has no idea what this means to me. "Oh, Malcolm!" I squeak. I stop dancing and wrap my arms around his torso, squeezing him tight. "Thank you," I choke out, sniffing loudly.

He carefully places his arms around my shoulders and gently comforts me. "Oh and just to say, you can call me Dad if you want to." He offers sweetly.

I squeeze my eyes shut. I feel my heart stitch back together just that last little bit – I feel like I'm finally healed. "Malcolm, you'll never know how much that means to me," I manage to whisper.

He squeezes my shoulders a little harder. "Actually I think I do, I know you have Tristan in your life, but I'm really looking forward to being a father to you."

The floodgates open and I cry like an idiot – *Now is not the time to have done this Malcolm!*

"Oh dear, I didn't mean to make you cry," he says, gently comforting me. "Would you like me to escort you to the bathroom?"

I pull out of his embrace and smile up at him. He looks very blurry right now. I reach up onto my tip-toes, place my hand on his shoulder and kiss his cheek, then do a little giggle-sob. "It's ok, I need to go upstairs and fix my make-up," I say, feeling slightly embarrassed I have cried so hard.

"Coral?" Tristan is at my side, looking anxious.

"Thank you, Malcolm, what you just said, it means a great deal to me." I reach up and kiss his cheek again. He nods once, smiling down at me. I look up at Tristan and take hold of his hand. "Escort me upstairs?"

"Of course," he says, glancing once at Malcolm. As we carefully climb the stairs, so I don't trip over my dress, I let Tristan know what Malcolm just said to me, he looks relieved.

"Why do you look relieved?" I ask, heading into our bedroom.

Tristan follows. "Because I thought he'd upset you, which would have meant I would have had to have words with him." He tells me in a firm tone as he locks the door.

I freeze. "You would have done that?" I squeak.

"I will always fight for your honour Coral, and protect you from anyone who wants to hurt you." He says his tone soft now.

"Oh." I smile lovingly at him. *I want him now!* I pull on his lapels, so his body is pressing hard against mine. "Are you going to fulfil your promise to me?" I ask, trying to seduce him.

Without a word, he bends down in front of me and takes hold of the bottom of my dress, and his warm hands clasp around my ankles, making me catch my breath. This feels different though, I guess that's because I can feel his wedding band on his left hand. Then he looks up at me through his long lashes, his eyes dark and seductive – *Whoa!*

"What do you want wife?" He asks, slowly skimming his hands up the back of my legs, the material of the dress hanging over his forearms.

I am hot and panting already.

"You, husband, inside me, now!" I manage to say.

His hands continue up behind my knees and keep going, he hasn't broken eye contact. His look is heated, calling to me on every level, and as his hands reach the top of my lacy stockings, he gasps aloud. Then he stands and tells me to turn around with his finger. I do so, smiling seductively at him, and he slowly pulls the zip down on my dress.

"We don't want to get this beautiful dress creased," he croakily says in that sexy, husky voice of his. He slowly and seductively pulls it off my shoulders. "And we don't want anyone knowing what we've been up to," he adds– *No, we certainly do not!*

Tristan kisses my scar and then takes hold of my hand so I can carefully step out of my dress. As I turn and look up at him, his mouth pops open, yet he just stands there, open-mouthed, blinking rapidly as he drinks me in. I have my brand new vintage ivory corset on, a pair of frilly, sexy ivory knickers with a matching suspender belt, and nude stockings that have a pretty, flowery pattern at the top. And my heels are high, which makes my legs look longer – so right now, I am feeling very sexy.

He swallows hard. "Good God you're wearing stockings." He eyes widen, and his cheeks flush as he continues to drink me in, then he shakes his head slightly, almost as though he's coming out of a trance. "Don't move an inch," he tells me, his voice low and raspy. I watch Tristan walk into the built-in closet and hang up my dress, and his jacket. My heart starts hammering against my chest, I am aching with want and need, Tristan slowly walks back over to me, he looks so sexy, so debonair.

"Oh Coral, you look so beautiful, so sexy." He says, gazing adoringly at me.

I don't think twice. I grab hold of his lapels and push him against the bed, then I sink to my knees, unzip his trousers, pull them down with his boxers and take his hard, heavy erection in my mouth.

"Coral..." He gasps. I look up and lock eyes with him. "I don't want to come," he firmly tells me. I nod as best I can and suck harder, twirling my tongue around, gently pulling my hand up and down, tasting him all of him. God, I'm so in love with him – he turns me on so much.

"Mmm..." I suck harder, keeping eye contact with him.

Tristan hisses then leans down, takes hold of my arms and gently pulls me to my feet.

"You have made me the happiest man alive today, do you know that?" Before I have time to answer, his lips swoop down, kissing me hard as his tongue moves in perfect symmetry with mine.

Tristan moans with desire which makes my blood pressure feel like it's spiked. He has his arms wrapped tightly around me, crushing me against his firm body. He suddenly spins me around, so my back is to his front. His hands skim across my shoulders, and then down over my breasts, my nipples are straining against the corset. He wraps his one arm around my waist, pulling me against his erection. His other hand skims down over my belly, across the skimpy material of my knickers, and then his fingers find my clitoris. He slowly circles his fingers. My head falls back, my eyes closed. I feel his lips hungrily kiss and nip along my neck and shoulder, making me shudder in the most delicious way.

He suddenly pulls back. "We need to be quick," he pants. "Sit down baby."

I sit on the edge of the bed. Tristan kneels down in front of me, and with the most panty-combusting smile, he takes hold of my knees and pulls my legs open wide.

"Keep your eyes open baby, I want to see you." He says, gazing up at me.

"Ok." I pant.

I place my hands on the bed, lean back, and watch as Tristan slowly moves my knickers to the side, his eyes on mine the whole time. He bobs his tongue out, making his intention clear and wiggles it up and down, then he smiles so sexily, I almost climax.

And then his tongue is on me, twirling around, up and down – *Oh god!*

"Husband..." I moan. My hand reaching down and

Forever With Him

gripping his hair, then his fingers are inside me, pushing in and out. "Argh!" My head falls back, my eyes closing.

"Open your eyes baby, I want to see you." My eyes dart open. He pulls his fingers from inside me, I take hold of his hand and gently suck his fingers. I can taste me.

He gasps aloud. "Oh Coral!"

"Take me husband," I softly mewl.

"With pleasure wife," he says.

Tristan places his hands under my knees and pulls me towards him. I can see his erection, hard and ready, his tip at my opening. Tristan teases me a couple of times, pushing just his tip inside me then pulling out.

I cannot take my eyes off his impressive length.

"I know it's sexy to watch," he breathes. "But I want you to look at *me* Coral."

"I am," I tease, then look him in the eye, grinning sexily at him.

"You are such a sexy tease." His eyes instantly darken, and with one smooth jolt, he slams into me. The feeling is exquisite, my husband inside me, skin to skin. He releases his right hand from my leg, his thumb starts circling my clitoris, round and round as he slowly pulls out and then rams into me again, my muscles contracting and squeezing him tight.

"Tristan!" I hiss – I am going to explode. *How can it be happening this fast?*

"Fast or slow baby?" He asks, slowly pulling out then slamming into me again, his eyes not leaving mine. *This is so hot!*

"Fast," I pant. Tristan really starts to move, pounding into me, over and over, it's relentless.

"Christ Coral," he hisses, his one hand gripping my thigh, his thumb continuing to circle my clitoris, bringing me closer to the edge.

"Tristan..." I can hardly breathe, watching him do this, it's so wild.

And I come – Hard and fast, pulsing around his erection. I haven't seen or touched him like this since yesterday evening. I manage to keep my eyes locked on his as he continues pounding into me. I gasp for breath, my skin heating all over, blood pounding in my ears.

"Come in me husband!" I garble. I can tell he's so close.

"Coral!" He cries out as he climaxes, pouring himself into me. Releasing my other leg, he collapses on top of me, his head buried in my neck and hair. I wrap my one arm around his shoulders, while my other hand runs back and forth through his thick, soft hair. We stay like that for a good five minutes, as we slowly catch our breath.

Suddenly, Tristan lifts his head. "I really fucking love you," he says.

It makes me laugh aloud. "And I really love fucking you!" I tease.

"Mrs Freeman!" He scolds playfully. Then he leans down, runs his thumb over my bottom lip, traces his tongue where his thumb was, then he softly kisses me. "I want you again and again and again, but we'd better get back," Tristan chuckles.

"I know," I whisper, staring up into his beautiful eyes. "Tristan?" I look down at our bodies, wondering if what I'm about to ask will upset him. "Are you ok?" I softly ask.

"Ok?" he laughs. "Coral, I am incandescently happy," he says, smiling broadly at me, his dimples deep.

"I just, I thought I saw a moment earlier...you were looking up at the pictures of your folks," I softly say.

"Oh...well, I was just..." He stops and runs his hand through his hair. "I just wish they could have been here today," he says, his voice raw.

"I...I think they are," I whisper.

"What makes you say that?" He softly says. I shake my head not wanting to share. Tristan cups his finger under my chin and raises my head. "Tell me," he says in his authoritative tone.

I sigh inwardly. "I'm not sure what I saw, I'm not sure if it was my mind making it up, or I really did...see them," I whisper.

Tristan gasps aloud. "See them?" He whispers, his eyes wide with shock. "Tell me Coral."

I take a deep breath. "Ok...well earlier, just before you laughed at whatever Rob had said, well I was watching you, and I was thinking about your folks, and wondering if you were very sad that they couldn't be here today?..." I take another deep breath. "And then they...well...appeared," I whisper.

Tristan's mouth is gaping open. "What? What exactly did you see?" He softly asks.

"They looked young, in their twenties maybe? They were right behind you Tristan, both of them' – he gasps again – 'Do you really want me to tell you this?" I question.

"Yes," he breathes.

"Ok...well, they were both looking at me and smiling, then your Gran...she put her hand on your shoulder and then they both nodded at me." I blink up at Tristan.

"They were here..." He breaks off. I watch a single tear flow down his cheek. Then he crushes me to him, squeezing me tight. "Thank you Coral," he breathes. "Thank you so much baby, you've made my day saying that."

I wrap my arms around his neck, kiss his cheek and just hold him tight. "I haven't upset you have I? Would you have preferred I didn't say?"

"No baby," he says, his voice muffled against my skin.

"Ok." I hold him to me for the longest time.

Tristan finally leans back and pecks me on the nose. "We'd better get back," he says.

"I guess," I mumble, which makes him grin.

"Come on gorgeous." Tristan slowly pulls out of me, and I follow him into the bathroom so we can clean up after our lovemaking. Back in the bedroom, Tristan helps me into my dress, zips me up and then shrugs his jacket on.

"I better sort my make-up," I say, remembering that Malcolm made me cry.

"I'll come with you," he says.

"Why?" I chuckle.

"I like watching you," he says, shrugging slightly. "You're fascinating to me Coral."

I blink up at him. "Fascinating?" Tristan nods reaches out and softly strokes my cheek. *Whoa!* Then he follows me into the bathroom and watches with amused fascination as I make myself look half decent again...

CHAPTER TWENTY-NINE

I WAKE, AND BEFORE I even open my eyes, I smile contentedly. It's Sunday morning, the day after the wedding and we are aboard the yacht, we've been travelling overnight to some unknown destination. I smile widely again, Tristan and his surprises. I stretch my body out, and with my eyes still closed, I reach out for Tristan, only to find he isn't next to me. I jolt upright and search the bedroom, he's nowhere to be seen, then I notice it, a scribbled note lying next to me – with a goofy grin on my face, I pick up the note.

> Wife-It is a beautiful day outside, why don't you come and meet me on deck for some breakfast.
> Your loving Husband, Tristan xxx

His note makes me smile a ridiculous ear to ear grin. I jump out of bed and head to the bathroom. Ten minutes later, I have showered, and I'm in my bikini. I'm about to walk out of the bedroom when I hear Tristan call out for me, but it stops me in my tracks. There's something strangely significant about it. I turn and face the full-length mirror in the bedroom. I'm in my khaki bikini – the one Tristan bought for me – I look back at my bronzed body and then look down at my toes – brown toes, pink toe-nails.

I take another step forward and open the door. Tristan calls to me again. Why does this feel so familiar? I look up at the wooden stairs and cock my head to the side, it's like I know, but I don't know. How odd. I climb the wooden stairs and reaching the top I step out onto the decking, the bright sunshine blinding me for a moment, he's right, it is a beautiful day.

Right at that moment, Tristan appears, he's dressed in a pair of navy blue combat shorts, his torso is bare, as are his feet, and he's wearing his aviator sunglasses. *Boy, he looks good!*

I look out at my surroundings, and see we are moored in a little cove that's surrounded by a beautiful rocky landscape – This is not Brighton. The sun is high, the sky a perfect blue, and the sea is sparkling. I turn to face Tristan, and he is beaming at me, a smile so wide, that his dimples are deeper than I've ever seen them. He reaches his hand out to me, I place my hand in his and then he leans down and softly kisses the back of my hand.

"Mrs Freeman," he coos. His smile is wide, then he leans forward, and his lips meet mine.

And that's when it hits me – *Oh my God!*

This is my dream, the dream I had of us on the boat – *Holy crap!* It must have been a premonition. I gasp aloud, making Tristan pull back, his face a worried picture. I have my mouth open in shock as I rapidly blink in my surroundings. Everything is the same, the colour of the sea, the rocks surrounding us, even down to what Tristan and I are wearing – It's all exactly the same. *Oh my God!*

My legs start shaking so badly I feel like I may just collapse.

"Coral!" Tristan whips me up into his arms, takes me under the shelter of the canopy and sits me down on one of the sofas. "What is it baby, what's wrong?" He asks, pulling his shades off.

"I..." I stare blankly at him, still in shock.

"Coral?" Tristan prompts.

I start to laugh, hysterically. I fall back onto the sofa, clutching my belly.

Tristan instantly relaxes and laughs along with me. "What are you laughing about?" He asks, in-between chuckles as he runs his hand up and down my hip.

When I finally manage to compose myself, I sit up and take his beautiful face in my hands. "Good morning Mr Freeman, my husband, my love." I lean forward and kiss his full soft lips.

"Good morning to you too," he says, reaching up and softly stroking my cheek. "Want to tell me why you almost gave me heart failure?" He adds sarcastically.

"I'm sorry baby," I say falling into his arms and embracing him tightly.

"It's ok, I'm just glad you're alright, but I would appreciate an explanation?" He says, softly stroking my back.

"You're not going to believe this," I say, pulling back and

grinning widely at him. Then I tell Tristan all about the dream. Now *he's* the one that looks like he's seen a ghost.

"No wonder you looked like you did," he says, shaking his head in surprise.

"I know. Spooky, right?" I say.

"Very spooky," he says, his eyes wide, and if I'm not mistaken, he's a little freaked out.

I look up again and check out the yacht and the cove. "Where are we?" I ask.

"Cornwall." Tristan beams from ear to ear, his dimples on full wattage. "That's Polzeath beach," he adds, pointing inland.

"Wow! It's beautiful," I say, still feeling strangely odd about the premonition.

"Still freaked out?" Tristan asks.

"Yeah..." I laugh, shaking my head slightly – I still can't believe it was going to come true.

"Me too!" He laughs. "Hungry?" He adds.

"Yes!" I beam, feeling ravenous. God knows what time we actually fell asleep this morning. Tristan and his sexing! Then again, I initiated it twice, so can't really blame him.

"Sore?" Tristan chuckles as we walk hand in hand over to the breakfast table.

"Dirty boy!" I chide playfully. "And yes, I am. No more sex for at least a couple of days," I tease. Tristan pouts, making me giggle aloud.

"Oh, I do love it when you giggle Mrs Freeman." He leans forward, takes my face in his hands and kisses me so softly I have to fight back the tears...

IF ALL NEWLY married couples have this much sex, I'm surprised they get anything done! The most blissful, with one very sad moment, month of my life has passed by in a whirl of activities. Gladys and Malcolm's wedding, Joyce's very, very tearful goodbye, Rob and Carlos flying to China and returning with Xiao-Mei, and according to Carlos its pronounced Shao-Mei, and she's the cutest little baby girl I have ever seen. I've been taking the cookery classes, had therapy with George, Hypnotherapy with Cindy, and instead of training with Will, which I'm still not allowed to do yet, I am swimming again, and I've had my weekly Physiotherapy.

I just love my Physiothcrapist's. His name is Raj, and he's a very dedicated Sikh, who wears a large turban and has a wicked strong Indian accent. He's one of the nicest, friendliest people

I have ever met, and he's really funny too, so when he's doing his thing with my shoulder, and I'm in pain, he makes some random joke that just has me laughing so hard that my belly hurts. In fact, he and his wife Amarjeet have been over for dinner a couple of times, sampling my cooking. They have also returned the offer and had Tristan, and I dine with them – they can cook a mean curry. It took a lot of persuading to get Raj to part with the family recipe, but eventually, he did.

Other news is that I no longer want to move to Cornwall – Tristan was right, again! I just don't think I could give up Brighton, my family or my friends. I'd miss them all too much, besides, now I'm the owner of a luxury motor yacht we can travel down there as much as we want – I still haven't got over the shock. Plus, Tristan and I are now godparents to little Mei, so what good would we be if we were never around, besides its good practice – at least we get to give her back.

Debs and Scott are still arguing about Spain, I'm not sure what decision they'll come to, I just hope they keep their shit together, for Lily's sake. I still haven't taken the sailing lessons yet, as I'm not quite healed enough for that. Tristan said next spring or summer, which isn't that far away. I'm very excited about it...and about Hawaii.

I look up at my desktop. I am at Chester House, and I'm sat at my desk scrolling through agencies for jobs. Even though I have loved seeing Tristan so much, at home and at work, I need my independence, and I think it's just as healthy to have time apart as it is to have quality time together – so I need a different job. But as I sit, in all honesty, getting bored with the agencies offerings, I can't help thinking back to last Friday when we all went out dancing. It was one last blow out for Rob and Carlos before they became parents, and an opportunity for us all to get out together. Debs and Scott joined us, as well as Joe, Claire and Karen, my new girlfriends, and we all had a blast. Rob was equally as impressed with Tristan's dance moves.

Hmm, Tristan's dance moves, and I drift off into another daydream...Tristan and I are in the club, practically having sex on the dance floor as we grind our bodies against one another in a very slow sexy tempo as Justin Timberlake sings Mirrors – Such a top tune! Debs, Rob and Joe have their mouths gaping open as we continue to bump and grind against each other – "Coral?" I look up, feeling quite startled.

Tristan is stood outside his office door, his hands on his hips – He doesn't look very happy.

"I've been calling you?" He says with his head cocked to the side.

"You have?" I squeak. *Damn, he looks hot today.* He's in his gunmetal grey suit, white shirt and dark blue tie – I'm swooning!

He shakes his head and laughs at me, then walks over to me. Unfortunately, in my mesmerised state, I haven't switched programmes. So the first thing Tristan notices as he steps behind me is the webpage with the job agency splattered all over it – *Uh-oh!*

"Job agency eh?" He says. I bite my bottom lip – *Oops!*

Caught at work doing something I shouldn't be doing! He frowns down at me, his one hand on his hip, the other hand rubbing his chin – He's contemplating something, but I'm not sure what it is? I immediately picture the sexy time we had last night and start to get breathless. I thought being blindfolded was sexy enough, but being tied up, teased until you can't take anymore, and then having hot, make your legs shake sexy sex, with a few sexy spankings in-between, is enough to make any girl drool over her man. Maybe he's considering doing that, a sexy punishment for being caught slacking on the job? My sex starts throbbing, my heart relocating to my throat – I can hardly breathe. In an effort to control myself, I press my thighs together, trying to stop the throbbing, and take several, deep calming breaths.

"Oh fuck it!" He finally says, reaching down and clasping my hand in his. In the next breathe, he has pulled me to my feet, and we are marching down the hallway, towards reception. I am struggling to keep up in my heels and tight pencil skirt.

"Tristan, what are you doing?" I protest.

"I want to show you something," he says, I am almost running as I try to keep up with his long strides.

"Joe. Take messages." Tristan orders as we march past reception. I give her a brief wave and an I-don't-know-what's-going-on look.

Tristan pushes the glass door open for me. "After you wife," he says, winking at me as I duck past him and out into the cloudy morning.

"Tristan, what's going on?" I question as he firmly clasps my hand in his and we continue walking, my heels clicking loudly against the pavement.

He doesn't answer me. I want to huff at him, but he seems slightly bemused by what he's doing. It's as though there's an internal battle raging. We make a right turn, taking us deeper into the block of offices, then a left, and finally he comes to an abrupt stop. We're only five minutes from the office, in the business sector. Then, standing behind me, he places his hands on my shoulders and turns me around, so I'm facing a sandwich shop called Arnie's Sarnies. *Is he trying to tell me he's hungry?*

"Tristan, why are' – "First impression, what do you think?" He asks.

"What?" I twist my head around to look up at him.

"Coral, just go with me on this – please?" He begs, his eyes dancing with mirth.

I shrug, wondering what he's up to, but decide to play along, I turn back around and stare up at the shop. "It's too dark," I say. I have been to this sandwich shop several times – they do nice sandwiches –it's small and quaint, but it seriously needs a lick of paint. The shop sign is painted in black, as is the door, and the interior makes you feel like you've just walked onto a navy ship; it's that military grey colour.

"What else?" Tristan asks, his lips inches from my ear, his breath on my cheek. I swoon for a moment, my legs slightly trembling, I want to pounce on him – How does my husband still do this to me? *Concentrate Coral!*

I take a deep, calming breath. "Um...well they have no board outside, so there's nothing to entice people in."

"Very good. What else?"

"They have the room, so why haven't they got two or three tables and chairs outside too?"

"Keep going," Tristan prompts.

"They could have a canopy fitted with the shop's logo on it. At least then, the people sitting outside won't get blasted by the sun – in summer!" I dryly add, because our beautiful summer is coming to an end, I can feel it. The wind is cooler, and the sun has lost its intense summer heat, autumn is on its way – and then there's the dreaded winter – I hate the cold!

Tristan is nodding along with me, but I still don't know what he's up to.

"Tristan, is this some sort of test?" I ask, glancing up at him.

"No." His eyes are narrowed and fixed on the shop. "Do you want to add anything else, before we go inside?" *We're going in? Maybe he does want to eat?*

I look at the shop again. "Yes." I firmly answer. "They could put a screen door up so the front door can stay open, which means the smell of the food would entice people in too."

Without a word, Tristan slowly spins me around 180

degrees; then he repeats the process, whispering in my ear as he does. "What do you see?" He says.

Apart from feeling a little dizzy from being spun around, and Tristan's close proximity, I take a good long look, trying to work out what he wants me to see. Lots and lots of office buildings?

"This is the only place to eat?" I guess, eyeing the sandwich shop. "Unless you go to Munchies, but that's ten minutes from here," I add.

"Excellent." Tristan clasps my hand again, and we walk over to the shop. He pulls the door open, I can tell it's stiff and heavy, and gestures for me to go first again. "After you wife," he says again, his eyes glinting wickedly at me.

"Why thank you husband," I tease, winking at him as I step inside. Yes, I was right. This place definitely looks like the inside of a battleship.

"So," Tristan says, standing behind me and placing his hands on my shoulders again. "What do you see now we are inside?"

"It is too dark, just like I remembered. Um...the lighting is really bad, and the chairs and tables definitely need changing." I look down at the four large tables that are in here, they look old and as though they should be in some greasy cafe. You could really modernise this place.

"Why do they need changing?" Tristan asks.

"Well, this is the business sector," I say. Tristan nods in agreement. "Most people go to lunch alone, or with one work colleague, two max' – "What makes you say that?" He interrupts.

"Because most businesses don't close for lunch, so somebody's got to stay behind to cover the phones?" I say shrugging slightly, wondering if I'm right? "Well, that seems to be how it is at Chester House," I add, turning to glance up at Tristan, surprised to see he has a very smug smile on his face. "What are you' – "Please, by all means, do continue," he interrupts, gesturing to the room and grinning widely at me.

I turn back around. Scanning the room, I decide it would be possible to put ten small tables and chairs comfortably into the space. "So get rid of the four tables," I say. "And replace them with more modern, small two-seater tables, I reckon you could probably get ten in here?" I say.

"So they could seat sixteen before, and now they can seat twenty?" He says, sounding proud.

I smile up at him. *What's this all about?*

"What else?" Tristan says.

"Hmm, it's quite a long, narrow space, so if you positioned the table and chairs correctly, you could get a long breakfast bar/ type counter along the back left wall. What do you think? You could get maybe...ten stools along there?" I ask.

Tristan shakes his head, in amazement, I think?

"Am I wrong?" I huff, frowning at him.

"No baby," he chuckles, leaning forward to kiss my temple. "What else stands out to you?"

I look around the shop. "They may have it, but there's no sign saying Wi-Fi available? Most people want to jump online at lunch, and free Wi-Fi is always a bonus!"

"And another enticement to eat here," Tristan adds.

"Yes," I smile, agreeing wholeheartedly.

"What else?" He asks, his eyes shining with love.

"It's too quiet," I whisper, because the people who have just been served have sat at the closest table to us, and no radio or music is playing so you can't hear other people's conversations.

"How would you change that?" Tristan whispers back.

"Well, that's a difficult one," I say, shaking my head in thought. "Well, you don't really want it to sound like a doctor's or a dentist's by playing classical music, but you don't want to push away the Radio Two lovers because Radio One is always playing or vice versa. So maybe, just playlists, you know, different kinds of music, catering to everyone's needs?" I suggest, still wondering what this is all about.

"Interesting," Tristan murmurs in my ear. His hands are still on my shoulders, so he slowly turns me to face the counter. "This is the part I'm most intrigued about," he adds.

"You are?" I chuckle.

"Yes. What do you think?" He asks.

"About what?" I ask, still baffled by what's going on.

"All of it, the menu, how it's displayed, what they offer..." Tristan trails off, his hand waving in front of him; I glance up at him again and narrow my eyes – *What is this all about?*

Not coming to any kind of conclusion, I take a deep breath and begin. "Ok, well they have a good selection," I say, perusing the menu.

"Meaning?" Tristan prompts.

I roll my eyes at him. "Of bread, you know, white, brown, granary, baguettes, ciabatta's, crusty or soft rolls, etc. etc..." I say, waving my hand in the air like Tristan did.

"And that's good?" He questions.

"Well yeah...if we all liked the same things, life would be very boring, don't you think?" I cock my head to the side and smile sweetly at him, it makes him chuckle.

"Ok, so they have that part right, but what's missing?" He questions. *Missing?*

I look up and scan the menu board again and see they have a good selection of fillings. Meats, fish, seafood and vegetarian options, but not everyone wants that. Where are the salads, soups, jacket potatoes? And why haven't they got ready-made sandwiches and meal deals going on?

"They haven't got any meal-deals," I say. I glance up at Tristan, he's grinning triumphantly at me. "Tristan' – "Go on," he interrupts.

I frown at his odd behaviour and continue. "They're not selling salads either," I point out. Tristan cocks his head to the side and has his one eyebrow arched. "People enjoy cold salads! Not everyone wants bread every day, I know I don't," I add.

"Cold salads?" Tristan questions, his eyebrows forming a v.

I roll my eyes, exasperated. "Yes, people like pasta salads, couscous salads, rice salads, bean salads." Tristan doesn't seem convinced. I cross my arms and arch an eyebrow. "They always sell out at the little M&S in town," I say a little pompously, trying to prove my point.

"Really?" Tristan is pulling an I-didn't-know-that-face and slowly nodding his head in approval. "So you would add salads and meal deals to the menu?" He questions.

"Yes and maybe ready-made sandwiches. Sometimes, if you're in a rush, you don't have time to wait in a queue. They could put a board outside advertising that fact. And they could keep one girl on the till here purely for that line, that way busy workers can dash in an out, and there's no waiting around."

Tristan nods once. "So you've added pre-made salads and sandwiches, would introduce meal deals, and free Wi-Fi, and you'd change the decor. Anything else?" He asks.

I shrug at him. "It's a sandwich shop," I say. "Tristan, what exactly are we doing here?" I add a little exasperated by it all.

"Humour me." He laughs, which makes me frown. "So you wouldn't change anything else?" He adds as I stare at his profile. *Yes, I'd add lots more, but that's not the point.*

With my arms still crossed, I start tapping my foot. "No!" I bite. He's up to something, but I'm not sure what? He turns and pulls me into his body. My beautiful husband, he smells divine, is head to toe handsome and happens to be the most

Forever With Him

well-mannered, chivalrous man I have ever known. I peek up at him through my lashes, he is gazing down at me, his eyes full of love and warmth.

"What?" I giggle.

Leaning down, so he's millimetres from my lips he whispers, "I want something hot!"

I blink up at him, his cheeks have flushed, and his eyes have darkened.

"Hot?" I breathe. Starting to feel *hot* and bothered myself!

"Yes, hot and spicy," he whispers seductively. I know there's a double meaning there.

"Like what?" I whisper breathlessly.

"What would you suggest?" He says, teasing me with his heated look.

I blink several times, trying to get my brain to fire. "Um... well..." I shake my head, and in an effort to kick start my brain, I look away from Tristan's molten lava look. I think I need to fan myself. "Hot and spicy?" I whisper, looking up at the menu. And then it hits me. "I'd make you a Cuban Sandwich!"

Tristan smiles widely at me. "How did I know you'd have the answer? Tell me, wife, what's in a Cuban Sandwich?"

I smile coyly at him. "Ham, slow roasted pork, Swiss cheese, pickles or jalapeños – depending on how *hot* you like it,' I say raising my eyebrows at him teasingly, 'and mustard, all toasted on a sandwich until the cheese is melted!" I say, teasing him with a wink.

"Sounds delicious," he says his eyes widening as he leans down, his lips almost brushing against mine. "And I like it hot!" He adds as a wicked – turn my bones to jelly – tempting, teasing smile spreads across his face. I swallow hard. How can he make me feel like this when he's not even touching me? Now I'm just a bag of sexual tension and frustration! I have no idea what this exercise has been about, and it's driving me crazy.

"I think you should add that to the menu," he says, chortling at my expression.

I stop breathing. "What!?"

"You heard me," he grins.

My mouth pops open. *Holy fuck!*

"Tell me Coral, what other choices of hot lunches would you offer?" I go to speak, but nothing comes out. What did he just say? 'I think *you* should add that to the menu'. "I'm waiting," he teases, grinning broadly – his dimples distracting me.

"Um..." I blink up at him and start blurting it out. "Panini's, toasted sandwiches, soup, um...Quesadillas?" I stop talking, my heart is hammering against my chest, and it's making it hard to breathe.

"What about Jacket Potatoes, people like those in the winter, don't they?" Tristan adds.

Mmm...hot jacket with melted butter and cheese. I'm drooling. "Yes, they do. But what's your point, Tristan?" I gripe.

He turns away from me grinning widely and steps up to the food counter. "Good morning," he says, smiling at the pretty blonde girl behind the counter, her cheeks instantly flush. I want to roll my eyes, but I don't.

"Hi," she squeaks – *Jeez, I hope I don't look that helpless when Tristan smiles at me?*

"Is Henrique in today?" Tristan asks. *Henrique? Who's Henrique?*

She nods once; she seems to have lost the power of speech too.

"Good. It's an unscheduled visit, but can you let him know Tristan Freeman is here?" He says.

She nods again, scuttles from behind the counter, runs past the tables and pushes through a door that clearly states 'staff only' – Tristan turns to me, he's wearing his smug smile. I narrow my eyes at him. I have my arms crossed, my eyebrow is arched, and my foot is tapping in annoyance – *What is he doing?*

"Mr Freeman!" I turn to see a young man with black hair, almost black eyes and European skin walking towards us; he looks really young too, twenties maybe? And has what I think is a Spanish accent.

"Henrique." Tristan greets him warmly, shaking his hand. "May I introduce my wife, Coral Freeman." My heart slams against my chest, I'm still not used to hearing that yet.

The young boy turns to me and smiles in recognition. "Of course, I've heard all about you," he says as I glance at him then glare at Tristan.

"You have?" I say, surprised.

"Yes." His white-toothed grin widens. "Please, take a seat." Tristan takes my hand, and we head over to one of the tables. "Can I get you anything?" Henrique asks.

"Coffee please, and a Cappuccino for the lady," Tristan says, winking at me.

I wait until Henrique is far enough away so he can't hear me. "What are you up to?" I hiss my voice low.

"Oh...just discussing buying a sandwich shop," he answers

wistfully, waving his hand in the air. Then he leans back, crosses his legs, and runs his forefinger across his bottom lip, just watching my reaction.

"For me?" I question, even though I know I'm right.

"Yes." He grins triumphantly.

"I don't want a sandwich shop," I say petulantly, crossing my arms.

"You don't?" His eyebrows raise, I have his complete attention.

"No, if I were going into the food industry, I would want a restaurant. But we've already discussed this, the hours are dreadful, especially at weekends – I'd never get to see you!" I add mournfully.

"Which is exactly why this place is perfect," He tells me. *Oh god!*

"You've already bought it, haven't you?" I choke out. Tristan simply grins at me because Henrique has arrived with our drinks. He places my Cappuccino down in front of me, passes Tristan his coffee, then sits next to him.

"I wasn't expecting to see you today," Henrique says, nervously biting his nails.

"Yes, sorry about the surprise visit, but something unexpected came up," Tristan says.

"Oh I see, is something wrong?" Henrique asks, looking even more concerned.

"No, not at all," Tristan replies, "Is everything set up your end?" He asks.

Henrique nods. "Yes, thanks to you Mr Freeman, I can finally get him home." *Huh?* I gaze quizzically at the young boy then glance at Tristan, who very subtly shakes his head at me. *Oh! What's that all about?*

I decide I will question it later, and silently sip my Cappuccino while Henrique and Tristan talk politics, profit margins, and the best coffee beans to use...

TWENTY MINUTES LATER, Tristan says his goodbye. "See you tomorrow to wrap everything up," he says, getting to his feet. I stand too and wait by the table.

Henrique warmly shakes his hand again. "Mr Freeman, I cannot thank you enough," he says, and before I can stop him, he has turned around and wrapped me up in a bear hug – *What the fuck!*

"You have the most wonderful husband," he gushes, I gaze wide-eyed at Tristan. "Take care of him," he adds, letting me go.

Feeling bemused, I say nothing and smile quizzically at the young boy.

"It was nice to meet you, Mrs Freeman," he adds, then walks down the shop and into the back room. Tristan clasps my hand in his, and we walk out of the shop without a word said, except for the goodbye he gives to the blonde girl, who instantly turns scarlet.

"Tristan, what the' – His lips meet mine, instantly silencing me. Pulling back, with his arms tightly wrapped around my waist he whispers, "Thank you."

"What for?" I breathe, staring at his lips.

"Playing the game, and not freaking out. Henrique's had it really rough since his dad died."

"His dad died?" I balk.

"Yes, unexpectedly. His mother wants to go home, back to Portugal, to bury him there. She has absolutely no idea about the business, so Henrique was pulled out of University to sort it all out, poor kid has spent months going through the books, only to find that his father was on the brink of bankruptcy."

My mouth pops open. "You've bought a shop that's doing so badly, it's almost,' – "No Coral, the shop isn't doing too badly, it needs renovating and the menu changing like you said. His father had a gambling problem, it's his personal finances that are in ruins," Tristan says, his brows pulling together. "The stress of being in so much debt is probably what gave him the heart attack!"

I hear Henrique talking again – '*Thanks to you Mr Freeman, I can finally get him home.*'

"What did you do Tristan?" I whisper, gazing up at my personal angel.

He smiles shyly at me. "I made a deal," he says.

"What kind of deal?" I whisper.

Tristan sighs heavily. "That he knocked the price down on the business and in return I would, well, pay his University fees," he says, shrugging slightly.

"And?" I prompt.

Tristan sighs again. "He's a good lad, and his mother...well she's devastated. Her dream was to retire in Portugal, go back to her roots, but she can't do that unless I...intervened." He says, his cheeks flaming.

I swallow hard against the lump that's formed. Tristan has to be an angel, who else would help complete strangers out?

"So he put the shop up for sale, and you enquired?" I quietly question.

"Yes, I told him if he slashed the price of the business, as it's going to need money investing to get it back into profit, that I would help him and his mother in exchange."

"How have you helped his mother?" I ask, reaching up to stroke his cheek, gazing adoringly at my man, my husband. Tristan smiles his shy smile. "Tell me," I push.

"I have bought a very small cottage for his mother in Portugal, and paid for his father's body to be shipped back to Portugal, so they can bury him there." He softly says.

"Tristan!" I gasp.

"It's just good business sense," he says, shrugging at me.

"No, it's not!" I swoon. "You could have gone in there and just made a deal on the shop, but you didn't! How did you find all this out?" I ask.

"He broke down...poor kid's missing his father, stressing about the shop and his mother, and well...he said he felt like his future was crashing down around him, that he'd never see University again." I look like a fish right now, my mouth opening and closing with no words coming out. "But none of that is important Coral," he adds.

"Not important!" I scoff.

"No, what is important," he says turning me around to look at the shop again. "Is whether you can see yourself here," he adds.

Whoa, my own place! Can I see myself here?

"It's only open during office hours darling, so no evenings or weekends. Unless you wanted to open weekends and have someone run it for you," Tristan suggests.

I am speechless.

"Coral, say something baby!" Tristan prompts.

"Tristan..." Tears pool in my eyes, I turn and look up at my wonderful, caring, simply irresistible husband. "It's magical Tristan," I add.

Tristan wraps his arms around me. I nuzzle my head into his chest and wrap my arms tightly around him. It is magical that he's done this, he's really thought about it, and to have done that for Henrique and his mother too - He is so sweet! I squeeze him tighter. *Wow! I have my own sandwich shop!*

The moment I think that ideas start flooding my mind, all

the little things we can do, the little touches, little changes that will make a huge difference to the place – I think I can make a success of this. I lift my head and gaze up at Tristan. *God, I'm so in love with him!* It's ridiculous to feel this way.

"Happy?" He asks, placing his hands on my cheeks.

"Very, but a little scared," I say.

"Why?" He asks his forehead creased in concern.

"I have no idea how to run a business Tristan, cooking food yes, but' – "You have no need to worry about that," He interrupts.

"I don't?" I squeak.

"No baby, you've got me," he says, smiling brightly at me. "Coral, do you really think I would just leave you to it?" I smile up at him feeling guilty. "Have a little faith," he adds, running a cool, soft finger across my bottom lip. "I'll teach you, but you'll be the owner baby. You choose the hours you work. I can help you hire the best staff, it's all up to you baby. It's all your choice," he adds.

"Ok," I whisper blinking up at his beautiful face. "Thank you husband, it's perfect," I add.

"You, my darling wife, are most welcome." His lips meet mine, kissing me sweetly.

Ok, so maybe this is what he's been up to over the past month, constantly in and out of his office at home, taking 'private' calls. He even banned me from going in there by teasing me and saying he had some top secret files I wasn't allowed to see. In fact, come to think of it, Stuart has been acting weird and secretive too. I'll bet it's all been about this, Tristan wouldn't have wanted me to find out and spoil the surprise.

I sigh blissfully, my loving husband – I still feel like I'm dreaming…

CHAPTER THIRTY

IS IT REALLY possible to be this happy? I mean, can you die of happiness? I have a wonderful husband, a man who I can now and forever call my home, a man I can completely be myself with and yet, he still loves me. We live in a wonderful house that shelters us, keeps us warm at night, and protects us from the elements. I have a career I never thought I would have, and a life full of love, family and friends. So I'll ask again, is it possible to die from being this blissfully happy? I can't help smiling at myself as I prop my feet up onto the table. I am in the sandwich shop, but I'm in the back room taking a break. I take a sip of my Cappuccino and marvel at the fact that I am here, and that I own this place. It makes me think of my old job, and how Joe's doing.

After careful consideration of my suggestion to give Joe a chance at taking over my position, Tristan agreed to give Joe a trial. I trained her for a couple of weeks before I left, and so far, so good. Tristan said she's doing really well. I think she's pleased as punch that she was even considered for the position. It's a lot more money than what she was earning, and she needs that now that her kids are home, but like Tristan, I think certain people in life deserve a break, and Joe is definitely one of them.

I close my eyes for a moment and sigh blissfully. I can't wait to see Tristan tonight. It's his birthday in a month, and tonight I'll be surprising him with my gift. A delicious shiver runs through me. I've bought him lots of little presents for on the day, and a weekends racing at Brand's Hatch, I think he'll love that. But only recently did I find out – from Edith – that Tristan's always wanted to learn how to fly, and that he's actually quite fascinated with planes and has been since he was a child.

I was really shocked when Edith told me this, and when I asked why he hasn't delved further into this passion, she said she didn't know. So, I'm really hoping he'll like the gift of flying lessons. It won't be here though, as winter will soon be upon us, so I wanted somewhere with warmer weather. Carlos was the one that suggested Spain, so that's where we are going for a week. Our flights are booked, Joe has secretly blocked out his diary, and the tickets for the weeks flying course arrived in the post today – I bite my bottom lip feeling nervous. I really hope he likes it.

I can't believe another month has passed by so quickly. However, I was wrong in thinking the sandwich shop surprise was what was taking Tristan away from me at home as he's still in and out of his office. I've never known him be so busy, and kind of tense, so I'm really pleased we have this break coming up, he needs it. I did ask him last night what he's up to though, hoping it's not more surprises – I still haven't got over the yacht - but apparently not. He said that he's working on several property deals, that some of them are abroad, and that time zones suck. I laughed at his expression and let him stalk off into his office...

IT'S JUST GONE 6pm by the time Stuart drops me outside the house and feeling too excited to wait for Stuart to open my door, I jump out of the car and head towards the front door. We were so busy today that I'm hoping it means we'll be back in profit soon, but honestly I have no idea. I'll have to ask Tristan to check it out for me. I put my key in the lock, twist it and open the door, but the moment I walk inside, I know something isn't right.

The house is eerily dark and silent, and there are no lights on. Edith isn't in the kitchen, which she normally is at this time of night, and Tristan hasn't come to greet me either, which he always does, if and when I arrive home before him. I frown and scan my surroundings, something...something's wrong, but what? Why do I feel worried, on edge, like all my senses should be on hyper-alert?

"Tristan?" I call out for him, my heart hammering against my chest.

I hear footsteps in the kitchen, and I'm about to take a step forward, but to my complete and utter horror, Kane comes waltzing around the breakfast bar, with a smug smile spread across his face.

Fuck! What is he doing in our house? I glance at the alarm, the cover is down, and there's no green light flashing. The police don't know we've intruders in our house – *Fuck!*

I should be afraid, for myself, for Tristan, for Edith, but I'm not. My body instantly floods with adrenaline, fight or flight kicking in. All I feel is pure rage flooding through my veins – Rage and hatred for this evil twisted freak. I grit my teeth and glare back at him – *What the fuck is he doing in my house!* I take a quick snapshot of the room, there's no sign of a struggle - so where are Edith and Tristan?

Kane stops at least four feet away from me. "So glad you're home," he says, smiling brightly.

I instantly realise I'm being flanked from behind. I drop my bag, clench my fists, and step my feet apart ready to fight them off – *Damn, I wish I wasn't in a skirt and heels right now!*

I don't panic though, because any minute now Stuart's going to come through that door, and they'll be screwed. I grit my teeth and glare at Kane. "Where's Tristan?" I growl.

He laughs and takes another step forward, so I take a step back in response.

"I thought you might ask that." He cracks a smile again. "Careful boys, this one knows how to fight," he adds, then nods to the men behind me.

The two men lunge and try to grab hold of me. Will always told me that screaming is useless, that it just wastes energy, so I fight, with all of my might. I manage to pull my arm free from the guy on my left, I turn and slam the heel of my hand into his nose. I don't think I shoved it into his brain, but he looks stunned for a moment as blood starts pouring out his nostrils, then he passes out on the floor – *One down!*

The other guy still has my other arm in his grip, so I crouch down, pulling his arm as I do, and go to flip him over my back, but he's evidently trained in this kind of fighting. So he counteracts me, by twisting back on my arm and kneeing me in the stomach – I groan as all the air leaves my lungs.

In the next second he flips me onto my stomach, smashing me to the floor, he crushes his knee in between my shoulder blades and pulls my arms back – *Fuck that hurts!*

But I don't scream, I won't scream. I pull my leg back, kicking him hard at the bottom of his spine with the heel of my foot, but he just twists and rams his foot down on the back of my knees. I'm pinned to the floor – *Fuck!*

Then I feel my hands being tied – *Shit!*

He pulls me up by my shoulders, pushes me onto my side and brings his fist down hard across my cheek, making me groan in pain – *Bastard!*

"That's enough!" Kane snaps.

I glare up at my attacker. I feel blood swill in my mouth, so I spit it back in his face. He reaches up to punch me again, but Kane shouts at him to stop. I take a good look at him. His eye is split, and there's a streak of dried blood that's run down the side of his face. His left cheek is swollen, his ear and his top lip are split, and bleeding.

And I know, I just know – he's fought with Tristan.

"Bring her down," Kane snaps.

Kane stomps across the hallway and heads down the stairs. I'm instantly pulled to my feet. I quickly kick off my heels. I'll fight better without them. He grabs me by the scruff of the neck and drags me along with him. We head down the stairs, and down into the basement. Kane is in front of me, but too far in front for me to kick him in the back. We bypass the cinema room, then Kane opens the door to the swimming pool, and I'm pushed through. All the air leaves my lungs when I see him. I feel my heart thud to a stop then begin racing out of control. Tristan is next to the pool. He's sitting on a chair, his arms and feet are bound to the chair with duct tape, and there are several free weights taped to his legs. His face is almost unrecognisable; he's been beaten so badly that he can barely hold his head up, his right socket is so swollen you can't see his eye at all.

A man is standing behind him, Tristan must have fought with him too because he has a split lip, a bloody nose, and his right cheekbone looks cracked. It's really swollen and has blood oozing out of it, and he's clutching his stomach as though he's in pain. I look down at the weights again, then at the swimming pool – And I know, it's to make him heavier, so he'll sink to the bottom of the pool – *Fuck!*

"Tristan!" I gasp. I'm shocked and horrified by what lies before me.

"Coral," Tristan says, his voice so torn, so ragged, it's as though he's being hung drawn and quartered. He takes a deep breath, wincing as he does. "RUN!" He roars wildly.

Kane laughs at Tristan and takes a seat on the bench by the wall. I hadn't realised before, but he's dressed smartly in a suit, it's almost as though this is some sort of business transaction for him, he crosses his legs, and straightens his tie, he looks very relaxed and serene. Then I notice another man, sitting in the far corner, his arms have been tied behind his back, and he looks as though he's in pain. The lighting is so dull in here that I struggle to work out who he is, then he leans forward, groaning in pain.

The spotlight above him suddenly illuminates his face. In that instance, I realise it's Kane's brother – Dillon.

"Let me go you fucker!" Dillon shouts.

My attacker pushes me further into the room. I'm only a few feet away from Tristan now. I try to struggle free and take a step towards Tristan, but Kane holds his leg up in front of me, effectively blocking me.

"Oh no you don't," He warns, and I'm yanked back again by my hair.

Kane nods to the man behind Tristan. He steps in front of Tristan, brings his fist up and slams it into Tristan's face.

"NO!" I launch myself towards him, but my attacker wraps his arms around me in a vice-like grip.

"Release her." Kane laughs.

My attacker throws me onto the floor, and with my arms bound behind me, I have no way to protect myself. My head glances off the corner of the wooden bench, I see white hot blotches in my vision, I feel like I'm losing consciousness, then as I hit the cold tiled floor, the searing pain brings me back, I can't help grimacing out loud, that hurt so much. My shoulder feels like it's been dislocated and my lungs feel like all the air's been knocked out of them. I feel something begin to trickle down my right cheek.

Stuart, where the fuck are you?

"What do you want Kane?" I shout, slightly disorientated.

He smiles widely at me then leans down towards me. "It would seem your husband has been meddling in other people's business. You should have told him Coral, don't try taking on the devil when you have something to lose." *What the fuck does that mean?*

I try to work it out but come to no conclusion. Tristan starts jumping up and down in the chair, howling with rage as he wildly thrashes about, trying to free himself.

"Finish him off," Kane spits, gesturing to the man that fought with me to help the other. The two men both stand in front of Tristan, fists raised.

All the air leaves my lungs – *No!*

"No!" I shout. "Please, I'll do whatever you want, just don't hurt him anymore, please," I beg, keeping my eyes locked with Kane's.

He smiles as though this is exactly what he wanted to hear then he starts to laugh again, and gestures for the two men to back off. Tristan is still thrashing about, his teeth bared, his one eye wide as he continues to struggle free. I look up at Tristan, and subtly shake my head at him, mentally pleading with him to stay calm, but it makes no difference.

"I'm gonna rip your fucking head off!" he growls at Kane.

I look back at Kane. "Why are you here? What do you want?" I snap.

He bends down in front of me. "A re-enactment," He smiles, his eyes alight with joy. "That's what I want, and that's why the little bro is here." I look up at Dillon, he has his eyes closed, and his head is hung low – I realise he has no part in this. I wonder if he will do what his brother wants?

"As for the why..." He cocks his head to the side as though I should know.

I frown up at him then glance at Tristan.

"Oh!" Kane laughs. "You don't know, do you?" He looks from me to Tristan, then back again.

"What do you mean?" I snap, trying to get my head around it.

Kane laughs again. "Shall I tell her Tristan?" He says turning to look at him.

"Get away from her!" Tristan growls, making Kane laugh again, he's enjoying this.

He turns and smiles widely at me. "My dad told me all about bumping into you again, as you can imagine, I was intrigued to know more, after all, it's been a good couple of years hasn't it." Kane stops and looks across at Tristan, who starts howling in rage again – *Tristan, please calm down!*

"You see Coral, it turns out daddy made one too many mistakes, he trusted people he shouldn't have trusted. Apparently, he's been under surveillance, and they've been investigating him for a couple of years now. They have a couple of witnesses, who of course won't testify, not if they value their families lives, but unfortunately, because of your dear husband here, and the very inquisitive Detective Annie Marsh, they have him on fraud and embezzlement charges again. So, they have shut down all his companies, frozen his shares and forensic accountants are going through the books as we speak."

I look up at Tristan, and he hangs his head in shame – *Oh Tristan, what have you done!* I blink back the tears, he lied to me. He promised me he wouldn't do anything about this. But he did, and now look what's happened. I stare down at the floor, I don't believe this.

Kane continues. "So, I thought, before I have to disappear

for good and because this was also a personal request from my father, that we'd all have a little fun." I swallow hard. "Release her," Kane snaps. I feel the bindings on my wrists being cut away.

It's my chance to run to Tristan, but I know it won't do any good. So I just stay where I am, on the cold floor, just biding my time. *Where the fuck are you Stuart?* Just as I think that he comes waltzing into the room. Tristan instantly stops struggling, and we both stare wide eyed and opened mouthed at Stuart casually walking into the room. *Why isn't he doing something? – I don't understand!*

"Ah, yes. I suppose you want your money," Kane says to Stuart, who nods once in return.

"YOU!" I bellow. I look across at Tristan, he's in complete shock. I don't think he can believe it. Stuart glances at Tristan, and then looks down at me, his eyes showing no remorse.

"Money talks," He simply says. I instantly realise that's how they got in, why the alarms haven't gone off and why they have got to Tristan and I so easily – He led them to us!

I don't even think about it, I launch to my feet to attack him. I go for a gut punch, but Stuart smacks my arm away, grabs me by the throat and slams me up against the wall. He's so much stronger than I am.

"For once in your life, why don't you shut the fuck up," He squeezes my throat tighter, crushing my windpipe. "Always whining," He adds, his jaw clenching.

I struggle furiously against him, kicking my legs and arms, trying to free myself – *I can't breathe!*

"Let her go." Kane snaps. Stuart releases me, and I fall to the floor, choking and gasping for air. *How the fuck didn't, I see this? Stuart of all people, Stuart!* Kane hands Stuart a black briefcase and reaches his hand out to shake. Stuart hesitates, then reaches forward and takes Kane's hand.

"Disappear," Kane tells him.

"I have every intention of doing just that," he says.

"Mother Fucker!" Tristan roars, trying to get to his feet. "I trusted you...I trusted you!" He yells, still trying to free himself.

Stuart winces slightly as he glances at Tristan, then turns and stalks out of the room. I shake my head in denial - *This is not happening!* It's all a dream, a very bad dream. I start to really panic now, with Stuart gone...what the fuck are we meant to do? I shake my head in disbelief. That did not just happen...this is just a bad dream...a very vivid and very frightening dream.

"Now where were we?" Kane says, smiling cynically as he looks from me to Tristan. Then he opens his suit jacket and pulls out a gun. It's a big black gun, like Mel Gibson uses in Lethal Weapon – I instantly stop breathing.

Kane smiles, loads the gun, clicks what I think is the safety and points it at Tristan.

"NO!" I scream in panic, my hands held up. "Not him, please...please - Kane!" I cannot allow Tristan to die, no way, not ever – I try to think of something to do, something to get us out of this. Kane turns and looks down at me. "If you want to kill someone, kill me, not him. I'm begging you..." I cry out.

"NO CORAL!" Tristan roars again, still thrashing wildly about.

Kane laughs again. "How very brave of you Coral, offering to give your life up for another? Hmm...I wonder?" He points the gun at my head. "Eenie." He turns and points it at Tristan. "Meenie." Then back to me – Bastard is toying with us. "Minie." Back to Tristan. "Mo." Finishing with me.

I squeeze my eyes shut. "Tristan I love you," I shout out, and stay still, waiting for the inevitable to happen, but nothing does so I look up at Kane.

He is laughing again, enjoying his game. "I'm only teasing!" He jests, "That part won't happen yet. I have plans for you," he says and kneels down in front of me.

He reaches forward, making me flinch, and runs his finger down my cheek. I want to slap it away, but I don't know what he'll do if I enrage him. His touch turns my stomach, it's making me want to gag. I fight back against the bile rising in my throat. My whole body starts to shake with rage. I want to kill him, I want him dead.

I grit my teeth. "Just get on with it," I snap. Not wanting to know what he's going to do, or what his plans are. If they are what I think they are, I will just disappear and blank it out like I did as a child. Either way, it doesn't matter, because I am reconciled with my fate.

My life for Tristan's - always.

"Something to remember you by," he adds, then looks up at the two men next to Tristan. "Go get the kit," he says with a jerk of his head. *Kit?*

I watch the two men leave the room. Kane walks over to Dillon and snaps the bindings on his wrists. "Time to do your part Bro' you should enjoy this, just like old times."

My stomach turns again.

Kane yanks Dillon forward until he's stood at Tristan's side, and keeping hold of his arm, Kane looks down at me, smiling widely. "You do remember, don't you Coral, what we all did together as kids? I want to see that again, I want to see him'- he jabs his finger at Dillon- 'Fuck you all over again, we just need the cameras. This room will make for an excellent scene, don't you think?" Dillon hangs his head. He looks like he may throw up. I think I'm going to throw up too. I stare down at the floor, blinking in horror.

Tristan is thrashing about again, if he doesn't stay still he's going to topple over in the chair, he's so close to the water...and I won't be able to save him.

"Keep still," I shout at Tristan. He stills, but he's breathing so heavily and so deeply. He grits his teeth, squeezes his eyes shut and screams out, almost like he's howling in rage.

Kane continues. "So, we're going to make a nice little porno, and then we're going to do something else. You see, sex sells Coral as I'm sure you are aware of, but nowadays it's nowhere near as lucrative as snuff movies, and this is good practice for me. You see, I'll be taking over the family business when I disappear." *Snuff movies?*

I glare up at Kane, I try not to let him see that his words have affected me, but I can't help it. My heart is going like the clappers, so I'm breathing like I've been running up a hill, literally gasping for air. I suddenly realise I don't want to die, not like this. I want to die an old woman in my bed, safely wrapped up in Tristan's arms. I stare down at the floor again...shaking my head in disbelief. This is about to happen, I'm probably going to be gang-raped, then have a bullet put through my head – unless they decide to torture me first.

I swallow back more bile.

"Now, you're not going to disappoint me, are you Coral?" I swallow hard and try to concentrate, but my head feels so woozy. Tristan is still howling with rage. I glance up at him then look across at Kane. "Answer me!" Kane shouts.

"I'll do whatever you want," I croak, feeling utterly defeated. Maybe, if I do, they'll let Tristan go, but somehow I doubt that – *Tristan, why did you investigate, why!*

"Oh, I know you will," Kane says, his voice dark and menacing.

He releases Dillon, bends down in front of me, and reaching forward he cups my chin in his fingers. His touch makes me gag, but I try my best to keep very still and keep him focused on me because Dillon has silently bent down behind Kane and has picked up the iron barbell that held the weights on Tristan's legs – this maybe our only chance.

"Can I ask you something?" I ask as timidly as I can, blinking up at Kane – I'm just giving Dillon more time so he can position himself correctly.

"What?" Kane asks, cocking his head to the side. Right at the moment, Dillon whacks the barbell across Kane's head.

Kane groans in pain and then his eyes roll into the back of his head, his body going limp. He almost falls on top of me as he hits the floor, but I manage to slide out of the way. I watch as the gun falls from his hand and goes skidding across the floor. I look down at him, trying to see if he's still alive, he's lying face down, and blood is oozing out of his head.

I think he's actually dead. I look up at Dillon. *What's he going to do?*

"I won't hurt you," he says and lunges for the gun.

"Get the door!" Tristan shouts.

I launch to my feet, run over to the door, slam it shut and lock it. Hoping that will keep the other men from getting to us – unless they have guns too? I run back over to Tristan, trying to free him. Dillon has the gun pointing at Kane, it's shaking rapidly in his hand as he begins to cry out in rage.

"You bastard, you mother fucker..." He shouts, bouncing up and down, jabbing the gun at Kane.

"I think he's dead," I tell him, but I get no response. "Dillon?" I shout.

He doesn't look at me or answer me. *Shit!*

I run back over to Kane, reach down and check for a pulse – nothing. I turn back around with my hands held up and look Dillon square in the eye. "Dillon, he can't hurt you anymore, he's dead, ok he's dead." Tears pool in Dillon's eyes, the gun continues to shake in his hands. "It's ok," I tell him. "It's ok."

A deafening bang makes me crouch down and cover my ears. I spin around and see a hole in the door handle. Fuck there getting in – *Tristan!*

I run back over to him, trying to free him, but I can't rip the tape of him.

"Go!" He shouts.

"No!" I growl back. I hear police sirens in the distance. *Please be coming to us!* Another loud bang goes off, and the two men burst through the door – I don't have time to think about it, I just do it.

"Breathe!" I scream to Tristan, then push him into the pool and launch myself in with him. I wrap myself around him, and we quickly sink to the bottom of the pool. I hear more muffled bangs going off above me, but I keep my eyes locked on Tristan's one good eye.

I give him the ok sign, and he nods. If there's one thing Tristan and I can do well, is to hold our breath longer than the average person, one of the many advantages of being a swimmer. And right now, I thank god that we are. I hear shouting, and what I think is fighting going on above us. Then I see an arm, a very bloody arm fall against the edge of the pool and slip into the water. The blood instantly mingles with the water, turning it red, and I know from that arm that it's Dillon – *God, please let him survive this!*

It suddenly goes deathly quiet above us. I look at Tristan and then at his legs, I need to get him out of this now. I give him the thumb up, letting him know I'm going up to the surface. He frowns and shakes his head at me. I widen my eyes as if to say we don't have another choice. Jesus, he's arguing with me now? He's going to run out of air soon, and I can't drag him up, he's too heavy, not with all this weight strapped to him – *Fuck!*

I frown at him and thumb up again. His eyes close in resignation, and he nods once. I have no idea what's going on, or who's up there, so I'm going to have to be as quiet as I can. I move towards him, kiss him hard on the forehead, and then swim to the edge of the pool. I slowly come up to the surface, blowing all the air out of my lungs as I do. When my face breaks through the surface of the water, I take a silent, deep breath in, just in case I need it. Then I silently pull myself up so I can scan the room.

Kane is still there on the floor and Dillon is still breathing, but struggling and I can see the guy that tried to attack me is lying on the floor by the door. I whip my head around, looking for the other man. He's not in here, but that doesn't mean he's not in the house. *Damn it!*

I need a knife or scissors, something to cut Tristan free with, and the only place I'll find that is upstairs in the kitchen. Tristan's going to run out of air soon. I have no time. I need to do this now, no matter the consequences. I swim to the shallow end and run up the few steps, my bare feet slipping as I try to get a grip. When I'm out of the water, I yank my skirt right up to my thighs and just go for it. I run out of the room, take the stairs two at a time, belt it down the hallway, and come skidding to a stop in the kitchen. I grab one of my Global knives and a pair of scissors – just in case I need them – and turn to run back out – *Fuck!*

The guy I slammed my hand into is just stood there, blood oozing out of his nose, and down his lips. *Really bad timing!*

"Move!" I threaten. He pulls his lips back over his teeth, and I know he's going to lunge at me.

Ok fine! - He wants to do this, bring it on! My only priority is Tristan, and if I don't get back to him, right now, he might die. I can't fuck about with this. I need to take this guy down – Immediately!

I take a step back against the kitchen cabinets and beckon him forward. He lunges toward me, as I thought he would, but I sink down into a crouch and shove the knife up into his belly. The feeling of his soft flesh against the razor sharp knife turns my stomach, and I gag. Blood starts pouring out of him. He staggers back, his hands on the knife, and a look of shock on his face. *No time!*

I jump back up, grab another knife, dash around the other side of the breakfast bar and run like my life depends on it. I almost fall down the stairs as I'm running so fast to get to Tristan. I sprint down the hall, skid into the room, run to the edge of the pool and just dive into the water – Tristan isn't moving, or looking up at me – *No!*

I swim down to him, kicking my arms and legs as hard as I can so I can reach him. I grab hold of the chair, pull myself around and slice the tape open with the knife – *Thank god, it worked!* Then I slice the tape on both his legs, which frees the weights, I manage to push them off him, and they float down to the bottom of the pool. Then I carefully slice the tape binding his feet – *He's free!*

I pull Tristan into my arms, and with my feet firmly planted on the floor, I bend down into a squat and with as much force as I can, I launch myself up so I can get him to the surface. The moment my face breaks the water I get him onto his back, hold his chin up and swim to the steps. As I reach them I stand up, grab hold of him under his arms and try to pull him up, but he's so heavy, a dead weight in my weak arms.

"Come on!" I scream as I pull and pull, and pull. His body is still half in and half out the water. *No!* I need him lying flat. "Come on!" I scream again, and with one last screaming effort, I manage to pull him up onto the floor, stumbling onto my backside as I do.

I lunge forward and check his pulse – *No heartbeat!*

"No Tristan!" I immediately start CPR, pumping his heart hard.

One, two, three, four, five pumps. "Come on, breathe... breathe..." I take a deep breath, push his head up, pinch his nose and blow as much air as I can into his lungs, then I go back to his heart, pumping again. "One, two...come on, come on!" I scream, still pumping. I blow into his lungs again, then back to his heart, pushing and pumping as hard as I can.

"You're not dead...you're not dead..." I croak, fear gripping my very being – *He has to survive!*

I blow into his lungs again, then pump his heart, I start to feel weak, no energy.

"Don't you dare leave me!" I screech, tears pooling down my cheeks.

I blow more air into his lungs, then I go back to pumping his heart. "Come on Tristan...breathe, breathe..." I do the same again. "Come on!" I scream in panic. "You're not dead...you're not dead...You can't leave me!" Tristan gasps a loud rasping sound, then turns on his side and starts vomiting water.

"Tristan!" I screech. I reach down and slam his back. "Breathe...breathe..." He starts coughing and spluttering; choking up more water – *Oh god, thank you...thank you...*

"It's ok Tristan...breathe, you're ok...I'm right here." He's still struggling, his breath coming in sharp gusts, as he continues coughing up water. "It's ok...just breathe...just breathe..." I say, squeezing his arm, and smacking his back to help get the water out.

"Coral..." He chokes, and that's my cue. I cry out in relief, a choking sob bursting out of me.

"Tristan..." I squeeze my eyes shut, fall against him and just cry tears of relief.

"Coral..." He croaks, his voice raw, his breath still coming in sharp gusts.

"It's ok, we're ok..." I manage to choke out.

I hear the halo of an ambulance and police sirens above us, and then footsteps running down the stairs. Two policemen quickly followed by two paramedics come running into the room. I have never felt so relieved in my entire life. The Paramedics run over to us, kneel down next to Tristan, and they immediately start working on him.

"He drowned," I choke out, still fighting tears, then I look across at Dillon – *He saved us!*

"Help him!" I scream. One of the Paramedics looks over his shoulder, shouts for back-up on his radio and dashes over to Dillon. Then I remember – *Edith!*

I launch to my feet and run over to the policeman. "My housekeeper, Edith, she's still missing! Please...find her!" I shout in desperation.

"Is she in the house?" He asks.

"I don't know?" I manage to squeak. He nods once and speaks into his radio – *Dear God, please let her be ok!* I want to find her, but I don't want to leave Tristan, I dash back over to him.

"Found her." The policeman shouts. "She's ok." He tells me.

I sag with relief, and then everything just becomes blurry and muffled. Too many people, police, paramedics, too much noise. I blank them all out as I watch them lift Tristan onto a stretcher. I keep his hand in mine as we go through the garage and up to the waiting ambulance on the driveway.

"Coral!" I hear Edith shout out.

I turn and see the front door wide open and Edith running towards me. "Edith!" We crash into one another and hug fiercely. "Are you ok?" I ask, tears streaming down my cheeks, she's crying too, and unable to say anything she just nods. "Come on." I grab her by the hand, and we step into the ambulance, as I look down at Tristan, I see his eyes aren't open.

"What's happened?" I shout in panic.

"He's fine, just passed out. Probably the morphine, all his vital signs are good." He tells me.

I sag with relief once more. I keep Edith's hand tightly held in mine as we ride over to the hospital...

AS I SIT watching Tristan, I keep my eyes focused on the rise and fall of his chest as he breathes. The door flies open, I drag my eyes away from Tristan and look up. Dr Green walks over and checks his IV drip, then his readouts.

"Why hasn't he woken up yet?" I ask my voice cold and bleak.

"He'll come back when he's ready." She says, placing her hand on my shoulder – but it brings me no comfort. Tristan is still unconscious and has been for two days and nights now. I grip his hand in mine and close my eyes, saying a small prayer for all to be well when he does wake.

"All tests show there's no brain damage Coral," she tells me again. "He's had a traumatic experience. This is his way of processing it all and healing, just like you did. He's going to be fine, he just needs time, all he needs is time," She softly tells me.

I silently nod and stare down at Tristan. He's growing a beard again. I choke back the tears. *Fucking tears!* This is the fifth time today.

"I'll be back later to check on him. Try not to worry." Dr Green says.

I don't look up at her, even though she's tried to convince me all will be well, there's a part of me that's afraid. Like, if I look up at her, I'll see she's lying, and that will be it for me. Dr Green squeezes my shoulder once more.

When I know she's gone and the nurse on duty has disappeared back to her desk – and she won't be back for at least four hours – I pull back the sheet on the large hospital bed and climb in next to Tristan. He's flat on his back with his mouth slightly open, the cannula in his nose feeding him oxygen.

"Tristan," I whisper in his ear. "I love you, and I miss you, baby, so much…Please come back to me." I choke back the tears again, sniff loudly, close my eyes and rest my head on his shoulder.

I place my arm across his chest and squeeze his shoulder, trying my best not to cry. I need to sleep. I'm so exhausted, but every time I do I'm back in the pool room, trying to resuscitate Tristan, only I can't bring him back, he won't wake up…and Kane is stood over us, laughing, he has the gun in his hand, and he's pointing it at my head…

I STARTLE AWAKE and look up at Tristan, only to find his eyes wide open, watching me.

"Tristan!" I g

asp and sit up so I can see him properly.

He frowns back at me, and then closes his eyes for a moment, he swallows hard.

"Hey baby," I softly say.

He groggily opens his eyes again. "Thirsty," he whispers. I jump up from the bed, the pain making me wince from the beating I received and press the button for the Nurse.

"The nurse is coming baby, she's coming." I try not to cry as I gently stroke his hair, he still seems so out of it. His eye, his cheekbones and his lips are still so swollen. I don't know where to kiss him.

The nurse enters the room. "Hey Tristan, good to see you awake," she says.

"He's thirsty," I tell her.

"Ok. I'll let Dr Green know he's awake and I'll get you some crushed ice. Just a little at a time mind you," she says. I nod once, keeping my eyes fixed on Tristan. He reaches his hand up, but he's got an IV in his right hand, so I reach over and pick up his left. I clasp it hard in between my hands, then bring his hand up to my lips and kiss him.

"Coral, are you ok?" He croakily asks, reaching up to touch my swollen cheek.

"Don't worry about me," I tell him firmly.

His eyes close again. "You know I can't help doing that," he croaks.

"Tristan, please just relax, everything's ok." I sit back up on the edge of the bed and hover over him. I reach up and run my hands through his hair. "You look terrible," I tease.

"Thanks," he croaks. "What happened Coral?"

I frown back at him. "You don't remember?"

"Some of it…I know you wouldn't leave when I told you to." He tries to narrow his eyes at me, but with his face so bruised it kind of doesn't work.

"Hey, let's fight about it when you're better, ok?" I whisper softly. I'm so happy he's awake. He tries to smile at me, but it makes him wince in pain.

I lean down and very carefully touch my lips to his. "I love you, Tristan Freeman."

"Coral…" He breathes, then reaches up and wraps his arms tightly around me. "Oh, baby…I thought…you're alive…oh I love you, so much." He grips me tighter. "You saved us, baby."

"No, Dillon did," I croak out. "Oh, Tristan…" I reach up and stroke his hair, his cheek.

Forever With Him

"What happened, tell me everything – Shit! Edith!" Tristan gasps.

"Shhh, she's ok, everyone's ok. Relax baby, relax. I'll tell you everything, but you need to get checked out first ok?" I tell him.

"Oh, Coral!" He crushes me to him again, constantly kissing the top of my head.

The door is opened. I look up and see Dr Green and the nurse walk in together. "Good afternoon Mr Freeman," Dr Green says, smiling at Tristan. "Let's get you checked out," she adds. I give Tristan one more gentle kiss on the lips and hop down from the bed.

"Don't go," he croaks.

I squeeze his hand tightly. "Hey, I'll be back in a couple of minutes ok. I want to let everyone know you're awake." I say.

"Ok," he croaks, trying to smile. I nod to Dr Green, and feeling utterly exhausted, but very elated, I head over to the waiting room. All our family and friends have been taking shifts here, to support me and wait for news on Tristan, and right now it's Gladys and Malcolm that are here, but when I round the corner, I see it's just Malcolm in the room, and the moment he sees me he stands up.

"Oh Coral...is?' – "He's awake," I manage to choke out, and burst into tears of relief.

Malcolm dashes over to me and wraps his arms around me, squeezing me tight, comforting me. "Oh...I'm so glad," he says, rocking me gently.

"Where's mom?" I manage to choke out.

"Ladies," He softly tells me.

"Will you tell her for me?" I choke. "I want to get back to him."

"Of course darling," He says, kissing the top of my head.

I reach up and kiss his cheek. "Thanks, dad," I croak.

Malcolm smiles warmly at me, squeezes my hand and then lets me go. In a sleep-deprived daze, I head back to Tristan's room. Dr Green is just finishing with him, and the Nurse is feeding him crushed ice.

"May I?" I say, holding my hands out to her so I can do it.

"Just a little more," The nurse tells me as she passes me the cup and spoon.

"Tristan, you're looking good, but you're going to be in here a few more days," Dr Green says. Tristan nods in recognition. I turn and smile at Dr Green. "See you both in a while," she adds and then she leaves the room with the nurse.

I sit on the edge of Tristan's bed and fill the spoon with more ice. "Open wide," I tease. Tristan does so, and slowly chews the ice.

"Coral...I'm so sorry." He says, tears pooling in his good eye.

"I know you are," I say. "But none of that matters now. You're alive, and you're safe – "I didn't break my promise to you," he interrupts.

"You didn't?" I say, filling up the spoon.

"No baby. You remember..." Tristan stops, wincing in pain.

"Tristan, you don't need to do this now' – "Yes, I do." He snaps – He hasn't changed, still my broody man.

"Fine!" I bite.

"Fine!" He bites back.

We both grin at one another. "Come on then, out with it!" I say.

"After you told me about Simon and I went for a walk, I called Detective Marsh, and we spoke for a while, I wasn't really sure why I was calling her. I think...I just needed to hear what could be done if..." Tristan trails off and takes a deep breath. "The next day, when you said you wanted nothing done about it, I called her back and told her of your decision. I never intended to have anything more to do with it, as I promised you. Then a couple of weeks later, Detective Marsh called me, she said she'd done some digging around, and it turned out Simon was already under investigation. She asked me if I wanted to be kept updated, I said yes. That's what all the phone calls were about, I didn't think for one second it would come back to us. I am so sorry baby...so sorry' – "Hey." I place my lips against his.

"It's ok Tristan, its ok. I've already spoken to Detective Marsh, and she told me that Simon was aware he was under investigation, so he had all the investigators lines tapped. He knew she'd been calling you, and she told me that..." I take a deep breath. "The witnesses didn't make it." I swallow hard. "She told me that he's involved in one of the biggest crime syndicates she has ever known, they're only just scraping the surface, and Tristan..." I take a deep breath and swallow hard. "They found Stuart's body."

Tristan glares back at me and clenches his jaw.

"They were never going to let him go, I guess." I swallow hard again. "But like I said, none of that matters. You're alive - you're a mess, but you're alive," I say, trying to tease. "Had enough ice?" I ask, giving him another spoonful.

He chews once, swallows and nods once. "Am I forgiven?" He asks.

"Tristan, there's nothing to forgive," I say, staring down at his good eye.

Tears pool in my eyes again – *God damn it!*

"Come here baby," he croaks. I lean forward and gently peck his lips. "Lie down with me," he adds.

"Ok." I pull my legs up, so I'm lying adjacent to him and rest my head on his chest. Tristan wraps his arms around me and squeezes me tight. I sigh inwardly – All is well in the world again.

Tristan is alive, and we both survived – again.

"I love you, Tristan," I mumble, sleep pulling me under.

"And I love you Coral Freeman, more than life itself – Forever," he whispers croakily.

"Forever," I breathe and slip into unconsciousness...

EPILOGUE

Two Years Later

TRISTAN SQUEEZES my hand as we walk into the house. It's Christmas Eve, and we've just had a very wet and windy walk on the beach. But I love that feeling of being frozen outside and coming home to a warm house. We head straight upstairs and change into dry clothes.

"Would you like a glass of wine darling?" Tristan asks.

I stop drying my hair with the towel for a moment as I try to think of the correct response so he doesn't get suspicious. "Um...later I think. I really want a hot chocolate," I say.

Tristan's brow becomes quizzical. "Are you feeling unwell Mrs Freeman? You always say yes to wine."

I gasp. "Mr Freeman, what are you implying?" I say in a teasing way.

"No implications, just fact Mrs Freeman." He teases back with wide playful eyes.

"Hot chocolate!" I say, narrowing my eyes at him.

"As you wish," He grins widely, leans forward and kisses me. His kiss still has the same effect, my whole body lights up, and I shiver from head to toe.

"See you downstairs," he adds, the cutest grin spreading across his face. I shake my head, laughing as I do.

With my hair dried, I head over to my handbag and find the chocolate coins for the Christmas tree. When Tristan told me a few weeks ago that he'd never had these as a child, I made sure I bought three bags of them. I head back down the stairs and into the living room. I hear music playing, Lonestar's Amazed – My man is such a softie!

Tristan surprises me by lifting me up into his arms and swinging me around, then dancing me around the room as he sings the words of the song to me, making me swoon up at him – I still can't quite believe he is mine, that I'm married to such a wonderful man.

When the song ends he leans down and kisses me softly, smiling against my lips.

"Hot chocolate?" He questions again, his eyebrows pulling together.

"Yes," I whisper, kissing him back. I can't help chuckling as he winks at me then heads into the kitchen – The man's definitely still got it.

I turn around and see the fire is blasting and the Christmas tree is twinkling sweetly. Dillon and Edith are in the kitchen, cooking something up for tea tonight. When Dillon saved us from near death, I promised myself I would do everything within my power to help him recover from his injuries. So he came here, and Edith helped me nurse him and Tristan back to full health.

In the time that we all spent together, I found out he'd run away from home when he was only thirteen years old, and that he had lived on the streets for a while until he found shelter. Eventually, he got a job, but he was so fucked up with everything that happened to him, that he turned to drink and drugs, which led to stealing cars to get money for the drugs and then to an arrest, court and time in prison.

When we met him, he'd been clean for five years and was struggling with work, but as he reminded me, not many people want to employ ex-convicts. So, after talking to Tristan, we gave him Stuart's job – Sound silly, I know, but I really would trust him with my life, and Tristan's. And he's done so well, and he's so happy, he really feels like part of our family now.

Tristan finds me hanging the coins on the tree. "Chocolate coins?" He asks, grinning from ear to ear.

"Yes, but you are not allowed to eat them all tonight, ok!" I tease.

Tristan pouts at me, then hands me my hot chocolate. "I have a present for you," I say.

"You do?" He quizzes.

"Well, it's not so much as a present, more like..." I shake my head. *What the hell am I on about?* I place my cup down on the coffee table, take both his hands and pull him in front of the fire, away from Edith and Dillon, where we are alone, and no-one can see us.

"I love you Tristan Freeman, Merry Christmas baby." I look down, lift up my top and place his right hand on my belly, and then I slowly look up at him through my lashes.

It takes a moment, but then his eyes widen as the penny drops. "Coral!" He gasps. I start laughing at his awed expression. "You're sure?" He whispers.

"Yes," I whisper, a few happy tears rolling down my cheeks.

"Oh, baby…" Tristan sinks to his knees, pulls my top further up and plants his lips there, right on my belly. He keeps his hands firmly planted on my hips as he kisses me there several times, then he pulls back and starts talking to Junior – to my belly.

"Now listen here, young man…or young lady. We'll have no bad behaviour, no sleepless nights, and no puking on mommy or me, or there will be trouble!" He kisses me there again, then looks up at me in that way of his, total admiration – then he looks at my belly and continues talking to junior.

"You are going to be so loved. You're going to have the best mommy in the world, you'll see when you meet her, she's amazing. She's kind and sweet, and funny and strong, and she'll protect you and love you unconditionally, forever, and so will I."

I blink back more tears, I feel like I'm in a dream again. I think I may have to pinch myself…

Six Years Later…

I CAN'T HELP myself. I know I shouldn't, but I love listening to Coral when she talks to Ethan, our amazing little man. It fills me with such a powerful, loving feeling that I just want to do it again and again. I creep along the hallway and stop outside his bedroom door. Ethan was five today, I know this is a monumental day to Coral, so much happened to her at that age, and she's done so well to protect Ethan from any kind of pain, especially in these young, impressionable years. And it was my turn to put Ethan to bed tonight, but Coral insisted she wanted to do it, so I relented, then again I always relent with Coral, whatever she wants, she will always have.

"Mommy, why do you kiss Daddy?"

"Because I love him, baby, just like I love you."

"But you kiss Daddy differently."

"Yeah, I know, but that's because we're grown-ups, and when you grow up you'll understand that."

"Lily said she kissed a boy like that and it was all wet and slimy." I hear Coral snigger, which makes me want to laugh aloud. He's really going through an inquisitive stage.

"Well, it probably does feel like that when you're little, but it feels very different when you're a grown-up."

"Mommy?"

"Yes..."

"Why do mommy's have boobies and daddies have willies?"

Coral laughs again. "Well because we're supposed to be different baby."

"Why?"

"Ethan!"

"Yes, mommy?"

"I love you very much."

"I love you too mommy."

"Did you have a nice birthday?"

"Yes."

"What did you like the most?"

"My chocolate cake."

Typical! He loved Coral's cake, not what I bought him, it makes me smile.

"You didn't like the electric car that Daddy bought you?"

"Daddy showed me how to drive it, but I want a big car like Daddy's."

"Can't have one of those yet baby."

"I have to be big like Daddy?"

"Yes."

"Mommy?"

"Yes..."

"Can I have a puppy instead?"

"You want a puppy instead of your car?"

"No mommy, I want to take the puppy in the car."

"Oh...I see, well, I'll talk to Daddy ok?"

"Mommy?"

I have to go in, or she'll be there all night otherwise. "What's all this noise I hear?" I say, walking into his room, Coral looks up at me trying to hide her smile.

"Daddy!" Ethan squeals, reaching up to me. Coral gives me a stern look, I know, I know, I'm waking him back up. I rush over to him and pull him up into my arms, then tickle him.

"What are you still doing up young man?" I say, trying not to laugh.

"Daddy...don't..." He laughs, wriggling about in his bed.

"You should be asleep." I scold, but lightly.

"Mommy said I can have a puppy!" He says his eyes wide with delight. *Nice try kid!*

"I don't think Mommy said yes," I say. I feel Coral run her fingers through the back of my hair. It never fails to move me. Just her presence alone moves me. I reach up, take her hand in mine, and kiss the back of her hand.

"Daddy?"

"Oh no, you don't!" I say, wagging my finger at him. "No more questions from you tonight young man, you need to sleep now." I stroke his forehead, and his hair. He's such a mix of us both. Medium brown hair, green eyes, cheeks that flush, but the best part is that he has his mother's smile. "Shall we read a story?" I ask.

"No, it's ok daddy." He yawns widely. "I'm tired now."

"Alright, well snuggle up." I pull the quilt over him and tuck him in either side. Coral is watching us both, I can tell. I reach down and kiss his warm cheek. "Night kiddo, I love you."

"Love you too daddy." He says.

He yawns widely, and I can tell he's struggling to keep his eyes open. I glance across at Coral, she smiles her shy smile that I utterly adore, and slightly shakes her head. I watch her lean down and kiss Ethan's cheek.

"Goodnight my sweet, baby boy. Sweet dreams."

He yawns again. "Night mommy..."

We both sit there, watching him fall asleep. When we know he's drifted off, I take Coral's hand, and we head out of his room. I pull the door closed behind me, but leave a tiny gap. Ethan is like his mother when he wakes in the night and needs the bathroom – zombie – so he doesn't do too well with door handles.

Then taking Coral by surprise, I push her up against the wall and press my body against hers. I reach up and take her face in my hands. It never fails to amaze me that she is mine. She smiles that shy smile again – It takes my breath away, she takes my breath away, in everything that she does.

I lean down, acting as though I'm going to kiss her, but I stop just as our lips are about to touch. Coral arches a brow at me, it makes me smile widely, she smiles back flashing her perfect teeth.

"I want to tell you something," I whisper – *Don't want to wake the kid up!*

"Do you now," she whispers back, teasing me.

I smile wryly at her. "I think you are the most wonderful mother, wife...lover." I gently press my lips to hers, because they are just too kissable, I pull back and lean my forehead against hers. "No man has ever loved a woman as much as I love you," I tell her, stroking her cheek, gazing at her perfect, fragile features.

Coral reaches up and places her hands on my cheeks. "And no woman has ever loved a man as much as I love you." She reaches up onto her tip-toes and kisses me, hard.

I lift her up, she wraps her legs around me, and we continue into our perfect, blissful little piece of heaven...

THE END

Thank you to very reader who has travelled this journey with Coral and Tristan.

Hi There!
Did you enjoy this book?
If so, you can make a big difference.

Reviews are the most powerful tools in my arsenal when it comes to getting attention for my books. Much as I'd like to, I don't have the financial muscle of a New York Publisher. I can't take out full page ads in the newspaper, or put posters on the subway. But I do have something more powerful than that, and it's something that those publishers would kill to get their hands on.

A committed and loyal bunch of readers.

Honest reviews of my books help bring them to the attention of other readers like you. If you've enjoyed this book I would be very grateful if you could spend just five minutes leaving a review (it can be as short as you like) or simply rating the book on Amazon. I wholeheartedly thank you in advance.

Find Out What Happens Next In…
A Christmas Wish
Darkest Fears Christmas Special Book Four

A Contemporary Feel Good Christmas Romance

Coral and Tristan have faced many challenges in the short time they have known each other and have come out stronger than ever. They managed to find love against odds so steep, it would scare those of lesser hearts, yet they have held strong through trauma, the past, death and violence. Now settled in their Brighton home together, they face their final challenge - Christmas.
It's the one time of year full of heart warming reunions with family and friends, when love is in the air and people are full of festive cheer. Christmas carols are played in stores, Christmas lights decorate the shops and towns and the countdown to Christmas has begun.
So with Christmas fast approaching, Coral and Tristan must decide what to do for their very first Christmas together. However Coral has a Christmas wish, and she is determined to

make it come true. But as events unfold, Coral comes to realise that sometimes, the one thing you think you really want, isn't always what you truly need.

Grab a mug of hot chocolate, sit back and relax with Coral and Tristan once again...

5 stars – Kobo
5 stars – iBooks
5 stars – Barnes & Noble
5 stars – Scribd
Avg 4.5 stars - Goodreads

Join My Mailing List

Join my mailing list via my website www.clairdelaneyauthor.com for exclusive offers and competitions and to keep updated with future releases.

Connect with me

Also, you can connect with me via social media. Or contact me via the email address below. I would love to answer your questions, or simply read your feedback and comments.

FACEBOOK - Clair Delaney Author
TWITTER - @CDelaney_Author
INSTAGRAM – ClairDelaneyAuthor
PINTEREST – Clair Delaney Author
WEBSITE - www.clairdelaneyauthor.com
EMAIL - clairdelaneyauthor@gmail.com

ABOUT THE AUTHOR

CLAIR DELANEY is a former P.A who currently lives in rural Wales in the UK. From a very young age, Clair would always be found drawing pictures and writing an exciting story to go with those picture books. At five years of age she told her mother she wanted to work for Disney, that dream didn't pan out, but eventually, she found the courage to put pen to paper and write her first romance novel Fallen For Him. She is also the author of Freed By Him, Forever With Him and A Christmas Wish, Darkest Fears Christmas Special. When she is not writing Clair loves to read, listen to music, keep fit and take long walks with her dogs in the countryside.

FOREVER WITH HIM - Copyright © 2018 Clair Delaney

The moral rights of the author have been asserted. All characters and events in this e-book other than those clearly in the public domain are fictitious and any resemblance to real persons, living or dead is purely coincidence - All right reserved. This e-book is copyright material and must not be copied, reproduced, transferred, distributed or used in any way except as specifically permitted in writing by the author, as allowed under the terms and conditions under which it was purchased or as strictly permitted by applicable law. Any unauthorised distribution or use of this text, maybe a direct infringement of the authors rights, and those responsible maybe liable in law accordingly.

Printed in Great Britain
by Amazon